Selected Works of H. G. Wells

Selected Works
of
H. G. Wells

Word Cloud Classics
San Diego

Canterbury Classics
An imprint of Printers Row Publishing Group
9717 Pacific Heights Blvd, San Diego, CA 92121
www.canterburyclassicsbooks.com • mail@canterburyclassicsbooks.com

All correspondence concerning the content of this book should be sent to Canterbury Classics, Editorial Department, at the above address.

Publisher: Peter Norton • Associate Publisher: Ana Parker
Art Director: Charles McStravick
Senior Developmental Editor: April Graham Farr
Editor: Traci Douglas
Production Team: Julie Greene, Rusty von Dyl

Cover design: Rosemary Rae
Image credits: Vectorcarrot/Shutterstock

Library of Congress Control Number: 2021932483

ISBN: 978-1-64517-743-2

Printed in China

25 24 23 22 21 1 2 3 4 5

Editor's Note: The pieces in this book have been published in their original form to preserve the author's intent and style.

CONTENTS

The War in the Air

Foreword

Modern readers view H. G. Wells (1866–1946) as one of the "Fathers of Science Fiction." Though they appreciate how prophetic Wells's work has proven to be, few may realize how prolific the author was, and how complicated his publishing history has been.

The Time Machine, included within this book, originated as a short story titled "The Chronic Argonauts" in a self-published literary journal Wells formed during his early twenties in 1888. After appearing, in part, in a revised form six years later as "The Time Traveler's Story" in the *National Observer*, the story was revised and serialized yet again in 1895 within the periodical *The New Review*, this time with the title "The Time Machine." Each iteration of the story was so well received that Wells approached the American publisher Henry Holt to print it as a novel by the same name, which was accomplished at the beginning of May that year. While that publication was in the works, Wells also solicited another publisher in London—William Heinemann—who, just three weeks after the American release, published a different version of the novel, titled *The Time Machine, An Invention.* In scholarly circles, these novels have become known as the "Holt text" and the "Heinemann text," respectively. Even though the two books include the same story and were published nearly concurrently, the bodies of text contain notable differences. In 1924, Wells revised the Heinemann edition of the story yet again, removing chapter titles and reducing the body to twelve chapters plus an epilogue. Although it was not to be the absolute final version, this condensed text was published within a twenty-eight-volume set titled *The Atlantic Edition of the Works of H. G. Wells.* It

is the most published edition in modern times, and is the one we have chosen to include in this collection.

In a similar vein, Wells later saw multiple reprints of *The War in the Air*. Whereas his earlier *War of the Worlds* had been categorized as a romantic, albeit dark, "what if" idea of alien invasion, *The War in the Air* took a more satirical, "if we continue like this" tone, promising dystopia as the only logical outcome of social ignorance and indifference. It was first released in several parts in *Pall Mall Magazine* in 1908; the novel followed that fall, and garnered impressive sales. Reprint editions issued in 1917 and 1921 each contained their own preface from Wells, who was desperate to impart that "war has no winners." Yet another reprint edition followed in 1941, in which Wells's new preface distills his message to a proposed epitaph: "I told you so. You *damned* fools." We have included the 1908 version of *The War in the Air* in this volume, accompanied by the prefaces printed with the 1917 and 1921 editions of the book.

The Time Machine

Chapter I

The Time Traveller (for so it will be convenient to speak of him) was expounding a recondite matter to us. His grey eyes shone and twinkled, and his usually pale face was flushed and animated. The fire burned brightly, and the soft radiance of the incandescent lights in the lilies of silver caught the bubbles that flashed and passed in our glasses. Our chairs, being his patents, embraced and caressed us rather than submitted to be sat upon, and there was that luxurious after-dinner atmosphere when thought roams gracefully free of the trammels of precision. And he put it to us in this way—marking the points with a lean forefinger—as we sat and lazily admired his earnestness over this new paradox (as we thought it) and his fecundity.

"You must follow me carefully. I shall have to controvert one or two ideas that are almost universally accepted. The geometry, for instance, they taught you at school is founded on a misconception."

"Is not that rather a large thing to expect us to begin upon?" said Filby, an argumentative person with red hair.

"I do not mean to ask you to accept anything without reasonable ground for it. You will soon admit as much as I need from you. You know of course that a mathematical line, a line of thickness *nil*, has no real existence. They taught you that? Neither has a mathematical plane. These things are mere abstractions."

"That is all right," said the Psychologist.

"Nor, having only length, breadth, and thickness, can a cube have a real existence."

"There I object," said Filby. "Of course a solid body may exist. All real things—"

"So most people think. But wait a moment. Can an *instantaneous* cube exist?"

"Don't follow you," said Filby.

"Can a cube that does not last for any time at all, have a real existence?"

Filby became pensive. "Clearly," the Time Traveller proceeded, "any real body must have extension in *four* directions: it must have Length, Breadth, Thickness, and—Duration. But through a natural infirmity of the flesh, which I will explain to you in a moment, we incline to overlook this fact. There are really four dimensions, three which we call the three planes of Space, and a fourth, Time. There is, however, a tendency to draw an unreal distinction between the former three dimensions and the latter, because it happens that our consciousness moves intermittently in one direction along the latter from the beginning to the end of our lives."

"That," said a very young man, making spasmodic efforts to relight his cigar over the lamp; "that . . . very clear indeed."

"Now, it is very remarkable that this is so extensively overlooked," continued the Time Traveller, with a slight accession of cheerfulness. "Really this is what is meant by the Fourth Dimension, though some people who talk about the Fourth Dimension do not know they mean it. It is only another way of looking at Time. *There is no difference between Time and any of the three dimensions of Space except that our consciousness moves along it.* But some foolish people have got hold of the wrong side of that idea. You have all heard what they have to say about this Fourth Dimension?"

"*I* have not," said the Provincial Mayor.

"It is simply this. That Space, as our mathematicians have it, is spoken of as having three dimensions, which one may call Length, Breadth, and Thickness, and is always definable by reference to three planes, each at right angles to the others. But some philosophical people have been asking why *three* dimensions particularly—why not another direction at right angles to the other three?—and have even tried to construct a Four-Dimension geometry. Professor Simon Newcomb was expounding this to the New York Mathematical Society only

a month or so ago. You know how on a flat surface, which has only two dimensions, we can represent a figure of a three-dimensional solid, and similarly they think that by models of three dimensions they could represent one of four—if they could master the perspective of the thing. See?"

"I think so," murmured the Provincial Mayor; and, knitting his brows, he lapsed into an introspective state, his lips moving as one who repeats mystic words. "Yes, I think I see it now," he said after some time, brightening in a quite transitory manner.

"Well, I do not mind telling you I have been at work upon this geometry of Four Dimensions for some time. Some of my results are curious. For instance, here is a portrait of a man at eight years old, another at fifteen, another at seventeen, another at twenty-three, and so on. All these are evidently sections, as it were, Three-Dimensional representations of his Four-Dimensioned being, which is a fixed and unalterable thing.

"Scientific people," proceeded the Time Traveller, after the pause required for the proper assimilation of this, "know very well that Time is only a kind of Space. Here is a popular scientific diagram, a weather record. This line I trace with my finger shows the movement of the barometer. Yesterday it was so high, yesterday night it fell, then this morning it rose again, and so gently upward to here. Surely the mercury did not trace this line in any of the dimensions of Space generally recognized? But certainly it traced such a line, and that line, therefore, we must conclude was along the Time-Dimension."

"But," said the Medical Man, staring hard at a coal in the fire, "if Time is really only a fourth dimension of Space, why is it, and why has it always been, regarded as something different? And why cannot we move in Time as we move about in the other dimensions of Space?"

The Time Traveller smiled. "Are you sure we can move freely in Space? Right and left we can go, backward and forward freely enough, and men always have done so. I admit we move freely in

two dimensions. But how about up and down? Gravitation limits us there."

"Not exactly," said the Medical Man. "There are balloons."

"But before the balloons, save for spasmodic jumping and the inequalities of the surface, man had no freedom of vertical movement."

"Still they could move a little up and down," said the Medical Man.

"Easier, far easier down than up."

"And you cannot move at all in Time, you cannot get away from the present moment."

"My dear sir, that is just where you are wrong. That is just where the whole world has gone wrong. We are always getting away from the present moment. Our mental existences, which are immaterial and have no dimensions, are passing along the Time-Dimension with a uniform velocity from the cradle to the grave. Just as we should *travel* down if we began our existence fifty miles above the earth's surface."

"But the great difficulty is this," interrupted the Psychologist. "You *can* move about in all directions of Space, but you cannot move about in Time."

"That is the germ of my great discovery. But you are wrong to say that we cannot move about in Time. For instance, if I am recalling an incident very vividly I go back to the instant of its occurrence: I become absent-minded, as you say. I jump back for a moment. Of course we have no means of staying back for any length of Time, any more than a savage or an animal has of staying six feet above the ground. But a civilized man is better off than the savage in this respect. He can go up against gravitation in a balloon, and why should he not hope that ultimately he may be able to stop or accelerate his drift along the Time-Dimension, or even turn about and travel the other way?"

"Oh, *this*," began Filby, "is all—"

"Why not?" said the Time Traveller.

"It's against reason," said Filby.

"What reason?" said the Time Traveller.

"You can show black is white by argument," said Filby, "but you will never convince me."

"Possibly not," said the Time Traveller. "But now you begin to see the object of my investigations into the geometry of Four Dimensions. Long ago I had a vague inkling of a machine—"

"To travel through Time!" exclaimed the Very Young Man.

"That shall travel indifferently in any direction of Space and Time, as the driver determines."

Filby contented himself with laughter.

"But I have experimental verification," said the Time Traveller.

"It would be remarkably convenient for the historian," the Psychologist suggested. "One might travel back and verify the accepted account of the Battle of Hastings, for instance!"

"Don't you think you would attract attention?" said the Medical Man. "Our ancestors had no great tolerance for anachronisms."

"One might get one's Greek from the very lips of Homer and Plato," the Very Young Man thought.

"In which case they would certainly plough you for the Little-go. The German scholars have improved Greek so much."

"Then there is the future," said the Very Young Man. "Just think! One might invest all one's money, leave it to accumulate at interest, and hurry on ahead!"

"To discover a society," said I, "erected on a strictly communistic basis."

"Of all the wild extravagant theories!" began the Psychologist.

"Yes, so it seemed to me, and so I never talked of it until—"

"Experimental verification!" cried I. "You are going to verify *that*?"

"The experiment!" cried Filby, who was getting brain-weary.

"Let's see your experiment anyhow," said the Psychologist, "though it's all humbug, you know."

The Time Traveller smiled round at us. Then, still smiling faintly, and with his hands deep in his trousers pockets, he walked slowly out of the room, and we heard his slippers shuffling down the long passage to his laboratory.

The Psychologist looked at us. "I wonder what he's got?"

"Some sleight-of-hand trick or other," said the Medical Man, and Filby tried to tell us about a conjurer he had seen at Burslem; but before he had finished his preface the Time Traveller came back, and Filby's anecdote collapsed.

The thing the Time Traveller held in his hand was a glittering metallic framework, scarcely larger than a small clock, and very delicately made. There was ivory in it, and some transparent crystalline substance. And now I must be explicit, for this that follows—unless his explanation is to be accepted—is an absolutely unaccountable thing. He took one of the small octagonal tables that were scattered about the room, and set it in front of the fire, with two legs on the hearthrug. On this table he placed the mechanism. Then he drew up a chair, and sat down. The only other object on the table was a small shaded lamp, the bright light of which fell upon the model. There were also perhaps a dozen candles about, two in brass candlesticks upon the mantel and several in sconces, so that the room was brilliantly illuminated. I sat in a low arm-chair nearest the fire, and I drew this forward so as to be almost between the Time Traveller and the fireplace. Filby sat behind him, looking over his shoulder. The Medical Man and the Provincial Mayor watched him in profile from the right, the Psychologist from the left. The Very Young Man stood behind the Psychologist. We were all on the alert. It appears incredible to me that any kind of trick, however subtly conceived and however adroitly done, could have been played upon us under these conditions.

The Time Traveller looked at us, and then at the mechanism. "Well?" said the Psychologist.

"This little affair," said the Time Traveller, resting his elbows upon the table and pressing his hands together above the apparatus, "is only a model. It is my plan for a machine to travel through time. You will notice that it looks singularly askew,

and that there is an odd twinkling appearance about this bar, as though it was in some way unreal." He pointed to the part with his finger. "Also, here is one little white lever, and here is another."

The Medical Man got up out of his chair and peered into the thing. "It's beautifully made," he said.

"It took two years to make," retorted the Time Traveller. Then, when we had all imitated the action of the Medical Man, he said: "Now I want you clearly to understand that this lever, being pressed over, sends the machine gliding into the future, and this other reverses the motion. This saddle represents the seat of a time traveller. Presently I am going to press the lever, and off the machine will go. It will vanish, pass into future Time, and disappear. Have a good look at the thing. Look at the table too, and satisfy yourselves there is no trickery. I don't want to waste this model, and then be told I'm a quack."

There was a minute's pause perhaps. The Psychologist seemed about to speak to me, but changed his mind. Then the Time Traveller put forth his finger towards the lever. "No," he said suddenly. "Lend me your hand." And turning to the Psychologist, he took that individual's hand in his own and told him to put out his forefinger. So that it was the Psychologist himself who sent forth the model Time Machine on its interminable voyage. We all saw the lever turn. I am absolutely certain there was no trickery. There was a breath of wind, and the lamp flame jumped. One of the candles on the mantel was blown out, and the little machine suddenly swung round, became indistinct, was seen as a ghost for a second perhaps, as an eddy of faintly glittering brass and ivory; and it was gone—vanished! Save for the lamp the table was bare.

Everyone was silent for a minute. Then Filby said he was damned.

The Psychologist recovered from his stupor, and suddenly looked under the table. At that the Time Traveller laughed cheerfully. "Well?" he said, with a reminiscence of the

Psychologist. Then, getting up, he went to the tobacco jar on the mantel, and with his back to us began to fill his pipe.

We stared at each other. "Look here," said the Medical Man, "are you in earnest about this? Do you seriously believe that that machine has travelled into time?"

"Certainly," said the Time Traveller, stooping to light a spill at the fire. Then he turned, lighting his pipe, to look at the Psychologist's face. (The Psychologist, to show that he was not unhinged, helped himself to a cigar and tried to light it uncut.) "What is more, I have a big machine nearly finished in there"—he indicated the laboratory—"and when that is put together I mean to have a journey on my own account."

"You mean to say that that machine has travelled into the future?" said Filby.

"Into the future or the past—I don't, for certain, know which."

After an interval the Psychologist had an inspiration. "It must have gone into the past if it has gone anywhere," he said.

"Why?" said the Time Traveller.

"Because I presume that it has not moved in space, and if it travelled into the future it would still be here all this time, since it must have travelled through this time."

"But," I said, "if it travelled into the past it would have been visible when we came first into this room; and last Thursday when we were here; and the Thursday before that; and so forth!"

"Serious objections," remarked the Provincial Mayor, with an air of impartiality, turning towards the Time Traveller.

"Not a bit," said the Time Traveller, and, to the Psychologist: "You think. *You* can explain that. It's presentation below the threshold, you know, diluted presentation."

"Of course," said the Psychologist, and reassured us. "That's a simple point of psychology. I should have thought of it. It's plain enough, and helps the paradox delightfully. We cannot see it, nor can we appreciate this machine, any more than we can the spoke of a wheel spinning, or a bullet flying through the air. If

it is travelling through time fifty times or a hundred times faster than we are, if it gets through a minute while we get through a second, the impression it creates will of course be only one-fiftieth or one-hundredth of what it would make if it were not travelling in time. That's plain enough." He passed his hand through the space in which the machine had been. "You see?" he said, laughing.

We sat and stared at the vacant table for a minute or so. Then the Time Traveller asked us what we thought of it all.

"It sounds plausible enough to-night," said the Medical Man; "but wait until to-morrow. Wait for the common sense of the morning."

"Would you like to see the Time Machine itself?" asked the Time Traveller. And therewith, taking the lamp in his hand, he led the way down the long, draughty corridor to his laboratory. I remember vividly the flickering light, his queer, broad head in silhouette, the dance of the shadows, how we all followed him, puzzled but incredulous, and how there in the laboratory we beheld a larger edition of the little mechanism which we had seen vanish from before our eyes. Parts were of nickel, parts of ivory, parts had certainly been filed or sawn out of rock crystal. The thing was generally complete, but the twisted crystalline bars lay unfinished upon the bench beside some sheets of drawings, and I took one up for a better look at it. Quartz it seemed to be.

"Look here," said the Medical Man, "are you perfectly serious? Or is this a trick—like that ghost you showed us last Christmas?"

"Upon that machine," said the Time Traveller, holding the lamp aloft, "I intend to explore time. Is that plain? I was never more serious in my life."

None of us quite knew how to take it.

I caught Filby's eye over the shoulder of the Medical Man, and he winked at me solemnly.

Chapter II

I think that at that time none of us quite believed in the Time Machine. The fact is, the Time Traveller was one of those men who are too clever to be believed: you never felt that you saw all round him; you always suspected some subtle reserve, some ingenuity in ambush, behind his lucid frankness. Had Filby shown the model and explained the matter in the Time Traveller's words, we should have shown *him* far less scepticism. For we should have perceived his motives; a pork butcher could understand Filby. But the Time Traveller had more than a touch of whim among his elements, and we distrusted him. Things that would have made the fame of a less clever man seemed tricks in his hands. It is a mistake to do things too easily. The serious people who took him seriously never felt quite sure of his deportment; they were somehow aware that trusting their reputations for judgment with him was like furnishing a nursery with egg-shell china. So I don't think any of us said very much about time travelling in the interval between that Thursday and the next, though its odd potentialities ran, no doubt, in most of our minds: its plausibility, that is, its practical incredibleness, the curious possibilities of anachronism and of utter confusion it suggested. For my own part, I was particularly preoccupied with the trick of the model. That I remember discussing with the Medical Man, whom I met on Friday at the Linnaean. He said he had seen a similar thing at Tübingen, and laid considerable stress on the blowing out of the candle. But how the trick was done he could not explain.

The next Thursday I went again to Richmond—I suppose I was one of the Time Traveller's most constant guests—and, arriving late, found four or five men already assembled in his drawing-room. The Medical Man was standing before the fire with a sheet of paper in one hand and his watch in the other. I looked round

for the Time Traveller, and—"It's half-past seven now," said the Medical Man. "I suppose we'd better have dinner?"

"Where's ——?" said I, naming our host.

"You've just come? It's rather odd. He's unavoidably detained. He asks me in this note to lead off with dinner at seven if he's not back. Says he'll explain when he comes."

"It seems a pity to let the dinner spoil," said the Editor of a well-known daily paper; and thereupon the Doctor rang the bell.

The Psychologist was the only person besides the Doctor and myself who had attended the previous dinner. The other men were Blank, the Editor aforementioned, a certain journalist, and another—a quiet, shy man with a beard—whom I didn't know, and who, as far as my observation went, never opened his mouth all the evening. There was some speculation at the dinner-table about the Time Traveller's absence, and I suggested time travelling, in a half-jocular spirit. The Editor wanted that explained to him, and the Psychologist volunteered a wooden account of the "ingenious paradox and trick" we had witnessed that day week. He was in the midst of his exposition when the door from the corridor opened slowly and without noise. I was facing the door, and saw it first. "Hallo!" I said. "At last!" And the door opened wider, and the Time Traveller stood before us. I gave a cry of surprise. "Good heavens! Man, what's the matter?" cried the Medical Man, who saw him next. And the whole tableful turned towards the door.

He was in an amazing plight. His coat was dusty and dirty, and smeared with green down the sleeves; his hair disordered, and as it seemed to me greyer—either with dust and dirt or because its colour had actually faded. His face was ghastly pale; his chin had a brown cut on it—a cut half healed; his expression was haggard and drawn, as by intense suffering. For a moment he hesitated in the doorway, as if he had been dazzled by the light. Then he came into the room. He walked with just such a limp as I have seen in footsore tramps. We stared at him in silence, expecting him to speak.

He said not a word, but came painfully to the table, and made a motion towards the wine. The Editor filled a glass of champagne, and pushed it towards him. He drained it, and it seemed to do him good: for he looked round the table, and the ghost of his old smile flickered across his face. "What on earth have you been up to, man?" said the Doctor. The Time Traveller did not seem to hear. "Don't let me disturb you," he said, with a certain faltering articulation. "I'm all right." He stopped, held out his glass for more, and took it off at a draught. "That's good," he said. His eyes grew brighter, and a faint colour came into his cheeks. His glance flickered over our faces with a certain dull approval, and then went round the warm and comfortable room. Then he spoke again, still as it were feeling his way among his words. "I'm going to wash and dress, and then I'll come down and explain things . . . Save me some of that mutton. I'm starving for a bit of meat."

He looked across at the Editor, who was a rare visitor, and hoped he was all right. The Editor began a question. "Tell you presently," said the Time Traveller. "I'm—funny! Be all right in a minute."

He put down his glass, and walked towards the staircase door. Again I remarked his lameness and the soft padding sound of his footfall, and standing up in my place, I saw his feet as he went out. He had nothing on them but a pair of tattered, blood-stained socks. Then the door closed upon him. I had half a mind to follow, till I remembered how he detested any fuss about himself. For a minute, perhaps, my mind was wool-gathering. Then, "Remarkable Behaviour of an Eminent Scientist," I heard the Editor say, thinking (after his wont) in headlines. And this brought my attention back to the bright dinner-table.

"What's the game?" said the Journalist. "Has he been doing the Amateur Cadger? I don't follow." I met the eye of the Psychologist, and read my own interpretation in his face. I thought of the Time Traveller limping painfully upstairs. I don't think any one else had noticed his lameness.

The first to recover completely from this surprise was the Medical Man, who rang the bell—the Time Traveller hated to have servants waiting at dinner—for a hot plate. At that the Editor turned to his knife and fork with a grunt, and the Silent Man followed suit. The dinner was resumed. Conversation was exclamatory for a little while, with gaps of wonderment; and then the Editor got fervent in his curiosity. "Does our friend eke out his modest income with a crossing? Or has he his Nebuchadnezzar phases?" he inquired. "I feel assured it's this business of the Time Machine," I said, and took up the Psychologist's account of our previous meeting. The new guests were frankly incredulous. The Editor raised objections. "What was this time travelling? A man couldn't cover himself with dust by rolling in a paradox, could he?" And then, as the idea came home to him, he resorted to caricature. Hadn't they any clothes-brushes in the Future? The Journalist too, would not believe at any price, and joined the Editor in the easy work of heaping ridicule on the whole thing. They were both the new kind of journalist—very joyous, irreverent young men. "Our Special Correspondent in the Day after To-morrow reports," the Journalist was saying—or rather shouting—when the Time Traveller came back. He was dressed in ordinary evening clothes, and nothing save his haggard look remained of the change that had startled me.

"I say," said the Editor hilariously, "These chaps here say you have been travelling into the middle of next week! Tell us all about little Rosebery, will you? What will you take for the lot?"

The Time Traveller came to the place reserved for him without a word. He smiled quietly, in his old way. "Where's my mutton?" he said. "What a treat it is to stick a fork into meat again!"

"Story!" cried the Editor.

"Story be damned!" said the Time Traveller. "I want something to eat. I won't say a word until I get some peptone into my arteries. Thanks. And the salt."

"One word," said I. "Have you been time travelling?"

"Yes," said the Time Traveller, with his mouth full, nodding his head.

"I'd give a shilling a line for a verbatim note," said the Editor. The Time Traveller pushed his glass towards the Silent Man and rang it with his fingernail; at which the Silent Man, who had been staring at his face, started convulsively, and poured him wine. The rest of the dinner was uncomfortable. For my own part, sudden questions kept on rising to my lips, and I dare say it was the same with the others. The Journalist tried to relieve the tension by telling anecdotes of Hettie Potter. The Time Traveller devoted his attention to his dinner, and displayed the appetite of a tramp. The Medical Man smoked a cigarette, and watched the Time Traveller through his eyelashes. The Silent Man seemed even more clumsy than usual, and drank champagne with regularity and determination out of sheer nervousness. At last the Time Traveller pushed his plate away, and looked round us. "I suppose I must apologize," he said. "I was simply starving. I've had a most amazing time." He reached out his hand for a cigar, and cut the end. "But come into the smoking-room. It's too long a story to tell over greasy plates." And ringing the bell in passing, he led the way into the adjoining room.

"You have told Blank, and Dash, and Chose about the machine?" he said to me, leaning back in his easy-chair and naming the three new guests.

"But the thing's a mere paradox," said the Editor.

"I can't argue to-night. I don't mind telling you the story, but I can't argue. I will," he went on, "tell you the story of what has happened to me, if you like, but you must refrain from interruptions. I want to tell it. Badly. Most of it will sound like lying. So be it! It's true—every word of it, all the same. I was in my laboratory at four o'clock, and since then . . . I've lived eight days . . . such days as no human being ever lived before! I'm nearly worn out, but I shan't sleep till I've told this thing over to you. Then I shall go to bed. But no interruptions! Is it agreed?"

"Agreed," said the Editor, and the rest of us echoed "Agreed." And with that the Time Traveller began his story as I have set it forth. He sat back in his chair at first, and spoke like a weary man. Afterwards he got more animated. In writing it down I feel with only too much keenness the inadequacy of pen and ink—and, above all, my own inadequacy—to express its quality. You read, I will suppose, attentively enough; but you cannot see the speaker's white, sincere face in the bright circle of the little lamp, nor hear the intonation of his voice. You cannot know how his expression followed the turns of his story! Most of us hearers were in shadow, for the candles in the smoking-room had not been lighted, and only the face of the Journalist and the legs of the Silent Man from the knees downward were illuminated. At first we glanced now and again at each other. After a time we ceased to do that, and looked only at the Time Traveller's face.

Chapter III

I told some of you last Thursday of the principles of the Time Machine, and showed you the actual thing itself, incomplete in the workshop. There it is now, a little travel-worn, truly; and one of the ivory bars is cracked, and a brass rail bent; but the rest of it's sound enough. I expected to finish it on Friday, but on Friday, when the putting together was nearly done, I found that one of the nickel bars was exactly one inch too short, and this I had to get remade; so that the thing was not complete until this morning. It was at ten o'clock to-day that the first of all Time Machines began its career. I gave it a last tap, tried all the screws again, put one more drop of oil on the quartz rod, and sat myself in the saddle. I suppose a suicide who holds a pistol to his skull feels much the same wonder at what will come next as I felt then. I took the starting lever in one hand and the stopping one in the other, pressed the first, and almost immediately the second. I seemed to reel; I felt a nightmare sensation of falling; and, looking round, I saw the laboratory exactly as before. Had anything happened? For a moment I suspected that my intellect had tricked me. Then I noted the clock. A moment before, as it seemed, it had stood at a minute or so past ten; now it was nearly half-past three!

"I drew a breath, set my teeth, gripped the starting lever with both hands, and went off with a thud. The laboratory got hazy and went dark. Mrs. Watchett came in and walked, apparently without seeing me, towards the garden door. I suppose it took her a minute or so to traverse the place, but to me she seemed to shoot across the room like a rocket. I pressed the lever over to its extreme position. The night came like the turning out of a lamp, and in another moment came to-morrow. The laboratory grew faint and hazy, then fainter and ever fainter. Tomorrow night came black, then day again, night again, day again, faster

and faster still. An eddying murmur filled my ears, and a strange, dumb confusedness descended on my mind.

"I am afraid I cannot convey the peculiar sensations of time travelling. They are excessively unpleasant. There is a feeling exactly like that one has upon a switchback—of a helpless headlong motion! I felt the same horrible anticipation, too, of an imminent smash. As I put on pace, night followed day like the flapping of a black wing. The dim suggestion of the laboratory seemed presently to fall away from me, and I saw the sun hopping swiftly across the sky, leaping it every minute, and every minute marking a day. I supposed the laboratory had been destroyed and I had come into the open air. I had a dim impression of scaffolding, but I was already going too fast to be conscious of any moving things. The slowest snail that ever crawled dashed by too fast for me. The twinkling succession of darkness and light was excessively painful to the eye. Then, in the intermittent darknesses, I saw the moon spinning swiftly through her quarters from new to full, and had a faint glimpse of the circling stars. Presently, as I went on, still gaining velocity, the palpitation of night and day merged into one continuous greyness; the sky took on a wonderful deepness of blue, a splendid luminous color like that of early twilight; the jerking sun became a streak of fire, a brilliant arch, in space; the moon a fainter fluctuating band; and I could see nothing of the stars, save now and then a brighter circle flickering in the blue.

"The landscape was misty and vague. I was still on the hill-side upon which this house now stands, and the shoulder rose above me grey and dim. I saw trees growing and changing like puffs of vapour, now brown, now green; they grew, spread, shivered, and passed away. I saw huge buildings rise up faint and fair, and pass like dreams. The whole surface of the earth seemed changed—melting and flowing under my eyes. The little hands upon the dials that registered my speed raced round faster and faster. Presently I noted that the sun belt swayed up and down, from solstice to solstice, in a minute or less, and that

consequently my pace was over a year a minute; and minute by minute the white snow flashed across the world, and vanished, and was followed by the bright, brief green of spring.

"The unpleasant sensations of the start were less poignant now. They merged at last into a kind of hysterical exhilaration. I remarked indeed a clumsy swaying of the machine, for which I was unable to account. But my mind was too confused to attend to it, so with a kind of madness growing upon me, I flung myself into futurity. At first I scarce thought of stopping, scarce thought of anything but these new sensations. But presently a fresh series of impressions grew up in my mind—a certain curiosity and therewith a certain dread—until at last they took complete possession of me. What strange developments of humanity, what wonderful advances upon our rudimentary civilization, I thought, might not appear when I came to look nearly into the dim elusive world that raced and fluctuated before my eyes! I saw great and splendid architecture rising about me, more massive than any buildings of our own time, and yet, as it seemed, built of glimmer and mist. I saw a richer green flow up the hill-side, and remain there, without any wintry intermission. Even through the veil of my confusion the earth seemed very fair. And so my mind came round to the business of stopping.

"The peculiar risk lay in the possibility of my finding some substance in the space which I, or the machine, occupied. So long as I travelled at a high velocity through time, this scarcely mattered; I was, so to speak, attenuated—was slipping like a vapour through the interstices of intervening substances! But to come to a stop involved the jamming of myself, molecule by molecule, into whatever lay in my way; meant bringing my atoms into such intimate contact with those of the obstacle that a profound chemical reaction—possibly a far-reaching explosion—would result, and blow myself and my apparatus out of all possible dimensions—into the Unknown. This possibility had occurred to me again and again while I was making the machine; but then I had cheerfully accepted it as an unavoidable

risk—one of the risks a man has got to take! Now the risk was inevitable, I no longer saw it in the same cheerful light. The fact is that, insensibly, the absolute strangeness of everything, the sickly jarring and swaying of the machine, above all, the feeling of prolonged falling, had absolutely upset my nerve. I told myself that I could never stop, and with a gust of petulance I resolved to stop forthwith. Like an impatient fool, I lugged over the lever, and incontinently the thing went reeling over, and I was flung headlong through the air.

"There was the sound of a clap of thunder in my ears. I may have been stunned for a moment. A pitiless hail was hissing round me, and I was sitting on soft turf in front of the overset machine. Everything still seemed grey, but presently I remarked that the confusion in my ears was gone. I looked round me. I was on what seemed to be a little lawn in a garden, surrounded by rhododendron bushes, and I noticed that their mauve and purple blossoms were dropping in a shower under the beating of the hail-stones. The rebounding, dancing hail hung in a cloud over the machine, and drove along the ground like smoke. In a moment I was wet to the skin. 'Fine hospitality,' said I, 'to a man who has travelled innumerable years to see you.'

"Presently I thought what a fool I was to get wet. I stood up and looked round me. A colossal figure, carved apparently in some white stone, loomed indistinctly beyond the rhododendrons through the hazy downpour. But all else of the world was invisible.

"My sensations would be hard to describe. As the columns of hail grew thinner, I saw the white figure more distinctly. It was very large, for a silver birch-tree touched its shoulder. It was of white marble, in shape something like a winged sphinx, but the wings, instead of being carried vertically at the sides, were spread so that it seemed to hover. The pedestal, it appeared to me, was of bronze, and was thick with verdigris. It chanced that the face was towards me; the sightless eyes seemed to watch me; there was the faint shadow of a smile on the lips. It was greatly weather-worn, and that imparted an unpleasant suggestion of disease. I stood looking at it for a little space—half a minute, perhaps, or half an hour. It seemed to advance and to recede as the hail drove before it denser or thinner. At last I tore my eyes from it for a moment and saw that the hail curtain had worn threadbare, and that the sky was lightening with the promise of the sun.

"I looked up again at the crouching white shape, and the full temerity of my voyage came suddenly upon me. What might appear when that hazy curtain was altogether withdrawn? What might not have happened to men? What if cruelty had grown into a common passion? What if in this interval the race had lost its manliness and had developed into something inhuman, unsympathetic, and overwhelmingly powerful? I might seem some old-world savage animal, only the more dreadful and disgusting for our common likeness—a foul creature to be incontinently slain.

"Already I saw other vast shapes—huge buildings with intricate parapets and tall columns, with a wooded hill-side dimly creeping in upon me through the lessening storm. I was seized with a panic fear. I turned frantically to the Time Machine, and strove hard to readjust it. As I did so the shafts of the sun smote through the thunderstorm. The grey downpour was swept aside and vanished like the trailing garments of a ghost. Above me, in the intense blue of the summer sky, some faint brown shreds of cloud whirled into nothingness. The great buildings about me stood out clear and distinct, shining with the wet of the thunderstorm, and picked out in white by the unmelted hailstones piled along their courses. I felt naked in a strange world. I felt as perhaps a bird may feel in the clear air, knowing the hawk wings above and will swoop. My fear grew to frenzy. I took a breathing space, set my teeth, and again grappled fiercely, wrist and knee, with the machine. It gave under my desperate onset and turned over. It struck my chin violently. One hand on the saddle, the other on the lever, I stood panting heavily in attitude to mount again.

"But with this recovery of a prompt retreat my courage recovered. I looked more curiously and less fearfully at this world of the remote future. In a circular opening, high up in the wall of the nearer house, I saw a group of figures clad in rich soft robes. They had seen me, and their faces were directed towards me.

"Then I heard voices approaching me. Coming through the bushes by the White Sphinx were the heads and shoulders of men running. One of these emerged in a pathway leading straight to the little lawn upon which I stood with my machine. He was a slight creature—perhaps four feet high—clad in a purple tunic, girdled at the waist with a leather belt. Sandals or buskins—I could not clearly distinguish which—were on his feet; his legs were bare to the knees, and his head was bare. Noticing that, I noticed for the first time how warm the air was.

"He struck me as being a very beautiful and graceful creature, but indescribably frail. His flushed face reminded me of the more beautiful kind of consumptive—that hectic beauty of which we used to hear so much. At the sight of him I suddenly regained confidence. I took my hands from the machine."

Chapter IV

In another moment we were standing face to face, I and this fragile thing out of futurity. He came straight up to me and laughed into my eyes. The absence from his bearing of any sign of fear struck me at once. Then he turned to the two others who were following him and spoke to them in a strange and very sweet and liquid tongue.

"There were others coming, and presently a little group of perhaps eight or ten of these exquisite creatures were about me. One of them addressed me. It came into my head, oddly enough, that my voice was too harsh and deep for them. So I shook my head, and, pointing to my ears, shook it again. He came a step forward, hesitated, and then touched my hand. Then I felt other soft little tentacles upon my back and shoulders. They wanted to make sure I was real. There was nothing in this at all alarming. Indeed, there was something in these pretty little people that inspired confidence—a graceful gentleness, a certain childlike ease. And besides, they looked so frail that I could fancy myself flinging the whole dozen of them about like nine-pins. But I made a sudden motion to warn them when I saw their little pink hands feeling at the Time Machine. Happily then, when it was not too late, I thought of a danger I had hitherto forgotten, and reaching over the bars of the machine I unscrewed the little levers that would set it in motion, and put these in my pocket. Then I turned again to see what I could do in the way of communication.

"And then, looking more nearly into their features, I saw some further peculiarities in their Dresden china type of prettiness. Their hair, which was uniformly curly, came to a sharp end at the neck and cheek; there was not the faintest suggestion of it on the face, and their ears were singularly minute. The mouths were small, with bright red, rather thin lips, and the little chins ran

to a point. The eyes were large and mild; and—this may seem egotism on my part—I fancied even that there was a certain lack of the interest I might have expected in them.

"As they made no effort to communicate with me, but simply stood round me smiling and speaking in soft cooing notes to each other, I began the conversation. I pointed to the Time Machine and to myself. Then hesitating for a moment how to express time, I pointed to the sun. At once a quaintly pretty little figure in chequered purple and white followed my gesture, and then astonished me by imitating the sound of thunder.

"For a moment I was staggered, though the import of his gesture was plain enough. The question had come into my mind abruptly: were these creatures fools? You may hardly understand how it took me. You see I had always anticipated that the people of the year Eight Hundred and Two Thousand odd would be incredibly in front of us in knowledge, art, everything. Then one of them suddenly asked me a question that showed him to be on the intellectual level of one of our five-year-old children—asked me, in fact, if I had come from the sun in a thunderstorm! It let loose the judgment I had suspended upon their clothes, their frail light limbs, and fragile features. A flow of disappointment rushed across my mind. For a moment I felt that I had built the Time Machine in vain.

"I nodded, pointed to the sun, and gave them such a vivid rendering of a thunderclap as startled them. They all withdrew a pace or so and bowed. Then came one laughing towards me, carrying a chain of beautiful flowers altogether new to me, and put it about my neck. The idea was received with melodious applause; and presently they were all running to and fro for flowers, and laughingly flinging them upon me until I was almost smothered with blossom. You who have never seen the like can scarcely imagine what delicate and wonderful flowers countless years of culture had created. Then someone suggested that their plaything should be exhibited in the nearest building, and so I was led past the sphinx of white marble, which had seemed to watch me all the while with a smile at my astonishment, towards a vast grey edifice of fretted stone. As I went with them the memory of my confident anticipations of a profoundly grave and intellectual posterity came, with irresistible merriment, to my mind.

"The building had a huge entry, and was altogether of colossal dimensions. I was naturally most occupied with the growing crowd of little people, and with the big open portals that yawned before me shadowy and mysterious. My general impression of the world I saw over their heads was a tangled waste of beautiful bushes and flowers, a long neglected and yet weedless garden. I saw a number of tall spikes of strange white flowers, measuring a foot perhaps across the spread of the waxen petals. They grew scattered, as if wild, among the variegated shrubs, but, as I say, I did not examine them closely at this time. The Time Machine was left deserted on the turf among the rhododendrons.

"The arch of the doorway was richly carved, but naturally I did not observe the carving very narrowly, though I fancied I saw suggestions of old Phoenician decorations as I passed through, and it struck me that they were very badly broken and weather-worn. Several more brightly clad people met me in the doorway, and so we entered, I, dressed in dingy nineteenth-century garments, looking grotesque enough, garlanded with flowers, and surrounded by an eddying mass of bright, soft-colored robes and shining white limbs, in a melodious whirl of laughter and laughing speech.

"The big doorway opened into a proportionately great hall hung with brown. The roof was in shadow, and the windows, partially glazed with coloured glass and partially unglazed, admitted a tempered light. The floor was made up of huge blocks of some very hard white metal, not plates nor slabs—blocks, and it was so much worn, as I judged by the going to and fro of past generations, as to be deeply channelled along the more frequented ways. Transverse to the length were innumerable tables made of slabs of polished stone, raised perhaps a foot

from the floor, and upon these were heaps of fruits. Some I recognized as a kind of hypertrophied raspberry and orange, but for the most part they were strange.

"Between the tables was scattered a great number of cushions. Upon these my conductors seated themselves, signing for me to do likewise. With a pretty absence of ceremony they began to eat the fruit with their hands, flinging peel and stalks, and so forth, into the round openings in the sides of the tables. I was not loath to follow their example, for I felt thirsty and hungry. As I did so I surveyed the hall at my leisure.

"And perhaps the thing that struck me most was its dilapidated look. The stained-glass windows, which displayed only a geometrical pattern, were broken in many places, and the curtains that hung across the lower end were thick with dust. And it caught my eye that the corner of the marble table near me was fractured. Nevertheless, the general effect was extremely rich and picturesque. There were, perhaps, a couple of hundred people dining in the hall, and most of them, seated as near to me as they could come, were watching me with interest, their little eyes shining over the fruit they were eating. All were clad in the same soft and yet strong, silky material.

"Fruit, by the by, was all their diet. These people of the remote future were strict vegetarians, and while I was with them, in spite of some carnal cravings, I had to be frugivorous also. Indeed, I found afterwards that horses, cattle, sheep, dogs, had followed the Ichthyosaurus into extinction. But the fruits were very delightful; one, in particular, that seemed to be in season all the time I was there—a floury thing in a three-sided husk—was especially good, and I made it my staple. At first I was puzzled by all these strange fruits, and by the strange flowers I saw, but later I began to perceive their import.

"However, I am telling you of my fruit dinner in the distant future now. So soon as my appetite was a little checked, I determined to make a resolute attempt to learn the speech of these new men of mine. Clearly that was the next thing to do. The fruits seemed a convenient thing to begin upon, and holding one of these up I began a series of interrogative sounds and gestures. I had some considerable difficulty in conveying my meaning. At first my efforts met with a stare of surprise or inextinguishable laughter, but presently a fair-haired little creature seemed to grasp my intention and repeated a name. They had to chatter and explain the business at great length to each other, and my first attempts to make the exquisite little sounds of their language caused an immense amount of amusement. However, I felt like a schoolmaster amidst children, and persisted, and presently I had a score of noun substantives at least at my command; and then I got to demonstrative pronouns, and even the verb 'to eat.' But it was slow work, and the little people soon tired and wanted to get away from my interrogations, so I determined, rather of necessity, to let them give their lessons in little doses when they felt inclined. And very little doses I found they were before long, for I never met people more indolent or more easily fatigued.

"A queer thing I soon discovered about my little hosts, and that was their lack of interest. They would come to me with eager cries of astonishment, like children, but like children they would soon stop examining me and wander away after some other toy. The dinner and my conversational beginnings ended, I noted for the first time that almost all those who had surrounded me at first were gone. It is odd, too, how speedily I came to disregard these little people. I went out through the portal into the sunlit world again as soon as my hunger was satisfied. I was continually meeting more of these men of the future, who would follow me a little distance, chatter and laugh about me, and, having smiled and gesticulated in a friendly way, leave me again to my own devices.

"The calm of evening was upon the world as I emerged from the great hall, and the scene was lit by the warm glow of the setting sun. At first things were very confusing. Everything was so entirely different from the world I had known—even the flowers. The big building I had left was situated on the slope of

a broad river valley, but the Thames had shifted perhaps a mile from its present position. I resolved to mount to the summit of a crest, perhaps a mile and a half away, from which I could get a wider view of this our planet in the year Eight Hundred and Two Thousand Seven Hundred and One A.D. For that, I should explain, was the date the little dials of my machine recorded.

"As I walked I was watching for every impression that could possibly help to explain the condition of ruinous splendour in which I found the world—for ruinous it was. A little way up the hill, for instance, was a great heap of granite, bound together by masses of aluminium, a vast labyrinth of precipitous walls and crumpled heaps, amidst which were thick heaps of very beautiful pagoda-like plants—nettles possibly—but wonderfully tinted with brown about the leaves, and incapable of stinging. It was evidently the derelict remains of some vast structure, to what end built I could not determine. It was here that I was destined, at a later date, to have a very strange experience—the first intimation of a still stranger discovery—but of that I will speak in its proper place.

"Looking round with a sudden thought, from a terrace on which I rested for a while, I realised that there were no small houses to be seen. Apparently the single house, and possibly even the household, had vanished. Here and there among the greenery were palace-like buildings, but the house and the cottage, which form such characteristic features of our own English landscape, had disappeared.

"'Communism,' said I to myself.

"And on the heels of that came another thought. I looked at the half-dozen little figures that were following me. Then, in a flash, I perceived that all had the same form of costume, the same soft hairless visage, and the same girlish rotundity of limb. It may seem strange, perhaps, that I had not noticed this before. But everything was so strange. Now, I saw the fact plainly enough. In costume, and in all the differences of texture and bearing that now mark off the sexes from each other, these

people of the future were alike. And the children seemed to my eyes to be but the miniatures of their parents. I judged, then, that the children of that time were extremely precocious, physically at least, and I found afterwards abundant verification of my opinion.

"Seeing the ease and security in which these people were living, I felt that this close resemblance of the sexes was after all what one would expect; for the strength of a man and the softness of a woman, the institution of the family, and the differentiation of occupations are mere militant necessities of an age of physical force; where population is balanced and abundant, much childbearing becomes an evil rather than a blessing to the State; where violence comes but rarely and off-spring are secure, there is less necessity—indeed there is no necessity—for an efficient family, and the specialization of the sexes with reference to their children's needs disappears. We see some beginnings of this even in our own time, and in this future age it was complete. This, I must remind you, was my speculation at the time. Later, I was to appreciate how far it fell short of the reality.

"While I was musing upon these things, my attention was attracted by a pretty little structure, like a well under a cupola. I thought in a transitory way of the oddness of wells still existing, and then resumed the thread of my speculations. There were no large buildings towards the top of the hill, and as my walking powers were evidently miraculous, I was presently left alone for the first time. With a strange sense of freedom and adventure I pushed on up to the crest.

"There I found a seat of some yellow metal that I did not recognize, corroded in places with a kind of pinkish rust and half smothered in soft moss, the arm-rests cast and filed into the resemblance of griffins' heads. I sat down on it, and I surveyed the broad view of our old world under the sunset of that long day. It was as sweet and fair a view as I have ever seen. The sun had already gone below the horizon and the west was flaming gold, touched with some horizontal bars of purple and crimson.

Below was the valley of the Thames, in which the river lay like a band of burnished steel. I have already spoken of the great palaces dotted about among the variegated greenery, some in ruins and some still occupied. Here and there rose a white or silvery figure in the waste garden of the earth, here and there came the sharp vertical line of some cupola or obelisk. There were no hedges, no signs of proprietary rights, no evidences of agriculture; the whole earth had become a garden.

"So watching, I began to put my interpretation upon the things I had seen, and as it shaped itself to me that evening, my interpretation was something in this way. (Afterwards I found I had got only a half-truth—or only a glimpse of one facet of the truth.)

"It seemed to me that I had happened upon humanity upon the wane. The ruddy sunset set me thinking of the sunset of mankind. For the first time I began to realize an odd consequence of the social effort in which we are at present engaged. And yet, come to think, it is a logical consequence enough. Strength is the outcome of need; security sets a premium on feebleness. The work of ameliorating the conditions of life—the true civilizing process that makes life more and more secure—had gone steadily on to a climax. One triumph of a united humanity over Nature had followed another. Things that are now mere dreams had become projects deliberately put in hand and carried forward. And the harvest was what I saw!

"After all, the sanitation and the agriculture of to-day are still in the rudimentary stage. The science of our time has attacked but a little department of the field of human disease, but even so, it spreads its operations very steadily and persistently. Our agriculture and horticulture destroy a weed just here and there and cultivate perhaps a score or so of wholesome plants, leaving the greater number to fight out a balance as they can. We improve our favourite plants and animals—and how few they are—gradually by selective breeding; now a new and better peach, now a seedless grape, now a sweeter and larger flower, now a more convenient breed of cattle. We improve them gradually, because our ideals are vague and tentative, and our knowledge is very limited; because Nature, too, is shy and slow in our clumsy hands. Some day all this will be better organized, and still better. That is the drift of the current in spite of the eddies. The whole world will be intelligent, educated, and cooperating; things will move faster and faster towards the subjugation of Nature. In the end, wisely and carefully we shall readjust the balance of animal and vegetable life to suit our human needs.

"This adjustment, I say, must have been done, and done well; done indeed for all Time, in the space of Time across which my machine had leaped. The air was free from gnats, the earth from weeds or fungi; everywhere were fruits and sweet and delightful flowers; brilliant butterflies flew hither and thither. The ideal of preventive medicine was attained. Diseases had been stamped out. I saw no evidence of any contagious diseases during all my stay. And I shall have to tell you later that even the processes of putrefaction and decay had been profoundly affected by these changes.

"Social triumphs, too, had been effected. I saw mankind housed in splendid shelters, gloriously clothed, and as yet I had found them engaged in no toil. There were no signs of struggle, neither social nor economical struggle. The shop, the advertisement, traffic, all that commerce which constitutes the body of our world, was gone. It was natural on that golden evening that I should jump at the idea of a social paradise. The difficulty of increasing population had been met, I guessed, and population had ceased to increase.

"But with this change in condition comes inevitably adaptations to the change. What, unless biological science is a mass of errors, is the cause of human intelligence and vigour? Hardship and freedom: conditions under which the active, strong, and subtle survive and the weaker go to the wall; conditions that put a premium upon the loyal alliance of capable men, upon self-restraint, patience, and decision. And the institution of the

family, and the emotions that arise therein, the fierce jealousy, the tenderness for offspring, parental self-devotion, all found their justification and support in the imminent dangers of the young. *Now*, where are these imminent dangers? There is a sentiment arising, and it will grow, against connubial jealousy, against fierce maternity, against passion of all sorts; unnecessary things now, and things that make us uncomfortable, savage survivals, discords in a refined and pleasant life.

"I thought of the physical slightness of the people, their lack of intelligence, and those big abundant ruins, and it strengthened my belief in a perfect conquest of Nature. For after the battle comes Quiet. Humanity had been strong, energetic, and intelligent, and had used all its abundant vitality to alter the conditions under which it lived. And now came the reaction of the altered conditions.

"Under the new conditions of perfect comfort and security, that restless energy, that with us is strength, would become weakness. Even in our own time certain tendencies and desires, once necessary to survival, are a constant source of failure. Physical courage and the love of battle, for instance, are no great help—may even be hindrances—to a civilized man. And in a state of physical balance and security, power, intellectual as well as physical, would be out of place. For countless years I judged there had been no danger of war or solitary violence, no danger from wild beasts, no wasting disease to require strength of constitution, no need of toil. For such a life, what we should call the weak are as well equipped as the strong, are indeed no longer weak. Better equipped indeed they are, for the strong would be fretted by an energy for which there was no outlet. No doubt the exquisite beauty of the buildings I saw was the outcome of the last surgings of the now purposeless energy of mankind before it settled down into perfect harmony with the conditions under which it lived—the flourish of that triumph which began the last great peace. This has ever been the fate of energy in security; it takes to art and to eroticism, and then come languor and decay.

"Even this artistic impetus would at last die away—had almost died in the Time I saw. To adorn themselves with flowers, to dance, to sing in the sunlight: so much was left of the artistic spirit, and no more. Even that would fade in the end into a contented inactivity. We are kept keen on the grindstone of pain and necessity, and, it seemed to me, that here was that hateful grindstone broken at last!

"As I stood there in the gathering dark I thought that in this simple explanation I had mastered the problem of the world—mastered the whole secret of these delicious people. Possibly the checks they had devised for the increase of population had succeeded too well, and their numbers had rather diminished than kept stationary. That would account for the abandoned ruins. Very simple was my explanation, and plausible enough—as most wrong theories are!"

Chapter V

As I stood there musing over this too perfect triumph of man, the full moon, yellow and gibbous, came up out of an overflow of silver light in the north-east. The bright little figures ceased to move about below, a noiseless owl flitted by, and I shivered with the chill of the night. I determined to descend and find where I could sleep.

"I looked for the building I knew. Then my eye travelled along to the figure of the White Sphinx upon the pedestal of bronze, growing distinct as the light of the rising moon grew brighter. I could see the silver birch against it. There was the tangle of rhododendron bushes, black in the pale light, and there was the little lawn. I looked at the lawn again. A queer doubt chilled my complacency. "No," said I stoutly to myself, "that was not the lawn."

"But it was the lawn. For the white leprous face of the sphinx was towards it. Can you imagine what I felt as this conviction came home to me? But you cannot. The Time Machine was gone!

"At once, like a lash across the face, came the possibility of losing my own age, of being left helpless in this strange new world. The bare thought of it was an actual physical sensation. I could feel it grip me at the throat and stop my breathing. In another moment I was in a passion of fear and running with great leaping strides down the slope. Once I fell headlong and cut my face; I lost no time in stanching the blood, but jumped up and ran on, with a warm trickle down my cheek and chin. All the time I ran I was saying to myself: 'They have moved it a little, pushed it under the bushes out of the way.' Nevertheless, I ran with all my might. All the time, with the certainty that sometimes comes with excessive dread, I knew that such assurance was folly, knew instinctively that the machine was removed out of my reach. My breath came with pain. I suppose I covered the whole distance from the hill crest to the little lawn, two miles perhaps, in ten minutes. And I am not a young man. I cursed aloud, as I ran, at my confident folly in leaving the machine, wasting good breath thereby. I cried aloud, and none answered. Not a creature seemed to be stirring in that moonlit world.

"When I reached the lawn my worst fears were realised. Not a trace of the thing was to be seen. I felt faint and cold when I faced the empty space among the black tangle of bushes. I ran round it furiously, as if the thing might be hidden in a corner, and then stopped abruptly, with my hands clutching my hair. Above me towered the sphinx, upon the bronze pedestal, white, shining, leprous, in the light of the rising moon. It seemed to smile in mockery of my dismay.

"I might have consoled myself by imagining the little people had put the mechanism in some shelter for me, had I not felt assured of their physical and intellectual inadequacy. That is what dismayed me: the sense of some hitherto unsuspected power, through whose intervention my invention had vanished. Yet, for one thing I felt assured: unless some other age had produced its exact duplicate, the machine could not have moved in time. The attachment of the levers—I will show you the method later—prevented anyone from tampering with it in that way when they were removed. It had moved, and was hid, only in space. But then, where could it be?

"I think I must have had a kind of frenzy. I remember running violently in and out among the moonlit bushes all round the sphinx, and startling some white animal that, in the dim light, I took for a small deer. I remember, too, late that night, beating the bushes with my clenched fist until my knuckles were gashed and bleeding from the broken twigs. Then, sobbing and raving in my anguish of mind, I went down to the great building of stone. The big hall was dark, silent, and deserted. I slipped on the uneven floor, and fell over one of the malachite tables, almost breaking my shin. I lit a match and went on past the dusty curtains, of which I have told you.

"There I found a second great hall covered with cushions, upon which, perhaps, a score or so of the little people were sleeping. I have no doubt they found my second appearance strange enough, coming suddenly out of the quiet darkness with inarticulate noises and the splutter and flare of a match. For they had forgotten about matches. 'Where is my Time Machine?' I began, bawling like an angry child, laying hands upon them and shaking them up together. It must have been very queer to them. Some laughed, most of them looked sorely frightened. When I saw them standing round me, it came into my head that I was doing as foolish a thing as it was possible for me to do under the circumstances, in trying to revive the sensation of fear. For, reasoning from their daylight behaviour, I thought that fear must be forgotten.

"Abruptly, I dashed down the match, and, knocking one of the people over in my course, went blundering across the big dining-hall again, out under the moonlight. I heard cries of terror and their little feet running and stumbling this way and that. I do not remember all I did as the moon crept up the sky. I suppose it was the unexpected nature of my loss that maddened me. I felt hopelessly cut off from my own kind—a strange animal in an unknown world. I must have raved to and fro, screaming and crying upon God and Fate. I have a memory of horrible fatigue, as the long night of despair wore away; of looking in this impossible place and that; of groping among moonlit ruins and touching strange creatures in the black shadows; at last, of lying on the ground near the sphinx and weeping with absolute wretchedness. I had nothing left but misery. Then I slept, and when I woke again it was full day, and a couple of sparrows were hopping round me on the turf within reach of my arm.

"I sat up in the freshness of the morning, trying to remember how I had got there, and why I had such a profound sense of desertion and despair. Then things came clear in my mind. With the plain, reasonable daylight, I could look my circumstances fairly in the face. I saw the wild folly of my frenzy overnight, and

I could reason with myself. 'Suppose the worst?' I said. 'Suppose the machine altogether lost—perhaps destroyed? It behoves me to be calm and patient, to learn the way of the people, to get a clear idea of the method of my loss, and the means of getting materials and tools; so that in the end, perhaps, I may make another.' That would be my only hope, perhaps, but better than despair. And, after all, it was a beautiful and curious world.

"But probably the machine had only been taken away. Still, I must be calm and patient, find its hiding-place, and recover it by force or cunning. And with that I scrambled to my feet and looked about me, wondering where I could bathe. I felt weary, stiff, and travel-soiled. The freshness of the morning made me desire an equal freshness. I had exhausted my emotion. Indeed, as I went about my business, I found myself wondering at my intense excitement overnight. I made a careful examination of the ground about the little lawn. I wasted some time in futile questionings, conveyed, as well as I was able, to such of the little people as came by. They all failed to understand my gestures; some were simply stolid, some thought it was a jest and laughed at me. I had the hardest task in the world to keep my hands off their pretty laughing faces. It was a foolish impulse, but the devil begotten of fear and blind anger was ill curbed and still eager to take advantage of my perplexity. The turf gave better counsel. I found a groove ripped in it, about midway between the pedestal of the sphinx and the marks of my feet where, on arrival, I had struggled with the overturned machine. There were other signs of removal about, with queer narrow footprints like those I could imagine made by a sloth. This directed my closer attention to the pedestal. It was, as I think I have said, of bronze. It was not a mere block, but highly decorated with deep framed panels on either side. I went and rapped at these. The pedestal was hollow. Examining the panels with care I found them discontinuous with the frames. There were no handles or keyholes, but possibly the panels, if they were doors, as I supposed, opened from within. One thing was clear enough to

my mind. It took no very great mental effort to infer that my Time Machine was inside that pedestal. But how it got there was a different problem.

"I saw the heads of two orange-clad people coming through the bushes and under some blossom-covered apple-trees towards me. I turned smiling to them and beckoned them to me. They came, and then, pointing to the bronze pedestal, I tried to intimate my wish to open it. But at my first gesture towards this they behaved very oddly. I don't know how to convey their expression to you. Suppose you were to use a grossly improper gesture to a delicate-minded woman—it is how she would look. They went off as if they had received the last possible insult. I tried a sweet-looking little chap in white next, with exactly the same result. Somehow, his manner made me feel ashamed of myself. But, as you know, I wanted the Time Machine, and I tried him once more. As he turned off, like the others, my temper got the better of me. In three strides I was after him, had him by the loose part of his robe round the neck, and began dragging him towards the sphinx. Then I saw the horror and repugnance of his face, and all of a sudden I let him go.

"But I was not beaten yet. I banged with my fist at the bronze panels. I thought I heard something stir inside—to be explicit, I thought I heard a sound like a chuckle—but I must have been mistaken. Then I got a big pebble from the river, and came and hammered till I had flattened a coil in the decorations, and the verdigris came off in powdery flakes. The delicate little people must have heard me hammering in gusty outbreaks a mile away on either hand, but nothing came of it. I saw a crowd of them upon the slopes, looking furtively at me. At last, hot and tired, I sat down to watch the place. But I was too restless to watch long; I am too Occidental for a long vigil. I could work at a problem for years, but to wait inactive for twenty-four hours—that is another matter.

"I got up after a time, and began walking aimlessly through the bushes towards the hill again. 'Patience,' said I to myself.

'If you want your machine again you must leave that sphinx alone. If they mean to take your machine away, it's little good your wrecking their bronze panels, and if they don't, you will get it back as soon as you can ask for it. To sit among all those unknown things before a puzzle like that is hopeless. That way lies monomania. Face this world. Learn its ways, watch it, be careful of too hasty guesses at its meaning. In the end you will find clues to it all.' Then suddenly the humour of the situation came into my mind: the thought of the years I had spent in study and toil to get into the future age, and now my passion of anxiety to get out of it. I had made myself the most complicated and the most hopeless trap that ever a man devised. Although it was at my own expense, I could not help myself. I laughed aloud.

"Going through the big palace, it seemed to me that the little people avoided me. It may have been my fancy, or it may have had something to do with my hammering at the gates of bronze. Yet I felt tolerably sure of the avoidance. I was careful, however, to show no concern and to abstain from any pursuit of them, and in the course of a day or two things got back to the old footing. I made what progress I could in the language, and in addition I pushed my explorations here and there. Either I missed some subtle point or their language was excessively simple—almost exclusively composed of concrete substantives and verbs. There seemed to be few, if any, abstract terms, or little use of figurative language. Their sentences were usually simple and of two words, and I failed to convey or understand any but the simplest propositions. I determined to put the thought of my Time Machine and the mystery of the bronze doors under the sphinx as much as possible in a corner of memory, until my growing knowledge would lead me back to them in a natural way. Yet a certain feeling, you may understand, tethered me in a circle of a few miles round the point of my arrival.

"So far as I could see, all the world displayed the same exuberant richness as the Thames valley. From every hill I

climbed I saw the same abundance of splendid buildings, endlessly varied in material and style, the same clustering thickets of evergreens, the same blossom-laden trees and tree-ferns. Here and there water shone like silver, and beyond, the land rose into blue undulating hills, and so faded into the serenity of the sky. A peculiar feature, which presently attracted my attention, was the presence of certain circular wells, several, as it seemed to me, of a very great depth. One lay by the path up the hill, which I had followed during my first walk. Like the others, it was rimmed with bronze, curiously wrought, and protected by a little cupola from the rain. Sitting by the side of these wells, and peering down into the shafted darkness, I could see no gleam of water, nor could I start any reflection with a lighted match. But in all of them I heard a certain sound: a thud—thud—thud, like the beating of some big engine; and I discovered, from the flaring of my matches, that a steady current of air set down the shafts. Further, I threw a scrap of paper into the throat of one, and, instead of fluttering slowly down, it was at once sucked swiftly out of sight.

"After a time, too, I came to connect these wells with tall towers standing here and there upon the slopes; for above them there was often just such a flicker in the air as one sees on a hot day above a sun-scorched beach. Putting things together, I reached a strong suggestion of an extensive system of subterranean ventilation, whose true import it was difficult to imagine. I was at first inclined to associate it with the sanitary apparatus of these people. It was an obvious conclusion, but it was absolutely wrong.

"And here I must admit that I learned very little of drains and bells and modes of conveyance, and the like conveniences, during my time in this real future. In some of these visions of Utopias and coming times which I have read, there is a vast amount of detail about building, and social arrangements, and so forth. But while such details are easy enough to obtain when the whole world is contained in one's imagination, they are altogether inaccessible to a real traveller amid such realities as I found here. Conceive the tale of London which a negro, fresh from Central Africa, would take back to his tribe! What would he know of railway companies, of social movements, of telephone and telegraph wires, of the Parcels Delivery Company, and postal orders and the like? Yet we, at least, should be willing enough to explain these things to him! And even of what he knew, how much could he make his untravelled friend either apprehend or believe? Then, think how narrow the gap between a negro and a white man of our own times, and how wide the interval between myself and these of the Golden Age! I was sensible of much which was unseen, and which contributed to my comfort; but save for a general impression of automatic organization, I fear I can convey very little of the difference to your mind.

"In the matter of sepulture, for instance, I could see no signs of crematoria nor anything suggestive of tombs. But it occurred to me that, possibly, there might be cemeteries (or crematoria) somewhere beyond the range of my explorings. This, again, was a question I deliberately put to myself, and my curiosity was at first entirely defeated upon the point. The thing puzzled me, and I was led to make a further remark, which puzzled me still more: that aged and infirm among this people there were none.

"I must confess that my satisfaction with my first theories of an automatic civilization and a decadent humanity did not long endure. Yet I could think of no other. Let me put my difficulties. The several big palaces I had explored were mere living places, great dining-halls and sleeping apartments. I could find no machinery, no appliances of any kind. Yet these people were clothed in pleasant fabrics that must at times need renewal, and their sandals, though undecorated, were fairly complex specimens of metalwork. Somehow such things must be made. And the little people displayed no vestige of a creative tendency. There were no shops, no workshops, no sign of importations among them. They spent all their time in playing gently, in bathing in the river, in making love in a half-playful fashion, in

eating fruit and sleeping. I could not see how things were kept going.

"Then, again, about the Time Machine: something, I knew not what, had taken it into the hollow pedestal of the White Sphinx. Why? For the life of me I could not imagine. Those waterless wells, too, those flickering pillars. I felt I lacked a clue. I felt—how shall I put it? Suppose you found an inscription, with sentences here and there in excellent plain English, and interpolated therewith, others made up of words, of letters even, absolutely unknown to you? Well, on the third day of my visit, that was how the world of Eight Hundred and Two Thousand Seven Hundred and One presented itself to me!

"That day, too, I made a friend—of a sort. It happened that, as I was watching some of the little people bathing in a shallow, one of them was seized with cramp and began drifting downstream. The main current ran rather swiftly, but not too strongly for even a moderate swimmer. It will give you an idea, therefore, of the strange deficiency in these creatures, when I tell you that none made the slightest attempt to rescue the weakly crying little thing which was drowning before their eyes. When I realised this, I hurriedly slipped off my clothes, and, wading in at a point lower down, I caught the poor mite and drew her safe to land. A little rubbing of the limbs soon brought her round, and I had the satisfaction of seeing she was all right before I left her. I had got to such a low estimate of her kind that I did not expect any gratitude from her. In that, however, I was wrong.

"This happened in the morning. In the afternoon I met my little woman, as I believe it was, as I was returning towards my centre from an exploration, and she received me with cries of delight and presented me with a big garland of flowers—evidently made for me and me alone. The thing took my imagination. Very possibly I had been feeling desolate. At any rate I did my best to display my appreciation of the gift. We were soon seated together in a little stone arbour, engaged in conversation, chiefly of smiles. The creature's friendliness affected me exactly as a child's might have done. We passed each other flowers, and she kissed my hands. I did the same to hers. Then I tried talk, and found that her name was Weena, which, though I don't know what it meant, somehow seemed appropriate enough. That was the beginning of a queer friendship which lasted a week, and ended—as I will tell you!

"She was exactly like a child. She wanted to be with me always. She tried to follow me everywhere, and on my next journey out and about it went to my heart to tire her down, and leave her at last, exhausted and calling after me rather plaintively. But the problems of the world had to be mastered. I had not, I said to myself, come into the future to carry on a miniature flirtation. Yet her distress when I left her was very great, her expostulations at the parting were sometimes frantic, and I think, altogether, I had as much trouble as comfort from her devotion. Nevertheless she was, somehow, a very great comfort. I thought it was mere childish affection that made her cling to me. Until it was too late, I did not clearly know what I had inflicted upon her when I left her. Nor until it was too late did I clearly understand what she was to me. For, by merely seeming fond of me, and showing in her weak, futile way that she cared for me, the little doll of a creature presently gave my return to the neighbourhood of the White Sphinx almost the feeling of coming home; and I would watch for her tiny figure of white and gold so soon as I came over the hill.

"It was from her, too, that I learned that fear had not yet left the world. She was fearless enough in the daylight, and she had the oddest confidence in me; for once, in a foolish moment, I made threatening grimaces at her, and she simply laughed at them. But she dreaded the dark, dreaded shadows, dreaded black things. Darkness to her was the one thing dreadful. It was a singularly passionate emotion, and it set me thinking and observing. I discovered then, among other things, that these little people gathered into the great houses after dark, and slept in droves. To enter upon them without a light was to put them

into a tumult of apprehension. I never found one out of doors, or one sleeping alone within doors, after dark. Yet I was still such a blockhead that I missed the lesson of that fear, and in spite of Weena's distress I insisted upon sleeping away from these slumbering multitudes.

"It troubled her greatly, but in the end her odd affection for me triumphed, and for five of the nights of our acquaintance, including the last night of all, she slept with her head pillowed on my arm. But my story slips away from me as I speak of her. It must have been the night before her rescue that I was awakened about dawn. I had been restless, dreaming most disagreeably that I was drowned, and that sea anemones were feeling over my face with their soft palps. I woke with a start, and with an odd fancy that some greyish animal had just rushed out of the chamber. I tried to get to sleep again, but I felt restless and uncomfortable. It was that dim grey hour when things are just creeping out of darkness, when everything is colourless and clear cut, and yet unreal. I got up, and went down into the great hall, and so out upon the flagstones in front of the palace. I thought I would make a virtue of necessity, and see the sunrise.

"The moon was setting, and the dying moonlight and the first pallor of dawn were mingled in a ghastly half-light. The bushes were inky black, the ground a sombre grey, the sky colourless and cheerless. And up the hill I thought I could see ghosts. There several times, as I scanned the slope, I saw white figures. Twice I fancied I saw a solitary white, ape-like creature running rather quickly up the hill, and once near the ruins I saw a leash of them carrying some dark body. They moved hastily. I did not see what became of them. It seemed that they vanished among the bushes. The dawn was still indistinct, you must understand. I was feeling that chill, uncertain, early-morning feeling you may have known. I doubted my eyes.

"As the eastern sky grew brighter, and the light of the day came on and its vivid colouring returned upon the world once more, I scanned the view keenly. But I saw no vestige of my white figures. They were mere creatures of the half light. 'They must have been ghosts,' I said; 'I wonder whence they dated.' For a queer notion of Grant Allen's came into my head, and amused me. If each generation die and leave ghosts, he argued, the world at last will get overcrowded with them. On that theory they would have grown innumerable some Eight Hundred Thousand Years hence, and it was no great wonder to see four at once. But the jest was unsatisfying, and I was thinking of these figures all the morning, until Weena's rescue drove them out of my head. I associated them in some indefinite way with the white animal I had startled in my first passionate search for the Time Machine. But Weena was a pleasant substitute. Yet all the same, they were soon destined to take far deadlier possession of my mind.

"I think I have said how much hotter than our own was the weather of this Golden Age. I cannot account for it. It may be that the sun was hotter, or the earth nearer the sun. It is usual to assume that the sun will go on cooling steadily in the future. But people, unfamiliar with such speculations as those of the younger Darwin, forget that the planets must ultimately fall back one by one into the parent body. As these catastrophes occur, the sun will blaze with renewed energy; and it may be that some inner planet had suffered this fate. Whatever the reason, the fact remains that the sun was very much hotter than we know it.

"Well, one very hot morning—my fourth, I think—as I was seeking shelter from the heat and glare in a colossal ruin near the great house where I slept and fed, there happened this strange thing: Clambering among these heaps of masonry, I found a narrow gallery, whose end and side windows were blocked by fallen masses of stone. By contrast with the brilliancy outside, it seemed at first impenetrably dark to me. I entered it groping, for the change from light to blackness made spots of colour swim before me. Suddenly I halted spellbound. A pair of eyes, luminous by reflection against the daylight without, was watching me out of the darkness.

"The old instinctive dread of wild beasts came upon me. I clenched my hands and steadfastly looked into the glaring eyeballs. I was afraid to turn. Then the thought of the absolute security in which humanity appeared to be living came to my mind. And then I remembered that strange terror of the dark. Overcoming my fear to some extent, I advanced a step and spoke. I will admit that my voice was harsh and ill-controlled. I put out my hand and touched something soft. At once the eyes darted sideways, and something white ran past me. I turned with my heart in my mouth, and saw a queer little ape-like figure, its head held down in a peculiar manner, running across the sunlit space behind me. It blundered against a block of granite, staggered aside, and in a moment was hidden in a black shadow beneath another pile of ruined masonry.

"My impression of it is, of course, imperfect; but I know it was a dull white, and had strange large greyish-red eyes; also that there was flaxen hair on its head and down its back. But, as I say, it went too fast for me to see distinctly. I cannot even say whether it ran on all-fours, or only with its forearms held very low. After an instant's pause I followed it into the second heap of ruins. I could not find it at first; but, after a time in the profound obscurity, I came upon one of those round well-like openings of which I have told you, half closed by a fallen pillar. A sudden thought came to me. Could this Thing have vanished down the shaft? I lit a match, and, looking down, I saw a small, white, moving creature, with large bright eyes which regarded me steadfastly as it retreated. It made me shudder. It was so like a human spider! It was clambering down the wall, and now I saw for the first time a number of metal foot and hand rests forming a kind of ladder down the shaft. Then the light burned my fingers and fell out of my hand, going out as it dropped, and when I had lit another the little monster had disappeared.

"I do not know how long I sat peering down that well. It was not for some time that I could succeed in persuading myself that the thing I had seen was human. But, gradually, the truth dawned on me: that Man had not remained one species, but had differentiated into two distinct animals: that my graceful children of the Upper World were not the sole descendants of our generation, but that this bleached, obscene, nocturnal Thing, which had flashed before me, was also heir to all the ages.

"I thought of the flickering pillars and of my theory of an underground ventilation. I began to suspect their true import. And what, I wondered, was this Lemur doing in my scheme of a perfectly balanced organization? How was it related to the indolent serenity of the beautiful Upper Worlders? And what was hidden down there, at the foot of that shaft? I sat upon the edge of the well telling myself that, at any rate, there was nothing to fear, and that there I must descend for the solution of my difficulties. And withal I was absolutely afraid to go! As I hesitated, two of the beautiful Upper World people came running in their amorous sport across the daylight in the shadow. The male pursued the female, flinging flowers at her as he ran.

"They seemed distressed to find me, my arm against the overturned pillar, peering down the well. Apparently it was considered bad form to remark these apertures; for when I pointed to this one, and tried to frame a question about it in their tongue, they were still more visibly distressed and turned away. But they were interested by my matches, and I struck some to amuse them. I tried them again about the well, and again I failed. So presently I left them, meaning to go back to Weena, and see what I could get from her. But my mind was already in revolution; my guesses and impressions were slipping and sliding to a new adjustment. I had now a clue to the import of these wells, to the ventilating towers, to the mystery of the ghosts; to say nothing of a hint at the meaning of the bronze gates and the fate of the Time Machine! And very vaguely there came a suggestion towards the solution of the economic problem that had puzzled me.

"Here was the new view. Plainly, this second species of Man was subterranean. There were three circumstances in particular

which made me think that its rare emergence above ground was the outcome of a long-continued underground habit. In the first place, there was the bleached look common in most animals that live largely in the dark—the white fish of the Kentucky caves, for instance. Then, those large eyes, with that capacity for reflecting light, are common features of nocturnal things—witness the owl and the cat. And last of all, that evident confusion in the sunshine, that hasty yet fumbling awkward flight towards dark shadow, and that peculiar carriage of the head while in the light—all reinforced the theory of an extreme sensitiveness of the retina.

"Beneath my feet, then, the earth must be tunnelled enormously, and these tunnellings were the habitat of the new race. The presence of ventilating shafts and wells along the hill slopes—everywhere, in fact, except along the river valley—showed how universal were its ramifications. What so natural, then, as to assume that it was in this artificial Underworld that such work as was necessary to the comfort of the daylight race was done? The notion was so plausible that I at once accepted it, and went on to assume the *how* of this splitting of the human species. I dare say you will anticipate the shape of my theory; though, for myself, I very soon felt that it fell far short of the truth.

"At first, proceeding from the problems of our own age, it seemed clear as daylight to me that the gradual widening of the present merely temporary and social difference between the Capitalist and the Labourer, was the key to the whole position. No doubt it will seem grotesque enough to you—and wildly incredible!—and yet even now there are existing circumstances to point that way. There is a tendency to utilize underground space for the less ornamental purposes of civilization; there is the Metropolitan Railway in London, for instance, there are new electric railways, there are subways, there are underground workrooms and restaurants, and they increase and multiply. Evidently, I thought, this tendency had increased till Industry

had gradually lost its birthright in the sky. I mean that it had gone deeper and deeper into larger and ever larger underground factories, spending a still-increasing amount of its time therein, till, in the end—! Even now, does not an East-end worker live in such artificial conditions as practically to be cut off from the natural surface of the earth?

"Again, the exclusive tendency of richer people—due, no doubt, to the increasing refinement of their education, and the widening gulf between them and the rude violence of the poor—is already leading to the closing, in their interest, of considerable portions of the surface of the land. About London, for instance, perhaps half the prettier country is shut in against intrusion. And this same widening gulf—which is due to the length and expense of the higher educational process and the increased facilities for and temptations towards refined habits on the part of the rich—will make that exchange between class and class, that promotion by intermarriage which at present retards the splitting of our species along lines of social stratification, less and less frequent. So, in the end, above ground you must have the Haves, pursuing pleasure and comfort and beauty, and below ground the Have-nots, the Workers getting continually adapted to the conditions of their labour. Once they were there, they would no doubt have to pay rent, and not a little of it, for the ventilation of their caverns; and if they refused, they would starve or be suffocated for arrears. Such of them as were so constituted as to be miserable and rebellious would die; and, in the end, the balance being permanent, the survivors would become as well adapted to the conditions of underground life, and as happy in their way, as the Upper World people were to theirs. As it seemed to me, the refined beauty and the etiolated pallor followed naturally enough.

"The great triumph of Humanity I had dreamed of took a different shape in my mind. It had been no such triumph of moral education and general cooperation as I had imagined. Instead, I saw a real aristocracy, armed with a perfected science

and working to a logical conclusion the industrial system of to-day. Its triumph had not been simply a triumph over Nature, but a triumph over Nature and the fellow-man. This, I must warn you, was my theory at the time. I had no convenient cicerone in the pattern of the Utopian books. My explanation may be absolutely wrong. I still think it is the most plausible one. But even on this supposition the balanced civilization that was at last attained must have long since passed its zenith, and was now far fallen into decay. The too-perfect security of the Upper-worlders had led them to a slow movement of degeneration, to a general dwindling in size, strength, and intelligence. That I could see clearly enough already. What had happened to the Undergrounders I did not yet suspect; but from what I had seen of the 'Morlocks'—that, by the by, was the name by which these creatures were called—I could imagine that the modification of the human type was even far more profound than among the 'Eloi,' the beautiful race that I already knew.

"Then came troublesome doubts. Why had the Morlocks taken my Time Machine? For I felt sure it was they who had taken it. Why, too, if the Eloi were masters, could they not restore the machine to me? And why were they so terribly afraid of the dark? I proceeded, as I have said, to question Weena about this Under-world, but here again I was disappointed. At first she would not understand my questions, and presently she refused to answer them. She shivered as though the topic was unendurable. And when I pressed her, perhaps a little harshly, she burst into tears. They were the only tears, except my own, I ever saw in that Golden Age. When I saw them I ceased abruptly to trouble about the Morlocks, and was only concerned in banishing these signs of the human inheritance from Weena's eyes. And very soon she was smiling and clapping her hands, while I solemnly burned a match."

Chapter VI

It may seem odd to you, but it was two days before I could follow up the newfound clue in what was manifestly the proper way. I felt a peculiar shrinking from those pallid bodies. They were just the half-bleached colour of the worms and things one sees preserved in spirit in a zoological museum. And they were filthily cold to the touch. Probably my shrinking was largely due to the sympathetic influence of the Eloi, whose disgust of the Morlocks I now began to appreciate.

"The next night I did not sleep well. Probably my health was a little disordered. I was oppressed with perplexity and doubt. Once or twice I had a feeling of intense fear for which I could perceive no definite reason. I remember creeping noiselessly into the great hall where the little people were sleeping in the moonlight—that night Weena was among them—and feeling reassured by their presence. It occurred to me even then, that in the course of a few days the moon must pass through its last quarter, and the nights grow dark, when the appearances of these unpleasant creatures from below, these whitened Lemurs, this new vermin that had replaced the old, might be more abundant. And on both these days I had the restless feeling of one who shirks an inevitable duty. I felt assured that the Time Machine was only to be recovered by boldly penetrating these underground mysteries. Yet I could not face the mystery. If only I had had a companion it would have been different. But I was so horribly alone, and even to clamber down into the darkness of the well appalled me. I don't know if you will understand my feeling, but I never felt quite safe at my back.

"It was this restlessness, this insecurity, perhaps, that drove me further and further afield in my exploring expeditions. Going to the south-westward towards the rising country that is now called Combe Wood, I observed far off, in the direction of nineteenth-

century Banstead, a vast green structure, different in character from any I had hitherto seen. It was larger than the largest of the palaces or ruins I knew, and the façade had an Oriental look: the face of it having the lustre, as well as the pale-green tint, a kind of bluish-green, of a certain type of Chinese porcelain. This difference in aspect suggested a difference in use, and I was minded to push on and explore. But the day was growing late, and I had come upon the sight of the place after a long and tiring circuit; so I resolved to hold over the adventure for the following day, and I returned to the welcome and the caresses of little Weena. But next morning I perceived clearly enough that my curiosity regarding the Palace of Green Porcelain was a piece of self-deception, to enable me to shirk, by another day, an experience I dreaded. I resolved I would make the descent without further waste of time, and started out in the early morning towards a well near the ruins of granite and aluminium.

"Little Weena ran with me. She danced beside me to the well, but when she saw me lean over the mouth and look downward, she seemed strangely disconcerted. 'Good-bye, little Weena,' I said, kissing her; and then putting her down, I began to feel over the parapet for the climbing hooks. Rather hastily, I may as well confess, for I feared my courage might leak away! At first she watched me in amazement. Then she gave a most piteous cry, and running to me, she began to pull at me with her little hands. I think her opposition nerved me rather to proceed. I shook her off, perhaps a little roughly, and in another moment I was in the throat of the well. I saw her agonized face over the parapet, and smiled to reassure her. Then I had to look down at the unstable hooks to which I clung.

"I had to clamber down a shaft of perhaps two hundred yards. The descent was effected by means of metallic bars projecting from the sides of the well, and these being adapted to the needs of a creature much smaller and lighter than myself, I was speedily cramped and fatigued by the descent. And not simply fatigued! One of the bars bent suddenly under my weight, and almost swung me off into the blackness beneath. For a moment I hung by one hand, and after that experience I did not dare to rest again. Though my arms and back were presently acutely painful, I went on clambering down the sheer descent with as quick a motion as possible. Glancing upward, I saw the aperture, a small blue disk, in which a star was visible, while little Weena's head showed as a round black projection. The thudding sound of a machine below grew louder and more oppressive. Everything save that little disk above was profoundly dark, and when I looked up again Weena had disappeared.

"I was in an agony of discomfort. I had some thought of trying to go up the shaft again, and leave the Under-world alone. But even while I turned this over in my mind I continued to descend. At last, with intense relief, I saw dimly coming up, a foot to the right of me, a slender loophole in the wall. Swinging myself in, I found it was the aperture of a narrow horizontal tunnel in which I could lie down and rest. It was not too soon. My arms ached, my back was cramped, and I was trembling with the prolonged terror of a fall. Besides this, the unbroken darkness had had a distressing effect upon my eyes. The air was full of the throb and hum of machinery pumping air down the shaft.

"I do not know how long I lay. I was roused by a soft hand touching my face. Starting up in the darkness I snatched at my matches and, hastily striking one, I saw three stooping white creatures similar to the one I had seen above ground in the ruin, hastily retreating before the light. Living, as they did, in what appeared to me impenetrable darkness, their eyes were abnormally large and sensitive, just as are the pupils of the abysmal fishes, and they reflected the light in the same way. I have no doubt they could see me in that rayless obscurity, and they did not seem to have any fear of me apart from the light. But, so soon as I struck a match in order to see them, they fled incontinently, vanishing into dark gutters and tunnels, from which their eyes glared at me in the strangest fashion.

"I tried to call to them, but the language they had was apparently different from that of the Over-world people; so that I was needs left to my own unaided efforts, and the thought of flight before exploration was even then in my mind. But I said to myself, 'You are in for it now,' and, feeling my way along the tunnel, I found the noise of machinery grow louder. Presently the walls fell away from me, and I came to a large open space, and striking another match, saw that I had entered a vast arched cavern, which stretched into utter darkness beyond the range of my light. The view I had of it was as much as one could see in the burning of a match.

"Necessarily my memory is vague. Great shapes like big machines rose out of the dimness, and cast grotesque black shadows, in which dim spectral Morlocks sheltered from the glare. The place, by the by, was very stuffy and oppressive, and the faint halitus of freshly shed blood was in the air. Some way down the central vista was a little table of white metal, laid with what seemed a meal. The Morlocks at any rate were carnivorous! Even at the time, I remember wondering what large animal could have survived to furnish the red joint I saw. It was all very indistinct: the heavy smell, the big unmeaning shapes, the obscene figures lurking in the shadows, and only waiting for the darkness to come at me again! Then the match burned down, and stung my fingers, and fell, a wriggling red spot in the blackness.

"I have thought since how particularly ill-equipped I was for such an experience. When I had started with the Time Machine, I had started with the absurd assumption that the men of the Future would certainly be infinitely ahead of ourselves in all their appliances. I had come without arms, without medicine, without anything to smoke—at times I missed tobacco frightfully—even without enough matches. If only I had thought of a Kodak! I could have flashed that glimpse of the Under-world in a second, and examined it at leisure. But, as it was, I stood there with only the weapons and the powers that Nature had endowed me with—hands, feet, and teeth; these, and four safety-matches that still remained to me.

"I was afraid to push my way in among all this machinery in the dark, and it was only with my last glimpse of light I discovered that my store of matches had run low. It had never occurred to me until that moment that there was any need to economize them, and I had wasted almost half the box in astonishing the Upper Worlders, to whom fire was a novelty. Now, as I say, I had four left, and while I stood in the dark, a hand touched mine, lank fingers came feeling over my face, and I was sensible of a peculiar unpleasant odour. I fancied I heard the breathing of a crowd of those dreadful little beings about me. I felt the box of matches in my hand being gently disengaged, and other hands behind me plucking at my clothing. The sense of these unseen creatures examining me was indescribably unpleasant. The sudden realization of my ignorance of their ways of thinking and doing came home to me very vividly in the darkness. I shouted at them as loudly as I could. They started away, and then I could feel them approaching me again. They clutched at me more boldly, whispering odd sounds to each other. I shivered violently, and shouted again—rather discordantly. This time they were not so seriously alarmed, and they made a queer laughing noise as they came back at me. I will confess I was horribly frightened. I determined to strike another match and escape under the protection of its glare. I did so, and eking out the flicker with a scrap of paper from my pocket, I made good my retreat to the narrow tunnel. But I had scarce entered this when my light was blown out and in the blackness I could hear the Morlocks rustling like wind among leaves, and pattering like the rain, as they hurried after me.

"In a moment I was clutched by several hands, and there was no mistaking that they were trying to haul me back. I struck another light, and waved it in their dazzled faces. You can scarce imagine how nauseatingly inhuman they looked—those pale, chinless faces and great, lidless, pinkish-grey eyes!—as they

stared in their blindness and bewilderment. But I did not stay to look, I promise you: I retreated again, and when my second match had ended, I struck my third. It had almost burned through when I reached the opening into the shaft. I lay down on the edge, for the throb of the great pump below made me giddy. Then I felt sideways for the projecting hooks, and, as I did so, my feet were grasped from behind, and I was violently tugged backward. I lit my last match . . . and it incontinently went out. But I had my hand on the climbing bars now, and, kicking violently, I disengaged myself from the clutches of the Morlocks and was speedily clambering up the shaft, while they stayed peering and blinking up at me: all but one little wretch who followed me for some way, and well-nigh secured my boot as a trophy.

"That climb seemed interminable to me. With the last twenty or thirty feet of it a deadly nausea came upon me. I had the greatest difficulty in keeping my hold. The last few yards was a frightful struggle against this faintness. Several times my head swam, and I felt all the sensations of falling. At last, however, I got over the well-mouth somehow, and staggered out of the ruin into the blinding sunlight. I fell upon my face. Even the soil smelt sweet and clean. Then I remember Weena kissing my hands and ears, and the voices of others among the Eloi. Then, for a time, I was insensible."

Chapter VII

Now, indeed, I seemed in a worse case than before. Hitherto, except during my night's anguish at the loss of the Time Machine, I had felt a sustaining hope of ultimate escape, but that hope was staggered by these new discoveries. Hitherto I had merely thought myself impeded by the childish simplicity of the little people, and by some unknown forces which I had only to understand to overcome; but there was an altogether new element in the sickening quality of the Morlocks—a something inhuman and malign. Instinctively I loathed them. Before, I had felt as a man might feel who had fallen into a pit: my concern was with the pit and how to get out of it. Now I felt like a beast in a trap, whose enemy would come upon him soon.

"The enemy I dreaded may surprise you. It was the darkness of the new moon. Weena had put this into my head by some at first incomprehensible remarks about the Dark Nights. It was not now such a very difficult problem to guess what the coming Dark Nights might mean. The moon was on the wane: each night there was a longer interval of darkness. And I now understood to some slight degree at least the reason of the fear of the little Upper World people for the dark. I wondered vaguely what foul villainy it might be that the Morlocks did under the new moon. I felt pretty sure now that my second hypothesis was all wrong. The Upper World people might once have been the favoured aristocracy, and the Morlocks their mechanical servants: but that had long since passed away. The two species that had resulted from the evolution of man were sliding down towards, or had already arrived at, an altogether new relationship. The Eloi, like the Carolingian kings, had decayed to a mere beautiful futility. They still possessed the earth on sufferance: since the Morlocks, subterranean for innumerable generations, had come at last to find the daylit surface intolerable. And the Morlocks made

their garments, I inferred, and maintained them in their habitual needs, perhaps through the survival of an old habit of service. They did it as a standing horse paws with his foot, or as a man enjoys killing animals in sport: because ancient and departed necessities had impressed it on the organism. But, clearly, the old order was already in part reversed. The Nemesis of the delicate ones was creeping on apace. Ages ago, thousands of generations ago, man had thrust his brother man out of the ease and the sunshine. And now that brother was coming back changed! Already the Eloi had begun to learn one old lesson anew. They were becoming reacquainted with Fear. And suddenly there came into my head the memory of the meat I had seen in the Under-world. It seemed odd how it floated into my mind: not stirred up as it were by the current of my meditations, but coming in almost like a question from outside. I tried to recall the form of it. I had a vague sense of something familiar, but I could not tell what it was at the time.

"Still, however helpless the little people in the presence of their mysterious Fear, I was differently constituted. I came out of this age of ours, this ripe prime of the human race, when Fear does not paralyse and mystery has lost its terrors. I at least would defend myself. Without further delay I determined to make myself arms and a fastness where I might sleep. With that refuge as a base, I could face this strange world with some of that confidence I had lost in realizing to what creatures night by night I lay exposed. I felt I could never sleep again until my bed was secure from them. I shuddered with horror to think how they must already have examined me.

"I wandered during the afternoon along the valley of the Thames, but found nothing that commended itself to my mind as inaccessible. All the buildings and trees seemed easily practicable to such dexterous climbers as the Morlocks, to judge by their wells, must be. Then the tall pinnacles of the Palace of Green Porcelain and the polished gleam of its walls came back to my memory; and in the evening, taking Weena like a child upon my shoulder, I went up the hills towards the south-west. The distance, I had reckoned, was seven or eight miles, but it must have been nearer eighteen. I had first seen the place on a moist afternoon when distances are deceptively diminished. In addition, the heel of one of my shoes was loose, and a nail was working through the sole—they were comfortable old shoes I wore about indoors—so that I was lame. And it was already long past sunset when I came in sight of the palace, silhouetted black against the pale yellow of the sky.

"Weena had been hugely delighted when I began to carry her, but after a while she desired me to let her down, and ran along by the side of me, occasionally darting off on either hand to pick flowers to stick in my pockets. My pockets had always puzzled Weena, but at the last she had concluded that they were an eccentric kind of vase for floral decoration. At least she utilized them for that purpose. And that reminds me! In changing my jacket I found . . ."

The Time Traveller paused, put his hand into his pocket, and silently placed two withered flowers, not unlike very large white mallows, upon the little table. Then he resumed his narrative.

"As the hush of evening crept over the world and we proceeded over the hill crest towards Wimbledon, Weena grew tired and wanted to return to the house of grey stone. But I pointed out the distant pinnacles of the Palace of Green Porcelain to her, and contrived to make her understand that we were seeking a refuge there from her Fear. You know that great pause that comes upon things before the dusk? Even the breeze stops in the trees. To me there is always an air of expectation about that evening stillness. The sky was clear, remote, and empty save for a few horizontal bars far down in the sunset. Well, that night the expectation took the colour of my fears. In that darkling calm my senses seemed preternaturally sharpened. I fancied I could even feel the hollowness of the ground beneath my feet: could, indeed, almost see through it the Morlocks on their ant-hill going hither and thither and waiting for the dark. In

my excitement I fancied that they would receive my invasion of their burrows as a declaration of war. And why had they taken my Time Machine?

"So we went on in the quiet, and the twilight deepened into night. The clear blue of the distance faded, and one star after another came out. The ground grew dim and the trees black. Weena's fears and her fatigue grew upon her. I took her in my arms and talked to her and caressed her. Then, as the darkness grew deeper, she put her arms round my neck, and, closing her eyes, tightly pressed her face against my shoulder. So we went down a long slope into a valley, and there in the dimness I almost walked into a little river. This I waded, and went up the opposite side of the valley, past a number of sleeping houses, and by a statue—a Faun, or some such figure, minus the head. Here too were acacias. So far I had seen nothing of the Morlocks, but it was yet early in the night, and the darker hours before the old moon rose were still to come.

"From the brow of the next hill I saw a thick wood spreading wide and black before me. I hesitated at this. I could see no end to it, either to the right or the left. Feeling tired—my feet, in particular, were very sore—I carefully lowered Weena from my shoulder as I halted, and sat down upon the turf. I could no longer see the Palace of Green Porcelain, and I was in doubt of my direction. I looked into the thickness of the wood and thought of what it might hide. Under that dense tangle of branches one would be out of sight of the stars. Even were there no other lurking danger—a danger I did not care to let my imagination loose upon—there would still be all the roots to stumble over and the tree-boles to strike against. I was very tired, too, after the excitements of the day; so I decided that I would not face it, but would pass the night upon the open hill.

"Weena, I was glad to find, was fast asleep. I carefully wrapped her in my jacket, and sat down beside her to wait for the moonrise. The hill-side was quiet and deserted, but from the black of the wood there came now and then a stir of living

things. Above me shone the stars, for the night was very clear. I felt a certain sense of friendly comfort in their twinkling. All the old constellations had gone from the sky, however: that slow movement which is imperceptible in a hundred human lifetimes, had long since rearranged them in unfamiliar groupings. But the Milky Way, it seemed to me, was still the same tattered streamer of star-dust as of yore. Southward (as I judged it) was a very bright red star that was new to me; it was even more splendid than our own green Sirius. And amid all these scintillating points of light one bright planet shone kindly and steadily like the face of an old friend.

"Looking at these stars suddenly dwarfed my own troubles and all the gravities of terrestrial life. I thought of their unfathomable distance, and the slow inevitable drift of their movements out of the unknown past into the unknown future. I thought of the great precessional cycle that the pole of the earth describes. Only forty times had that silent revolution occurred during all the years that I had traversed. And during these few revolutions all the activity, all the traditions, the complex organizations, the nations, languages, literatures, aspirations, even the mere memory of Man as I knew him, had been swept out of existence. Instead were these frail creatures who had forgotten their high ancestry, and the white Things of which I went in terror. Then I thought of the Great Fear that was between the two species, and for the first time, with a sudden shiver, came the clear knowledge of what the meat I had seen might be. Yet it was too horrible! I looked at little Weena sleeping beside me, her face white and starlike under the stars, and forthwith dismissed the thought.

"Through that long night I held my mind off the Morlocks as well as I could, and whiled away the time by trying to fancy I could find signs of the old constellations in the new confusion. The sky kept very clear, except for a hazy cloud or so. No doubt I dozed at times. Then, as my vigil wore on, came a faintness in the eastward sky, like the reflection of some colourless fire, and the old moon rose, thin and peaked and white. And close

behind, and overtaking it, and overflowing it, the dawn came, pale at first, and then growing pink and warm. No Morlocks had approached us. Indeed, I had seen none upon the hill that night. And in the confidence of renewed day it almost seemed to me that my fear had been unreasonable. I stood up and found my foot with the loose heel swollen at the ankle and painful under the heel; so I sat down again, took off my shoes, and flung them away.

"I awakened Weena, and we went down into the wood, now green and pleasant instead of black and forbidding. We found some fruit wherewith to break our fast. We soon met others of the dainty ones, laughing and dancing in the sunlight as though there was no such thing in nature as the night. And then I thought once more of the meat that I had seen. I felt assured now of what it was, and from the bottom of my heart I pitied this last feeble rill from the great flood of humanity. Clearly, at some time in the Long-Ago of human decay the Morlocks' food had run short. Possibly they had lived on rats and such-like vermin. Even now man is far less discriminating and exclusive in his food than he was—far less than any monkey. His prejudice against human flesh is no deep-seated instinct. And so these inhuman sons of men—! I tried to look at the thing in a scientific spirit. After all, they were less human and more remote than our cannibal ancestors of three or four thousand years ago. And the intelligence that would have made this state of things a torment had gone. Why should I trouble myself? These Eloi were mere fatted cattle, which the ant-like Morlocks preserved and preyed upon—probably saw to the breeding of. And there was Weena dancing at my side!

"Then I tried to preserve myself from the horror that was coming upon me, by regarding it as a rigorous punishment of human selfishness. Man had been content to live in ease and delight upon the labours of his fellow-man, had taken Necessity as his watchword and excuse, and in the fullness of time Necessity had come home to him. I even tried a Carlyle-like scorn of this wretched aristocracy in decay. But this attitude of mind was impossible. However great their intellectual degradation, the Eloi had kept too much of the human form not to claim my sympathy, and to make me perforce a sharer in their degradation and their Fear.

"I had at that time very vague ideas as to the course I should pursue. My first was to secure some safe place of refuge, and to make myself such arms of metal or stone as I could contrive. That necessity was immediate. In the next place, I hoped to procure some means of fire, so that I should have the weapon of a torch at hand, for nothing, I knew, would be more efficient against these Morlocks. Then I wanted to arrange some contrivance to break open the doors of bronze under the White Sphinx. I had in mind a battering ram. I had a persuasion that if I could enter those doors and carry a blaze of light before me I should discover the Time Machine and escape. I could not imagine the Morlocks were strong enough to move it far away. Weena I had resolved to bring with me to our own time. And turning such schemes over in my mind I pursued our way towards the building which my fancy had chosen as our dwelling."

Chapter VIII

I found the Palace of Green Porcelain, when we approached it about noon, deserted and falling into ruin. Only ragged vestiges of glass remained in its windows, and great sheets of the green facing had fallen away from the corroded metallic framework. It lay very high upon a turfy down, and looking north-eastward before I entered it, I was surprised to see a large estuary, or even creek, where I judged Wandsworth and Battersea must once have been. I thought then—though I never followed up the thought—of what might have happened, or might be happening, to the living things in the sea.

"The material of the Palace proved on examination to be indeed porcelain, and along the face of it I saw an inscription in some unknown character. I thought, rather foolishly, that Weena might help me to interpret this, but I only learned that the bare idea of writing had never entered her head. She always seemed to me, I fancy, more human than she was, perhaps because her affection was so human.

"Within the big valves of the door—which were open and broken—we found, instead of the customary hall, a long gallery lit by many side windows. At the first glance I was reminded of a museum. The tiled floor was thick with dust, and a remarkable array of miscellaneous objects was shrouded in the same grey covering. Then I perceived, standing strange and gaunt in the centre of the hall, what was clearly the lower part of a huge skeleton. I recognized by the oblique feet that it was some extinct creature after the fashion of the Megatherium. The skull and the upper bones lay beside it in the thick dust, and in one place, where rain-water had dropped through a leak in the roof, the thing itself had been worn away. Further in the gallery was the huge skeleton barrel of a Brontosaurus. My museum hypothesis was confirmed. Going towards the side I found what appeared to be sloping shelves, and clearing away the thick dust, I found the old familiar glass cases of our own time. But they must have been air-tight to judge from the fair preservation of some of their contents.

"Clearly we stood among the ruins of some latter-day South Kensington! Here, apparently, was the Palaeontological Section, and a very splendid array of fossils it must have been, though the inevitable process of decay that had been staved off for a time, and had, through the extinction of bacteria and fungi, lost ninety-nine hundredths of its force, was nevertheless, with extreme sureness if with extreme slowness at work again upon all its treasures. Here and there I found traces of the little people in the shape of rare fossils broken to pieces or threaded in strings upon reeds. And the cases had in some instances been bodily removed—by the Morlocks as I judged. The place was very silent. The thick dust deadened our footsteps. Weena, who had been rolling a sea urchin down the sloping glass of a case, presently came, as I stared about me, and very quietly took my hand and stood beside me.

"And at first I was so much surprised by this ancient monument of an intellectual age, that I gave no thought to the possibilities it presented. Even my preoccupation about the Time Machine receded a little from my mind.

"To judge from the size of the place, this Palace of Green Porcelain had a great deal more in it than a Gallery of Palaeontology; possibly historical galleries; it might be, even a library! To me, at least in my present circumstances, these would be vastly more interesting than this spectacle of old-time geology in decay. Exploring, I found another short gallery running transversely to the first. This appeared to be devoted to minerals, and the sight of a block of sulphur set my mind running on gunpowder. But I could find no saltpeter; indeed, no nitrates of any kind. Doubtless they had deliquesced ages ago. Yet the sulphur hung in my mind, and set up a train of thinking. As for the rest of the contents of that gallery, though

on the whole they were the best preserved of all I saw, I had little interest. I am no specialist in mineralogy, and I went on down a very ruinous aisle running parallel to the first hall I had entered. Apparently this section had been devoted to natural history, but everything had long since passed out of recognition. A few shrivelled and blackened vestiges of what had once been stuffed animals, desiccated mummies in jars that had once held spirit, a brown dust of departed plants: that was all! I was sorry for that, because I should have been glad to trace the patent readjustments by which the conquest of animated nature had been attained. Then we came to a gallery of simply colossal proportions, but singularly ill-lit, the floor of it running downward at a slight angle from the end at which I entered. At intervals white globes hung from the ceiling—many of them cracked and smashed—which suggested that originally the place had been artificially lit. Here I was more in my element, for rising on either side of me were the huge bulks of big machines, all greatly corroded and many broken down, but some still fairly complete. You know I have a certain weakness for mechanism, and I was inclined to linger among these; the more so as for the most part they had the interest of puzzles, and I could make only the vaguest guesses at what they were for. I fancied that if I could solve their puzzles I should find myself in possession of powers that might be of use against the Morlocks.

"Suddenly Weena came very close to my side. So suddenly that she startled me. Had it not been for her I do not think I should have noticed that the floor of the gallery sloped at all. The end I had come in at was quite above ground, and was lit by rare slit-like windows. As you went down the length, the ground came up against these windows, until at last there was a pit like the 'area' of a London house before each, and only a narrow line of daylight at the top. I went slowly along, puzzling about the machines, and had been too intent upon them to notice the gradual diminution of the light, until Weena's increasing apprehensions drew my attention. Then I saw that the gallery

ran down at last into a thick darkness. I hesitated, and then, as I looked round me, I saw that the dust was less abundant and its surface less even. Further away towards the dimness, it appeared to be broken by a number of small narrow footprints. My sense of the immediate presence of the Morlocks revived at that. I felt that I was wasting my time in the academic examination of machinery. I called to mind that it was already far advanced in the afternoon, and that I had still no weapon, no refuge, and no means of making a fire. And then down in the remote blackness of the gallery I heard a peculiar pattering, and the same odd noises I had heard down the well.

"I took Weena's hand. Then, struck with a sudden idea, I left her and turned to a machine from which projected a lever not unlike those in a signal-box. Clambering upon the stand, and grasping this lever in my hands, I put all my weight upon it sideways. Suddenly Weena, deserted in the central aisle, began to whimper. I had judged the strength of the lever pretty correctly, for it snapped after a minute's strain, and I rejoined her with a mace in my hand more than sufficient, I judged, for any Morlock skull I might encounter. And I longed very much to kill a Morlock or so. Very inhuman, you may think, to want to go killing one's own descendants! But it was impossible, somehow, to feel any humanity in the things. Only my disinclination to leave Weena, and a persuasion that if I began to slake my thirst for murder my Time Machine might suffer, restrained me from going straight down the gallery and killing the brutes I heard.

"Well, mace in one hand and Weena in the other, I went out of that gallery and into another and still larger one, which at the first glance reminded me of a military chapel hung with tattered flags. The brown and charred rags that hung from the sides of it, I presently recognized as the decaying vestiges of books. They had long since dropped to pieces, and every semblance of print had left them. But here and there were warped boards and cracked metallic clasps that told the tale well enough. Had I been a literary man I might, perhaps, have moralized upon the

futility of all ambition. But as it was, the thing that struck me with keenest force was the enormous waste of labour to which this sombre wilderness of rotting paper testified. At the time I will confess that I thought chiefly of the *Philosophical Transactions* and my own seventeen papers upon physical optics.

"Then, going up a broad staircase, we came to what may once have been a gallery of technical chemistry. And here I had not a little hope of useful discoveries. Except at one end where the roof had collapsed, this gallery was well preserved. I went eagerly to every unbroken case. And at last, in one of the really air-tight cases, I found a box of matches. Very eagerly I tried them. They were perfectly good. They were not even damp. I turned to Weena. 'Dance,' I cried to her in her own tongue. For now I had a weapon indeed against the horrible creatures we feared. And so, in that derelict museum, upon the thick soft carpeting of dust, to Weena's huge delight, I solemnly performed a kind of composite dance, whistling *The Land of the Leal* as cheerfully as I could. In part it was a modest *cancan*, in part a step-dance, in part a skirt-dance (so far as my tail-coat permitted), and in part original. For I am naturally inventive, as you know.

"Now, I still think that for this box of matches to have escaped the wear of time for immemorial years was a most strange, as for me it was a most fortunate thing. Yet, oddly enough, I found a far unlikelier substance, and that was camphor. I found it in a sealed jar, that by chance, I suppose, had been really hermetically sealed. I fancied at first that it was paraffin wax, and smashed the glass accordingly. But the odour of camphor was unmistakable. In the universal decay this volatile substance had chanced to survive, perhaps through many thousands of centuries. It reminded me of a sepia painting I had once seen done from the ink of a fossil Belemnite that must have perished and become fossilized millions of years ago. I was about to throw it away, but I remembered that it was inflammable and burned with a good bright flame—was, in fact, an excellent candle—and I put it in my pocket. I found no explosives, however, nor any means of breaking down the bronze doors. As yet my iron crowbar was the most helpful thing I had chanced upon. Nevertheless I left that gallery greatly elated.

"I cannot tell you all the story of that long afternoon. It would require a great effort of memory to recall my explorations in at all the proper order. I remember a long gallery of rusting stands of arms, and how I hesitated between my crowbar and a hatchet or a sword. I could not carry both, however, and my bar of iron promised best against the bronze gates. There were numbers of guns, pistols, and rifles. The most were masses of rust, but many were of some new metal, and still fairly sound. But any cartridges or powder there may once have been had rotted into dust. One corner I saw was charred and shattered; perhaps, I thought, by an explosion among the specimens. In another place was a vast array of idols—Polynesian, Mexican, Grecian, Phoenician, every country on earth I should think. And here, yielding to an irresistible impulse, I wrote my name upon the nose of a steatite monster from South America that particularly took my fancy.

"As the evening drew on, my interest waned. I went through gallery after gallery, dusty, silent, often ruinous, the exhibits sometimes mere heaps of rust and lignite, sometimes fresher. In one place I suddenly found myself near the model of a tin-mine, and then by the merest accident I discovered, in an air-tight case, two dynamite cartridges! I shouted 'Eureka!' and smashed the case with joy. Then came a doubt. I hesitated. Then, selecting a little side gallery, I made my essay. I never felt such a disappointment as I did in waiting five, ten, fifteen minutes for an explosion that never came. Of course the things were dummies, as I might have guessed from their presence. I really believe that had they not been so, I should have rushed off incontinently and blown Sphinx, bronze doors, and (as it proved) my chances of finding the Time Machine, all together into non-existence.

"It was after that, I think, that we came to a little open court

within the palace. It was turfed, and had three fruit-trees. So we rested and refreshed ourselves. Towards sunset I began to consider our position. Night was creeping upon us, and my inaccessible hiding-place had still to be found. But that troubled me very little now. I had in my possession a thing that was, perhaps, the best of all defences against the Morlocks—I had matches! I had the camphor in my pocket, too, if a blaze were needed. It seemed to me that the best thing we could do would be to pass the night in the open, protected by a fire. In the morning there was the getting of the Time Machine. Towards that, as yet, I had only my iron mace. But now, with my growing knowledge, I felt very differently towards those bronze doors. Up to this, I had refrained from forcing them, largely because of the mystery on the other side. They had never impressed me as being very strong, and I hoped to find my bar of iron not altogether inadequate for the work."

Chapter IX

We emerged from the palace while the sun was still in part above the horizon. I was determined to reach the White Sphinx early the next morning, and ere the dusk I purposed pushing through the woods that had stopped me on the previous journey. My plan was to go as far as possible that night, and then, building a fire, to sleep in the protection of its glare. Accordingly, as we went along I gathered any sticks or dried grass I saw, and presently had my arms full of such litter. Thus loaded, our progress was slower than I had anticipated, and besides Weena was tired. And I began to suffer from sleepiness too; so that it was full night before we reached the wood. Upon the shrubby hill of its edge Weena would have stopped, fearing the darkness before us; but a singular sense of impending calamity, that should indeed have served me as a warning, drove me onward. I had been without sleep for a night and two days, and I was feverish and irritable. I felt sleep coming upon me, and the Morlocks with it.

"While we hesitated, among the black bushes behind us, and dim against their blackness, I saw three crouching figures. There was scrub and long grass all about us, and I did not feel safe from their insidious approach. The forest, I calculated, was rather less than a mile across. If we could get through it to the bare hill-side, there, as it seemed to me, was an altogether safer resting-place; I thought that with my matches and my camphor I could contrive to keep my path illuminated through the woods. Yet it was evident that if I was to flourish matches with my hands I should have to abandon my firewood; so, rather reluctantly, I put it down. And then it came into my head that I would amaze our friends behind by lighting it. I was to discover the atrocious folly of this proceeding, but it came to my mind as an ingenious move for covering our retreat.

"I don't know if you have ever thought what a rare thing flame must be in the absence of man and in a temperate climate. The sun's heat is rarely strong enough to burn, even when it is focused by dewdrops, as is sometimes the case in more tropical districts. Lightning may blast and blacken, but it rarely gives rise to widespread fire. Decaying vegetation may occasionally smoulder with the heat of its fermentation, but this rarely results in flame. In this decadence, too, the art of fire-making had been forgotten on the earth. The red tongues that went licking up my heap of wood were an altogether new and strange thing to Weena.

"She wanted to run to it and play with it. I believe she would have cast herself into it had I not restrained her. But I caught her up, and in spite of her struggles, plunged boldly before me into the wood. For a little way the glare of my fire lit the path. Looking back presently, I could see, through the crowded stems, that from my heap of sticks the blaze had spread to some bushes adjacent, and a curved line of fire was creeping up the grass of the hill. I laughed at that, and turned again to the dark trees before me. It was very black, and Weena clung to me convulsively, but there was still, as my eyes grew accustomed to the darkness, sufficient light for me to avoid the stems. Overhead it was simply black, except where a gap of remote blue sky shone down upon us here and there. I struck none of my matches because I had no hand free. Upon my left arm I carried my little one, in my right hand I had my iron bar.

"For some way I heard nothing but the crackling twigs under my feet, the faint rustle of the breeze above, and my own breathing and the throb of the blood-vessels in my ears. Then I seemed to know of a pattering about me. I pushed on grimly. The pattering grew more distinct, and then I caught the same queer sound and voices I had heard in the Under-world. There were evidently several of the Morlocks, and they were closing in upon me. Indeed, in another minute I felt a tug at my coat, then something at my arm. And Weena shivered violently, and became quite still.

"It was time for a match. But to get one I must put her down. I did so, and, as I fumbled with my pocket, a struggle began in the darkness about my knees, perfectly silent on her part and with the same peculiar cooing sounds from the Morlocks. Soft little hands, too, were creeping over my coat and back, touching even my neck. Then the match scratched and fizzed. I held it flaring, and saw the white backs of the Morlocks in flight amid the trees. I hastily took a lump of camphor from my pocket, and prepared to light it as soon as the match should wane. Then I looked at Weena. She was lying clutching my feet and quite motionless, with her face to the ground. With a sudden fright I stooped to her. She seemed scarcely to breathe. I lit the block of camphor and flung it to the ground, and as it split and flared up and drove back the Morlocks and the shadows, I knelt down and lifted her. The wood behind seemed full of the stir and murmur of a great company!

"She seemed to have fainted. I put her carefully upon my shoulder and rose to push on, and then there came a horrible realization. In manoeuvring with my matches and Weena, I had turned myself about several times, and now I had not the faintest idea in what direction lay my path. For all I knew, I might be facing back towards the Palace of Green Porcelain. I found myself in a cold sweat. I had to think rapidly what to do. I determined to build a fire and encamp where we were. I put Weena, still motionless, down upon a turfy bole, and very hastily, as my first lump of camphor waned, I began collecting sticks and leaves. Here and there out of the darkness round me the Morlocks' eyes shone like carbuncles.

"The camphor flickered and went out. I lit a match, and as I did so, two white forms that had been approaching Weena dashed hastily away. One was so blinded by the light that he came straight for me, and I felt his bones grind under the blow of my fist. He gave a whoop of dismay, staggered a little way, and fell down. I lit another piece of camphor, and went on gathering my bonfire. Presently I noticed how dry was some of the foliage

above me, for since my arrival on the Time Machine, a matter of a week, no rain had fallen. So, instead of casting about among the trees for fallen twigs, I began leaping up and dragging down branches. Very soon I had a choking smoky fire of green wood and dry sticks, and could economize my camphor. Then I turned to where Weena lay beside my iron mace. I tried what I could to revive her, but she lay like one dead. I could not even satisfy myself whether or not she breathed.

"Now, the smoke of the fire beat over towards me, and it must have made me heavy of a sudden. Moreover, the vapour of camphor was in the air. My fire would not need replenishing for an hour or so. I felt very weary after my exertion, and sat down. The wood, too, was full of a slumbrous murmur that I did not understand. I seemed just to nod and open my eyes. But all was dark, and the Morlocks had their hands upon me. Flinging off their clinging fingers I hastily felt in my pocket for the match-box, and—it had gone! Then they gripped and closed with me again. In a moment I knew what had happened. I had slept, and my fire had gone out, and the bitterness of death came over my soul. The forest seemed full of the smell of burning wood. I was caught by the neck, by the hair, by the arms, and pulled down. It was indescribably horrible in the darkness to feel all these soft creatures heaped upon me. I felt as if I was in a monstrous spider's web. I was overpowered, and went down. I felt little teeth nipping at my neck. I rolled over, and as I did so my hand came against my iron lever. It gave me strength. I struggled up, shaking the human rats from me, and, holding the bar short, I thrust where I judged their faces might be. I could feel the succulent giving of flesh and bone under my blows, and for a moment I was free.

"The strange exultation that so often seems to accompany hard fighting came upon me. I knew that both I and Weena were lost, but I determined to make the Morlocks pay for their meat. I stood with my back to a tree, swinging the iron bar before me. The whole wood was full of the stir and cries of them. A

minute passed. Their voices seemed to rise to a higher pitch of excitement, and their movements grew faster. Yet none came within reach. I stood glaring at the blackness. Then suddenly came hope. What if the Morlocks were afraid? And close on the heels of that came a strange thing. The darkness seemed to grow luminous. Very dimly I began to see the Morlocks about me—three battered at my feet—and then I recognized, with incredulous surprise, that the others were running, in an incessant stream, as it seemed, from behind me, and away through the wood in front. And their backs seemed no longer white, but reddish. As I stood agape, I saw a little red spark go drifting across a gap of starlight between the branches, and vanish. And at that I understood the smell of burning wood, the slumbrous murmur that was growing now into a gusty roar, the red glow, and the Morlocks' flight.

"Stepping out from behind my tree and looking back, I saw, through the black pillars of the nearer trees, the flames of the burning forest. It was my first fire coming after me. With that I looked for Weena, but she was gone. The hissing and crackling behind me, the explosive thud as each fresh tree burst into flame, left little time for reflection. My iron bar still gripped, I followed in the Morlocks' path. It was a close race. Once the flames crept forward so swiftly on my right as I ran that I was outflanked and had to strike off to the left. But at last I emerged upon a small open space, and as I did so, a Morlock came blundering towards me, and past me, and went on straight into the fire!

"And now I was to see the most weird and horrible thing, I think, of all that I beheld in that future age. This whole space was as bright as day with the reflection of the fire. In the centre was a hillock or tumulus, surmounted by a scorched hawthorn. Beyond this was another arm of the burning forest, with yellow tongues already writhing from it, completely encircling the space with a fence of fire. Upon the hill-side were some thirty or forty Morlocks, dazzled by the light and heat, and blundering hither and thither against each other in their bewilderment. At first I

did not realize their blindness, and struck furiously at them with my bar, in a frenzy of fear, as they approached me, killing one and crippling several more. But when I had watched the gestures of one of them groping under the hawthorn against the red sky, and heard their moans, I was assured of their absolute helplessness and misery in the glare, and I struck no more of them.

"Yet every now and then one would come straight towards me, setting loose a quivering horror that made me quick to elude him. At one time the flames died down somewhat, and I feared the foul creatures would presently be able to see me. I was thinking of beginning the fight by killing some of them before this should happen; but the fire burst out again brightly, and I stayed my hand. I walked about the hill among them and avoided them, looking for some trace of Weena. But Weena was gone.

"At last I sat down on the summit of the hillock, and watched this strange incredible company of blind things groping to and fro, and making uncanny noises to each other, as the glare of the fire beat on them. The coiling uprush of smoke streamed across the sky, and through the rare tatters of that red canopy, remote as though they belonged to another universe, shone the little stars. Two or three Morlocks came blundering into me, and I drove them off with blows of my fists, trembling as I did so.

"For the most part of that night I was persuaded it was a nightmare. I bit myself and screamed in a passionate desire to awake. I beat the ground with my hands, and got up and sat down again, and wandered here and there, and again sat down. Then I would fall to rubbing my eyes and calling upon God to let me awake. Thrice I saw Morlocks put their heads down in a kind of agony and rush into the flames. But, at last, above the subsiding red of the fire, above the streaming masses of black smoke and the whitening and blackening tree stumps, and the diminishing numbers of these dim creatures, came the white light of the day.

"I searched again for traces of Weena, but there were none. It was plain that they had left her poor little body in the forest. I cannot describe how it relieved me to think that it had escaped the awful fate to which it seemed destined. As I thought of that, I was almost moved to begin a massacre of the helpless abominations about me, but I contained myself. The hillock, as I have said, was a kind of island in the forest. From its summit I could now make out through a haze of smoke the Palace of Green Porcelain, and from that I could get my bearings for the White Sphinx. And so, leaving the remnant of these damned souls still going hither and thither and moaning, as the day grew clearer, I tied some grass about my feet and limped on across smoking ashes and among black stems, that still pulsated internally with fire, towards the hiding-place of the Time Machine. I walked slowly, for I was almost exhausted, as well as lame, and I felt the intensest wretchedness for the horrible death of little Weena. It seemed an overwhelming calamity. Now, in this old familiar room, it is more like the sorrow of a dream than an actual loss. But that morning it left me absolutely lonely again—terribly alone. I began to think of this house of mine, of this fireside, of some of you, and with such thoughts came a longing that was pain.

"But as I walked over the smoking ashes under the bright morning sky, I made a discovery. In my trouser pocket were still some loose matches. The box must have leaked before it was lost."

Chapter X

About eight or nine in the morning I came to the same seat of yellow metal from which I had viewed the world upon the evening of my arrival. I thought of my hasty conclusions upon that evening and could not refrain from laughing bitterly at my confidence. Here was the same beautiful scene, the same abundant foliage, the same splendid palaces and magnificent ruins, the same silver river running between its fertile banks. The gay robes of the beautiful people moved hither and thither among the trees. Some were bathing in exactly the place where I had saved Weena, and that suddenly gave me a keen stab of pain. And like blots upon the landscape rose the cupolas above the ways to the Under-world. I understood now what all the beauty of the Upper-world people covered. Very pleasant was their day, as pleasant as the day of the cattle in the field. Like the cattle, they knew of no enemies and provided against no needs. And their end was the same.

"I grieved to think how brief the dream of the human intellect had been. It had committed suicide. It had set itself steadfastly towards comfort and ease, a balanced society with security and permanency as its watchword, it had attained its hopes—to come to this at last. Once, life and property must have reached almost absolute safety. The rich had been assured of his wealth and comfort, the toiler assured of his life and work. No doubt in that perfect world there had been no unemployed problem, no social question left unsolved. And a great quiet had followed.

"It is a law of nature we overlook, that intellectual versatility is the compensation for change, danger, and trouble. An animal perfectly in harmony with its environment is a perfect mechanism. Nature never appeals to intelligence until habit and instinct are useless. There is no intelligence where there is no change and no need of change. Only those animals partake of intelligence that have to meet a huge variety of needs and dangers.

"So, as I see it, the Upper-world man had drifted towards his feeble prettiness, and the Under-world to mere mechanical industry. But that perfect state had lacked one thing even for mechanical perfection—absolute permanency. Apparently as time went on, the feeding of the Under-world, however it was effected, had become disjointed. Mother Necessity, who had been staved off for a few thousand years, came back again, and she began below. The Under-world being in contact with machinery, which, however perfect, still needs some little thought outside habit, had probably retained perforce rather more initiative, if less of every other human character, than the Upper. And when other meat failed them, they turned to what old habit had hitherto forbidden. So I say I saw it in my last view of the world of Eight Hundred and Two Thousand Seven Hundred and One. It may be as wrong an explanation as mortal wit could invent. It is how the thing shaped itself to me, and as that I give it to you.

"After the fatigues, excitements, and terrors of the past days, and in spite of my grief, this seat and the tranquil view and the warm sunlight were very pleasant. I was very tired and sleepy, and soon my theorizing passed into dozing. Catching myself at that, I took my own hint, and spreading myself out upon the turf I had a long and refreshing sleep.

"I awoke a little before sunsetting. I now felt safe against being caught napping by the Morlocks, and, stretching myself, I came on down the hill towards the White Sphinx. I had my crowbar in one hand, and the other hand played with the matches in my pocket.

"And now came a most unexpected thing. As I approached the pedestal of the sphinx I found the bronze valves were open. They had slid down into grooves.

"At that I stopped short before them, hesitating to enter.

"Within was a small apartment, and on a raised place in the

corner of this was the Time Machine. I had the small levers in my pocket. So here, after all my elaborate preparations for the siege of the White Sphinx, was a meek surrender. I threw my iron bar away, almost sorry not to use it.

"A sudden thought came into my head as I stooped towards the portal. For once, at least, I grasped the mental operations of the Morlocks. Suppressing a strong inclination to laugh, I stepped through the bronze frame and up to the Time Machine. I was surprised to find it had been carefully oiled and cleaned. I have suspected since that the Morlocks had even partially taken it to pieces while trying in their dim way to grasp its purpose.

"Now as I stood and examined it, finding a pleasure in the mere touch of the contrivance, the thing I had expected happened. The bronze panels suddenly slid up and struck the frame with a clang. I was in the dark—trapped. So the Morlocks thought. At that I chuckled gleefully.

"I could already hear their murmuring laughter as they came towards me. Very calmly I tried to strike the match. I had only to fix on the levers and depart then like a ghost. But I had overlooked one little thing. The matches were of that abominable kind that light only on the box.

"You may imagine how all my calm vanished. The little brutes were close upon me. One touched me. I made a sweeping blow in the dark at them with the levers, and began to scramble into the saddle of the machine. Then came one hand upon me and then another. Then I had simply to fight against their persistent fingers for my levers, and at the same time feel for the studs over which these fitted. One, indeed, they almost got away from me. As it slipped from my hand, I had to butt in the dark with my head—I could hear the Morlock's skull ring—to recover it. It was a nearer thing than the fight in the forest, I think, this last scramble.

"But at last the lever was fitted and pulled over. The clinging hands slipped from me. The darkness presently fell from my eyes. I found myself in the same grey light and tumult I have already described."

Chapter XI

I have already told you of the sickness and confusion that comes with time travelling. And this time I was not seated properly in the saddle, but sideways and in an unstable fashion. For an indefinite time I clung to the machine as it swayed and vibrated, quite unheeding how I went, and when I brought myself to look at the dials again I was amazed to find where I had arrived. One dial records days, and another thousands of days, another millions of days, and another thousands of millions. Now, instead of reversing the levers, I had pulled them over so as to go forward with them, and when I came to look at these indicators I found that the thousands hand was sweeping round as fast as the seconds hand of a watch—into futurity.

"As I drove on, a peculiar change crept over the appearance of things. The palpitating greyness grew darker; then—though I was still travelling with prodigious velocity—the blinking succession of day and night, which was usually indicative of a slower pace, returned, and grew more and more marked. This puzzled me very much at first. The alternations of night and day grew slower and slower, and so did the passage of the sun across the sky, until they seemed to stretch through centuries. At last a steady twilight brooded over the earth, a twilight only broken now and then when a comet glared across the darkling sky. The band of light that had indicated the sun had long since disappeared; for the sun had ceased to set—it simply rose and fell in the west, and grew ever broader and more red. All trace of the moon had vanished. The circling of the stars, growing slower and slower, had given place to creeping points of light. At last, some time before I stopped, the sun, red and very large, halted motionless upon the horizon, a vast dome glowing with a dull heat, and now and then suffering a momentary extinction. At one time it had for a little while glowed more brilliantly again,

but it speedily reverted to its sullen red heat. I perceived by this slowing down of its rising and setting that the work of the tidal drag was done. The earth had come to rest with one face to the sun, even as in our own time the moon faces the earth. Very cautiously, for I remembered my former headlong fall, I began to reverse my motion. Slower and slower went the circling hands until the thousands one seemed motionless and the daily one was no longer a mere mist upon its scale. Still slower, until the dim outlines of a desolate beach grew visible.

"I stopped very gently and sat upon the Time Machine, looking round. The sky was no longer blue. North-eastward it was inky black, and out of the blackness shone brightly and steadily the pale white stars. Overhead it was a deep Indian red and starless, and south-eastward it grew brighter to a glowing scarlet where, cut by the horizon, lay the huge hull of the sun, red and motionless. The rocks about me were of a harsh reddish colour, and all the trace of life that I could see at first was the intensely green vegetation that covered every projecting point on their south-eastern face. It was the same rich green that one sees on forest moss or on the lichen in caves: plants which like these grow in a perpetual twilight.

"The machine was standing on a sloping beach. The sea stretched away to the south-west, to rise into a sharp bright horizon against the wan sky. There were no breakers and no waves, for not a breath of wind was stirring. Only a slight oily swell rose and fell like a gentle breathing, and showed that the eternal sea was still moving and living. And along the margin where the water sometimes broke was a thick incrustation of salt—pink under the lurid sky. There was a sense of oppression in my head, and I noticed that I was breathing very fast. The sensation reminded me of my only experience of mountaineering, and from that I judged the air to be more rarefied than it is now.

"Far away up the desolate slope I heard a harsh scream, and saw a thing like a huge white butterfly go slanting and fluttering up into the sky and, circling, disappear over some low hillocks beyond. The sound of its voice was so dismal that I shivered and seated myself more firmly upon the machine. Looking round me again, I saw that, quite near, what I had taken to be a reddish mass of rock was moving slowly towards me. Then I saw the thing was really a monstrous crab-like creature. Can you imagine a crab as large as yonder table, with its many legs moving slowly and uncertainly, its big claws swaying, its long antennae, like carters' whips, waving and feeling, and its stalked eyes gleaming at you on either side of its metallic front? Its back was corrugated and ornamented with ungainly bosses, and a greenish incrustation blotched it here and there. I could see the many palps of its complicated mouth flickering and feeling as it moved.

"As I stared at this sinister apparition crawling towards me, I felt a tickling on my cheek as though a fly had lighted there. I tried to brush it away with my hand, but in a moment it returned, and almost immediately came another by my ear. I struck at this, and caught something threadlike. It was drawn swiftly out of my hand. With a frightful qualm, I turned, and I saw that I had grasped the antenna of another monster crab that stood just behind me. Its evil eyes were wriggling on their stalks, its mouth was all alive with appetite, and its vast ungainly claws, smeared with an algal slime, were descending upon me. In a moment my hand was on the lever, and I had placed a month between myself and these monsters. But I was still on the same beach, and I saw them distinctly now as soon as I stopped. Dozens of them seemed to be crawling here and there, in the sombre light, among the foliated sheets of intense green.

"I cannot convey the sense of abominable desolation that hung over the world. The red eastern sky, the northward blackness, the salt Dead Sea, the stony beach crawling with these foul, slow-stirring monsters, the uniform poisonous-looking green of the lichenous plants, the thin air that hurts one's lungs: all contributed to an appalling effect. I moved on a hundred years, and there was the same red sun—a little larger, a little duller—the same dying sea, the same chill air, and the same

crowd of earthy crustacea creeping in and out among the green weed and the red rocks. And in the westward sky, I saw a curved pale line like a vast new moon.

"So I travelled, stopping ever and again, in great strides of a thousand years or more, drawn on by the mystery of the earth's fate, watching with a strange fascination the sun grow larger and duller in the westward sky, and the life of the old earth ebb away. At last, more than thirty million years hence, the huge red-hot dome of the sun had come to obscure nearly a tenth part of the darkling heavens. Then I stopped once more, for the crawling multitude of crabs had disappeared, and the red beach, save for its livid green liverworts and lichens, seemed lifeless. And now it was flecked with white. A bitter cold assailed me. Rare white flakes ever and again came eddying down. To the north-eastward, the glare of snow lay under the starlight of the sable sky and I could see an undulating crest of hillocks pinkish white. There were fringes of ice along the sea margin, with drifting masses further out; but the main expanse of that salt ocean, all bloody under the eternal sunset, was still unfrozen.

"I looked about me to see if any traces of animal life remained. A certain indefinable apprehension still kept me in the saddle of the machine. But I saw nothing moving, in earth or sky or sea. The green slime on the rocks alone testified that life was not extinct. A shallow sandbank had appeared in the sea and the water had receded from the beach. I fancied I saw some black object flopping about upon this bank, but it became motionless as I looked at it, and I judged that my eye had been deceived, and that the black object was merely a rock. The stars in the sky were intensely bright and seemed to me to twinkle very little.

"Suddenly I noticed that the circular westward outline of the sun had changed; that a concavity, a bay, had appeared in the curve. I saw this grow larger. For a minute perhaps I stared aghast at this blackness that was creeping over the day, and then I realised that an eclipse was beginning. Either the moon or the planet Mercury was passing across the sun's disk. Naturally, at first I took it to be the moon, but there is much to incline me to believe that what I really saw was the transit of an inner planet passing very near to the earth.

"The darkness grew apace; a cold wind began to blow in freshening gusts from the east, and the showering white flakes in the air increased in number. From the edge of the sea came a ripple and whisper. Beyond these lifeless sounds the world was silent. Silent? It would be hard to convey the stillness of it. All the sounds of man, the bleating of sheep, the cries of birds, the hum of insects, the stir that makes the background of our lives—all that was over. As the darkness thickened, the eddying flakes grew more abundant, dancing before my eyes; and the cold of the air more intense. At last, one by one, swiftly, one after the other, the white peaks of the distant hills vanished into blackness. The breeze rose to a moaning wind. I saw the black central shadow of the eclipse sweeping towards me. In another moment the pale stars alone were visible. All else was rayless obscurity. The sky was absolutely black.

"A horror of this great darkness came on me. The cold, that smote to my marrow, and the pain I felt in breathing, overcame me. I shivered, and a deadly nausea seized me. Then like a red-hot bow in the sky appeared the edge of the sun. I got off the machine to recover myself. I felt giddy and incapable of facing the return journey. As I stood sick and confused I saw again the moving thing upon the shoal—there was no mistake now that it was a moving thing—against the red water of the sea. It was a round thing, the size of a football perhaps, or, it may be, bigger, and tentacles trailed down from it; it seemed black against the weltering blood-red water, and it was hopping fitfully about. Then I felt I was fainting. But a terrible dread of lying helpless in that remote and awful twilight sustained me while I clambered upon the saddle."

Chapter XII

So I came back. For a long time I must have been insensible upon the machine. The blinking succession of the days and nights was resumed, the sun got golden again, the sky blue. I breathed with greater freedom. The fluctuating contours of the land ebbed and flowed. The hands spun backward upon the dials. At last I saw again the dim shadows of houses, the evidences of decadent humanity. These, too, changed and passed, and others came. Presently, when the million dial was at zero, I slackened speed. I began to recognize our own pretty and familiar architecture, the thousands hand ran back to the starting-point, the night and day flapped slower and slower. Then the old walls of the laboratory came round me. Very gently, now, I slowed the mechanism down.

"I saw one little thing that seemed odd to me. I think I have told you that when I set out, before my velocity became very high, Mrs. Watchett had walked across the room, travelling, as it seemed to me, like a rocket. As I returned, I passed again across that minute when she traversed the laboratory. But now her every motion appeared to be the exact inversion of her previous ones. The door at the lower end opened, and she glided quietly up the laboratory, back foremost, and disappeared behind the door by which she had previously entered. Just before that I seemed to see Hillyer for a moment; but he passed like a flash.

"Then I stopped the machine, and saw about me again the old familiar laboratory, my tools, my appliances just as I had left them. I got off the thing very shakily, and sat down upon my bench. For several minutes I trembled violently. Then I became calmer. Around me was my old workshop again, exactly as it had been. I might have slept there, and the whole thing have been a dream.

"And yet, not exactly! The thing had started from the south-east corner of the laboratory. It had come to rest again in the

north-west, against the wall where you saw it. That gives you the exact distance from my little lawn to the pedestal of the White Sphinx, into which the Morlocks had carried my machine.

"For a time my brain went stagnant. Presently I got up and came through the passage here, limping, because my heel was still painful, and feeling sorely begrimed. I saw the *Pall Mall Gazette* on the table by the door. I found the date was indeed to-day, and looking at the timepiece, saw the hour was almost eight o'clock. I heard your voices and the clatter of plates. I hesitated—I felt so sick and weak. Then I sniffed good wholesome meat, and opened the door on you. You know the rest. I washed, and dined, and now I am telling you the story.

"I know," he said, after a pause, "that all this will be absolutely incredible to you. To me the one incredible thing is that I am here to-night in this old familiar room looking into your friendly faces and telling you these strange adventures."

He looked at the Medical Man. "No. I cannot expect you to believe it. Take it as a lie—or a prophecy. Say I dreamed it in the workshop. Consider I have been speculating upon the destinies of our race until I have hatched this fiction. Treat my assertion of its truth as a mere stroke of art to enhance its interest. And taking it as a story, what do you think of it?"

He took up his pipe, and began, in his old accustomed manner, to tap with it nervously upon the bars of the grate. There was a momentary stillness. Then chairs began to creak and shoes to scrape upon the carpet. I took my eyes off the Time Traveller's face, and looked round at his audience. They were in the dark, and little spots of colour swam before them. The Medical Man seemed absorbed in the contemplation of our host. The Editor was looking hard at the end of his cigar—the sixth. The Journalist fumbled for his watch. The others, as far as I remember, were motionless.

The Editor stood up with a sigh. "What a pity it is you're not a writer of stories!" he said, putting his hand on the Time Traveller's shoulder.

"You don't believe it?"

"Well—"

"I thought not."

The Time Traveller turned to us. "Where are the matches?" he said. He lit one and spoke over his pipe, puffing. "To tell you the truth . . . I hardly believe it myself . . . And yet . . ."

His eye fell with a mute inquiry upon the withered white flowers upon the little table. Then he turned over the hand holding his pipe, and I saw he was looking at some half-healed scars on his knuckles.

The Medical Man rose, came to the lamp, and examined the flowers. "The gynaeceum's odd," he said. The Psychologist leant forward to see, holding out his hand for a specimen.

"I'm hanged if it isn't a quarter to one," said the Journalist. "How shall we get home?"

"Plenty of cabs at the station," said the Psychologist.

"It's a curious thing," said the Medical Man; "but I certainly don't know the natural order of these flowers. May I have them?"

The Time Traveller hesitated. Then suddenly: "Certainly not."

"Where did you really get them?" said the Medical Man.

The Time Traveller put his hand to his head. He spoke like one who was trying to keep hold of an idea that eluded him. "They were put into my pocket by Weena, when I travelled into Time." He stared round the room. "I'm damned if it isn't all going. This room and you and the atmosphere of every day is too much for my memory. Did I ever make a Time Machine, or a model of a Time Machine? Or is it all only a dream? They say life is a dream, a precious poor dream at times—but I can't stand another that won't fit. It's madness. And where did the dream come from? . . . I must look at that machine. If there is one!"

He caught up the lamp swiftly, and carried it, flaring red, through the door into the corridor. We followed him. There in the flickering light of the lamp was the machine sure enough, squat, ugly, and askew; a thing of brass, ebony, ivory, and translucent glimmering quartz. Solid to the touch—for I put out my hand and felt the rail of it—and with brown spots and smears upon the ivory, and bits of grass and moss upon the lower parts, and one rail bent awry.

The Time Traveller put the lamp down on the bench, and ran his hand along the damaged rail. "It's all right now," he said. "The story I told you was true. I'm sorry to have brought you out here in the cold." He took up the lamp, and, in an absolute silence, we returned to the smoking-room.

He came into the hall with us and helped the Editor on with his coat. The Medical Man looked into his face and, with a certain hesitation, told him he was suffering from overwork, at which he laughed hugely. I remember him standing in the open doorway, bawling good night.

I shared a cab with the Editor. He thought the tale a "gaudy lie." For my own part I was unable to come to a conclusion. The story was so fantastic and incredible, the telling so credible and sober. I lay awake most of the night thinking about it. I determined to go next day and see the Time Traveller again. I was told he was in the laboratory, and being on easy terms in the house, I went up to him. The laboratory, however, was empty. I stared for a minute at the Time Machine and put out my hand and touched the lever. At that the squat substantial-looking mass swayed like a bough shaken by the wind. Its instability startled me extremely, and I had a queer reminiscence of the childish days when I used to be forbidden to meddle. I came back through the corridor. The Time Traveller met me in the smoking-room. He was coming from the house. He had a small camera under one arm and a knapsack under the other. He laughed when he saw me, and gave me an elbow to shake. "I'm frightfully busy," said he, "with that thing in there."

"But is it not some hoax?" I said. "Do you really travel through time?"

"Really and truly I do." And he looked frankly into my eyes. He hesitated. His eye wandered about the room. "I only want

half an hour," he said. "I know why you came, and it's awfully good of you. There's some magazines here. If you'll stop to lunch I'll prove you this time travelling up to the hilt, specimen and all. If you'll forgive my leaving you now?"

I consented, hardly comprehending then the full import of his words, and he nodded and went on down the corridor. I heard the door of the laboratory slam, seated myself in a chair, and took up a daily paper. What was he going to do before lunch-time? Then suddenly I was reminded by an advertisement that I had promised to meet Richardson, the publisher, at two. I looked at my watch, and saw that I could barely save that engagement. I got up and went down the passage to tell the Time Traveller.

As I took hold of the handle of the door I heard an exclamation, oddly truncated at the end, and a click and a thud. A gust of air whirled round me as I opened the door, and from within came the sound of broken glass falling on the floor. The Time Traveller was not there. I seemed to see a ghostly, indistinct figure sitting in a whirling mass of black and brass for a moment—a figure so transparent that the bench behind with its sheets of drawings was absolutely distinct; but this phantasm vanished as I rubbed my eyes. The Time Machine had gone. Save for a subsiding stir of dust, the further end of the laboratory was empty. A pane of the skylight had, apparently, just been blown in.

I felt an unreasonable amazement. I knew that something strange had happened, and for the moment could not distinguish what the strange thing might be. As I stood staring, the door into the garden opened, and the man-servant appeared.

We looked at each other. Then ideas began to come. "Has Mr. —— gone out that way?" said I.

"No, sir. No one has come out this way. I was expecting to find him here."

At that I understood. At the risk of disappointing Richardson I stayed on, waiting for the Time Traveller; waiting for the second,

perhaps still stranger story, and the specimens and photographs he would bring with him. But I am beginning now to fear that I must wait a lifetime. The Time Traveller vanished three years ago. And, as everybody knows now, he has never returned.

Epilogue

One cannot choose but wonder. Will he ever return? It may be that he swept back into the past, and fell among the blood-drinking, hairy savages of the Age of Unpolished Stone; into the abysses of the Cretaceous Sea; or among the grotesque saurians, the huge reptilian brutes of the Jurassic times. He may even now—if I may use the phrase—be wandering on some plesiosaurus-haunted Oolitic coral reef, or beside the lonely saline lakes of the Triassic Age. Or did he go forward, into one of the nearer ages, in which men are still men, but with the riddles of our own time answered and its wearisome problems solved? Into the manhood of the race: for I, for my own part, cannot think that these latter days of weak experiment, fragmentary theory, and mutual discord are indeed man's culminating time! I say, for my own part. He, I know—for the question had been discussed among us long before the Time Machine was made—thought but cheerlessly of the Advancement of Mankind, and saw in the growing pile of civilization only a foolish heaping that must inevitably fall back upon and destroy its makers in the end. If that is so, it remains for us to live as though it were not so. But to me the future is still black and blank—is a vast ignorance, lit at a few casual places by the memory of his story. And I have by me, for my comfort, two strange white flowers—shrivelled now, and brown and flat and brittle—to witness that even when mind and strength had gone, gratitude and a mutual tenderness still lived on in the heart of man.

The Invisible Man

Chapter I

THE STRANGE MAN'S ARRIVAL

The stranger came early in February one wintry day, through a biting wind and a driving snow, the last snowfall of the year, over the down, walking as it seemed from Bramblehurst railway station, and carrying a little black portmanteau in his thickly gloved hand. He was wrapped up from head to foot, and the brim of his soft felt hat hid every inch of his face but the shiny tip of his nose; the snow had piled itself against his shoulders and chest, and added a white crest to the burden he carried. He staggered into the Coach and Horses more dead than alive, and flung his portmanteau down. "A fire," he cried, "in the name of human charity! A room and a fire!" He stamped and shook the snow from off himself in the bar, and followed Mrs. Hall into her guest parlour to strike his bargain. And with that much introduction, that and a couple of sovereigns flung upon the table, he took up his quarters in the inn.

Mrs. Hall lit the fire and left him there while she went to prepare him a meal with her own hands. A guest to stop at Iping in the wintertime was an unheard-of piece of luck, let alone a guest who was no "haggler," and she was resolved to show herself worthy of her good fortune. As soon as the bacon was well under way, and Millie, her lymphatic aid, had been brisked up a bit by a few deftly chosen expressions of contempt, she carried the cloth, plates, and glasses into the parlour and began to lay them with the utmost *éclat*. Although the fire was burning up briskly, she was surprised to see that her visitor still wore his hat and coat, standing with his back to her and staring out of the window at the falling snow in the yard. His gloved hands were clasped behind him, and he seemed to be lost in thought. She noticed that the melting snow that still sprinkled his shoulders

dripped upon her carpet. "Can I take your hat and coat, sir," she said, "and give them a good dry in the kitchen?"

"No," he said without turning.

She was not sure she had heard him, and was about to repeat her question.

He turned his head and looked at her over his shoulder. "I prefer to keep them on," he said with emphasis, and she noticed that he wore big blue spectacles with sidelights, and had a bush side-whisker over his coat-collar that completely hid his cheeks and face.

"Very well, sir," she said. "*As* you like. In a bit the room will be warmer."

He made no answer, and had turned his face away from her again, and Mrs. Hall, feeling that her conversational advances were ill-timed, laid the rest of the table things in a quick staccato and whisked out of the room. When she returned he was still standing there, like a man of stone, his back hunched, his collar turned up, his dripping hat-brim turned down, hiding his face and ears completely. She put down the eggs and bacon with considerable emphasis, and called rather than said to him, "Your lunch is served, sir."

"Thank you," he said at the same time, and did not stir until she was closing the door. Then he swung round and approached the table.

As she went behind the bar to the kitchen she heard a sound repeated at regular intervals. Chirk, chirk, chirk, it went, the sound of a spoon being rapidly whisked round a basin. "That girl!" she said. "There! I clean forgot it. It's her being so long!" And while she herself finished mixing the mustard, she gave Millie a few verbal stabs for her excessive slowness. She had cooked the ham and eggs, laid the table, and done everything, while Millie (help indeed!) had only succeeded in delaying the mustard. And him a new guest and wanting to stay! Then she filled the mustard pot, and, putting it with a certain stateliness upon a gold and black tea-tray, carried it into the parlour.

She rapped and entered promptly. As she did so her visitor moved quickly, so that she got but a glimpse of a white object disappearing behind the table. It would seem he was picking something from the floor. She rapped down the mustard pot on the table, and then she noticed the overcoat and hat had been taken off and put over a chair in front of the fire, and a pair of wet boots threatened rust to her steel fender. She went to these things resolutely. "I suppose I may have them to dry now," she said in a voice that brooked no denial.

"Leave the hat," said her visitor in a muffled voice, and turning she saw he had raised his head and was sitting and looking at her.

For a moment she stood gaping at him, too surprised to speak.

He held a white cloth—it was a serviette he had brought with him—over the lower part of his face, so that his mouth and jaws were completely hidden, and that was the reason of his muffled voice. But it was not that which startled Mrs. Hall. It was the fact that all his forehead above his blue glasses was covered by a white bandage, and that another covered his ears, leaving not a scrap of his face exposed excepting only his pink, peaked nose. It was bright, pink, and shiny just as it had been at first. He wore a dark-brown velvet jacket with a high, black, linen-lined collar turned up about his neck. The thick black hair, escaping as it could below and between the cross bandages, projected in curious tails and horns, giving him the strangest appearance conceivable. This muffled and bandaged head was so unlike what she had anticipated, that for a moment she was rigid.

He did not remove the serviette, but remained holding it, as she saw now, with a brown gloved hand, and regarding her with his inscrutable blue glasses. "Leave the hat," he said, speaking very distinctly through the white cloth.

Her nerves began to recover from the shock they had received. She placed the hat on the chair again by the fire. "I didn't know, sir," she began, "that—" and she stopped embarrassed.

"Thank you," he said drily, glancing from her to the door and then at her again.

"I'll have them nicely dried, sir, at once," she said, and carried his clothes out of the room. She glanced at his white-swathed head and blue goggles again as she was going out of the door; but his napkin was still in front of his face. She shivered a little as she closed the door behind her, and her face was eloquent of her surprise and perplexity. "I *never*," she whispered. "There!" She went quite softly to the kitchen, and was too preoccupied to ask Millie what she was messing about with *now*, when she got there.

The visitor sat and listened to her retreating feet. He glanced inquiringly at the window before he removed his serviette, and resumed his meal. He took a mouthful, glanced suspiciously at the window, took another mouthful, then rose and, taking the serviette in his hand, walked across the room and pulled the blind down to the top of the white muslin that obscured the lower panes. This left the room in a twilight. This done, he returned with an easier air to the table and his meal.

"The poor soul's had an accident or an op'ration or somethin'," said Mrs. Hall. "What a turn them bandages did give me, to be sure!"

She put on some more coal, unfolded the clothes-horse, and extended the traveller's coat upon this. "And they goggles! Why, he looked more like a divin' helmet than a human man!" She hung his muffler on a corner of the horse. "And holding that handkerchief over his mouth all the time. Talkin' through it! . . . Perhaps his mouth was hurt too—maybe."

She turned round, as one who suddenly remembers. "Bless my soul alive!" she said, going off at a tangent. "Ain't you done them taters *yet*, Millie?"

When Mrs. Hall went to clear away the stranger's lunch, her idea that his mouth must also have been cut or disfigured in the accident she supposed him to have suffered, was confirmed, for he was smoking a pipe, and all the time that she was in the room he never loosened the silk muffler he had wrapped round the lower part of his face to put the mouthpiece to his

lips. Yet it was not forgetfulness, for she saw he glanced at it as it smouldered out. He sat in the corner with his back to the window-blind and spoke now, having eaten and drunk and being comfortably warmed through, with less aggressive brevity than before. The reflection of the fire lent a kind of red animation to his big spectacles they had lacked hitherto.

"I have some luggage," he said, "at Bramblehurst station," and he asked her how he could have it sent. He bowed his bandaged head quite politely in acknowledgment of her explanation. "To-morrow?" he said. "There is no speedier delivery?" and seemed quite disappointed when she answered, "No." Was she quite sure? No man with a trap who would go over?

Mrs. Hall, nothing loath, answered his questions and developed a conversation. "It's a steep road by the down, sir," she said in answer to the question about a trap; and then, snatching at an opening, said, "It was there a carriage was up-settled, a year ago and more. A gentleman killed, besides his coachman. Accidents, sir, happen in a moment, don't they?"

But the visitor was not to be drawn so easily. "They do," he said through his muffler, eyeing her quietly through his impenetrable glasses.

"But they take long enough to get well, don't they? . . . There was my sister's son, Tom, jest cut his arm with a scythe, tumbled on it in the 'ayfield, and, bless me! he was three months tied up sir. You'd hardly believe it. It's regular given me a dread of a scythe, sir."

"I can quite understand that," said the visitor.

"He was afraid, one time, that he'd have to have an op'ration—he was that bad, sir."

The visitor laughed abruptly, a bark of a laugh that he seemed to bite and kill in his mouth. "*Was* he?" he said.

"He was, sir. And no laughing matter to them as had the doing for him, as I had—my sister being took up with her little ones so much. There was bandages to do, sir, and bandages to undo. So that if I may make so bold as to say it, sir—"

"Will you get me some matches?" said the visitor, quite abruptly. "My pipe is out."

Mrs. Hall was pulled up suddenly. It was certainly rude of him, after telling him all she had done. She gasped at him for a moment, and remembered the two sovereigns. She went for the matches.

"Thanks," he said concisely, as she put them down, and turned his shoulder upon her and stared out of the window again. It was altogether too discouraging. Evidently he was sensitive on the topic of operations and bandages. She did not "make so bold as to say," however, after all. But his snubbing way had irritated her, and Millie had a hot time of it that afternoon.

The visitor remained in the parlour until four o'clock, without giving the ghost of an excuse for an intrusion. For the most part he was quite still during that time; it would seem he sat in the growing darkness smoking in the firelight, perhaps dozing.

Once or twice a curious listener might have heard him at the coals, and for the space of five minutes he was audible pacing the room. He seemed to be talking to himself. Then the armchair creaked as he sat down again.

Chapter II

MR. TEDDY HENFREY'S FIRST IMPRESSIONS

At four o'clock, when it was fairly dark and Mrs. Hall was screwing up her courage to go in and ask her visitor if he would take some tea, Teddy Henfrey, the clock-jobber, came into the bar. "My sakes! Mrs. Hall," said he, "but this is terrible weather for thin boots!" The snow outside was falling faster.

Mrs. Hall agreed, and then noticed he had his bag with him. "Now you're here, Mr. Teddy," said she, "I'd be glad if you'd give th' old clock in the parlour a bit of a look. 'Tis going, and it strikes well and hearty; but the hour-hand won't do nuthin' but point at six."

And leading the way, she went across to the parlour door and rapped and entered.

Her visitor, she saw as she opened the door, was seated in the armchair before the fire, dozing it would seem, with his bandaged head drooping on one side. The only light in the room was the red glow from the fire—which lit his eyes like adverse railway signals, but left his downcast face in darkness—and the scanty vestiges of the day that came in through the open door. Everything was ruddy, shadowy, and indistinct to her, the more so since she had just been lighting the bar lamp, and her eyes were dazzled. But for a second it seemed to her that the man she looked at had an enormous mouth wide open—a vast and incredible mouth that swallowed the whole of the lower portion of his face. It was the sensation of a moment: the white-bound head, the monstrous goggle eyes, and this huge yawn below it. Then he stirred, started up in his chair, put up his hand. She opened the door wide, so that the room was lighter, and she

saw him more clearly, with the muffler held up to his face just as she had seen him hold the serviette before. The shadows, she fancied, had tricked her.

"Would you mind, sir, this man a-coming to look at the clock, sir?" she said, recovering from the momentary shock.

"Look at the clock?" he said, staring round in a drowsy manner, and speaking over his hand, and then, getting more fully awake, "Certainly."

Mrs. Hall went away to get a lamp, and he rose and stretched himself. Then came the light, and Mr. Teddy Henfrey, entering, was confronted by this bandaged person. He was, he says, "taken aback."

"Good afternoon," said the stranger, regarding him, as Mr. Henfrey says, with a vivid sense of the dark spectacles, "like a lobster."

"I hope," said Mr. Henfrey, "that it's no intrusion."

"None whatever," said the stranger. "Though, I understand," he said turning to Mrs. Hall, "that this room is really to be mine for my own private use."

"I thought, sir," said Mrs. Hall, "you'd prefer the clock—" She was going to say "mended."

"Certainly," said the stranger, "certainly—but, as a rule, I like to be alone and undisturbed.

"But I'm really glad to have the clock seen to," he said, seeing a certain hesitation in Mr. Henfrey's manner. "Very glad." Mr. Henfrey had intended to apologise and withdraw, but this anticipation reassured him. The stranger turned round with his back to the fireplace and put his hands behind his back. "And presently," he said, "when the clock-mending is over, I think I should like to have some tea. But not till the clock-mending is over."

Mrs. Hall was about to leave the room—she made no conversational advances this time, because she did not want to be snubbed in front of Mr. Henfrey—when her visitor asked her if she had made any arrangements about his boxes at

Bramblehurst. She told him she had mentioned the matter to the postman, and that the carrier could bring them over on the morrow. "You are certain that is the earliest?" he said.

She was certain, with a marked coldness.

"I should explain," he added, "what I was really too cold and fatigued to do before, that I am an experimental investigator."

"Indeed, sir," said Mrs. Hall, much impressed.

"And my baggage contains apparatus and appliances."

"Very useful things indeed they are, sir," said Mrs. Hall.

"And I'm very naturally anxious to get on with my inquiries."

"Of course, sir."

"My reason for coming to Iping," he proceeded, with a certain deliberation of manner, "was—a desire for solitude. I do not wish to be disturbed in my work. In addition to my work, an accident—"

"I thought as much," said Mrs. Hall to herself.

"—necessitates a certain retirement. My eyes—are sometimes so weak and painful that I have to shut myself up in the dark for hours together. Lock myself up. Sometimes—now and then. Not at present, certainly. At such times the slightest disturbance, the entry of a stranger into the room, is a source of excruciating annoyance to me—it is well these things should be understood."

"Certainly, sir," said Mrs. Hall. "And if I might make so bold as to ask—"

"That I think, is all," said the stranger, with that quietly irresistible air of finality he could assume at will. Mrs. Hall reserved her question and sympathy for a better occasion.

After Mrs. Hall had left the room, he remained standing in front of the fire, glaring, so Mr. Henfrey puts it, at the clock-mending. Mr. Henfrey not only took off the hands of the clock, and the face, but extracted the works; and he tried to work in as slow and quiet and unassuming a manner as possible. He worked with the lamp close to him, and the green shade threw a brilliant light upon his hands, and upon the frame and wheels, and left the rest of the room shadowy. When he looked up, coloured patches swam in his eyes. Being constitutionally of a curious nature, he had removed the works—a quite unnecessary proceeding—with the idea of delaying his departure and perhaps falling into conversation with the stranger. But the stranger stood there, perfectly silent and still. So still, it got on Henfrey's nerves. He felt alone in the room and looked up, and there, grey and dim, was the bandaged head and huge blue lenses staring fixedly, with a mist of green spots drifting in front of them. It was so uncanny to Henfrey that for a minute they remained staring blankly at one another. Then Henfrey looked down again. Very uncomfortable position! One would like to say something. Should he remark that the weather was very cold for the time of year?

He looked up as if to take aim with that introductory shot. "The weather—" he began.

"Why don't you finish and go?" said the rigid figure, evidently in a state of painfully suppressed rage. "All you've got to do is to fix the hour-hand on its axle. You're simply humbugging—"

"Certainly, sir—one minute more. I overlooked—" and Mr. Henfrey finished and went.

But he went feeling excessively annoyed. "Damn it!" said Mr. Henfrey to himself, trudging down the village through the thawing snow. "A man must do a clock at times, sure lie."

And again, "Can't a man look at you? Ugly!"

And yet again, "Seemingly not. If the police was wanting you you couldn't be more wropped and bandaged."

At Gleeson's corner he saw Hall, who had recently married the stranger's hostess at the Coach and Horses, and who now drove the Iping conveyance, when occasional people required it, to Sidderbridge Junction, coming towards him on his return from that place. Hall had evidently been "stopping a bit" at Sidderbridge, to judge by his driving. "'ow do, Teddy?" he said, passing.

"You got a rum un up home!" said Teddy.

Hall very sociably pulled up. "What's that?" he asked.

"Rum-looking customer stopping at the Coach and Horses," said Teddy. "My sakes!"

And he proceeded to give Hall a vivid description of his grotesque guest. "Looks a bit like a disguise, don't it? I'd like to see a man's face if I had him stopping in *my* place," said Henfrey. "But women are that trustful—where strangers are concerned. He's took your rooms and he ain't even given a name, Hall."

"You don't say so!" said Hall, who was a man of sluggish apprehension.

"Yes," said Teddy. "By the week. Whatever he is, you can't get rid of him under the week. And he's got a lot of luggage coming to-morrow, so he says. Let's hope it won't be stones in boxes, Hall."

He told Hall how his aunt at Hastings had been swindled by a stranger with empty portmanteaux. Altogether he left Hall vaguely suspicious. "Get up, old girl," said Hall. "I s'pose I must see 'bout this."

Teddy trudged on his way with his mind considerably relieved.

Instead of "seeing 'bout it," however, Hall on his return was severely rated by his wife on the length of time he had spent in Sidderbridge, and his mild inquiries were answered snappishly and in a manner not to the point. But the seed of suspicion Teddy had sown germinated in the mind of Mr. Hall in spite of these discouragements. "You wim' don't know everything," said Mr. Hall, resolved to ascertain more about the personality of his guest at the earliest possible opportunity. And after the stranger had gone to bed, which he did about half-past nine, Mr. Hall went very aggressively into the parlour and looked very hard at his wife's furniture, just to show that the stranger wasn't master there, and scrutinised closely and a little contemptuously a sheet of mathematical computations the stranger had left. When retiring for the night he instructed Mrs. Hall to look very closely at the stranger's luggage when it came next day.

"You mind you own business, Hall," said Mrs. Hall, "and I'll mind mine."

She was all the more inclined to snap at Hall because the stranger was undoubtedly an unusually strange sort of stranger, and she was by no means assured about him in her own mind. In the middle of the night she woke up dreaming of huge white heads like turnips, that came trailing after her, at the end of interminable necks, and with vast black eyes. But being a sensible woman, she subdued her terrors and turned over and went to sleep again.

Chapter III

THE THOUSAND AND ONE BOTTLES

So it was that on the ninth day of February, at the beginning of the thaw, this singular person fell out of infinity into Iping Village. Next day his luggage arrived through the slush—and very remarkable luggage it was. There were a couple of trunks indeed, such as a rational man might need, but in addition there were a box of books,—big, fat books, of which some were just in an incomprehensible handwriting,—and a dozen or more crates, boxes, and cases, containing objects packed in straw, as it seemed to Hall, tugging with a casual curiosity at the straw—glass bottles. The stranger, muffled in hat, coat, gloves, and wrapper, came out impatiently to meet Fearenside's cart, while Hall was having a word or so of gossip preparatory to helping bring them in. Out he came, not noticing Fearenside's dog, who was sniffing in a *dilettante* spirit at Hall's legs. "Come along with those boxes," he said. "I've been waiting long enough."

And he came down the steps towards the tail of the cart as if to lay hands on the smaller crate.

No sooner had Fearenside's dog caught sight of him, however, than it began to bristle and growl savagely, and when he rushed down the steps it gave an undecided hop, and then sprang straight at his hand. "Whup!" cried Hall, jumping back, for he was no hero with dogs, and Fearenside howled, "Lie down!" and snatched his whip.

They saw the dog's teeth had slipped the hand, heard a kick, saw the dog execute a flanking jump and get home on the stranger's leg, and heard the rip of his trousering. Then the finer end of Fearenside's whip reached his property, and the dog, yelping with dismay, retreated under the wheels of the waggon.

It was all the business of a swift half-minute. No one spoke, everyone shouted. The stranger glanced swiftly at his torn glove and at his leg, made as if he would stoop to the latter, then turned and rushed swiftly up the steps into the inn. They heard him go headlong across the passage and up the uncarpeted stairs to his bedroom.

"You brute, you!" said Fearenside, climbing off the waggon with his whip in his hand, while the dog watched him through the wheel. "Come here," said Fearenside—"You'd better."

Hall had stood gaping. "He wuz bit," said Hall. "I'd better go and see to en," and he trotted after the stranger. He met Mrs. Hall in the passage. "Carrier's darg," he said, "bit en."

He went straight upstairs, and the stranger's door being ajar, he pushed it open and was entering without any ceremony, being of a naturally sympathetic turn of mind.

The blind was down and the room dim. He caught a glimpse of a most singular thing, what seemed a handless arm waving towards him, and a face of three huge indeterminate spots on white, very like the face of a pale pansy. Then he was struck violently in the chest, hurled back, and the door slammed in his face and locked. It was so rapid that it gave him no time to observe. A waving of indecipherable shapes, a blow, and a concussion. There he stood on the dark little landing, wondering what it might be that he had seen.

A couple of minutes after, he joined the little group that had formed outside the Coach and Horses. There was Fearenside telling about it all over again for the second time; there was Mrs. Hall saying his dog didn't have no business to bite her guests; there was Huxter, the general dealer from over the road, interrogative; and Sandy Wadgers from the forge, judicial; besides women and children—all of them saying fatuities: "Wouldn't let en bite *me*, I knows"; "'Tasn't right *have* such dargs"; "Whad *'e* bite 'n for, than?" and so forth.

Mr. Hall, staring at them from the steps and listening, found it incredible that he had seen anything so very remarkable happen

upstairs. Besides, his vocabulary was altogether too limited to express his impressions.

"He don't want no help, he says," he said in answer to his wife's inquiry. "We'd better be a-takin' of his luggage in."

"He ought to have it cauterised at once," said Mr. Huxter; "especially if it's at all inflamed."

"I'd shoot en, that's what I'd do," said a lady in the group.

Suddenly the dog began growling again.

"Come along," cried an angry voice in the doorway, and there stood the muffled stranger with his collar turned up, and his hat-brim bent down. "The sooner you get those things in the better I'll be pleased." It is stated by an anonymous bystander that his trousers and gloves had been changed.

"Was you hurt, sir?" said Fearenside. "I'm rare sorry the darg—"

"Not a bit," said the stranger. "Never broke the skin. Hurry up with those things."

He then swore to himself, so Mr. Hall asserts.

Directly the first crate was carried into the parlour, in accordance with his directons, the stranger flung himself upon it with extraordinary eagerness, and began to unpack it, scattering the straw with an utter disregard of Mrs. Hall's carpet. And from it he began to produce bottles—little fat bottles containing powders, small and slender bottles containing coloured and white fluids, fluted blue bottles labeled *Poison*, bottles with round bodies and slender necks, large green-glass bottles, large white-glass bottles, bottles with glass stoppers and frosted labels, bottles with fine corks, bottles with bungs, bottles with wooden caps, wine bottles, salad-oil bottles—putting them in rows on the chiffonnier, on the mantel, on the table under the window, round the floor, on the bookshelf,—everywhere. The chemist's shop in Bramblehurst could not boast half so many. Quite a sight it was. Crate after crate yielded bottles, until all six were empty and the table high with straw; the only things that came out of these crates

besides the bottles were a number of test-tubes and a carefully packed balance.

And directly the crates were unpacked, the stranger went to the window and set to work, not troubling in the least about the litter of straw, the fire which had gone out, the box of books outside, nor for the trunks and other luggage that had gone upstairs.

When Mrs. Hall took his dinner in to him, he was already so absorbed in his work, pouring little drops out of the bottles into test-tubes, that he did not hear her until she had swept away the bulk of the straw and put the tray on the table, with some little emphasis perhaps, seeing the state that the floor was in. Then he half turned his head and immediately turned it away again. But she saw he had removed his glasses; they were beside him on the table, and it seemed to her that his eye sockets were extraordinarily hollow. He put on his spectacles again, and then turned and faced her. She was about to complain of the straw on the floor when he anticipated her.

"I wish you wouldn't come in without knocking," he said in the tone of abnormal exasperation that seemed so characteristic of him.

"I knocked, but seemingly—"

"Perhaps you did. But in my investigations—my really very urgent and necessary investigations—the slightest disturbance, the jar of a door—I must ask you—"

"Certainly, sir. You can turn the lock if you're like that, you know—anytime."

"A very good idea," said the stranger.

"This stror, sir, if I might make so bold as to remark—"

"Don't. If the straw makes trouble put it down in the bill." And he mumbled at her—words suspiciously like curses.

He was so odd, standing there, so aggressive and explosive, bottle in one hand and test-tube in the other, that Mrs. Hall was quite alarmed. But she was a resolute woman. "In which case, I should like to know, sir, what you consider—"

"A shilling—put down a shilling. Surely a shilling's enough?"

"So be it," said Mrs. Hall, taking up the table-cloth and beginning to spread it over the table. "If you're satisfied, of course—"

He turned and sat down, with his coat-collar toward her.

All the afternoon he worked with the door locked and, as Mrs. Hall testifies, for the most part in silence. But once there was a concussion and a sound of bottles ringing together as though the table had been hit, and the smash of a bottle flung violently down, and then a rapid pacing athwart the room. Fearing "something was the matter," she went to the door and listened, not caring to knock.

"I can't go on," he was raving. "I can't go on. Three hundred thousand, four hundred thousand! The huge multitude! Cheated! All my life it may take me! Patience! Patience indeed! Fool and liar!"

There was a noise of hobnails on the bricks in the bar, and Mrs. Hall had very reluctantly to leave the rest of his soliloquy. When she returned the room was silent again, save for the faint crepitation of his chair and the occasional clink of a bottle. It was all over. The stranger had resumed work.

When she took in his tea she saw broken glass in the corner of the room under the concave mirror, and a golden stain that had been carelessly wiped. She called attention to it.

"Put it down in the bill," snapped her visitor. "For God's sake don't worry me. If there's damage done, put it down in the bill," and he went on ticking a list in the exercise book before him.

"I'll tell you something," said Fearenside mysteriously. It was late in the afternoon, and they were in the little beer-shop of Iping Hanger.

"Well?" said Teddy Henfrey.

"This chap you're speaking of, what my dog bit. Well—he's black. Leastways, his legs are. I seed through the tear of his trousers and the tear of his glove. You'd have expected a sort

of pinky to show, wouldn't you? Well—there wasn't none. Just blackness. I tell you, he's as black as my hat."

"My sakes!" said Henfrey. "It's a rummy case altogether. Why, his nose is as pink as paint!"

"That's true," said Fearenside. "I knows that. And I tell 'ee what I'm thinking. That marn's a piebald, Teddy. Black here and white there—in patches. And he's ashamed of it. He's a kind of half-breed, and the colour's come off patchy instead of mixing. I've heard of such things before. And it's the common way with horses, as anyone can see."

Chapter IV

MR. CUSS INTERVIEWS THE STRANGER

I have told the circumstances of the stranger's arrival in Iping with a certain fulness of detail, in order that the curious impression he created may be understood by the reader. But excepting two odd incidents, the circumstances of his stay until the extraordinary day of the club festival may be passed over very cursorily. There were a number of skirmishes with Mrs. Hall on matters of domestic discipline, but in every case until late April, when the first signs of penury began, he over-rode her by the easy expedient of an extra payment. Hall did not like him, and whenever he dared he talked of the advisability of getting rid of him; but he showed his dislike chiefly by concealing it ostentatiously, and avoiding his visitor as much as possible. "Wait till the summer," said Mrs. Hall sagely, "when the artisks are beginning to come. Then we'll see. He may be a bit overbearing, but bills settled punctual is bills settled punctual, whatever you'd like to say."

The stranger did not go to church, and indeed made no difference between Sunday and the irreligious days, even in costume. He worked, as Mrs. Hall thought, very fitfully. Some days he would come down early and be continuously busy. On others he would rise late, pace his room, fretting audibly for hours together, smoke, sleep in the armchair by the fire. Communication with the world beyond the village he had none. His temper continued very uncertain; for the most part his manner was that of a man suffering under almost unendurable provocation, and once or twice things were snapped, torn, crushed, or broken in spasmodic gusts of violence. He seemed under a chronic irritation of the greatest intensity. His habit of talking to himself in a low voice grew steadily upon him,

but though Mrs. Hall listened conscientiously she could make neither head nor tail of what she heard.

He rarely went abroad by daylight, but at twilight he would go out muffled up invisibly, whether the weather were cold or not, and he chose the loneliest paths and those most overshadowed by trees and banks. His goggling spectacles and ghastly bandaged face under the penthouse of his hat, came with a disagreeable suddenness out of the darkness upon one or two home-going labourers, and Teddy Henfrey, tumbling out of the Scarlet Coat one night, at half-past nine, was scared shamefully by the stranger's skull-like head (he was walking hat in hand) lit by the sudden light of the opened inn door. Such children as saw him at nightfall dreamt of bogies, and it seemed doubtful whether he disliked boys more than they disliked him, or the reverse—but there was certainly a vivid enough dislike on either side.

It was inevitable that a person of so remarkable an appearance and bearing should form a frequent topic in such a village as Iping. Opinion was greatly divided about his occupation. Mrs. Hall was sensitive on the point. When questioned, she explained very carefully that he was an "experimental investigator," going gingerly over the syllables as one who dreads pitfalls. When asked what an experimental investigator was, she would say with a touch of superiority that most educated people knew such things as that, and would thus explain that he "discovered things." Her visitor had had an accident, she said, which temporarily discoloured his face and hands, and being of a sensitive disposition, he was averse to any public notice of the fact.

Out of her hearing there was a view largely entertained that he was a criminal trying to escape from justice by wrapping himself up so as to conceal himself altogether from the eye of the police. This idea sprang from the brain of Mr. Teddy Henfrey. No crime of any magnitude dating from the middle or end of February was known to have occurred. Elaborated in the imagination of Mr. Gould, the probationary assistant in the

National School, this theory took the form that the stranger was an Anarchist in disguise, preparing explosives, and he resolved to undertake such detective operations as his time permitted. These consisted for the most part in looking very hard at the stranger whenever they met, or in asking people who had never seen the stranger, leading questions about him. But he detected nothing.

Another school of opinion followed Mr. Fearenside, and either accepted the piebald view or some modification of it; as, for instance, Silas Durgan, who was heard to assert that "if he choses to show enself at fairs he'd make his fortune in no time," and being a bit of a theologian, compared the stranger to the man with the one talent. Yet another view explained the entire matter by regarding the stranger as a harmless lunatic. That had the advantage of accounting for everything straight away.

Between these main groups there were waverers and compromisers. Sussex folk have few superstitions, and it was only after the events of early April that the thought of the supernatural was first whispered in the village. Even then it was only credited among the women folks.

But whatever they thought of him, people in Iping, on the whole, agreed in disliking him. His irritability, though it might have been comprehensible to an urban brain-worker, was an amazing thing to these quiet Sussex villagers. The frantic gesticulations they surprised now and then, the headlong pace after nightfall that swept him upon them round quiet corners, the inhuman bludgeoning of all tentative advances of curiosity, the taste for twilight that led to the closing of doors, the pulling down of blinds, the extinction of candles and lamps—who could agree with such goings on? They drew aside as he passed down the village, and when he had gone by, young humourists would up with coat-collars and down with hat-brims, and go pacing nervously after him in imitation of his occult bearing. There was a song popular at that time called the "Bogey Man." Miss Statchell sang it at the schoolroom concert (in aid of the

church lamps), and thereafter whenever one or two of the villagers were gathered together and the stranger appeared, a bar or so of this tune, more or less sharp or flat, was whistled in the midst of them. Also belated little children would call "Bogey Man!" after him, and make off tremulously elated.

Cuss, the general practitioner, was devoured by curiosity. The bandages excited his professional interest, the report of the thousand and one bottles aroused his jealous regard. All through April and May he coveted an opportunity of talking to the stranger, and at last, towards Whitsuntide, he could stand it no longer, but hit upon the subscription-list for a village nurse as an excuse. He was surprised to find that Mr. Hall did not know his guest's name. "He give a name," said Mrs. Hall—an assertion which was quite unfounded—"but I didn't rightly hear it." She thought it seemed so silly not to know the man's name.

Cuss rapped at the parlour door and entered. There was a fairly audible imprecation from within. "Pardon my intrusion," said Cuss, and then the door closed and cut Mrs. Hall off from the rest of the conversation.

She could hear the murmur of voices for the next ten minutes, then a cry of surprise, a stirring of feet, a chair flung aside, a bark of laughter, quick steps to the door, and Cuss appeared, his face white, his eyes staring over his shoulder. He left the door open behind him, and without looking at her strode across the hall and went down the steps, and she heard his feet hurrying along the road. He carried his hat in his hand. She stood behind the door, looking at the open door of the parlour. Then she heard the stranger laughing quietly, and then his footsteps came across the room. She could not see his face where she stood. The parlour door slammed, and the place was silent again.

Cuss went straight up the village to Bunting the vicar. "Am I mad?" Cuss began abruptly, as he entered the shabby little study. "Do I look like an insane person?"

"What's happened?" said the vicar, putting the ammonite on the loose sheets of his forthcoming sermon.

"That chap at the inn—"

"Well?"

"Give me something to drink," said Cuss, and he sat down.

When his nerves had been steadied by a glass of cheap sherry—the only drink the good vicar had available—he told him of the interview he had just had. "Went in," he gasped, "and began to demand a subscription for that Nurse Fund. He'd stuck his hands in his pockets as I came in, and he sat down lumpily in his chair. Sniffed. I told him I'd heard he took an interest in scientific things. He said yes. Sniffed again. Kept on sniffing all the time; evidently recently caught an infernal cold. No wonder, wrapped up like that! I developed the nurse idea, and all the while kept my eyes open. Bottles—chemicals—everywhere. Balance, test-tubes in stands, and a smell of—evening primrose. Would he subscribe? Said he'd consider it. Asked him, point-blank, was he researching. Said he was. A long research? Got quite cross. 'A damnable long research,' said he, blowing the cork out, so to speak. 'Oh,' said I. And out came the grievance. The man was just on the boil, and my question boiled him over. He had been given a prescription, most valuable prescription—what for he wouldn't say. Was it medical? 'Damn you! What are you fishing after?' I apologised. Dignified sniff and cough. He resumed. He'd read it. Five ingredients. Put it down; turned his head. Draught of air from window lifted the paper. Swish, rustle. He was working in a room with an open fireplace, he said. Saw a flicker, and there was the prescription burning and lifting chimneyward. Rushed towards it just as it whisked up the chimney. So! Just at that point, to illustrate his story, out came his arm."

"Well?"

"No hand—just an empty sleeve. Lord! I thought, that's a deformity! Got a cork arm, I suppose, and has taken it off. Then, I thought, there's something odd in that. What the devil keeps that sleeve up and open, if there's nothing in it? There was nothing in it, I tell you. Nothing down it, right down to the joint.

I could see right down it to the elbow, and there was a glimmer of light shining through a tear of the cloth. 'Good God!' I said. Then he stopped. Stared at me with those black goggles of his, and then at his sleeve."

"Well?"

"That's all. He never said a word; just glared, and put his sleeve back in his pocket quickly. 'I was saying,' said he, 'that there was the prescription burning, wasn't I?' Interrogative cough. 'How the devil,' said I, 'can you move an empty sleeve like that?' 'Empty sleeve?' 'Yes,' said I, 'an empty sleeve.'

"'It's an empty sleeve, is it? You saw it was an empty sleeve?' He stood up right away. I stood up too. He came towards me in three very slow steps, and stood quite close. Sniffed venomously. I didn't flinch, though I'm hanged if that bandaged knob of his, and those blinkers, aren't enough to unnerve anyone, coming quietly up to you.

"'You said it was an empty sleeve?' he said. 'Certainly,' I said. At staring and saying nothing a barefaced man, unspectacled, starts scratch. Then very quietly he pulled his sleeve out of his pocket again, and raised his arm towards me as though he would show it to me again. He did it very, very slowly. I looked at it. Seemed an age. 'Well?' said I, clearing my throat, 'there's nothing in it.' Had to say something. I was beginning to feel frightened. I could see right down it. He extended it straight towards me, slowly, slowly—just like that—until the cuff was six inches from my face. Queer thing to see an empty sleeve come at you like that! And then—"

"Well?"

"Something—exactly like a finger and thumb it felt—nipped my nose."

Bunting began to laugh.

"There wasn't anything there!" said Cuss, his voice running up into a shriek at the "there." "It's all very well for you to laugh, but I tell you I was so startled, I hit his cuff hard, and turned around, and cut out of the room—I left him—"

Cuss stopped. There was no mistaking the sincerity of his panic. He turned round in a helpless way and took a second glass of the excellent vicar's very inferior sherry. "When I hit his cuff," said Cuss, "I tell you, it felt exactly like hitting an arm. And there wasn't an arm! There wasn't the ghost of an arm!"

Mr. Bunting thought it over. He looked suspiciously at Cuss. "It's a most remarkable story," he said. He looked very wise and grave indeed. "It's really," said Mr. Bunting with judicial emphasis, "a most remarkable story."

Chapter V

THE BURGLARY AT THE VICARAGE

The facts of the burglary at the vicarage came to us chiefly through the medium of the vicar and his wife. It occurred in the small hours of Whitmonday, the day devoted in Iping to the Club festivities. Mrs. Bunting, it seems, woke up suddenly in the stillness that comes before the dawn, with the strong impression that the door of their bedroom had opened and closed. She did not arouse her husband at first, but sat up in bed listening. She then distinctly heard the pad, pad, pad of bare feet coming out of the adjoining dressing-room and walking along the passage towards the staircase. As soon as she felt assured of this, she aroused the Rev. Mr. Bunting as quietly as possible. He did not strike a light, but putting on his spectacles, her dressing-gown and his bath slippers, he went out on the landing to listen. He heard quite distinctly a fumbling going on at his study desk downstairs, and then a violent sneeze.

At that he returned to his bedroom, armed himself with the most obvious weapon, the poker, and descended the staircase as noiselessly as possible. Mrs. Bunting came out on the landing.

The hour was about four, and the ultimate darkness of the night was past. There was a faint shimmer of light in the hall, but the study doorway yawned impenetrably black. Everything was still except the faint creaking of the stairs under Mr. Bunting's tread, and the slight movements in the study. Then something snapped, the drawer was opened, and there was a rustle of papers. Then came an imprecation, and a match was struck and the study was flooded with yellow light. Mr. Bunting was now in the hall, and through the crack of the door he could see the desk and the open drawer and a candle burning on the desk. But the robber he could not see. He stood there in the

hall undecided what to do, and Mrs. Bunting, her face white and intent, crept slowly downstairs after him. One thing kept Mr. Bunting's courage; the persuasion that this burglar was a resident in the village.

They heard the chink of money, and realised that the robber had found the housekeeping reserve of gold—two pounds ten in half sovereigns altogether. At that sound Mr. Bunting was nerved to abrupt action. Gripping the poker firmly, he rushed into the room, closely followed by Mrs. Bunting. "Surrender!" cried Mr. Bunting, fiercely, and then stooped amazed. Apparently the room was perfectly empty.

Yet their conviction that they had, that very moment, heard somebody moving in the room had amounted to a certainty. For half a minute, perhaps, they stood gaping, then Mrs. Bunting went across the room and looked behind the screen, while Mr. Bunting, by a kindred impulse, peered under the desk. Then Mrs. Bunting turned back the window-curtains, and Mr. Bunting looked up the chimney and probed it with the poker. Then Mrs. Bunting scrutinised the waste-paper basket and Mr. Bunting opened the lid of the coal-scuttle. Then they came to a stop and stood with eyes interrogating each other.

"I could have sworn—" said Mr. Bunting.

"The candle!" said Mr. Bunting. "Who lit the candle?"

"The drawer!" said Mrs. Bunting. "And the money's gone!" She went hastily to the doorway.

"Of all the extraordinary occurrences—"

There was a violent sneeze in the passage. They rushed out, and as they did so the kitchen door slammed. "Bring the candle," said Mr. Bunting, and led the way. They both heard a sound of bolts being hastily shot back.

As he opened the kitchen door he saw through the scullery that the back door was just opening, and the faint light of early dawn displayed the dark masses of the garden beyond. He is certain that nothing went out of the door. It opened, stood open for a moment, and then closed with a slam. As it did so, the candle Mrs. Bunting was carrying from the study flickered and flared. It was a minute or more before they entered the kitchen.

The place was empty. They refastened the back door, examined the kitchen, pantry, and scullery thoroughly, and at last went down into the cellar. There was not a soul to be found in the house, search as they would.

Daylight found the vicar and his wife, a quaintly costumed little couple, still marvelling about on their own ground floor by the unnecessary light of a guttering candle.

Chapter VI

THE FURNITURE THAT WENT MAD

Now it happened that in the early hours of Whit-Monday, before Millie was hunted out for the day, Mr. Hall and Mrs. Hall both rose and went noiselessly down into the cellar. Their business there was of a private nature, and had something to do with the specific gravity of their beer. They had hardly entered the cellar when Mrs. Hall found she had forgotten to bring down a bottle of sarsaparilla from their joint-room. As she was the expert and principal operator in this affair, Hall very properly went upstairs for it.

On the landing he was surprised to see that the stranger's door was ajar. He went on into his own room and found the bottle as he had been directed.

But returning with the bottle, he noticed that the bolts of the front door had been shot back, that the door was in fact simply on the latch. And with a flash of inspiration he connected this with the stranger's room upstairs and the suggestions of Mr. Teddy Henfrey. He distinctly remembered holding the candle while Mrs. Hall shot these bolts overnight. At the sight he stopped, gaping, then with the bottle still in his hand went upstairs again. He rapped at the stranger's door. There was no answer. He rapped again; then pushed the door wide open and entered.

It was as he expected. The bed, the room also, was empty. And what was stranger, even to his heavy intelligence, on the bedroom chair and along the rail of the bed were scattered the garments, the only garments so far as he knew, and the bandages of their guest. His big slouch hat even was cocked jauntily over the bedpost.

As Hall stood there he heard his wife's voice coming out

of the depth of the cellar, with that rapid telescoping of the syllables and interrogative cocking up of the final words to a high note, by which the West Sussex villager is wont to indicate a brisk impatience. "Gearge! You gart what a wand?"

At that he turned and hurried down to her. "Janny," he said, over the rail of the cellar steps, "'tas the truth what Henfrey sez. 'E's not in uz room, 'e ent. And the front door's unbolted."

At first Mrs. Hall did not understand, and as soon as she did she resolved to see the empty room for herself. Hall, still holding the bottle, went first. "If 'e ent there," he said, "his cloes are. And what's 'e doin' without his cloes, then? 'Tas a most curious basness."

As they came up the cellar steps they both, it was afterwards ascertained, fancied they heard the front door open and shut, but seeing it closed and nothing there, neither said a word to the other about it at the time. Mrs. Hall passed her husband in the passage and ran on first upstairs. Someone sneezed on the staircase. Hall, following six steps behind, thought that he heard her sneeze. She, going on first, was under the impression that Hall was sneezing. She flung open the door and stood regarding the room. "Of all the curious!" she said.

She heard a sniff close behind her head as it seemed, and turning, was surprised to see Hall a dozen feet off on the topmost stair. But in another moment he was beside her. She bent forward and put her hand on the pillow and then under the clothes.

"Cold," she said. "He's been up this hour or more."

As she did so, a most extraordinary thing happened,—the bed-clothes gathered themselves together, leapt up suddenly into a sort of peak, and then jumped headlong over the bottom rail. It was exactly as if a hand had clutched them in the centre and flung them aside. Immediately after, the stranger's hat hopped off the bed-post, described a whirling flight in the air through the better part of a circle, and then dashed straight at Mrs. Hall's face. Then as swiftly came the sponge from the washstand; and

then the chair, flinging the stranger's coat and trousers carelessly aside, and laughing drily in a voice singularly like the stranger's, turned itself up with its four legs at Mrs. Hall, seemed to take aim at her for a moment, and charged at her. She screamed and turned, and then the chair legs came gently but firmly against her back and impelled her and Hall out of the room. The door slammed violently and was locked. The chair and bed seemed to be executing a dance of triumph for a moment, and then abruptly everything was still.

Mrs. Hall was left almost in a fainting condition in Mr. Hall's arms on the landing. It was with the greatest difficulty that Mr. Hall and Millie, who had been roused by her scream of alarm, succeeded in getting her downstairs, and applying the restoratives customary in such cases.

"'Tas sperits," said Mrs. Hall. "I know 'tas sperits. I've read in papers of en. Tables and chairs leaping and dancing!—"

"Take a drop more, Janny," said Hall. "'Twill steady ye."

"Lock him out," said Mrs. Hall. "Don't let him come in again. I half guessed—I might ha' known. With them goggling eyes and bandaged head, and never going to church of a Sunday. And all they bottles—more'n it's right for anyone to have. He's put the sperits into the furniture . . . My good old furniture! 'Twas in that very chair my poor dear mother used to sit when I was a little girl. To think it should rise up against me now!"

"Just a drop more, Janny," said Hall. "Your nerves is all upset."

They sent Millie across the street through the golden five o'clock sunshine to rouse up Mr. Sandy Wadgers, the blacksmith. Mr. Hall's compliments and the furniture upstairs was behaving most extraordinary. Would Mr. Wadgers come round? He was a knowing man, was Mr. Wadgers, and very resourceful. He took quite a grave view of the case. "Arm darmed ef thet ent witchcraft," was the view of Mr. Sandy Wadgers. "You warnt horseshoes for such gentry as he."

He came round greatly concerned. They wanted him to lead the way upstairs to the room, but he didn't seem to be in any hurry. He preferred to talk in the passage. Over the way Huxter's apprentice came out and began taking down the shutters of the tobacco window. He was called over to join the discussion. Mr. Huxter naturally followed over in the course of a few minutes. The Anglo-Saxon genius for parliamentary government asserted itself; there was a great deal of talk and no decisive action. "Let's have the facts first," insisted Mr. Sandy Wadgers. "Let's be sure we'd be acting perfectly right in bustin' that there door open. A door onbust is always open to bustin', but ye can't onbust a door once you've busted en."

And suddenly and most wonderfully the door of the room upstairs opened of its own accord, and as they looked up in amazement, they saw descending the stairs the muffled figure of the stranger staring more blackly and blankly than ever with those unreasonably large blue glass eyes of his. He came down stiffly and slowly, staring all the time; he walked across the passage staring, then stopped.

"Look there!" he said, and their eyes followed the direction of his gloved finger and saw a bottle of sarsaparilla hard by the cellar door. Then he entered the parlour, and suddenly, swiftly, viciously, slammed the door in their faces.

Not a word was spoken until the last echoes of the slam had died away. They stared at one another. "Well, if that don't lick everything!" said Mr. Wadgers, and left the alternative unsaid.

"I'd go in and ask'n 'bout it," said Wadgers, to Mr. Hall. "I'd d'mand an explanation."

It took some time to bring the landlady's husband up to that pitch. At last he rapped, opened the door, and got as far as, "Excuse me—"

"Go to the devil!" said the stranger in a tremendous voice, and, "Shut that door after you." So that brief interview terminated.

Chapter VII

THE UNVEILING OF THE STRANGER

The stranger went into the little parlour of the Coach and Horses about half-past five in the morning, and there he remained until near midday, the blinds down, the door shut, and none, after Hall's repulse, venturing near him.

All that time he must have fasted. Thrice he rang his bell, the third time furiously and continuously, but no one answered him. "Him and his 'go to the devil' indeed!" said Mrs. Hall. Presently came an imperfect rumour of the burglary at the vicarage, and two and two were put together. Hall, assisted by Wadgers, went off to find Mr. Shuckleforth, the magistrate, and take his advice. No one ventured upstairs. How the stranger occupied himself is unknown. Now and then he would stride violently up and down, and twice came an outburst of curses, a tearing of paper, and a violent smashing of bottles.

The little group of scared but curious people increased. Mrs. Huxter came over; some gay young fellows resplendent in black ready-made jackets and *piqué* paper ties, for it was Whit-Monday, joined the group with confused interrogations. Young Archie Harker distinguished himself by going up the yard and trying to peep under the window-blinds. He could see nothing, but gave reason for supposing that he did, and others of the Iping youth presently joined him.

It was the finest of all possible Whit-Mondays, and down the village street stood a row of nearly a dozen booths, a shooting gallery, and on the grass by the forge were three yellow and chocolate waggons and some picturesque strangers of both sexes putting up a cocoanut shy. The gentlemen wore blue jerseys, the ladies white aprons and quite fashionable hats with heavy plumes. Woodyer, of the Purple Fawn, and Mr. Jaggers, the cobbler, who

also sold second-hand ordinary bicycles, were stretching a string of union-jacks and royal ensigns (which had originally celebrated the first Victorian Jubilee) across the road. . . .

And inside, in the artificial darkness of the parlour, into which only one thin jet of sunlight penetrated, the stranger, hungry we must suppose, and fearful, hidden in his uncomfortable hot wrappings, pored through his dark glasses upon his paper or chinked his dirty little bottles, and occasionally swore savagely at the boys, audible if invisible, outside the windows. In the corner by the fireplace lay the fragments of half a dozen smashed bottles, and a pungent twang of chlorine tainted the air. So much we know from what was heard at the time and from what was subsequently seen in the room.

About noon he suddenly opened his parlour door and stood glaring fixedly at the three or four people in the bar. "Mrs. Hall," he said. Somebody went sheepishly and called for Mrs. Hall.

Mrs. Hall appeared after an interval, a little short of breath, but all the fiercer for that. Hall was still out. She had deliberated over this scene, and she came holding a little tray with an unsettled bill upon it. "Is it your bill you're wanting, sir?" she said.

"Why wasn't my breakfast laid? Why haven't you prepared my meals and answered my bell? Do you think I live without eating?"

"Why isn't my bill paid?" said Mrs. Hall. "That's what I want to know."

"I told you three days ago I was awaiting a remittance—"

"I told you two days ago I wasn't going to await no remittances. You can't grumble if your breakfast waits a bit, if my bill's been waiting these five days, can you?"

The stranger swore briefly but vividly.

"Nar, nar!" from the bar.

"And I'd thank you kindly, sir, if you'd keep your swearing to yourself, sir," said Mrs. Hall.

The stranger stood looking more like an angry diving-helmet

than ever. It was universally felt in the bar that Mrs. Hall had the better of him. His next words showed as much.

"Look here, my good woman—" he began.

"Don't 'good woman' *me*," said Mrs. Hall.

"I've told you my remittance hasn't come."

"Remittance indeed!" said Mrs. Hall.

"Still, I daresay in my pocket—"

"You told me three days ago that you hadn't anything but a sovereign's worth of silver upon you."

"Well, I've found some more—"

"'Ul-*lo!*" from the bar.

"I wonder where you found it!" said Mrs. Hall.

That seemed to annoy the stranger very much. He stamped his foot. "What do you mean?" he said.

"That I wonder where you found it," said Mrs. Hall. "And before I take any bills or get any breakfasts, or do any such things whatsoever, you got to tell me one or two things I don't understand, and what nobody don't understand, and what everybody is very anxious to understand. I want to know what you been doing t' my chair upstairs, and I want to know how 'tis your room was empty, and how you got in again. Them as stops in this house comes in by the doors—that's the rule of the house, and that you *didn't* do, and what I want to know is how you *did* come in. And I want to know—"

Suddenly the stranger raised his gloved hands clenched, stamped his foot, and said, "Stop!" with such extraordinary violence that he silenced her instantly.

"You don't understand," he said, "who I am or what I am. I'll show you. By Heaven! I'll show you." Then he put his open palm over his face and withdrew it. The centre of his face became a black cavity. "Here," he said. He stepped forward and handed Mrs. Hall something which she, staring at his metamorphosed face, accepted automatically. Then, when she saw what it was, she screamed loudly, dropped it, and staggered back. The nose—it was the stranger's nose! pink and shining—rolled on the floor.

Then he removed his spectacles, and everyone in the bar gasped. He took off his hat, and with a violent gesture tore at his whiskers and bandages. For a moment they resisted him. A flash of horrible anticipation passed through the bar. "Oh, my Gard!" said someone. Then off they came.

It was worse than anything. Mrs. Hall, standing open-mouthed and horror-struck, shrieked at what she saw, and made for the door of the house. Everyone began to move. They were prepared for scars, disfigurements, tangible horrors, but *nothing!* The bandages and false hair flew across the passage into the bar, making a hobbledehoy jump to avoid them. Everyone tumbled on everyone else down the steps. For the man who stood there shouting some incoherent explanation, was a solid gesticulating figure up to the coat-collar of him, and then—nothingness, no visible thing at all!

People down the village heard shouts and shrieks, and looking up the street saw the Coach and Horses violently firing out its humanity. They saw Mrs. Hall fall down and Mr. Teddy Henfrey jump to avoid tumbling over her, and then they heard the frightful screams of Millie, who, emerging suddenly from the kitchen at the noise of the tumult, had come upon the headless stranger from behind. These ceased suddenly.

Forthwith everyone all down the street, the sweetstuff seller, cocoanut shy proprietor and his assistant, the swing man, little boys and girls, rustic dandies, smart wenches, smocked elders and aproned gipsies, began running towards the inn, and in a miraculously short space of time a crowd of perhaps forty people, and rapidly increasing, swayed and hooted and inquired and exclaimed and suggested, in front of Mrs. Hall's establishment. Everyone seemed eager to talk at once, and the result was babel. A small group supported Mrs. Hall, who was picked up in a state of collapse. There was a conference, and the incredible evidence of a vociferous eye-witness. "O Bogey!" "What's he been doin', then?" "Ain't hurt the girl, 'as 'e?" "Run at en with a knife, I believe." "No 'ed, I tell ye. I don't mean no

manner of speaking. I mean *marn 'ithout a 'ed!*" "Narnsense! 'Tis some conjuring trick." "Fetched off 'is wrappin's, 'e did—"

In its struggles to see in through the open door, the crowd formed itself into a straggling wedge, with the more adventurous apex nearest the inn. "He stood for a moment, I heerd the gal scream, and he turned. I saw her skirts whisk, and he went after her. Didn't take ten seconds. Back he comes with a knife in uz hand and a loaf; stood just as if he was staring. Not a moment ago. Went in that there door. I tell 'e, 'e ain't gart no 'ed 't all. You just missed en—"

There was a disturbance behind, and the speaker stopped to step aside for a little procession that was marching very resolutely towards the house—first Mr. Hall, very red and determined, then Mr. Bobby Jaffers, the village constable, and then the wary Mr. Wadgers. They had come now armed with a warrant.

People shouted conflicting information of the recent circumstances. "'Ed or no 'ed," said Jaffers, "I got to 'rest en, and 'rest en I *will*."

Mr. Hall marched up the steps, marched straight to the door of the parlour and flung it open. "Constable," he said, "do your duty."

Jaffers marched in. Hall next, Wadgers last. They saw in the dim light the headless figure facing them, with a gnawed crust of bread in one gloved hand and a chunk of cheese in the other.

"That's him!" said Hall.

"What the devil's this?" came in a tone of angry expostulation from above the collar of the figure.

"You're a damned rum customer, mister," said Mr. Jaffers. "But 'ed or no 'ed, the warrant says 'body,' and duty's duty—"

"Keep off!" said the figure, starting back.

Abruptly he whipped down the bread and cheese, and Mr. Hall just grasped the knife on the table in time to save it. Off came the stranger's left glove and was slapped in Jaffers' face. In another moment Jaffers, cutting short some statement concerning a warrant, had gripped him by the handless wrist and

caught his invisible throat. He got a sounding kick on the shin that made him shout, but he kept his grip. Hall sent the knife sliding along the table to Wadgers, who acted as goal-keeper for the offensive, so to speak, and then stepped forward as Jaffers and the stranger swayed and staggered towards him, clutching and hitting in. A chair stood in the way, and went aside with a crash as they came down together.

"Get the feet," said Jaffers between his teeth.

Mr. Hall, endeavouring to act on instructions, received a sounding kick in the ribs that disposed of him for a moment, and Mr. Wadgers, seeing the decapitated stranger had rolled over and got the upper side of Jaffers, retreated towards the door, knife in hand, and so collided with Mr. Huxter and the Siddermorton carter coming to the rescue of law and order. At the same moment down came three or four bottles from the chiffonnier and shot a web of pungency into the air of the room.

"I'll surrender," cried the stranger, though he had Jaffers down, and in another moment he stood up panting, a strange figure, headless and handless—for he had pulled off his right glove now as well as his left. "It's no good," he said, as if sobbing for breath.

It was the strangest thing in the world to hear that voice coming as if out of empty space, but the Sussex peasants are perhaps the most matter-of-fact people under the sun. Jaffers got up also and produced a pair of handcuffs. Then he stared.

"I say!" said Jaffers, brought up short by a dim realization of the incongruity of the whole business, "Darn it! Can't use 'em as I can see."

The stranger ran his arm down his waistcoat, and as if by a miracle the buttons to which his empty sleeve pointed became undone. Then he said something about his shin, and stooped down. He seemed to be fumbling with his shoes and socks.

"Why!" said Huxter, suddenly. "That's not a man at all. It's just empty clothes. Look! You can see down his collar and the linings of his clothes. I could put my arm—"

He extended his hand; it seemed to meet something in mid-air, and he drew it back with a sharp exclamation. "I wish you'd keep your fingers out of my eye," said the aerial voice, in a tone of savage expostulation. "The fact is, I'm all here—head, hands, legs, and all the rest of it, but it happens I'm invisible. It's a confounded nuisance, but I am. That's no reason why I should be poked to pieces by every stupid bumpkin in Iping, is it?"

The suit of clothes, now all unbuttoned and hanging loosely upon its unseen supports, stood up, arms akimbo.

Several other of the men folks had now entered the room, so that it was closely crowded. "Invisible, eh?" said Huxter, ignoring the stranger's abuse. "Who ever heard the likes of that?"

"It's strange, perhaps, but it's not a crime. Why am I assaulted by a policeman in this fashion?"

"Ah! That's a different matter," said Jaffers. "No doubt you are a bit difficult to see in this light, but I got a warrant and it's all correct. What I'm after ain't no invisibility—it's burglary. There's a house been broke into and money took."

"Well?"

"And circumstances certainly point—"

"Stuff and nonsense!" said the Invisible Man.

"I hope so, sir; but I've got my instructions."

"Well," said the stranger, "I'll come. I'll *come*. But no handcuffs."

"It's the regular thing," said Jaffers.

"No handcuffs," stipulated the stranger.

"Pardon me," said Jaffers.

Abruptly the figure sat down, and before anyone could realise was was being done, the slippers, socks, and trousers had been kicked off under the table. Then he sprang up again and flung off his coat.

"Here, stop that," said Jaffers, suddenly realising what was happening. He gripped at the waistcoat; it struggled, and the shirt slipped out of it and left it limply and empty in his hand. "Hold him!" said Jaffers loudly. "Once he gets the things off—"

"Hold him!" cried everyone, and there was a rush at the fluttering white shirt which was now all that was visible of the stranger.

The shirt-sleeve planted a shrewd blow in Hall's face that stopped his open-armed advance, and sent him backward into old Toothsome the sexton, and in another moment the garment was lifted up and became convulsed and vacantly flapping about the arms, even as a shirt that is being thrust over a man's head. Jaffers clutched at it, and only helped to pull it off; he was struck in the mouth out of the air, and incontinently threw his truncheon and smote Teddy Henfrey savagely upon the crown of his head.

"Look out!" said everybody, fencing at random and hitting at nothing. "Hold him! Shut the door! Don't let him loose! I got something! Here he is!" A perfect babel of noises they made. Everybody, it seemed, was being hit all at once, and Sandy Wadgers, knowing as ever and his wits sharpened by a frightful blow in the nose, reopened the door and led the rout. The others, following incontinently, were jammed for a moment in the corner by the doorway. The hitting continued. Phipps, the Unitarian, had a front tooth broken, and Henfrey was injured in the cartilage of his ear. Jaffers was struck under the jaw, and, turning, caught at something that intervened between him and Huxter in the *mêlée*, and prevented their coming together. He felt a muscular chest, and in another moment the whole mass of struggling, excited men shot out into the crowded hall.

"I got him!" shouted Jaffers, choking and reeling through them all, and wrestling with purple face and swelling veins against his unseen enemy.

Men staggered right and left as the extraordinary conflict swayed swiftly towards the house door, and went spinning down the half-dozen steps of the inn. Jaffers cried in a strangled voice—holding tight, nevertheless, and making play with his knee—spun around, and fell heavily undermost with his head on the gravel. Only then did his fingers relax.

There were excited cries of "Hold him!" "Invisible!" and so forth, and a young fellow, a stranger in the place whose name did not come to light, rushed in at once, caught something, missed his hold, and fell over the constable's prostrate body. Half-way across the road a woman screamed as something pushed by her; a dog, kicked apparently, yelped and ran howling into Huxter's yard, and with that the transit of the Invisible Man was accomplished. For a space people stood amazed and gesticulating, and then came panic, and scattered them abroad through the village as a gust scatters dead leaves.

But Jaffers lay quite still, face upward and knees bent, at the foot of the steps of the inn.

Chapter VIII

IN TRANSIT

The eighth chapter is exceedingly brief, and relates that Gibbons, the amateur naturalist of the district, while lying out on the spacious open downs without a soul within a couple of miles of him, as he thought, and almost dozing, heard close to him the sound as of a man coughing, sneezing, and then swearing savagely to himself; and looking, beheld nothing. Yet the voice was indisputable. It continued to swear with that breadth and variety that distinguishes the swearing of a cultivated man. It grew to a climax, diminished again, and died away in the distance, going as it seemed to him in the direction of Adderdean. It lifted to a spasmodic sneeze and ended. Gibbons had heard nothing of the morning's occurrences, but the phenomenon was so striking and disturbing that his philosophical tranquillity vanished; he got up hastily, and hurried down the steepness of the hill towards the village, as fast as he could go.

Chapter IX

MR. THOMAS MARVEL

You must picture Mr. Thomas Marvel as a person of copious, flexible visage, a nose of cylindrical protrusion, a liquorish, ample, fluctuating mouth, and a beard of bristling eccentricity. His figure inclined to embonpoint; his short limbs accentuated this inclination. He wore a furry silk hat, and the frequent substitution of twine and shoe-laces for buttons, apparent at critical points of his costume, marked a man essentially bachelor.

Mr. Thomas Marvel was sitting with his feet in a ditch by the roadside over the down towards Adderdean, about a mile and a half out of Iping. His feet, save for socks of irregular open-work, were bare, his big toes were broad, and pricked like the ears of a watchful dog. In a leisurely manner—he did everything in a leisurely manner—he was contemplating trying on a pair of boots. They were the soundest boots he had come across for a long time, but too large for him; whereas the ones he had were, in dry weather, a very comfortable fit, but too thin-soled for damp. Mr. Thomas Marvel hated roomy shoes, but then he hated damp. He had never properly thought out which he hated most, and it was a pleasant day, and there was nothing better to do. So he put the four shoes in a graceful group on the turf and looked at them. And seeing them there among the grass and springing agrimony, it suddenly occurred to him that both pairs were exceedingly ugly to see. He was not at all startled by a voice behind him.

"They're boots, anyhow," said the Voice.

"They are—charity boots," said Mr. Thomas Marvel, with his head on one side regarding them distastefully; "and which is the ugliest pair in the whole blessed universe, I'm darned if I know!"

"H'm," said the Voice.

"I've worn worse—in fact, I've worn none. But none so owdacious ugly—if you'll allow the expression. I've been cadging boots—in particular—for days. Because I was sick of *them.* They're sound enough, of course. But a gentleman on tramp sees such a thundering lot of his boots. And if you'll believe me, I've raised nothing in the whole blessed country, try as I would, but them. Look at 'em! And a good country for boots, too, in a general way. But it's just my promiscuous luck. I've got my boots in this country ten years or more. And then they treat you like this."

"It's a beast of a country," said the Voice. "And pigs for people."

"Ain't it?" said Mr. Thomas Marvel. "Lord! But them boots! It beats it."

He turned his head over his shoulder to the right, to look at the boots of his interlocutor with a view to comparisons, and lo! where the boots of his interlocutor should have been were neither legs nor boots. He was irradiated by the dawn of a great amazement. "Where *are* yer?" said Mr. Thomas Marvel over his shoulder and coming on all fours. He saw a stretch of empty downs with the wind swaying the remote green-pointed furze bushes.

"Am I drunk?" said Mr. Marvel. "Have I had visions? Was I talking to myself? What the—"

"Don't be alarmed," said a voice.

"None of your ventriloquising *me*," said Mr. Thomas Marvel, rising sharply to his feet. "Where *are* yer? Alarmed, indeed!"

"Don't be alarmed," repeated the Voice.

"*You'll* be alarmed in a minute, you silly fool," said Mr. Thomas Marvel. "Where *are* yer? Lemme get my mark on yer—

"Are yer *buried*?" said Mr. Thomas Marvel, after an interval.

There was no answer. Mr. Thomas Marvel stood bootless and amazed, his jacket nearly thrown off.

"Peewit," said a peewit, very remote.

"Peewit, indeed!" said Mr. Thomas Marvel. "This ain't no

time for foolery." The down was desolate, east and west, north and south; the road with its shallow ditches and white bordering stakes, ran smooth and empty north and south, and, save for that peewit, the blue sky was empty too. "So help me," said Mr. Thomas Marvel, shuffling his coat on to his shoulders again. "It's the drink! I might ha' known."

"It's not the drink," said the Voice. "You keep your nerves steady."

"Ow!" said Mr. Marvel, and his face grew white amidst its patches. "It's the drink!" his lips repeated noiselessly. He remained staring about him, rotating slowly backwards. "I could have *swore* I heard a voice," he whispered.

"Of course you did."

"It's there again," said Mr. Marvel, closing his eyes and clasping his hand on his brow with a tragic gesture. He was suddenly taken by the collar and shaken violently, and left more dazed than ever. "Don't be a fool," said the Voice.

"I'm—off—my—blooming—chump," said Mr. Marvel. "It's no good. It's fretting about them blarsted boots. I'm off my blessed blooming chump. Or it's spirits."

"Neither one thing nor the other," said the Voice. "Listen!"

"Chump," said Mr. Marvel.

"One minute," said the Voice, penetratingly, tremulous with self-control.

"Well?" said Mr. Thomas Marvel, with a strange feeling of having been dug in the chest by a finger.

"You think I'm just imagination? Just imagination?"

"What else *can* you be?" said Mr. Thomas Marvel, rubbing the back of his neck.

"Very well," said the Voice, in a tone of relief. "Then I'm going to throw flints at you till you think differently."

"But where *are* yer?"

The Voice made no answer. Whizz came a flint, apparently out of the air, and missed Mr. Marvel's shoulder by a hair's-breadth. Mr. Marvel, turning, saw a flint jerk up into the air, trace a complicated path, hang for a moment, and then fling at his feet with almost invisible rapidity. He was too amazed to dodge. Whizz it came, and ricocheted from a bare toe into the ditch. Mr. Thomas Marvel jumped a foot and howled aloud. Then he started to run, tripped over an unseen obstacle, and came head over heels into a sitting position.

"*Now*," said the Voice, as a third stone curved upward and hung in the air above the tramp. "Am I imagination?"

Mr. Marvel by way of reply struggled to his feet, and was immediately rolled over again. He lay quiet for a moment. "If you struggle anymore," said the Voice, "I shall throw the flint at your head."

"It's a fair do," said Mr. Thomas Marvel, sitting up, taking his wounded toe in hand and fixing his eye on the third missile. "I don't understand it. Stones flinging themselves. Stones talking. Put yourself down. Rot away. I'm done."

The third flint fell.

"It's very simple," said the Voice. "I'm an invisible man."

"Tell us something I don't know," said Mr. Marvel, gasping with pain. "Where you've hid—how you do it—I *don't* know. I'm beat."

"That's all," said the Voice. "I'm invisible. That's what I want you to understand."

"Anyone could see that. There is no need for you to be so confounded impatient, mister. *Now* then. Give us a notion. How are you hid?"

"I'm invisible. That's the great point. And what I want you to understand is this—"

"But whereabouts?" interrupted Mr. Marvel.

"Here! Six yards in front of you."

"Oh, *come*! I ain't blind. You'll be telling me next you're just thin air. I'm not one of your ignorant tramps—"

"Yes, I am—thin air. You're looking through me."

"What! Ain't there any stuff to you? *Vox et*—what is it?—jabber. Is it that?"

"I am just a human being—solid, needing food and drink, needing covering too—But I'm invisible. You see? Invisible. Simple idea. Invisible."

"What, real like?"

"Yes, real."

"Let's have a hand of you," said Marvel, "if you *are* real. It won't be so darn out-of-the-way like, then—*Lord*!" he said, "How you made me jump! Gripping me like that!"

He felt the hand that had closed round his wrist with his disengaged fingers, and his fingers went timorously up the arm, patted a muscular chest, and explored a bearded face. Marvel's face was astonishment.

"I'm dashed!" he said. "If this don't beat cock-fighting! Most remarkable! And there I can see a rabbit clean through you, 'arf a mile away! Not a bit of you visible—except—"

He scrutinised the apparently empty space keenly. "You 'aven't been eatin' bread and cheese?" he asked, holding the invisible arm.

"You're quite right, and it's not quite assimilated into the system."

"Ah!" said Mr. Marvel. "Sort of ghostly, though."

"Of course, all this isn't half so wonderful as you think."

"It's quite wonderful enough for *my* modest wants," said Mr. Thomas Marvel. "Howjer manage it! How the dooce is it done?"

"It's too long a story. And besides—"

"I tell you, the whole business fairly beats me," said Mr. Marvel.

"What I want to say at present is this: I need help. I have come to that—I came upon you suddenly. I was wandering, mad with rage, naked, impotent. I could have murdered. And I saw you—"

"*Lord*!" said Mr. Marvel.

"I came up behind you—hesitated—went on—"

Mr. Marvel's expression was eloquent.

"—then stopped. 'Here,' I said, 'is an out-cast like myself.

This is the man for me.' So I turned back and came to you—you. And—"

"*Lord*!" said Mr. Marvel. "But I'm all in a dizzy. May I ask—How is it? And what you may be requiring in the way of help? Invisible!"

"I want you to help me get clothes—and shelter—and then, with other things. I've left them long enough. If you won't—well! But you *will—must*."

"Look here," said Mr. Marvel. "I'm too flabbergasted. Don't knock me about any more. And leave me go. I must get steady a bit. And you've pretty near broken my toe. It's all so unreasonable. Empty downs, empty sky. Nothing visible for miles except the bosom of Nature. And then comes a voice. A voice out of heaven! And stones! And a fist—Lord!"

"Pull yourself together," said the Voice, "for you have to do the job I've chosen for you."

Mr. Marvel blew out his cheeks, and his eyes were round.

"I've chosen you," said the Voice. "You are the only man except some of those fools down there, who knows there is such a thing as an invisible man. You have to be my helper. Help me—and I will do great things for you. An invisible man is a man of power." He stopped for a moment to sneeze violently.

"But if you betray me," he said, "if you fail to do as I direct you—"

He paused and tapped Mr. Marvel's shoulder smartly. Mr. Marvel gave a yelp of terror at the touch. "*I* don't want to betray you," said Mr. Marvel, edging away from the direction of the fingers. "Don't you go a-thinking that, whatever you do. All I want to do is to help you—just tell me what I got to do. (Lord!) Whatever you want done, that I'm most willing to do."

Chapter X

MR. MARVEL'S VISIT TO IPING

After the first gusty panic had spent itself Iping became argumentative. Scepticism suddenly reared its head—rather nervous scepticism, not at all assured of its back, but scepticism nevertheless. It is so much easier not to believe in an invisible man; and those who had actually seen him dissolve into air, or felt the strength of his arm, could be counted on the fingers of two hands. And of these witnesses Mr. Wadgers was presently missing, having retired impregnably behind the bolts and bars of his own house, and Jaffers was lying stunned in the parlour of the Coach and Horses. Great and strange ideas transcending experience often have less effect upon men and women than smaller, more tangible considerations. Iping was gay with bunting, and everybody was in gala dress. Whit-Monday had been looked forward to for a month or more. By the afternoon even those who believed in the Unseen were beginning to resume their little amusements in a tentative fashion, on the supposition that he had quite gone away, and with the sceptics he was already a jest. But people, sceptics and believers alike, were remarkably sociable all that day.

Haysman's meadow was gay with a tent, in which Mrs. Bunting and other ladies were preparing tea, while, without, the Sunday-school children ran races and played games under the noisy guidance of the curate and the Misses Cuss and Sackbut. No doubt there was a slight uneasiness in the air, but people for the most part had the sense to conceal whatever imaginative qualms they experienced. On the village green an inclined strong, down which, clinging the while to a pulley-swung handle, one could be hurled violently against a sack at the other end, came in for considerable favour among the adolescent, as also did the swings and the cocoanut shies. There was also promenading, and the steam organ attached to a small roundabout filled the air with a pungent flavour of oil and with equally pungent music. Members of the club, who had attended church in the morning, were splendid in badges of pink and green, and some of the gayer-minded had also adorned their bowler hats with brilliant-coloured favours of ribbon. Old Fletcher, whose conceptions of holiday-making were severe, was visible through the jasmine about his window or through the open door (whichever way you chose to look), poised delicately on a plank supported on two chairs, and whitewashing the ceiling of his front-room.

About four o'clock a stranger entered the village from the direction of the downs. He was a short, stout person in an extraordinarily shabby top hat, and he appeared to be very much out of breath. His cheeks were alternately limp and tightly puffed. His mottled face was apprehensive, and he moved with a sort of reluctant alacrity. He turned the corner of the church, and directed his way to the Coach and Horses. Among others old Fletcher remembers seeing him, and indeed the old gentleman was so struck by his peculiar agitation that he inadvertently allowed a quantity of whitewash to run down the brush into the sleeve of his coat while regarding him.

This stranger, to the perceptions of the proprietor of the cocoanut shy, appeared to be talking to himself, and Mr. Huxter remarked the same thing. He stopped at the foot of the Coach and Horses steps, and, according to Mr. Huxter, appeared to undergo a severe internal struggle before he could induce himself to enter the house. Finally he marched up the steps, and was seen by Mr. Huxter to turn to the left and open the door of the parlour. Mr. Huxter heard voices from within the room and from the bar apprising the man of his error. "That room's private!" said Hall, and the stranger shut the door clumsily and went into the bar.

In the course of a few minutes he reappeared, wiping his lips with the back of his hand with an air of quiet satisfaction that

somehow impressed Mr. Huxter as assumed. He stood looking about him for some moments, and then Mr. Huxter saw him walk in an oddly furtive manner towards the gates of the yard, upon which the parlour window opened. The stranger, after some hesitation, leant against one of the gate-posts, produced a short clay pipe, and prepared to fill it. His fingers trembled while doing so. He lit it clumsily, and folding his arms began to smoke in a languid attitude, an attitude which his occasional glances up the yard altogether belied.

All this Mr. Huxter saw over the canisters of the tobacco window, and the singularity of the man's behaviour prompted him to maintain his observation.

Presently the stranger stood up abruptly and put his pipe in his pocket. Then he vanished into the yard. Forthwith Mr. Huxter, conceiving he was witness of some petty larceny, leapt round his counter and ran out into the road to intercept the thief. As he did so, Mr. Marvel reappeared, his hat askew, a big bundle in a blue table-cloth in one hand, and three books tied together—as it proved afterwards with the Vicar's braces—in the other. Directly he saw Huxter he gave a sort of gasp, and turning sharply to the left, began to run. "Stop, thief!" cried Huxter, and set off after him. Mr. Huxter's sensations were vivid but brief. He saw the man just before him and spurting briskly for the church corner and the hill road. He saw the village flags and festivities beyond, and a face or so turned towards him. He bawled, "Stop!" again. He had hardly gone ten strides before his shin was caught in some mysterious fashion, and he was no longer running, but flying with inconceivable rapidity through the air. He saw the ground suddenly close to his face. The world seemed to splash into a million whirling specks of light, and subsequent proceedings interested him no more.

Chapter XI

IN THE COACH AND HORSES

Now in order clearly to understand what had happened in the inn, it is necessary to go back to the moment when Mr. Marvel first came into view of Mr. Huxter's window. At that precise moment Mr. Cuss and Mr. Bunting were in the parlour. They were seriously investigating the strange occurrences of the morning, and were, with Mr. Hall's permission, making a thorough examination of the Invisible Man's belongings. Jaffers had partially recovered from his fall and had gone home in the charge of his sympathetic friends. The stranger's scattered garments had been removed by Mrs. Hall and the room tidied up. And on the table under the window where the stranger had been wont to work, Cuss had hit almost at once on three big books in manuscript labelled "Diary."

"Diary!" said Cuss, putting the three books on the table. "Now, at any rate, we shall learn something." The Vicar stood with his hands on the table.

"Diary," repeated Cuss, sitting down, putting two volumes to support the third, and opening it. "H'm—no name on the flyleaf. Bother! Cypher. And figures."

The vicar came round to look over his shoulder.

Cuss turned the pages over with a face suddenly disappointed. "I'm—dear me! It's all cypher, Bunting."

"There are no diagrams?" asked Mr. Bunting. "No illustrations throwing light—"

"See for yourself," said Mr. Cuss. "Some of it's mathematical and some of it's Russian or some such language (to judge by the letters), and some of it's Greek. Now the Greek I thought *you*—"

"Of course," said Mr. Bunting, taking out and wiping his

spectacles and feeling suddenly very uncomfortable—for he had no Greek left in his mind worth talking about; "yes—the Greek, of course, may furnish a clue."

"I'll find you a place."

"I'd rather glance through the volumes first," said Mr. Bunting, still wiping. "A general impression first, Cuss, and *then*, you know, we can go looking for clues."

He coughed, put on his glasses, arranged them fastidiously, coughed again, and wished something would happen to avert the seemingly inevitable exposure. Then he took the volume Cuss handed him in a leisurely manner. And then something did happen.

The door opened suddenly.

Both gentlemen started violently, looked round, and were relieved to see a sporadically rosy face beneath a furry silk hat. "Tap?" asked the face, and stood staring.

"No," said both gentlemen at once.

"Over the other side, my man," said Mr. Bunting. And "Please shut that door," said Mr. Cuss, irritably.

"All right," said the intruder, as it seemed in a low voice curiously different from the huskiness of its first inquiry. "Right you are," said the intruder in the former voice. "Stand clear!" and he vanished and closed the door.

"A sailor, I should judge," said Mr. Bunting. "Amusing fellows, they are. Stand clear! Indeed. A nautical term, referring to his getting back out of the room, I suppose."

"I daresay so," said Cuss. "My nerves are all loose to-day. It quite made me jump—the door opening like that."

Mr. Bunting smiled as if he had not jumped. "And now," he said with a sigh, "these books."

Someone sniffed as he did so.

"One thing is indisputable," said Bunting, drawing up a chair next to that of Cuss. "There certainly have been very strange things happen in Iping during the last few days—very strange. I cannot of course believe in this absurd invisibility story—"

"It's incredible," said Cuss—"incredible. But the fact remains that I saw—I certainly saw right down his sleeve—"

"But did you—are you sure? Suppose a mirror, for instance—hallucinations are so easily produced. I don't know if you have ever seen a really good conjuror—"

"I won't argue again," said Cuss. "We've thrashed that out, Bunting. And just now there's these books—ah! Here's some of what I take to be Greek! Greek letters certainly."

He pointed to the middle of the page. Mr. Bunting flushed slightly and brought his face nearer, apparently finding some difficulty with his glasses. Suddenly he became aware of a strange feeling at the nape of his neck. He tried to raise his head, and encountered an immovable resistance. The feeling was a curious pressure, the grip of a heavy, firm hand, and it bore his chin irresistibly to the table. "*Don't move, little men,*" whispered a voice, "*or I'll brain you both!*" He looked into the face of Cuss, close to his own, and each saw a horrified reflection of his own sickly astonishment.

"I'm sorry to handle you so roughly," said the Voice, "but it's unavoidable."

"Since when did you learn to pry into an investigator's private memoranda?" said the Voice; and two chins struck the table simultaneously, and two sets of teeth rattled.

"Since when did you learn to invade the private rooms of a man in misfortune?" and the concussion was repeated.

"Where have they put my clothes?"

"Listen," said the Voice. "The windows are fastened and I've taken the key out of the door. I am a fairly strong man, and I have the poker handy—besides being invisible. There's not the slightest doubt that I could kill you both and get away quite easily if I wanted to—do you understand? Very well. If I let you go will you promise not to try any nonsense and do what I tell you?"

The Vicar and the Doctor looked at one another, and the doctor pulled a face. "Yes," said Mr. Bunting, and the Doctor

repeated it. Then the pressure on the necks relaxed, and the Doctor and the Vicar sat up, both very red in the face and wriggling their heads.

"Please keep sitting where you are," said the Invisible Man. "Here's the poker, you see."

"When I came into this room," continued the Invisible Man, after presenting the poker to the tip of the nose of each of his visitors, "I did not expect to find it occupied, and I expected to find, in addition to my books of memoranda, an outfit of clothing. Where is it? No—don't rise. I can see it's gone. Now, just at present, though the days are quite warm enough for an invisible man to run about stark, the evenings are quite chilly. I want clothing—and other accommodation; and I must also have those three books."

Chapter XII

THE INVISIBLE MAN LOSES HIS TEMPER

It is unavoidable that at this point the narrative should break off again, for a certain very painful reason that will presently be apparent. While these things were going on in the parlour, and while Mr. Huxter was watching Mr. Marvel smoking his pipe against the gate, not a dozen yards away were Mr. Hall and Teddy Henfrey discussing in a state of cloudy puzzlement the one Iping topic.

Suddenly there came a violent thud against the door of the parlour, a sharp cry, and then—silence.

"*Hul*-lo!" said Teddy Henfrey.

"Hul-*lo!*" from the Tap.

Mr. Hall took things in slowly but surely. "That ain't right," he said, and came round from behind the bar towards the parlour door.

He and Teddy approached the door together, with intent faces. Their eyes considered. "Summat wrong," said Hall, and Henfrey nodded agreement. Whiffs of an unpleasant chemical odour met them, and there was a muffled sound of conversation, very rapid and subdued.

"You all raight thur?" asked Hall, rapping.

The muttered conversation ceased abruptly, for a moment silence, then the conversation was resumed, in hissing whispers, then a sharp cry of "No! No, you don't!" There came a sudden motion and the oversetting of a chair, a brief struggle. Silence again.

"What the dooce?" exclaimed Henfrey, *sotto voce.*

"You—all—raight thur?" asked Mr. Hall sharply, again.

The Vicar's voice answered with a curious jerking intonation: "Quite ri—right. Please don't—interrupt."

"Odd!" said Mr. Henfrey.

"Odd!" said Mr. Hall.

"Says, 'Don't interrupt,'" said Henfrey.

"I heerd'n," said Hall.

"And a sniff," said Henfrey.

They remained listening. The conversation was rapid and subdued. "I *can't*," said Mr. Bunting, his voice rising; "I tell you, sir, I *will* not."

"What was that?" asked Henfrey.

"Says he wi' nart," said Hall. "Warn't speaking to us, wuz he?"

"Disgraceful!" said Mr. Bunting, within.

"'Disgraceful,'" said Mr. Henfrey. "I heard it—*distinct*."

"Who's that speaking now?" asked Henfrey.

"Mr. Cuss, I s'pose," said Hall. "Can you hear—anything?"

Silence. The sounds within indistinct and perplexing.

"Sounds like throwing the table-cloth about," said Hall.

Mrs. Hall appeared behind the bar. Hall made gestures of silence and invitation. This aroused Mrs. Hall's wifely opposition. "What yer listenin' there for, Hall?" she asked. "Ain't you nothin' better to do—busy day like this?"

Hall tried to convey everything by grimaces and dumb show, but Mrs. Hall was obdurate. She raised her voice. So Hall and Henfrey, rather crestfallen, tiptoed back to the bar, gesticulating to explain to her.

At first she refused to see anything in what they had heard at all. Then she insisted on Hall keeping silence, while Henfrey told her his story. She was inclined to think the whole business nonsense—perhaps they were just moving the furniture about. "I heerd'n say 'disgraceful'; *that* I did," said Hall.

"*I* heerd that, Mrs. Hall," said Henfrey.

"Like as not—" began Mrs. Hall.

"Hsh!" said Mr. Teddy Henfrey. "Didn't I hear the window?"

"What window?" asked Mrs. Hall.

"Parlour window," said Henfrey.

Everyone stood listening intently. Mrs. Hall's eyes, directed straight before her, saw without seeing the brilliant oblong of the inn door, the road white and vivid, and Huxter's shop-front blistering in the June sun. Abruptly Huxter's door opened and Huxter appeared, eyes staring with excitement, arms gesticulating. "*Yap!*" cried Huxter. "Stop, thief!" and he ran obliquely across the oblong towards the yard gates, and vanished.

Simultaneously came a tumult from the parlour, and a sound of windows being closed.

Hall, Henfrey, and the human contents of the Tap rushed out at once pell-mell into the street. They saw someone whisk round the corner towards the road, and Mr. Huxter executing a complicated leap in the air that ended on his face and shoulder. Down the street people were standing astonished or running towards them.

Mr. Huxter was stunned. Henfrey stopped to discover this, but Hall and the two labourers from the Tap rushed at once to the corner, shouting incoherent things, and saw Mr. Marvel vanishing by the corner of the church wall. They appear to have jumped to the impossible conclusion that this was the Invisible Man suddenly become visible, and set off at once along the lane in pursuit. But Hall had hardly run a dozen yards before he gave a loud shout of astonishment and went flying headlong sideways, clutching one of the labourers and bringing him to the ground. He had been charged just as one charges a man at football. The second labourer came round in a circle, stared, and conceiving that Hall had tumbled over of his own accord, turned to resume the pursuit, only to be tripped by the ankle just as Huxter had been. Then, as the first labourer struggled to his feet, he was kicked sideways by a blow that might have felled an ox.

As he went down, the rush from the direction of the village green came round the corner. The first to appear was the proprietor of the cocoanut shy, a burly man in a blue jersey. He was astonished to see the lane empty save for three men sprawling absurdly on the ground. And then something happened to his rear-most foot, and he went headlong and rolled sideways just

in time to graze the feet of his brother and partner, following headlong. The two were then kicked, knelt on, fallen over, and cursed by quite a number of over-hasty people.

Now when Hall and Henfrey and the labourers ran out of the house, Mrs. Hall, who had been disciplined by years of experience, remained in the bar next the till. And suddenly the parlour door was opened, and Mr. Cuss appeared, and without glancing at her rushed at once down the steps toward the corner. "Hold him!" he cried. "Don't let him drop that parcel! You can see him so long as he holds that parcel."

He knew nothing of the existence of Marvel. For the Invisible Man had handed over the books and bundle in the yard. The face of Mr. Cuss was angry and resolute, but his costume was defective, a sort of limp white kilt that could only have passed muster in Greece. "Hold him!" he bawled. "He's got my trousers! And every stitch of the Vicar's clothes!"

"'Tend to him in a minute!" he cried to Henfrey as he passed the prostrate Huxter, and, coming round the corner to join the tumult, was promptly knocked off his feet into an indecorous sprawl. Somebody in full flight trod heavily on his finger. He yelled, struggled to regain his feet, was knocked against and thrown on all fours again, and became aware that he was involved not in a capture, but a rout. Everyone was running back to the village. He rose again and was hit severely behind the ear. He staggered and set off back to the Coach and Horses forthwith, leaping over the deserted Huxter, who was now sitting up, on his way.

Behind him as he was halfway up the inn steps he heard a sudden yell of rage, rising sharply out of the confusion of cries, and a sounding smack in someone's face. He recognised the Voice as that of the Invisible Man, and the note was that of a man suddenly infuriated by a painful blow.

In another moment Mr. Cuss was back in the parlour. "He's coming back, Bunting!" he said, rushing in. "Save yourself! He's gone mad!"

Mr. Bunting was standing in the window engaged in an attempt to clothe himself in the hearth-rug and a West Surrey Gazette. "Who's coming?" he said, so startled that his costume narrowly escaped disintegration.

"Invisible Man," said Cuss, and rushed on to the window. "We'd better clear out from here! He's fighting mad! Mad!"

In another moment he was out in the yard.

"Good heavens!" said Mr. Bunting, hesitating between two horrible alternatives. He heard a frightful struggle in the passage of the inn, and his decision was made. He clambered out of the window, adjusted his costume hastily, and fled up the village as fast as his fat little legs would carry him.

From the moment when the Invisible Man screamed with rage and Mr. Bunting made his memorable flight up the village, it became impossible to give a consecutive account of affairs in Iping. Possibly the Invisible Man's original intention was simply to cover Marvel's retreat with the clothes and books. But his temper, at no time very good, seems to have gone completely at some chance blow, and forthwith he set to smiting and overthrowing, for the mere satisfaction of hurting.

You must figure the street full of running figures, of doors slamming and fights for hiding-places. You must figure the tumult suddenly striking on the unstable equilibrium of old Fletcher's planks and two chairs—with cataclysmic results. You must figure an appalled couple caught dismally in a swing. And then the whole tumultuous rush has passed and the Iping street with its gauds and flags is deserted save for the still raging unseen, and littered with cocoanuts, overthrown canvas screens, and the scattered stock in trade of a sweetstuff stall. Everywhere there is a sound of closing shutters and shoving bolts, and the only visible humanity is an occasional flitting eye under a raised eyebrow in the corner of a windowpane.

The Invisible Man amused himself for a little while by breaking all the windows in the Coach and Horses, and then he thrust a street lamp through the parlour window of Mrs.

Gribble. He it must have been who cut the telegraph wire to Adderdean just beyond Higgins' cottage on the Adderdean road. And after that, as his peculiar qualities allowed, he passed out of human perceptions altogether, and he was neither heard, seen, nor felt in Iping anymore. He vanished absolutely.

But it was the best part of two hours before any human being ventured out again into the desolation of Iping street.

Chapter XIII

MR. MARVEL DISCUSSES HIS RESIGNATION

When the dusk was gathering and Iping was just beginning to peep timorously forth again upon the shattered wreckage of its Bank Holiday, a short, thick-set man in a shabby silk hat was marching painfully through the twilight behind the beechwoods on the road to Bramblehurst. He carried three books bound together by some sort of ornamental elastic ligature, and a bundle wrapped in a blue table-cloth. His rubicund face expressed consternation and fatigue; he appeared to be in a spasmodic sort of hurry. He was accompanied by a voice other than his own, and ever and again he winced under the touch of unseen hands.

"If you give me the slip again," said the Voice, "if you attempt to give me the slip again—"

"Lord!" said Mr. Marvel. "That shoulder's a mass of bruises as it is."

"On my honour," said the Voice, "I will kill you."

"I didn't try to give you the slip," said Marvel, in a voice that was not far remote from tears. "I swear I didn't. I didn't know the blessed turning, that was all! How the devil was I to know the blessed turning? As it is, I've been knocked about—"

"You'll get knocked about a great deal more if you don't mind," said the Voice, and Mr. Marvel abruptly became silent. He blew out his cheeks, and his eyes were eloquent of despair.

"It's bad enough to let these floundering yokels explode my little secret, without *your* cutting off with my books. It's lucky for some of them they cut and ran when they did! Here am I—no one knew I was invisible! And now what am I to do?"

"What am *I* to do?" asked Marvel, *sotto voce.*

"It's all about. It will be in the papers! Everybody will be looking for me; everyone on their guard—" The Voice broke off into vivid curses and ceased.

The despair of Mr. Marvel's face deepened, and his pace slackened.

"Go on!" said the Voice.

Mr. Marvel's face assumed a greyish tint between the ruddier patches.

"Don't drop those books, stupid," said the Voice, sharply—overtaking him.

"The fact is," said the Voice, "I shall have to make use of you. You're a poor tool, but I must."

"I'm a *miserable* tool," said Marvel.

"You are," said the Voice.

"I'm the worst possible tool you could have," said Marvel.

"I'm not strong," he said after a discouraging silence.

"I'm not over strong," he repeated.

"No?"

"And my heart's weak. That little business—I pulled it through, of course—but bless you! I could have dropped."

"Well?"

"I haven't the nerve and strength for the sort of thing you want."

"*I'll* stimulate you."

"I wish you wouldn't. I wouldn't like to mess up your plans, you know. But I might—out of sheer funk and misery."

"You'd better not," said the Voice, with quiet emphasis.

"I wish I was dead," said Marvel.

"It ain't justice," he said; "you must admit—it seems to me I've a perfect right—"

"*Get* on!" said the Voice.

Mr. Marvel mended his pace, and for a time they went in silence again.

"It's devilish hard," said Mr. Marvel.

This was quite ineffectual. He tried another tack.

"What do I make by it?" he began again in a tone of unendurable wrong.

"Oh! *shut up!*" said the Voice, with sudden amazing vigour. "I'll see to you all right. You do what you're told. You'll do it all right. You're a fool and all that, but you'll do—"

"I tell you, sir, I'm not the man for it. Respectfully—but it is so—"

"If you don't shut up I shall twist your wrist again," said the Invisible Man. "I want to think."

Presently two oblongs of yellow light appeared through the trees, and the square tower of a church loomed through the gloaming. "I shall keep my hand on your shoulder," said the Voice, "all through the village. Go straight through and try no foolery. It will be the worse for you if you do."

"I know that," sighed Mr. Marvel, "I know all that."

The unhappy-looking figure in the obsolete silk hat passed up the street of the little village with his burdens, and vanished into the gathering darkness beyond the lights of the windows.

Chapter XIV

AT PORT STOWE

Ten o'clock the next morning found Mr. Marvel, unshaven, dirty, and travel-stained, sitting with the books beside him and his hands deep in his pockets, looking very weary, nervous, and uncomfortable, and inflating his cheeks at infrequent intervals, on the bench outside a little inn on the outskirts of Port Stowe. Beside him were the books, but now they were tied with string. The bundle had been abandoned in the pine-woods beyond Bramblehurst, in accordance with a change in the plans of the Invisible Man. Mr. Marvel sat on the bench, and although no one took the slightest notice of him, his agitation remained at fever heat. His hands would go ever and again to his various pockets with a curious nervous fumbling.

When he had been sitting for the best part of an hour, however, an elderly mariner, carrying a newspaper, came out of the inn and sat down beside him. "Pleasant day," said the mariner.

Mr. Marvel glanced about him with something very like terror. "Very," he said.

"Just seasonable weather for the time of year," said the mariner, taking no denial.

"Quite," said Mr. Marvel.

The mariner produced a toothpick, and (saving his regard) was engrossed thereby for some minutes. His eyes meanwhile were at liberty to examine Mr. Marvel's dusty figure, and the books beside him. As he had approached Mr. Marvel he had heard a sound like the dropping of coins into a pocket. He was struck by the contrast of Mr. Marvel's appearance with this suggestion of opulence. Thence his mind wandered back again to a topic that had taken a curiously firm hold of his imagination.

"Books?" he said suddenly, noisily finishing with the toothpick.

Mr. Marvel started and looked at them. "Oh, yes," he said. "Yes, they're books."

"There's some ex-traordinary things in books," said the mariner.

"I believe you," said Mr. Marvel.

"And some extra-ordinary things out of 'em," said the mariner.

"True likewise," said Mr. Marvel. He eyed his interlocutor, and then glanced about him.

"There's some extraordinary things in newspapers, for example," said the mariner.

"There are."

"In this newspaper," said the mariner.

"Ah!" said Mr. Marvel.

"There's a story," said the mariner, fixing Mr. Marvel with an eye that was firm and deliberate; "there's a story about an Invisible Man, for instance."

Mr. Marvel pulled his mouth askew and scratched his cheek and felt his ears glowing. "What will they be writing next?" he asked faintly. "Ostria, or America?"

"Neither," said the mariner. "*Here.*"

"Lord!" said Mr. Marvel, starting.

"When I say *here*," said the mariner, to Mr. Marvel's intense relief, "I don't of course mean here in this place, I mean hereabouts."

"An Invisible Man!" said Mr. Marvel. "And what's he been up to?"

"Everything," said the mariner, controlling Marvel with his eye, and then amplifying: "Every Blessed Thing."

"I ain't seen a paper these four days," said Marvel.

"Iping's the place he started at," said the mariner.

"In-*deed!*" said Mr. Marvel.

"He started there. And where he came from, nobody don't

seem to know. Here it is: 'Pe Culiar Story from Iping.' And it says in this paper that the evidence is extraordinary strong—extra-ordinary."

"Lord!" said Mr. Marvel.

"But then, it's a extra-ordinary story. There is a clergyman and a medical gent witnesses—saw 'im all right and proper—or leastways didn't see 'im. He was staying, it says, at the Coach an' Horses, and no one don't seem to have been aware of his misfortune, it says, aware of his misfortune, until in an Alteration in the inn, it says, his bandages on his head was torn off. It was then ob-served that his head was invisible. Attempts were At Once made to secure him, but casting off his garments, it says, he succeeded in escaping, but not until after a desperate struggle, In Which he had inflicted serious injuries, it says, on our worthy and able constable, Mr. J. A. Jaffers. Pretty straight story, eigh? Names and everything."

"Lord!" said Mr. Marvel, looking nervously about him, trying to count the money in his pockets by his unaided sense of touch, and full of a strange and novel idea. "It sounds most astonishing."

"Don't it? Extra-ordinary, *I* call it. Never heard tell of Invisible Men before, I haven't, but nowadays one hears such a lot of extra-ordinary things—that—"

"That all he did?" asked Marvel, trying to seem at his ease.

"It's enough, ain't it?" said the mariner.

"Didn't go Back by any chance?" asked Marvel. "Just escaped and that's all, eh?"

"All!" said the mariner. "Why!—ain't it enough?"

"Quite enough," said Marvel.

"I should think it was enough," said the mariner. "I should think it was enough."

"He didn't have any pals—it don't say he had any pals, does it?" asked Mr. Marvel, anxious.

"Ain't one of a sort enough for you?" asked the mariner. "No, thank Heaven, as one might say, he didn't."

He nodded his head slowly. "It makes me regular uncomfortable, the bare thought of that chap running about the country! He is at present At Large, and from certain evidence it is supposed that he has—taken—*took*, I suppose they mean—the road to Port Stowe. You see we're right *in* it! None of your American wonders, this time. And just think of the things he might do! Where'd you be, if he took a drop over and above, and had a fancy to go for you? Suppose he wants to rob—who can prevent him? He can trespass, he can burgle, he could walk through a cordon of policemen as easy as me or you could give the slip to a blind man! Easier! For these here blind chaps hear uncommon sharp, I'm told. And wherever there was liquor he fancied—"

"He's got a tremenjous advantage, certainly," said Mr. Marvel. "And—well."

"You're right," said the mariner. "He *has*."

All this time Mr. Marvel had been glancing about him intently, listening for faint footfalls, trying to detect imperceptible movements. He seemed on the point of some great resolution. He coughed behind his hand.

He looked about him again, listened, bent towards the mariner, and lowered his voice: "The fact of it is—I happen—to know just a thing or two about this Invisible Man. From private sources."

"Oh!" said the mariner, interested. "*You?*"

"Yes," said Mr. Marvel. "Me."

"Indeed!" said the mariner. "And may I ask—"

"You'll be astonished," said Mr. Marvel behind his hand. "It's tremenjous."

"Indeed!" said the mariner.

"The fact is," began Mr. Marvel eagerly in a confidential undertone. Suddenly his expression changed marvellously. "Ow!" he said. He rose stiffly in his seat. His face was eloquent of physical suffering. "Wow!" he said.

"What's up?" said the mariner, concerned.

"Toothache," said Mr. Marvel, and put his hand to his ear. He caught hold of his books. "I must be getting on, I think," he said. He edged in a curious way along the seat away from his interlocutor. "But you was just a-going to tell me about this here Invisible Man!" protested the mariner. Mr. Marvel seemed to consult with himself. "Hoax," said a Voice. "It's a hoax," said Mr. Marvel.

"But it's in the paper," said the mariner.

"Hoax all the same," said Marvel. "I know the chap that started the lie. There ain't no Invisible Man whatsoever—Blimey."

"But how 'bout this paper? D'you mean to say—?"

"Not a word of it," said Marvel, stoutly.

The mariner stared, paper in hand. Mr. Marvel jerkily faced about. "Wait a bit," said the mariner, rising and speaking slowly. "D'you mean to say—?"

"I do," said Mr. Marvel.

"Then why did you let me go on and tell you all this blarsted stuff, then? What d'yer mean by letting a man make a fool of himself like that for? Eigh?"

Mr. Marvel blew out his cheeks. The mariner was suddenly very red indeed; he clenched his hands. "I been talking here this ten minutes," he said; "and you, you little pot-bellied, leathery-faced son of an old boot, couldn't have the elementary manners—"

"Don't you come bandying words with *me*," said Mr. Marvel.

"Bandying words! I'm a jolly good mind—"

"Come up," said a Voice, and Mr. Marvel was suddenly whirled about and started marching off in a curious spasmodic manner. "You'd better move on," said the mariner. "*Who's* moving on?" said Mr. Marvel. He was receding obliquely with a curious hurrying gait, with occasional violent jerks forward. Some way along the road he began a muttered monologue, protests and recriminations.

"Silly devil!" said the mariner, legs wide apart, elbows akimbo, watching the receding figure. "I'll show you, you silly ass—hoaxing *me!* It's here—on the paper!"

Mr. Marvel retorted incoherently and, receding, was hidden by a bend in the road, but the mariner still stood magnificent in the midst of the way, until the approach of a butcher's cart dislodged him. Then he turned himself towards Port Stowe. "Full of extra-ordinary asses," he said softly to himself. "Just to take me down a bit—that was his silly game—It's on the paper!"

And there was another extraordinary thing he was presently to hear, that had happened quite close to him. And that was a vision of a "fist full of money" (no less) travelling without visible agency, along by the wall at the corner of St. Michael's Lane. A brother mariner had seen this wonderful sight that very morning. He had snatched at the money forthwith and had been knocked headlong, and when he had got to his feet the butterfly money had vanished. Our mariner was in the mood to believe anything, he declared, but that was a bit too stiff. Afterwards, however, he began to think things over.

The story of the flying money was true. And all about that neighbourhood, even from the august London and Country Banking Company, from the tills of shops and inns—doors standing that sunny weather entirely open—money had been quietly and dexterously making off that day in handfuls and rouleaux, floating quietly along by walls and shady places, dodging quickly from the approaching eyes of men. And it had, though no man had traced it, invariably ended its mysterious flight in the pocket of that agitated gentleman in the obsolete silk hat, sitting outside the little inn on the outskirts of Port Stowe.

Chapter XV

THE MAN WHO WAS RUNNING

In the early evening time Doctor Kemp was sitting in his study in the belvedere on the hill overlooking Burdock. It was a pleasant little room, with three windows—north, west, and south—and bookshelves covered with books and scientific publications, and a broad writing-table, and, under the north window, a microscope, glass slips, minute instruments, some cultures, and scattered bottles of reagents. Doctor Kemp's solar lamp was lit, albeit the sky was still bright with the sunset light, and his blinds were up because there was no offence of peering outsiders to require them pulled down. Doctor Kemp was a tall and slender young man, with flaxen hair and a moustache almost white, and the work he was upon would earn him, he hoped, the fellowship of the Royal Society, so highly did he think of it.

And his eye, presently wandering from his work, caught the sunset blazing at the back of the hill that is over against his own. For a minute perhaps he sat, pen in mouth, admiring the rich golden colour above the crest, and then his attention was attracted by the little figure of a man, inky black, running over the hill-brow towards him. He was a shortish little man, and he wore a high hat, and he was running so fast that his legs verily twinkled.

"Another of those fools," said Doctor Kemp. "Like that ass who ran into me this morning round a corner, with the ''Visible Man a-coming, sir!' I can't imagine what possesses people. One might think we were in the thirteenth century."

He got up, went to the window, and stared at the dusky hillside, and the dark little figure tearing down it. "He seems in a confounded hurry," said Doctor Kemp, "but he doesn't seem to be getting on. If his pockets were full of lead, he couldn't run heavier."

"Spurted, sir," said Doctor Kemp.

In another moment the higher of the villas that had clambered up the hill from Burdock had occulted the running figure. He was visible again for a moment, and again, and then again, three times between the three detached houses that came next, and the terrace hid him.

"Asses!" said Doctor Kemp, swinging round on his heel and walking back to his writing-table.

But those who saw the fugitive nearer, and perceived the abject terror on his perspiring face, being themselves in the open roadway, did not share in the doctor's contempt. By the man pounded, and as he ran he chinked like a well-filled purse that is tossed to and fro. He looked neither to the right nor the left, but his dilated eyes stared straight downhill to where the lamps were being lit, and the people were crowded in the street. And his ill-shaped mouth fell apart, and a glairy foam lay on his lips, and his breath came hoarse and noisy. All he passed stopped and began staring up the road and down, and interrogating one another with an inkling of discomfort for the reason of his haste.

And then presently, far up the hill, a dog playing in the road yelped and ran under a gate, and as they still wondered something,—a wind—a pad, pad, pad—a sound like a panting breathing—rushed by.

People screamed. People sprang off the pavement: It passed in shouts, it passed by instinct down the hill. They were shouting in the street before Marvel was halfway there. They were bolting into houses and slamming the doors behind them, with the news. He heard it and made one last desperate spurt. Fear came striding by, rushed ahead of him, and in a moment had seized the town.

"The Invisible Man is coming! *The Invisible Man!*"

Chapter XVI

IN THE JOLLY CRICKETERS

The Jolly Cricketers is just at the bottom of the hill, where the tram-lines begin. The barman leant his fat red arms on the counter and talked of horses with an anaemic cabman, while a black-bearded man in grey snapped up biscuit and cheese, drank Burton, and conversed in American with a policeman off duty.

"What's the shouting about!" said the anaemic cabman, going off at a tangent, trying to see up the hill over the dirty yellow blind in the low window of the inn. Somebody ran by outside. "Fire, perhaps," said the barman.

Footsteps approached, running heavily, the door was pushed open violently, and Marvel, weeping and dishevelled, his hat gone, the neck of his coat torn open, rushed in, made a convulsive turn, and attempted to shut the door. It was held half open by a strap.

"Coming!" he bawled, his voice shrieking with terror. "He's coming. The 'Visible Man! After me! For Gawd's sake! 'Elp! 'Elp! 'Elp! 'Elp!"

"Shut the doors," said the policeman. "Who's coming? What's the row?" He went to the door, released the strap, and it slammed. The American closed the other door.

"Lemme go inside," said Marvel, staggering and weeping, but still clutching the books. "Lemme go inside. Lock me in—somewhere. I tell you he's after me. I give him the slip. He said he'd kill me and he will."

"*You're* safe," said the man with the black beard. "The door's shut. What's it all about?"

"Lemme go inside," said Marvel, and shrieked aloud as a blow suddenly made the fastened door shiver and was followed by a hurried rapping and a shouting outside. "Hullo," cried the

policeman, "who's there?" Mr. Marvel began to make frantic dives at panels that looked like doors. "He'll kill me—he's got a knife or something. For Gawd's sake!"

"Here you are," said the barman. "Come in here." And he held up the flap of the bar.

Mr. Marvel rushed behind the bar as the summons outside was repeated. "Don't open the door," he screamed. "*Please* don't open the door. *Where* shall I hide?"

"This, this Invisible Man, then?" asked the man with the black beard, with one hand behind him. "I guess it's about time we saw him."

The window of the inn was suddenly smashed in, and there was a screaming and running to and fro in the street. The policeman had been standing on the settee staring out, craning to see who was at the door. He got down with raised eyebrows. "It's that," he said. The barman stood in front of the bar-parlour door which was now locked on Mr. Marvel, stared at the smashed window, and came round to the two other men.

Everything was suddenly quiet. "I wish I had my truncheon," said the policeman, going irresolutely to the door. "Once we open, in he comes. There's no stopping him."

"Don't you be in too much hurry about that door," said the anaemic cabman, anxiously.

"Draw the bolts," said the man with the black beard, "and if he comes—" He showed a revolver in his hand.

"That won't do," said the policeman; "that's murder."

"I know what country I'm in," said the man with the beard. "I'm going to let off at his legs. Draw the bolts."

"Not with that blinking thing going off behind me," said the barman, craning over the blind.

"Very well," said the man with the black beard, and stooping down, revolver ready, drew them himself. Barman, cabman, and policeman faced about.

"Come in," said the bearded man in an undertone, standing back and facing the unbolted doors with his pistol behind

him. No one came in, the door remained closed. Five minutes afterwards when a second cabman pushed his head in cautiously, they were still waiting, and an anxious face peered out of the bar-parlour and supplied information. "Are all the doors of the house shut?" asked Marvel. "He's going round—prowling round. He's as artful as the devil."

"Good Lord!" said the burly barman. "There's the back! Just watch them doors! I say—!" He looked about him helplessly. The bar-parlour door slammed and they heard the key turn. "There's the yard door and the private door. The yard door—"

He rushed out of the bar.

In a minute he reappeared with a carving-knife in his hand. "The yard door was open!" he said, and his fat underlip dropped.

"He may be in the house now!" said the first cabman.

"He's not in the kitchen," said the barman. "There's two women there, and I've stabbed every inch of it with this little beef slicer. And they don't think he's come in. They haven't noticed—"

"Have you fastened it?" asked the first cabman.

"I'm out of frocks," said the barman.

The man with the beard replaced his revolver. And even as he did so the flap of the bar was shut down and the bolt clicked, and then with a tremendous thud the catch of the door snapped and the bar-parlour door burst open. They heard Marvel squeal like a caught leveret, and forthwith they were clambering over the bar to his rescue. The bearded man's revolver cracked and the looking-glass at the back of the parlour starred and came smashing and tinkling down.

As the barman entered the room he saw Marvel, curiously crumpled up and struggling against the door that led to the yard and kitchen. The door flew open while the barman hesitated, and Marvel was dragged into the kitchen. There was a scream and a clatter of pans. Marvel, head down, and lugging back obstinately, was forced to the kitchen door, and the bolts were drawn.

Then the policeman, who had been trying to pass the barman, rushed in, followed by one of the cabmen, gripped the wrist of the invisible hand that collared Marvel, was hit in the face and went reeling back. The door opened, and Marvel made a frantic effort to obtain a lodgment behind it. Then the cabman collared something. "I got him," said the cabman. The barman's red hands came clawing at the unseen. "Here he is!" said the barman.

Mr. Marvel, released, suddenly dropped to the ground and made an attempt to crawl behind the legs of the fighting men. The struggle blundered round the edge of the door. The voice of the Invisible Man was heard for the first time, yelling out sharply, as the policeman trod on his foot. Then he cried out passionately and his fists flew round like flails. The cabman suddenly whooped and doubled up, kicked under the diaphragm. The door into the bar-parlour from the kitchen slammed and covered Mr. Marvel's retreat. The men in the kitchen found themselves clutching at and struggling with empty air.

"Where's he gone?" cried the man with the beard. "Out?"

"This way," said the policeman, stepping into the yard and stopping.

A piece of tile whizzed by his head and smashed among the crockery on the kitchen table.

"I'll show him," shouted the man with the black beard, and suddenly a steel barrel shone over the policeman's shoulder, and five bullets had followed one another into the twilight whence the missile had come. As he fired, the man with the beard moved his hand in a horizontal curve, so that his shots radiated out into the narrow yard like spokes from a wheel.

A silence followed. "Five cartridges," said the man with the black beard. "That's the best of all. Four aces and a joker. Get a lantern, someone, and come and feel about for his body."

Chapter XVII

DOCTOR KEMP'S VISITOR

Doctor Kemp had continued writing in his study until the shots aroused him. Crack, crack, crack, they came one after the other.

"Hullo!" said Doctor Kemp, putting his pen into his mouth again and listening. "Who's letting off revolvers in Burdock? What are the asses at now?"

He went to the south window, threw it up, and leaning out stared down on the network of windows, beaded gas-lamps and shops, with its black interstices of roof and yard that made up the town at night. "Looks like a crowd down the hill," he said, "by the Cricketers," and remained watching. Thence his eyes wandered over the town to far away where the ships' lights shone, and the pier glowed—a little illuminated, faceted pavilion like a gem of yellow light. The moon in its first quarter hung over the westward hill, and the stars were clear and almost tropically bright.

After five minutes, during which his mind had travelled into a remote speculation of social conditions of the future, and lost itself at last over the time dimension, Doctor Kemp roused himself with a sigh, pulled down the window again, and returned to his writing-desk.

It must have been about an hour after this that the front-door bell rang. He had been writing slackly, and with intervals of abstraction, since the shots. He sat listening. He heard the servant answer the door, and waited for her feet on the staircase, but she did not come. "Wonder what that was," said Doctor Kemp.

He tried to resume his work, failed, got up, went downstairs from his study to the landing, rang, and called over the balustrade to the housemaid as she appeared in the hall below. "Was that a letter?" he asked.

"Only a runaway ring, sir," she answered.

"I'm restless to-night," he said to himself. He went back to his study, and this time attacked his work resolutely. In a little while he was hard at work again, and the only sounds in the room were the ticking of the clock and the subdued shrillness of his quill, hurrying in the very centre of the circle of light his lampshade threw on his table.

It was two o'clock before Doctor Kemp had finished his work for the night. He rose, yawned, and went downstairs to bed. He had already removed his coat and vest, when he noticed that he was thirsty. He took a candle and went down to the dining-room in search of a syphon and whiskey.

Doctor Kemp's scientific pursuits have made him a very observant man, and as he recrossed the hall, he noticed a dark spot on the linoleum near the mat at the foot of the stairs. He went on upstairs, and then it suddenly occurred to him to ask himself what the spot on the linoleum might be. Apparently some subconscious element was at work. At any rate, he turned with his burden, went back to the hall, put down the syphon and whiskey, and bending down, touched the spot. Without any great surprise he found it had the stickiness and colour of drying blood.

He took up his burden again, and returned upstairs, looking about him and trying to account for the blood-spot. On the landing he saw something and stopped astonished. The door-handle of his own room was bloodstained.

He looked at his own hand. It was quite clean, and then he remembered that the door of his room had been open when he came down from his study, and that consequently he had not touched the handle at all. He went straight into his room, his face quite calm—perhaps a trifle more resolute than usual. His glance, wandering inquisitively, fell on the bed. On the counterpane was a mess of blood, and the sheet had been torn.

He had not noticed this before because he had walked straight to the dressing-table. On the further side the bedclothes were depressed as if someone had been recently sitting there.

Then he had an odd impression that he had heard a low voice say, "Good Heavens! *Kemp!*" But Doctor Kemp was no believer in Voices.

He stood staring at the tumbled sheets. Was that really a voice? He looked about again, but noticed nothing further than the disordered and bloodstained bed. Then he distinctly heard a movement across the room, near the wash-hand stand. All men, however highly educated, retain some superstitious inklings. The feeling that is called "eerie" came upon him. He closed the door of the room, came forward to the dressing-table, and put down his burdens. Suddenly, with a start, he perceived a coiled and bloodstained bandage of linen rag hanging in mid-air, between him and the wash-hand stand.

He stared at this in amazement. It was an empty bandage, a bandage properly tied but quite empty. He would have advanced to grasp it, but a touch arrested him, and a voice speaking quite close to him.

"Kemp!" said the Voice.

"Eh?" said Kemp, with his mouth open.

"Keep your nerve," said the Voice. "I'm an Invisible Man."

Kemp made no answer for a space, simply stared at the bandage. "Invisible Man," he said.

"I am an Invisible Man," repeated the Voice.

The story he had been active to ridicule only that morning rushed through Kemp's brain. He does not appear to have been either very much frightened or very greatly surprised at the moment. Realisation came later.

"I thought it was all a lie," he said. The thought uppermost in his mind was the reiterated arguments of the morning. "Have you a bandage on?" he asked.

"Yes," said the Invisible Man.

"Oh!" said Kemp, and then roused himself. "I say!" he said.

"But this is nonsense. It's some trick." He stepped forward suddenly, and his hand, extended towards the bandage, met invisible fingers.

He recoiled at the touch and his colour changed.

"Keep steady, Kemp, for God's sake! I want help badly. Stop!"

The hand gripped his arm. He struck at it.

"Kemp!" cried the Voice. "Kemp! Keep steady!" and the grip tightened.

A frantic desire to free himself took possession of Kemp. The hand of the bandaged arm gripped his shoulder, and he was suddenly tripped and flung backwards upon the bed. He opened his mouth to shout, and the corner of the sheet was thrust between his teeth. The Invisible Man had him down grimly, but his arms were free and he struck and tried to kick savagely.

"Listen to reason, will you?" said the Invisible Man, sticking to him in spite of a pounding in the ribs. "By Heaven! You'll madden me in a minute!

"Lie still, you fool!" bawled the Invisible Man in Kemp's ear.

Kemp struggled for another moment and then lay still.

"If you shout, I'll smash your face," said the Invisible Man, relieving his mouth.

"I'm an Invisible Man. It's no foolishness, and no magic. I really am an Invisible Man. And I want your help. I don't want to hurt you, but if you behave like a frantic rustic, I must. Don't you remember me, Kemp? Griffin, of University College?"

"Let me get up," said Kemp. "I'll stop where I am. And let me sit quiet for a minute."

He sat up and felt his neck.

"I am Griffin, of University College, and I have made myself invisible. I am just an ordinary man—a man you have known—made invisible."

"Griffin?" said Kemp.

"Griffin," answered the Voice. "A younger student than you were, almost an albino, six feet high, and broad, with a pink and white face and red eyes, who won the medal for chemistry."

"I am confused," said Kemp. "My brain is rioting. What has this to do with Griffin?"

"I *am* Griffin."

Kemp thought. "It's horrible," he said. "But what devilry must happen to make a man invisible?"

"It's no devilry. It's a process, sane and intelligible enough—"

"It's horrible!" said Kemp. "How on earth—?"

"It's horrible enough. But I'm wounded and in pain, and tired—Great God! Kemp, you are a man. Take it steady. Give me some food and drink, and let me sit down here."

Kemp stared at the bandage as it moved across the room, then saw a basket chair dragged across the floor and come to rest near the bed. It creaked, and the seat was depressed the quarter of an inch or so. He rubbed his eyes and felt his neck again. "This beats ghosts," he said, and laughed stupidly.

"That's better. Thank Heaven, you're getting sensible!"

"Or silly," said Kemp, and knuckled his eyes.

"Give me some whiskey. I'm near dead."

"It didn't feel so. Where are you? If I get up shall I run into you? *There!* All right. Whiskey? Here. Where shall I give it to you?"

The chair creaked and Kemp felt the glass drawn away from him. He let go by an effort; his instinct was all against it. It came to rest poised twenty inches above the front edge of the seat of the chair. He stared at it in infinite perplexity. "This is—this *must* be—hypnotism. You have suggested you are invisible."

"Nonsense," said the Voice.

"It's frantic."

"Listen to me."

"I demonstrated conclusively this morning," began Kemp, "that invisibility—"

"Never mind what you've demonstrated! I'm starving," said the Voice, "and the night is chilly to a man without clothes."

"Food?" said Kemp.

The tumbler of whiskey tilted itself. "Yes," said the Invisible Man rapping it down. "Have you a dressing-gown?"

Kemp made some exclamation in an undertone. He walked to a wardrobe and produced a robe of dingy scarlet. "This do?" he asked. It was taken from him. It hung limp for a moment in mid-air, fluttered weirdly, stood full and decorous buttoning itself, and sat down in his chair. "Drawers, socks, slippers would be a comfort," said the Unseen, curtly. "And food."

"Anything. But this is the insanest thing I ever was in, in my life!"

He turned out his drawers for the articles, and then went downstairs to ransack his larder. He came back with some cold cutlets and bread, pulled up a light table, and placed them before his guest. "Never mind knives," said his visitor, and a cutlet hung in mid-air, with a sound of gnawing.

"Invisible!" said Kemp, and sat down on a bedroom chair.

"I always like to get something about me before I eat," said the Invisible Man, with a full mouth, eating greedily. "Queer fancy!"

"I suppose that wrist is all right," said Kemp.

"Trust me," said the Invisible Man.

"Of *all* the strange and wonderful—"

"Exactly. But it's odd I should blunder into *your* house to get my bandaging. My first stroke of luck! Anyhow I meant to sleep in this house to-night. You must stand that! It's a filthy nuisance, my blood showing, isn't it? Quite a clot over there. Gets visible as it coagulates, I see. I've been in the house three hours."

"But how's it done?" began Kemp, in a tone of exasperation. "Confound it! The whole business—it's unreasonable from beginning to end."

"Quite reasonable," said the Invisible Man. "Perfectly reasonable."

He reached over and secured the whiskey bottle. Kemp stared at the devouring dressing gown. A ray of candlelight penetrating a torn patch in the right shoulder, made a triangle of light under the left ribs. "What were the shots?" he asked. "How did the shooting begin?"

"There was a real fool of a man—a sort of confederate of mine—curse him!—who tried to steal my money. *Has* done so."

"Is *he* invisible too?"

"No."

"Well?"

"Can't I have some more to eat before I tell you all that? I'm hungry—in pain. And you want me to tell stories!"

Kemp got up. "*You* didn't do any shooting?" he asked.

"Not me," said his visitor. "Some fool I'd never seen fired at random. A lot of them got scared. They all got scared at me. Curse them! I say—I want more to eat than this, Kemp."

"I'll see what there is to eat downstairs," said Kemp. "Not much, I'm afraid."

After he had done eating, and he made a heavy meal, the Invisible Man demanded a cigar. He bit the end savagely before Kemp could find a knife, and cursed when the outer leaf loosened. It was strange to see him smoking; his mouth, and throat, pharynx and nares, became visible as a sort of whirling smoke cast.

"This blessed gift of smoking!" he said, and puffed vigorously. "I'm lucky to have fallen upon you, Kemp. You must help me. Fancy tumbling on you just now! I'm in a devilish scrape—I've been mad, I think. The things I have been through! But we will do things yet. Let me tell you—"

He helped himself to more whiskey and soda. Kemp got up, looked about him, and fetched a glass from his spare room. "It's wild—but I suppose I may drink."

"You haven't changed much, Kemp, these dozen years. You fair men don't. Cool and methodical—after the first collapse. I must tell you. We will work together!"

"But how was it all done?" said Kemp. "And how did you get like this?"

"For God's sake, let me smoke in peace for a little while! And then I will begin to tell you."

But the story was not told that night. The Invisible Man's

wrist was growing painful; he was feverish, exhausted, and his mind came round to brood upon his chase down the hill and the struggle about the inn. He spoke in fragments of Marvel, he smoked faster, his voice grew angry. Kemp tried to gather what he could.

"He was afraid of me, I could see that he was afraid of me," said the Invisible Man many times over. "He meant to give me the slip—he was always casting about! What a fool I was!

"The cur!

"I should have killed him!"

"Where did you get the money?" asked Kemp, abruptly.

The Invisible Man was silent for a space. "I can't tell you to-night," he said.

He groaned suddenly and leant forward, supporting his invisible head on invisible hands. "Kemp," he said, "I've had no sleep for near three days, except a couple of dozes of an hour or so. I must sleep soon."

"Well, have my room—have this room."

"But how can I sleep? If I sleep—he will get away. Ugh! What does it matter?"

"What's the shot wound?" asked Kemp, abruptly.

"Nothing—scratch and blood. Oh, God! How I want sleep!"

"Why not?"

The Invisible Man appeared to be regarding Kemp. "Because I've a particular objection to being caught by my fellow-men," he said slowly.

Kemp started.

"Fool that I am!" said the Invisible Man, striking the table smartly. "I've put the idea into your head."

Chapter XVIII

THE INVISIBLE MAN SLEEPS

Exhausted and wounded as the Invisible Man was, he refused to accept Kemp's word that his freedom should be respected. He examined the two windows of the bedroom, drew up the blinds and opened the sashes, to confirm Kemp's statement that a retreat by them would be possible. Outside the night was very quiet and still, and the new moon was setting over the down. Then he examined the keys of the bedroom and the two dressing-room doors, to satisfy himself that these also could be made an assurance of freedom. Finally he expressed himself satisfied. He stood on the hearth rug and Kemp heard the sound of a yawn.

"I'm sorry," said the Invisible Man, "if I cannot tell you all that I have done to-night. But I am worn out. It's grotesque, no doubt. It's horrible! But believe me, Kemp, in spite of your arguments of this morning, it is quite a possible thing. I have made a discovery. I meant to keep it to myself. I can't. I must have a partner. And you—we can do such things—but to-morrow. Now, Kemp, I feel as though I must sleep or perish."

Kemp stood in the middle of the room staring at the headless garment. "I suppose I must leave you," he said. "It's—incredible. Three things happening like this, overturning all my preconceptions—would make me insane. But it's real! Is there anything more that I can get you?"

"Only bid me good-night," said Griffin.

"Good-night," said Kemp, and shook an invisible hand. He walked sideways to the door. Suddenly the dressing-gown walked quickly towards him. "Understand me!" said the dressing-gown. "No attempts to hamper me, or capture me! Or—"

Kemp's face changed a little. "I thought I gave you my word," he said.

Kemp closed the door softly behind him, and the key was turned upon him forthwith. Then, as he stood with an expression of passive amazement on his face, the rapid feet came to the door of the dressing-room and that too was locked. Kemp slapped his brow with his hand. "Am I dreaming? Has the world gone mad—or have I?"

He laughed, and put his hand to the locked door. "Barred out of my own bedroom, by a flagrant absurdity!" he said.

He walked to the head of the staircase, turned, and stared at the locked doors. "It's fact," he said. He put his fingers to his slightly bruised neck. "Undeniable fact!

"But—"

He shook his head hopelessly, turned, and went downstairs.

He lit the dining-room lamp, got out a cigar, and began pacing the room, ejaculating. Now and then he would argue with himself.

"Invisible!" he said.

"Is there such a thing as an invisible animal? In the sea, yes. Thousands—millions. All the larvae, all the little nauplii and tornarias, all the microscopic things, the jelly-fish. In the sea there are more things invisible than visible! I never thought of that before. And in the ponds too! All those little pond-life things—specks of colourless translucent jelly! But in air? No!

"It can't be.

"But after all—why not?

"If a man was made of glass he would still be visible."

His meditation became profound. The bulk of three cigars had passed into the invisible or diffused as a white ash over the carpet before he spoke again. Then it was merely an exclamation. He turned aside, walked out of the room, and went into his little consulting-room and lit the gas there. It was a little room, because Doctor Kemp did not live by practice, and in it were the day's newspapers. The morning's paper lay carelessly opened and thrown aside. He caught it up, turned it over, and read the account of a "Strange Story from Iping" that the mariner at

Port Stowe had spelt over so painfully to Mr. Marvel. Kemp read it swiftly.

"Wrapped up!" said Kemp. "Disguised! Hiding it! 'No one seems to have been aware of his misfortune.' What the devil *is* his game?"

He dropped the paper, and his eye went seeking. "Ah!" he said, and caught up the *St. James' Gazette*, lying folded up as it arrived. "Now we shall get at the truth," said Doctor Kemp. He rent the paper open; a couple of columns confronted him. "An Entire Village in Sussex goes Mad" was the heading.

"Good Heavens!" said Kemp, reading eagerly an incredulous account of the events in Iping, of the previous afternoon, that have already been described. Over the leaf the report in the morning paper had been reprinted.

He reread it. "Ran through the streets striking right and left. Jaffers insensible. Mr. Huxter in great pain—still unable to describe what he saw. Painful humiliation—vicar. Woman ill with terror! Windows smashed. This extraordinary story probably a fabrication. Too good not to print—*cum grano!*"

He dropped the paper and stared blankly in front of him. "Probably a fabrication!"

He caught up the paper again, and reread the whole business. "But when does the Tramp come in? Why the deuce was he chasing a Tramp?"

He sat down abruptly on the surgical bench. "He's not only invisible," he said, "but he's mad! Homicidal!"

When dawn came to mingle its pallor with the lamp-light and cigar smoke of the dining-room, Kemp was still pacing up and down, trying to grasp the incredible.

He was altogether too excited to sleep. His servants, descending sleepily, discovered him, and were inclined to think that over-study had worked this ill on him. He gave them extraordinary but quite explicit instructions to lay breakfast for two in the belvedere study—and then to confine themselves to the basement and ground-floor. Then he continued to pace the

dining-room until the morning's paper came. That had much to say and little to tell, beyond the confirmation of the evening before, and a very badly written account of another remarkable tale from Port Burdock. This gave Kemp the essence of the happenings at the Jolly Cricketers, and the name of Marvel. "He has made me keep with him twenty-four hours," Marvel testified. Certain minor facts were added to the Iping story, notably the cutting of the village telegraph-wire. But there was nothing to throw light on the connexion between the Invisible Man and the Tramp; for Mr. Marvel had supplied no information about the three books, or the money with which he was lined. The incredulous tone had vanished and a shoal of reporters and inquirers were already at work elaborating the matter.

Kemp read every scrap of the report and sent his housemaid out to get everyone of the morning papers she could. These also he devoured.

"He is invisible!" he said. "And it reads like rage growing to mania! The things he may do! The things he may do! And he's upstairs free as the air. What on earth ought I to do?"

"For instance, would it be a breach of faith if—? No."

He went to a little untidy desk in the corner, and began a note. He tore this up half written, and wrote another. He read it over and considered it. Then he took an envelope and addressed it to "Colonel Adye, Port Burdock."

The Invisible Man awoke even as Kemp was doing this. He awoke in an evil temper, and Kemp, alert for every sound, heard his pattering feet rush suddenly across the bedroom overhead. Then a chair was flung over and the wash-hand stand tumbler smashed. Kemp hurried upstairs and rapped eagerly.

Chapter XIX

CERTAIN FIRST PRINCIPLES

What's the matter?" asked Kemp, when the Invisible Man admitted him.

"Nothing," was the answer.

"But, confound it! The smash?"

"Fit of temper," said the Invisible Man. "Forgot this arm; and it's sore."

"You're rather liable to that sort of thing."

"I am."

Kemp walked across the room and picked up the fragments of broken glass. "All the facts are out about you," said Kemp, standing up with the glass in his hand; "all that happened in Iping, and down the hill. The world has become aware of its invisible citizen. But no one knows you are here."

The Invisible Man swore.

"The secret's out. I gather it was a secret. I don't know what your plans are, but of course I'm anxious to help you."

The Invisible Man sat down on the bed.

"There's breakfast upstairs," said Kemp, speaking as easily as possible, and he was delighted to find his strange guest rose willingly. Kemp led the way up the narrow staircase to the belvedere.

"Before we can do anything else," said Kemp, "I must understand a little more about this invisibility of yours." He had sat down, after one nervous glance out of the window, with the air of a man who has talking to do. His doubts of the sanity of the entire business flashed and vanished again as he looked across to where Griffin sat at the breakfast-table—a headless, handless dressing-gown, wiping unseen lips on a miraculously held serviette.

"It's simple enough—and credible enough," said Griffin, putting the serviette aside and leaning the invisible head on an invisible hand.

"No doubt, to you, but—" Kemp laughed.

"Well, yes; to me it seemed wonderful at first, no doubt. But now, great God! But we will do great things yet! I came on the stuff first at Chesilstowe."

"Chesilstowe?"

"I went there after I left London. You know I dropped medicine and took up physics? No?—well, I did. Light—fascinated me."

"Ah!"

"Optical density! The whole subject is a network of riddles—a network with solutions glimmering elusively through. And being but two and twenty and full of enthusiasm, I said, 'I will devote my life to this. This is worthwhile.' You know what fools we are at two and twenty?"

"Fools then or fools now," said Kemp.

"As though knowing could be any satisfaction to a man!

"But I went to work—like a nigger. And I had hardly worked and thought about the matter six months before light came through one of the meshes suddenly—blindingly! I found a general principle of pigments and refraction—a formula, a geometrical expression involving four dimensions. Fools, common men, even common mathematicians, do not know anything of what some general expression may mean to the student of molecular physics. In the books—the books that tramp has hidden—there are marvels, miracles! But this was not a method, it was an idea, that might lead to a method by which it would be possible, without changing any other property of matter—except, in some instances colours—to lower the refractive index of a substance, solid or liquid, to that of air—so far as all practical purposes are concerned."

"Phew!" said Kemp. "That's odd! But still I don't see quite—I can understand that thereby you could spoil a valuable stone, but personal invisibility is a far cry."

"Precisely," said Griffin. "But consider: Visibility depends on the action of the visible bodies on light. Either a body absorbs light, or it reflects or refracts it, or does all these things. If it neither reflects nor refracts nor absorbs light, it cannot of itself be visible. You see an opaque red box, for instance, because the colour absorbs some of the light and reflects the rest, all the red part of the light, to you. If it did not absorb any particular part of the light, but reflected it all, then it would be a shining white box. Silver! A diamond box would neither absorb much of the light nor reflect much from the general surface, but just here and there where the surfaces were favourable the light would be reflected and refracted, so that you would get a brilliant appearance of flashing reflections and translucencies—a sort of skeleton of light. A glass box would not be so brilliant, not so clearly visible, as a diamond box, because there would be less refraction and reflection. See that? From certain points of view you would see quite clearly through it. Some kinds of glass would be more visible than others, a box of flint glass would be brighter than a box of ordinary window glass. A box of very thin common glass would be hard to see in a bad light, because it would absorb hardly any light and refract and reflect very little. And if you put a sheet of common white glass in water, still more if you put it in some denser liquid than water, it would vanish almost altogether, because light passing from water to glass is only slightly refracted or reflected or indeed affected in any way. It is almost as invisible as a jet of coal gas or hydrogen is in air. And for precisely the same reason!"

"Yes," said Kemp, "that is pretty plain sailing."

"And here is another fact you will know to be true. If a sheet of glass is smashed, Kemp, and beaten into a powder, it becomes much more visible while it is in the air; it becomes at last an opaque white powder. This is because the powdering multiplies the surfaces of the glass at which refraction and reflection occur. In the sheet of glass there are only two surfaces; in the powder the light is reflected or refracted by each grain it passes through, and very little gets right through the powder. But if the white powdered glass is put into water, it forthwith vanishes. The powdered glass and water have much the same refractive index; that is, the light undergoes very little refraction or reflection in passing from one to the other.

"You make the glass invisible by putting it into a liquid of nearly the same refractive index; a transparent thing becomes invisible if it is put in any medium of almost the same refractive index. And if you will consider only a second, you will see also that the powder of glass might be made to vanish in air, if its refractive index could be made the same as that of air; for then there would be no refraction or reflection as the light passed from glass to air."

"Yes, yes," said Kemp. "But a man's not powdered glass!"

"No," said Griffin. "*He's more transparent!*"

"Nonsense!"

"That from a doctor! How one forgets! Have you already forgotten your physics, in ten years? Just think of all the things that are transparent and seem not to be so. Paper, for instance, is made up of transparent fibres, and it is white and opaque only for the same reason that a powder of glass is white and opaque. Oil white paper, fill up the interstices between the particles with oil so that there is no longer refraction or reflection except at the surfaces, and it becomes as transparent as glass. And not only paper, but cotton fibre, linen fibre, wool fibre, woody fibre, and *bone*, Kemp, *flesh*, Kemp, *hair*, Kemp, *nails* and *nerves*, Kemp, in fact the whole fabric of a man except the red of his blood and the black pigment of hair, are all made up of transparent, colourless tissue. So little suffices to make us visible one to the other. For the most part the fibres of a living creature are no more opaque than water."

"Great Heavens!" cried Kemp. "Of course, of course! I was thinking only last night of the sea larvae and all jelly-fish!"

"*Now* you have me! And all that I knew and had in mind a year after I left London—six years ago. But I kept it to myself.

I had to do my work under frightful disadvantages. Oliver, my professor, was a scientific bounder, a journalist by instinct, a thief of ideas—he was always prying! And you know the knavish system of the scientific world. I simply would not publish, and let him share my credit. I went on working; I got nearer and nearer making my formula into an experiment, a reality. I told no living soul, because I meant to flash my work upon the world with crushing effect and become famous at a blow. I took up the question of pigments to fill up certain gaps. And suddenly, not by design but by accident, I made a discovery in physiology."

"Yes?"

"You know the red colouring matter of blood; it can be made white—colourless—and remain with all the functions it has now!"

Kemp gave a cry of incredulous amazement.

The Invisible Man rose and began pacing the little study. "You may well exclaim. I remember that night. It was late at night—in the daytime one was bothered with the gaping, silly students—and I worked then sometimes till dawn. It came suddenly, splendid and complete in my mind. I was alone; the laboratory was still, with the tall lights burning brightly and silently. In all my great moments I have been alone. 'One could make an animal—a tissue—transparent! One could make it invisible! All except the pigments—I could be invisible!' I said, suddenly realising what it meant to be an albino with such knowledge. It was overwhelming. I left the filtering I was doing, and went and stared out of the great window at the stars. 'I could be invisible!' I repeated.

"To do such a thing would be to transcend magic. And I beheld, unclouded by doubt, a magnificent vision of all that invisibility might mean to a man—the mystery, the power, the freedom. Drawbacks I saw none. You have only to think! And I, a shabby, poverty-struck, hemmed-in demonstrator, teaching fools in a provincial college, might suddenly become—this. I ask you, Kemp if *you*—anyone, I tell you, would have flung himself upon that research. And I worked three years, and every mountain of difficulty I toiled over showed another from its summit. The infinite details! And the exasperation—a professor, a provincial professor, always prying. 'When are you going to publish this work of yours?' was his everlasting question. And the students, the cramped means! Three years I had of it—

"And after three years of secrecy and exasperation, I found that to complete it was impossible—impossible."

"How?" asked Kemp.

"Money," said the Invisible Man, and went again to stare out of the window.

He turned around abruptly. "I robbed the old man—robbed my father.

"The money was not his, and he shot himself."

Chapter XX

AT THE HOUSE IN GREAT PORTLAND STREET

For a moment Kemp sat in silence, staring at the back of the headless figure at the window. Then he started, struck by a thought, rose, took the Invisible Man's arm, and turned him away from the outlook.

"You are tired," he said, "and while I sit, you walk about. Have my chair."

He placed himself between Griffin and the nearest window. For a space Griffin sat silent, and then he resumed abruptly:

"I had left the Chesilstowe cottage already," he said, "when that happened. It was last December. I had taken a room in London, a large unfurnished room in a big ill-managed lodging-house in a slum near Great Portland Street. The room was soon full of the appliances I had bought with his money; the work was going on steadily, successfully, drawing near an end. I was like a man emerging from a thicket, and suddenly coming on some unmeaning tragedy. I went to bury him. My mind was still on this research, and I did not lift a finger to save his character. I remember the funeral, the cheap hearse, the scant ceremony, the windy frost-bitten hillside, and the old college friend of his who read the service over him—a shabby, black, bent old man with a snivelling cold.

"I remember walking back to the empty house, through the place that had once been a village and was now patched and tinkered by the jerry builders into the ugly likeness of a town. Every way the roads ran out at last into the desecrated fields and ended in rubble heaps and rank wet weeds. I remember myself as a gaunt black figure, going along the slippery, shiny pavement, and the strange sense of detachment I felt from the squalid respectability, the sordid commercialism of the place.

"I did not feel a bit sorry for my father. He seemed to me to be the victim of his own foolish sentimentality. The current cant required my attendance at his funeral, but it was really not my affair.

"But going along the High Street, my old life came back to me for a space, for I met the girl I had known ten years since. Our eyes met.

"Something moved me to turn back and talk to her. She was a very ordinary person.

"It was all like a dream, that visit to the old places. I did not feel then that I was lonely, that I had come out from the world into a desolate place. I appreciated my loss of sympathy, but I put it down to the general inanity of things. Re-entering my room seemed like the recovery of reality. There were the things I knew and loved. There stood the apparatus, the experiments arranged and waiting. And now there was scarcely a difficulty left, beyond the planning of details.

"I will tell you, Kemp, sooner or later, all the complicated processes. We need not go into that now. For the most part, saving certain gaps I chose to remember, they are written in cypher in those books that tramp has hidden. We must hunt him down. We must get those books again. But the essential phase was to place the transparent object whose refractive index was to be lowered between two radiating centres of a sort of ethereal vibration, of which I will tell you more fully later. No, not those Röntgen vibrations—I don't know that these others of mine have been described. Yet they are obvious enough. I needed two little dynamos, and these I worked with a cheap gas engine. My first experiment was with a bit of white wool fabric. It was the strangest thing in the world to see it in the flicker of the flashes soft and white, and then to watch it fade like a wreath of smoke and vanish.

"I could scarcely believe I had done it. I put my hand into

the emptiness, and there was the thing as solid as ever. I felt it awkwardly, and threw it on the floor. I had a little trouble finding it again.

"And then came a curious experience. I heard a miaow behind me, and turning, saw a lean white cat, very dirty, on the cistern cover outside the window. A thought came into my head. 'Everything ready for you,' I said, and went to the window, opened it, and called softly. She came in, purring—the poor beast was starving—and I gave her some milk. All my food was in a cupboard in the corner of the room. After that she went smelling round the room, evidently with the idea of making herself at home. The invisible rag upset her a bit; you should have seen her spit at it! But I made her comfortable on the pillow of my truckle-bed. And I gave her butter to get her to wash."

"And you processed her?"

"I processed her. But giving drugs to a cat is no joke, Kemp! And the process failed."

"Failed!"

"In two particulars. These were the claws and the pigment stuff, what is it?At the back of the eye in a cat. You know?"

"*Tapetum*."

"Yes, the *tapetum*. It didn't go. After I'd given the stuff to bleach the blood and done certain other things to her, I gave the beast opium, and put her and the pillow she was sleeping on, on the apparatus. And after all the rest had faded and vanished, there remained two little ghosts of her eyes."

"Odd!"

"I can't explain it. She was bandaged and clamped, of course—so I had her safe; but she woke while she was still misty, and miaowed dismally, and someone came knocking. It was an old woman from downstairs, who suspected me of vivisecting—a drink-sodden old creature, with only a white cat to care for in all the world. I whipped out some chloroform, applied it, and answered the door. 'Did I hear a cat?' she asked. 'My cat?' 'Not here,' said I, very politely. She was a little doubtful and tried to peer past me into the room; strange enough to her no doubt—bare walls, uncurtained windows, truckle-bed, with the gas engine vibrating, and the seethe of the radiant points, and that faint ghastly stinging of chloroform in the air. She had to be satisfied at last and went away again."

"How long did it take?" asked Kemp.

"Three or four hours—the cat. The bones and sinews and the fat were the last to go, and the tips of the coloured hairs. And, as I say, the back part of the eye, tough, iridescent stuff it is, wouldn't go at all.

"It was night outside long before the business was over, and nothing was to be seen but the dim eyes and the claws. I stopped the gas engine, felt for and stroked the beast, which was still insensible, and then, being tired, left it sleeping on the invisible pillow and went to bed. I found it hard to sleep. I lay awake thinking weak aimless stuff, going over the experiment over and over again, or dreaming feverishly of things growing misty and vanishing about me, until everything, the ground I stood on, vanished, and so I came to that sickly falling nightmare one gets. About two, the cat began miaowing about the room. I tried to hush it by talking to it, and then I decided to turn it out. I remember the shock I had when striking a light—there were just the round eyes shining green—and nothing round them. I would have given it milk, but I hadn't any. It wouldn't be quiet, it just sat down and miaowed at the door. I tried to catch it, with an idea of putting it out of the window, but it wouldn't be caught, it vanished. Then it began miaowing in different parts of the room. At last I opened the window and made a bustle. I suppose it went out at last. I never saw anymore of it.

"Then—Heaven knows why—I fell thinking of my father's funeral again, and the dismal windy hillside, until the day had come. I found sleeping was hopeless, and, locking my door after me, wandered out into the morning streets."

"You don't mean to say there's an invisible cat at large!" said Kemp.

"If it hasn't been killed," said the Invisible Man. "Why not?"

"Why not?" said Kemp. "I didn't mean to interrupt."

"It's very probably been killed," said the Invisible Man. "It was alive four days after, I know, and down a grating in Great Titchfield Street; because I saw a crowd round the place, trying to see whence the miaowing came."

He was silent for the best part of a minute. Then he resumed abruptly:

"I remember that morning before the change very vividly. I must have gone up Great Portland Street. I remember the barracks in Albany Street, and the horse soldiers coming out, and at last I found the summit of Primrose Hill. It was a sunny day in January—one of those sunny, frosty days that came before the snow this year. My weary brain tried to formulate the position, to plot out a plan of action.

"I was surprised to find, now that my prize was within my grasp, how inconclusive its attainment seemed. As a matter of fact I was worked out; the intense stress of nearly four years' continuous work left me incapable of any strength of feeling. I was apathetic, and I tried in vain to recover the enthusiasm of my first inquiries, the passion of discovery that had enabled me to compass even the downfall of my father's grey hairs. Nothing seemed to matter. I saw pretty clearly this was a transient mood, due to overwork and want of sleep, and that either by drugs or rest it would be possible to recover my energies.

"All I could think clearly was that the thing had to be carried through; the fixed idea still ruled me. And soon, for the money I had was almost exhausted. I looked about me at the hillside, with children playing and girls watching them, and tried to think of all the fantastic advantages an invisible man would have in the world. After a time I crawled home, took some food and a strong dose of strychnine, and went to sleep in my clothes on my unmade bed. Strychnine is a grand tonic, Kemp, to take the flabbiness out of a man."

"It's the devil," said Kemp. "It's the palaeolithic in a bottle."

"I awoke vastly invigorated and rather irritable. You know?"

"I know the stuff."

"And there was someone rapping at the door. It was my landlord with threats and inquiries, an old Polish Jew in a long grey coat and greasy slippers. I had been tormenting a cat in the night, he was sure—the old woman's tongue had been busy. He insisted on knowing all about it. The laws in this country against vivisection were very severe—he might be liable. I denied the cat. Then the vibration of the little gas engine could be felt all over the house, he said. That was true, certainly. He edged round me into the room, peering about over his German-silver spectacles, and a sudden dread came into my mind that he might carry away something of my secret. I tried to keep between him and the concentrating apparatus I had arranged, and that only made him more curious. What was I doing? Why was I always alone and secretive? Was it legal? Was it dangerous? I paid nothing but the usual rent. His had always been a most respectable house—in a disreputable neighbourhood. Suddenly my temper gave way. I told him to get out. He began to protest, to jabber of his right of entry. In a moment I had him by the collar; something ripped, and he went spinning out into his own passage. I slammed and locked the door and sat down quivering.

"He made a fuss outside, which I disregarded, and after a time he went away.

"But this brought matters to a crisis. I did not know what he would do, nor even what he had the power to do. To move to fresh apartments would have meant delay; altogether I had barely twenty pounds left in the world, for the most part in a bank—and I could not afford that. Vanish! It was irresistible. Then there would be an inquiry, the sacking of my room.

"At the thought of the possibility of my work being exposed or interrupted at its very climax, I became very angry and active. I hurried out with my three books of notes, my cheque-book—the tramp has them now—and directed them from the nearest Post Office to a house of call for letters and parcels in Great

Portland Street. I tried to go out noiselessly. Coming in, I found my landlord going quietly upstairs; he had heard the door close, I suppose. You would have laughed to see him jump aside on the landing as I came tearing after him. He glared at me as I went by him, and I made the house quiver with the slamming of my door. I heard him come shuffling up to my floor, hesitate, and go down. I set to work upon my preparations forthwith.

"It was all done that evening and night. While I was still sitting under the sickly, drowsy influence of the drugs that decolourise blood, there came a repeated knocking at the door. It ceased, footsteps went away and returned, and the knocking was resumed. There was an attempt to push something under the door—a blue paper. Then in a fit of irritation I rose and went and flung the door wide open. 'Now then?' said I.

"It was my landlord, with a notice of ejectment or something. He held it out to me, saw something odd about my hands, I expect, and lifted his eyes to my face.

"For a moment he gaped. Then he gave a sort of inarticulate cry, dropped candle and writ together, and went blundering down the dark passage to the stairs. I shut the door, locked it, and went to the looking-glass. Then I understood his terror . . . My face was white—like white stone.

"But it was all horrible. I had not expected the suffering. A night of racking anguish, sickness and fainting. I set my teeth, though my skin was presently afire, all my body afire; but I lay there like grim death. I understood now how it was the cat had howled until I chloroformed it. Lucky it was I lived alone and untended in my room. There were times when I sobbed and groaned and talked. But I stuck to it . . . I became insensible and woke languid in the darkness.

"The pain had passed. I thought I was killing myself and I did not care. I shall never forget that dawn, and the strange horror of seeing that my hands had become as clouded glass, and watching them grow clearer and thinner as the day went by, until at last I could see the sickly disorder of my room through

them, though I closed my transparent eyelids. My limbs became glassy, the bones and arteries faded, vanished, and the little white nerves went last. I gritted my teeth and stayed there to the end. At last only the dead tips of the fingernails remained, pallid and white, and the brown stain of some acid upon my fingers.

"I struggled up. At first I was as incapable as a swathed infant—stepping with limbs I could not see. I was weak and very hungry. I went and stared at nothing in my shaving-glass, at nothing save where an attenuated pigment still remained behind the retina of my eyes, fainter than mist. I had to hang on to the table and press my forehead against the glass.

"It was only by a frantic effort of will that I dragged myself back to the apparatus and completed the process.

"I slept during the forenoon, pulling the sheet over my eyes to shut out the light, and about midday I was awakened again by a knocking. My strength had returned. I sat up and listened and heard a whispering. I sprang to my feet and as noiselessly as possible began to detach the connections of my apparatus, and to distribute it about the room, so as to destroy the suggestions of its arrangement. Presently the knocking was renewed and voices called, first my landlord's, and then two others. To gain time I answered them. The invisible rag and pillow came to hand and I opened the window and pitched them out on to the cistern cover. As the window opened, a heavy crash came at the door. Someone had charged it with the idea of smashing the lock. But the stout bolts I had screwed up some days before stopped him. That startled me, made me angry. I began to tremble and do things hurriedly.

"I tossed together some loose paper, straw, packing paper and so forth, in the middle of the room, and turned on the gas. Heavy blows began to rain upon the door. I could not find the matches. I beat my hands on the wall with rage. I turned down the gas again, stepped out of the window on the cistern cover, very softly lowered the sash, and sat down, secure and invisible, but quivering with anger, to watch events. They split a panel, I

saw, and in another moment they had broken away the staples of the bolts and stood in the open doorway. It was the landlord and his two step-sons, sturdy young men of three or four and twenty. Behind them fluttered the old hag of a woman from downstairs.

"You may imagine their astonishment to find the room empty. One of the younger men rushed to the window at once, flung it up and stared out. His staring eyes and thick-lipped bearded face came a foot from my face. I was half minded to hit his silly countenance, but I arrested my doubled fist. He stared right through me. So did the others as they joined him. The old man went and peered under the bed, and then they all made a rush for the cupboard. They had to argue about it at length in Yiddish and Cockney English. They concluded I had not answered them, that their imagination had deceived them. A feeling of extraordinary elation took the place of my anger as I sat outside the window and watched these four people—for the old lady came in, glancing suspiciously about her like a cat, trying to understand the riddle of my behaviour.

"The old man, so far as I could understand his *patois*, agreed with the old lady that I was a vivisectionist. The sons protested in garbled English that I was an electrician, and appealed to the dynamos and radiators. They were all nervous about my arrival, although I found subsequently that they had bolted the front door. The old lady peered into the cupboard and under the bed, and one of the young men pushed up the register and stared up the chimney. One of my fellow lodgers, a coster-monger who shared the opposite room with a butcher, appeared on the landing, and he was called in and told incoherent things.

"It occurred to me that the radiators, if they fell into the hands of some acute well-educated person, would give me away too much, and watching my opportunity, I came into the room and tilted one of the little dynamos off its fellow on which it was standing, and smashed both apparatus. Then, while they were trying to explain the smash, I dodged out of the room and went softly downstairs.

"I went into one of the sitting-rooms and waited until they came down, still speculating and argumentative, all a little disappointed at finding no 'horrors,' and all a little puzzled how they stood legally towards me. Then I slipped up again with a box of matches, fired my heap of paper and rubbish, put the chairs and bedding thereby, led the gas to the affair, by means of an india-rubber tube, and waving a farewell to the room left it for the last time."

"You fired the house!" exclaimed Kemp.

"Fired the house. It was the only way to cover my trail—and no doubt it was insured. I slipped the bolts of the front door quietly and went out into the street. I was invisible, and I was only just beginning to realise the extraordinary advantage my invisibility gave me. My head was already teeming with plans of all the wild and wonderful things I had now impunity to do."

Chapter XXI

IN OXFORD STREET

In going downstairs the first time I found an unexpected difficulty because I could not see my feet; indeed I stumbled twice, and there was an unaccustomed clumsiness in gripping the bolt. By not looking down, however, I managed to walk on the level passably well.

"My mood, I say, was one of exaltation. I felt as a seeing man might do, with padded feet and noiseless clothes, in a city of the blind. I experienced a wild impulse to jest, to startle people, to clap men on the back, fling people's hats astray, and generally revel in my extraordinary advantage.

"But hardly had I emerged upon Great Portland Street, however (my lodging was close to the big draper's shop there), when I heard a clashing concussion and was hit violently behind, and turning saw a man carrying a basket of soda-water syphons, and looking in amazement at his burden. Although the blow had really hurt me, I found something so irresistible in his astonishment that I laughed aloud. 'The devil's in the basket,' I said, and suddenly twisted it out of his hand. He let go incontinently, and I swung the whole weight into the air.

"But a fool of a cabman, standing outside a public house, made a sudden rush for this, and his extending fingers took me with excruciating violence under the ear. I let the whole down with a smash on the cabman, and then, with shouts and the clatter of feet about me, people coming out of shops, vehicles pulling up, I realised what I had done for myself, and cursing my folly, backed against a shop window and prepared to dodge out of the confusion. In a moment I should be wedged into a crowd and inevitably discovered. I pushed by a butcher boy, who luckily did not turn to see the nothingness that shoved him aside, and dodged behind the cabman's four-wheeler. I do not know how they settled the business, I hurried straight across the road, which was happily clear, and hardly heeding which way I went, in the fright of detection the incident had given me, plunged into the afternoon throng of Oxford Street.

"I tried to get into the stream of people, but they were too thick for me, and in a moment my heels were being trodden upon. I took to the gutter, the roughness of which I found painful to my feet, and forthwith the shaft of a crawling hansom dug me forcibly under the shoulder blade, reminding me that I was already bruised severely. I staggered out of the way of the cab, avoided a perambulator by a convulsive movement, and found myself behind the hansom. A happy thought saved me, and as this drove slowly along I followed in its immediate wake, trembling and astonished at the turn of my adventure. And not only trembling, but shivering. It was a bright day in January and I was stark naked and the thin slime of mud that covered the road was freezing. Foolish as it seems to me now, I had not reckoned that, transparent or not, I was still amenable to the weather and all its consequences.

"Then suddenly a bright idea came into my head. I ran round and got into the cab. And so, shivering, scared, and sniffing with the first intimations of a cold, and with the bruises in the small of my back growing upon my attention, I drove slowly along Oxford Street and past Tottenham Court Road. My mood was as different from that in which I had sallied forth ten minutes ago as it is possible to imagine. This invisibility indeed! The one thought that possessed me was—how was I to get out of the scrape I was in.

"We crawled past Mudie's, and there a tall woman with five or six yellow-labelled books hailed my cab, and I sprang out just in time to escape her, shaving a railway van narrowly in my flight. I made off up the roadway to Bloomsbury Square, intending to strike north past the Museum and so get into the quiet district. I was now cruelly chilled, and the strangeness of my situation so

unnerved me that I whimpered as I ran. At the northward corner of the Square a little white dog ran out of the Pharmaceutical Society's offices, and incontinently made for me, nose down.

"I had never realised it before, but the nose is to the mind of a dog what the eye is to the mind of a seeing man. Dogs perceive the scent of a man moving as men perceive his vision. This brute began barking and leaping, showing, as it seemed to me, only too plainly that he was aware of me. I crossed Great Russell Street, glancing over my shoulder as I did so, and went some way along Montague Street before I realised what I was running towards.

"Then I became aware of a blare of music, and looking along the street saw a number of people advancing out of Russell Square, red shirts, and the banner of the Salvation Army to the fore. Such a crowd, chanting in the roadway and scoffing on the pavement, I could not hope to penetrate, and dreading to go back and farther from home again, and deciding on the spur of the moment, I ran up the white steps of a house facing the museum railings, and stood there until the crowd should have passed. Happily the dog stopped at the noise of the band too, hesitated, and turned tail, running back to Bloomsbury Square again.

"On came the band, bawling with unconscious irony some hymn about 'When shall we see His face?' and it seemed an interminable time to me before the tide of the crowd washed along the pavement by me. Thud, thud, thud, came the drum with a vibrating resonance, and for the moment I did not notice two urchins stopping at the railings by me. 'See 'em,' said one. 'See what?' said the other. 'Why—them footmarks—*bare*. Like what you makes in mud.'

"I looked down and saw the youngsters had stopped and were gaping at the muddy footmarks I had left behind me up the newly whitened steps. The passing people elbowed and jostled them, but their confounded intelligence was arrested. 'Thud, thud, thud, when, thud, shall we see, thud, his face, thud, thud.'

'There's a barefoot man gone up them steps, or I don't know nothing,' said one. 'And he ain't never come down again. And his foot was a-bleeding.'

"The thick of the crowd had already passed. 'Looky there, Ted,' quoth the younger of the detectives, with the sharpness of surprise in his voice, and pointed straight to my feet. I looked down and saw at once the dim suggestion of their outline sketched in splashes of mud. For a moment I was paralysed.

" 'Why, that's rum,' said the elder. 'Dashed rum! It's just like the ghost of a foot, ain't it?' He hesitated and advanced with outstretched hand. A man pulled up short to see what he was catching, and then a girl. In another moment he would have touched me. Then I saw what to do. I made a step, the boy started back with an exclamation, and with a rapid movement I swung myself over into the portico of the next house. But the smaller boy was sharp-eyed enough to follow the movement, and before I was well down the steps and upon the pavement, he had recovered from his momentary astonishment and was shouting out that the feet had gone over the wall.

"They rushed round and saw my new footmarks flash into being on the lower step and upon the pavement. 'What's up?' asked someone. 'Feet! Look! Feet running!' Everybody in the road, except my three pursuers, was pouring along after the Salvation Army, and this blow not only impeded me but them. There was an eddy of surprise and interrogation. At the cost of bowling over one young fellow I got through, and in another moment I was rushing headlong round the circuit of Russell Square, with six or seven astonished people following my footmarks. There was no time for explanation, or else the whole host would have been after me.

"Twice I doubled round corners, thrice I crossed the road and came back upon my tracks, and then, as my feet grew hot and dry, the damp impressions began to fade. At last I had a breathing space and rubbed my feet clean with my hands, and so got away altogether. The last I saw of the chase was a little group

of a dozen people perhaps, studying with infinite perplexity a slowly drying footprint that had resulted from a puddle in Tavistock Square, a footprint as isolated and incomprehensible to them as Crusoe's solitary discovery.

"This running warmed me to a certain extent, and I went on with a better courage through the maze of less frequented roads that runs hereabouts. My back had now become very stiff and sore, my tonsils were painful from the cabman's fingers, and the skin of my neck had been scratched by his nails; my feet hurt exceedingly and I was lame from a little cut on one foot. I saw in time a blind man approaching me, and fled limping, for I feared his subtle intuitions. Once or twice accidental collisions occurred and I left people amazed, with unaccountable curses ringing in their ears. Then came something silent and quiet against my face, and across the Square fell a thin veil of slowly falling flakes of snow. I had caught a cold, and do as I would I could not avoid an occasional sneeze. And every dog that came in sight, with its pointing nose and curious sniffing, was a terror to me.

"Then came men and boys running, first one and then others, and shouting as they ran. It was a fire. They ran in the direction of my lodging, and looking back down a street I saw a mass of black smoke streaming up above the roofs and telephone wires. It was my lodging burning; my clothes, my apparatus, all my resources indeed, except my cheque-book and the three volumes of memoranda that awaited me in Great Portland Street, were there. Burning! I had burnt my boats—if ever a man did! The place was blazing."

The Invisible Man paused and thought. Kemp glanced nervously out of the window. "Yes?" he said. "Go on."

Chapter XXII

IN THE EMPORIUM

So last January, with the beginning of a snowstorm in the air about me—and if it settled on me it would betray me!—weary, cold, painful, inexpressibly wretched, and still but half convinced of my invisible quality, I began this new life to which I am committed. I had no refuge, no appliances, no human being in the world in whom I could confide. To have told my secret would have given me away—made a mere show and rarity of me. Nevertheless, I was half-minded to accost some passer-by and throw myself upon his mercy. But I knew too clearly the terror and brutal cruelty my advances would evoke. I made no plans in the street. My sole object was to get shelter from the snow, to get myself covered and warm; then I might hope to plan. But even to me, an Invisible Man, the rows of London houses stood latched, barred, and bolted impregnably.

"Only one thing could I see clearly before me—the cold exposure and misery of the snowstorm and the night.

"And then I had a brilliant idea. I turned down one of the roads leading from Gower Street to Tottenham Court Road, and found myself outside Omniums, the big establishment where everything is to be bought—you know the place: meat, grocery, linen, furniture, clothing, oil paintings even—a huge meandering collection of shops rather than a shop. I had thought I should find the doors open, but they were closed, and as I stood in the wide entrance a carriage stopped outside, and a man in uniform—you know the kind of personage with 'Omnium' on his cap—flung open the door. I contrived to enter, and walking down the shop—it was a department where they were selling ribbons and gloves and stockings and that kind of thing—came to a more spacious region devoted to picnic baskets and wicker furniture.

"I did not feel safe there, however; people were going to and fro, and I prowled restlessly about until I came upon a huge section in an upper floor containing multitudes of bedsteads, and over these I clambered, and found a resting-place at last among a huge pile of folded flock mattresses. The place was already lit up and agreeably warm, and I decided to remain where I was, keeping a cautious eye on the two or three sets of shopmen and customers who were meandering through the place, until closing time came. Then I should be able, I thought, to rob the place for food and clothing, and disguised, prowl through it and examine its resources, perhaps sleep on some of the bedding. That seemed an acceptable plan. My idea was to procure clothing to make myself a muffled but acceptable figure, to get money, and then to recover my books and parcels where they awaited me, take a lodging somewhere and elaborate plans for the complete realisation of the advantages my invisibility gave me (as I still imagined) over my fellow-men.

"Closing time arrived quickly enough. It could not have been more than an hour after I took up my position on the mattresses before I noticed the blinds of the windows being drawn, and customers being marched doorward. And then a number of brisk young men began with remarkable alacrity to tidy up the goods that remained disturbed. I left my lair as the crowds diminished, and prowled cautiously out into the less desolate parts of the shop. I was really surprised to observe how rapidly the young men and women whipped away the goods displayed for sale during the day. All the boxes of goods, the hanging fabrics, the festoons of lace, the boxes of sweets in the grocery section, the displays of this and that, were being whipped down, folded up, slapped into tidy receptacles, and everything that could not be taken down and put away had sheets of some coarse stuff like sacking flung over them. Finally all the chairs were turned up on to the counters, leaving the floor clear. Directly each of these young people had done, he or she made promptly for the door with such an expression of animation as I have rarely observed in a shop assistant before. Then came a lot of youngsters scattering sawdust and carrying pails and brooms. I had to dodge to get out of the way, and as it was, my ankle got stung with the sawdust. For some time, wandering through the swathed and darkened departments, I could hear the brooms at work. And at last a good hour or more after the shop had been closed, came a noise of locking doors. Silence came upon the place, and I found myself wandering through the vast and intricate shops, galleries, show-rooms of the place, alone. It was very still; in one place I remember passing near one of the Tottenham Court Road entrances and listening to the tapping of boot-heels of the passers-by.

"My first visit was to the place where I had seen stockings and gloves for sale. It was dark, and I had the devil of a hunt after matches, which I found at last in the drawer of the little cash desk. Then I had to get a candle. I had to tear down wrappings and ransack a number of boxes and drawers, but at last I managed to turn out what I sought; the box label called them lambswool pants, and lambswool vests. Then socks, a thick comforter, and then I went to the clothing place and got trousers, a lounge jacket, an overcoat and a slouch hat—a clerical sort of hat with the brim turned down. I began to feel a human being again, and my next thought was food.

"Upstairs was a refreshment department, and there I got cold meat. There was coffee still in the urn, and I lit the gas and warmed it up again, and altogether I did not do badly. Afterwards, prowling through the place in search of blankets—I had to put up at last with a heap of down quilts—I came upon a grocery section with a lot of chocolate and candied fruits, more than was good for me indeed—and some white burgundy. And near that was a toy department, and I had a brilliant idea. I found some artificial noses—dummy noses, you know, and I thought of dark spectacles. But Omniums had no optical department. My nose had been a difficulty indeed—I had thought of paint. But the discovery set my mind running on wigs and masks and

the like. Finally I went to sleep in a heap of down quilts, very warm and comfortable.

"My last thoughts before sleeping were the most agreeable I had had since the change. I was in a state of physical serenity, and that was reflected in my mind. I thought that I should be able to slip out unobserved in the morning with my clothes upon me, muffling my face with a white wrapper I had taken, purchase, with the money I had taken, spectacles and so forth, and so complete my disguise. I lapsed into disorderly dreams of all the fantastic things that had happened during the last few days. I saw the ugly little Jew of a landlord vociferating in his rooms; I saw his two sons marvelling, and the wrinkled old woman's gnarled face as she asked for her cat. I experienced again the strange sensation of seeing the cloth disappear, and so I came round to the windy hillside and the sniffing old clergyman mumbling 'Earth to earth, ashes to ashes, dust to dust,' at my father's open grave.

"'You also,' said a voice, and suddenly I was being forced towards the grave. I struggled, shouted, appealed to the mourners, but they continued stonily following the service; the old clergyman, too, never faltered droning and sniffing through the ritual. I realised I was invisible and inaudible, that overwhelming forces had their grip on me. I struggled in vain, I was forced over the brink, the coffin rang hollow as I fell upon it, and the gravel came flying after me in spadefuls. Nobody heeded me, nobody was aware of me. I made convulsive struggles and awoke.

"The pale London dawn had come, the place was full of a chilly grey light that filtered round the edges of the window blinds. I sat up, and for a time I could not think where this ample apartment, with its counters, its piles of rolled stuff, its heap of quilts and cushions, its iron pillars, might be. Then, as recollection came back to me, I heard voices in conversation.

"Then far down the place, in the brighter light of some department which had already raised its blinds, I saw two men approaching. I scrambled to my feet, looking about me for some way of escape, and even as I did so the sound of my movement made them aware of me. I suppose they saw merely a figure moving quietly and quickly away. 'Who's that?' cried one, and 'Stop, there!' shouted the other. I dashed around a corner and came full tilt—a faceless figure, mind you!—on a lanky lad of fifteen. He yelled and I bowled him over, rushed past him, turned another corner, and by a happy inspiration threw myself behind a counter. In another moment feet went running past and I heard voices shouting, 'All hands to the doors!' asking what was 'up,' and giving one another advice how to catch me.

"Lying on the ground, I felt scared out of my wits. But—odd as it may seem—it did not occur to me at the moment to take off my clothes as I should have done. I had made up my mind, I suppose, to get away in them, and that ruled me. And then down the vista of the counters came a bawling of 'Here he is!'

"I sprang to my feet, whipped a chair off the counter, and sent it whirling at the fool who had shouted, turned, came into another round a corner, sent him spinning, and rushed up the stairs. He kept his footing, gave a view hallo, and came up the staircase hot after me. Up the staircase were piled a multitude of those bright-coloured pot things—what are they?"

"Art pots," suggested Kemp.

"That's it! Art pots. Well, I turned at the top step and swung round, plucked one out of a pile and smashed it on his silly head as he came at me. The whole pile of pots went headlong, and I heard shouting and footsteps running from all parts. I made a mad rush for the refreshment place, and there was a man in white like a man cook, who took up the chase. I made one last desperate turn and found myself among lamps and ironmongery. I went behind the counter of this, and waited for my cook, and as he bolted in at the head of the chase, I doubled him up with a lamp. Down he went, and I crouched down behind the counter and began whipping off my clothes as fast as I could. Coat, jacket, trousers, shoes were all right, but a lambswool vest

fits a man like a skin. I heard more men coming, my cook was lying quiet on the other side of the counter, stunned or scared speechless, and I had to make another dash for it, like a rabbit hunted out of a wood-pile.

"'This way, policeman!' I heard someone shouting. I found myself in my bedstead storeroom again, and at the end of a wilderness of wardrobes. I rushed among them, went flat, got rid of my vest after infinite wriggling, and stood a free man again, panting and scared, as the policeman and three of the shopmen came round the corner. They made a rush for the vest and pants, and collared the trousers. 'He's dropping his plunder,' said one of the young men. 'He *must* be somewhere here.'

"But they did not find me all the same.

"I stood watching them hunt for me for a time, and cursing my ill-luck in losing the clothes. Then I went into the refreshment-room, drank a little milk I found there, and sat down by the fire to consider my position.

"In a little while two assistants came in and began to talk over the business very excitedly and like the fools they were. I heard a magnified account of my depredations, and other speculations as to my whereabouts. Then I fell to scheming again. The insurmountable difficulty of the place, especially now it was alarmed, was to get any plunder out of it. I went down into the warehouse to see if there was any chance of packing and addressing a parcel, but I could not understand the system of checking. About eleven o'clock, the snow having thawed as it fell, and the day being finer and a little warmer than the previous one, I decided that the Emporium was hopeless, and went out again, exasperated at my want of success, with only the vaguest plans of action in my mind."

Chapter XXIII

IN DRURY LANE

"But you begin now to realise," said the Invisible Man, "the full disadvantage of my condition. I had no shelter, no covering. To get clothing was to forego all my advantage, to make myself a strange and terrible thing. I was fasting; for to eat, to fill myself with unassimilated matter, would be to become grotesquely visible again."

"I never thought of that," said Kemp.

"Nor had I. And the snow had warned me of other dangers. I could not go abroad in snow—it would settle on me and expose me. Rain, too, would make me a watery outline, a glistening surface of a man—a bubble. And fog—I should be like a fainter bubble in a fog, a surface, a greasy glimmer of humanity. Moreover, as I went abroad—in the London air—I gathered dirt about my ankles, floating smuts and dust upon my skin. I did not know how long it would be before I should become visible from that cause also. But I saw clearly it could not be for long.

"Not in London at any rate.

"I went into the slums towards Great Portland Street, and found myself at the end of the street in which I had lodged. I did not go that way, because of the crowd halfway down it opposite to the still smoking ruins of the house I had fired. My most immediate problem was to get clothing. What to do with my face puzzled me. Then I saw in one of those little miscellaneous shops—news, sweets, toys, stationery, belated Christmas tomfoolery, and so forth—an array of masks and noses. I realised that problem was solved. In a flash I saw my course. I turned about, no longer aimless, and went—circuitously in order to avoid the busy ways, towards the back streets north

of the Strand; for I remembered, though not very distinctly where, that some theatrical costumiers had shops in that district.

"The day was cold, with a nipping wind down the northward running streets. I walked fast to avoid being overtaken. Every crossing was a danger, every passenger a thing to watch alertly. One man as I was about to pass him at the top of Bedford Street, turned upon me abruptly and came into me, sending me into the road and almost under the wheel of a passing hansom. The verdict of the cab-rank was that he had had some sort of stroke. I was so unnerved by this encounter that I went into Covent Garden Market and sat down for some time in a quiet corner by a stall of violets, panting and trembling. I found I had caught a fresh cold, and had to turn out after a time lest my sneezes should attract attention.

"At last I reached the object of my quest, a dirty, fly-blown little shop in a by-way near Drury Lane, with a window full of tinsel robes, sham jewels, wigs, slippers, dominoes and theatrical photographs. The shop was old-fashioned and low and dark, and the house rose above it for four storeys, dark and dismal. I peered through the window and, seeing no one within, entered. The opening of the door set a clanking bell ringing. I left it open, and walked round a bare costume stand, into a corner behind a cheval glass. For a minute or so no one came. Then I heard heavy feet striding across a room, and a man appeared down the shop.

"My plans were now perfectly definite. I proposed to make my way into the house, secrete myself upstairs, watch my opportunity, and when everything was quiet, rummage out a wig, mask, spectacles, and costume, and go into the world, perhaps a grotesque but still a credible figure. And incidentally of course I could rob the house of any available money.

"The man who had just entered the shop was a short, slight, hunched, beetle-browed man, with long arms and very short bandy legs. Apparently I had interrupted a meal. He stared about the shop with an expression of expectation. This gave way to surprise, and then to anger, as he saw the shop empty. 'Damn the boys!' he said. He went to stare up and down the street. He came in again in a minute, kicked the door to with his foot spitefully, and went muttering back to the house door.

"I came forward to follow him, and at the noise of my movement he stopped dead. I did so too, startled by his quickness of ear. He slammed the house door in my face.

"I stood hesitating. Suddenly I heard his quick footsteps returning, and the door reopened. He stood looking about the shop like one who was still not satisfied. Then, murmuring to himself, he examined the back of the counter and peered behind some fixtures. Then he stood doubtful. He had left the house door open and I slipped into the inner room.

"It was a queer little room, poorly furnished and with a number of big masks in the corner. On the table was his belated breakfast, and it was a confoundedly exasperating thing for me, Kemp, to have to sniff his coffee and stand watching while he came in and resumed his meal. And his table manners were irritating. Three doors opened into the little room, one going upstairs and one down, but they were all shut. I could not get out of the room while he was there; I could scarcely move because of his alertness, and there was a draught down my back. Twice I strangled a sneeze just in time.

"The spectacular quality of my sensations was curious and novel, but for all that I was heartily tired and angry long before he had done his eating. But at last he made an end and putting his beggarly crockery on the black tin tray upon which he had had his teapot, and gathering all the crumbs up on the mustard stained cloth, he took the whole lot of things after him. His burden prevented his shutting the door behind him—as he would have done; I never saw such a man for shutting doors—and I followed him into a very dirty underground kitchen and scullery. I had the pleasure of seeing him begin to wash up, and then, finding no good in keeping down there, and the brick floor being cold on my feet, I returned upstairs and sat in his chair by

the fire. It was burning low, and scarcely thinking, I put on a little coal. The noise of this brought him up at once, and he stood aglare. He peered about the room and was within an ace of touching me. Even after that examination, he scarcely seemed satisfied. He stopped in the doorway and took a final inspection before he went down.

"I waited in the little parlour for an age, and at last he came up and opened the upstairs door. I just managed to get by him.

"On the staircase he stopped suddenly, so that I very nearly blundered into him. He stood looking back right into my face and listening. 'I could have sworn,' he said. His long hairy hand pulled at his lower lip. His eye went up and down the staircase. Then he grunted and went on up again.

"His hand was on the handle of a door, and then he stopped again with the same puzzled anger on his face. He was becoming aware of the faint sounds of my movements about him. The man must have had diabolically acute hearing. He suddenly flashed into rage. 'If there's anyone in this house—' he cried with an oath, and left the threat unfinished. He put his hand in his pocket, failed to find what he wanted, and rushing past me went blundering noisily and pugnaciously downstairs. But I did not follow him. I sat on the head of the staircase until his return.

"Presently he came up again, still muttering. He opened the door of the room, and before I could enter, slammed it in my face.

"I resolved to explore the house, and spent some time in doing so as noiselessly as possible. The house was very old and tumble-down, damp so that the paper in the attics was peeling from the walls, and rat infested. Some of the door handles were stiff and I was afraid to turn them. Several rooms I did inspect were unfurnished, and others were littered with theatrical lumber, bought second-hand, I judged, from its appearance. In one room next to his I found a lot of old clothes. I began routing among these, and in my eagerness forgot again the evident sharpness of his ears. I heard a stealthy footstep and, looking up just in time,

saw him peering in at the tumbled heap and holding an old-fashioned revolver in his hand. I stood perfectly still while he stared about open-mouthed and suspicious. 'It must have been her,' he said slowly. 'Damn her!'

"He shut the door quietly, and immediately I heard the key turn in the lock. Then his footsteps retreated. I realised abruptly that I was locked in. For a minute I did not know what to do. I walked from door to window and back, and stood perplexed. A gust of anger came upon me. But I decided to inspect the clothes before I did anything further, and my first attempt brought down a pile from an upper shelf. This brought him back, more sinister than ever. That time he actually touched me, jumped back with amazement and stood astonished in the middle of the room.

"Presently he calmed a little. 'Rats,' he said in an undertone, fingers on lips. He was evidently a little scared. I edged quietly out of the room, but a plank creaked. Then the infernal little brute started going all over the house, revolver in hand and locking door after door and pocketing the keys. When I realised what he was up to I had a fit of rage—I could hardly control myself sufficiently to watch my opportunity. By this time I knew he was alone in the house, and so I made no more ado, but knocked him on the head."

"Knocked him on the head?" exclaimed Kemp.

"Yes—stunned him—as he was going downstairs. Hit him from behind with a stool that stood on the landing. He went downstairs like a bag of old boots."

"But—I say! The common conventions of humanity—"

"Are all very well for common people. But the point was, Kemp, that I had to get out of that house in a disguise without his seeing me. I couldn't think of any other way of doing it. And then I gagged him with a Louis Quatorze vest and tied him up in a sheet."

"Tied him up in a sheet!"

"Made a sort of bag of it. It was rather a good idea to keep

the idiot scared and quiet, and a devilish hard thing to get out of—head away from the string. My dear Kemp, it's no good your sitting glaring as though I was a murderer. It had to be done. He had his revolver. If once he saw me he would be able to describe me—"

"But still," said Kemp, "in England—to-day. And the man was in his own house, and you were—well, robbing."

"Robbing! Confound it! You'll call me a thief next! Surely, Kemp, you're not fool enough to dance on the old strings. Can't you see my position?"

"And his too," said Kemp.

The Invisible Man stood up sharply. "What do you mean to say?"

Kemp's face grew a trifle hard. He was about to speak and checked himself. "I suppose, after all," he said with a sudden change of manner, "the thing had to be done. You were in a fix. But still—"

"Of course I was in a fix—an infernal fix. And he made me wild too—hunting me about the house, fooling about with his revolver, locking and unlocking doors. He was simply exasperating. You don't blame me, do you? You don't blame me?"

"I never blame anyone," said Kemp. "It's quite out of fashion. What did you do next?"

"I was hungry. Downstairs I found a loaf and some rank cheese—more than sufficient to satisfy my hunger. I took some brandy and water, and then went up past my impromptu bag—he was lying quite still—to the room containing the old clothes. This looked out upon the street, two lace curtains brown with dirt guarding the window. I went and peered out through their interstices. Outside the day was bright—by contrast with the brown shadows of the dismal house in which I found myself, dazzlingly bright. A brisk traffic was going by, fruit carts, a hansom, a four-wheeler with a pile of boxes, a fishmonger's cart. I turned with spots of colour swimming before my eyes to the shadowy fixtures behind me. My excitement was giving place to a clear apprehension of my position again. The room was full of a faint scent of benzoline, used, I suppose, in cleaning the garments.

"I began a systematic search of the place. I should judge the hunchback had been alone in the house for some time. He was a curious person. Everything that could possibly be of service to me I collected in the clothes storeroom, and then I made a deliberate selection. I found a handbag I thought a suitable possession, and some powder, rouge, and sticking-plaster.

"I had thought of painting and powdering my face and all that there was to show of me, in order to render myself visible, but the disadvantage of this lay in the fact that I should require turpentine and other appliances and a considerable amount of time before I could vanish again. Finally I chose a mask of the better type, slightly grotesque but not more so than many human beings, dark glasses, greyish whiskers, and a wig. I could find no underclothing, but that I could buy subsequently, and for the time I swathed myself in calico dominoes and some white cashmere scarfs. I could find no socks, but the hunchback's boots were rather a loose fit and sufficed. In a desk in the shop were three sovereigns and about thirty shillings' worth of silver, and in a locked cupboard I burst in the inner room were eight pounds in gold. I could go forth into the world again, equipped.

"Then came a curious hesitation. Was my appearance really credible? I tried myself with a little bedroom looking-glass, inspecting myself from every point of view to discover any forgotten chink, but it all seemed sound. I was grotesque to the theatrical pitch, a stage miser, but I was certainly not a physical impossibility. Gathering confidence, I took my looking-glass down into the shop, pulled down the shop blinds, and surveyed myself from every point of view with the help of the cheval glass in the corner.

"I spent some minutes screwing up my courage and then unlocked the shop door and marched out into the street, leaving

the little man to get out of his sheet again when he liked. In five minutes a dozen turnings intervened between me and the costumier's shop. No one appeared to notice me very pointedly. My last difficulty seemed overcome."

He stopped again.

"And you troubled no more about the hunchback?" said Kemp.

"No," said the Invisible Man. "Nor have I heard what became of him. I suppose he untied himself or kicked himself out. The knots were pretty tight."

He became silent and went to the window and stared out.

"What happened when you went out into the Strand?"

"Oh! Disillusionment again. I thought my troubles were over. Practically I thought I had impunity to do whatever I chose, everything—save to give away my secret. So I thought. Whatever I did, whatever the consequences might be, was nothing to me. I had merely to fling aside my garments and vanish. No person could hold me. I could take my money where I found it. I decided to treat myself to a sumptuous feast, and then put up at a good hotel, and accumulate a new outfit of property. I felt amazingly confident—it's not particularly pleasant recalling that I was an ass. I went into a place and was already ordering lunch, when it occurred to me that I could not eat unless I exposed my invisible face. I finished ordering the lunch, told the man I should be back in ten minutes, and went out exasperated. I don't know if you have ever been disappointed in your appetite."

"Not quite so badly," said Kemp, "but I can imagine it."

"I could have smashed the silly devils. At last, faint with the desire for tasteful food, I went into another place and demanded a private room. 'I am disfigured,' I said. 'Badly.' They looked at me curiously, but of course it was not their affair—and so at last I got my lunch. It was not particularly well served, but it sufficed; and when I had had it, I sat over a cigar, trying to plan my line of action. And outside a snowstorm was beginning.

"The more I thought it over, Kemp, the more I realised

what a helpless absurdity an Invisible Man was—in a cold and dirty climate and a crowded civilised city. Before I made this mad experiment I had dreamt of a thousand advantages. That afternoon it seemed all disappointment. I went over the heads of the things a man reckons desirable. No doubt invisibility made it possible to get them, but it made it impossible to enjoy them when they are got. Ambition—what is the good of pride of place when you cannot appear there? What is the good of the love of woman when her name must needs be Delilah? I have no taste for politics, for the blackguardisms of fame, for philanthropy, for sport. What was I to do? And for this I had become a wrapped-up mystery, a swathed and bandaged caricature of a man!"

He paused, and his attitude suggested a roving glance at the window.

"But how did you get to Iping?" said Kemp, anxious to keep his guest busy talking.

"I went there to work. I had one hope. It was a half idea! I have it still. It is a full-blown idea now. A way of getting back! Of restoring what I have done. When I choose. When I have done all I mean to do invisibly. And that is what I chiefly want to talk to you about now."

"You went straight to Iping?"

"Yes. I had simply to get my three volumes of memoranda and my cheque-book, my luggage and underclothing, order a quantity of chemicals to work out this idea of mine—I will show you the calculations as soon as I get my books—and then I started. Jove! I remember the snowstorm now, and the accursed bother it was to keep the snow from damping my pasteboard nose."

"At the end," said Kemp, "the day before yesterday, when they found you out, you rather—to judge by the papers—"

"I did. Rather. Did I kill that fool of a constable?"

"No," said Kemp. "He's expected to recover."

"That's his luck, then. I clean lost my temper, the fools! Why couldn't they leave me alone? And that grocer lout?"

"There are no deaths expected," said Kemp.

"I don't know about that tramp of mine," said the Invisible Man, with an unpleasant laugh.

"By Heaven, Kemp, you don't know what rage *is*! To have worked for years, to have planned and plotted, and then to get some fumbling purblind idiot messing across your course! Every conceivable sort of silly creature that has ever been created has been sent to cross me.

"If I have much more of it, I shall go wild—I shall start mowing 'em.

"As it is, they've made things a thousand times more difficult."

"No doubt it's exasperating," said Kemp, drily.

Chapter XXIV

THE PLAN THAT FAILED

"But now," said Kemp, with a side glance out of the window, "what are we to do?"

He moved nearer his guest as he spoke in such a manner as to prevent the possibility of a sudden glimpse of the three men who were advancing up the hill road—with an intolerable slowness, as it seemed to Kemp.

"What were you planning to do when you were heading for Port Burdock? *Had* you any plan?"

"I was going to clear out of the country. But I have altered that plan rather since seeing you. I thought it would be wise, now the weather is hot and invisibility possible, to make for the South. Especially as my secret was known, and everyone would be on the lookout for a masked and muffled man. You have a line of steamers from here to France. My idea was to get aboard one and run the risks of the passage. Thence I could go by train into Spain, or else get to Algiers. It would not be difficult. There a man might always be invisible—and yet live. And do things. I was using that tramp as a money box and luggage carrier, until I decided how to get my books and things sent over to meet me."

"That's clear."

"And then the filthy brute must needs try and rob me! He has hidden my books, Kemp. Hidden my books! If I can lay my hands on him!"

"Best plan to get the books out of him first."

"But where is he? Do you know?"

"He's in the town police station, locked up, by his own request, in the strongest cell in the place."

"Cur!" said the Invisible Man.

"But that hangs up your plans a little."

"We must get those books; those books are vital."

"Certainly," said Kemp, a little nervously, wondering if he heard footsteps outside. "Certainly we must get those books. But that won't be difficult, if he doesn't know they're for you."

"No," said the Invisible Man, and thought.

Kemp tried to think of something to keep the talk going, but the Invisible Man resumed of his own accord.

"Blundering into your house, Kemp," he said, "changes all my plans. For you are a man that can understand. In spite of all that has happened, in spite of this publicity, of the loss of my books, of what I have suffered, there still remain great possibilities, huge possibilities—"

"You have told no one I am here?" he asked abruptly.

Kemp hesitated. "That was implied," he said.

"No one?" insisted Griffin.

"Not a soul."

"Ah! Now—" The Invisible Man stood up, and sticking his arms akimbo began to pace the study.

"I made a mistake, Kemp, a huge mistake, in carrying this thing through alone. I have wasted strength, time, opportunities. Alone—it is wonderful how little a man can do alone! To rob a little, to hurt a little, and there is the end.

"What I want, Kemp, is a goal-keeper, a helper, and a hiding-place, an arrangement whereby I can sleep and eat and rest in peace, and unsuspected. I must have a confederate. With a confederate, with food and rest—a thousand things are possible.

"Hitherto I have gone on vague lines. We have to consider all that invisibility means, all that it does not mean. It means little advantage for eavesdropping and so forth—one makes sounds. It's of little help—a little help perhaps—in housebreaking and so forth. Once you've caught me you could easily imprison me. But on the other hand I am hard to catch. This invisibility, in fact, is only good in two cases: It's useful in getting away, it's useful in approaching. It's particularly useful, therefore, in killing. I can walk round a man, whatever weapon he has, choose my point, strike as I like. Dodge as I like. Escape as I like."

Kemp's hand went to his moustache. Was that a movement downstairs?

"And it is killing we must do, Kemp."

"It is killing we must do," repeated Kemp. "I'm listening to your plan, Griffin, but I'm not agreeing, mind. Why killing?"

"Not wanton killing, but a judicious slaying. The point is, they know there is an Invisible Man—as well as we know there is an Invisible Man. And that Invisible Man, Kemp, must now establish a Reign of Terror. Yes; no doubt it's startling. But I mean it. A Reign of Terror. He must take some town like your Burdock and terrify and dominate it. He must issue his orders. He can do that in a thousand ways—scraps of paper thrust under doors would suffice. And all who disobey his orders he must kill, and kill all who would defend the disobedient."

"Humph!" said Kemp, no longer listening to Griffin but to the sound of his front door opening and closing.

"It seems to me, Griffin," he said, to cover his wandering attention, "that your confederate would be in a difficult position."

"No one would know he was a confederate," said the Invisible Man, eagerly. And then suddenly, "*Hush!* What's that downstairs?"

"Nothing," said Kemp, and suddenly began to speak loud and fast. "I don't agree to this, Griffin," he said. "Understand me, I don't agree to this. Why dream of playing a game against the race? How can you hope to gain happiness? Don't be a lone wolf. Publish your results; take the world—take the nation at least—into your confidence. Think what you might do with a million helpers—"

The Invisible Man interrupted Kemp. "There are footsteps coming upstairs," he said in a low voice.

"Nonsense," said Kemp.

"Let me see," said the Invisible Man, and advanced, arm extended, to the door.

Kemp hesitated for a second and then moved to intercept him. The Invisible Man started and stood still. "Traitor!" cried the Voice, and suddenly the dressing-gown opened, and sitting down the Unseen began to disrobe. Kemp made three swift steps to the door, and forthwith the Invisible Man—his legs had vanished—sprang to his feet with a shout. Kemp flung the door open.

As it opened, there came a sound of hurrying feet downstairs and voices.

With a quick movement Kemp thrust the Invisible Man back, sprang aside, and slammed the door. The key was outside and ready. In another moment Griffin would have been alone in the belvedere study, a prisoner. Save for one little thing. The key had been slipped in hastily that morning. As Kemp slammed the door it fell noisily upon the carpet.

Kemp's face became white. He tried to grip the door handle with both hands. For a moment he stood lugging. Then the door gave six inches. But he got it closed again. The second time it was jerked a foot wide, and the dressing-gown came wedging itself into the opening. His throat was gripped by invisible fingers, and he left his hold on the handle to defend himself. He was forced back, tripped and pitched heavily into the corner of the landing. The empty dressing-gown was flung on the top of him.

Halfway up the staircase was Colonel Adye, the recipient of Kemp's letter, the chief of the Burdock police. He was staring aghast at the sudden appearance of Kemp, followed by the extraordinary sight of clothing tossing empty in the air. He saw Kemp felled, and struggling to his feet. He saw him rush forward, and go down again, felled like an ox.

Then suddenly he was struck violently. By nothing! A vast weight, it seemed, leapt upon him, and he was hurled headlong down the staircase, with a grip on his throat and a knee in his groin. An invisible foot trod on his back, a ghostly patter passed downstairs, he heard the two police officers in the hall shout and run, and the front door of the house slammed violently.

He rolled over and sat up staring. He saw, staggering down the staircase, Kemp, dusty and disheveled, one side of his face white from a blow, his lip bleeding, and a pink dressing-gown and some underclothing held in his arms.

"My God!" cried Kemp. "The game's up! He's gone!"

Chapter XXV

THE HUNTING OF THE INVISIBLE MAN

For a space Kemp was too inarticulate to make Adye understand the swift things that had just happened. They stood on the landing, Kemp speaking swiftly, the grotesque swathings of Griffin still on his arm. But presently Adye began to grasp something of the situation.

"He is mad," said Kemp; "inhuman. He is pure selfishness. He thinks of nothing but his own advantage, his own safety. I have listened to such a story this morning of brutal self-seeking! He has wounded men. He will kill them unless we can prevent him. He will create a panic. Nothing can stop him. He is going out now—furious!"

"He must be caught," said Adye. "That is certain."

"But how?" cried Kemp, and suddenly became full of ideas. "You must begin at once. You must set every available man to work; you must prevent his leaving this district. Once he gets away, he may go through the country-side as he wills, killing and maiming. He dreams of a reign of terror! A reign of terror, I tell you. You must set a watch on trains and roads and shipping. The garrison must help. You must wire for help. The only thing that may keep him here is the thought of recovering some books of notes he counts of value. I will tell you of that! There is a man in your police station—Marvel."

"I know," said Adye, "I know. Those books—yes."

"And you must prevent him from eating or sleeping; day and night the country must be astir for him. Food must be locked up and secured, all food, so that he will have to break his way to it. The houses everywhere must be barred against him. Heaven send us cold nights and rain! The whole country-side must begin hunting and keep hunting. I tell you, Adye, he is a danger, a disaster; unless he is pinned and secured, it is frightful to think of the things that may happen."

"What else can we do?" said Adye. "I must go down at once and begin organising. But why not come? Yes—you come too! Come, and we must hold a sort of council of war—get Hopps to help—and the railway managers. By Jove! It's urgent. Come along—tell me as we go. What else is there we can do? Put that stuff down."

In another moment Adye was leading the way downstairs. They found the front door open and the policemen standing outside staring at empty air. "He's got away, sir," said one.

"We must go to the central station at once," said Adye. "One of you go on down and get a cab to come up and meet us—quickly. And now, Kemp, what else?"

"Dogs," said Kemp. "Get dogs. They don't see him, but they wind him. Get dogs."

"Good," said Adye. "It's not generally known, but the prison officials over at Halstead know a man with bloodhounds. Dogs. What else?"

"Bear in mind," said Kemp, "his food shows. After eating, his food shows until it is assimilated. So that he has to hide after eating. You must keep on beating. Every thicket, every quiet corner. And put all weapons—all implements that might be weapons, away. He can't carry such things for long. And what he can snatch up and strike men with must be hidden away."

"Good again," said Adye. "We shall have him yet!"

"And on the roads," said Kemp, and hesitated.

"Yes?" said Adye.

"Powdered glass," said Kemp. "It's cruel, I know. But think of what he may do!"

Adye drew the air in sharply between his teeth. "It's unsportsmanlike. I don't know. But I'll have powdered glass got ready. If he goes too far—"

"The man's become inhuman, I tell you," said Kemp. "I am as sure he will establish a Reign of Terror—so soon as he has

got over the emotions of this escape—as I am sure I am talking to you. Our only chance is to be ahead. He has cut himself off from his kind. His blood be upon his own head."

Chapter XXVI

THE WICKSTEED MURDER

The Invisible Man seems to have rushed out of Kemp's house in a state of blind fury. A little child playing near Kemp's gateway was violently caught up and thrown aside, so that its ankle was broken, and thereafter for some hours the Invisible Man passed out of human perceptions. No one knows where he went nor what he did. But one can imagine him hurrying through the hot June forenoon, up the hill and on to the open downland behind Port Burdock, raging and despairing at his intolerable fate, and sheltering at last, heated and weary, amid the thickets of Hintondean, to piece together again his shattered schemes against his species. That seems the most probable refuge for him, for there it was he re-asserted himself in a grimly tragical manner about two in the afternoon.

One wonders what his state of mind may have been during that time, and what plans he devised. No doubt he was almost ecstatically exasperated by Kemp's treachery, and though we may be able to understand the motives that led to that deceit, we may still imagine and even sympathise a little with the fury the attempted surprise must have occasioned. Perhaps something of the stunned astonishment of his Oxford Street experiences may have returned to him, for he had evidently counted on Kemp's co-operation in his brutal dream of a terrorised world. At any rate he vanished from human ken about midday, and no living witness can tell what he did until about half-past two. It was a fortunate thing, perhaps, for humanity, but for him it was a fatal inaction.

During that time a growing multitude of men scattered over the country-side were busy. In the morning he had still been simply a legend, a terror; in the afternoon, by virtue chiefly of

Kemp's drily worded proclamation, he was presented as a tangible antagonist, to be wounded, captured, or overcome, and the country-side began organising itself with inconceivable rapidity. By two o'clock even he might still have removed himself out of the district by getting aboard a train, but after two that became impossible. Every passenger train along the lines on a great parallelogram between Southampton, Manchester, Brighton and Horsham, travelled with locked doors, and the goods traffic was almost entirely suspended. And in a great circle of twenty miles round Port Burdock, men armed with guns and bludgeons were presently setting out in groups of three and four, with dogs, to beat the roads and fields.

Mounted policemen rode along the country lanes, stopping at every cottage and warning the people to lock up their houses, and keep indoors unless they were armed, and all the elementary schools had broken up by three o'clock, and the children, scared and keeping together in groups, were hurrying home. Kemp's proclamation—signed indeed by Adye—was posted over almost the whole district by four or five o'clock in the afternoon. It gave briefly but clearly all the conditions of the struggle, the necessity of keeping the Invisible Man from food and sleep, the necessity for incessant watchfulness and for a prompt attention to any evidence of his movements. And so swift and decided was the action of the authorities, so prompt and universal was the belief in this strange being, that before nightfall an area of several hundred square miles was in a stringent state of siege. And before nightfall, too, a thrill of horror went through the whole watching nervous country-side. Going from whispering mouth to mouth, swift and certain over the length and breadth of the country, passed the story of the murder of Mr. Wicksteed.

If our supposition that the Invisible Man's refuge was the Hintondean thickets, then we must suppose that in the early afternoon he sallied out again bent upon some project that involved the use of a weapon. We cannot know what the project was, but the evidence that he had the iron rod in hand before he met Wicksteed is to me at least overwhelming.

We can know nothing of the details of that encounter. It occurred on the edge of a gravel pit, not two hundred yards from Lord Burdock's lodge gate. Everything points to a desperate struggle—the trampled ground, the numerous wounds Mr. Wicksteed received, his splintered walking-stick; but why the attack was made—save in a murderous frenzy, it is impossible to imagine. Indeed the theory of madness is almost unavoidable. Mr. Wicksteed was a man of forty-five or forty-six, steward to Lord Burdock, of inoffensive habits and appearance, the very last person in the world to provoke such a terrible antagonist. Against him it would seem the Invisible Man used an iron rod dragged from a broken piece of fence. He stopped this quiet man, going quietly home to his midday meal, attacked him, beat down his feeble defences, broke his arm, felled him, and smashed his head to a jelly.

He must have dragged this rod out of the fencing before he met his victim; he must have been carrying it ready in his hand. Only two details beyond what has already been stated seem to bear on the matter. One is the circumstance that the gravel pit was not in Mr. Wicksteed's direct path home, but nearly a couple of hundred yards out of his way. The other is the assertion of a little girl to the effect that, going to her afternoon school, she saw the murdered man "trotting" in a peculiar manner across a field towards the gravel pit. Her pantomime of his action suggests a man pursuing something on the ground before him and striking at it ever and again with his walking-stick. She was the last person to see him alive. He passed out of her sight to his death, the struggle being hidden from her only by a clump of beech trees and a slight depression in the ground.

Now this, to the present writer's mind at least, lifts the murder out of the realm of the absolutely wanton. We may imagine that Griffin had taken the rod as a weapon indeed, but without any deliberate intention of using it in murder. Wicksteed may

then have come by and noticed this rod inexplicably moving through the air. Without any thought of the Invisible Man—for Port Burdock is ten miles away—he may have pursued it. It is quite conceivable that he may not even have heard of the Invisible Man. One can then imagine the Invisible Man making off—quietly in order to avoid discovering his presence in the neighbourhood, and Wicksteed, excited and curious, pursuing this unaccountably locomotive object—finally striking at it.

No doubt the Invisible Man could easily have distanced his middle-aged pursuer under ordinary circumstances, but the position in which Wicksteed's body was found suggests that he had the ill luck to drive his quarry into a corner between a drift of stinging nettles and the gravel pit. To those who appreciate the extraordinary irascibility of the Invisible Man, the rest of the encounter will be easy to imagine.

But this is pure hypothesis. The only undeniable facts—for stories of children are often unreliable—are the discovery of Wicksteed's body, done to death, and of the bloodstained iron rod flung among the nettles. The abandonment of the rod by Griffin, suggests that in the emotional excitement of the affair, the purpose for which he took it—if he had a purpose—was abandoned. He was certainly an intensely egotistical and unfeeling man, but the sight of his victim, his first victim, bloody and pitiful at his feet, may have released some long pent fountain of remorse which for a time may have flooded whatever scheme of action he had contrived.

After the murder of Mr. Wicksteed, he would seem to have struck across the country towards the downland. There is a story of a voice heard about sunset by a couple of men in a field near Fern Bottom. It was wailing and laughing, sobbing and groaning, and ever and again it shouted. It must have been queer hearing. It drove up across the middle of a clover field and died away towards the hills.

That afternoon the Invisible Man must have learnt something of the rapid use Kemp had made of his confidences. He must

have found houses locked and secured; he may have loitered about railway stations and prowled about inns, and no doubt he read the proclamations and realised something of the nature of the campaign against him. And as the evening advanced, the fields became dotted here and there with groups of three or four men, and noisy with the yelping of dogs. These men-hunters had particular instructions in the case of an encounter as to the way they should support one another. But he avoided them all. We may understand something of his exasperation, and it could have been none the less because he himself had supplied the information that was being used so remorselessly against him. For that day at least he lost heart; for nearly twenty-four hours, save when he turned on Wicksteed, he was a hunted man. In the night, he must have eaten and slept; for in the morning he was himself again, active, powerful, angry, and malignant, prepared for his last great struggle against the world.

Chapter XXVII

THE SIEGE OF KEMP'S HOUSE

Kemp read a strange missive, written in pencil on a greasy sheet of paper.

"You have been amazingly energetic and clever," this letter ran, "though what you stand to gain by it I cannot imagine. You are against me. For a whole day you have chased me; you have tried to rob me of a night's rest. But I have had food in spite of you, I have slept in spite of you, and the game is only beginning. The game is only beginning. There is nothing for it, but to start the Terror. This announces the first day of the Terror. Port Burdock is no longer under the Queen, tell your Colonel of Police, and the rest of them; it is under me—the Terror! This is day one of year one of the new epoch—the Epoch of the Invisible Man. I am Invisible Man the First. To begin with the rule will be easy. The first day there will be one execution for the sake of example—a man named Kemp. Death starts for him to-day. He may lock himself away, hide himself away, get guards about him, put on armour if he likes—Death, the unseen Death, is coming. Let him take precautions; it will impress my people. Death starts from the pillar box by midday. The letter will fall in as the postman comes along, then off! The game begins. Death starts. Help him not, my people, lest Death fall upon you also. Today Kemp is to die."

Kemp read this letter twice, "It's no hoax," he said. "That's his voice! And he means it."

He turned the folded sheet over and saw on the addressed side of it the postmark Hintondean, and the prosaic detail "*2d. to pay.*"

He got up slowly, leaving his lunch unfinished—the letter had come by the one o'clock post—and went into his study. He

rang for his housekeeper, and told her to go round the house at once, examine all the fastenings of the windows, and close all the shutters. He closed the shutters of his study himself. From a locked drawer in his bedroom he took a little revolver, examined it carefully, and put it into the pocket of his lounge jacket. He wrote a number of brief notes, one to Colonel Adye, gave them to his servant to take, with explicit instructions as to her way of leaving the house. "There is no danger," he said, and added a mental reservation, "to you." He remained meditative for a space after doing this, and then returned to his cooling lunch.

He ate with gaps of thought. Finally he struck the table sharply. "We will have him!" he said. "And I am the bait. He will come too far."

He went up to the belvedere, carefully shutting every door after him. "It's a game," he said, "an odd game—but the chances are all for me, Mr. Griffin, in spite of your invisibility. Griffin *contra mundum*—with a vengeance."

He stood at the window staring at the hot hillside. "He must get food every day—and I don't envy him. Did he really sleep last night? Out in the open somewhere—secure from collisions. I wish we could get some good cold wet weather instead of the heat.

"He may be watching me now."

He went close to the window. Something rapped smartly against the brickwork over the frame, and made him start violently.

"I'm getting nervous," said Kemp. But it was five minutes before he went to the window again. "It must have been a sparrow," he said.

Presently he heard the front-door bell ringing, and hurried downstairs. He unbolted and unlocked the door, examined the chain, put it up, and opened cautiously without showing himself. A familiar voice hailed him. It was Adye.

"Your servant's been assaulted, Kemp," he said round the door.

"What!" exclaimed Kemp.

"Had that note of yours taken away from her. He's close about here. Let me in."

Kemp released the chain, and Adye entered through as narrow an opening as possible. He stood in the hall, looking with infinite relief at Kemp refastening the door. "Note was snatched out of her hand. Scared her horribly. She's down at the station. Hysterics. He's close here. What was it about?"

Kemp swore.

"What a fool I was," said Kemp. "I might have known. It's not an hour's walk from Hintondean. Already!"

"What's up?" said Adye.

"Look here!" said Kemp, and led the way into his study. He handed Adye the Invisible Man's letter. Adye read it and whistled softly. "And you—?" said Adye.

"Proposed a trap—like a fool," said Kemp, "and sent my proposal out by a maidservant. To him."

Adye followed Kemp's profanity.

"He'll clear out," said Adye.

"Not he," said Kemp.

A resounding smash of glass came from upstairs. Adye had a silvery glimpse of a little revolver half out of Kemp's pocket. "It's a window, upstairs!" said Kemp, and led the way up. There came a second smash while they were still on the staircase. When they reached the study they found two of the three windows smashed, half the room littered with splintered glass, and one big flint lying on the writing table. The two men stopped in the doorway, contemplating the wreckage. Kemp swore again, and as he did so the third window went with a snap like a pistol, hung starred for a moment, and collapsed in jagged, shivering triangles into the room.

"What's this for?" said Adye.

"It's a beginning," said Kemp.

"There's no way of climbing up here?"

"Not for a cat," said Kemp.

"No shutters?"

"Not here. All the downstairs rooms—hullo!"

Smash, and then whack of boards hit hard came from downstairs. "Confound him!" said Kemp. "That must be—yes—it's one of the bedrooms. He's going to do all the house. But he's a fool. The shutters are up, and the glass will fall outside. He'll cut his feet."

Another window proclaimed its destruction. The two men stood on the landing perplexed. "I have it!" said Adye. "Let me have a stick or something, and I'll go down to the station and get the bloodhounds put on. That ought to settle him! They're hard by—not ten minutes—"

Another window went the way of its fellows.

"You haven't a revolver?" asked Adye.

Kemp's hand went to his pocket. Then he hesitated. "I haven't one—at least to spare."

"I'll bring it back," said Adye, "you'll be safe here."

Kemp, ashamed of his momentary lapse from truthfulness, handed him the weapon.

"Now for the door," said Adye.

As they stood hesitating in the hall, they heard one of the first-floor bedroom windows crack and clash. Kemp went to the door and began to slip the bolts as silently as possible. His face was a little paler than usual. "You must step straight out," said Kemp. In another moment Adye was on the doorstep and the bolts were dropping back into the staples. He hesitated for a moment, feeling more comfortable with his back against the door. Then he marched, upright and square, down the steps. He crossed the lawn and approached the gate. A little breeze seemed to ripple over the grass. Something moved near him. "Stop a bit," said a Voice, and Adye stopped dead and his hand tightened on the revolver.

"Well?" said Adye, white and grim, and every nerve tense.

"Oblige me by going back to the house," said the Voice, as tense and grim as Adye's.

"Sorry," said Adye a little hoarsely, and moistened his lips with his tongue. The Voice was on his left front, he thought. Suppose he were to take his luck with a shot?

"What are you going for?" said the Voice, and there was a quick movement of the two, and a flash of sunlight from the open lip of Adye's pocket.

Adye desisted and thought. "Where I go," he said slowly, "is my own business." The words were still on his lips, when an arm came round his neck, his back felt a knee, and he was sprawling backward. He drew clumsily and fired absurdly, and in another moment he was struck in the mouth and the revolver wrested from his grip. He made a vain clutch at a slippery limb, tried to struggle up and fell back. "Damn!" said Adye. The Voice laughed. "I'd kill you now if it wasn't the waste of a bullet," it said. He saw the revolver in mid-air, six feet off, covering him.

"Well?" said Adye, sitting up.

"Get up," said the Voice.

Adye stood up.

"Attention," said the Voice, and then fiercely, "Don't try any games. Remember I can see your face if you can't see mine. You've got to go back to the house."

"He won't let me in," said Adye.

"That's a pity," said the Invisible Man. "I've got no quarrel with you."

Adye moistened his lips again. He glanced away from the barrel of the revolver and saw the sea far off very blue and dark under the midday sun, the smooth green down, the white cliff of the Head, and the multitudinous town, and suddenly he knew that life was very sweet. His eyes came back to this little metal thing hanging between heaven and earth, six yards away. "What am I to do?" he said sullenly.

"What am *I* to do?" asked the Invisible Man. "You will get help. The only thing is for you to go back."

"I will try. If he lets me in will you promise not to rush the door?"

"I've got no quarrel with you," said the Voice.

Kemp had hurried upstairs after letting Adye out, and now crouching among the broken glass and peering cautiously over the edge of the study window sill, he saw Adye stand parleying with the Unseen. "Why doesn't he fire?" whispered Kemp to himself. Then the revolver moved a little and the glint of the sunlight flashed in Kemp's eyes. He shaded his eyes and tried to see the source of the blinding beam.

"Surely!" he said, "Adye has given up the revolver."

"Promise not to rush the door," Adye was saying. "Don't push a winning game too far. Give a man a chance."

"You go back to the house. I tell you flatly I will not promise anything."

Adye's decision seemed suddenly made. He turned towards the house, walking slowly with his hands behind him. Kemp watched him—puzzled. The revolver vanished, flashed again into sight, vanished again, and became evident on a closer scrutiny as a little dark object following Adye. Then things happened very quickly. Adye leapt backwards, swung around, clutched at this little object, missed it, threw up his hands and fell forward on his face, leaving a little puff of blue in the air. Kemp did not hear the sound of the shot. Adye writhed, raised himself on one arm, fell forward, and lay still.

For a space Kemp remained staring at the quiet carelessness of Adye's attitude. The afternoon was very hot and still, nothing seemed stirring in all the world save a couple of yellow butterflies chasing each other through the shrubbery between the house and the road gate. Adye lay on the lawn near the gate. The blinds of all the villas down the hill-road were drawn, but in one little green summer-house was a white figure, apparently an old man asleep. Kemp scrutinised the surroundings of the house for a glimpse of the revolver, but it had vanished. His eyes came back to Adye. The game was opening well.

Then came a ringing and knocking at the front door, that grew at last tumultuous, but pursuant to Kemp's instructions

the servants had locked themselves into their rooms. This was followed by a silence. Kemp sat listening and then began peering cautiously out of the three windows, one after another. He went to the staircase head and stood listening uneasily. He armed himself with his bedroom poker, and went to examine the interior fastenings of the ground-floor windows again. Everything was safe and quiet. He returned to the belvedere. Adye lay motionless over the edge of the gravel just as he had fallen. Coming along the road by the villas were the housemaid and two policemen.

Everything was deadly still. The three people seemed very slow in approaching. He wondered what his antagonist was doing.

He started. There was a smash from below. He hesitated and went downstairs again. Suddenly the house resounded with heavy blows and the splintering of wood. He heard a smash and the destructive clang of the iron fastenings of the shutters. He turned the key and opened the kitchen door. As he did so, the shutters, split and splintering, came flying inward. He stood aghast. The window frame, save for one crossbar, was still intact, but only little teeth of glass remained in the frame. The shutters had been driven in with an axe, and now the axe was descending in sweeping blows upon the window frame and the iron bars defending it. Then suddenly it leapt aside and vanished. He saw the revolver lying on the path outside, and then the little weapon sprang into the air. He dodged back. The revolver cracked just too late, and a splinter from the edge of the closing door flashed over his head. He slammed and locked the door, and as he stood outside he heard Griffin shouting and laughing. Then the blows of the axe, with its splitting and smashing consequences, were resumed.

Kemp stood in the passage trying to think. In a moment the Invisible Man would be in the kitchen. This door would not keep him a moment, and then—

A ringing came at the front door again. It would be the

policemen. He ran into the hall, put up the chain, and drew the bolts. He made the girl speak before he dropped the chain, and the three people blundered into the house in a heap, and Kemp slammed the door again.

"The Invisible Man!" said Kemp. "He has a revolver, with two shots—left. He's killed Adye. Shot him anyhow. Didn't you see him on the lawn? He's lying there."

"Who?" said one of the policemen.

"Adye," said Kemp.

"We came in the back way," said the girl.

"What's that smashing?" asked one of the policemen.

"He's in the kitchen—or will be. He has found an axe—"

Suddenly the house was full of the Invisible Man's resounding blows on the kitchen door. The girl stared towards the kitchen, shuddered, and retreated into the dining-room. Kemp tried to explain in broken sentences. They heard the kitchen door give.

"This way," said Kemp, starting into activity, and bundled the policemen into the dining-room doorway.

"Poker," said Kemp, and rushed to the fender. He handed the poker he had carried to the policeman and the dining-room one to the other. He suddenly flung himself backward.

"Whup!" said one policeman, ducked, and caught the axe on his poker. The pistol snapped its penultimate shot and ripped a valuable Sidney Cooper. The second policeman brought his poker down on the little weapon, as one might knock down a wasp, and sent it rattling to the floor.

At the first clash the girl screamed, stood screaming for a moment by the fireplace, and then ran to open the shutters—possibly with an idea of escaping by the shattered window.

The axe receded into the passage, and fell to a position about two feet from the ground. They could hear the Invisible Man breathing. "Stand away, you two," he said. "I want that man Kemp."

"We want you," said the first policeman, making a quick step forward and wiping with his poker at the Voice. The Invisible

Man must have started back, and he blundered into the umbrella stand. Then, as the policeman staggered with the swing of the blow he had aimed, the Invisible Man countered with the axe, the helmet crumpled like paper, and the blow sent the man spinning to the floor at the head of the kitchen stairs. But the second policeman, aiming behind the axe with his poker, hit something soft that snapped. There was a sharp exclamation of pain and then the axe fell to the ground. The policeman wiped again at vacancy and hit nothing; he put his foot on the axe, and struck again. Then he stood, poker clubbed, listening intent for the slightest movement.

He heard the dining-room window open, and a quick rush of feet within. His companion rolled over and sat up, with the blood running down between his eye and ear. "Where is he?" asked the man on the floor.

"Don't know. I've hit him. He's standing somewhere in the hall. Unless he's slipped past you. Doctor Kemp—sir."

Pause.

"Doctor Kemp," cried the policeman again.

The second policeman began struggling to his feet. He stood up. Suddenly the faint pad of bare feet on the kitchen stairs could be heard. "Yap!" cried the first policeman, and incontinently flung his poker. It smashed a little gas bracket.

He made as if he would pursue the Invisible Man downstairs. Then he thought better of it and stepped into the dining-room.

"Doctor Kemp—" he began, and stopped short—

"Doctor Kemp's in here," he said, as his companion looked over his shoulder.

The dining-room window was wide open, and neither housemaid nor Kemp was to be seen.

The second policeman's opinion of Kemp was terse and vivid.

Chapter XXVIII

THE HUNTER HUNTED

Mr. Heelas, Mr. Kemp's nearest neighbour among the villa holders, was asleep in his summer house when the siege of Kemp's house began. Mr. Heelas was one of the sturdy minority who refused to believe "in all this nonsense" about an Invisible Man. His wife, however, as he was subsequently to be reminded, did. He insisted upon walking about his garden just as if nothing was the matter, and he went to sleep in the afternoon in accordance with the custom of years. He slept through the smashing of the windows, and then woke up suddenly with a curious persuasion of something wrong. He looked across at Kemp's house, rubbed his eyes and looked again. Then he put his feet to the ground, and sat listening. He said he was damned, but still the strange thing was visible. The house looked as though it had been deserted for weeks—after a violent riot. Every window was broken, and every window, save those of the belvedere study, was blinded by the internal shutters.

"I could have sworn it was all right"—he looked at his watch—"twenty minutes ago."

He became aware of a measured concussion and the clash of glass, far away in the distance. And then, as he sat open-mouthed, came a still more wonderful thing. The shutters of the drawing-room window were flung open violently, and the housemaid in her outdoor hat and garments, appeared struggling in a frantic manner to throw up the sash. Suddenly a man appeared beside her, helping her—Doctor Kemp! In another moment the window was open, and the housemaid was struggling out; she pitched forward and vanished among the shrubs. Mr. Heelas stood up, exclaiming vaguely and vehemently at all these wonderful things. He saw Kemp stand on the sill,

spring from the window, and reappear almost instantaneously running along a path in the shrubbery and stooping as he ran, like a man who evades observation. He vanished behind a laburnum, and appeared again clambering over a fence that abutted on the open down. In a second he had tumbled over and was running at a tremendous pace down the slope towards Mr. Heelas.

"Lord!" cried Mr. Heelas, struck with an idea; "it's that Invisible Man brute! It's right, after all!"

With Mr. Heelas to think things like that was to act, and his cook watching him from the top window was amazed to see him come pelting towards the house at a good nine miles an hour. There was a slamming of doors, a ringing of bells, and the voice of Mr. Heelas bellowing like a bull. "Shut the doors, shut the windows, shut everything! The Invisible Man is coming!" Instantly the house was full of screams and directions, and scurrying feet. He ran himself to shut the French windows that opened on the veranda; as he did so Kemp's head and shoulders and knee appeared over the edge of the garden fence. In another moment Kemp had ploughed through the asparagus, and was running across the tennis lawn to the house.

"You can't come in," said Mr. Heelas, shutting the bolts. "I'm very sorry if he's after you, but you can't come in!"

Kemp appeared with a face of terror close to the glass, rapping and then shaking frantically at the French window. Then, seeing his efforts were useless, he ran along the veranda, vaulted the end, and went to hammer at the side door. Then he ran round by the side gate to the front of the house, and so into the hill-road. And Mr. Heelas staring from his window—a face of horror—had scarcely witnessed Kemp vanish, ere the asparagus was being trampled this way and that by feet unseen. At that Mr. Heelas fled precipitately upstairs, and the rest of the chase is beyond his purview. But as he passed the staircase window, he heard the side gate slam.

Emerging into the hill-road, Kemp naturally took the

downward direction, and so it was he came to run in his own person the very race he had watched with such a critical eye from the belvedere study only four days ago. He ran it well, for a man out of training, and though his face was white and wet, his wits were cool to the last. He ran with wide strides, and wherever a patch of rough ground intervened, wherever there came a patch of raw flints, or a bit of broken glass shone dazzling, he crossed it and left the bare invisible feet that followed to take what line they would.

For the first time in his life Kemp discovered that the hill-road was indescribably vast and desolate, and that the beginnings of the town far below at the hill foot were strangely remote. Never had there been a slower or more painful method of progression than running. All the gaunt villas, sleeping in the afternoon sun, looked locked and barred; no doubt they were locked and barred—by his own orders. But at any rate they might have kept a lookout for an eventuality like this! The town was rising up now, the sea had dropped out of sight behind it, and people down below were stirring. A tram was just arriving at the hill foot. Beyond that was the police station. Was that footsteps he heard behind him? Spurt.

The people below were staring at him, one or two were running, and his breath was beginning to saw in his throat. The tram was quite near now, and the Jolly Cricketers was noisily barring its doors. Beyond the tram were posts and heaps of gravel—the drainage works. He had a transitory idea of jumping into the tram and slamming the doors, and then he resolved to go for the police station. In another moment he had passed the door of the Jolly Cricketers, and was in the blistering fag end of the street, with human beings about him. The tram driver and his helper—arrested by the sight of his furious haste—stood staring with the tram horses unhitched. Further on the astonished features of navvies appeared above the mounds of gravel.

His pace broke a little, and then he heard the swift pad of

his pursuer, and leapt forward again. "The Invisible Man!" he cried to the navvies, with a vague indicative gesture, and by an inspiration leapt the excavation and placed a burly group between him and the chase. Then abandoning the idea of the police station he turned into a little side street, rushed by a greengrocer's cart, hesitated for the tenth of a second at the door of a sweetstuff shop, and then made for the mouth of an alley that ran back into the main Hill Street again. Two or three little children were playing here, and shrieked and scattered at his apparition, and forthwith doors and windows opened and excited mothers revealed their hearts. Out he shot into Hill Street again, three hundred yards from the tram-line end, and immediately he became aware of a tumultuous vociferation and running people.

He glanced up the street towards the hill. Hardly a dozen yards off ran a huge navvy, cursing in fragments and slashing viciously with a spade, and hard behind him came the tram conductor with his fists clenched. Up the street others followed these two, striking and shouting. Down towards the town, men and women were running, and he noticed clearly one man coming out of a shop-door with a stick in his hand. "Spread out! Spread out!" cried someone. Kemp suddenly grasped the altered condition of the chase. He stopped, and looked round, panting. "He's close here!" he cried. "Form a line across—"

He was hit hard under the ear, and went reeling, trying to face round towards his unseen antagonist. He just managed to keep his feet, and he struck a vain counter in the air. Then he was hit again under the jaw, and sprawled headlong on the ground. In another moment a knee compressed his diaphragm, and a couple of eager hands gripped his throat, but the grip of one was weaker than the other; he grasped the wrists, heard a cry of pain from his assailant, and then the spade of the navvy came whirling through the air above him, and struck something with a dull thud. He felt a drop of moisture on his face. The grip at his throat suddenly relaxed, and with a convulsive effort, Kemp loosed himself, grasped a limp shoulder, and rolled uppermost. He gripped the unseen elbows near the ground. "I've got him!" screamed Kemp. "Help! Help! Hold! He's down! Hold his feet!"

In another second there was a simultaneous rush upon the struggle, and a stranger coming into the road suddenly might have thought an exceptionally savage game of Rugby football was in progress. And there was no shouting after Kemp's cry—only a sound of blows and feet and heavy breathing.

Then came a mighty effort, and the Invisible Man threw off a couple of his antagonists and rose to his knees. Kemp clung to him in front like a hound to a stag, and a dozen hands gripped, clutched, and tore at the Unseen. The tram conductor suddenly got the neck and shoulders and lugged him back.

Down went the heap of struggling men again and rolled over. There was, I am afraid, some savage kicking. Then suddenly a wild scream of "Mercy! Mercy!" that died down swiftly to a sound like choking.

"Get back, you fools!" cried the muffled voice of Kemp, and there was a vigorous shoving back of stalwart forms. "He's hurt, I tell you. Stand back!"

There was a brief struggle to clear a space, and then the circle of eager faces saw the doctor kneeling, as it seemed, fifteen inches in the air, and holding invisible arms to the ground. Behind him a constable gripped invisible ankles.

"Don't you leave go of en," cried the big navvy, holding a bloodstained spade; "he's shamming."

"He's not shamming," said the doctor, cautiously raising his knee; "and I'll hold him." His face was bruised and already going red; he spoke thickly because of a bleeding lip. He released one hand and seemed to be feeling at the face. "The mouth's all wet," he said. And then, "Good God!"

He stood up abruptly and then knelt down on the ground by the side of the thing unseen. There was a pushing and shuffling, a sound of heavy feet as fresh people turned up to increase the pressure of the crowd. People now were coming out of the

houses. The doors of the Jolly Cricketers stood suddenly wide open. Very little was said.

Kemp felt about, his hand seeming to pass through empty air. "He's not breathing," he said, and then, "I can't feel his heart. His side—ugh!"

Suddenly an old woman, peering under the arm of the big navvy, screamed sharply. "Looky there!" she said, and thrust out a wrinkled finger.

And looking where she pointed, everyone saw, faint and transparent as though it was made of glass, so that veins and arteries and bones and nerves could be distinguished, the outline of a hand, a hand limp and prone. It grew clouded and opaque even as they stared.

"Hullo!" cried the constable. "Here's his feet a-showing!"

And so, slowly, beginning at his hands and feet and creeping along his limbs to the vital centres of his body, that strange change continued. It was like the slow spreading of a poison. First came the little white nerves, a hazy grey sketch of a limb, then the glassy bones and intricate arteries, then the flesh and skin, first a faint fogginess, and then growing rapidly dense and opaque. Presently they could see his crushed chest and his shoulders, and the dim outline of his drawn and battered features.

When at last the crowd made way for Kemp to stand erect, there lay, naked and pitiful on the ground, the bruised and broken body of a young man about thirty. His hair and brow were white—not grey with age, but white with the whiteness of albinism—and his eyes were like garnets. His hands were clenched, his eyes wide open, and his expression was one of anger and dismay.

"Cover his face!" said a man. "For Gawd's sake, cover that face!" and three little children, pushing forward through the crowd, were suddenly twisted round and sent packing off again.

Someone brought a sheet from the Jolly Cricketers, and having covered him, they carried him into that house.

The Epilogue

So ends the story of the strange and evil experiments of the Invisible Man. And if you would learn more of him you must go to a little inn near Port Stowe and talk to the landlord. The sign of the inn is an empty board save for a hat and boots, and the name is the title of this story. The landlord is a short and corpulent little man with a nose of cylindrical proportions, wiry hair, and a sporadic rosiness of visage. Drink generously, and he will tell you generously of all the things that happened to him after that time, and of how the lawyers tried to do him out of the treasure found upon him.

"When they found they couldn't prove who's money was which, I'm blessed," he says, "if they didn't try to make me out a blooming treasure trove! Do I *look* like a Treasure Trove? And then a gentleman gave me a guinea a night to tell the story at the Empire Music 'all—just to tell 'em in my own words—barring one."

And if you want to cut off the flow of his reminiscences abruptly, you can always do so by asking if there weren't three manuscript books in the story. He admits there were and proceeds to explain, with asseverations that everybody thinks *he* has 'em! But bless you! He hasn't. "The Invisible Man it was took 'em off to hide 'em when I cut and ran for Port Stowe. It's that Mr. Kemp put people on with the idea of *my* having 'em."

And then he subsides into a pensive state, watches you furtively, bustles nervously with glasses, and presently leaves the bar.

He is a bachelor man—his tastes were ever bachelor, and there are no women folk in the house. Outwardly he buttons—it is expected of him—but in his more vital privacies, in the matter of braces for example, he still turns to string. He conducts his house without enterprise, but with eminent decorum. His

movements are slow, and he is a great thinker. But he has a reputation for wisdom and for a respectable parsimony in the village, and his knowledge of the roads of the South of England would beat Cobbett.

And on Sunday mornings, every Sunday morning, all the year round, while he is closed to the outer world, and every night after ten, he goes into his bar parlour, bearing a glass of gin faintly tinged with water, and having placed this down, he locks the door and examines the blinds, and even looks under the table. And then, being satisfied of his solitude, he unlocks the cupboard and a box in the cupboard and a drawer in that box, and produces three volumes bound in brown leather, and places them solemnly in the middle of the table. The covers are weather-worn and tinged with an algal green—for once they sojourned in a ditch and some of the pages have been washed blank by dirty water. The landlord sits down in an armchair, fills a long clay pipe slowly—gloating over the books the while. Then he pulls one towards him and opens it, and begins to study it—turning over the leaves backwards and forwards.

His brows are knit and his lips move painfully. "Hex, little two up in the air, cross and a fiddle-de-dee. Lord! What a one he was for intellect!"

Presently he relaxes and leans back, and blinks through his smoke across the room at things invisible to other eyes. "Full of secrets," he says. "Wonderful secrets!

"Once I get the haul of them—*Lord!*

"I wouldn't do what *he* did; I'd just—well!" He pulls at his pipe.

So he lapses into a dream, the undying wonderful dream of his life. And though Kemp has fished unceasingly, no human being save the landlord knows those books are there, with the subtle secret of invisibility and a dozen other strange secrets written therein. And none other will know of them until he dies.

The War in the Air

Preface to Reprint Edition (1917)

The reader should grasp clearly the date at which this book was written. It was done in 1907: it appeared in various magazines as a serial in 1908 and it was published in the Fall of that year. At that time the aeroplane was, for most people, merely a rumour and the "Sausage" held the air. The contemporary reader has all the advantage of ten years' experience since this story was imagined. He can correct his author at a dozen points and estimate the value of these warnings by the standard of a decade of realities. The book is weak on anti-aircraft guns, for example, and still more negligent of submarines. Much, no doubt, will strike the reader as quaint and limited but upon much the writer may not unreasonably plume himself. The interpretation of the German spirit must have read as a caricature in 1908. Was it a caricature? Prince Karl seemed a fantasy then. Reality has since copied Prince Karl with an astonishing faithfulness. Is it too much to hope that some democratic "Bert" may not ultimately get even with his Highness? Our author tells us in this book, as he has told us in others, more especially in *The World Set Free*, and as he has been telling us this year in his *War and the Future*, that if mankind goes on with war, the smash-up of civilization is inevitable. It is chaos or the United States of the World for mankind. There is no other choice. Ten years have but added an enormous conviction to the message of this book. It remains essentially right, a pamphlet story—in support of the League to Enforce Peace.

K.

Preface to the 1921 Reprint Edition

A short preface to *The War in the Air* has become necessary if the reader is to do justice to that book. It is one of a series of stories I have written at different times; *The World Set Free* is another, and *When the Sleeper Wakes* a third; which are usually spoken of as "scientific romances" or "futurist romances," but which it would be far better to call "fantasias of possibility." They take some developing possibility in human affairs and work it out so as to develop the broad consequences of that possibility. This *War in the Air* was written, the reader should note, in 1907, and it began to appear as a serial story in the *Pall Mall Magazine* in January, 1908. This was before the days of the flying machine; Bleriot did not cross the Channel until July, 1909; and the Zeppelin airship was still in its infancy. The reader will find it amusing now to compare the guesses and notions of the author with the achieved realities of to-day.

But the book, I venture to think, has not been altogether superseded. The main idea is not that men will fly, or to show how they will fly; the main idea is a thesis that the experiences of the intervening years strengthen rather than supersede. The thesis is this; that with the flying machine war alters in its character; it ceases to be an affair of "fronts" and becomes an affair of "areas"; neither side, victor or loser, remains immune from the gravest injuries, and while there is a vast increase in the destructiveness of war, there is also an increased indecisive- ness. Consequently "War in the Air" means social destruction instead of victory as the end of war. It not only alters the methods of war but the consequences of war. After all that has happened since this fantasia of possibility was written, I do not think that there is much wrong with that thesis. And after a recent journey to Russia, of which I have given an account in *Russia in the Shadows*, I am inclined to think very well of myself as I re-read

the entirely imaginary account of the collapse of civilisation under the strain of modern war which forms the Epilogue of this story. In 1907 this chapter was read with hearty laughter as the production of an "imaginative novelist's" distempered brain. Is it quite so wildly funny to-day?

And I ask the reader to remember that date of 1907 also when he reads of Prince Karl Albert and the Graf von Winterfeld. Seven years before the Great War, its shadow stood out upon our sunny world as plainly as all that, for the "imaginative novelist"—or any one else with ordinary common sense—to see. The great catastrophe marched upon us in the daylight. But everybody thought that somebody else would stop it before it really arrived. Behind that great catastrophe march others to-day. The steady deterioration of currency, the shrinkage of production, the ebb of educational energy in Europe, work out to consequences that are obvious to every clear-headed man. National and imperialist rivalries march whole nations at the quickstep towards social collapse. The process goes on as plainly as the militarist process was going on in the years when *The War in the Air* was written.

Do we still trust to somebody else?

H. G. Wells.
Easton Glebe, 1921.

Chapter I

OF PROGRESS AND THE SMALLWAYS FAMILY

§1

"This here Progress," said Mr. Tom Smallways, "it keeps on."

"You'd hardly think it *could* keep on," said Mr. Tom Smallways.

It was long before the War in the Air began that Mr. Smallways made this remark. He was sitting on the fence at the end of his garden and surveying the great Bun Hill gas-works with an eye that neither praised nor blamed. Above the clustering gasometers three unfamiliar shapes appeared, thin, wallowing bladders that flapped and rolled about, and grew bigger and bigger and rounder and rounder—balloons in course of inflation for the South of England Aero Club's Saturday-afternoon ascent.

"They goes up every Saturday," said his neighbour, Mr. Stringer, the milkman. "It's only yestiday, so to speak, when all London turned out to see a balloon go over, and now every little place in the country has its weekly outings—uppings, rather. It's been the salvation of them gas companies."

"Larst Satiday I got three barrer-loads of gravel off my petaters," said Mr. Tom Smallways. "Three barrer-loads! What they dropped as ballase. Some of the plants was broke, and some was buried."

"Ladies, they say, goes up!"

"I suppose we got to call 'em ladies," said Mr. Tom Smallways. "Still, it ain't hardly my idea of a lady—flying about in the air, and throwing gravel at people. It ain't what I been accustomed to consider ladylike, whether or no."

Mr. Stringer nodded his head approvingly, and for a time they continued to regard the swelling bulks with expressions that had changed from indifference to disapproval.

Mr. Tom Smallways was a greengrocer by trade and a gardener by disposition; his little wife Jessica saw to the shop, and Heaven had planned him for a peaceful world. Unfortunately Heaven had not planned a peaceful world for him. He lived in a world of obstinate and incessant change, and in parts where its operations were unsparingly conspicuous. Vicissitude was in the very soil he tilled; even his garden was upon a yearly tenancy, and overshadowed by a huge board that proclaimed it not so much a garden as an eligible building-site. He was horticulture under notice to quit, the last patch of country in a district flooded by new and urban things. He did his best to console himself, to imagine matters near the turn of the tide.

"You'd hardly think it could keep on," he said.

Mr. Smallways' aged father could remember Bun Hill as an idyllic Kentish village. He had driven Sir Peter Bone until he was fifty and then he took to drink a little, and driving the station bus, which lasted him until he was seventy-eight. Then he retired. He sat by the fireside, a shrivelled, very, very old coachman, full charged with reminiscences, and ready for any careless stranger. He could tell you of the vanished estate of Sir Peter Bone, long since cut up for building, and how that magnate ruled the country-side when it was country-side, of shooting and hunting, and of caches along the high road, of how "where the gas-works is" was a cricket-field, and of the coming of the Crystal Palace. The Crystal Palace was six miles away from Bun Hill, a great façade that glittered in the morning, and was a clear blue outline against the sky in the afternoon, and at night a source of gratuitous fireworks for all the population of Bun Hill. And then had come the railway, and then villas and villas, and then the gas-works and the water-works, and a great ugly sea of workmen's houses, and then drainage, and the water vanished out of the Otterbourne and left it a dreadful ditch, and

then a second railway station, Bun Hill South, and more houses and more, more shops, more competition, plate-glass shops, a board-school, rates, omnibuses, tramcars—going right away into London itself—bicycles, motor-cars and then more motor-cars, a Carnegie library.

"You'd hardly think it could keep on," said Mr. Tom Smallways, growing up among these marvels.

But it kept on. Even from the first the greengrocer's shop which he had set up in one of the smallest of the old surviving village houses in the tail of the High Street had a submerged air, an air of hiding from something that was looking for it. When they had made up the pavement of the High Street, they levelled that up so that one had to go down three steps into the shop. Tom did his best to sell only his own excellent but limited range of produce; but Progress came shoving things into his window, French artichokes and aubergines, foreign apples—apples from the State of New York, apples from California, apples from Canada, apples from New Zealand, "pretty lookin' fruit, but not what I should call English apples," said Tom—bananas, unfamiliar nuts, grape fruits, mangoes.

The motor-cars that went by northward and southward grew more and more powerful and efficient, whizzed faster and smelt worse; there appeared great clangorous petrol trolleys delivering coal and parcels in the place of vanishing horse-vans; motor-omnibuses ousted the horse-omnibuses, even the Kentish strawberries going Londonward in the night took to machinery and clattered instead of creaking, and became affected in flavour by progress and petrol.

And then young Bert Smallways got a motor bicycle. . . .

§2

Bert, it is necessary to explain, was a progressive Smallways.

Nothing speaks more eloquently of the pitiless insistence of progress and expansion in our time than that it should get into the Smallways blood. But there was something advanced

and enterprising about young Smallways before he was out of short frocks. He was lost for a whole day before he was five, and nearly drowned in the reservoir of the new water-works before he was seven. He had a real pistol taken away from him by a real policeman when he was ten. And he learnt to smoke, not with pipes and brown paper and cane as Tom had done, but with a penny packet of Boys of England American cigarettes. His language shocked his father before he was twelve, and by that age, what with touting for parcels at the station and selling the Bun Hill *Weekly Express*, he was making three shillings a week, or more, and spending it on *Chips, Comic Cuts, Ally Sloper's Half-holiday*, cigarettes, and all the concomitants of a life of pleasure and enlightenment. All of this without hindrance to his literary studies, which carried him up to the seventh standard at an exceptionally early age. I mention these things so that you may have no doubt at all concerning the sort of stuff Bert had in him.

He was six years younger than Tom, and for a time there was an attempt to utilise him in the greengrocer's shop when Tom at twenty-one married Jessica—who was thirty, and had saved a little money in service. But it was not Bert's *forte* to be utilised. He hated digging, and when he was given a basket of stuff to deliver, a nomadic instinct arose irresistibly, it became his pack and he did not seem to care how heavy it was nor where he took it, so long as he did not take it to its destination. Glamour filled the world, and he strayed after it, basket and all. So Tom took his goods out himself, and sought employers for Bert who did not know of this strain of poetry in his nature. And Bert touched the fringe of a number of trades in succession—draper's porter, chemist's boy, doctor's page, junior assistant gas-fitter, envelope addresser, milk-cart assistant, golf caddie, and at last helper in a bicycle shop. Here, apparently, he found the progressive quality his nature had craved. His employer was a pirate-souled young man named Grubb, with a black-smeared face by day, and a music-hall side in the evening, who dreamt of a patent

lever chain; and it seemed to Bert that he was the perfect model of a gentleman of spirit. He hired out quite the dirtiest and unsafest bicycles in the whole south of England, and conducted the subsequent discussions with astonishing verve. Bert and he settled down very well together. Bert lived in, became almost a trick rider—he could ride bicycles for miles that would have come to pieces instantly under you or me—took to washing his face after business, and spent his surplus money upon remarkable ties and collars, cigarettes, and shorthand classes at the Bun Hill Institute.

He would go round to Tom at times, and look and talk so brilliantly that Tom and Jessie, who both had a natural tendency to be respectful to anybody or anything, looked up to him immensely.

"He's a go-ahead chap, is Bert," said Tom. "He knows a thing or two."

"Let's hope he don't know too much," said Jessica, who had a fine sense of limitations.

"It's go-ahead Times," said Tom. "Noo petaters, and English at that; we'll be having 'em in March if things go on as they do go. I never see such Times. See his tie last night?"

"It wasn't suited to him, Tom. It was a gentleman's tie. He wasn't up to it—not the rest of him, It wasn't becoming". . .

Then presently Bert got a cyclist's suit, cap, badge, and all; and to see him and Grubb going down to Brighton (and back)—heads down, handle-bars down, backbones curved—was a revelation in the possibilities of the Smallways blood.

Go-ahead Times!

Old Smallways would sit over the fire mumbling of the greatness of other days, of old Sir Peter, who drove his coach to Brighton and back in eight-and-twenty hours, of old Sir Peter's white top-hats, of Lady Bone, who never set foot to ground except to walk in the garden, of the great prize-fights at Crawley. He talked of pink and pig-skin breeches, of foxes at Ring's Bottom, where now the County Council pauper lunatics were enclosed, of Lady Bone's chintzes and crinolines. Nobody heeded him. The world had thrown up a new type of gentleman altogether—a gentleman of most ungentlemanly energy, a gentleman in dusty oilskins and motor goggles and a wonderful cap, a stink-making gentleman, a swift, high-class badger, who fled perpetually along high roads from the dust and stink he perpetually made. And his lady, as they were able to see her at Bun Hill, was a weather-bitten goddess, as free from refinement as a gipsy—not so much dressed as packed for transit at a high velocity.

So Bert grew up, filled with ideals of speed and enterprise, and became, so far as he became anything, a kind of bicycle engineer of the let's-'ave-a-look-at-it and enamel chipping variety. Even a road-racer, geared to a hundred and twenty, failed to satisfy him, and for a time he pined in vain at twenty miles an hour along roads that were continually more dusty and more crowded with mechanical traffic. But at last his savings accumulated, and his chance came. The hire-purchase system bridged a financial gap, and one bright and memorable Sunday morning he wheeled his new possession through the shop into the road, got on to it with the advice and assistance of Grubb, and teuf-teuffed off into the haze of the traffic-tortured high road, to add himself as one more voluntary public danger to the amenities of the south of England.

"Orf to Brighton!" said old Smallways, regarding his youngest son from the sitting-room window over the greengrocer's shop with something between pride and reprobation. "When I was 'is age, I'd never been to London, never bin south of Crawley—never bin anywhere on my own where I couldn't walk. And nobody didn't go. Not unless they was gentry. Now everybody's orf everywhere; the whole dratted country sims flying to pieces. Wonder they all get back. Orf to Brighton indeed! Anybody want to buy 'orses?"

"You can't say *I* bin to Brighton, father," said Tom.

"Nor don't want to go," said Jessica sharply; " 'creering about and spendin' your money."

§3

For a time the possibilities of the motor-bicycle so occupied Bert's mind that he remained regardless of the new direction in which the striving soul of man was finding exercise and refreshment. He failed to observe that the type of motor-car, like the type of bicycle, was settling-down and losing its adventurous quality. Indeed, it is as true as it is remarkable that Tom was the first to observe the new development. But his gardening made him attentive to the heavens, and the proximity of the Bun Hill gas-works and the Crystal Palace, from which ascents were continually being made, and presently the descent of ballast upon his potatoes, conspired to bear in upon his unwilling mind the fact that the Goddess of Change was turning her disturbing attention to the sky. The first great boom in aeronautics was beginning.

Grubb and Bert heard of it in a music-hall, then it was driven home to their minds by the cinematograph, then Bert's imagination was stimulated by a sixpenny edition of that aeronautic classic, Mr. George Griffith's "Clipper of the Clouds," and so the thing really got hold of them.

At first the most obvious aspect was the multiplication of balloons. The sky of Bun Hill began to be infested by balloons. On Wednesday and Saturday afternoons particularly you could scarcely look skyward for a quarter of an hour without discovering a balloon somewhere. And then one bright day Bert, motoring toward Croydon, was arrested by the insurgence of a huge, bolster-shaped monster from the Crystal Palace grounds, and obliged to dismount and watch it. It was like a bolster with a broken nose, and below it, and comparatively small, was a stiff framework bearing a man and an engine with a screw that whizzed round in front and a sort of canvas rudder behind. The framework had an air of dragging the reluctant gas-cylinder after it like a brisk little terrier towing a shy, gas-distended elephant into society. The combined monster certainly travelled and steered. It went overhead perhaps a thousand feet up (Bert

heard the engine), sailed away southward, vanished over the hills, reappeared a little blue outline far off in the east, going now very fast before a gentle south-west gale, returned above the Crystal Palace towers, circled round them, chose a position for descent, and sank down out of sight.

Bert sighed deeply, and turned to his motor-bicycle again.

And that was only the beginning of a succession of strange phenomena in the heavens—cylinders, cones, pear-shaped monsters, even at last a thing of aluminium that glittered wonderfully, and that Grubb, through some confusion of ideas about armour plates, was inclined to consider a war machine.

There followed actual flight.

This, however, was not an affair that was visible from Bun Hill; it was something that occurred in private grounds or other enclosed places and, under favourable conditions, and it was brought home to Grubb and Bert Smallways only by means of the magazine page of the half-penny newspapers or by cinematograph records. But it was brought home very insistently, and in those days if, ever one heard a man saying in a public place in a loud, reassuring, confident tone, "It's bound to come," the chances were ten to one he was talking of flying. And Bert got a box lid and wrote out in correct window-ticket style, and Grubb put in the window this inscription, "Aeroplanes made and repaired." It quite upset Tom—it seemed taking one's shop so lightly; but most of the neighbours, and all the sporting ones, approved of it as being very good indeed.

Everybody talked of flying, everybody repeated over and over again, "Bound to come," and then you know it didn't come. There was a hitch. They flew—that was all right; they flew in machines heavier than air. But they smashed. Sometimes they smashed the engine, sometimes they smashed the aeronaut, usually they smashed both. Machines that made flights of three or four miles and came down safely, went up the next time to headlong disaster. There seemed no possible trusting to them. The breeze upset them, the eddies near the ground upset them,

a passing thought in the mind of the aeronaut upset them. Also they upset—simply.

"It's this 'stability' does 'em," said Grubb, repeating his newspaper. "They pitch and they pitch, till they pitch themselves to pieces."

Experiments fell away after two expectant years of this sort of success, the public and then the newspapers tired of the expensive photographic reproductions, the optimistic reports, the perpetual sequence of triumph and disaster and silence. Flying slumped, even ballooning fell away to some extent, though it remained a fairly popular sport, and continued to lift gravel from the wharf of the Bun Hill gas-works and drop it upon deserving people's lawns and gardens. There were half a dozen reassuring years for Tom—at least so far as flying was concerned. But that was the great time of mono-rail development, and his anxiety was only diverted from the high heavens by the most urgent threats and symptoms of change in the lower sky.

There had been talk of mono-rails for several years. But the real mischief began when Brennan sprang his gyroscopic mono-rail car upon the Royal Society. It was the leading sensation of the 1907 soirées; that celebrated demonstration-room was all too small for its exhibition. Brave soldiers, leading Zionists, deserving novelists, noble ladies, congested the narrow passage and thrust distinguished elbows into ribs the world would not willingly let break, deeming themselves fortunate if they could see "just a little bit of the rail." Inaudible, but convincing, the great inventor expounded his discovery, and sent his obedient little model of the trains of the future up gradients, round curves, and across a sagging wire. It ran along its single rail, on its single wheels, simple and sufficient; it stopped, reversed stood still, balancing perfectly. It maintained its astounding equilibrium amidst a thunder of applause. The audience dispersed at last, discussing how far they would enjoy crossing an abyss on a wire cable. "Suppose the gyroscope stopped!" Few of them

anticipated a tithe of what the Brennan mono-rail would do for their railway securities and the face of the world.

In a few, years they realised better. In a little while no one thought anything of crossing an abyss on a wire, and the mono-rail was superseding the tram-lines, railways: and indeed every form of track for mechanical locomotion. Where land was cheap the rail ran along the ground, where it was dear the rail lifted up on iron standards and passed overhead; its swift, convenient cars went everywhere and did everything that had once been done along made tracks upon the ground.

When old Smallways died, Tom could think of nothing more striking to say of him than that, "When he was a boy, there wasn't nothing higher than your chimbleys—there wasn't a wire nor a cable in the sky!"

Old Smallways went to his grave under an intricate network of wires and cables, for Bun Hill became not only a sort of minor centre of power distribution—the Home Counties Power Distribution Company set up transformers and a generating station close beside the old gas-works—but, also a junction on the suburban mono-rail system. Moreover, every tradesman in the place, and indeed nearly every house, had its own telephone.

The mono-rail cable standard became a striking fact in urban landscape, for the most part stout iron erections rather like tapering trestles, and painted a bright bluish green. One, it happened, bestrode Tom's house, which looked still more retiring and apologetic beneath its immensity; and another giant stood just inside the corner of his garden, which was still not built upon and unchanged, except for a couple of advertisement boards, one recommending a two-and-sixpenny watch, and one a nerve restorer. These, by the bye, were placed almost horizontally to catch the eye of the passing mono-rail passengers above, and so served admirably to roof over a tool-shed and a mushroom-shed for Tom. All day and all night the fast cars from Brighton and Hastings went murmuring by overhead—long, broad, comfortable-looking cars, that were brightly lit after

dusk. As they flew by at night, transient flares of light and a rumbling sound of passage, they kept up a perpetual summer lightning and thunderstorm in the street below.

Presently the English Channel was bridged—a series of great iron Eiffel Tower pillars carrying mono-rail cables at a height of a hundred and fifty feet above the water, except near the middle, where they rose higher to allow the passage of the London and Antwerp shipping and the Hamburg-America liners.

Then heavy motor-cars began to run about on only a couple of wheels, one behind the other, which for some reason upset Tom dreadfully, and made him gloomy for days after the first one passed the shop. . . .

All this gyroscopic and mono-rail development naturally absorbed a vast amount of public attention, and there was also a huge excitement consequent upon the amazing gold discoveries off the coast of Anglesea made by a submarine prospector, Miss Patricia Giddy. She had taken her degree in geology and mineralogy in the University of London, and while working upon the auriferous rocks of North Wales, after a brief holiday spent in agitating for women's suffrage, she had been struck by the possibility of these reefs cropping up again under the water. She had set herself to verify this supposition by the use of the submarine crawler invented by Doctor Alberto Cassini. By a happy mingling of reasoning and intuition peculiar to her sex she found gold at her first descent, and emerged after three hours' submersion with about two hundredweight of ore containing gold in the unparalleled quantity of seventeen ounces to the ton. But the whole story of her submarine mining, intensely interesting as it is, must be told at some other time; suffice it now to remark simply that it was during the consequent great rise of prices, confidence, and enterprise that the revival of interest in flying occurred.

§4

It is curious how the final boom of flying began. It was like

the coming of a breeze on a quiet day; nothing started it, it came. People began to talk of flying with an air of never having for one moment dropped the subject. Pictures of flying and flying machines returned to the newspapers; articles and allusions increased and multiplied in the serious magazines. People asked in mono-rail trains, "When are we going to fly?" A new crop of inventors sprang up in a night or so like fungi. The Aero Club announced the project of a great Flying Exhibition in a large area of ground that the removal of slums in Whitechapel had rendered available.

The advancing wave soon produced a sympathetic ripple in the Bun Hill establishment. Grubb routed out his flying-machine model again, tried it in the yard behind the shop, got a kind of flight out of it, and broke seventeen panes of glass and nine flower-pots in the greenhouse that occupied the next yard but one.

And then, springing from nowhere, sustained one knew not how, came a persistent, disturbing rumour that the problem had been solved, that the secret was known. Bert met it one early-closing afternoon as he refreshed himself in an inn near Nutfield, whither his motor-bicycle had brought him. There smoked and meditated a person in khaki, an engineer, who presently took an interest in Bert's machine. It was a sturdy piece of apparatus, and it had acquired a kind of documentary value in these quick-changing times; it was now nearly eight years old. Its points discussed, the soldier broke into a new topic with, "My next's going to be an aeroplane, so far as I can see. I've had enough of roads and ways."

"They *tork*," said Bert.

"They talk—and they do," said the soldier.

"The thing's coming—"

"It keeps *on* coming," said Bert; "I shall believe when I see it."

"That won't be long," said the soldier.

The conversation seemed degenerating into an amiable wrangle of contradiction.

"I tell you they *are* flying," the soldier insisted. "I see it myself."

"We've all seen it," said Bert.

"I don't mean flap up and smash up; I mean real, safe, steady, controlled flying, against the wind, good and right."

"You ain't seen that!"

"I *'ave!* Aldershot. They try to keep it a secret. They got it right enough. You bet—our War Office isn't going to be caught napping this time."

Bert's incredulity was shaken. He asked questions—and the soldier expanded.

"I tell you they got nearly a square mile fenced in—a sort of valley. Fences of barbed wire ten feet high, and inside that they do things. Chaps about the camp—now and then we get a peep. It isn't only us neither. There's the Japanese; you bet they got it too—and the Germans! And I never knowed anything of this sort yet that the Frencheys didn't get ahead with—after their manner! They started ironclads, they started submarines, they started navigables, and you bet they won't be far be'ind at this."

The soldier stood with his legs very wide apart, and filled his pipe thoughtfully. Bert sat on the low wall against which his motor-bicycle was leaning.

"Funny thing fighting'll be," he said.

"Flying's going to break out," said the soldier. "When it *does* come, when the curtain does go up, I tell you you'll find every one on the stage—busy. . . . Such fighting, too!. . . I suppose you don't read the papers about this sort of thing?"

"I read 'em a bit," said Bert.

"Well, have you noticed what one might call the remarkable case of the disappearing inventor—the inventor who turns up in a blaze of publicity, fires off a few successful experiments, and vanishes?"

"Can't say I 'ave," said Bert.

"Well, I 'ave, anyhow. You get anybody come along who does anything striking in this line, and, you bet, he vanishes. Just goes off quietly out of sight. After a bit, you don't hear anything more of 'em at all. See? They disappear. Gone—no address. First—oh! it's an old story now—there was those Wright Brothers out in America. They glided—they glided miles and miles. Finally they glided off stage. Why, it must be nineteen hundred and four, or five, *they* vanished! Then there was those people in Ireland—no, I forget their names. Everybody said they could fly. *They* went. They ain't dead that I've heard tell; but you can't say they're alive. Not a feather of 'em can you see. Then that chap who flew round Paris and upset in the Seine. De Booley, was it? I forget. That was a grand fly, in spite of the accident; but where's he got to? The accident didn't hurt him. Eh? *'E's* gone to cover."

The soldier prepared to light his pipe.

"Looks like a secret society got hold of them," said Bert.

"Secret society! *Naw!*"

The soldier lit his match, and drew. "Secret society," he repeated, with his pipe between his teeth and the match flaring, in response to his words. "War Departments; that's more like it." He threw his match aside, and walked to his machine. "I tell you, sir," he said, "there isn't a big Power in Europe, *or* Asia, *or* America, *or* Africa, that hasn't got at least one or two flying machines hidden up its sleeve at the present time. Not one. Real, workable, flying machines. And the spying! The spying and manoeuvring to find out what the others have got. I tell you, sir, a foreigner, or, for the matter of that, an unaccredited native, can't get within four miles of Lydd nowadays—not to mention our little circus at Aldershot, and the experimental camp in Galway. No!"

"Well," said Bert, "I'd like to see one of them, anyhow. Jest to help believing. I'll believe when I see, that I'll promise you."

"You'll see 'em, fast enough," said the soldier, and led his machine out into the road.

He left Bert on his wall, grave and pensive, with his cap on the back of his head, and a cigarette smouldering in the corner of his mouth.

"If what he says is true," said Bert, "me and Grubb, we been

wasting our blessed old time. Besides incurring expense with thet green'ouse."

§5

It was while this mysterious talk with the soldier still stirred in Bert Smallways' imagination that the most astounding incident in the whole of that dramatic chapter of human history, the coming of flying, occurred. People talk glibly enough of epoch-making events; this was an epoch-making event. It was the unanticipated and entirely successful flight of Mr. Alfred Butteridge from the Crystal Palace to Glasgow and back in a small businesslike-looking machine heavier than air—an entirely manageable and controllable machine that could fly as well as a pigeon.

It wasn't, one felt, a fresh step forward in the matter so much as a giant stride, a leap. Mr. Butteridge remained in the air altogether for about nine hours, and during that time he flew with the ease and assurance of a bird. His machine was, however neither bird-like nor butterfly-like, nor had it the wide, lateral expansion of the ordinary aeroplane. The effect upon the observer was rather something in the nature of a bee or wasp. Parts of the apparatus were spinning very rapidly, and gave one a hazy effect of transparent wings; but parts, including two peculiarly curved "wing-cases"—if one may borrow a figure from the flying beetles—remained expanded stiffly. In the middle was a long rounded body like the body of a moth, and on this Mr. Butteridge could be seen sitting astride, much as a man bestrides a horse. The wasp-like resemblance was increased by the fact that the apparatus flew with a deep booming hum, exactly the sound made by a wasp at a windowpane.

Mr. Butteridge took the world by surprise. He was one of those gentlemen from nowhere Fate still succeeds in producing for the stimulation of mankind. He came, it was variously said, from Australia and America and the South of France. He was also described quite incorrectly as the son of a man who had

amassed a comfortable fortune in the manufacture of gold nibs and the Butteridge fountain pens. But this was an entirely different strain of Butteridges. For some years, in spite of a loud voice, a large presence, an aggressive swagger, and an implacable manner, he had been an undistinguished member of most of the existing aeronautical associations. Then one day he wrote to all the London papers to announce that he had made arrangements for an ascent from the Crystal Palace of a machine that would demonstrate satisfactorily that the outstanding difficulties in the way of flying were finally solved. Few of the papers printed his letter, still fewer were the people who believed in his claim. No one was excited even when a fracas on the steps of a leading hotel in Piccadilly, in which he tried to horse-whip a prominent German musician upon some personal account, delayed his promised ascent. The quarrel was inadequately reported, and his name spelt variously Betteridge and Betridge. Until his flight indeed, he did not and could not contrive to exist in the public mind. There were scarcely thirty people on the look-out for him, in spite of all his clamour, when about six o'clock one summer morning the doors of the big shed in which he had been putting together his apparatus opened—it was near the big model of a megatherium in the Crystal Palace grounds—and his giant insect came droning out into a negligent and incredulous world.

But before he had made his second circuit of the Crystal Palace towers, Fame was lifting her trumpet, she drew a deep breath as the startled tramps who sleep on the seats of Trafalgar Square were roused by his buzz and awoke to discover him circling the Nelson column, and by the time he had got to Birmingham, which place he crossed about half-past ten, her deafening blast was echoing throughout the country. The despaired-of thing was done.

A man was flying securely and well.

Scotland was agape for his coming. Glasgow he reached by one o'clock, and it is related that scarcely a ship-yard or factory in that busy hive of industry resumed work before half-past

two. The public mind was just sufficiently educated in the impossibility of flying to appreciate Mr. Butteridge at his proper value. He circled the University buildings, and dropped to within shouting distance of the crowds in West End Park and on the slope of Gilmorehill. The thing flew quite steadily at a pace of about three miles an hour, in a wide circle, making a deep hum that would have drowned his full, rich voice completely had he not provided himself with a megaphone. He avoided churches, buildings, and mono-rail cables with consummate ease as he conversed.

"Me name's Butteridge," he shouted; "B-U-T-T-E-R-I-D-G-E.—Got it? Me mother was Scotch."

And having assured himself that he had been understood, he rose amidst cheers and shouting and patriotic cries, and then flew up very swiftly and easily into the south-eastern sky, rising and falling with long, easy undulations in an extraordinarily wasp-like manner.

His return to London—he visited and hovered over Manchester and Liverpool and Oxford on his way, and spelt his name out to each place—was an occasion of unparalleled excitement. Every one was staring heavenward. More people were run over in the streets upon that one day, than in the previous three months, and a County Council steamboat, the *Isaac Walton*, collided with a pier of Westminster Bridge, and narrowly escaped disaster by running ashore—it was low water—on the mud on the south side. He returned to the Crystal Palace grounds, that classic starting-point of aeronautical adventure, about sunset, re-entered his shed without disaster, and had the doors locked immediately upon the photographers and journalists who been waiting his return.

"Look here, you chaps," he said, as his assistant did so, "I'm tired to death, and saddle sore. I can't give you a word of talk. I'm too—done. My name's Butteridge. B-U-T-T-E-R-I-D-G-E. Get that right. I'm an Imperial Englishman. I'll talk to you all to-morrow."

Foggy snapshots still survive to record that incident. His assistant struggles in a sea of aggressive young men carrying note-books or upholding cameras and wearing bowler hats and enterprising ties. He himself towers up in the doorway, a big figure with a mouth—an eloquent cavity beneath a vast black moustache—distorted by his shout to these relentless agents of publicity. He towers there, the most famous man in the country.

Almost symbolically he holds and gesticulates with a megaphone in his left hand.

§6

Tom and Bert Smallways both saw that return. They watched from the crest of Bun Hill, from which they had so often surveyed the pyrotechnics of the Crystal Palace. Bert was excited, Tom kept calm and lumpish, but neither of them realised how their own lives were to be invaded by the fruits of that beginning. "P'raps old Grubb'll mind the shop a bit now," he said, "and put his blessed model in the fire. Not that that can save us, if we don't tide over with Steinhart's account."

Bert knew enough of things and the problem of aeronautics to realise that this gigantic imitation of a bee would, to use his own idiom, "give the newspapers fits." The next day it was clear the fits had been given even as he said: their magazine pages were black with hasty photographs, their prose was convulsive, they foamed at the headline. The next day they were worse. Before the week was out they were not so much published as carried screaming into the street.

The dominant fact in the uproar was the exceptional personality of Mr. Butteridge, and the extraordinary terms he demanded for the secret of his machine.

For it was a secret and he kept it secret in the most elaborate fashion. He built his apparatus himself in the safe privacy of the great Crystal Palace sheds, with the assistance of inattentive workmen, and the day next following his flight he took it to pieces single handed, packed certain portions, and then secured

unintelligent assistance in packing and dispersing the rest. Sealed packing-cases went north and east and west to various pantechnicons, and the engines were boxed with peculiar care. It became evident these precautions were not inadvisable in view of the violent demand for any sort of photograph or impressions of his machine. But Mr. Butteridge, having once made his demonstration, intended to keep his secret safe from any further risk of leakage. He faced the British public now with the question whether they wanted his secret or not; he was, he said perpetually, an "Imperial Englishman," and his first wish and his last was to see his invention the privilege and monopoly of the Empire. Only—

It was there the difficulty began.

Mr. Butteridge, it became evident, was a man singularly free from any false modesty—indeed, from any modesty of any kind—singularly willing to see interviewers, answer questions upon any topic except aeronautics, volunteer opinions, criticisms, and autobiography, supply portraits and photographs of himself, and generally spread his personality across the terrestrial sky. The published portraits insisted primarily upon an immense black moustache, and secondarily upon a fierceness behind the moustache. The general impression upon the public was that Butteridge was a small man. No one big, it was felt, could have so virulently aggressive an expression, though, as a matter of fact, Butteridge had a height of six feet two inches, and a weight altogether proportionate to that. Moreover, he had a love affair of large and unusual dimensions and irregular circumstances and the still largely decorous British public learnt with reluctance and alarm that a sympathetic treatment of this affair was inseparable from the exclusive acquisition of the priceless secret of aerial stability by the British Empire. The exact particulars of the similarity never came to light, but apparently the lady had, in a fit of high-minded inadvertence, had gone through the ceremony of marriage with, one quotes the unpublished discourse of Mr. Butteridge—"a white-livered skunk," and this zoological aberration did in some legal and vexatious manner mar her social happiness. He wanted to talk about the business, to show the splendour of her nature in the light of its complications. It was really most embarrassing to a press that has always possessed a considerable turn for reticence, that wanted things personal indeed in the modern fashion. Yet not too personal. It was embarrassing, I say, to be inexorably confronted with Mr. Butteridge's great heart, to see it laid open in relentlesss self-vivisection, and its pulsating dissepiments adorned with emphatic flag labels.

Confronted they were, and there was no getting away from it. He would make this appalling viscus beat and throb before the shrinking journalists—no uncle with a big watch and a little baby ever harped upon it so relentlessly; whatever evasion they attempted he set aside. He "gloried in his love," he said, and compelled them to write it down.

"That's of course a private affair, Mr. Butteridge," they would object.

"The injustice, sorr, is public. I do not care either I am up against institutions or individuals. I do not care if I am up against the universal All. I am pleading the cause of a woman, a woman I lurve, sorr—a noble woman—misunderstood. I intend to vindicate her, sorr, to the four winds of heaven!"

"I lurve England," he used to say—"lurve England, but Puritanism, sorr, I abhor. It fills me with loathing. It raises my gorge. Take my own case."

He insisted relentlessly upon his heart, and upon seeing proofs of the interview. If they had not done justice to his erotic bellowings and gesticulations, he stuck in, in a large inky scrawl, all and more than they had omitted.

It was a strangely embarrassing thing for British journalism. Never was there a more obvious or uninteresting affair; never had the world heard the story of erratic affection with less appetite or sympathy. On the other hand it was extremely curious about Mr. Butteridge's invention. But when Mr. Butteridge

could be deflected for a moment from the cause of the lady he championed, then he talked chiefly, and usually with tears of tenderness in his voice, about his mother and his childhood—his mother who crowned a complete encyclopedia of maternal virtue by being "largely Scotch." She was not quite neat, but nearly so. "I owe everything in me to me mother," he asserted—"everything. Eh!" and—"ask any man who's done anything. You'll hear the same story. All we have we owe to women. They are the species, sorr. Man is but a dream. He comes and goes. The woman's soul leadeth us upward and on!"

He was always going on like that.

What in particular he wanted from the Government for his secret did not appear, nor what beyond a money payment could be expected from a modern state in such an affair. The general effect upon judicious observers, indeed, was not that he was treating for anything, but that he was using an unexampled opportunity to bellow and show off to an attentive world. Rumours of his real identity spread abroad. It was said that he had been the landlord of an ambiguous hotel in Cape Town, and had there given shelter to, and witnessed, the experiments and finally stolen the papers and plans of, an extremely shy and friendless young inventor named Palliser, who had come to South Africa from England in an advanced stage of consumption, and died there. This, at any rate, was the allegation of the more outspoken American press. But the proof or disproof of that never reached the public.

Mr. Butteridge also involved himself passionately in a tangle of disputes for the possession of a great number of valuable money prizes. Some of these had been offered so long ago as 1906 for successful mechanical flight. By the time of Mr. Butteridge's success a really very considerable number of newspapers, tempted by the impunity of the pioneers in this direction, had pledged themselves to pay in some cases, quite overwhelming sums to the first person to fly from Manchester to Glasgow, from London to Manchester, one hundred miles,

two hundred miles in England, and the like. Most had hedged a little with ambiguous conditions, and now offered resistance; one or two paid at once, and vehemently called attention to the fact; and Mr. Butteridge plunged into litigation with the more recalcitrant, while at the same time sustaining a vigorous agitation and canvass to induce the Government to purchase his invention.

One fact, however, remained permanent throughout all the developments of this affair behind Butteridge's preposterous love interest, his politics and personality, and all his shouting and boasting, and that was that, so far as the mass of people knew, he was in sole possession of the secret of the practicable aeroplane in which, for all one could tell to the contrary, the key of the future empire of the world resided. And presently, to the great consternation of innumerable people, including among others Mr. Bert Smallways, it became apparent that whatever negotiations were in progress for the acquisition of this precious secret by the British Government were in danger of falling through. The London *Daily Requiem* first voiced the universal alarm, and published an interview under the terrific caption of, "Mr. Butteridge Speaks his Mind."

Therein the inventor—if he was an inventor—poured out his heart.

"I came from the end of the earth," he said, which rather seemed to confirm the Cape Town story, "bringing me Motherland the secret that would give her the empire of the world. And what do I get?" He paused. "I am sniffed at by elderly mandarins!. . . And the woman I love is treated like a leper!"

"I am an Imperial Englishman," he went on in a splendid outburst, subsequently written into the interview by his own hand; "but there there are limits to the human heart! There are younger nations—living nations! Nations that do not snore and gurgle helplessly in paroxysms of plethora upon beds of formality and red tape! There are nations that will not fling away

the empire of earth in order to slight an unknown man and insult a noble woman whose boots they are not fitted to unlatch. There are nations not blinded to Science, not given over hand and foot to effete snobocracies and Degenerate Decadents. In short, mark my words—*there are other nations!"*. . .

This speech it was that particularly impressed Bert Smallways. "If them Germans or them Americans get hold of this," he said impressively to his brother, "the British Empire's done. It's U-P. The Union Jack, so to speak, won't be worth the paper it's written on, Tom."

"I suppose you couldn't lend us a hand this morning," said Jessica, in his impressive pause. "Everybody in Bun Hill seems wanting early potatoes at once. Tom can't carry half of them."

"We're living on a volcano," said Bert, disregarding the suggestion. "At any moment war may come—such a war!"

He shook his head portentously.

"You'd better take this lot first, Tom," said Jessica. She turned briskly on Bert. "Can you spare us a morning?" she asked.

"I dessay I can," said Bert. "The shop's very quiet s'morning. Though all this danger to the Empire worries me something frightful."

"Work'll take it off your mind," said Jessica.

And presently he too was going out into a world of change and wonder, bowed beneath a load of potatoes and patriotic insecurity, that merged at last into a very definite irritation at the weight and want of style of the potatoes and a very clear conception of the entire detestableness of Jessica.

Chapter II

HOW BERT SMALLWAYS GOT INTO DIFFICULTIES

It did not occur to either Tom or Bert Smallways that this remarkable aerial performance of Mr. Butteridge was likely to affect either of their lives in any special manner, that it would in any way single them out from the millions about them; and when they had witnessed it from the crest of Bun Hill and seen the fly-like mechanism, its rotating planes a golden haze in the sunset, sink humming to the harbour of its shed again, they turned back towards the sunken greengrocery beneath the great iron standard of the London to Brighton mono-rail, and their minds reverted to the discussion that had engaged them before Mr. Butteridge's triumph had come in sight out of the London haze.

It was a difficult and unsuccessful discussion. They had to carry it on in shouts because of the moaning and roaring of the gyroscopic motor-cars that traversed the High Street, and in its nature it was contentious and private. The Grubb business was in difficulties, and Grubb in a moment of financial eloquence had given a half-share in it to Bert, whose relations with his employer had been for some time unsalaried and pallish and informal.

Bert was trying to impress Tom with the idea that the reconstructed Grubb & Smallways offered unprecedented and unparalleled opportunities to the judicious small investor. It was coming home to Bert, as though it were an entirely new fact, that Tom was singularly impervious to ideas. In the end he put the financial issues on one side, and, making the thing entirely a matter of fraternal affection, succeeded in borrowing a sovereign on the security of his word of honour.

The firm of Grubb & Smallways, formerly Grubb, had indeed been singularly unlucky in the last year or so. For many years the business had struggled along with a flavour of romantic insecurity in a small, dissolute-looking shop in the High Street, adorned with brilliantly coloured advertisements of cycles, a display of bells, trouser-clips, oil-cans, pump-clips, frame-cases, wallets, and other accessories, and the announcement of "Bicycles on Hire," "Repairs," "Free inflation," "Petrol," and similar attractions. They were agents for several obscure makes of bicycle,—two samples constituted the stock,—and occasionally they effected a sale; they also repaired punctures and did their best—though luck was not always on their side—with any other repairing that was brought to them. They handled a line of cheap gramophones, and did a little with musical boxes.

The staple of their business was, however, the letting of bicycles on hire. It was a singular trade, obeying no known commercial or economic principles—indeed, no principles. There was a stock of ladies' and gentlemen's bicycles in a state of disrepair that passes description, and these, the hiring stock, were let to unexacting and reckless people, inexpert in the things of this world, at a nominal rate of one shilling for the first hour and sixpence per hour afterwards. But really there were no fixed prices, and insistent boys could get bicycles and the thrill of danger for an hour for so low a sum as threepence, provided they could convince Grubb that that was all they had. The saddle and handle-bar were then sketchily adjusted by Grubb, a deposit exacted, except in the case of familiar boys, the machine lubricated, and the adventurer started upon his career. Usually he or she came back, but at times, when the accident was serious, Bert or Grubb had to go out and fetch the machine home. Hire was always charged up to the hour of return to the shop and deducted from the deposit. It was rare that a bicycle started out from their hands in a state of pedantic efficiency. Romantic possibilities of accident lurked in the worn thread of the screw that adjusted the saddle, in the precarious pedals, in the loose-knit chain, in the handle-bars, above all in the brakes and tyres. Tappings and clankings and strange rhythmic creakings awoke as the intrepid hirer pedalled out into the country. Then perhaps the bell would jam or a brake fail to act on a hill; or the seat-pillar would get loose, and the saddle drop three or four inches with a disconcerting bump; or the loose and rattling chain would jump the cogs of the chain-wheel as the machine ran downhill, and so bring the mechanism to an abrupt and disastrous stop without at the same time arresting the forward momentum of the rider; or a tyre would bang, or sigh quietly, and give up the struggle for efficiency.

When the hirer returned, a heated pedestrian, Grubb would ignore all verbal complaints, and examine the machine gravely.

"This ain't 'ad fair usage," he used to begin.

He became a mild embodiment of the spirit of reason. "You can't expect a bicycle to take you up in its arms and carry you," he used to say. "You got to show intelligence. After all—it's machinery."

Sometimes the process of liquidating the consequent claims bordered on violence. It was always a very rhetorical and often a trying affair, but in these progressive times you have to make a noise to get a living. It was often hard work, but nevertheless this hiring was a fairly steady source of profit, until one day all the panes in the window and door were broken and the stock on sale in the window greatly damaged and disordered by two over-critical hirers with no sense of rhetorical irrelevance. They were big, coarse stokers from Gravesend. One was annoyed because his left pedal had come off, and the other because his tyre had become deflated, small and indeed negligible accidents by Bun Hill standards, due entirely to the ungentle handling of the delicate machines entrusted to them—and they failed to see clearly how they put themselves in the wrong by this method of argument. It is a poor way of convincing a man that he has let you a defective machine to throw his foot-pump about his shop, and take his stock of gongs outside in order to return

them through the window-panes. It carried no real conviction to the minds of either Grubb or Bert; it only irritated and vexed them. One quarrel makes many, and this unpleasantness led to a violent dispute between Grubb and the landlord upon the moral aspects of and legal responsibility for the consequent re-glazing. In the end Grubb and Smallways were put to the expense of a strategic nocturnal removal to another position.

It was a position they had long considered. It was a small, shed-like shop with a plate-glass window and one room behind, just at the sharp bend in the road at the bottom of Bun Hill; and here they struggled along bravely, in spite of persistent annoyance from their former landlord, hoping for certain eventualities the peculiar situation of the shop seemed to promise. Here, too, they were doomed to disappointment.

The High Road from London to Brighton that ran through Bun Hill was like the British Empire or the British Constitution—a thing that had grown to its present importance. Unlike any other roads in Europe the British high roads have never been subjected to any organised attempts to grade or straighten them out, and to that no doubt their peculiar picturesqueness is to be ascribed. The old Bun Hill High Street drops at its end for perhaps eighty or a hundred feet of descent at an angle of one in five, turns at right angles to the left, runs in a curve for about thirty yards to a brick bridge over the dry ditch that had once been the Otterbourne, and then bends sharply to the right again round a dense clump of trees and goes on, a simple, straightforward, peaceful high road. There had been one or two horse-and-van and bicycle accidents in the place before the shop Bert and Grubb took was built, and, to be frank, it was the probability of others that attracted them to it.

Its possibilities had come to them first with a humorous flavour.

"Here's one of the places where a chap might get a living by keeping hens," said Grubb.

"You can't get a living by keeping hens," said Bert.

"You'd keep the hen and have it spatch-cocked," said Grubb. "The motor chaps would pay for it."

When they really came to take the place they remembered this conversation. Hens, however, were out of the question; there was no place for a run unless they had it in the shop. It would have been obviously out of place there. The shop was much more modern than their former one, and had a plate-glass front. "Sooner or later," said Bert, "we shall get a motor-car through this."

"That's all right," said Grubb. "Compensation. I don't mind when that motor-car comes along. I don't mind even if it gives me a shock to the system."

"And meanwhile," said Bert, with great artfulness, "*I'm* going to buy myself a dog."

He did. He bought three in succession. He surprised the people at the Dogs' Home in Battersea by demanding a deaf retriever, and rejecting every candidate that pricked up its ears. "I want a good, deaf, slow-moving dog," he said. "A dog that doesn't put himself out for things."

They displayed inconvenient curiosity; they declared a great scarcity of deaf dogs.

"You see," they said, "dogs aren't deaf."

"Mine's got to be," said Bert. "I've *had* dogs that aren't deaf. All I want. It's like this, you see—I sell gramophones. Naturally I got to make 'em talk and tootle a bit to show 'em orf. Well, a dog that isn't deaf doesn't like it—gets excited, smells round, barks, growls. That upsets the customer. See? Then a dog that has his hearing fancies things. Makes burglars out of passing tramps. Wants to fight every motor that makes a whizz. All very well if you want livening up, but our place is lively enough. I don't want a dog of that sort. I want a quiet dog."

In the end he got three in succession, but none of them turned out well. The first strayed off into the infinite, heeding no appeals; the second was killed in the night by a fruit motor-waggon which fled before Grubb could get down; the third got

itself entangled in the front wheel of a passing cyclist, who came through the plate glass, and proved to be an actor out of work and an undischarged bankrupt. He demanded compensation for some fancied injury, would hear nothing of the valuable dog he had killed or the window he had broken, obliged Grubb by sheer physical obduracy to straighten his buckled front wheel, and pestered the struggling firm with a series of inhumanly worded solicitor's letters. Grubb answered them—stingingly, and put himself, Bert thought, in the wrong.

Affairs got more and more exasperating and strained under these pressures. The window was boarded up, and an unpleasant altercation about their delay in repairing it with the new landlord, a Bun Hill butcher—and a loud, bellowing, unreasonable person at that—served to remind them of their unsettled troubles with the old. Things were at this pitch when Bert bethought himself of creating a sort of debenture capital in the business for the benefit of Tom. But, as I have said, Tom had no enterprise in his composition. His idea of investment was the stocking; he bribed his brother not to keep the offer open.

And then ill-luck made its last lunge at their crumbling business and brought it to the ground.

§2

It is a poor heart that never rejoices, and Whitsuntide had an air of coming as an agreeable break in the business complications of Grubb & Smallways. Encouraged by the practical outcome of Bert's negotiations with his brother, and by the fact that half the hiring-stock was out from Saturday to Monday, they decided to ignore the residuum of hiring-trade on Sunday and devote that day to much-needed relaxation and refreshment—to have, in fact, an unstinted good time, a beano on Whit Sunday and return invigorated to grapple with their difficulties and the Bank Holiday repairs on the Monday. No good thing was ever done by exhausted and dispirited men. It happened that they had made the acquaintance of two young ladies in employment in

Clapham, Miss Flossie Bright and Miss Edna Bunthorne, and it was resolved therefore to make a cheerful little cyclist party of four into the heart of Kent, and to picnic and spend an indolent afternoon and evening among the trees and bracken between Ashford and Maidstone.

Miss Bright could ride a bicycle, and a machine was found for her, not among the hiring stock, but specially, in the sample held for sale. Miss Bunthorne, whom Bert particularly affected, could not ride, and so with some difficulty he hired a basket-work trailer from the big business of Wray's in the Clapham Road.

To see our young men, brightly dressed and cigarettes alight, wheeling off to the rendezvous, Grubb guiding the lady's machine beside him with one skilful hand and Bert teuf-teuffing steadily, was to realise how pluck may triumph even over insolvency. Their landlord, the butcher, said, "Gurr," as they passed, and shouted, "Go it!" in a loud, savage tone to their receding backs.

Much they cared!

The weather was fine, and though they were on their way southward before nine o'clock, there was already a great multitude of holiday people abroad upon the roads. There were quantities of young men and women on bicycles and motor-bicycles, and a majority of gyroscopic motor-cars running bicycle-fashion on two wheels, mingled with old-fashioned four-wheeled traffic. Bank Holiday times always bring out old stored-away vehicles and odd people; one saw tricars and electric broughams and dilapidated old racing motors with huge pneumatic tyres. Once our holiday-makers saw a horse and cart, and once a youth riding a black horse amidst the badinage of the passersby. And there were several navigable gas air-ships, not to mention balloons, in the air. It was all immensely interesting and refreshing after the dark anxieties of the shop. Edna wore a brown straw hat with poppies, that suited her admirably, and sat in the trailer like a queen, and the eight-year-old motor-bicycle ran like a thing of yesterday.

Little it seemed to matter to Mr. Bert Smallways that a newspaper placard proclaimed:—

GERMANY DENOUNCES THE
MONROE DOCTRINE.

AMBIGUOUS ATTITUDE OF JAPAN.

WHAT WILL BRITAIN DO? IS IT WAR?

This sort of thing was alvays going on, and on holidays one disregarded it as a matter of course. Week-davs, in the slack time after the midday meal, then perhaps one might worry about the Empire and international politics; but not on a sunny Sunday, with a pretty girl trailing behind one, and envious cyclists trying to race you. Nor did our young people attach any great importance to the flitting suggestions of military activity they glimpsed ever and again. Near Maidstone they came on a string of eleven motor-guns of peculiar construction halted by the roadside, with a number of businesslike engineers grouped about them watching through field-glasses some sort of entrenchment that was going on near the crest of the downs. It signified nothing to Bert.

"What's up?" said Edna.

"Oh!—manoeuvres," said Bert.

"Oh! I thought they did them at Easter," said Edna, and troubled no more.

The last great British war, the Boer war, was over and forgotten, and the public had lost the fashion of expert military criticism.

Our four young people picnicked cheerfully, and were happy in the manner of a happiness that was an ancient mode in Nineveh. Eyes were bright, Grubb was funny and almost witty, and Bert achieved epigrams; the hedges were full of honeysuckle and dog-roses; in the woods the distant toot-toot-toot of the traffic on the dust-hazy high road might have been no more than the horns of elf-land. They laughed and gossiped and

picked flowers and made love and talked, and the girls smoked cigarettes. Also they scuffled playfully. Among other things they talked aeronautics, and how thev would come for a picnic together in Bert's flying-machine before ten years were out. The world seemed full of amusing possibilities that afternoon. They wondered what their great-grandparents would have thought of aeronautics. In the evening, about seven, the party turned homeward, expecting no disaster, and it was only on the crest of the downs between Wrotham and Kingsdown that disaster came.

They had come up the hill in the twilight; Bert was anxious to get as far as possible before he lit—or attempted to light, for the issue was a doubtful one—his lamps, and they had scorched past a number of cyclists, and by a four-wheeled motor-car of the old style lamed by a deflated tyre. Some dust had penetrated Bert's horn, and the result was a curious, amusing, wheezing sound had got into his "honk, honk." For the sake of merriment and glory he was making this sound as much as possible, and Edna was in fits of laughter in the trailer. They made a sort of rushing cheerfulness along the road that affected their fellow travellers variously, according to their temperaments. She did notice a good lot of bluish, evil-smelling smoke coming from about the bearings between his feet, but she thought this was one of the natural concomitants of motor-traction, and troubled no more about it, until abruptly it burst into a little yellow-tipped flame.

"Bert!" she screamed.

But Bert had put on the brakes with such suddenness that she found herself involved with his leg as he dismounted. She got to the side of the road and hastily readjusted her hat, which had suffered.

"Gaw!" said Bert.

He stood for some fatal seconds watching the petrol drip and catch, and the flame, which was now beginning to smell of enamel as well as oil, spread and grew. His chief idea was the sorrowful one that he had not sold the machine second-hand a

year ago, and that he ought to have done so—a good idea in its way, but not immediately helpful. He turned upon Edna sharply. "Get a lot of wet sand," he said. Then he wheeled the machine a little towards the side of the roadway, and laid it down and looked about for a supply of wet sand. The flames received this as a helpful attention, and made the most of it. They seemed to brighten and the twilight to deepen about them. The road was a flinty road in the chalk country, and ill-provided with sand.

Edna accosted a short, fat cyclist. "We want wet sand," she said, and added, "our motor's on fire." The short, fat cyclist stared blankly for a moment, then with a helpful cry began to scrabble in the road-grit. Whereupon Bert and Edna also scrabbled in the road-grit. Other cyclists arrived, dismounted and stood about, and their flame-lit faces expressed satisfaction, interest, curiosity. "Wet sand," said the short, fat man, scrabbling terribly—"wet sand." One joined him. They threw hard-earned handfuls of road-grit upon the flames, which accepted them with enthusiasm.

Grubb arrived, riding hard. He was shouting something. He sprang off and threw his bicycle into the hedge. "Don't throw water on it!" he said—"don't throw water on it!" He displayed commanding presence of mind. He became captain of the occasion. Others were glad to repeat the things he said and imitate his actions.

"Don't throw water on it!" they cried. Also there was no water.

"Beat it out, you fools!" he said.

He seized a rug from the trailer (it was an Austrian blanket, and Bert's winter coverlet) and began to beat at the burning petrol. For a wonderful minute he seemed to succeed. But he scattered burning pools of petrol on the road, and others, fired by his enthusiasm, imitated his action. Bert caught up a trailer-cushion and began to beat; there was another cushion and a table-cloth, and these also were seized. A young hero pulled off his jacket and joined the beating. For a moment there was less talking than hard breathing, and a tremendous flapping. Flossie, arriving on the outskirts of the crowd, cried, "Oh, my God!" and burst loudly into tears. "Help!" she said, and "Fire!"

The lame motor-car arrived, and stopped in consternation. A tall, goggled, grey-haired man who was driving inquired with an Oxford intonation and a clear, careful enunciation, "Can *we* help at all?"

It became manifest that the rug, the table-cloth, the cushions, the jacket, were getting smeared with petrol and burning. The soul seemed to go out of the cushion Bert was swaying, and the air was full of feathers, like a snowstorm in the still twilight.

Bert had got very dusty and sweaty and strenuous. It seemed to him his weapon had been wrested from him at the moment of victory. The fire lay like a dying thing, close to the ground and wicked; it gave a leap of anguish at every whack of the beaters. But now Grubb had gone off to stamp out the burning blanket; the others were lacking just at the moment of victory. One had dropped the cushion and was running to the motor-car. " *'Ere!*" cried Bert; "keep on!"

He flung the deflated burning rags of cushion aside, whipped off his jacket and sprang at the flames with a shout. He stamped into the ruin until flames ran up his boots. Edna saw him, a red-lit hero, and thought it was good to be a man.

A bystander was hit by a hot halfpenny flying out of the air. Then Bert thought of the papers in his pockets, and staggered back, trying to extinguish his burning jacket—checked, repulsed, dismayed.

Edna was struck by the benevolent appearance of an elderly spectator in a silk hat and Sabbatical garments. "Oh!" she cried to him. "Help this young man! How can you stand and see it?"

A cry of "The tarpauling!" arose.

An earnest-looking man in a very light grey cycling-suit had suddenly appeared at the side of the lame motor-car and addressed the owner. "Have you a tarpauling?" he said.

"Yes," said the gentlemanly man. "Yes. We've got a tarpauling."

"That's it," said the earnest-looking man, suddenly shouting. "Let's have it, quick!"

The gentlemanly man, with feeble and deprecatory gestures, and in the manner of a hypnotised person, produced an excellent large tarpauling.

"Here!" cried the earnest-looking man to Grubb. "Ketch holt!"

Then everybody realised that a new method was to be tried. A number of willing hands seized upon the Oxford gentleman's tarpauling. The others stood away with approving noises. The tarpauling was held over the burning bicycle like a canopy, and then smothered down upon it.

"We ought to have done this before," panted Grubb.

There was a moment of triumph. The flames vanished. Every one who could contrive to do so touched the edge of the tarpauling. Bert held down a corner with two hands and a foot. The tarpauling, bulged up in the centre, seemed to be suppressing triumphant exultation. Then its self-approval became too much for it; it burst into a bright red smile in the centre. It was exactly like the opening of a mouth. It laughed with a gust of flames. They were reflected redly in the observant goggles of the gentleman who owned the tarpauling. Everybody recoiled.

"Save the trailer!" cried some one, and that was the last round in the battle. But the trailer could not be detached; its wicker-work had caught, and it was the last thing to burn. A sort of hush fell upon the gathering. The petrol burnt low, the wicker-work trailer banged and crackled. The crowd divided itself into an outer circle of critics, advisers, and secondary characters, who had played undistinguished parts or no parts at all in the affair, and a central group of heated and distressed principals. A young man with an inquiring mind and a considerable knowledge of motor-bicycles fixed on to Grubb and wanted to argue that the thing could not have happened. Grubb was short and inattentive with him, and the young

man withdrew to the back of the crowd, and there told the benevolent old gentleman in the silk hat that people who went out with machines they didn't understand had only themselves to blame if things went wrong.

The old gentleman let him talk for some time, and then remarked, in a tone of rapturous enjoyment: "Stone deaf," and added, "Nasty things."

A rosy-faced man in a straw hat claimed attention. "I *did* save the front wheel," he said; "you'd have had that tyre catch, too, if I hadn't kept turning it round." It became manifest that this was so. The front wheel had retained its tyre, was intact, was still rotating slowly among the blackened and twisted ruins of the rest of the machine. It had something of that air of conscious virtue, of unimpeachable respectability, that distinguishes a rent collector in a low neighbourhood. "That wheel's worth a pound," said the rosy-faced man, making a song of it. "I kep' turning it round."

Newcomers kept arriving from the south with the question, "What's up?" until it got on Grubb's nerves. Londonward the crowd was constantly losing people; they would mount their various wheels with the satisfied manner of spectators who have had the best. Their voices would recede into the twilight; one would hear a laugh at the memory of this particularly salient incident or that.

"I'm afraid," said the gentleman of the motor-car, "my tarpauling's a bit done for."

Grubb admitted that the owner was the best judge of that.

"Nothin, else I can do for you?" said the gentleman of the motor-car, it may be with a suspicion of irony.

Bert was roused to action. "Look here," he said. "There's my young lady. If she ain't 'ome by ten they lock her out. See? Well, all my money was in my jacket pocket, and it's all mixed up with the burnt stuff, and that's too 'ot to touch. *Is* Clapham out of your way?"

"All in the day's work," said the gentleman with the motor-

car, and turned to Edna. "Very pleased indeed," he said, "if you'll come with us. We're late for dinner as it is, so it won't make much difference for us to go home by way of Clapham. We've got to get to Surbiton, anyhow. I'm afraid you'll find us a little slow."

"But what's Bert going to do?" said Edna.

"I don't know that we can accommodate Bert," said the motor-car gentleman, "though we're tremendously anxious to oblige."

"You couldn't take the whole lot?" said Bert, waving his hand at the deboshed and blackened ruins on the ground.

"I'm awfully afraid I can't," said the Oxford man. "Awfully sorry, you know."

"Then I'll have to stick 'ere for a bit," said Bert. "I got to see the thing through. You go on, Edna."

"Don't like leavin' you, Bert."

"You can't 'elp it, Edna.". . .

The last Edna saw of Bert was his figure, in charred and blackened shirtsleeves, standing in the dusk. He was musing deeply by the mixed ironwork and ashes of his vanished motor-bicycle, a melancholy figure. His retinue of spectators had shrunk now to half a dozen figures. Flossie and Grubb were preparing to follow her desertion.

"Cheer up, old Bert!" cried Edna, with artificial cheerfulness. "So long."

"So long, Edna," said Bert.

"See you to-morrer."

"See you to-morrer," said Bert, though he was destined, as a matter of fact, to see much of the habitable globe before he saw her again.

Bert began to light matches from a borrowed boxful, and search for a half-crown that still eluded him among the charred remains.

His face was grave and melancholy.

"I *wish* that 'adn't 'appened," said Flossie, riding on with Grubb. . . .

And at last Bert was left almost alone, a sad, blackened Promethean figure, cursed by the gift of fire. He had entertained vague ideas of hiring a cart, of achieving miraculous repairs, of still snatching some residual value from his one chief possession. Now, in the darkening night, he perceived the vanity of such intentions. Truth came to him bleakly, and laid her chill conviction upon him. He took hold of the handle-bar, stood the thing up, tried to push it forward. The tyreless hind-wheel was jammed hopelessly, even as he feared. For a minute or so he stood upholding his machine, a motionless despair. Then with a great effort he thrust the ruins from him into the ditch, kicked at it once, regarded it for a moment, and turned his face resolutely Londonward.

He did not once look back.

"That's the end of *that* game!" said Bert. "No more teuf-teuf-teuf for Bert Smallways for a year or two. Good-bye 'olidays!. . . Oh! I ought to 'ave sold the blasted thing when I had a chance three years ago."

§3

The next morning found the firm of Grubb & Smallways in a state of profound despondency. It seemed a small matter to them that the newspaper and cigarette shop opposite displayed such placards as this:—

REPORTED AMERICAN ULTIMATUM

BRITAIN MUST FIGHT

OUR INFATUATED WAR OFFICE STILL REFUSES
TO LISTEN TO MR. BUTTERIDGE

GREAT MONO-RAIL DISASTER AT TIMBUCTOO

or this:—

WAR A QUESTION OF HOURS

NEW YORK CALM

EXCITEMENT IN BERLIN

or again:—

WASHINGTON STILL SILENT

WHAT WILL PARIS DO?

THE PANIC ON THE BOURSE

THE KING'S GARDEN PARTY TO THE MASKED TWAREGS

MR. BUTTERIDGE MAKES AN OFFER

LATEST BETTING FROM TEHERAN

or this:—

WILL AMERICA FIGHT?

ANTI-GERMAN RIOT IN BAGDAD.

THE MUNICIPAL SCANDALS AT DAMASCUS

MR. BUTTERIDGE'S INVENTION FOR AMERICA

Bert stared at these over the card of pump-clips in the pane in the door with unseeing eyes. He wore a blackened flannel shirt, and the jacketless ruins of the holiday suit of yesterday. The

boarded-up shop was dark and depressing beyond words, the few scandalous hiring machines had never looked so hopelessly disreputable. He thought of their fellows who were "out," and of the approaching disputations of the afternoon. He thought of their new landlord, and of their old landlord, and of bills and claims. Life presented itself for the first time as a hopeless fight against fate. . . .

"Grubb, O' man," he said, distilling the quintessence, "I'm fair sick of this shop."

"So'm I," said Grubb.

"I'm out of conceit with it. I don't seem to care ever to speak to a customer again."

"There's that trailer," said Grubb, after a pause.

"Blow the trailer!" said Bert. "Anyhow, I didn't leave a deposit on it. I didn't do that. Still—"

He turned round on his friend. "Look 'ere," he said, "we aren't gettin' on here. We been losing money hand over fist. We got things tied up in fifty knots."

"What can we do?" said Grubb.

"Clear out. Sell what we can for what it will fetch, and quit. See? It's no good 'anging on to a losing concern. No sort of good. Jest foolishness."

"That's all right," said Grubb—"that's all right; but it ain't your capital been sunk in it."

"No need for us to sink after our capital," said Bert, ignoring the point.

"I'm not going to be held responsible for that trailer, anyhow. That ain't my affair."

"Nobody arst you to make it your affair. If you like to stick on here, well and good. I'm quitting. I'll see Bank Holiday through, and then I'm O-R-P-H. See?"

"Leavin' me?"

"Leavin' you. If you must be left."

Grubb looked round the shop. It certainly had become distasteful. Once upon a time it had been bright with hope and

new beginnings and stock and the prospect of credit. Now—now it was failure and dust. Very likely the landlord would be round presently to go on with the row about the window. . . . "Where d'you think of going, Bert?" Grubb asked.

Bert turned round and regarded him. "I thought it out as I was walking 'ome, and in bed. I couldn't sleep a wink."

"What did you think out?"

"Plans."

"What plans?"

"Oh! You're for sticking here."

"Not if anything better was to offer."

"It's only an ideer," said Bert.

"You made the girls laugh yestiday, that song you sang."

"Seems a long time ago now," said Grubb.

"And old Edna nearly cried—over that bit of mine."

"She got a fly in her eye," said Grubb; "I saw it. But what's this got to do with your plan?"

"No end," said Bert.

" 'Ow?"

"Don't you see?"

"Not singing in the streets?"

"Streets! No fear! But 'ow about the Tour of the Waterin' Places of England, Grubb? Singing! Young men of family doing it for a lark? You ain't got a bad voice, you know, and mine's all right. I never see a chap singing on the beach yet that I couldn't 'ave sung into a cocked hat. And we both know how to put on the toff a bit. Eh? Well, that's my ideer. Me and you, Grubb, with a refined song and a breakdown. Like we was doing for foolery yestiday. That was what put it into my 'ead. Easy make up a programme—easy. Six choice items, and one or two for encores and patter. I'm all right for the patter anyhow."

Grubb remained regarding his darkened and disheartening shop; he thought of his former landlord and his present landlord, and of the general disgustingness of business in an age which re-echoes to The Bitter Cry of the Middle Class;

and then it seemed to him that afar off he heard the twankle, twankle of a banjo, and the voice of a stranded siren singing. He had a sense of hot sunshine upon sand, of the children of at least transiently opulent holiday makers in a circle round about him, of the whisper, "They are really gentlemen," and then dollop, dollop came the coppers in the hat. Sometimes even silver. It was all income; no outgoings, no bills. "I'm on, Bert," he said.

"Right O!" said Bert, and, "Now we shan't be long."

"We needn't start without capital neither," said Grubb. "If we take the best of these machines up to the Bicycle Mart in Finsbury we'd raise six or seven pounds on 'em. We could easy do that to-morrow before anybody much was about. . . ."

"Nice to think of old Suet-and-Bones coming round to make his usual row with us, and finding a card up 'Closed for Repairs.'"

"We'll do that," said Grubb with zest—"we'll do that. And we'll put up another notice, and jest arst all inquirers to go round to 'im and inquire. See? Then they'll know all about us."

Before the day was out the whole enterprise was planned. They decided at first that they would call themselves the Naval Mr. O's, a plagiarism, and not perhaps a very good one, from the title of the well-known troupe of "Scarlet Mr. E's," and Bert rather clung to the idea of a uniform of bright blue serge, with a lot of gold lace and cord and ornamentation, rather like a naval officer's, but more so. But that had to be abandoned as impracticable, it would have taken too much time and money to prepare. They perceived they must wear some cheaper and more readily prepared costume, and Grubb fell back on white dominoes. They entertained the notion for a time of selecting the two worst machines from the hiring-stock, painting them over with crimson enamel paint, replacing the bells by the loudest sort of motor-horn, and doing a ride about to begin and end the entertainment. They doubted the advisability of this step.

"There's people in the world," said Bert, "who wouldn't

recognise us, who'd know them bicycles again like a shot, and we don't want to go on with no old stories. We want a fresh start."

"*I* do," said Grubb, "badly."

"We want to forget things—and cut all these rotten old worries. They ain't doin' us good."

Nevertheless, they decided to take the risk of these bicycles, and they decided their costumes should be brown stockings and sandals, and cheap unbleached sheets with a hole cut in the middle, and wigs and beards of tow. The rest their normal selves! "The Desert Dervishes," they would call themselves, and their chief songs would be those popular ditties, "In my Trailer," and "What Price Hair-pins Now?"

They decided to begin with small seaside places, and gradually, as they gained confidence, attack larger centres. To begin with they selected Littlestone in Kent, chiefly because of its unassuming name.

So they planned, and it seemed a small and unimportant thing to them that as they clattered the governments of half the world and more were drifting into war. About midday they became aware of the first of the evening-paper placards shouting to them across the street:—

THE WAR-CLOUD DARKENS

Nothing else but that.

"Always rottin' about war now," said Bert.

"They'll get it in the neck in real earnest one of these days, if they ain't precious careful."

§4

So you will understand the sudden apparition that surprised rather than delighted the quiet informality of Dymchurch sands. Dymchurch was one of the last places on the coast of England to be reached by the mono-rail, and so its spacious sands were still, at the time of this story, the secret and delight of quite a limited number of people. They went there to flee vulgarity and extravagances, and to bathe and sit and talk and play with their children in peace, and the Desert Dervishes did not please them at all.

The two white figures on scarlet wheels came upon them out of the infinite along the sands from Littlestone, grew nearer and larger and more audible, honk-honking and emitting weird cries, and generally threatening liveliness of the most aggressive type. "Good heavens!" said Dymchurch, "what's this?"

Then our young men, according to a preconcerted plan, wheeled round from file to line, dismounted and stood it attention. "Ladies and gentlemen," they said, "we beg to present ourselves—the Desert Dervishes." They bowed profoundly.

The few scattered groups upon the beach regarded them with horror for the most part, but some of the children and young people were interested and drew nearer. "There ain't a bob on the beach," said Grubb in an undertone, and the Desert Dervishes plied their bicycles with comic "business," that got a laugh from one very unsophisticated little boy. Then they took a deep breath and struck into the cheerful strain of "What Price Hair-pins Now?" Grubb sang the song, Bert did his best to make the chorus a rousing one, and it the end of each verse they danced certain steps, skirts in hand, that they had carefully rehearsed.

> *"Ting-a-ling-a-ting-a-ling-a-ting-a-ling-a-tang. . .*
> *What Price Hair-pins Now?"*

So they chanted and danced their steps in the sunshine on Dymchurch beach, and the children drew near these foolish young men, marvelling that they should behave in this way, and the older people looked cold and unfriendly.

All round the coasts of Europe that morning banjos were ringing, voices were bawling and singing, children were playing in the sun, pleasure-boats went to and fro; the common abundant

life of the time, unsuspicious of all dangers that gathered darkly against it, flowed on its cheerful aimless way. In the cities men fussed about their businesses and engagements. The newspaper placards that had cried "wolf!" so often, cried "wolf!" now in vain.

§5

Now as Bert and Grubb bawled their chorus for the third time, they became aware of a very big, golden-brown balloon low in the sky to the north-west, and coming rapidly towards them. "Jest as we're gettin' hold of 'em," muttered Grubb, "up comes a counter-attraction. Go it, Bert!"

> *"Ting-a-ling-a-ting-a-ling-a-ting-a-ling-a-tang. . .*
> *What Price Hair-pins Now?"*

The balloon rose and fell, went out of sight—"landed, thank goodness," said Grubb—re-appeared with a leap. " *'eng!*" said Grubb. "Step it, Bert, or they'll see it!"

They finished their dance, and then stood frankly staring.

"There's something wrong with that balloon," said Bert.

Everybody now was looking at the balloon, drawing rapidly nearer before a brisk north-westerly breeze. The song and dance were a "dead frost." Nobody thought any more about it. Even Bert and Grubb forgot it, and ignored the next item on the programme altogether. The balloon was bumping as though its occupants were trying to land; it would approach, sinking slowly, touch the ground, and instantly jump fifty feet or so in the air and immediately begin to fall again. Its car touched a clump of trees, and the black figure that had been struggling in the ropes fell back, or jumped back, into the car. In another moment it was quite close. It seemed a huge affair, as big as a house, and it floated down swiftly towards the sands; a long rope trailed behind it, and enormous shouts came from the man in the car. He seemed to be taking off his clothes, then his head came over the side of the car. "Catch hold of the rope!" they heard, quite plain.

"Salvage, Bert!" cried Grubb, and started to head off the rope.

Bert followed him, and collided, without upsetting, with a fisherman bent upon a similar errand. A woman carrying a baby in her arms, two small boys with toy spades, and a stout gentleman in flannels all got to the trailing rope at about the same time, and began to dance over it in their attempts to secure it. Bert came up to this wriggling, elusive serpent and got his foot on it, went down on all fours and achieved a grip. In half a dozen seconds the whole diffused population of the beach had, as it were, crystallised on the rope, and was pulling against the balloon under the vehement and stimulating directions of the man in the car. "Pull, I tell you!" said the man in the car—"pull!"

For a second or so the balloon obeyed its momentum and the wind and tugged its human anchor seaward. It dropped, touched the water, and made a flat, silvery splash, and recoiled as one's finger recoils when one touches anything hot. "Pull her in," said the man in the car. "*She's fainted!*"

He occupied himself with some unseen object while the people on the rope pulled him in. Bert was nearest the balloon, and much excited and interested. He kept stumbling over the tail of the Dervish costume in his zeal. He had never imagined before what a big, light, wallowing thing a balloon was. The car was of brown coarse wicker-work, and comparatively small. The rope he tugged at was fastened to a stout-looking ring, four or five feet above the car. At each tug he drew in a yard or so of rope, and the waggling wicker-work was drawn so much nearer. Out of the car came wrathful bellowings: "Fainted, she has!" and then: "It's her heart—broken with all she's had to go through."

The balloon ceased to struggle, and sank downward. Bert dropped the rope, and ran forward to catch it in a new place. In another moment he had his hand on the car. "Lay hold of it," said the man in the car, and his face appeared close to Bert's—a strangely familiar face, fierce eyebrows, a flattish nose, a huge black moustache. He had discarded coat and waistcoat—perhaps

with some idea of presently having to swim for his life—and his black hair was extraordinarily disordered. "Will all you people get hold round the car?" he said. "There's a lady here fainted—or got failure of the heart. Heaven alone knows which! My name is Butteridge. Butteridge, my name is—in a balloon. Now please, all on to the edge. This is the last time I trust myself to one of these paleolithic contrivances. The ripping-cord failed, and the valve wouldn't act. If ever I meet the scoundrel who ought to have seen—"

He stuck his head out between the ropes abruptly, and said, in a note of earnest expostulation: "Get some brandy!—some neat brandy!" Some one went up the beach for it.

In the car, sprawling upon a sort of bed-bench, in an attitude of elaborate self-abandonment, was a large, blond lady, wearing a fur coat and a big floriferous hat. Her head lolled back against the padded corner of the car, and her eyes were shut and her mouth open. "Me dear!" said Mr. Butteridge, in a common, loud voice, "we're safe!"

She gave no sign.

"Me dear!" said Mr. Butteridge, in a greatly intensified loud voice, "we're safe!"

She was still quite impassive.

Then Mr. Butteridge showed the fiery core of his soul. "If she is dead," he said, slowly lifting a fist towards the balloon above him, and speaking in an immense tremulous bellow—"if she is dead, I will r-r-rend the heavens like a garment! I must get her out," he cried, his nostrils dilated with emotion—"I must get her out. I cannot have her die in a wicker-work basket nine feet square—she who was made for kings' palaces! Keep holt of this car! Is there a strong man among ye to take her if I hand her out?"

He swept the lady together by a powerful movement of his arms, and lifted her. "Keep the car from jumping," he said to those who clustered about him. "Keep your weight on it. She is no light woman, and when she is out of it—it will be relieved."

Bert leapt lightly into a sitting position on the edge of the car. The others took a firmer grip upon the ropes and ring.

"Are you ready?" said Mr. Butteridge.

He stood upon the bed-bench and lifted the lady carefully. Then he sat down on the wicker edge opposite to Bert, and put one leg over to dangle outside. A rope or so seemed to incommode him. "Will some one assist me?" he said. "If they would take this lady?"

It was just at this moment, with Mr. Butteridge and the lady balanced finely on the basket brim, that she came-to. She came-to suddenly and violently with a loud, heart-rending cry of "Alfred! Save me!" And she waved her arms searchingly, and then clasped Mr. Butteridge about.

It seemed to Bert that the car swayed for a moment and then buck-jumped and kicked him. Also he saw the boots of the lady and the right leg of the gentleman describing arcs through the air, preparatory to vanishing over the side of the car. His impressions were complex, but they also comprehended the fact that he had lost his balance, and was going to stand on his head inside this creaking basket. He spread out clutching arms. He did stand on his head, more or less, his tow-beard came off and got in his mouth, and his cheek slid along against padding. His nose buried itself in a bag of sand. The car gave a violent lurch, and became still.

"Confound it!" he said.

He had an impression he must be stunned because of a surging in his ears, and because all the voices of the people about him had become small and remote. They were shouting like elves inside a hill.

He found it a little difficult to get on his feet. His limbs were mixed up with the garments Mr. Butteridge had discarded when that gentleman had thought he must needs plunge into the sea. Bert bawled out half angry, half rueful, "You might have said you were going to tip the basket." Then he stood up and clutched the ropes of the car convulsively.

Below him, far below him, shining blue, were the waters of the English Channel. Far off, a little thing in the sunshine, and rushing down as if some one was bending it hollow, was the beach and the irregular cluster of houses that constitutes Dymchurch. He could see the little crowd of people he had so abruptly left. Grubb, in the white wrapper of a Desert Dervish, was running along the edge of the sea. Mr. Butteridge was knee-deep in the water, bawling immensely. The lady was sitting up with her floriferous hat in her lap, shockingly neglected. The beach, east and west, was dotted with little people—they seemed all heads and feet—looking up. And the balloon, released from the twenty-five stone or so of Mr. Butteridge and his lady, was rushing up into the sky at the pace of a racing motor-car. "My crikey!" said Bert; "here's a go!"

He looked down with a pinched face at the receding beach, and reflected that he wasn't giddy; then he made a superficial survey of the cords and ropes about him with a vague idea of "doing something." "I'm not going to mess about with the thing," he said at last, and sat down upon the mattress. "I'm not going to touch it. . . . I wonder what one ought to do?"

Soon he got up again and stared for a long time at the sinking world below, at white cliffs to the east and flattening marsh to the left, at a minute wide prospect of weald and downland, at dim towns and harbours, and rivers and ribbon-like roads, at ships and ships' decks and foreshortened funnels upon the ever-widening sea, and at the great mono-rail bridge that straddled the Channel from Folkestone to Boulogne, until at last, first little wisps and then a veil of filmy cloud hid the prospect from his eyes. He wasn't at all giddy nor very much frightened, only in a state of enormous consternation.

Chapter III.

THE BALLOON

§1

Bert Smallways was a vulgar little creature, the sort of pert, limited soul that the old civilisation of the early twentieth century produced by the million in every country of the world. He had lived all his life in narrow streets, and between mean houses he could not look over, and in a narrow circle of ideas from which there was no escape. He thought the whole duty of man was to be smarter than his fellows, get his hands, as he put it, "on the dibs," and have a good time. He was, in fact, the sort of man who had made England and America what they were. The luck had been against him so far, but that was by the way. He was a mere aggressive and acquisitive individual with no sense of the State, no habitual loyalty, no devotion, no code of honour, no code even of courage. Now by a curious accident he found himself lifted out of his marvellous modern world for a time, out of all the rush and confused appeals of it, and floating like a thing dead and disembodied between sea and sky. It was as if Heaven was experimenting with him, had picked him out as a sample from the English millions, to look at him more nearly, and to see what was happening to the soul of man. But what Heaven made of him in that case I cannot profess to imagine, for I have long since abandoned all theories about the ideals and satisfactions of Heaven.

To be alone in a balloon at a height of fourteen or fifteen thousand feet—and to that height Bert Smallways presently rose is like nothing else in human experience. It is one of the supreme things possible to man. No flying machine can ever better it. It is to pass extraordinarily out of human things. It is

to be still and alone to an unprecedented degree. It is solitude without the suggestion of intervention; it is calm without a single irrelevant murmur. It is to see the sky. No sound reaches one of all the roar and jar of humanity, the air is clear and sweet beyond the thought of defilement. No bird, no insect comes so high. No wind blows ever in a balloon, no breeze rustles, for it moves with the wind and is itself a part of the atmosphere. Once started, it does not rock nor sway; you cannot feel whether it rises or falls. Bert felt acutely cold, but he wasn't mountain-sick; he put on the coat and overcoat and gloves Butteridge had discarded—put them over the "Desert Dervish" sheet that covered his cheap best suit—and sat very still for a long, time, overawed by the new-found quiet of the world. Above him was the light, translucent, billowing globe of shining brown oiled silk and the blazing sunlight and the great deep blue dome of the sky.

Below, far below, was a torn floor of sunlit cloud slashed by enormous rents through which he saw the sea.

If you had been watching him from below, you would have seen his head, a motionless little black knob, sticking out from the car first of all for a long time on one side, and then vanishing to reappear after a time at some other point.

He wasn't in the least degree uncomfortable nor afraid. He did think that as this uncontrollable thing had thus rushed up the sky with him it might presently rush down again, but this consideration did not trouble him very much. Essentially his state was wonder. There is no fear nor trouble in balloons—until they descend.

"Gollys!" he said at last, feeling a need for talking; "it's better than a motor-bike."

"It's all right!"

"I suppose they're telegraphing about, about me.". . .

The second hour found him examining the equipment of the car with great particularity. Above him was the throat of the balloon bunched and tied together, but with an open

lumen through which Bert could peer up into a vast, empty, quiet interior, and out of which descended two fine cords of unknown import, one white, one crimson, to pockets below the ring. The netting about the balloon-ended in cords attached to the ring, a big steel-bound hoop to which the car was slung by ropes. From it depended the trail rope and grapnel, and over the sides of the car were a number of canvas bags that Bert decided must be ballast to "chuck down" if the balloon fell. ("Not much falling just yet," said Bert.)

There were an aneroid and another box-shaped instrument hanging from the ring. The latter had an ivory plate bearing "statoscope" and other words in French, and a little indicator quivered and waggled, between *Montee* and *Descente.* "That's all right," said Bert. "That tells if you're going up or down." On the crimson padded seat of the balloon there lay a couple of rugs and a Kodak, and in opposite corners of the bottom of the car were an empty champagne bottle and a glass. "Refreshments," said Bert meditatively, tilting the empty bottle. Then he had a brilliant idea. The two padded bed-like seats, each with blankets and mattress, he perceived, were boxes, and within he found Mr. Butteridge's conception of an adequate equipment for a balloon ascent: a hamper which included a game pie, a Roman pie, a cold fowl, tomatoes, lettuce, ham sandwiches, shrimp sandwiches, a large cake, knives and forks and paper plates, self-heating tins of coffee and cocoa, bread, butter, and marmalade, several carefully packed bottles of champagne, bottles of Perrier water, and a big jar of water for washing, a portfolio, maps, and a compass, a rucksack containing a number of conveniences, including curling-tongs and hair-pins, a cap with ear-flaps, and so forth.

"A 'ome from 'ome," said Bert, surveying this provision as he tied the ear-flaps under his chin. He looked over the side of the car. Far below were the shining clouds. They had thickened so that the whole world was hidden. Southward they were piled in great snowy masses, so that he was half disposed to think them

mountains; northward and eastward they were in wavelike levels, and blindingly sunlit.

"Wonder how long a balloon keeps up?" he said.

He imagined he was not moving, so insensibly did the monster drift with the air about it. "No good coming down till we shift a bit," he said.

He consulted the statoscope.

"Still Monty," he said.

"Wonder what would happen if you pulled a cord?"

"No," he decided. "I ain't going to mess it about."

Afterwards he did pull both the ripping- and the valve-cords, but, as Mr. Butteridge had already discovered, they had fouled a fold of silk in the throat. Nothing happened. But for that little hitch the ripping-cord would have torn the balloon open as though it had been slashed by a sword, and hurled Mr. Smallways to eternity at the rate of some thousand feet a second. "No go!" he said, giving it a final tug. Then he lunched.

He opened a bottle of champagne, which, as soon as he cut the wire, blew its cork out with incredible violence, and for the most part followed it into space. Bert, however, got about a tumblerful. "Atmospheric pressure," said Bert, finding a use at last for the elementary physiography of his seventh-standard days. "I'll have to be more careful next time. No good wastin' drink."

Then he routed about for matches to utilise Mr. Butteridge's cigars; but here again luck was on his side, and he couldn't find any wherewith to set light to the gas above him. Or else he would have dropped in a flare, a splendid but transitory pyrotechnic display. "'eng old Grubb!" said Bert, slapping unproductive pockets. "'e didn't ought to 'ave kep' my box. 'e's always sneaking matches."

He reposed for a time. Then he got up, paddled about, rearranged the ballast bags on the floor, watched the clouds for a time, and turned over the maps on the locker. Bert liked maps, and he spent some time in trying to find one of France or the Channel; but they were all British ordnance maps of English counties. That set him thinking about languages and trying to recall his seventh-standard French. "Je suis Anglais. C'est une méprise. Je suis arrivé par accident ici," he decided upon as convenient phrases. Then it occurred to him that he would entertain himself by reading Mr. Butteridge's letters and examining his pocket-book, and in this manner he whiled away the afternoon.

§2

He sat upon the padded locker, wrapped about very carefully, for the air, though calm, was exhilaratingly cold and clear. He was wearing first a modest suit of blue serge and all the unpretending underwear of a suburban young man of fashion, with sandal-like cycling-shoes and brown stockings drawn over his trouser ends; then the perforated sheet proper to a Desert Dervish; then the coat and waistcoat and big fur-trimmed overcoat of Mr. Butteridge; then a lady's large fur cloak, and round his knees a blanket. Over his head was a tow wig, surmounted by a large cap of Mr. Butteridge's with the flaps down over his ears. And some fur sleeping-boots of Mr. Butteridge's warmed his feet. The car of the balloon was small and neat, some bags of ballast the untidiest of its contents, and he had found a light folding-table and put it at his elbow, and on that was a glass with champagne. And about him, above and below, was space—such a clear emptiness and silence of space as only the aeronaut can experience.

He did not know where he might be drifting, or what might happen next. He accepted this state of affairs with a serenity creditable to the Smallways' courage, which one might reasonably have expected to be of a more degenerate and contemptible quality altogether. His impression was that he was bound to come down somewhere, and that then, if he wasn't smashed, some one, some "society" perhaps, would probably pack him and the balloon back to England. If not, he would ask very

firmly for the British Consul. "Le consuelo Britannique," he decided this would be. "Apportez moi à le consuelo Britannique, s'il vous plait," he would say, for he was by no means ignorant of French. In the meanwhile, he found the intimate aspects of Mr. Butteridge an interesting study.

There were letters of an entirely private character addressed to Mr. Butteridge, and among others several love-letters of a devouring sort in a large feminine hand. These are no business of ours, and one remarks with regret that Bert read them.

When he had read them he remarked, "Gollys!" in an awestricken tone, and then, after a long interval, "I wonder if that was her?

"Lord!"

He mused for a time.

He resumed his exploration of the Butteridge interior. It included a number of press cuttings of interviews and also several letters in German, then some in the same German handwriting, but in English. "Hul-*lo*!" said Bert.

One of the latter, the first he took, began with an apology to Butteridge for not writing to him in English before, and for the inconvenience and delay that had been caused him by that, and went on to matter that Bert found exciting in, the highest degree. "We can understand entirely the difficulties of your position, and that you shall possibly be watched at the present juncture.— But, sir, we do not believe that any serious obstacles will be put in your way if you wished to endeavour to leave the country and come to us with your plans by the customary routes—either via Dover, Ostend, Boulogne, or Dieppe. We find it difficult to think you are right in supposing yourself to be in danger of murder for your invaluable invention."

"Funny!" said Bert, and meditated.

Then he went through the other letters.

"They seem to want him to come," said Bert, "but they don't seem hurting themselves to get 'im. Or else they're shamming don't care to get his prices down.

"They don't quite seem to be the gov'ment," he reflected, after an interval. "It's more like some firm's paper. All this printed stuff at the top. *Drachenflieger. Drachenballons. Ballonstoffe. Kugelballons.* Greek to me.

"But he was trying to sell his blessed secret abroad. That's all right. No Greek about that! Gollys! Here *is* the secret!"

He tumbled off the seat, opened the locker, and had the portfolio open before him on the folding-table. It was full of drawings done in the peculiar flat style and conventional colours engineers adopt. And, in, addition there were some rather under-exposed photographs, obviously done by an amateur, at close quarters, of the actual machine's mutterings had made, in its shed near the Crystal Palace. Bert found he was trembling. "Lord" he said, "here am I and the whole blessed secret of flying—lost up here on the roof of everywhere.

"Let's see!" He fell to studying the drawings and comparing them with the photographs. They puzzled him. Half of them seemed to be missing. He tried to imagine how they fitted together, and found the effort too great for his mind.

"It's tryin'," said Bert. "I wish I'd been brought up to the engineering. If I could only make it out!"

He went to the side of the car and remained for a time staring with unseeing eyes at a huge cluster of great clouds—a cluster of slowly dissolving Monte Rosas, sunlit below. His attention was arrested by a strange black spot that moved over them. It alarmed him. It was a black spot moving slowly with him far below, following him down there, indefatigably, over the cloud mountains. Why should such a thing follow him? What could it be?. . .

He had an inspiration. "Uv course!" he said. It was the shadow of the balloon. But he still watched it dubiously for a time.

He returned to the plans on the table.

He spent a long afternoon between his struggles to understand them and fits of meditation. He evolved a remarkable new sentence in French.

"Voici, Mossoo!—Je suis un inventeur Anglais. Mon nom est Butteridge. Beh. oo. teh. teh. eh. arr. E. deh. ghe. eh. J'avais ici pour vendre le secret de le *flying-machine*. Comprenez? Vendre pour l'argent tout suite, l'argent en main. Comprenez? C'est le machine à jouer dans l'air. Comprenez? C'est le machine a faire l'oiseau. Comprenez? Balancer? Oui, exactement! Battir l'oiseau en fait, à son propre jeu. Je désire de vendre ceci à votre government national. Voulez vous me directer la?

"Bit rummy, I expect, from the point of view of grammar," said Bert, "but they ought to get the hang of it all right.

"But then, if they arst me to explain the blessed thing?"

He returned in a worried way to the plans. "I don't believe it's all here!" he said. . . .

He got more and more perplexed up there among the clouds as to what he should do with this wonderful find of his. At any moment, so far as he knew he might descend among he knew not what foreign people.

"It's the chance of my life!" he said.

It became more and more manifest to him that it wasn't. "Directly I come down they'll telegraph—put it in the papers. Butteridge'll know of it and come along—on my track."

Butteridge would be a terrible person to be on any one's track. Bert thought of the great black moustaches, the triangular nose, the searching bellow and the glare. His afternoon's dream of a marvellous seizure and sale of the great Butteridge secret crumpled up in his mind, dissolved, and vanished. He awoke to sanity again.

"Wouldn't do. What's the good of thinking of it?" He proceeded slowly and reluctantly to replace the Butteridge papers in pockets and portfolio as he had found them. He became aware of a splendid golden light upon the balloon above him, and of a new warmth in the blue dome of the sky. He stood up and beheld the sun, a great ball of blinding gold, setting upon a tumbled sea of gold-edged crimson and purple clouds, strange and wonderful beyond imagining. Eastward cloudland stretched for ever, darkling blue, and it seemed to Bert the whole round hemisphere of the world was under his eyes.

Then far, away over the blue he caught sight of three long, dark shapes like hurrying fish that drove one after the other, as porpoises follow one another in the water. They were very fish-like indeed—with tails. It was an unconvincing impression in that light. He blinked his eyes, stared again, and they had vanished. For a long time he scrutinised those remote blue levels and saw no more. . . .

"Wonder if I ever saw anything," he said, and then: "There ain't such things. . . ."

Down went the sun and down, not diving steeply, but passing northward as it sank, and then suddenly daylight and the expansive warmth of daylight had gone altogether, and the index of the statoscope quivered over to *Descente.*

§3

"*Now* what's going to 'appen?" said Bert.

He found the cold, grey cloud wilderness rising towards him with a wide, slow steadiness. As he sank down among them the clouds ceased to seem the snowclad mountain-slopes they had resembled heretofore, became unsubstantial, confessed an immense silent drift and eddy in their substance. For a moment, when he was nearly among their twilight masses, his descent was checked. Then abruptly the sky was hidden, the last vestiges of daylight gone, and he was falling rapidly in an evening twilight through a whirl of fine snowflakes that streamed past him towards the zenith, that drifted in upon the things about him and melted, that touched his face with ghostly fingers. He shivered. His breath came smoking from his lips, and everything was instantly bedewed and wet.

He had an impression of a snowstorm pouring with unexampled and increasing fury *upward*; then he realised that he was falling faster and faster.

Imperceptibly a sound grew upon his ears. The great silence of the world was at an end. What was this confused sound?

He craned his head over the side, concerned, perplexed.

First he seemed to see, and then not to see. Then he saw clearly little edges of foam pursuing each other, and a wide waste of weltering waters below him. Far away was a pilot boat with a big sail bearing dim black letters, and a little pinkish-yellow light, and it was rolling and pitching, rolling and pitching in a gale, while he could feel no wind at, all. Soon the sound of waters was loud and near. He was dropping, dropping—into the sea!

He became convulsively active.

"Ballast!" he cried, and seized a little sack from the floor, and heaved it overboard. He did not wait for the effect of that, but sent another after it. He looked over in time to see a minute white splash in the dim waters below him, and then he was back in the snow and clouds again.

He sent out quite needlessly a third sack of ballast and a fourth, and presently had the immense satisfaction of soaring up out of the damp and chill into the clear, cold, upper air in which the day still lingered. "Thang-God!" he said, with all his heart.

A few stars now had pierced the blue, and in the east there shone brightly a prolate moon.

§4

That first downward plunge filled Bert with a haunting sense of boundless waters below. It was a summer's night, but it seemed to him, nevertheless, extraordinarily long. He had a feeling of insecurity that he fancied quite irrationally the sunrise would dispel. Also he was hungry. He felt, in the dark, in the locker, put his fingers in the Roman pie, and got some sandwiches, and he also opened rather successfully a half-bottle of champagne. That warmed and restored him, he grumbled at Grubb about the matches, wrapped himself up warmly on the locker, and dozed for a time. He got up once or twice to make sure that he

was still securely high above the sea. The first time the moonlit clouds were white and dense, and the shadow of the balloon ran athwart them like a dog that followed; afterwards they seemed thinner. As he lay still, staring up at the huge dark balloon above, he made a discovery. His—or rather Mr. Butteridge's—waistcoat rustled as he breathed. It was lined with papers. But Bert could not see to get them out or examine them, much as he wished to do so. . . .

He was awakened by the crowing of cocks, the barking of dogs, and a clamour of birds. He was driving slowly at a low level over a broad land lit golden by sunrise under a clear sky. He stared out upon hedgeless, well-cultivated fields intersected by roads, each lined with cable-bearing red poles. He had just passed over a compact, whitewashed, village with a straight church tower and steep red-tiled roofs. A number of peasants, men and women, in shiny blouses and lumpish footwear, stood regarding him, arrested on their way to work. He was so low that the end of his rope was trailing.

He stared out at these people. "I wonder how you land," he thought.

"S'pose I *ought* to land?"

He found himself drifting down towards a mono-rail line, and hastily flung out two or three handfuls of ballast to clear it.

"Lemme see! One might say just 'Prenez'! Wish I knew the French for take hold of the rope!. . . I suppose they are French?"

He surveyed the country again. "Might be Holland. Or Luxembourg. Or Lorraine 's far as *I* know. Wonder what those big affairs over there are? Some sort of kiln. Prosperous-looking country. . ."

The respectability of the country's appearance awakened answering chords in his nature.

"Make myself a bit ship-shape first," he said.

He resolved to rise a little and get rid of his wig (which now felt hot on his head), and so forth. He threw out a bag of ballast,

and was astonished to find himself careering up through the air very rapidly.

"Blow!" said Mr. Smallways. "I've over-done the ballast trick. . . . Wonder when I shall get down again?. . . brekfus' on board, anyhow."

He removed his cap and wig, for the air was warm, and an improvident impulse made him cast the latter object overboard. The statoscope responded with a vigorous swing to *Montée.*

"The blessed thing goes up if you only *look* overboard," he remarked, and assailed the locker. He found among other items several tins of liquid cocoa containing explicit directions for opening that he followed with minute care. He pierced the bottom with the key provided in the holes indicated, and forthwith the can grew from cold to hotter and hotter, until at last he could scarcely touch it, and then he opened the can at the other end, and there was his cocoa smoking, without the use of match or flame of any sort. It was an old invention, but new to Bert. There was also ham and marmalade and bread, so that he had a really very tolerable breakfast indeed.

Then he took off his overcoat, for the sunshine was now inclined to be hot, and that reminded him of the rustling he had heard in the night. He took off the waistcoat and examined it. "Old Butteridge won't like me unpicking this." He hesitated, and finally proceeded to unpick it. He found the missing drawings of the lateral rotating planes, on which the whole stability of the flying machine depended.

An observant angel would have seen Bert sitting for a long time after this discovery in a state of intense meditation. Then at last he rose with an air of inspiration, took Mr. Butteridge's ripped, demolished, and ransacked waistcoat, and hurled it from the balloon whence it fluttered down slowly and eddyingly until at last it came to rest with a contented flop upon the face of German tourist sleeping peacefully beside the Hohenweg near Wildbad. Also this sent the balloon higher, and so into a position still more convenient for observation by our imaginary angel

who would next have seen Mr. Smallways tear open his own jacket and waistcoat, remove his collar, open his shirt, thrust his hand into his bosom, and tear his heart out—or at least, if not his heart, some large bright scarlet object. If the observer, overcoming a thrill of celestial horror, had scrutinised this scarlet object more narrowly, one of Bert's most cherished secrets, one of his essential weaknesses, would have been laid bare. It was a red-flannel chest-protector, one of those large quasi-hygienic objects that with pills and medicines take the place of beneficial relics and images among the Protestant peoples of Christendom. Always Bert wore this thing; it was his cherished delusion, based on the advice of a shilling fortune-teller at Margate, that he was weak in the lungs.

He now proceeded to unbutton his fetish, to attack it with a penknife, and to thrust the new-found plans between the two layers of imitation Saxony flannel of which it was made. Then with the help of Mr. Butteridge's small shaving mirror and his folding canvas basin he readjusted his costume with the gravity of a man who has taken an irrevocable step in life, buttoned up his jacket, cast the white sheet of the Desert Dervish on one side, washed temperately, shaved, resumed the big cap and the fur overcoat, and, much refreshed by these exercises, surveyed the country below him.

It was indeed a spectacle of incredible magnificence. If perhaps it was not so strange and magnificent as the sunlit cloudland of the previous day, it was at any rate infinitely more interesting. The air was at its utmost clearness and except to the south and south-west there was not a cloud in the sky. The country was hilly, with occasional fir plantations and bleak upland spaces, but also with numerous farms, and the hills were deeply intersected by the gorges of several winding rivers interrupted at intervals by the banked-up ponds and weirs of electric generating wheels. It was dotted with bright-looking, steep-roofed villages, and each showed a distinctive and interesting church beside its wireless telegraph steeple; here and there were large chateaux and parks

and white roads, and paths lined with red and white cable posts were extremely conspicuous in the landscape. There were walled enclosures like gardens and rickyards and great roofs of barns and many electric dairy centres. The uplands were mottled with cattle. At places he would see the track of one of the old railroads (converted now to mono-rails) dodging through tunnels and crossing embankments, and a rushing hum would mark the passing of a train. Everything was extraordinarily clear as well as minute. Once or twice he saw guns and soldiers, and was reminded of the stir of military preparations he had witnessed on the Bank Holiday in England; but there was nothing to tell him that these military preparations were abnormal or to explain an occasional faint irregular firing of guns that drifted up to him.

"Wish I knew how to get down," said Bert, ten thousand feet or so above it all, and gave himself to much futile tugging at the red and white cords. Afterwards he made a sort of inventory of the provisions. Life in the high air was giving him an appalling appetite, and it seemed to him discreet at this stage to portion out his supply into rations. So far as he could see he might pass a week in the air.

At first all the vast panorama below had been as silent as a painted picture. But as the day wore on and the gas diffused slowly from the balloon, it sank earthward again, details increased, men became more visible, and he began to hear the whistle and moan of trains and cars, sounds of cattle, bugles and kettle drums, and presently even men's voices. And at last his guide-rope was trailing again, and he found it possible to attempt a landing. Once or twice as the rope dragged over cables he found his hair erect with electricity, and once he had a slight shock, and sparks snapped about the car. He took these things among the chances of the voyage. He had one idea now very clear in his mind, and that was to drop the iron grapnel that hung from the ring.

From the first this attempt was unfortunate, perhaps because the place for descent was ill-chosen. A balloon should come down in an empty open space, and he chose a crowd. He made his decision suddenly, and without proper reflection. As he trailed, Bert saw ahead of him one of the most attractive little towns in the world—a cluster of steep gables surmounted by a high church tower and diversified with trees, walled, and with a fine, large gateway opening out upon a tree-lined high road. All the wires and cables of the country-side converged upon it like guests to entertainment. It had a most home-like and comfortable quality, and it was made gayer by abundant flags. Along the road a quantity of peasant folk, in big pair-wheeled carts and afoot, were coming and going, besides an occasional mono-rail car; and at the car-junction, under the trees outside the town, was a busy little fair of booths. It seemed a warm, human, well-rooted, and altogether delightful place to Bert. He came low over the tree-tops, with his grapnel ready to throw and so anchor him—a curious, interested, and interesting guest, so his imagination figured it, in the very middle of it all.

He thought of himself performing feats with the sign language and chance linguistics amidst a circle of admiring rustics. . . .

And then the chapter of adverse accidents began.

The rope made itself unpopular long before the crowd had fully realised his advent over the trees. An elderly and apparently intoxicated peasant in a shiny black hat, and carrying a large crimson umbrella, caught sight of it first as it trailed past him, and was seized with a discreditable ambition to kill it. He pursued it, briskly with unpleasant cries. It crossed the road obliquely, splashed into a pail of milk upon a stall, and slapped its milky tail athwart a motor-car load of factory girls halted outside the town gates. They screamed loudly. People looked up and saw Bert making what he meant to be genial salutations, but what they considered, in view of the feminine outcry, to be insulting gestures. Then the car hit the roof of the gatehouse smartly, snapped a flag staff, played a tune upon some telegraph wires, and sent a broken wire like a whip-lash to do its share in

accumulating unpopularity. Bert, by clutching convulsively, just escaped being pitched headlong. Two young soldiers and several peasants shouted things up to him and shook fists at him and began to run in pursuit as he disappeared over the wall into the town.

Admiring rustics, indeed!

The balloon leapt at once, in the manner of balloons when part of their weight is released by touching down, with a sort of flippancy, and in another moment Bert was over a street crowded with peasants and soldiers, that opened into a busy market-square. The wave of unfriendliness pursued him.

"Grapnel," said Bert, and then with an afterthought shouted, "*Têtes* there, you! I say! I say! *Têtes.* 'eng it!"

The grapnel smashed down a steeply sloping roof, followed by an avalanche of broken tiles, jumped the street amidst shrieks and cries, and smashed into a plate-glass window with an immense and sickening impact. The balloon rolled nauseatingly, and the car pitched. But the grapnel had not held. It emerged at once bearing on one fluke, with a ridiculous air of fastidious selection, a small child's chair, and pursued by a maddened shopman. It lifted its catch, swung about with an appearance of painful indecision amidst a roar of wrath, and dropped it at last neatly, and as if by inspiration, over the head of a peasant woman in charge of an assortment of cabbages in the market-place.

Everybody now was aware of the balloon. Everybody was either trying to dodge the grapnel or catch the trail rope. With a pendulum-like swoop through the crowd, that sent people flying right and left the grapnel came to earth again, tried for and missed a stout gentleman in a blue suit and a straw hat, smacked away a trestle from under a stall of haberdashery, made a cyclist soldier in knickerbockers leap like a chamois, and secured itself uncertainly among the hind-legs of a sheep—which made convulsive, ungenerous efforts to free itself, and was dragged into a position of rest against a stone cross in the middle of the place. The balloon pulled up with a jerk. In another moment a score of willing hands were tugging it earthward. At the same instant Bert became aware for the first time of a fresh breeze blowing about him.

For some seconds he stood staggering in the car, which now swayed sickeningly, surveying the exasperated crowd below him and trying to collect his mind. He was extraordinarily astonished at this run of mishaps. Were the people really so annoyed? Everybody seemed angry with him. No one seemed interested or amused by his arrival. A disproportionate amount of the outcry had the flavour of imprecation—had, indeed a strong flavour of riot. Several greatly uniformed officials in cocked hats struggled in vain to control the crowd. Fists and sticks were shaken. And when Bert saw a man on the outskirts of the crowd run to a haycart and get a brightly pronged pitch-fork, and a blue-clad soldier unbuckle his belt, his rising doubt whether this little town was after all such a good place for a landing became a certainty.

He had clung to the fancy that they would make something of a hero of him. Now he knew that he was mistaken.

He was perhaps ten feet above the people when he made his decision. His paralysis ceased. He leapt up on the seat, and, at imminent risk of falling headlong, released the grapnel-rope from the toggle that held it, sprang on to the trail rope and disengaged that also. A hoarse shout of disgust greeted the descent of the grapnel-rope and the swift leap of the balloon, and something—he fancied afterwards it was a turnip—whizzed by his head. The trail-rope followed its fellow. The crowd seemed to jump away from him. With an immense and horrifying rustle the balloon brushed against a telephone pole, and for a tense instant he anticipated either an electric explosion or a bursting of the oiled silk, or both. But fortune was with him.

In another second he was cowering in the bottom of the car, and released from the weight of the grapnel and the two ropes, rushing up once more through the air. For a time he remained

crouching, and when at last he looked out again the little town was very small and travelling, with the rest of lower Germany, in a circular orbit round and round the car—or at least it appeared to be doing that. When he got used to it, he found this rotation of the balloon rather convenient; it saved moving about in the car.

§5

Late in the afternoon of a pleasant summer day in the year 191-, if one may borrow a mode of phrasing that once found favour with the readers of the late G. P. R. James, a solitary balloonist—replacing the solitary horseman of the classic romances—might have been observed wending his way across Franconia in a north-easterly direction, and at a height of about eleven thousand feet above the sea and still spindling slowly. His head was craned over the side of the car, and he surveyed the country below with an expression of profound perplexity; ever and again his lips shaped inaudible words. "Shootin' at a chap," for example, and "I'll come down right enough soon as I find out 'ow." Over the side of the basket the robe of the Desert Dervish was hanging, an appeal for consideration, an ineffectual white flag.

He was now very distinctly aware that the world below him, so far from being the naive country-side of his earlier imaginings that day, sleepily unconscious of him and capable of being amazed and nearly reverential at his descent, was acutely irritated by his career, and extremely impatient with the course he was taking.—But indeed it was not he who took that course, but his masters, the winds of heaven. Mysterious voices spoke to him in his ear, jerking the words up to him by means of megaphones, in a weird and startling manner, in a great variety of languages. Official-looking persons had signalled to him by means of flag flapping and arm waving. On the whole a guttural variant of English prevailed in the sentences that alighted upon the balloon; chiefly he was told to "gome down or you will be shot."

"All very well," said Bert, "but *'ow?*"

Then they shot a little wide of the car. Latterly he had been shot at six or seven times, and once the bullet had gone by with a sound so persuasively like the tearing of silk that he had resigned himself to the prospect of a headlong fall. But either they were aiming near him or they had missed, and as yet nothing was torn but the air about him—and his anxious soul.

He was now enjoying a respite from these attentions, but he felt it was at best an interlude, and he was doing what he could to appreciate his position. Incidentally he was having some hot coffee and pie in an untidy inadvertent manner, with an eye fluttering nervously over the side of the car. At first he had ascribed the growing interest in his career to his ill-conceived attempt to land in the bright little upland town, but now he was beginning to realise that the military rather than the civil arm was concerned about him.

He was quite involuntarily playing that weird mysterious part—the part of an International Spy. He was seeing secret things. He had, in fact, crossed the designs of no less a power than the German Empire, he had blundered into the hot focus of Welt-Politik, he was drifting helplessly towards the great Imperial secret, the immense aeronautic park that had been established at a headlong pace in Franconia to develop silently, swiftly, and on an immense scale the great discoveries of Hunstedt and Stossel, and so to give Germany before all other nations a fleet of airships, the air power and the Empire of the world.

Later, just before they shot him down altogether, Bert saw that great area of passionate work, warm lit in the evening light, a great area of upland on which the airships lay like a herd of grazing monsters at their feed. It was a vast busy space stretching away northward as far as he could see, methodically cut up into numbered sheds, gasometers, squad encampments, storage areas, interlaced with the omnipresent mono-rail lines, and altogether free from overhead wires or cables. Everywhere was the white,

black and yellow of Imperial Germany, everywhere the black eagles spread their wings. Even without these indications, the large vigorous neatness of everything would have marked it German. Vast multitudes of men went to and fro, many in white and drab fatigue uniforms busy about the balloons, others drilling in sensible drab. Here and there a full uniform glittered. The airships chiefly engaged his attention, and he knew at once it was three of these he had seen on the previous night, taking advantage of the cloud welkin to manoeuvre unobserved. They were altogether fish-like. For the great airships with which Germany attacked New York in her last gigantic effort for world supremacy—before humanity realised that world supremacy was a dream—were the lineal descendants of the Zeppelin airship that flew over Lake Constance in 1906, and of the Lebaudy navigables that made their memorable excursions over Paris in 1907 and 1908.

These German airships were held together by rib-like skeletons of steel and aluminium and a stout inelastic canvas outer-skin, within which was an impervious rubber gas-bag, cut up by transverse dissepiments into from fifty to a hundred compartments. These were all absolutely gas tight and filled with hydrogen, and the entire aerostat was kept at any level by means of a long internal balloonette of oiled and toughened silk canvas, into which air could be forced and from which it could be pumped. So the airship could be made either heavier or lighter than air, and losses of weight through the consumption of fuel, the casting of bombs and so forth, could also be compensated by admitting air to sections of the general gas-bag. Ultimately that made a highly explosive mixture; but in all these matters risks must be taken and guarded against. There was a steel axis to the whole affair, a central backbone which terminated in the engine and propeller, and the men and magazines were forward in a series of cabins under the expanded headlike forepart. The engine, which was of the extraordinarily powerful Pforzheim type, that supreme triumph of German invention, was worked by wires from this forepart, which was indeed the only really habitable part of the ship. If anything went wrong, the engineers went aft along a rope ladder beneath the frame. The tendency of the whole affair to roll was partly corrected by a horizontal lateral fin on either side, and steering was chiefly effected by two vertical fins, which normally lay back like gill-flaps on either side of the head. It was indeed a most complete adaptation of the fish form to aerial conditions, the position of swimming bladder, eyes, and brain being, however, below instead of above. A striking, and unfish-like feature was the apparatus for wireless telegraphy that dangled from the forward cabin—that is to say, under the chin of the fish.

These monsters were capable of ninety miles an hour in a calm, so that they could face and make headway against nearly everything except the fiercest tornado. They varied in length from eight hundred to two thousand feet, and they had a carrying power of from seventy to two hundred tons. How many Germany possessed history does not record, but Bert counted nearly eighty great bulks receding in perspective during his brief inspection. Such were the instruments on which she chiefly relied to sustain her in her repudiation of the Monroe Doctrine and her bold bid for a share in the empire of the New World. But not altogether did she rely on these; she had also a one-man bomb-throwing *Drachenflieger* of unknown value among the resources.

But the *Drachenflieger* were away in the second great aeronautic park east of Hamburg, and Bert Smallways saw nothing of them in the bird's-eye view he took of the Franconian establishment before they shot him down very neatly. The bullet tore past him and made a sort of pop as it pierced his balloon—a pop that was followed by a rustling sigh and a steady downward movement. And when in the confusion of the moment he dropped a bag of ballast, the Germans, very politely but firmly overcame his scruples by shooting his balloon again twice.

Chapter IV

THE GERMAN AIR-FLEET

§1

Of all the productions of the human imagination that make the world in which Mr. Bert Smallways lived confusingly wonderful, there was none quite so strange, so headlong and disturbing, so noisy and persuasive and dangerous, as the modernisations of patriotism produced by imperial and international politics. In the soul of all men is a liking for kind, a pride in one's own atmosphere, a tenderness for one's mother speech and one's familiar land. Before the coming of the Scientific Age this group of gentle and noble emotions had been a fine factor in the equipment of every worthy human being, a fine factor that had its less amiable aspect in a usually harmless hostility to strange people, and a usually harmless detraction of strange lands. But with the wild rush of change in the pace, scope, materials, scale, and possibilities of human life that then occurred, the old boundaries, the old seclusions and separations were violently broken down. All the old settled mental habits and traditions of men found themselves not simply confronted by new conditions, but by constantly renewed and changing new conditions. They had no chance of adapting themselves. They were annihilated or perverted or inflamed beyond recognition.

Bert Smallways' grandfather, in the days when Bun Hill was a village under the sway of Sir Peter Bone's parent, had "known his place" to the uttermost farthing, touched his hat to his betters, despised and condescended to his inferiors, and hadn't changed an idea from the cradle to the grave. He was Kentish and English, and that meant hops, beer, dog-rose's, and the sort of sunshine that was best in the world. Newspapers and politics

and visits to "Lunnon" weren't for the likes of him. Then came the change. These earlier chapters have given an idea of what happened to Bun Hill, and how the flood of novel things had poured over its devoted rusticity. Bert Smallways was only one of countless millions in Europe and America and Asia who, instead of being born rooted in the soil, were born struggling in a torrent they never clearly understood. All the faiths of their fathers had been taken by surprise, and startled into the strangest forms and reactions. Particularly did the fine old tradition of patriotism get perverted and distorted in the rush of the new times. Instead of the sturdy establishment in prejudice of Bert's grandfather, to whom the word "Frenchified" was the ultimate term of contempt, there flowed through Bert's brain a squittering succession of thinly violent ideas about German competition, about the Yellow Danger, about the Black Peril, about the White Man's Burthen—that is to say, Bert's preposterous right to muddle further the naturally very muddled politics of the entirely similar little cads to himself (except for a smear of brown) who smoked cigarettes and rode bicycles in Buluwayo, Kingston (Jamaica), or Bombay. These were Bert's "Subject Races," and he was ready to die—by proxy in the person of any one who cared to enlist—to maintain his hold upon that right. It kept him awake at nights to think that he might lose it.

The essential fact of the politics of the age in which Bert Smallways lived—the age that blundered at last into the catastrophe of the War in the Air—was a very simple one, if only people had had the intelligence to be simple about it. The development of Science had altered the scale of human affairs. By means of rapid mechanical traction, it had brought men nearer together, so much nearer socially, economically, physically, that the old separations into nations and kingdoms were no longer possible, a newer, wider synthesis was not only needed, but imperatively demanded. Just as the once independent dukedoms of France had to fuse into a nation, so now the nations had to adapt themselves to a wider coalescence, they had to keep what

was precious and possible, and concede what was obsolete and dangerous. A saner world would have perceived this patent need for a reasonable synthesis, would have discussed it temperately, achieved and gone on to organise the great civilisation that was manifestly possible to mankind. The world of Bert Smallways did nothing of the sort. Its national governments, its national interests, would not hear of anything so obvious; they were too suspicious of each other, too wanting in generous imaginations. They began to behave like ill-bred people in a crowded public car, to squeeze against one another, elbow, thrust, dispute and quarrel. Vain to point out to them that they had only to rearrange themselves to be comfortable. Everywhere, all over the world, the historian of the early twentieth century finds the same thing, the flow and rearrangement of human affairs inextricably entangled by the old areas, the old prejudices and a sort of heated irascible stupidity, and everywhere congested nations in inconvenient areas, slopping population and produce into each other, annoying each other with tariffs, and every possible commercial vexation, and threatening each other with navies and armies that grew every year more portentous.

It is impossible now to estimate how much of the intellectual and physical energy of the world was wasted in military preparation and equipment, but it was an enormous proportion. Great Britain spent upon army and navy money and capacity, that directed into the channels of physical culture and education would have made the British the aristocracy of the world. Her rulers could have kept the whole population learning and exercising up to the age of eighteen and made a broad-chested and intelligent man of every Bert Smallways in the islands, had they given the resources they spent in war material to the making of men. Instead of which they waggled flags at him until he was fourteen, incited him to cheer, and then turned him out of school to begin that career of private enterprise we have compactly recorded. France achieved similar imbecilities; Germany was, if possible worse; Russia under the waste and stresses of militarism festered towards bankruptcy and decay. All Europe was producing big guns and countless swarms of little Smallways. The Asiatic peoples had been forced in self-defence into a like diversion of the new powers science had brought them. On the eve of the outbreak of the war there were six great powers in the world and a cluster of smaller ones, each armed to the teeth and straining every nerve to get ahead of the others in deadliness of equipment and military efficiency. The great powers were first the United States, a nation addicted to commerce, but roused to military necessities by the efforts of Germany to expand into South America, and by the natural consequences of her own unwary annexations of land in the very teeth of Japan. She maintained two immense fleets east and west, and internally she was in violent conflict between Federal and State governments upon the question of universal service in a defensive militia. Next came the great alliance of Eastern Asia, a close-knit coalescence of China and Japan, advancing with rapid strides year by year to predominance in the world's affairs. Then the German alliance still struggled to achieve its dream of imperial expansion, and its imposition of the German language upon a forcibly united Europe. These were the three most spirited and aggressive powers in the world. Far more pacific was the British Empire, perilously scattered over the globe, and distracted now by insurrectionary movements in Ireland and among all its Subject Races. It had given these subject races cigarettes, boots, bowler hats, cricket, race meetings, cheap revolvers, petroleum, the factory system of industry, halfpenny newspapers in both English and the vernacular, inexpensive university degrees, motor-bicycles and electric trams; it had produced a considerable literature expressing contempt for the Subject Races, and rendered it freely accessible to them, and it had been content to believe that nothing would result from these stimulants because somebody once wrote "the immemorial east"; and also, in the inspired words of Kipling—

East is east and west is west,
And never the twain shall meet.

Instead of which, Egypt, India, and the subject countries generally had produced new generations in a state of passionate indignation and the utmost energy, activity and modernity. The governing class in Great Britain was slowly adapting itself to a new conception, of the Subject Races as waking peoples, and finding its efforts to keep the Empire together under these strains and changing ideas greatly impeded by the entirely sporting spirit with which Bert Smallways at home (by the million) cast his vote, and by the tendency of his more highly coloured equivalents to be disrespectful to irascible officials. Their impertinence was excessive; it was no mere stone-throwing and shouting. They would quote Burns at them and Mill and Darwin and confute them in arguments.

Even more pacific than the British Empire were France and its allies, the Latin powers, heavily armed states indeed, but reluctant warriors, and in many ways socially and politically leading western civilisation. Russia was a pacific power perforce, divided within itself, torn between revolutionaries and reactionaries who were equally incapable of social reconstruction, and so sinking towards a tragic disorder of chronic political vendetta. Wedged in among these portentous larger bulks, swayed and threatened by them, the smaller states of the world maintained a precarious independence, each keeping itself armed as dangerously as its utmost ability could contrive.

So it came about that in every country a great and growing body of energetic and inventive men was busied either for offensive or defensive ends, in elaborating the apparatus of war, until the accumulating tensions should reach the breaking-point. Each power sought to keep its preparations secret, to hold new weapons in reserve, to anticipate and learn the preparations of its rivals. The feeling of danger from fresh discoveries affected the patriotic imagination of every people in the world. Now it was rumoured the British had an overwhelming gun, now the

French an invincible rifle, now the Japanese a new explosive, now the Americans a submarine that would drive every ironclad from the seas. Each time there would be a war panic.

The strength and heart of the nations was given to the thought of war, and yet the mass of their citizens was a teeming democracy as heedless of and unfitted for fighting, mentally, morally, physically, as any population has ever been—or, one ventures to add, could ever be. That was the paradox of the time. It was a period altogether unique in the world's history. The apparatus of warfare, the art and method of fighting, changed absolutely every dozen years in a stupendous progress towards perfection, and people grew less and less warlike, and there was no war.

And then at last it came. It came as a surprise to all the world because its real causes were hidden. Relations were strained between Germany and the United States because of the intense exasperation of a tariff conflict and the ambiguous attitude of the former power towards the Monroe Doctrine, and they were strained between the United States and Japan because of the perennial citizenship question. But in both cases these were standing causes of offence. The real deciding cause, it is now known, was the perfecting of the Pforzheim engine by Germany and the consequent possibility of a rapid and entirely practicable airship. At that time Germany was by far the most efficient power in the world, better organised for swift and secret action, better equipped with the resources of modern science, and with her official and administrative classes at a higher level of education and training. These things she knew, and she exaggerated that knowledge to the pitch of contempt for the secret counsels of her neighbours. It may be that with the habit of self-confidence her spying upon them had grown less thorough. Moreover, she had a tradition of unsentimental and unscrupulous action that vitiated her international outlook profoundly. With the coming of these new weapons her collective intelligence thrilled with the sense that now her moment had come. Once again in the history

of progress it seemed she held the decisive weapon. Now she might strike and conquer—before the others had anything but experiments in the air.

Particularly she must strike America, swiftly, because there, if anywhere, lay the chance of an aerial rival. It was known that America possessed a flying-machine of considerable practical value, developed out of the Wright model; but it was not supposed that the Washington War Office had made any wholesale attempts to create an aerial navy. It was necessary to strike before they could do so. France had a fleet of slow navigables, several dating from 1908, that could make no possible headway against the new type. They had been built solely for reconnoitring purposes on the eastern frontier, they were mostly too small to carry more than a couple of dozen men without arms or provisions, and not one could do forty miles an hour. Great Britain, it seemed, in an access of meanness, temporised and wrangled with the imperial-spirited Butteridge and his extraordinary invention. That also was not in play—and could not be for some months at the earliest. From Asia there came no sign. The Germans explained this by saying the yellow peoples were without invention. No other competitor was worth considering. "Now or never," said the Germans—"now or never we may seize the air—as once the British seized the seas! While all the other powers are still experimenting."

Swift and systematic and secret were their preparations, and their plan most excellent. So far as their knowledge went, America was the only dangerous possibility; America, which was also now the leading trade rival of Germany and one of the chief barriers to her Imperial expansion. So at once they would strike at America. They would fling a great force across the Atlantic heavens and bear America down unwarned and unprepared.

Altogether it was a well-imagined and most hopeful and spirited enterprise, having regard to the information in the possession of the German government. The chances of it being a successful surprise were very great. The airship and the flying-machine were very different things from ironclads, which take a couple of years to build. Given hands, given plant, they could be made innumerably in a few weeks. Once the needful parks and foundries were organised, air-ships and *Drachenflieger* could be poured into the sky. Indeed, when the time came, they did pour into the sky like, as a bitter French writer put it, flies roused from filth.

The attack upon America was to be the first move in this tremendous game. But no sooner had it started than instantly the aeronautic parks were to proceed to put together and inflate the second fleet which was to dominate Europe and manoeuvre significantly over London, Paris, Rome, St. Petersburg, or wherever else its moral effect was required. A World Surprise it was to be—no less a World Conquest; and it is wonderful how near the calmly adventurous minds that planned it came to succeeding in their colossal design.

Von Sternberg was the Moltke of this War in the Air, but it was the curious hard romanticism of Prince Karl Albert that won over the hesitating Emperor to the scheme. Prince Karl Albert was indeed the central figure of the world drama. He was the darling of the Imperialist spirit in Germany, and the ideal of the new aristocratic feeling—the new Chivalry, as it was called—that followed the overthrow of Socialism through its internal divisions and lack of discipline, and the concentration of wealth in the hands of a few great families. He was compared by obsequious flatterers to the Black Prince, to Alcibiades, to the young Caesar. To many he seemed Nietzsche's Overman revealed. He was big and blond and virile, and splendidly non-moral. The first great feat that startled Europe, and almost brought about a new Trojan war, was his abduction of the Princess Helena of Norway and his blank refusal to marry her. Then followed his marriage with Gretchen Krass, a Swiss girl of peerless beauty. Then came the gallant rescue, which almost cost him his life, of three drowning tailors whose boat had upset in the sea near

Heligoland. For that and his victory over the American yacht *Defender*, C.C.I., the Emperor forgave him and placed him in control of the new aeronautic arm of the German forces. This he developed with marvellous energy and ability, being resolved, as he said, to give to Germany land and sea and sky. The national passion for aggression found in him its supreme exponent, and achieved through him its realisation in this astounding war. But his fascination was more than national; all over the world his ruthless strength dominated minds as the Napoleonic legend had dominated minds. Englishmen turned in disgust from the slow, complex, civilised methods of their national politics to this uncompromising, forceful figure. Frenchmen believed in him. Poems were written to him in American.

He made the war.

Quite equally with the rest of the world, the general German population was taken by surprise by the swift vigour of the Imperial government. A considerable literature of military forecasts, beginning as early as 1906 with Rudolf Martin, the author not merely of a brilliant book of anticipations, but of a proverb, "The future of Germany lies in the air," had, however, partially prepared the German imagination for some such enterprise.

§2

Of all these world-forces and gigantic designs Bert Smallways knew nothing until he found himself in the very focus of it all and gaped down amazed on the spectacle of that giant herd of air-ships. Each one seemed as long as the Strand, and as big about as Trafalgar Square. Some must have been a third of a mile in length. He had never before seen anything so vast and disciplined as this tremendous park. For the first time in his life he really had an intimation of the extraordinary and quite important things of which a contemporary may go in ignorance. He had always clung to the illusion that Germans were fat, absurd men, who smoked china pipes, and were addicted to knowledge and horseflesh and sauerkraut and indigestible things generally.

His bird's-eye view was quite transitory. He ducked at the first shot; and directly his balloon began to drop, his mind ran confusedly upon how he might explain himself, and whether he should pretend to be Butteridge or not. "O Lord!" he groaned, in an agony of indecision. Then his eye caught his sandals, and he felt a spasm of self-disgust. "They'll think I'm a bloomin' idiot," he said, and then it was he rose up desperately and threw over the sand-bag and provoked the second and third shots.

It flashed into his head, as he cowered in the bottom of the car, that he might avoid all sorts of disagreeable and complicated explanations by pretending to be mad.

That was his last idea before the airships seemed to rush up about him as if to look at him, and his car hit the ground and bounded and pitched him out on his head. . . .

He awoke to find himself famous, and to hear a voice crying, "Booteraidge! Ja! Ja! Herr Booteraidge! Selbst!"

He was lying on a little patch of grass beside one of the main avenues of the aeronautic park. The airships receded down a great vista, an immense perspective, and the blunt prow of each was adorned with a black eagle of a hundred feet or so spread. Down the other side of the avenue ran a series of gas generators, and big hose-pipes trailed everywhere across the intervening space. Close at hand was his now nearly deflated balloon and the car on its side looking minutely small, a mere broken toy, a shrivelled bubble, in contrast with the gigantic bulk of the nearer airship. This he saw almost end-on, rising like a cliff and sloping forward towards its fellow on the other side so as to overshadow the alley between them. There was a crowd of excited people about him, big men mostly in tight uniforms. Everybody was talking, and several were shouting, in German; he knew that because they splashed and aspirated sounds like startled kittens.

Only one phrase, repeated again and again could he recognize—the name of "Herr Booteraidge."

"Gollys!" said Bert. "They've spotted it."

"Besser," said some one, and some rapid German followed.

He perceived that close at hand was a field telephone, and that a tall officer in blue was talking thereat about him. Another stood close beside him with the portfolio of drawings and photographs in his hand. They looked round at him.

"Do you spik Cherman, Herr Booteraidge?"

Bert decided that he had better be dazed. He did his best to seem thoroughly dazed. "Where *am* I?" he asked.

Volubility prevailed. "Der Prinz," was mentioned. A bugle sounded far away, and its call was taken up by one nearer, and then by one close at hand. This seemed to increase the excitement greatly. A mono-rail car bumbled past. The telephone bell rang passionately, and the tall officer seemed to engage in a heated altercation. Then he approached the group about Bert, calling out something about "mitbringen."

An earnest-faced, emaciated man with a white moustache appealed to Bert. "Herr Booteraidge, sir, we are chust to start!"

"Where am I?" Bert repeated.

Some one shook him by the other shoulder. "Are you Herr Booteraidge?" he asked.

"Herr Booteraidge, we are chust to start!" repeated the white moustache, and then helplessly, "What is de goot? What can we do?"

The officer from the telephone repeated his sentence about "Der Prinz" and "mitbringen." The man with the moustache stared for a moment, grasped an idea and became violently energetic, stood up and bawled directions at unseen people. Questions were asked, and the doctor at Bert's side answered, "Ja! Ja!" several times, also something about "Kopf." With a certain urgency he got Bert rather unwillingly to his feet. Two huge soldiers in grey advanced upon Bert and seized hold of him. "'ullo!" said Bert, startled. "What's up?"

"It is all right," the doctor explained; "they are to carry you."

"Where?" asked Bert, unanswered.

"Put your arms roundt their—*hals*—round them!"

"Yes! but where?"

"Hold tight!"

Before Bert could decide to say anything more he was whisked up by the two soldiers. They joined hands to seat him, and his arms were put about their necks. "Vorwarts!" Some one ran before him with the portfolio, and he was borne rapidly along the broad avenue between the gas generators and the airships, rapidly and on the whole smoothly except that once or twice his bearers stumbled over hose-pipes and nearly let him down.

He was wearing Mr. Butteridge's Alpine cap, and his little shoulders were in Mr. Butteridge's fur-lined overcoat, and he had responded to Mr. Butteridge's name. The sandals dangled helplessly. Gaw! Everybody seemed in a devil of a hurry. Why? He was carried joggling and gaping through the twilight, marvelling beyond measure.

The systematic arrangement of wide convenient spaces, the quantities of business-like soldiers everywhere, the occasional neat piles of material, the ubiquitous mono-rail lines, and the towering ship-like hulls about him, reminded him a little of impressions he had got as a boy on a visit to Woolwich Dockyard. The whole camp reflected the colossal power of modern science that had created it. A peculiar strangeness was produced by the lowness of the electric light, which lay upon the ground, casting all shadows upwards and making a grotesque shadow figure of himself and his bearers on the airship sides, fusing all three of them into a monstrous animal with attenuated legs and an immense fan-like humped body. The lights were on the ground because as far as possible all poles and standards had been dispensed with to prevent complications when the airships rose.

It was deep twilight now, a tranquil blue-skyed evening; everything rose out from the splashes of light upon the ground into dim translucent tall masses; within the cavities of the airships small inspecting lamps glowed like cloud-veiled stars, and made them seem marvellously unsubstantial. Each airship

had its name in black letters on white on either flank, and forward the Imperial eagle sprawled, an overwhelming bird in the dimness.

Bugles sounded, mono-rail cars of quiet soldiers slithered burbling by. The cabins under the heads of the airships were being lit up; doors opened in them, and revealed padded passages.

Now and then a voice gave directions to workers indistinctly seen.

There was a matter of sentinels, gangways and a long narrow passage, a scramble over a disorder of baggage, and then Bert found himself lowered to the ground and standing in the doorway of a spacious cabin—it was perhaps ten feet square and eight high, furnished with crimson padding and aluminium. A tall, bird-like young man with a small head, a long nose, and very pale hair, with his hands full of things like shaving-strops, boot-trees, hair-brushes, and toilet tidies, was saying things about Gott and thunder and Dummer Booteraidge as Bert entered. He was apparently an evicted occupant. Then he vanished, and Bert was lying back on a couch in the corner with a pillow under his head and the door of the cabin shut upon him. He was alone. Everybody had hurried out again astonishingly.

"Gollys!" said Bert. "What next?"

He stared about him at the room.

"Butteridge! Shall I try to keep it up, or shan't I?"

The room he was in puzzled him. " 'Tisn't a prison and 'tisn't a norfis?" Then the old trouble came uppermost. "I wish to 'eaven I 'adn't these silly sandals on," he cried querulously to the universe. "They give the whole blessed show away."

§3

His door was flung open, and a compact young man in uniform appeared, carrying Mr. Butteridge's portfolio, rucksac, and shaving-glass.

"I say!" he said in faultless English as he entered. He had

a beaming face, and a sort of pinkish blond hair. "Fancy you being Butteridge." He slapped Bert's meagre luggage down.

"We'd have started," he said, "in another half-hour! You didn't give yourself much time!"

He surveyed Bert curiously. His gaze rested for a fraction of a moment on the sandals. "You ought to have come on your flying-machine, Mr. Butteridge."

He didn't wait for an answer. "The Prince says I've got to look after you. Naturally he can't see you now, but he thinks your coming's providential. Last grace of Heaven. Like a sign. Hullo!"

He stood still and listened.

Outside there was a going to and fro of feet, a sound of distant bugles suddenly taken up and echoed close at hand, men called out in loud tones short, sharp, seemingly vital things, and were answered distantly. A bell jangled, and feet went down the corridor. Then came a stillness more distracting than sound, and then a great gurgling and rushing and splashing of water. The young man's eyebrows lifted. He hesitated, and dashed out of the room. Presently came a stupendous bang to vary the noises without, then a distant cheering. The young man re-appeared.

"They're running the water out of the ballonette already."

"What water?" asked Bert.

"The water that anchored us. Artful dodge. Eh?"

Bert tried to take it in.

"Of course!" said the compact young man. "You don't understand."

A gentle quivering crept upon Bert's senses. "That's the engine," said the compact young man approvingly. "Now we shan't be long."

Another long listening interval.

The cabin swayed. "By Jove! we're starting already;" he cried. "We're starting!"

"Starting!" cried Bert, sitting up. "Where?"

But the young man was out of the room again. There were

noises of German in the passage, and other nerve-shaking sounds.

The swaying increased. The young man reappeared. "We're off, right enough!"

"I say!" said Bert, "where are we starting? I wish you'd explain. What's this place? I don't understand."

"What!" cried the young man, "you don't understand?"

"No. I'm all dazed-like from that crack on the nob I got. Where *are* we? *Where* are we starting?"

"Don't you know where you are—what this is?"

"Not a bit of it! What's all the swaying and the row?"

"What a lark!" cried the young man. "I say! What a thundering lark! Don't you know? We're off to America, and you haven't realised. You've just caught us by a neck. You're on the blessed old flagship with the Prince. You won't miss anything. Whatever's on, you bet the *Vaterland* will be there."

"Us!—off to America?"

"Ra—ther!"

"In an airship?"

"What do *you* think?"

"Me! going to America on an airship! After that balloon! 'ere! I say—I don't want to go! I want to walk about on my legs. Let me get out! I didn't understand."

He made a dive for the door.

The young man arrested Bert with a gesture, took hold of a strap, lifted up a panel in the padded wall, and a window appeared. "Look!" he said. Side by side they looked out.

"Gaw!" said Bert. "We're going up!"

"We are!" said the young man, cheerfully; "fast!"

They were rising in the air smoothly and quietly, and moving slowly to the throb of the engine athwart the aeronautic park. Down below it stretched, dimly geometrical in the darkness, picked out at regular intervals by glow-worm spangles of light. One black gap in the long line of grey, round-backed airships marked the position from which the *Vaterland* had come. Beside it a second monster now rose softly, released from its bonds and cables into the air. Then, taking a beautifully exact distance, a third ascended, and then a fourth.

"Too late, Mr. Butteridge!" the young man remarked. "We're off! I daresay it is a bit of a shock to you, but there you are! The Prince said you'd have to come."

"Look 'ere," said Bert. "I really *am* dazed. What's this thing? Where are we going?"

"This, Mr. Butteridge," said the young man, taking pains to be explicit, "is an airship. It's the flagship of Prince Karl Albert. This is the German air-fleet, and it is going over to America, to give that spirited people 'what for.' The only thing we were at all uneasy about was your invention. And here you are!"

"But!—you a German?" asked Bert.

"Lieutenant Kurt. Luft-lieutenant Kurt, at your service."

"But you speak English!"

"Mother was English—went to school in England. Afterwards, Rhodes scholar. German none the less for that. Detailed for the present, Mr. Butteridge, to look after you. You're shaken by your fall. It's all right, really. They're going to buy your machine and everything. You sit down, and take it quite calmly. You'll soon get the hang of the position."

§4

Bert sat down on the locker, collecting his mind, and the young man talked to him about the airship.

He was really a very tactful young man indeed, in a natural sort of way. "Daresay all this is new to you," he said; "not your sort of machine. These cabins aren't half bad."

He got up and walked round the little apartment, showing its points.

"Here is the bed," he said, whipping down a couch from the wall and throwing it back again with a click. "Here are toilet things," and he opened a neatly arranged cupboard. "Not much washing. No water we've got; no water at all except for drinking.

No baths or anything until we get to America and land. Rub over with loofah. One pint of hot for shaving. That's all. In the locker below you are rugs and blankets; you will need them presently. They say it gets cold. I don't know. Never been up before. Except a little work with gliders—which is mostly going down. Three-quarters of the chaps in the fleet haven't. Here's a folding-chair and table behind the door. Compact, eh?"

He took the chair and balanced it on his little finger. "Pretty light, eh? Aluminium and magnesium alloy and a vacuum inside. All these cushions stuffed with hydrogen. Foxy! The whole ship's like that. And not a man in the fleet, except the Prince and one or two others, over eleven stone. Couldn't sweat the Prince, you know. We'll go all over the thing to-morrow. I'm frightfully keen on it."

He beamed at Bert. "You *do* look young," he remarked. "I always thought you'd be an old man with a beard—a sort of philosopher. I don't know why one should expect clever people always to be old. I do."

Bert parried that compliment a little awkwardly, and then the lieutenant was struck with the riddle why Herr Butteridge had not come in his own flying machine.

"It's a long story," said Bert. "Look here!" he said abruptly, "I wish you'd lend me a pair of slippers, or something. I'm regular sick of these sandals. They're rotten things. I've been trying them for a friend."

"Right O!"

The ex-Rhodes scholar whisked out of the room and reappeared with a considerable choice of footwear—pumps, cloth bath-slippers, and a purple pair adorned with golden sunflowers.

But these he repented of at the last moment.

"I don't even wear them myself," he said. "Only brought 'em in the zeal of the moment." He laughed confidentially. "Had 'em worked for me—in Oxford. By a friend. Take 'em everywhere."

So Bert chose the pumps.

The lieutenant broke into a cheerful snigger. "Here we are trying on slippers," he said, "and the world going by like a panorama below. Rather a lark, eh? Look!"

Bert peeped with him out of the window, looking from the bright pettiness of the red-and-silver cabin into a dark immensity. The land below, except for a lake, was black and featureless, and the other airships were hidden. "See more outside," said the lieutenant. "Let's go! There's a sort of little gallery."

He led the way into the long passage, which was lit by one small electric light, past some notices in German, to an open balcony and a light ladder and gallery of metal lattice overhanging, empty space. Bert followed his leader down to the gallery slowly and cautiously. From it he was able to watch the wonderful spectacle of the first air-fleet flying through the night. They flew in a wedge-shaped formation, the *Vaterland* highest and leading, the tail receding into the corners of the sky. They flew in long, regular undulations, great dark fish-like shapes, showing hardly any light at all, the engines making a throb-throb-throbbing sound that was very audible out on the gallery. They were going at a level of five or six thousand feet, and rising steadily. Below, the country lay silent, a clear darkness dotted and lined out with clusters of furnaces, and the lit streets of a group of big towns. The world seemed to lie in a bowl; the overhanging bulk of the airship above hid all but the lowest levels of the sky.

They watched the landscape for a space.

"Jolly it must be to invent things," said the lieutenant suddenly. "How did you come to think of your machine first?"

"Worked it out," said Bert, after a pause. "Jest ground away at it."

"Our people are frightfully keen on you. They thought the British had got you. Weren't the British keen?"

"In a way," said Bert. "Still—it's a long story."

"I think it's an immense thing—to invent. I couldn't invent a thing to save my life."

They both fell silent, watching the darkened world and

following their thoughts until a bugle summoned them to a belated dinner. Bert was suddenly alarmed. "Don't you 'ave to dress and things?" he said. "I've always been too hard at Science and things to go into Society and all that."

"No fear," said Kurt. "Nobody's got more than the clothes they wear. We're travelling light. You might perhaps take your overcoat off. They've an electric radiator each end of the room."

And so presently Bert found himself sitting to eat in the presence of the "German Alexander"—that great and puissant Prince, Prince Karl Albert, the War Lord, the hero of two hemispheres. He was a handsome blond man, with deep-set eyes, a snub nose, upturned moustache, and long white hands. He sat higher than the others, under a black eagle with widespread wings and the German Imperial flags; he was, as it were, enthroned, and it struck Bert greatly that as he ate he did not look at people, but over their heads like one who sees visions. Twenty officers of various ranks stood about the table—and Bert. They all seemed extremely curious to see the famous Butteridge, and their astonishment at his appearance was ill-controlled. The Prince gave him a dignified salutation, to which, by an inspiration, he bowed. Standing next the Prince was a brown-faced, wrinkled man with silver spectacles and fluffy, dingy-grey side-whiskers, who regarded Bert with a peculiar and disconcerting attention. The company sat after ceremonies Bert could not understand. At the other end of the table was the bird-faced officer Bert had dispossessed, still looking hostile and whispering about Bert to his neighbour. Two soldiers waited. The dinner was a plain one—a soup, some fresh mutton, and cheese—and there was very little talk.

A curious solemnity indeed brooded over every one. Partly this was reaction after the intense toil and restrained excitement of starting; partly it was the overwhelming sense of strange new experiences, of portentous adventure. The Prince was lost in thought. He roused himself to drink to the Emperor in

champagne, and the company cried "Hoch!" like men repeating responses in church.

No smoking was permitted, but some of the officers went down to the little open gallery to chew tobacco. No lights whatever were safe amidst that bundle of inflammable things. Bert suddenly fell yawning and shivering. He was overwhelmed by a sense of his own insignificance amidst these great rushing monsters of the air. He felt life was too big for him—too much for him altogether.

He said something to Kurt about his head, went up the steep ladder from the swaying little gallery into the airship again, and so, as if it were a refuge, to bed.

§5

Bert slept for a time, and then his sleep was broken by dreams. Mostly he was fleeing from formless terrors down an interminable passage in an airship—a passage paved at first with ravenous trap-doors, and then with openwork canvas of the most careless description.

"Gaw!" said Bert, turning over after his seventh fall through infinite space that night.

He sat up in the darkness and nursed his knees. The progress of the airship was not nearly so smooth as a balloon; he could feel a regular swaying up, up, up and then down, down, down, and the throbbing and tremulous quiver of the engines.

His mind began to teem with memories—more memories and more.

Through them, like a struggling swimmer in broken water, came the perplexing question, what am I to do to-morrow? To-morrow, Kurt had told him, the Prince's secretary, the Graf Von Winterfeld, would come to him and discuss his flying-machine, and then he would see the Prince. He would have to stick it out now that he was Butteridge, and sell his invention. And then, if they found him out! He had a vision of infuriated Butteridges. . . . Suppose after all he owned up? Pretended it

was their misunderstanding? He began to scheme devices for selling the secret and circumventing Butteridge.

What should he ask for the thing? Somehow twenty thousand pounds struck him as about the sum indicated.

He fell into that despondency that lies in wait in the small hours. He had got too big a job on—too big a job. . . .

Memories swamped his scheming.

"Where was I this time last night?"

He recapitulated his evenings tediously and lengthily. Last night he had been up above the clouds in Butteridge's balloon. He thought of the moment when he dropped through them and saw the cold twilight sea close below. He still remembered that disagreeable incident with a nightmare vividness. And the night before he and Grubb had been looking for cheap lodgings at Littlestone in Kent. How remote that seemed now. It might be years ago. For the first time he thought of his fellow Desert Dervish, left with the two red-painted bicycles on Dymchurch sands. "'E won't make much of a show of it, not without me. Any'ow 'e did 'ave the treasury—such as it was—in his pocket!" . . . The night before that was Bank Holiday night and they had sat discussing their minstrel enterprise, drawing up a programme and rehearsing steps. And the night before was Whit Sunday. "Lord!" cried Bert, "what a doing that motor-bicycle give me!" He recalled the empty flapping of the eviscerated cushion, the feeling of impotence as the flames rose again. From among the confused memories of that tragic flare one little figure emerged very bright and poignantly sweet, Edna, crying back reluctantly from the departing motor-car, "See you to-morrer, Bert?"

Other memories of Edna clustered round that impression. They led Bert's mind step by step to an agreeable state that found expression in "I'll marry *'er* if she don't look out." And then in a flash it followed in his mind that if he sold the Butteridge secret he could! Suppose after all he did get twenty thousand pounds; such sums have been paid! With that he could buy house and garden, buy new clothes beyond dreaming, buy a

motor, travel, have every delight of the civilised life as he knew it, for himself and Edna. Of course, risks were involved. "I'll 'ave old Butteridge on my track, I expect!"

He meditated upon that. He declined again to despondency. As yet he was only in the beginning of the adventure. He had still to deliver the goods and draw the cash. And before that—Just now he was by no means on his way home. He was flying off to America to fight there. "Not much fighting," he considered; "all our own way." Still, if a shell did happen to hit the *Vaterland* on the underside! . . .

"S'pose I ought to make my will."

He lay back for some time composing wills—chiefly in favour of Edna. He had settled now it was to be twenty thousand pounds. He left a number of minor legacies. The wills became more and more meandering and extravagant. . . .

He woke from the eighth repetition of his nightmare fall through space. "This flying gets on one's nerves," he said.

He could feel the airship diving down, down, down, then slowly swinging to up, up, up. Throb, throb, throb, throb, quivered the engine.

He got up presently and wrapped himself about with Mr. Butteridge's overcoat and all the blankets, for the air was very keen. Then he peeped out of the window to see a grey dawn breaking over clouds, then turned up his light and bolted his door, sat down to the table, and produced his chest-protector.

He smoothed the crumpled plans with his hand, and contemplated them. Then he referred to the other drawings in the portfolio. Twenty thousand pounds. If he worked it right! It was worth trying, anyhow.

Presently he opened the drawer in which Kurt had put paper and writing-materials.

Bert Smallways was by no means a stupid person, and up to a certain limit he had not been badly educated. His board school had taught him to draw up to certain limits, taught him to calculate and understand a specification. If at that point his

country had tired of its efforts, and handed him over unfinished to scramble for a living in an atmosphere of advertisments and individual enterprise, that was really not his fault. He was as his State had made him, and the reader must not imagine because he was a little Cockney cad, that he was absolutely incapable of grasping the idea of the Butteridge flying-machine. But he found it stiff and perplexing. His motor-bicycle and Grubb's experiments and the "mechanical drawing" he had done in standard seven all helped him out; and, moreover, the maker of these drawings, whoever he was, had been anxious to make his intentions plain. Bert copied sketches, he made notes, he made a quite tolerable and intelligent copy of the essential drawings and sketches of the others. Then he fell into a meditation upon them.

At last he rose with a sigh, folded up the originals that had formerly been in his chest-protector and put them into the breast-pocket of his jacket, and then very carefully deposited the copies he had made in the place of the originals. He had no very clear plan in his mind in doing this, except that he hated the idea of altogether parting with the secret. For a long time he meditated profoundly—nodding. Then he turned out his light and went to bed again and schemed himself to sleep.

§6

The hochgeboren Graf von Winterfeld was also a light sleeper that night, but then he was one of these people who sleep little and play chess problems in their heads to while away the time—and that night he had a particularly difficult problem to solve.

He came in upon Bert while he was still in bed in the glow of the sunlight reflected from the North Sea below, consuming the rolls and coffee a soldier had brought him. He had a portfolio under his arm, and in the clear, early morning light his dingy grey hair and heavy, silver-rimmed spectacles made him look almost benevolent. He spoke English fluently, but with a strong German flavour. He was particularly bad with his "b's," and his

"th's" softened towards weak "z'ds." He called Bert explosively, "Pooterage." He began with some indistinct civilities, bowed, took a folding-table and chair from behind the door, put the former between himself and Bert, sat down on the latter, coughed drily, and opened his portfolio. Then he put his elbows on the table, pinched his lower lip with his two fore-fingers, and regarded Bert disconcertingly with magnified eyes. "You came to us, Herr Pooterage, against your will," he said at last.

"'Ow d'you make that out?" asked Bert, after a pause of astonishment.

"I chuge by ze maps in your car. They were all English. And your provisions. They were all picnic. Also your cords were entangled. You haf been tugging—but no good. You could not manage ze balloon, and anuzzer power than yours prought you to us. Is it not so?"

Bert thought.

"Also—where is ze laty?"

"'Ere!—what lady?"

"You started with a laty. That is evident. You shtarted for an afternoon excursion—a picnic. A man of your temperament—he would take a laty. She was not wiz you in your balloon when you came down at Dornhof. No! Only her chacket! It is your affair. Still, I am curious."

Bert reflected. "'ow d'you know that?"

"I chuge by ze nature of your farious provisions. I cannot account, Mr. Pooterage, for ze laty, what you haf done with her. Nor can I tell why you should wear nature-sandals, nor why you should wear such cheap plue clothes. These are outside my instructions. Trifles, perhaps. Officially they are to be ignored. Laties come and go—I am a man of ze worldt. I haf known wise men wear sandals and efen practice vegetarian habits. I haf known men—or at any rate, I haf known chemists—who did not schmoke. You haf, no doubt, put ze laty down somewhere. Well. Let us get to—business. A higher power"—his voice changed its emotional quality, his magnified eyes seemed to dilate—"has

prought you and your secret straight to us. So!"—he bowed his head—"so pe it. It is ze Destiny of Chermany and my Prince. I can undershtandt you always carry zat secret. You are afraidt of roppers and spies. So it comes wiz you—to us. Mr. Pooterage, Chermany will puy it."

"Will she?"

"She will," said the secretary, looking hard at Bert's abandoned sandals in the corner of the locker. He roused himself, consulted a paper of notes for a moment, and Bert eyed his brown and wrinkled face with expectation and terror. "Chermany, I am instructed to say," said the secretary, with his eyes on the table and his notes spread out, "has always been willing to puy your secret. We haf indeed peen eager to acquire it—fery eager; and it was only ze fear that you might be, on patriotic groundts, acting in collusion with your Pritish War Office zat has made us discreet in offering for your marvellous invention through intermediaries. We haf no hesitation whatefer now, I am instructed, in agreeing to your proposal of a hundert tousand poundts."

"Crikey!" said Bert, overwhelmed.

"I peg your pardon?"

"Jest a twinge," said Bert, raising his hand to his bandaged head.

"Ah! Also I am instructed to say that as for that noble, unrightly accused laty you haf championed so brafely against Pritish hypocrisy and coldness, all ze chivalry of Chermany is on her site."

"Lady?" said Bert faintly, and then recalled the great Butteridge love story. Had the old chap also read the letters? He must think him a scorcher if he had. "Oh! that's aw-right," he said, "about 'er. I 'adn't any doubts about that. I—"

He stopped. The secretary certainly had a most appalling stare. It seemed ages before he looked down again. "Well, ze laty as you please. She is your affair. I haf performt my instructions. And ze title of Paron, zat also can pe done. It can all pe done, Herr Pooterage."

He drummed on the table for a second or so, and resumed. "I haf to tell you, sir, zat you come to us at a crisis in—Welt-Politik. There can be no harm now for me to put our plans before you. Pefore you leafe this ship again they will be manifest to all ze worldt. War is perhaps already declared. We go—to America. Our fleet will descend out of ze air upon ze United States—it is a country quite unprepared for war eferywhere—eferywhere. Zey have always relied on ze Atlantic. And their navy. We have selected a certain point—it is at present ze secret of our commanders—which we shall seize, and zen we shall establish a depot—a sort of inland Gibraltar. It will be—what will it be?—an eagle's nest. Zere our airships will gazzer and repair, and thence they will fly to and fro ofer ze United States, terrorising cities, dominating Washington, levying what is necessary, until ze terms we dictate are accepted. You follow me?"

"Go on!" said Bert.

"We could haf done all zis wiz such *Luftschiffe* and *Drachenflieger* as we possess, but ze accession of your machine renders our project complete. It not only gifs us a better *Drachenflieger*, but it remofes our last uneasiness as to Great Pritain. Wizout you, sir, Great Pritain, ze land you lofed so well and zat has requited you so ill, zat land of Pharisees and reptiles, can do nozzing!—nozzing! You see, I am perfectly frank wiz you. Well, I am instructed that Chermany recognises all this. We want you to place yourself at our disposal. We want you to become our Chief Head Flight Engineer. We want you to manufacture, we want to equip a swarm of hornets under your direction. We want you to direct this force. And it is at our depot in America we want you. So we offer you simply, and without haggling, ze full terms you demanded weeks ago—one hundert tousand poundts in cash, a salary of three tousand poundts a year, a pension of one tousand poundts a year, and ze title of Paron as you desired. These are my instructions."

He resumed his scrutiny of Bert's face.

"That's all right, of course," said Bert, a little short of breath,

but otherwise resolute and calm; and it seemed to him that now was the time to bring his nocturnal scheming to the issue.

The secretary contemplated Bert's collar with sustained attention. Only for one moment did his gaze move to the sandals and back.

"Jes' lemme think a bit," said Bert, finding the stare debilitating. "Look 'ere!" he said at last, with an air of great explicitness, "I *got* the secret."

"Yes."

"But I don't want the name of Butteridge to appear—see? I been thinking that over."

"A little delicacy?"

"Exactly. You buy the secret—leastways, I give it you—from Bearer—see?"

His voice failed him a little, and the stare continued. "I want to do the thing Enonymously. See?"

Still staring. Bert drifted on like a swimmer caught by a current. "Fact is, I'm going to edop' the name of Smallways. I don't want no title of Baron; I've altered my mind. And I want the money quiet-like. I want the hundred thousand pounds paid into benks—thirty thousand into the London and County Benk Branch at Bun Hill in Kent directly I 'and over the plans; twenty thousand into the Benk of England; 'arf the rest into a good French bank, the other 'arf the German National Bank, see? I want it put there, right away. I don't want it put in the name of Butteridge. I want it put in the name of Albert Peter Smallways; that's the name I'm going to edop'. That's condition one."

"Go on!" said the secretary.

"The nex condition," said Bert, "is that you don't make any inquiries as to title. I mean what English gentlemen do when they sell or let you land. You don't arst 'ow I got it. See? 'ere I am—I deliver you the goods—that's all right. Some people 'ave the cheek to say this isn't my invention, see? It is, you know—*that's* all right; but I don't want that gone into. I want a fair and square agreement saying that's all right. See?"

His "See?" faded into a profound silence.

The secretary sighed at last, leant back in his chair and produced a tooth-pick, and used it, to assist his meditation on Bert's case. "What was that name?" he asked at last, putting away the tooth-pick; "I must write it down."

"Albert Peter Smallways," said Bert, in a mild tone.

The secretary wrote it down, after a little difficulty about the spelling because of the different names of the letters of the alphabet in the two languages.

"And now, Mr. Schmallvays," he said at last, leaning back and resuming the stare, "tell me: how did you ket hold of Mister Pooterage's balloon?"

§7

When at last the Graf von Winterfold left Bert Smallways, he left him in an extremely deflated condition, with all his little story told.

He had, as people say, made a clean breast of it. He had been pursued into details. He had had to explain the blue suit, the sandals, the Desert Dervishes—everything. For a time scientific zeal consumed the secretary, and the question of the plans remained in suspense. He even went into speculation about the previous occupants of the balloon. "I suppose," he said, "the laty *was* the laty. Bot that is not our affair.

"It is fery curious and amusing, yes: but I am afraid the Prince may be annoyt. He acted wiz his usual decision—always he acts wiz wonterful decision. Like Napoleon. Directly he was tolt of your descent into the camp at Dornhof, he said, 'Pring him!—pring him! It is my schtar!' His schtar of Destiny! You see? He will be dthwarted. He directed you to come as Herr Pooterage, and you haf not done so. You haf triet, of course; but it has peen a poor try. His chugments of men are fery just and right, and it is better for men to act up to them—gompletely. Especially now. Particularly now."

He resumed that attitude of his, with his underlip pinched

between his forefingers. He spoke almost confidentially. "It will be awkward. I triet to suggest some doubt, but I was overruled. The Prince does not listen. He is impatient in the high air. Perhaps he will think his schtar has been making a fool of him. Perhaps he will think *I* haf been making a fool of him."

He wrinkled his forehead, and drew in the corners of his mouth.

"I got the plans," said Bert.

"Yes. There is that! Yes. But you see the Prince was interested in Herr Pooterage because of his romantic seit. Herr Pooterage was so much more—ah!—in the picture. I am afraid you are not equal to controlling the flying machine department of our aerial park as he wished you to do. He hadt promised himself that. . . .

"And der was also the prestige—the worldt prestige of Pooterage with us . . . .. Well, we must see what we can do." He held out his hand. "Gif me the plans."

A terrible chill ran through the being of Mr. Smallways. To this day he is not clear in his mind whether he wept or no, but certainly there was weeping in his voice. "'Ere, I say!" he protested. "Ain't I to 'ave—nothin' for 'em?"

The secretary regarded him with benevolent eyes. "You do not deserve anyzing!" he said.

"I might 'ave tore 'em up."

"Zey are not yours!"

"They weren't Butteridge's!"

"No need to pay anyzing."

Bert's being seemed to tighten towards desperate deeds. "Gaw!" he said, clutching his coat, "*ain't* there?"

"Pe galm," said the secretary. "Listen! You shall haf five hundert poundts. You shall haf it on my promise. I will do that for you, and that is all I can do. Take it from me. Gif me the name of that bank. Write it down. So! I tell you the Prince—is no choke. I do not think he approffed of your appearance last night. No! I can't answer for him. He wanted Pooterage, and you haf spoilt it. The Prince—I do not understand quite, he is in a strange state. It is the excitement of the starting and this great soaring in the air. I cannot account for what he does. But if all goes well I will see to it—you shall haf five hundert poundts. Will that do? Then gif me the plans."

"Old beggar!" said Bert, as the door clicked. "Gaw!—what an ole beggar!—*Sharp!*"

He sat down in the folding-chair, and whistled noiselessly for a time.

"Nice 'old swindle for 'im if I tore 'em up! I could 'ave."

He rubbed the bridge of his nose thoughtfully. "I gave the whole blessed show away. If I'd j'es' kep quiet about being Enonymous . . . .. Gaw! . . . Too soon, Bert, my boy—too soon and too rushy. I'd like to kick my silly self.

"I couldn't 'ave kep' it up.

"After all, it ain't so very bad," he said.

"After all, five 'undred pounds. . . . It isn't *my* secret, anyhow. It's jes' a pickup on the road. Five 'undred.

"Wonder what the fare is from America back 'ome?"

§8

And later in the day an extremely shattered and disorganised Bert Smallways stood in the presence of the Prince Karl Albert.

The proceedings were in German. The Prince was in his own cabin, the end room of the airship, a charming apartment furnished in wicker-work with a long window across its entire breadth, looking forward. He was sitting at a folding-table of green baize, with Von Winterfeld and two officers sitting beside him, and littered before them was a number of American maps and Mr. Butteridge's letters and his portfolio and a number of loose papers. Bert was not asked to sit down, and remained standing throughout the interview. Von Winterfeld told his story, and every now and then the words Ballon and Pooterage struck on Bert's ears. The Prince's face remained stern and ominous and the two officers watched it cautiously or glanced

at Bert. There was something a little strange in their scrutiny of the Prince—a curiosity, an apprehension. Then presently he was struck by an idea, and they fell discussing the plans. The Prince asked Bert abruptly in English. "Did you ever see this thing go op?"

Bert jumped. "Saw it from Bun 'ill, your Royal Highness."

Von Winterfeld made some explanation.

"How fast did it go?"

"Couldn't say, your Royal Highness. The papers, leastways the *Daily Courier*, said eighty miles an hour."

They talked German over that for a time.

"Couldt it standt still? Op in the air? That is what I want to know."

"It could 'ovver, your Royal Highness, like a wasp," said Bert.

"*Viel besser, nicht wahr?*" said the Prince to Von Winterfeld, and then went on in German for a time.

Presently they came to an end, and the two officers looked at Bert. One rang a bell, and the portfolio was handed to an attendant, who took it away.

Then they reverted to the case of Bert, and it was evident the Prince was inclined to be hard with him. Von Winterfeld protested. Apparently theological considerations came in, for there were several mentions of "Gott!" Some conclusions emerged, and it was apparent that Von Winterfeld was instructed to convey them to Bert.

"Mr. Schmallvays, you haf obtained a footing in this airship," he said, "by disgraceful and systematic lying."

"'Ardly systematic," said Bert. "I—"

The Prince silenced him by a gesture.

"And it is within the power of his Highness to dispose of you as a spy."

"'Ere!—I came to sell—"

"Ssh!" said one of the officers.

"However, in consideration of the happy chance that mate you the instrument unter Gott of this Pooterage flying-machine reaching his Highness's hand, you haf been spared. Yes,—you were the pearer of goot tidings. You will be allowed to remain on this ship until it is convenient to dispose of you. Do you understandt?"

"We will bring him," said the Prince, and added terribly with a terrible glare, "*als Ballast.*"

"You are to come with us," said Winterfeld, "as pallast. Do you understandt?"

Bert opened his mouth to ask about the five hundred pounds, and then a saving gleam of wisdom silenced him. He met Von Winterfeld's eye, and it seemed to him the secretary nodded slightly.

"Go!" said the Prince, with a sweep of the great arm and hand towards the door. Bert went out like a leaf before a gale.

§9

But in between the time when the Graf von Winterfeld had talked to him and this alarming conference with the Prince, Bert had explored the *Vaterland* from end to end. He had found it interesting in spite of grave preoccupations. Kurt, like the greater number of the men upon the German air-fleet, had known hardly anything of aeronautics before his appointment to the new flagship. But he was extremely keen upon this wonderful new weapon Germany had assumed so suddenly and dramatically. He showed things to Bert with a boyish eagerness and appreciation. It was as if he showed them over again to himself, like a child showing a new toy. "Let's go all over the ship," he said with zest. He pointed out particularly the lightness of everything, the use of exhausted aluminium tubing, of springy cushions inflated with compressed hydrogen; the partitions were hydrogen bags covered with light imitation leather, the very crockery was a light biscuit glazed in a vacuum, and weighed next to nothing. Where strength was needed there was the new Charlottenburg alloy, German steel as it was called, the toughest and most resistant metal in the world.

There was no lack of space. Space did not matter, so long as load did not grow. The habitable part of the ship was two hundred and fifty feet long, and the rooms in two tiers; above these one could go up into remarkable little white-metal turrets with big windows and airtight double doors that enabled one to inspect the vast cavity of the gas-chambers. This inside view impressed Bert very much. He had never realised before that an airship was not one simple continuous gas-bag containing nothing but gas. Now he saw far above him the backbone of the apparatus and its big ribs, "like the neural and haemal canals," said Kurt, who had dabbled in biology.

"Rather!" said Bert appreciatively, though he had not the ghost of an idea what these phrases meant.

Little electric lights could be switched on up there if anything went wrong in the night. There were even ladders across the space. "But you can't go into the gas," protested Bert. "You can't breve it."

The lieutenant opened a cupboard door and displayed a diver's suit, only that it was made of oiled silk, and both its compressed-air knapsack and its helmet were of an alloy of aluminium and some light metal. "We can go all over the inside netting and stick up bullet holes or leaks," he explained. "There's netting inside and out. The whole outer-case is rope ladder, so to speak."

Aft of the habitable part of the airship was the magazine of explosives, coming near the middle of its length. They were all bombs of various types mostly in glass—none of the German airships carried any guns at all except one small pom-pom (to use the old English nickname dating from the Boer war), which was forward in the gallery upon the shield at the heart of the eagle. From the magazine amidships a covered canvas gallery with aluminium treads on its floor and a hand-rope, ran back underneath the gas-chamber to the engine-room at the tail; but along this Bert did not go, and from first to last he never saw the engines. But he went up a ladder against a gale of ventilation—a

ladder that was encased in a kind of gas-tight fire escape—and ran right athwart the great forward air-chamber to the little look-out gallery with a telephone, that gallery that bore the light pom-pom of German steel and its locker of shells. This gallery was all of aluminium magnesium alloy, the tight front of the air-ship swelled cliff-like above and below, and the black eagle sprawled overwhelmingly gigantic, its extremities all hidden by the bulge of the gas-bag. And far down, under the soaring eagles, was England, four thousand feet below perhaps, and looking very small and defenceless indeed in the morning sunlight.

The realisation that there was England gave Bert sudden and unexpected qualms of patriotic compunction. He was struck by a quite novel idea. After all, he might have torn up those plans and thrown them away. These people could not have done so very much to him. And even if they did, ought not an Englishman to die for his country? It was an idea that had hitherto been rather smothered up by the cares of a competitive civilisation. He became violently depressed. He ought, he perceived, to have seen it in that light before. Why hadn't he seen it in that light before?

Indeed, wasn't he a sort of traitor? . . .

He wondered how the aerial fleet must look from down there. Tremendous, no doubt, and dwarfing all the buildings.

He was passing between Manchester and Liverpool, Kurt told him; a gleaming band across the prospect was the Ship Canal, and a weltering ditch of shipping far away ahead, the Mersey estuary. Bert was a Southerner; he had never been north of the Midland counties, and the multitude of factories and chimneys—the latter for the most part obsolete and smokeless now, superseded by huge electric generating stations that consumed their own reek—old railway viaducts, mono-rail net-works and goods yards, and the vast areas of dingy homes and narrow streets, spreading aimlessly, struck him as though Camberwell and Rotherhithe had run to seed. Here and there, as if caught in a net, were fields and agricultural fragments. It was

a sprawl of undistinguished population. There were, no doubt, museums and town halls and even cathedrals of a sort to mark theoretical centres of municipal and religious organisation in this confusion; but Bert could not see them, they did not stand out at all in that wide disorderly vision of congested workers' houses and places to work, and shops and meanly conceived chapels and churches. And across this landscape of an industrial civilisation swept the shadows of the German airships like a hurrying shoal of fishes. . . .

Kurt and he fell talking of aerial tactics, and presently went down to the undergallery in order that Bert might see the *Drachenflieger* that the airships of the right wing had picked up overnight and were towing behind them; each airship towing three or four. They looked, like big box-kites of an exaggerated form, soaring at the ends of invisible cords. They had long, square heads and flattened tails, with lateral propellers.

"Much skill is required for those!—much skill!"

"Rather!"

Pause.

"Your machine is different from that, Mr. Butteridge?"

"Quite different," said Bert. "More like an insect, and less like a bird. And it buzzes, and don't drive about so. What can those things do?"

Kurt was not very clear upon that himself, and was still explaining when Bert was called to the conference we have recorded with the Prince. . . .

And after that was over, the last traces of Butteridge fell from Bert like a garment, and he became Smallways to all on board. The soldiers ceased to salute him, and the officers ceased to seem aware of his existence, except Lieutenant Kurt. He was turned out of his nice cabin, and packed in with his belongings to share that of Lieutenant Kurt, whose luck it was to be junior, and the bird-headed officer, still swearing slightly, and carrying strops and aluminium boot-trees and weightless hair-brushes and hand-mirrors and pomade in his hands, resumed possession.

Bert was put in with Kurt because there was nowhere else for him to lay his bandaged head in that close-packed vessel. He was to mess, he was told, with the men.

Kurt came and stood with his legs wide apart and surveyed, him for a moment as he sat despondent in his new quarters.

"What's your real name, then?" said Kurt, who was only imperfectly informed of the new state of affairs.

"Smallways."

"I thought you were a bit of a fraud—even when I thought you were Butteridge. You're jolly lucky the Prince took it calmly. He's a pretty tidy blazer when he's roused. He wouldn't stick a moment at pitching a chap of your sort overboard if he thought fit. No!. . . They've shoved you on to me, but it's my cabin, you know."

"I won't forget," said Bert.

Kurt left him, and when he came to look about him the first thing he saw pasted on the padded wall was a reproduction, of the great picture by Siegfried Schmalz of the War God, that terrible, trampling figure with the viking helmet and the scarlet cloak, wading through destruction, sword in hand, which had so strong a resemblance to Karl Albert, the prince it was painted to please.

Chapter V

THE BATTLE OF THE NORTH ATLANTIC

§1

The Prince Karl Albert had made a profound impression upon Bert. He was quite the most terrifying person Bert had ever encountered. He filled the Smallways soul with passionate dread and antipathy. For a long time Bert sat alone in Kurt's cabin, doing nothing and not venturing even to open the door lest he should be by that much nearer that appalling presence.

So it came about that he was probably the last person on board to hear the news that wireless telegraphy was bringing to the airship in throbs and fragments of a great naval battle in progress in mid-Atlantic.

He learnt it at last from Kurt.

Kurt came in with a general air of ignoring Bert, but muttering to himself in English nevertheless. "Stupendous!" Bert heard him say. "Here!" he said, "get off this locker." And he proceeded to rout out two books and a case of maps. He spread them on the folding-table, and stood regarding them. For a time his Germanic discipline struggled with his English informality and his natural kindliness and talkativeness, and at last lost.

"They're at it, Smallways," he said.

"At what, sir?" said Bert, broken and respectful.

"Fighting! The American North Atlantic squadron and pretty nearly the whole of our fleet. Our *Eiserne Kreuz* has had a gruelling and is sinking, and their *Miles Standish*—she's one of their biggest—has sunk with all hands. Torpedoes, I suppose. She was a bigger ship than the *Karl der Grosse*, but five or six years older. Gods! I wish we could see it, Smallways; a square fight in blue water, guns or nothing, and all of 'em steaming ahead!"

He spread his maps, he had to talk, and so he delivered a lecture on the naval situation to Bert.

"Here it is," he said, "latitude 30° 50′ N.—longitude 30° 50′ W. It's a good day off us, anyhow, and they're all going south-west by south at full pelt as hard as they can go. We shan't see a bit of it, worse luck! Not a sniff we shan't get!"

§2

The naval situation in the North Atlantic at that time was a peculiar one. The United States was by far the stronger of the two powers upon the sea, but the bulk of the American fleet was still in the Pacific. It was in the direction of Asia that war had been most feared, for the situation between Asiatic and white had become unusually violent and dangerous, and the Japanese government had shown itself quite unprecedentedly difficult. The German attack therefore found half the American strength at Manila, and what was called the Second Fleet strung out across the Pacific in wireless contact between the Asiatic station and San Francisco. The North Atlantic squadron was the sole American force on her eastern shore; it was returning from a friendly visit to France and Spain, and was pumping oil-fuel from tenders in mid-Atlantic—for most of its ships were steamships—when the international situation became acute. It was made up of four battleships and five armoured cruisers ranking almost with battleships, not one of which was of a later date than 1913. The Americans had indeed grown so accustomed to the idea that Great Britain could be trusted to keep the peace of the Atlantic that a naval attack on the eastern seaboard found them unprepared even in their imaginations. But long before the declaration of war—indeed, on Whit Monday—the whole German fleet of eighteen battleships, with a flotilla of fuel tenders and converted liners containing stores to be used in support of the air-fleet, had passed through the straits of Dover and headed boldly for New York. Not only did these German battleships outnumber the Americans two

to one, but they were more heavily armed and more modern in construction—seven of them having high explosive engines built of Charlottenburg steel, and all carrying Charlottenburg steel guns.

The fleets came into contact on Wednesday before any actual declaration of war. The Americans had strung out in the modern fashion at distances of thirty miles or so, and were steaming to keep themselves between the Germans and either the eastern states or Panama; because, vital as it was to defend the seaboard cities and particularly New York, it was still more vital to save the canal from any attack that might prevent the return of the main fleet from the Pacific. No doubt, said Kurt, this was now making records across that ocean, "unless the Japanese have had the same idea as the Germans." It was obviously beyond human possibility that the American North Atlantic fleet could hope to meet and defeat the German; but, on the other hand, with luck it might fight a delaying action and inflict such damage as to greatly weaken the attack upon the coast defences. Its duty, indeed, was not victory but devotion, the severest task in the world. Meanwhile the submarine defences of New York, Panama, and the other more vital points could be put in some sort of order.

This was the naval situation, and until Wednesday in Whit week it was the only situation the American people had realised. It was then they heard for the first time of the real scale of the Dornhof aeronautic park and the possibility of an attack coming upon them not only by sea, but by the air. But it is curious that so discredited were the newspapers of that period that a large majority of New Yorkers, for example, did not believe the most copious and circumstantial accounts of the German air-fleet until it was actually in sight of New York.

Kurt's talk was half soliloquy. He stood with a map on Mercator's projection before him, swaying to the swinging of the ship and talking of guns and tonnage, of ships and their build and powers and speed, of strategic points, and bases of operation. A certain shyness that reduced him to the status of a listener at the officers' table no longer silenced him.

Bert stood by, saying very little, but watching Kurt's finger on the map. "They've been saying things like this in the papers for a long time," he remarked. "Fancy it coming real!"

Kurt had a detailed knowledge of the *Miles Standish.* "She used to be a crack ship for gunnery—held the record. I wonder if we beat her shooting, or how? I wish I was in it. I wonder which of our ships beat her. Maybe she got a shell in her engines. It's a running fight! I wonder what the *Barbarossa* is doing," he went on, "She's my old ship. Not a first-rater, but good stuff. I bet she's got a shot or two home by now if old Schneider's up to form. Just think of it! There they are whacking away at each other, great guns going, shells exploding, magazines bursting, ironwork flying about like straw in a gale, all we've been dreaming of for years! I suppose we shall fly right away to New York—just as though it wasn't anything at all. I suppose we shall reckon we aren't wanted down there. It's no more than a covering fight on our side. All those tenders and store-ships of ours are going on southwest by west to New York to make a floating depot for us. See?" He dabbed his forefinger on the map. "Here we are. Our train of stores goes there, our battleships elbow the Americans out of our way there." . . .

When Bert went down to the men's mess-room to get his evening ration, hardly any one took notice of him except just to point him out for an instant. Every one was talking of the battle, suggesting, contradicting—at times, until the petty officers hushed them, it rose to a great uproar. There was a new bulletin, but what it said he did not gather except that it concerned the *Barbarossa.* Some of the men stared at him, and he heard the name of "Booteraidge" several times; but no one molested him, and there was no difficulty about his soup and bread when his turn at the end of the queue came. He had feared there might be no ration for him, and if so he did not know what he would have done.

Afterwards he ventured out upon the little hanging gallery with the solitary sentinel. The weather was still fine, but the wind was rising and the rolling swing of the airship increasing. He clutched the rail tightly and felt rather giddy. They were now out of sight of land, and over blue water rising and falling in great masses. A dingy old brigantine under the British flag rose and plunged amid the broad blue waves—the only ship in sight.

§3

In the evening it began to blow and the air-ship to roll like a porpoise as it swung through the air. Kurt said that several of the men were sea-sick, but the motion did not inconvenience Bert, whose luck it was to be of that mysterious gastric disposition which constitutes a good sailor. He slept well, but in the small hours the light awoke him, and he found Kurt staggering about in search of something. He found it at last in the locker, and held it in his hand unsteadily—a compass. Then he compared his map.

"We've changed our direction," he said, "and come into the wind. I can't make it out. We've turned away from New York to the south. Almost as if we were going to take a hand—"

He continued talking to himself for some time.

Day came, wet and windy. The window was bedewed externally, and they could see nothing through it. It was also very cold, and Bert decided to keep rolled up in his blankets on the locker until the bugle summoned him to his morning ration. That consumed, he went out on the little gallery; but he could see nothing but eddying clouds driving headlong by, and the dim outlines of the nearer airships. Only at rare intervals could he get a glimpse of grey sea through the pouring cloud-drift.

Later in the morning the *Vaterland* changed altitude, and soared up suddenly in a high, clear sky, going, Kurt said, to a height of nearly thirteen thousand feet.

Bert was in his cabin, and chanced to see the dew vanish from the window and caught the gleam of sunlight outside. He

looked out, and saw once more that sunlit cloud floor he had seen first from the balloon, and the ships of the German air-fleet rising one by one from the white, as fish might rise and become visible from deep water. He stared for a moment and then ran out to the little gallery to see this wonder better. Below was cloudland and storm, a great drift of tumbled weather going hard away to the north-east, and the air about him was clear and cold and serene save for the faintest chill breeze and a rare, drifting snow-flake. Throb, throb, throb, throb, went the engines in the stillness. That huge herd of airships rising one after another had an effect of strange, portentous monsters breaking into an altogether unfamiliar world....

Either there was no news of the naval battle that morning, or the Prince kept to himself whatever came until past midday. Then the bulletins came with a rush, bulletins that made the lieutenant wild with excitement.

"*Barbarossa* disabled and sinking," he cried. "Gott im Himmel! *Der alte Barbarossa! Aber welch ein braver krieger!*"

He walked about the swinging cabin, and for a time he was wholly German.

Then he became English again. "Think of it, Smallways! The old ship we kept so clean and tidy! All smashed about, and the iron flying about in fragments, and the chaps one knew—Gott!—flying about too! Scalding water squirting, fire, and the smash, smash of the guns! They smash when you're near! Like everything bursting to pieces! Wool won't stop it—nothing! And me up here—so near and so far! *Der alte Barbarossa!*"

"Any other ships?" asked Smallways, presently.

"Gott! Yes! We've lost the *Karl der Grosse*, our best and biggest. Run down in the night by a British liner that blundered into the fighting—in trying to blunder out. They're fighting in a gale. The liner's afloat with her nose broken, sagging about! There never was such a battle!—never before! Good ships and good men on both sides—and a storm and the night and the dawn and all in the open ocean full steam ahead! No stabbing!

No submarines! Guns and shooting! Half our ships we don't hear of any more, because their masts are shot away. Latitude, 30° 38′ N.—longitude, 40° 31′ W.—where's that?"

He routed out his map again, and stared at it with eyes that did not see.

"*Der alte Barbarossa!* I can't get it out of my head—with shells in her engine-room, and the fires flying out of her furnaces, and the stokers and engineers scalded and dead. Men I've messed with, Smallways—men I've talked to close! And they've had their day at last! And it wasn't all luck for them!

"Disabled and sinking! I suppose everybody can't have all the luck in a battle. Poor old Schneider! I bet he gave 'em something back!"

So it was the news of the battle came filtering through to them all that morning. The Americans had lost a second ship, name unknown; the *Hermann* had been damaged in covering the Barbarossa.... Kurt fretted like an imprisoned animal about the airship, now going up to the forward gallery under the eagle, now down into the swinging gallery, now poring over his maps. He infected Smallways with a sense of the immediacy of this battle that was going on just over the curve of the earth. But when Bert went down to the gallery the world was empty and still, a clear inky-blue sky above and a rippled veil of still, thin sunlit cirrus below, through which one saw a racing drift of rain-cloud, and never a glimpse of sea. Throb, throb, throb, throb, went the engines, and the long, undulating wedge of airships hurried after the flagship like a flight of swans after their leader. Save for the quiver of the engines it was as noiseless as a dream. And down there, somewhere in the wind and rain, guns roared, shells crashed home, and, after the old manner of warfare, men toiled and died.

§4

As the afternoon wore on the lower weather abated, and the sea became intermittently visible again. The air-fleet dropped

slowly to the middle air, and towards sunset they had a glimpse of the disabled *Barbarossa* far away to the east. Smallways heard men hurrying along the passage, and was drawn out to the gallery, where he found nearly a dozen officers collected and scrutinising the helpless ruins of the battleship through field-glasses. Two other vessels stood by her, one an exhausted petrol tank, very high out of the water, and the other a converted liner. Kurt was at the end of the gallery, a little apart from the others.

"Gott!" he said at last, lowering his binocular, "it is like seeing an old friend with his nose cut off—waiting to be finished. Der *Barbarossa*!"

With a sudden impulse he handed his glass to Bert, who had peered beneath his hands, ignored by every one, seeing the three ships merely as three brown-black lines upon the sea.

Never had Bert seen the like of that magnified slightly hazy image before. It was not simply a battered ironclad that wallowed helpless, it was a mangled ironclad. It seemed wonderful she still floated. Her powerful engines had been her ruin. In the long chase of the night she had got out of line with her consorts, and nipped in between the *Susquehanna* and the *Kansas City*. They discovered her proximity, dropped back until she was nearly broadside on to the former battleship, and signalled up the *Theodore Roosevelt* and the little *Monitor*. As dawn broke she had found herself hostess of a circle. The fight had not lasted five minutes before the appearance of the *Hermann* to the east, and immediately after of the *Fürst Bismarck* in the west, forced the Americans to leave her, but in that time they had smashed her iron to rags. They had vented the accumulated tensions of their hard day's retreat upon her. As Bert saw her, she seemed a mere metal-worker's fantasy of frozen metal writhings. He could not tell part from part of her, except by its position.

"Gott!" murmured Kurt, taking the glasses Bert restored to him—"Gott! Da waren Albrecht—der gute Albrecht und der alte Zimmermann—und von Rosen!" . . .

Long after the *Barbarossa* had been swallowed up in the twilight and distance he remained on the gallery peering through his glasses, and when he came back to his cabin he was unusually silent and thoughtful.

"This is a rough game, Smallways," he said at last—"this war is a rough game. Somehow one sees it different after a thing like that. Many men there were worked to make that Barbarossa, and there were men in it—one does not meet the like of them every day. Albrecht—there was a man named Albrecht—played the zither and improvised; I keep on wondering what has happened to him. He and I—we were very close friends, after the German fashion."

§5

Smallways woke the next night to discover the cabin in darkness, a draught blowing through it, and Kurt talking to himself in German. He could see him dimly by the window, which he had unscrewed and opened, peering down. That cold, clear, attenuated light which is not so much light as a going of darkness, which casts inky shadows and so often heralds the dawn in the high air, was on his face.

"What's the row?" said Bert.

"Shut up!" said the lieutenant. "Can't you hear?"

Into the stillness came the repeated heavy thud of guns, one, two, a pause, then three in quick succession.

"Gaw!" said Bert—"guns!" and was instantly at the lieutenant's side. The airship was still very high and the sea below was masked by a thin veil of clouds. The wind had fallen, and Bert, following Kurt's pointing finger, saw dimly through the colourless veil first a red glow, then a quick red flash, and then at a little distance from it another. They were, it seemed for a while, silent flashes, and seconds after, when one had ceased to expect them, came the belated thuds—thud, thud. Kurt spoke in German, very quickly.

A bugle call rang through the airship.

Kurt sprang to his feet, saying something in an excited tone, still using German, and went to the door.

"I say! What's up?" cried Bert. "What's that?"

The lieutenant stopped for an instant in the doorway, dark against the light passage. "You stay where you are, Smallways. You keep there and do nothing. We're going into action," he explained, and vanished.

Bert's heart began to beat rapidly. He felt himself poised over the fighting vessels far below. In a moment, were they to drop like a hawk striking a bird? "Gaw!" he whispered at last, in awestricken tones.

Thud!… thud! He discovered far away a second ruddy flare flashing guns back at the first. He perceived some difference on the *Vaterland* for which he could not account, and then he realised that the engines had slowed to an almost inaudible beat. He stuck his head out of the window—it was a tight fit—and saw in the bleak air the other airships slowed down to a scarcely perceptible motion.

A second bugle sounded, was taken up faintly from ship to ship. Out went the lights; the fleet became dim, dark bulks against an intense blue sky that still retained an occasional star. For a long time they hung, for an interminable time it seemed to him, and then began the sound of air being pumped into the balloonette, and slowly, slowly the *Vaterland* sank down towards the clouds.

He craned his neck, but he could not see if the rest of the fleet was following them; the overhang of the gas-chambers intervened. There was something that stirred his imagination deeply in that stealthy, noiseless descent. The obscurity deepened for a time, the last fading star on the horizon vanished, and he felt the cold presence of cloud. Then suddenly the glow beneath assumed distinct outlines, became flames, and the *Vaterland* ceased to descend and hung observant, and it would seem unobserved, just beneath a drifting stratum of cloud, a thousand feet, perhaps, over the battle below.

In the night the struggling naval battle and retreat had entered upon a new phase. The Americans had drawn together the ends of the flying line skilfully and dexterously, until at last it was a column and well to the south of the lax sweeping pursuit of the Germans. Then in the darkness before the dawn they had come about and steamed northward in close order with the idea of passing through the German battle-line and falling upon the flotilla that was making for New York in support of the German air-fleet. Much had altered since the first contact of the fleets. By this time the American admiral, O'Connor, was fully informed of the existence of the airships, and he was no longer vitally concerned for Panama, since the submarine flotilla was reported arrived there from Key West, and the *Delaware* and *Abraham Lincoln*, two powerful and entirely modern ships, were already at Rio Grande, on the Pacific side of the canal. His manoeuvre was, however, delayed by a boiler explosion on board the *Susquehanna*, and dawn found this ship in sight of and indeed so close to the *Bremen* and *Weimar* that they instantly engaged. There was no alternative to her abandonment but a fleet engagement. O'Connor chose the latter course. It was by no means a hopeless fight. The Germans, though much more numerous and powerful than the Americans, were in a dispersed line measuring nearly forty-five miles from end to end, and there were many chances that before they could gather in for the fight the column of seven Americans would have ripped them from end to end.

The day broke dim and overcast, and neither the *Bremen* nor the *Weimar* realised they had to deal with more than the *Susquehanna* until the whole column drew out from behind her at a distance of a mile or less and bore down on them. This was the position of affairs when the *Vaterland* appeared in the sky. The red glow Bert had seen through the column of clouds came from the luckless *Susquehanna*; she lay almost immediately below, burning fore and aft, but still fighting two of her guns and steaming slowly southward. The *Bremen* and the *Weimar*, both

hit in several places, were going west by south and away from her. The American fleet, headed by the *Theodore Roosevelt*, was crossing behind them, pounding them in succession, steaming in between them and the big modern *Fürst Bismarck*, which was coming up from the west. To Bert, however, the names of all these ships were unknown, and for a considerable time indeed, misled by the direction in which the combatants were moving, he imagined the Germans to be Americans and the Americans Germans. He saw what appeared to him to be a column of six battleships pursuing three others who were supported by a newcomer, until the fact that the *Bremen* and *Weimar* were firing into the *Susquehanna* upset his calculations. Then for a time he was hopelessly at a loss. The noise of the guns, too, confused him, they no longer seemed to boom; they went whack, whack, whack, whack, and each faint flash made his heart jump in anticipation of the instant impact. He saw these ironclads, too, not in profile, as he was accustomed to see ironclads in pictures, but in plan and curiously foreshortened. For the most part they presented empty decks, but here and there little knots of men sheltered behind steel bulwarks. The long, agitated noses of their big guns, jetting thin transparent flashes and the broadside activity of the quick-firers, were the chief facts in this bird's-eye view. The Americans being steam-turbine ships, had from two to four blast funnels each; the Germans lay lower in the water, having explosive engines, which now for some reason made an unwonted muttering roar. Because of their steam propulsion, the American ships were larger and with a more graceful outline. He saw all these foreshortened ships rolling considerably and fighting their guns over a sea of huge low waves and under the cold, explicit light of dawn. The whole spectacle waved slowly with the long rhythmic rising and beat of the airship.

At first only the *Vaterland* of all the flying fleet appeared upon the scene below. She hovered high, over the *Theodore Roosevelt*, keeping pace with the full speed of that ship. From that ship she must have been intermittently visible through the drifting

clouds. The rest of the German fleet remained above the cloud canopy at a height of six or seven thousand feet, communicating with the flagship by wireless telegraphy, but risking no exposure to the artillery below.

It is doubtful at what particular time the unlucky Americans realised the presence of this new factor in the fight. No account now survives of their experience. We have to imagine as well as we can what it must have been to a battled-strained sailor suddenly glancing upward to discover that huge long silent shape overhead, vaster than any battleship, and trailing now from its hinder quarter a big German flag. Presently, as the sky cleared, more of such ships appeared in the blue through the dissolving clouds, and more, all disdainfully free of guns or armour, all flying fast to keep pace with the running fight below.

From first to last no gun whatever was fired at the *Vaterland*, and only a few rifle shots. It was a mere adverse stroke of chance that she had a man killed aboard her. Nor did she take any direct share in the fight until the end. She flew above the doomed American fleet while the Prince by wireless telegraphy directed the movements of her consorts. Meanwhile the *Vogel-stern* and *Preussen*, each with half a dozen drachenflieger in tow, went full speed ahead and then dropped through the clouds, perhaps five miles ahead of the Americans. The *Theodore Roosevelt* let fly at once with the big guns in her forward barbette, but the shells burst far below the *Vogel-stern*, and forthwith a dozen single-man drachenflieger were swooping down to make their attack.

Bert, craning his neck through the cabin port-hole, saw the whole of that incident, that first encounter of aeroplane and ironclad. He saw the queer German drachenflieger, with their wide flat wings and square box-shaped heads, their wheeled bodies, and their single-man riders, soar down the air like a flight of birds. "Gaw!" he said. One to the right pitched extravagantly, shot steeply up into the air, burst with a loud report, and flamed down into the sea; another plunged nose forward into the water and seemed to fly to pieces as it hit the waves. He saw little men on the deck of the *Theodore Roosevelt* below, men foreshortened in plan into mere heads and feet, running out preparing to shoot at the others. Then the foremost flying-machine was rushing between Bert and the American's deck, and then bang! came the thunder of its bomb flung neatly at the forward barbette, and a thin little crackling of rifle shots in reply. Whack, whack, whack, went the quick-firing guns of the Americans' battery, and smash came an answering shell from the *Fürst Bismarck*. Then a second and third flying-machine passed between Bert and the American ironclad, dropping bombs also, and a fourth, its rider hit by a bullet, reeled down and dashed itself to pieces and exploded between the shot-torn funnels, blowing them apart. Bert had a momentary glimpse of a little black creature jumping from the crumpling frame of the flying-machine, hitting the funnel, and falling limply, to be instantly caught and driven to nothingness by the blaze and rush of the explosion.

Smash! came a vast explosion in the forward part of the flagship, and a huge piece of metalwork seemed to lift out of her and dump itself into the sea, dropping men and leaving a gap into which a prompt drachenflieger planted a flaring bomb. And then for an instant Bert perceived only too clearly in the growing, pitiless light a number of minute, convulsively active animalcula scorched and struggling in the *Theodore Roosevelt's* foaming wake. What were they? Not men—surely not men? Those drowning, mangled little creatures tore with their clutching fingers at Bert's soul. "Oh, Gord!" he cried, "Oh, Gord!" almost whimpering. He looked again and they had gone, and the black stem of the *Andrew Jackson*, a little disfigured by the sinking *Bremen's* last shot, was parting the water that had swallowed them into two neatly symmetrical waves. For some moments sheer blank horror blinded Bert to the destruction below.

Then, with an immense rushing sound, bearing as it were a straggling volley of crashing minor explosions on its back, the *Susquehanna*, three miles and more now to the east, blew up and vanished abruptly in a boiling, steaming welter. For a moment

nothing was to be seen but tumbled water, and—then there came belching up from below, with immense gulping noises, eructations of steam and air and petrol and fragments of canvas and woodwork and men.

That made a distinct pause in the fight. It seemed a long pause to Bert. He found himself looking for the drachenflieger. The flattened ruin of one was floating abeam of the *Monitor*, the rest had passed, dropping bombs down the American column; several were in the water and apparently uninjured, and three or four were still in the air and coming round now in a wide circle to return to their mother airships. The American ironclads were no longer in column formation; the *Theodore Roosevelt*, badly damaged, had turned to the southeast, and the *Andrew Jackson*, greatly battered but uninjured in any fighting part was passing between her and the still fresh and vigorous *Fürst Bismarck* to intercept and meet the latter's fire. Away to the west the *Hermann* and the *Germanicus* had appeared and were coming into action.

In the pause, after the *Susquehanna's* disaster Bert became aware of a trivial sound like the noise of an ill-greased, ill-hung door that falls ajar—the sound of the men in the *Fürst Bismarck* cheering.

And in that pause in the uproar too, the sun rose, the dark waters became luminously blue, and a torrent of golden light irradiated the world. It came like a sudden smile in a scene of hate and terror. The cloud veil had vanished as if by magic, and the whole immensity of the German air-fleet was revealed in the sky; the air-fleet stooping now upon its prey.

"Whack-bang, whack-bang," the guns resumed, but ironclads were not built to fight the zenith, and the only hits the Americans scored were a few lucky chances in a generally ineffectual rifle fire. Their column was now badly broken, the *Susquehanna* had gone, the *Theodore Roosevelt* had fallen astern out of the line, with her forward guns disabled, in a heap of wreckage, and the *Monitor* was in some grave trouble. These two had ceased

fire altogether, and so had the *Bremen* and *Weimar*, all four ships lying within shot of each other in an involuntary truce and with their respective flags still displayed. Only four American ships now, with the *Andrew Jackson* leading, kept to the south-easterly course. And the *Fürst Bismarck*, the *Hermann*, and the *Germanicus* steamed parallel to them and drew ahead of them, fighting heavily. The *Vaterland* rose slowly in the air in preparation for the concluding act of the drama.

Then, falling into place one behind the other, a string of a dozen airships dropped with unhurrying swiftness down the air in pursuit of the American fleet. They kept at a height of two thousand feet or more until they were over and a little in advance of the rearmost ironclad, and then stooped swiftly down into a fountain of bullets, and going just a little faster than the ship below, pelted her thinly protected decks with bombs until they became sheets of detonating flame. So the airships passed one after the other along the American column as it sought to keep up its fight with the *Fürst Bismarck*, the *Hermann*, and the *Germanicus*, and each airship added to the destruction and confusion its predecessor had made. The American gunfire ceased, except for a few heroic shots, but they still steamed on, obstinately unsubdued, bloody, battered, and wrathfully resistant, spitting bullets at the airships and unmercifully pounded by the German ironclads. But now Bert had but intermittent glimpses of them between the nearer bulks of the airships that assailed them. . . .

It struck Bert suddenly that the whole battle was receding and growing small and less thunderously noisy. The *Vaterland* was rising in the air, steadily and silently, until the impact of the guns no longer smote upon the heart but came to the ear dulled by distance, until the four silenced ships to the eastward were little distant things: but were there four? Bert now could see only three of those floating, blackened, and smoking rafts of ruin against the sun. But the *Bremen* had two boats out; the *Theodore Roosevelt* was also dropping boats to where the drift of minute objects struggled, rising and falling on the big, broad Atlantic

waves. . . . The *Vaterland* was no longer following the fight. The whole of that hurrying tumult drove away to the south-eastward, growing smaller and less audible as it passed. One of the airships lay on the water burning, a remote monstrous fount of flames, and far in the south-west appeared first one and then three other German ironclads hurrying in support of their consorts. . . .

§6

Steadily the Vaterland soared, and the air-fleet soared with her and came round to head for New York, and the battle became a little thing far away, an incident before the breakfast. It dwindled to a string of dark shapes and one smoking yellow flare that presently became a mere indistinct smear upon the vast horizon and the bright new day, that was at last altogether lost to sight. . .

So it was that Bert Smallways saw the first fight of the airship and the last fight of those strangest things in the whole history of war: the ironclad battleships, which began their career with the floating batteries of the Emperor Napoleon III in the Crimean war and lasted, with an enormous expenditure of human energy and resources, for seventy years. In that space of time the world produced over twelve thousand five hundred of these strange monsters, in schools, in types, in series, each larger and heavier and more deadly than its predecessors. Each in its turn was hailed as the last birth of time, most in their turn were sold for old iron. Only about five per cent of them ever fought in a battle. Some foundered, some went ashore, and broke up, several rammed one another by accident and sank. The lives of countless men were spent in their service, the splendid genius and patience of thousands of engineers and inventors, wealth and material beyond estimating; to their account we must put stunted and starved lives on land, millions of children sent to toil unduly, innumerable opportunities of fine living undeveloped and lost. Money had to be found for them at any cost—that was the law of a nation's existence during that strange time. Surely they were

the weirdest, most destructive and wasteful megatheria in the whole history of mechanical invention.

And then cheap things of gas and basket-work made an end of them altogether, smiting out of the sky!. . .

Never before had Bert Smallways seen pure destruction, never had he realised the mischief and waste of war. His startled mind rose to the conception; this also is in life. Out of all this fierce torrent of sensation one impression rose and became cardinal—the impression of the men of the *Theodore Roosevelt* who had struggled in the water after the explosion of the first bomb. "Gaw!" he said at the memory; "it might 'ave been me and Grubb!. . . I suppose you kick about and get the water in your mouf. I don't suppose it lasts long."

He became anxious to see how Kurt was affected by these things. Also he perceived he was hungry. He hesitated towards the door of the cabin and peeped out into the passage. Down forward, near the gangway to the men's mess, stood a little group of air sailors looking at something that was hidden from him in a recess. One of them was in the light diver's costume Bert had already seen in the gas chamber turret, and he was moved to walk along and look at this person more closely and examine the helmet he carried under his arm. But he forgot about the helmet when he got to the recess, because there he found lying on the floor the dead body of the boy who had been killed by a bullet from the *Theodore Roosevelt.*

Bert had not observed that any bullets at all had reached the *Vaterland* or, indeed, imagined himself under fire. He could not understand for a time what had killed the lad, and no one explained to him.

The boy lay just as he had fallen and died, with his jacket torn and scorched, his shoulder-blade smashed and burst away from his body and all the left side of his body ripped and rent. There was much blood. The sailors stood listening to the man with the helmet, who made explanations and pointed to the round bullet hole in the floor and the smash in the panel of the passage

upon which the still vicious missile had spent the residue of its energy. All the faces were grave and earnest: they were the faces of sober, blond, blue-eyed men accustomed to obedience and an orderly life, to whom this waste, wet, painful thing that had been a comrade came almost as strangely as it did to Bert.

A peal of wild laughter sounded down the passage in the direction of the little gallery and something spoke—almost shouted—in German, in tones of exultation.

Other voices at a lower, more respectful pitch replied.

"*Der Prinz*," said a voice, and all the men became stiffer and less natural. Down the passage appeared a group of figures, Lieutenant Kurt walking in front carrying a packet of papers.

He stopped point blank when he saw the thing in the recess, and his ruddy face went white.

"So!" said he in surprise.

The Prince was following him, talking over his shoulder to Von Winterfeld and the Kapitan.

"Eh?" he said to Kurt, stopping in mid-sentence, and followed the gesture of Kurt's hand. He glared at the crumpled object in the recess and seemed to think for a moment.

He made a slight, careless gesture towards the boy's body and turned to the Kapitan.

"Dispose of that," he said in German, and passed on, finishing his sentence to Von Winterfeld in the same cheerful tone in which it had begun.

§7

The deep impression of helplessly drowning men that Bert had brought from the actual fight in the Atlantic mixed itself up inextricably with that of the lordly figure of Prince Karl Albert gesturing aside the dead body of the *Vaterland* sailor. Hitherto he had rather liked the idea of war as being a jolly, smashing, exciting affair, something like a Bank Holiday rag on a large scale, and on the whole agreeable and exhilarating. Now he knew it a little better.

The next day there was added to his growing disillusionment a third ugly impression, trivial indeed to describe, a mere necessary everyday incident of a state of war, but very distressing to his urbanised imagination. One writes "urbanised" to express the distinctive gentleness of the period. It was quite peculiar to the crowded townsmen of that time, and different altogether from the normal experience of any preceding age, that they never saw anything killed, never encountered, save through the mitigating media of book or picture, the fact of lethal violence that underlies all life. Three times in his existence, and three times only, had Bert seen a dead human being, and he had never assisted at the killing of anything bigger than a new-born kitten.

The incident that gave him his third shock was the execution of one of the men on the *Adler* for carrying a box of matches. The case was a flagrant one. The man had forgotten he had it upon him when coming aboard. Ample notice had been given to every one of the gravity of this offence, and notices appeared at numerous points all over the airships. The man's defence was that he had grown so used to the notices and had been so preoccupied with his work that he hadn't applied them to himself; he pleaded, in his defence, what is indeed in military affairs another serious crime, inadvertency. He was tried by his captain, and the sentence confirmed by wireless telegraphy by the Prince, and it was decided to make his death an example to the whole fleet. "The Germans," the Prince declared, "hadn't crossed the Atlantic to go wool gathering." And in order that this lesson in discipline and obedience might be visible to every one, it was determined not to electrocute or drown but hang the offender.

Accordingly the air-fleet came clustering round the flagship like carp in a pond at feeding time. The *Adler* hung at the zenith immediately alongside the flagship. The whole crew of the *Vaterland* assembled upon the hanging gallery; the crews of the other airships manned the air-chambers, that is to say, clambered up the outer netting to the upper sides. The officers appeared

upon the machine-gun platforms. Bert thought it an altogether stupendous sight, looking down, as he was, upon the entire fleet. Far off below two steamers on the rippled blue water, one British and the other flying the American flag, seemed the minutest objects, and marked the scale. They were immensely distant. Bert stood on the gallery, curious to see the execution, but uncomfortable, because that terrible blond Prince was within a dozen feet of him, glaring terribly, with his arms folded, and his heels together in military fashion.

They hung the man from the *Adler*. They gave him sixty feet of rope, so, that he should hang and dangle in the sight of all evil-doers who might be hiding matches or contemplating any kindred disobedience. Bert saw the man standing, a living, reluctant man, no doubt scared and rebellious enough in his heart, but outwardly erect and obedient, on the lower gallery of the *Adler* about a hundred yards away. Then they had thrust him overboard.

Down he fell, hands and feet extending, until with a jerk he was at the end of the rope. Then he ought to have died and swung edifyingly, but instead a more terrible thing happened; his head came right off, and down the body went spinning to the sea, feeble, grotesque, fantastic, with the head racing it in its fall.

"Ugh!" said Bert, clutching the rail before him, and a sympathetic grunt came from several of the men beside him.

"So!" said the Prince, stiffer and sterner, glared for some seconds, then turned to the gang way up into the airship.

For a long time Bert remained clinging to the railing of the gallery. He was almost physically sick with the horror of this trifling incident. He found it far more dreadful than the battle. He was indeed a very degenerate, latter-day, civilised person.

Late that afternoon Kurt came into the cabin and found him curled up on his locker, and looking very white and miserable. Kurt had also lost something of his pristine freshness.

"Sea-sick?" he asked.

"No!"

"We ought to reach New York this evening. There's a good breeze coming up under our tails. Then we shall see things."

Bert did not answer.

Kurt opened out folding chair and table, and rustled for a time with his maps. Then he fell thinking darkly. He roused himself presently, and looked at his companion. "What's the matter?" he said.

"Nothing!"

Kurt stared threateningly. "What's the matter?"

"I saw them kill that chap. I saw that flying-machine man hit the funnels of the big ironclad. I saw that dead chap in the passage. I seen too much smashing and killing lately. That's the matter. I don't like it. I didn't know war was this sort of thing. I'm a civilian. I don't like it."

"*I* don't like it," said Kurt. "By Jove, no!"

"I've read about war, and all that, but when you see it it's different. And I'm gettin' giddy. I'm gettin' giddy. I didn't mind a bit being up in that balloon at first, but all this looking down and floating over things and smashing up people, it's getting on my nerves. See?"

"It'll have to get off again. . . ."

Kurt thought. "You're not the only one. The men are all getting strung up. The flying—that's just flying. Naturally it makes one a little swimmy in the head at first. As for the killing, we've got to be blooded; that's all. We're tame, civilised men. And we've got to get blooded. I suppose there's not a dozen men on the ship who've really seen bloodshed. Nice, quiet, law-abiding Germans they've been so far. . . . Here they are—in for it. They're a bit squeamy now, but you wait till they've got their hands in."

He reflected. "Everybody's getting a bit strung up," he said.

He turned again to his maps. Bert sat crumpled up in the corner, apparently heedless of him. For some time both kept silence.

"What did the Prince want to go and 'ang that chap for?" asked Bert, suddenly.

"That was all right," said Kurt, "that was all right. *Quite* right. Here were the orders, plain as the nose on your face, and here was that fool going about with matches—"

"Gaw! I shan't forget that bit in a 'urry," said Bert irrelevantly.

Kurt did not answer him. He was measuring their distance from New York and speculating. "Wonder what the American aeroplanes are like?" he said. "Something like our drachenflieger. . . . We shall know by this time to-morrow. . . . I wonder what we shall know? I wonder. Suppose, after all, they put up a fight. . . . Rum sort of fight!"

He whistled softly and mused. Presently he fretted out of the cabin, and later Bert found him in the twilight upon the swinging platform, staring ahead, and speculating about the things that might happen on the morrow. Clouds veiled the sea again, and the long straggling wedge of air-ships rising and falling as they flew seemed like a flock of strange new births in a Chaos that had neither earth nor water but only mist and sky.

Chapter VI

HOW WAR CAME TO NEW YORK

§1

The City of New York was in the year of the German attack the largest, richest, in many respects the most splendid, and in some, the wickedest city the world had ever seen. She was the supreme type of the City of the Scientific Commercial Age; she displayed its greatness, its power, its ruthless anarchic enterprise, and its social disorganisation most strikingly and completely. She had long ousted London from her pride of place as the modern Babylon, she was the centre of the world's finance, the world's trade, and the world's pleasure; and men likened her to the apocalyptic cities of the ancient prophets. She sat drinking up the wealth of a continent as Rome once drank the wealth of the Mediterranean and Babylon the wealth of the east. In her streets one found the extremes of magnificence and misery, of civilisation and disorder. In one quarter, palaces of marble, laced and, crowned with light and flame and flowers, towered up into her marvellous twilights beautiful, beyond description; in another, a black and sinister polyglot population sweltered in indescribable congestion in warrens, and excavations beyond the power and knowledge of government. Her vice, her crime, her law alike were inspired by a fierce and terrible energy, and like the great cities of mediaeval Italy, her ways were dark and adventurous with private war.

It was the peculiar shape of Manhattan Island, pressed in by arms of the sea on either side, and incapable of comfortable expansion, except along a narrow northward belt, that first gave the New York architects their bias for extreme vertical dimensions. Every need was lavishly supplied them—money,

material, labour; only space was restricted. To begin, therefore, they built high perforce. But to do so was to discover a whole new world of architectural beauty, of exquisite ascendant lines, and long after the central congestion had been relieved by tunnels under the sea, four colossal bridges over the east river, and a dozen mono-rail cables east and west, the upward growth went on. In many ways New York and her gorgeous plutocracy repeated Venice in the magnificence of her architecture, painting, metal work and sculpture, for example, in the grim intensity of her political method, in her maritime and commercial ascendancy. But she repeated no previous state at all in the lax disorder of her internal administration, a laxity that made vast sections of her area lawless beyond precedent, so that it was possible for whole districts to be impassable, while civil war raged between street and street, and for Alsatias to exist in her midst in which the official police never set foot. She was an ethnic whirlpool. The flags of all nations flew in her harbour, and at the climax, the yearly coming and going overseas numbered together upwards of two million human beings. To Europe she was America, to America she was the gateway of the world. But to tell the story of New York would be to write a social history of the world; saints and martyrs, dreamers and scoundrels, the traditions of a thousand races and a thousand religions, went to her making and throbbed and jostled in her streets. And over all that torrential confusion of men and purposes fluttered that strange flag, the stars and stripes, that meant at once the noblest thing in life, and the least noble, that is to say, Liberty on the one hand, and on the other the base jealousy the individual self-seeker feels towards the common purpose of the State.

For many generations New York had taken no heed of war, save as a thing that happened far away, that affected prices and supplied the newspapers with exciting headlines and pictures. The New Yorkers felt perhaps even more certainly than the English had done that war in their own land was an impossible

thing. In that they shared the delusion of all North America. They felt as secure as spectators at a bullfight; they risked their money perhaps on the result, but that was all. And such ideas of war as the common Americans possessed were derived from the limited, picturesque, adventurous war of the past. They saw war as they saw history, through an iridescent mist, deodorised, scented indeed, with all its essential cruelties tactfully hidden away. They were inclined to regret it as something ennobling, to sigh that it could no longer come into their own private experience. They read with interest, if not with avidity, of their new guns, of their immense and still more immense ironclads, of their incredible and still more incredible explosives, but just what these tremendous engines of destruction might mean for their personal lives never entered their heads. They did not, so far as one can judge from their contemporary literature, think that they meant anything to their personal lives at all. They thought America was safe amidst all this piling up of explosives. They cheered the flag by habit and tradition, they despised other nations, and whenever there was an international difficulty they were intensely patriotic, that is to say, they were ardently against any native politician who did not say, threaten, and do harsh and uncompromising things to the antagonist people. They were spirited to Asia, spirited to Germany, so spirited to Great Britain that the international attitude of the mother country to her great daughter was constantly compared in contemporary caricature to that between a hen-pecked husband and a vicious young wife. And for the rest, they all went about their business and pleasure as if war had died out with the megatherium. . . .

And then suddenly, into a world peacefully busied for the most part upon armaments and the perfection of explosives, war came; came the shock of realising that the guns were going off, that the masses of inflammable material all over the world were at last ablaze.

§2

The immediate effect upon New York of the sudden onset of war was merely to intensify her normal vehemence.

The newspapers and magazines that fed the American mind—for books upon this impatient continent had become simply material for the energy of collectors—were instantly a coruscation of war pictures and of headlines that rose like rockets and burst like shells. To the normal high-strung energy of New York streets was added a touch of war-fever. Great crowds assembled, more especially in the dinner hour, in Madison Square about the Farragut monument, to listen to and cheer patriotic speeches, and a veritable epidemic of little flags and buttons swept through these great torrents of swiftly moving young people, who poured into New York of a morning by car and mono-rail and subway and train, to toil, and ebb home again between the hours of five and seven. It was dangerous not to wear a war button. The splendid music-halls of the time sank every topic in patriotism and evolved scenes of wild enthusiasm, strong men wept at the sight of the national banner sustained by the whole strength of the ballet, and special searchlights and illuminations amazed the watching angels. The churches re-echoed the national enthusiasm in graver key and slower measure, and the aerial and naval preparations on the East River were greatly incommoded by the multitude of excursion steamers which thronged, helpfully cheering, about them. The trade in small arms was enormously stimulated, and many overwrought citizens found an immediate relief for their emotions in letting off fireworks of a more or less heroic, dangerous, and national character in the public streets. Small children's air-balloons of the latest model attached to string became a serious check to the pedestrian in Central Park. And amidst scenes of indescribable emotion the Albany legislature in permanent session, and with a generous suspension of rules and precedents, passed through both Houses the long-disputed Bill for universal military service in New York State.

Critics of the American character are disposed to consider—that up to the actual impact of the German attack the people of New York dealt altogether too much with the war as if it was a political demonstration. Little or no damage, they urge, was done to either the German or Japanese forces by the wearing of buttons, the waving of small flags, the fireworks, or the songs. They forgot that, under the conditions of warfare a century of science had brought about, the non-military section of the population could do no serious damage in any form to their enemies, and that there was no reason, therefore, why they should not do as they did. The balance of military efficiency was shifting back from the many to the few, from the common to the specialised.

The days when the emotional infantryman decided battles had passed by for ever. War had become a matter of apparatus, of special training and skill of the most intricate kind. It had become undemocratic. And whatever the value of the popular excitement, there can be no denying that the small regular establishment of the United States Government, confronted by this totally unexpected emergency of an armed invasion from Europe, acted with vigour, science, and imagination. They were taken by surprise so far as the diplomatic situation was concerned, and their equipment for building either navigables or aeroplanes was contemptible in comparison with the huge German parks. Still they set to work at once to prove to the world that the spirit that had created the *Monitor* and the Southern submarines of 1864 was not dead. The chief of the aeronautic establishment near West Point was Cabot Sinclair, and he allowed himself but one single moment of the posturing that was so universal in that democratic time. "We have chosen our epitaphs," he said to a reporter, "and we are going to have, 'They did all they could.' Now run away!"

The curious thing is that they did all do all they could; there is no exception known. Their only defect indeed was a defect of style.

One of the most striking facts historically about this war, and the one that makes the complete separation that had arisen between the methods of warfare and the necessity of democratic support, is the effectual secrecy of the Washington authorities about their airships. They did not bother to confide a single fact of their preparations to the public. They did not even condescend to talk to Congress. They burked and suppressed every inquiry. The war was fought by the President and the Secretaries of State in an entirely autocratic manner. Such publicity as they sought was merely to anticipate and prevent inconvenient agitation to defend particular points. They realised that the chief danger in aerial warfare from an excitable and intelligent public would be a clamour for local airships and aeroplanes to defend local interests. This, with such resources as they possessed, might lead to a fatal division and distribution of the national forces. Particularly they feared that they might be forced into a premature action to defend New York. They realised with prophetic insight that this would be the particular advantage the Germans would seek. So they took great pains to direct the popular mind towards defensive artillery, and to divert it from any thought of aerial battle. Their real preparations they masked beneath ostensible ones. There was at Washington a large reserve of naval guns, and these were distributed rapidly, conspicuously, and with much press attention, among the Eastern cities. They were mounted for the most part upon hills and prominent crests around the threatened centres of population. They were mounted upon rough adaptations of the Doan swivel, which at that time gave the maximum vertical range to a heavy gun. Much of this artillery was still unmounted, and nearly all of it was unprotected when the German air-fleet reached New York. And down in the crowded streets, when that occurred, the readers of the New York papers were regaling themselves with wonderful and wonderfully illustrated accounts of such matters as:—

THE SECRET OF THE THUNDERBOLT

AGED SCIENTIST PERFECTS ELECTRIC GUN TO ELECTROCUTE AIRSHIP CREWS BY UPWARD LIGHTNING

WASHINGTON ORDERS FIVE HUNDRED

WAR SECRETARY LODGE DELIGHTED

SAYS THEY WILL SUIT THE GERMANS DOWN TO THE GROUND

PRESIDENT PUBLICLY APPLAUDS THIS MERRY QUIP

§3

The German fleet reached New York in advance of the news of the American naval disaster. It reached New York in the late afternoon and was first seen by watchers at Ocean Grove and Long Branch coming swiftly out of the southward sea and going away to the northwest. The flagship passed almost vertically over the Sandy Hook observation station, rising rapidly as it did so, and in a few minutes all New York was vibrating to the Staten Island guns.

Several of these guns, and especially that at Giffords and the one on Beacon Hill above Matawan, were remarkably well handled. The former, at a distance of five miles, and with an elevation of six thousand feet, sent a shell to burst so close to the *Vaterland* that a pane of the Prince's forward window was smashed by a fragment. This sudden explosion made Bert tuck in his head with the celerity of a startled tortoise. The whole air-fleet immediately went up steeply to a height of about twelve thousand feet and at that level passed unscathed over the ineffectual guns. The airships lined out as they moved forward into the form of a flattened V, with its apex towards the city,

and with the flagship going highest at the apex. The two ends of the V passed over Plumfield and Jamaica Bay, respectively, and the Prince directed his course a little to the east of the Narrows, soared over Upper Bay, and came to rest over Jersey City in a position that dominated lower New York. There the monsters hung, large and wonderful in the evening light, serenely regardless of the occasional rocket explosions and flashing shell-bursts in the lower air.

It was a pause of mutual inspection. For a time naive humanity swamped the conventions of warfare altogether; the interest of the millions below and of the thousands above alike was spectacular. The evening was unexpectedly fine—only a few thin level bands of clouds at seven or eight thousand feet broke its luminous clarity. The wind had dropped; it was an evening infinitely peaceful and still. The heavy concussions of the distant guns and those incidental harmless pyrotechnics at the level of the clouds seemed to have as little to do with killing and force, terror and submission, as a salute at a naval review. Below, every point of vantage bristled with spectators, the roofs of the towering buildings, the public squares, the active ferry boats, and every favourable street intersection had its crowds: all the river piers were dense with people, the Battery Park was solid black with east-side population, and every position of advantage in Central Park and along Riverside Drive had its peculiar and characteristic assembly from the adjacent streets. The footways of the great bridges over the East River were also closely packed and blocked. Everywhere shopkeepers had left their shops, men their work, and women and children their homes, to come out and see the marvel.

"It beat," they declared, "the newspapers."

And from above, many of the occupants of the airships stared with an equal curiosity. No city in the world was ever so finely placed as New York, so magnificently cut up by sea and bluff and river, so admirably disposed to display the tall effects of buildings, the complex immensities of bridges and

mono-railways and feats of engineering. London, Paris, Berlin, were shapeless, low agglomerations beside it. Its port reached to its heart like Venice, and, like Venice, it was obvious, dramatic, and proud. Seen from above it was alive with crawling trains and cars, and at a thousand points it was already breaking into quivering light. New York was altogether at its best that evening, its splendid best.

"Gaw! *What* a place!" said Bert.

It was so great, and in its collective effect so pacifically magnificent, that to make war upon it seemed incongruous beyond measure, like laying siege to the National Gallery or attacking respectable people in an hotel dining-room with battle-axe and mail. It was in its entirety so large, so complex, so delicately immense, that to bring it to the issue of warfare was like driving a crowbar into the mechanism of a clock. And the fish-like shoal of great airships hovering light and sunlit above, filling the sky, seemed equally remote from the ugly forcefulness of war. To Kurt, to Smallways, to I know not how many more of the people in the air-fleet came the distinctest apprehension of these incompatibilities. But in the head of the Prince Karl Albert were the vapours of romance: he was a conqueror, and this was the enemy's city. The greater the city, the greater the triumph. No doubt he had a time of tremendous exultation and sensed beyond all precedent the sense of power that night.

There came an end at last to that pause. Some wireless communications had failed of a satisfactory ending, and fleet and city remembered they were hostile powers. "Look!" cried the multitude; "look!"

"What are they doing?"

"What?". . . Down through the twilight sank five attacking airships, one to the Navy Yard on East River, one to City Hall, two over the great business buildings of Wall Street and Lower Broadway, one to the Brooklyn Bridge, dropping from among their fellows through the danger zone from the distant guns smoothly and rapidly to a safe proximity to the city masses. At

that descent all the cars in the streets stopped with dramatic suddenness, and all the lights that had been coming on in the streets and houses went out again. For the City Hall had awakened and was conferring by telephone with the Federal command and taking measures for defence. The City Hall was asking for airships, refusing to surrender as Washington advised, and developing into a centre of intense emotion, of hectic activity. Everywhere and hastily the police began to clear the assembled crowds. "Go to your homes," they said; and the word was passed from mouth to mouth, "There's going to be trouble." A chill of apprehension ran through the city, and men hurrying in the unwonted darkness across City Hall Park and Union Square came upon the dim forms of soldiers and guns, and were challenged and sent back. In half an hour New York had passed from serene sunset and gaping admiration to a troubled and threatening twilight.

The first loss of life occurred in the panic rush from Brooklyn Bridge as the airship approached it. With the cessation of the traffic an unusual stillness came upon New York, and the disturbing concussions of the futile defending guns on the hills about grew more and more audible. At last these ceased also. A pause of further negotiation followed. People sat in darkness, sought counsel from telephones that were dumb. Then into the expectant hush came a great crash and uproar, the breaking down of the Brooklyn Bridge, the rifle fire from the Navy Yard, and the bursting of bombs in Wall Street and the City Hall. New York as a whole could do nothing, could understand nothing. New York in the darkness peered and listened to these distant sounds until presently they died away as suddenly as they had begun. "What could be happening?" They asked it in vain.

A long, vague period intervened, and people looking out of the windows of upper rooms discovered the dark hulls of German airships, gliding slowly and noiselessly, quite close at hand. Then quietly the electric lights came on again, and an uproar of nocturnal newsvendors began in the streets.

The units of that vast and varied population bought and learnt what had happened; there had been a fight and New York had hoisted the white flag.

§4

The lamentable incidents that followed the surrender of New York seem now in the retrospect to be but the necessary and inevitable consequence of the clash of modern appliances and social conditions produced by the scientific century on the one hand, and the tradition of a crude, romantic patriotism on the other. At first people received the fact with an irresponsible detachment, much as they would have received the slowing down of the train in which they were travelling or the erection of a public monument by the city to which they belonged.

"We have surrendered. Dear me! *have* we?" was rather the manner in which the first news was met. They took it in the same spectacular spirit they had displayed at the first apparition of the air-fleet. Only slowly was this realisation of a capitulation suffused with the flush of passion, only with reflection did they make any personal application. "*We* have surrendered!" came later; "in us America is defeated." Then they began to burn and tingle.

The newspapers, which were issued about one in the morning contained no particulars of the terms upon which New York had yielded—nor did they give any intimation of the quality of the brief conflict that had preceded the capitulation. The later issues remedied these deficiencies. There came the explicit statement of the agreement to victual the German airships, to supply the complement of explosives to replace those employed in the fight and in the destruction of the North Atlantic fleet, to pay the enormous ransom of forty million dollars, and to surrender the flotilla in the East River. There came, too, longer and longer descriptions of the smashing up of the City Hall and the Navy Yard, and people began to realise faintly what those brief minutes of uproar had meant. They read the tale

of men blown to bits, of futile soldiers in that localised battle fighting against hope amidst an indescribable wreckage, of flags hauled down by weeping men. And these strange nocturnal editions contained also the first brief cables from Europe of the fleet disaster, the North Atlantic fleet for which New York had always felt an especial pride and solicitude. Slowly, hour by hour, the collective consciousness woke up, the tide of patriotic astonishment and humiliation came floating in. America had come upon disaster; suddenly New York discovered herself with amazement giving place to wrath unspeakable, a conquered city under the hand of her conqueror.

As that fact shaped itself in the public mind, there sprang up, as flames spring up, an angry repudiation. "No!" cried New York, waking in the dawn. "No! I am not defeated. This is a dream."

Before day broke the swift American anger was running through all the city, through every soul in those contagious millions. Before it took action, before it took shape, the men in the airships could feel the gigantic insurgence of emotion, as cattle and natural creatures feel, it is said, the coming of an earthquake. The newspapers of the Knype group first gave the thing words and a formula. "We do not agree," they said simply. "We have been betrayed!" Men took that up everywhere, it passed from mouth to mouth, at every street corner under the paling lights of dawn orators stood unchecked, calling upon the spirit of America to arise, making the shame a personal reality to every one who heard. To Bert, listening five hundred feet above, it seemed that the city, which had at first produced only confused noises, was now humming like a hive of bees—of very angry bees.

After the smashing of the City Hall and Post-Office, the white flag had been hoisted from a tower of the old Park Row building, and thither had gone Mayor O'Hagen, urged thither indeed by the terror-stricken property owners of lower New York, to negotiate the capitulation with Von Winterfeld.

The *Vaterland*, having dropped the secretary by a rope ladder, remained hovering, circling very slowly above the great buildings, old and new, that clustered round City Hall Park, while the *Helmholz*, which had done the fighting there, rose overhead to a height of perhaps two thousand feet. So Bert had a near view of all that occurred in that central place. The City Hall and Court House, the Post-Office and a mass of buildings on the west side of Broadway, had been badly damaged, and the three former were a heap of blackened ruins. In the case of the first two the loss of life had not been considerable, but a great multitude of workers, including many girls and women, had been caught in the destruction of the Post-Office, and a little army of volunteers with white badges entered behind the firemen, bringing out the often still living bodies, for the most part frightfully charred, and carrying them into the big Monson building close at hand. Everywhere the busy firemen were directing their bright streams of water upon the smouldering masses: their hose lay about the square, and long cordons of police held back the gathering black masses of people, chiefly from the east side, from these central activities.

In violent and extraordinary contrast with this scene of destruction, close at hand were the huge newspaper establishments of Park Row. They were all alight and working; they had not been abandoned even while the actual bomb throwing was going on, and now staff and presses were vehemently active, getting out the story, the immense and dreadful story of the night, developing comment and, in most cases, spreading the idea of resistance under the very noses of the airships. For a long time Bert could not imagine what these callously active offices could be, then he detected the noise of the presses and emitted his "Gaw!"

Beyond these newspaper buildings again, and partially hidden by the arches of the old Elevated Railway of New York (long since converted into a mono-rail), there was another cordon of police and a sort of encampment of ambulances and doctors,

busy with the dead and wounded who had been killed early in the night by the panic upon Brooklyn Bridge. All this he saw in the perspectives of a bird's-eye view, as things happening in a big, irregular-shaped pit below him, between cliffs of high building. Northward he looked along the steep canyon of Broadway, down whose length at intervals crowds were assembling about excited speakers; and when he lifted his eyes he saw the chimneys and cable-stacks and roof spaces of New York, and everywhere now over these the watching, debating people clustered, except where the fires raged and the jets of water flew. Everywhere, too, were flagstaffs devoid of flags; one white sheet drooped and flapped and drooped again over the Park Row buildings. And upon the lurid lights, the festering movement and intense shadows of this strange scene, there was breaking now the cold, impartial dawn.

For Bert Smallways all this was framed in the frame of the open porthole. It was a pale, dim world outside that dark and tangible rim. All night he had clutched at that rim, jumped and quivered at explosions, and watched phantom events. Now he had been high and now low; now almost beyond hearing, now flying close to crashings and shouts and outcries. He had seen airships flying low and swift over darkened and groaning streets; watched great buildings, suddenly red-lit amidst the shadows, crumple at the smashing impact of bombs; witnessed for the first time in his life the grotesque, swift onset of insatiable conflagrations. From it all he felt detached, disembodied. The *Vaterland* did not even fling a bomb; she watched and ruled. Then down they had come at last to hover over City Hall Park, and it had crept in upon his mind, chillingly, terrifyingly, that these illuminated black masses were great offices afire, and that the going to and fro of minute, dim spectres of lantern-lit grey and white was a harvesting of the wounded and the dead. As the light grew clearer he began to understand more and more what these crumpled black things signified. . . .

He had watched hour after hour since first New York had

risen out of the blue indistinctness of the landfall. With the daylight he experienced an intolerable fatigue.

He lifted weary eyes to the pink flush in the sky, yawned immensely, and crawled back whispering to himself across the cabin to the locker. He did not so much lie down upon that as fall upon it and instantly become asleep.

There, hours after, sprawling undignified and sleeping profoundly, Kurt found him, a very image of the democratic mind confronted with the problems of a time too complex for its apprehension. His face was pale and indifferent, his mouth wide open, and he snored. He snored disagreeably.

Kurt regarded him for a moment with a mild distaste. Then he kicked his ankle.

"Wake up," he said to Smallways' stare, "and lie down decent."

Bert sat up and rubbed his eyes.

"Any more fightin' yet?" he asked.

"No," said Kurt, and sat down, a tired man.

"Gott!" he cried presently, rubbing his hands over his face, "but I'd like a cold bath! I've been looking for stray bullet holes in the air-chambers all night until now." He yawned. "I must sleep. You'd better clear out, Smallways. I can't stand you here this morning. You're so infernally ugly and useless. Have you had your rations? No! Well, go in and get 'em, and don't come back. Stick in the gallery. . . ."

§5

So Bert, slightly refreshed by coffee and sleep, resumed his helpless co-operation in the War in the Air. He went down into the little gallery as the lieutenant had directed, and clung to the rail at the extreme end beyond the look-out man, trying to seem as inconspicuous and harmless a fragment of life as possible.

A wind was rising rather strongly from the south-east. It obliged the *Vaterland* to come about in that direction, and made her roll a great deal as she went to and fro over Manhattan Island. Away in the north-west clouds gathered. The throb-

throb of her slow screw working against the breeze was much more perceptible than when she was going full speed ahead; and the friction of the wind against the underside of the gas-chamber drove a series of shallow ripples along it and made a faint flapping sound like, but fainter than, the beating of ripples under the stem of a boat. She was stationed over the temporary City Hall in the Park Row building, and every now and then she would descend to resume communication with the mayor and with Washington. But the restlessness of the Prince would not suffer him to remain for long in any one place. Now he would circle over the Hudson and East River; now he would go up high, as if to peer away into the blue distances; once he ascended so swiftly and so far that mountain sickness overtook him and the crew and forced him down again; and Bert shared the dizziness and nausea.

The swaying view varied with these changes of altitude. Now they would be low and close, and he would distinguish in that steep, unusual perspective, windows, doors, street and sky signs, people and the minutest details, and watch the enigmatical behaviour of crowds and clusters upon the roofs and in the streets; then as they soared the details would shrink, the sides of streets draw together, the view widen, the people cease to be significant. At the highest the effect was that of a concave relief map; Bert saw the dark and crowded land everywhere intersected by shining waters, saw the Hudson River like a spear of silver, and Lower Island Sound like a shield. Even to Bert's unphilosophical mind the contrast of city below and fleet above pointed an opposition, the opposition of the adventurous American's tradition and character with German order and discipline. Below, the immense buildings, tremendous and fine as they were, seemed like the giant trees of a jungle fighting for life; their picturesque magnificence was as planless as the chances of crag and gorge, their casualty enhanced by the smoke and confusion of still unsubdued and spreading conflagrations. In the sky soared the German airships like beings in a different, entirely more orderly world, all oriented to the same angle of the horizon, uniform in build and appearance, moving accurately with one purpose as a pack of wolves will move, distributed with the most precise and effectual co-operation.

It dawned upon Bert that hardly a third of the fleet was visible. The others had gone upon errands he could not imagine, beyond the compass of that great circle of earth and sky. He wondered, but there was no one to ask. As the day wore on, about a dozen reappeared in the east with their stores replenished from the flotilla and towing a number of drachenflieger. Towards afternoon the weather thickened, driving clouds appeared in the south-west and ran together and seemed to engender more clouds, and the wind came round into that quarter and blew stronger. Towards the evening the wind became a gale into which the now tossing airships had to beat.

All that day the Prince was negotiating with Washington, while his detached scouts sought far and wide over the Eastern States looking for anything resembling an aeronautic park. A squadron of twenty airships detached overnight had dropped out of the air upon Niagara and was holding the town and power works.

Meanwhile the insurrectionary movement in the giant city grew uncontrollable. In spite of five great fires already involving many acres, and spreading steadily, New York was still not satisfied that she was beaten.

At first the rebellious spirit below found vent only in isolated shouts, street-crowd speeches, and newspaper suggestions; then it found much more definite expression in the appearance in the morning sunlight of American flags at point after point above the architectural cliffs of the city. It is quite possible that in many cases this spirited display of bunting by a city already surrendered was the outcome of the innocent informality of the American mind, but it is also undeniable that in many it was a deliberate indication that the people "felt wicked."

The German sense of correctitude was deeply shocked by this outbreak. The Graf von Winterfeld immediately communicated

with the mayor, and pointed out the irregularity, and the fire look-out stations were instructed in the matter. The New York police was speedily hard at work, and a foolish contest in full swing between impassioned citizens resolved to keep the flag flying, and irritated and worried officers instructed to pull it down.

The trouble became acute at last in the streets above Columbia University. The captain of the airship watching this quarter seems to have stooped to lasso and drag from its staff a flag hoisted upon Morgan Hall. As he did so a volley of rifle and revolver shots was fired from the upper windows of the huge apartment building that stands between the University and Riverside Drive.

Most of these were ineffectual, but two or three perforated gas-chambers, and one smashed the hand and arm of a man upon the forward platform; The sentinel on the lower gallery immediately replied, and the machine gun on the shield of the eagle let fly and promptly stopped any further shots. The airship rose and signalled the flagship and City Hall, police and militiamen were directed at once to the spot, and this particular incident closed.

But hard upon that came the desperate attempt of a party of young clubmen from New York, who, inspired by patriotic and adventurous imaginations, slipped off in half a dozen motor-cars to Beacon Hill, and set to work with remarkable vigour to improvise a fort about the Doan swivel gun that had been placed there. They found it still in the hands of the disgusted gunners, who had been ordered to cease fire at the capitulation, and it was easy to infect these men with their own spirit. They declared their gun hadn't had half a chance, and were burning to show what it could do. Directed by the newcomers, they made a trench and bank about the mounting of the piece, and constructed flimsy shelter-pits of corrugated iron.

They were actually loading the gun when they were observed by the airship *Preussen* and the shell they succeeded in firing before the bombs of the latter smashed them and their crude defences to fragments, burst over the middle gas-chambers of the *Bingen*, and brought her to earth, disabled, upon Staten Island. She was badly deflated, and dropped among trees, over which her empty central gas-bags spread in canopies and festoons. Nothing, however, had caught fire, and her men were speedily at work upon her repair. They behaved with a confidence that verged upon indiscretion. While most of them commenced patching the tears of the membrane, half a dozen of them started off for the nearest road in search of a gas main, and presently found themselves prisoners in the hands of a hostile crowd. Close at hand was a number of villa residences, whose occupants speedily developed from an unfriendly curiosity to aggression. At that time the police control of the large polyglot population of Staten Island had become very lax, and scarcely a household but had its rifle or pistols and ammunition. These were presently produced, and after two or three misses, one of the men at work was hit in the foot. Thereupon the Germans left their sewing and mending, took cover among the trees, and replied.

The crackling of shots speedily brought the *Preussen* and *Kiel* on the scene, and with a few hand grenades they made short work of every villa within a mile. A number of non-combatant American men, women, and children were killed and the actual assailants driven off. For a time the repairs went on in peace under the immediate protection of these two airships. Then when they returned to their quarters, an intermittent sniping and fighting round the stranded *Bingen* was resumed, and went on all the afternoon, and merged at last in the general combat of the evening. . . .

About eight the Bingen was rushed by an armed mob, and all its defenders killed after a fierce, disorderly struggle.

The difficulty of the Germans in both these cases came from the impossibility of landing any efficient force or, indeed, any force at all from the air-fleet. The airships were quite unequal to

the transport of any adequate landing parties; their complement of men was just sufficient to manoeuvre and fight them in the air. From above they could inflict immense damage; they could reduce any organised Government to a capitulation in the briefest space, but they could not disarm, much less could they occupy, the surrendered areas below. They had to trust to the pressure upon the authorities below of a threat to renew the bombardment. It was their sole resource. No doubt, with a highly organised and undamaged Government and a homogeneous and well-disciplined people that would have sufficed to keep the peace. But this was not the American case. Not only was the New York Government a weak one and insufficiently provided with police, but the destruction of the City Hall and Post-Office and other central ganglia had hopelessly disorganised the co-operation of part with part. The street cars and railways had ceased; the telephone service was out of gear and only worked intermittently. The Germans had struck at the head, and the head was conquered and stunned—only to release the body from its rule. New York had become a headless monster, no longer capable of collective submission. Everywhere it lifted itself rebelliously; everywhere authorities and officials left to their own initiative were joining in the arming and flag-hoisting and excitement of that afternoon.

§6

The disintegrating truce gave place to a definite general breach with the assassination of the *Wetterhorn*—for that is the only possible word for the act—above Union Square, and not a mile away from the exemplary ruins of City Hall. This occurred late in the afternoon, between five and six. By that time the weather had changed very much for the worse, and the operations of the airships were embarrassed by the necessity they were under of keeping head on to the gusts. A series of squalls, with hail and thunder, followed one another from the south by south-east, and in order to avoid these as much as possible, the air-fleet came low over the houses, diminishing its range of observation and exposing itself to a rifle attack.

Overnight there had been a gun placed in Union Square. It had never been mounted, much less fired, and in the darkness after the surrender it was taken with its supplies and put out of the way under the arches of the great Dexter building. Here late in the morning it was remarked by a number of patriotic spirits. They set to work to hoist and mount it inside the upper floors of the place. They made, in fact, a masked battery behind the decorous office blinds, and there lay in wait as simply excited as children until at last the stem of the luckless *Wetterhorn* appeared, beating and rolling at quarter speed over the recently reconstructed pinnacles of Tiffany's. Promptly that one-gun battery unmasked. The airship's look-out man must have seen the whole of the tenth story of the Dexter building crumble out and smash in the street below to discover the black muzzle looking out from the shadows behind. Then perhaps the shell hit him.

The gun fired two shells before the frame of the Dexter building collapsed, and each shell raked the *Wetterhorn* from stem to stern. They smashed her exhaustively. She crumpled up like a can that has been kicked by a heavy boot, her forepart came down in the square, and the rest of her length, with a great snapping and twisting of shafts and stays, descended, collapsing athwart Tammany Hall and the streets towards Second Avenue. Her gas escaped to mix with air, and the air of her rent balloonette poured into her deflating gas-chambers. Then with an immense impact she exploded. . . .

The *Vaterland* at that time was beating up to the south of City Hall from over the ruins of the Brooklyn Bridge, and the reports of the gun, followed by the first crashes of the collapsing Dexter building, brought Kurt and, Smallways to the cabin porthole. They were in time to see the flash of the exploding gun, and then they were first flattened against the window and then rolled head over heels across the floor of the cabin by the

air wave of the explosion. The *Vaterland* bounded like a football some one has kicked and when they looked out again, Union Square was small and remote and shattered, as though some cosmically vast giant had rolled over it. The buildings to the east of it were ablaze at a dozen points, under the flaming tatters and warping skeleton of the airship, and all the roofs and walls were ridiculously askew and crumbling as one looked. "Gaw!" said Bert. "What's happened? Look at the people!"

But before Kurt could produce an explanation, the shrill bells of the airship were ringing to quarters, and he had to go. Bert hesitated and stepped thoughtfully into the passage, looking back at the window as he did so. He was knocked off his feet at once by the Prince, who was rushing headlong from his cabin to the central magazine.

Bert had a momentary impression of the great figure of the Prince, white with rage, bristling with gigantic anger, his huge fist swinging. "Blut und Eisen!" cried the Prince, as one who swears. "Oh! Blut und Eisen!"

Some one fell over Bert—something in the manner of falling suggested Von Winterfeld—and some one else paused and kicked him spitefully and hard. Then he was sitting up in the passage, rubbing a freshly bruised cheek and readjusting the bandage he still wore on his head. "Dem that Prince," said Bert, indignant beyond measure. "'E 'asn't the menners of a 'og!"

He stood up, collected his wits for a minute, and then went slowly towards the gangway of the little gallery. As he did so he heard noises suggestive of the return of the Prince. The lot of them were coming back again. He shot into his cabin like a rabbit into its burrow, just in time to escape that shouting terror.

He shut the door, waited until the passage was still, then went across to the window and looked out. A drift of cloud made the prospect of the streets and squares hazy, and the rolling of the airship swung the picture up and down. A few people were running to and fro, but for the most part the aspect of the district was desertion. The streets seemed to broaden out, they became clearer, and the little dots that were people larger as the *Vaterland* came down again. Presently she was swaying along above the lower end of Broadway. The dots below, Bert saw, were not running now, but standing and looking up. Then suddenly they were all running again.

Something had dropped from the aeroplane, something that looked small and flimsy. It hit the pavement near a big archway just underneath Bert. A little man was sprinting along the sidewalk within half a dozen yards, and two or three others and one woman were bolting across the roadway. They were odd little figures, so very small were they about the heads, so very active about the elbows and legs. It was really funny to see their legs going. Foreshortened, humanity has no dignity. The little man on the pavement jumped comically—no doubt with terror, as the bomb fell beside him.

Then blinding flames squirted out in all directions from the point of impact, and the little man who had jumped became, for an instant, a flash of fire and vanished—vanished absolutely. The people running out into the road took preposterous clumsy leaps, then flopped down and lay still, with their torn clothes smouldering into flame. Then pieces of the archway began to drop, and the lower masonry of the building to fall in with the rumbling sound of coals being shot into a cellar. A faint screaming reached Bert, and then a crowd of people ran out into the street, one man limping and gesticulating awkwardly. He halted, and went back towards the building. A falling mass of brick-work hit him and sent him sprawling to lie still and crumpled where he fell. Dust and black smoke came pouring into the street, and were presently shot with red flame. . . .

In this manner the massacre of New York began. She was the first of the great cities of the Scientific Age to suffer by the enormous powers and grotesque limitations of aerial warfare. She was wrecked as in the previous century endless barbaric cities had been bombarded, because she was at once too strong to be occupied and too undisciplined and proud to surrender

in order to escape destruction. Given the circumstances, the thing had to be done. It was impossible for the Prince to desist, and own himself defeated, and it was impossible to subdue the city except by largely destroying it. The catastrophe was the logical outcome of the situation, created by the application of science to warfare. It was unavoidable that great cities should be destroyed. In spite of his intense exasperation with his dilemma, the Prince sought to be moderate even in massacre. He tried to give a memorable lesson with the minimum waste of life and the minimum expenditure of explosives. For that night he proposed only the wrecking of Broadway. He directed the air-fleet to move in column over the route of this thoroughfare, dropping bombs, the *Vaterland* leading. And so our Bert Smallways became a participant in one of the most cold-blooded slaughters in the world's history, in which men who were neither excited nor, except for the remotest chance of a bullet, in any danger, poured death and destruction upon homes and crowds below.

He clung to the frame of the porthole as the airship tossed and swayed, and stared down through the light rain that now drove before the wind, into the twilight streets, watching people running out of the houses, watching buildings collapse and fires begin. As the airships sailed along they smashed up the city as a child will shatter its cities of brick and card. Below, they left ruins and blazing conflagrations and heaped and scattered dead; men, women, and children mixed together as though they had been no more than Moors, or Zulus, or Chinese. Lower New York was soon a furnace of crimson flames, from which there was no escape. Cars, railways, ferries, all had ceased, and never a light lit the way of the distracted fugitives in that dusky confusion but the light of burning. He had glimpses of what it must mean to be down there—glimpses. And it came to him suddenly as an incredible discovery, that such disasters were not only possible now in this strange, gigantic, foreign New York, but also in London—in Bun Hill! that the little island in the

silver seas was at the end of its immunity, that nowhere in the world any more was there a place left where a Smallways might lift his head proudly and vote for war and a spirited foreign policy, and go secure from such horrible things.

Chapter VII

THE "*VATERLAND*" IS DISABLED

§1

And then above the flames of Manhattan Island came a battle, the first battle in the air. The Americans had realised the price their waiting game must cost, and struck with all the strength they had, if haply they might still save New York from this mad Prince of Blood and Iron, and from fire and death.

They came down upon the Germans on the wings of a great gale in the twilight, amidst thunder and rain. They came from the yards of Washington and Philadelphia, full tilt in two squadrons, and but for one sentinel airship hard by Trenton, the surprise would have been complete.

The Germans, sick and weary with destruction, and half empty of ammunition, were facing up into the weather when the news of this onset reached them. New York they had left behind to the south-eastward, a darkened city with one hideous red scar of flames. All the airships rolled and staggered, bursts of hailstorm bore them down and forced them to fight their way up again; the air had become bitterly cold. The Prince was on the point of issuing orders to drop earthward and trail copper lightning chains when the news of the aeroplane attack came to him. He faced his fleet in line abreast south, had the drachenflieger manned and held ready to cast loose, and ordered a general ascent into the freezing clearness above the wet and darkness.

The news of what was imminent came slowly to Bert's perceptions. He was standing in the messroom at the time and the evening rations were being served out. He had resumed Butteridge's coat and gloves, and in addition he had wrapped his blanket about him. He was dipping his bread into his soup

and was biting off big mouthfuls. His legs were wide apart, and he leant against the partition in order to steady himself amidst the pitching and oscillation of the airship. The men about him looked tired and depressed; a few talked, but most were sullen and thoughtful, and one or two were air-sick. They all seemed to share the peculiarly outcast feeling that had followed the murders of the evening, a sense of a land beneath them, and an outraged humanity grown more hostile than the Sea.

Then the news hit them. A red-faced sturdy man, a man with light eyelashes and a scar, appeared in the doorway and shouted something in German that manifestly startled every one. Bert felt the shock of the altered tone, though he could not understand a word that was said. The announcement was followed by a pause, and then a great outcry of questions and suggestions. Even the air-sick men flushed and spoke. For some minutes the mess-room was Bedlam, and then, as if it were a confirmation of the news, came the shrill ringing of the bells that called the men to their posts.

Bert with pantomime suddenness found himself alone.

"What's up?" he said, though he partly guessed.

He stayed only to gulp down the remainder of his soup, and then ran along the swaying passage and, clutching tightly, down the ladder to the little gallery. The weather hit him like cold water squirted from a hose. The airship engaged in some new feat of atmospheric Jiu-Jitsu. He drew his blanket closer about him, clutching with one straining hand. He found himself tossing in a wet twilight, with nothing to be seen but mist pouring past him. Above him the airship was warm with lights and busy with the movements of men going to their quarters. Then abruptly the lights went out, and the *Vaterland* with bounds and twists and strange writhings was fighting her way up the air.

He had a glimpse, as the *Vaterland* rolled over, of some large buildings burning close below them, a quivering acanthus of flames, and then he saw indistinctly through the driving weather another airship wallowing along like a porpoise, and also working

up. Presently the clouds swallowed her again for a time, and then she came back to sight as a dark and whale-like monster, amidst streaming weather. The air was full of flappings and pipings, of void, gusty shouts and noises; it buffeted him and confused him; ever and again his attention became rigid—a blind and deaf balancing and clutching.

"Wow!"

Something fell past him out of the vast darknesses above and vanished into the tumults below, going obliquely downward. It was a German drachenflieger. The thing was going so fast he had but an instant apprehension of the dark figure of the aeronaut crouched together clutching at his wheel. It might be a manoeuvre, but it looked like a catastrophe.

"Gaw!" said Bert.

"Pup-pup-pup" went a gun somewhere in the mirk ahead and suddenly and quite horribly the *Vaterland* lurched, and Bert and the sentinel were clinging to the rail for dear life. "Bang!" came a vast impact out of the zenith, followed by another huge roll, and all about him the tumbled clouds flashed red and lurid in response to flashes unseen, revealing immense gulfs. The rail went right overhead, and he was hanging loose in the air holding on to it.

For a time Bert's whole mind and being was given to clutching. "I'm going into the cabin," he said, as the airship righted again and brought back the gallery floor to his feet. He began to make his way cautiously towards the ladder. "Whee-wow!" he cried as the whole gallery reared itself up forward, and then plunged down like a desperate horse.

Crack! Bang! Bang! Bang! And then hard upon this little rattle of shots and bombs came, all about him, enveloping him, engulfing him, immense and overwhelming, a quivering white blaze of lightning and a thunder-clap that was like the bursting of a world.

Just for the instant before that explosion the universe seemed to be standing still in a shadowless glare.

It was then he saw the American aeroplane. He saw it in the light of the flash as a thing altogether motionless. Even its screw appeared still, and its men were rigid dolls. (For it was so near he could see the men upon it quite distinctly.) Its stern was tilting down, and the whole machine was heeling over. It was of the Colt-Coburn-Langley pattern, with double up-tilted wings and the screw ahead, and the men were in a boat-like body netted over. From this very light long body, magazine guns projected on either side. One thing that was strikingly odd and wonderful in that moment of revelation was that the left upper wing was burning *downward* with a reddish, smoky flame. But this was not the most wonderful thing about this apparition. The most wonderful thing was that it and a German airship five hundred yards below were threaded as it were on the lightning flash, which turned out of its path as if to take them, and, that out from the corners and projecting points of its huge wings everywhere, little branching thorn-trees of lightning were streaming.

Like a picture Bert saw these things, a picture a little blurred by a thin veil of wind-torn mist.

The crash of the thunder-clap followed the flash and seemed a part of it, so that it is hard to say whether Bert was the rather deafened or blinded in that instant.

And then darkness, utter darkness, and a heavy report and a thin small sound of voices that went wailing downward into the abyss below.

§ 2

There followed upon these things a long, deep swaying of the airship, and then Bert began a struggle to get back to his cabin. He was drenched and cold and terrified beyond measure, and now more than a little air-sick. It seemed to him that the strength had gone out of his knees and hands, and that his feet had become icily slippery over the metal they trod upon. But that was because a thin film of ice had frozen upon the gallery.

He never knew how long his ascent of the ladder back

into the airship took him, but in his dreams afterwards, when he recalled it, that experience seemed to last for hours. Below, above, around him were gulfs, monstrous gulfs of howling wind and eddies of dark, whirling snowflakes, and he was protected from it all by a little metal grating and a rail, a grating and rail that seemed madly infuriated with him, passionately eager to wrench him off and throw him into the tumult of space.

Once he had a fancy that a bullet tore by his ear, and that the clouds and snowflakes were lit by a flash, but he never even turned his head to see what new assailant whirled past them in the void. He wanted to get into the passage! He wanted to get into the passage! He wanted to get into the passage! Would the arm by which he was clinging hold out, or would it give way and snap? A handful of hail smacked him in the face, so that for a time he was breathless and nearly insensible. Hold tight, Bert! He renewed his efforts.

He found himself, with an enormous sense of relief and warmth, in the passage. The passage was behaving like a dice-box, its disposition was evidently to rattle him about and then throw him out again. He hung on with the convulsive clutch of instinct until the passage lurched down ahead. Then he would make a short run cabin-ward, and clutch again as the fore-end rose.

Behold! He was in the cabin!

He snapped-to the door, and for a time he was not a human being, he was a case of air-sickness. He wanted to get somewhere that would fix him, that he needn't clutch. He opened the locker and got inside among the loose articles, and sprawled there helplessly, with his head sometimes bumping one side and sometimes the other. The lid shut upon him with a click. He did not care then what was happening any more. He did not care who fought who, or what bullets were fired or explosions occurred. He did not care if presently he was shot or smashed to pieces. He was full of feeble, inarticulate rage and despair. "Foolery!" he said, his one exhaustive comment on human enterprise, adventure, war, and the chapter of accidents that had entangled him. "Foolery! Ugh!" He included the order of the universe in that comprehensive condemnation. He wished he was dead.

He saw nothing of the stars, as presently the *Vaterland* cleared the rush and confusion of the lower weather, nor of the duel she fought with two circling aeroplanes, how they shot her rearmost chambers through, and how she fought them off with explosive bullets and turned to run as she did so.

The rush and swoop of these wonderful night birds was all lost upon him; their heroic dash and self-sacrifice. The *Vaterland* was rammed, and for some moments she hung on the verge of destruction, and sinking swiftly, with the American aeroplane entangled with her smashed propeller, and the Americans trying to scramble aboard. It signified nothing to Bert. To him it conveyed itself simply as vehement swaying. Foolery! When the American airship dropped off at last, with most of its crew shot or fallen, Bert in his locker appreciated nothing but that the *Vaterland* had taken a hideous upward leap.

But then came infinite relief, incredibly blissful relief. The rolling, the pitching, the struggle ceased, ceased instantly and absolutely. The *Vaterland* was no longer fighting the gale; her smashed and exploded engines throbbed no more; she was disabled and driving before the wind as smoothly as a balloon, a huge, windspread, tattered cloud of aerial wreckage.

To Bert it was no more than the end of a series of disagreeable sensations. He was not curious to know what had happened to the airship, nor what had happened to the battle. For a long time he lay waiting apprehensively for the pitching and tossing and his qualms to return, and so, lying, boxed up in the locker, he presently fell asleep.

§3

He awoke tranquil but very stuffy, and at the same time very cold, and quite unable to recollect where he could be. His head

ached, and his breath was suffocated. He had been dreaming confusedly of Edna, and Desert Dervishes, and of riding bicycles in an extremely perilous manner through the upper air amidst a pyrotechnic display of crackers and Bengal lights—to the great annoyance of a sort of composite person made up of the Prince and Mr. Butteridge. Then for some reason Edna and he had begun to cry pitifully for each other, and he woke up with wet eye-lashes into this ill-ventilated darkness of the locker. He would never see Edna any more, never see Edna any more.

He thought he must be back in the bedroom behind the cycle shop at the bottom of Bun Hill, and he was sure the vision he had had of the destruction of a magnificent city, a city quite incredibly great and splendid, by means of bombs, was no more than a particularly vivid dream.

"Grubb!" he called, anxious to tell him.

The answering silence, and the dull resonance of the locker to his voice, supplementing the stifling quality of the air, set going a new train of ideas. He lifted up his hands and feet, and met an inflexible resistance. He was in a coffin, he thought! He had been buried alive! He gave way at once to wild panic. "'elp!" he screamed. "'elp!" and drummed with his feet, and kicked and struggled. "Let me out! Let me out!"

For some seconds he struggled with this intolerable horror, and then the side of his imagined coffin gave way, and he was flying out into daylight. Then he was rolling about on what seemed to be a padded floor with Kurt, and being punched and sworn at lustily.

He sat up. His head bandage had become loose and got over one eye, and he whipped the whole thing off. Kurt was also sitting up, a yard away from him, pink as ever, wrapped in blankets, and with an aluminium diver's helmet over his knee, staring at him with a severe expression, and rubbing his downy unshaven chin. They were both on a slanting floor of crimson padding, and above them was an opening like a long, low cellar flap that Bert by an effort perceived to be the cabin door in a

half-inverted condition. The whole cabin had in fact turned on its side.

"What the deuce do you mean by it, Smallways?" said Kurt, "jumping out of that locker when I was certain you had gone overboard with the rest of them? Where have you been?"

"What's up?" asked Bert.

"This end of the airship is up. Most other things are down."

"Was there a battle?"

"There was."

"Who won?"

"I haven't seen the papers, Smallways. We left before the finish. We got disabled and unmanageable, and our colleagues—consorts I mean—were too busy most of them to trouble about us, and the wind blew us—Heaven knows where the wind *is* blowing us. It blew us right out of action at the rate of eighty miles an hour or so. Gott! what a wind that was! What a fight! And here we are!"

"Where?"

"In the air, Smallways—in the air! When we get down on the earth again we shan't know what to do with our legs."

"But what's below us?"

"Canada, to the best of my knowledge—and a jolly bleak, empty, inhospitable country it looks."

"But why ain't we right ways up?"

Kurt made no answer for a space.

"Last I remember was seeing a sort of flying-machine in a lightning flash," said Bert. "Gaw! that was 'orrible. Guns going off! Things explodin'! Clouds and 'ail. Pitching and tossing. I got so scared and desperate—and sick. You don't know how the fight came off?"

"Not a bit of it. I was up with my squad in those divers' dresses, inside the gas-chambers, with sheets of silk for caulking. We couldn't see a thing outside except the lightning flashes. I never saw one of those American aeroplanes. Just saw the shots flicker through the chambers and sent off men for the tears.

We caught fire a bit—not much, you know. We were too wet, so the fires spluttered out before we banged. And then one of their infernal things dropped out of the air on us and rammed. Didn't you feel it?"

"I felt everything," said Bert. "I didn't notice any particular smash—"

"They must have been pretty desperate if they meant it. They slashed down on us like a knife; simply ripped the after gas-chambers like gutting herrings, crumpled up the engines and screw. Most of the engines dropped off as they fell off us—or we'd have grounded—but the rest is sort of dangling. We just turned up our nose to the heavens and stayed there. Eleven men rolled off us from various points, and poor old Winterfeld fell through the door of the Prince's cabin into the chart-room and broke his ankle. Also we got our electric gear shot or carried away—no one knows how. That's the position, Smallways. We're driving through the air like a common aerostat, at the mercy of the elements, almost due north—probably to the North Pole. We don't know what aeroplanes the Americans have, or anything at all about it. Very likely we have finished 'em up. One fouled us, one was struck by lightning, some of the men saw a third upset, apparently just for fun. They were going cheap anyhow. Also we've lost most of our drachenflieger. They just skated off into the night. No stability in 'em. That's all. We don't know if we've won or lost. We don't know if we're at war with the British Empire yet or at peace. Consequently, we daren't get down. We don't know what we are up to or what we are going to do. Our Napoleon is alone, forward, and I suppose he's rearranging his plans. Whether New York was our Moscow or not remains to be seen. We've had a high old time and murdered no end of people! War! Noble war! I'm sick of it this morning. I like sitting in rooms rightway up and not on slippery partitions. I'm a civilised man. I keep thinking of old Albrecht and the *Barbarossa*. . . . I feel I want a wash and kind words and a quiet home. When I look at you, I *know* I want a

wash. Gott!"—he stifled a vehement yawn—"What a Cockney tadpole of a ruffian you look!"

"Can we get any grub?" asked Bert.

"Heaven knows!" said Kurt.

He meditated upon Bert for a time. "So far as I can judge, Smallways," he said, "the Prince will probably want to throw you overboard—next time he thinks of you. He certainly will if he sees you. . . . After all, you know, you came *als Ballast.* . . . And we shall have to lighten ship extensively pretty soon. Unless I'm mistaken, the Prince will wake up presently and start doing things with tremendous vigour. . . . I've taken a fancy to you. It's the English strain in me. You're a rum little chap. I shan't like seeing you whizz down the air. . . . You'd better make yourself useful, Smallways. I think I shall requisition you for my squad. You'll have to work, you know, and be infernally intelligent and all that. And you'll have to hang about upside down a bit. Still, it's the best chance you have. We shan't carry passengers much farther this trip, I fancy. Ballast goes over-board—if we don't want to ground precious soon and be taken prisoners of war. The Prince won't do that anyhow. He'll be game to the last."

§4

By means of a folding chair, which was still in its place behind the door, they got to the window and looked out in turn and contemplated a sparsely wooded country below, with no railways nor roads, and only occasional signs of habitation. Then a bugle sounded, and Kurt interpreted it as a summons to food. They got through the door and clambered with some difficulty up the nearly vertical passage, holding on desperately with toes and finger-tips, to the ventilating perforations in its floor. The mess stewards had found their fireless heating arrangements intact, and there was hot cocoa for the officers and hot soup for the men.

Bert's sense of the queerness of this experience was so keen that it blotted out any fear he might have felt. Indeed, he was far more interested now than afraid. He seemed to have touched

down to the bottom of fear and abandonment overnight. He was growing accustomed to the idea that he would probably be killed presently, that this strange voyage in the air was in all probability his death journey. No human being can keep permanently afraid: fear goes at last to the back of one's mind, accepted, and shelved, and done with. He squatted over his soup, sopping it up with his bread, and contemplated his comrades. They were all rather yellow and dirty, with four-day beards, and they grouped themselves in the tired, unpremeditated manner of men on a wreck. They talked little. The situation perplexed them beyond any suggestion of ideas. Three had been hurt in the pitching up of the ship during the fight, and one had a bandaged bullet wound. It was incredible that this little band of men had committed murder and massacre on a scale beyond precedent. None of them who squatted on the sloping gas-padded partition, soup mug in hand, seemed really guilty of anything of the sort, seemed really capable of hurting a dog wantonly. They were all so manifestly built for homely chalets on the solid earth and carefully tilled fields and blond wives and cheery merrymaking. The red-faced, sturdy man with light eyelashes who had brought the first news of the air battle to the men's mess had finished his soup, and with an expression of maternal solicitude was readjusting the bandages of a youngster whose arm had been sprained.

Bert was crumbling the last of his bread into the last of his soup, eking it out as long as possible, when suddenly he became aware that every one was looking at a pair of feet that were dangling across the downturned open doorway. Kurt appeared and squatted across the hinge. In some mysterious way he had shaved his face and smoothed down his light golden hair. He looked extraordinarily cherubic. "Der Prinz," he said.

A second pair of boots followed, making wide and magnificent gestures in their attempts to feel the door frame. Kurt guided them to a foothold, and the Prince, shaved and brushed and beeswaxed and clean and big and terrible, slid

down into position astride of the door. All the men and Bert also stood up and saluted.

The Prince surveyed them with the gesture of a man who sits a steed. The head of the Kapitän appeared beside him.

Then Bert had a terrible moment. The blue blaze of the Prince's eye fell upon him, the great finger pointed, a question was asked. Kurt intervened with explanations.

"*So*," said the Prince, and Bert was disposed of.

Then the Prince addressed the men in short, heroic sentences, steadying himself on the hinge with one hand and waving the other in a fine variety of gesture. What he said Bert could not tell, but he perceived that their demeanor changed, their backs stiffened. They began to punctuate the Prince's discourse with cries of approval. At the end their leader burst into song and all the men with him. "Ein feste Burg ist unser Gott," they chanted in deep, strong tones, with an immense moral uplifting. It was glaringly inappropriate in a damaged, half-overturned, and sinking airship, which had been disabled and blown out of action after inflicting the cruellest bombardment in the world's history; but it was immensely stirring nevertheless. Bert was deeply moved. He could not sing any of the words of Luther's great hymn, but he opened his mouth and emitted loud, deep, and partially harmonious notes. . . .

Far below, this deep chanting struck on the ears of a little camp of Christianised half-breeds who were lumbering. They were breakfasting, but they rushed out cheerfully, quite prepared for the Second Advent. They stared at the shattered and twisted *Vaterland* driving before the gale, amazed beyond words. In so many respects it was like their idea of the Second Advent, and then again in so many respects it wasn't. They stared at its passage, awestricken and perplexed beyond their power of words. The hymn ceased. Then after a long interval a voice came out of heaven. "Vat id diss blace here galled itself; vat?"

They made no answer. Indeed they did not understand, though the question repeated itself.

And at last the monster drove away northward over a crest of pine woods and was no more seen. They fell into a hot and long disputation. . . .

The hymn ended. The Prince's legs dangled up the passage again, and every one was briskly prepared for heroic exertion and triumphant acts. "Smallways!" cried Kurt, "come here!"

§5

Then Bert, under Kurt's direction, had his first experience of the work of an air-sailor.

The immediate task before the captain of the *Vaterland* was a very simple one. He had to keep afloat. The wind, though it had fallen from its earlier violence, was still blowing strongly enough to render the grounding of so clumsy a mass extremely dangerous, even if it had been desirable for the Prince to land in inhabited country, and so risk capture. It was necessary to keep the airship up until the wind fell and then, if possible, to descend in some lonely district of the Territory where there would be a chance of repair or rescue by some searching consort. In order to do this weight had to be dropped, and Kurt was detailed with a dozen men to climb down among the wreckage of the deflated air-chambers and cut the stuff clear, portion by portion, as the airship sank. So Bert, armed with a sharp cutlass, found himself clambering about upon netting four thousand feet up in the air, trying to understand Kurt when he spoke in English and to divine him when he used German.

It was giddy work, but not nearly so giddy as a rather overnourished reader sitting in a warm room might imagine. Bert found it quite possible to look down and contemplate the wild sub-arctic landscape below, now devoid of any sign of habitation, a land of rocky cliffs and cascades and broad swirling desolate rivers, and of trees and thickets that grew more stunted and scrubby as the day wore on. Here and there on the hills were patches and pockets of snow. And over all this he worked, hacking away at the tough and slippery oiled silk and clinging

stoutly to the netting. Presently they cleared and dropped a tangle of bent steel rods and wires from the frame, and a big chunk of silk bladder. That was trying. The airship flew up at once as this loose hamper parted. It seemed almost as though they were dropping all Canada. The stuff spread out in the air and floated down and hit and twisted up in a nasty fashion on the lip of a gorge. Bert clung like a frozen monkey to his ropes and did not move a muscle for five minutes.

But there was something very exhilarating, he found, in this dangerous work, and above every thing else, there was the sense of fellowship. He was no longer an isolated and distrustful stranger among these others, he had now a common object with them, he worked with a friendly rivalry to get through with his share before them. And he developed a great respect and affection for Kurt, which had hitherto been only latent in him. Kurt with a job to direct was altogether admirable; he was resourceful, helpful, considerate, swift. He seemed to be everywhere. One forgot his pinkness, his light cheerfulness of manner. Directly one had trouble he was at hand with sound and confident advice. He was like an elder brother to his men.

All together they cleared three considerable chunks of wreckage, and then Bert was glad to clamber up into the cabins again and give place to a second squad. He and his companions were given hot coffee, and indeed, even gloved as they were, the job had been a cold one. They sat drinking it and regarding each other with satisfaction. One man spoke to Bert amiably in German, and Bert nodded and smiled. Through Kurt, Bert, whose ankles were almost frozen, succeeded in getting a pair of top-boots from one of the disabled men.

In the afternoon the wind abated greatly, and small, infrequent snowflakes came drifting by. Snow also spread more abundantly below, and the only trees were clumps of pine and spruce in the lower valleys. Kurt went with three men into the still intact gas-chambers, let out a certain quantity of gas from them, and prepared a series of ripping panels for the descent. Also the

residue of the bombs and explosives in the magazine were thrown overboard and fell, detonating loudly, in the wilderness below. And about four o'clock in the afternoon upon a wide and rocky plain within sight of snow-crested cliffs, the *Vaterland* ripped and grounded.

It was necessarily a difficult and violent affair, for the *Vaterland* had not been planned for the necessities of a balloon. The captain got one panel ripped too soon and the others not soon enough. She dropped heavily, bounced clumsily, and smashed the hanging gallery into the fore-part, mortally injuring Von Winterfeld, and then came down in a collapsing heap after dragging for some moments. The forward shield and its machine gun tumbled in upon the things below. Two men were hurt badly—one got a broken leg and one was internally injured—by flying rods and wires, and Bert was pinned for a time under the side. When at last he got clear and could take a view of the situation, the great black eagle that had started so splendidly from Franconia six evenings ago, sprawled deflated over the cabins of the airship and the frost-bitten rocks of this desolate place and looked a most unfortunate bird—as though some one had caught it and wrung its neck and cast it aside. Several of the crew of the airship were standing about in silence, contemplating the wreckage and the empty wilderness into which they had fallen. Others were busy under the imromptu tent made by the empty gas-chambers. The Prince had gone a little way off and was scrutinising the distant heights through his field-glass. They had the appearance of old sea cliffs; here and there were small clumps of conifers, and in two places tall cascades. The nearer ground was strewn with glaciated boulders and supported nothing but a stunted Alpine vegetation of compact clustering stems and stalkless flowers. No river was visible, but the air was full of the rush and babble of a torrent close at hand. A bleak and biting wind was blowing. Ever and again a snowflake drifted past. The springless frozen earth under Bert's feet felt strangely dead and heavy after the buoyant airship.

§6

So it came about that that great and powerful Prince Karl Albert was for a time thrust out of the stupendous conflict he chiefly had been instrumental in provoking. The chances of battle and the weather conspired to maroon him in Labrador, and there he raged for six long days, while war and wonder swept the world. Nation rose against nation and air-fleet grappled air-fleet, cities blazed and men died in multitudes; but in Labrador one might have dreamt that, except for a little noise of hammering, the world was at peace.

There the encampment lay; from a distance the cabins, covered over with the silk of the balloon part, looked like a gipsy's tent on a rather exceptional scale, and all the available hands were busy in building out of the steel of the framework a mast from which the *Vaterland*'s electricians might hang the long conductors of the apparatus for wireless telegraphy that was to link the Prince to the world again. There were times when it seemed they would never rig that mast. From the outset the party suffered hardship. They were not too abundantly provisioned, and they were put on short rations, and for all the thick garments they had, they were but ill-equipped against the piercing wind and inhospitable violence of this wilderness. The first night was spent in darkness and without fires. The engines that had supplied power were smashed and dropped far away to the south, and there was never a match among the company. It had been death to carry matches. All the explosives had been thrown out of the magazine, and it was only towards morning that the bird-faced man whose cabin Bert had taken in the beginning confessed to a brace of duelling pistols and cartridges, with which a fire could be started. Afterwards the lockers of the machine gun were found to contain a supply of unused ammunition.

The night was a distressing one and seemed almost interminable. Hardly any one slept. There were seven wounded men aboard, and Von Winterfeld's head had been injured, and he

was shivering and in delirium, struggling with his attendant and shouting strange things about the burning of New York. The men crept together in the mess-room in the darkling, wrapped in what they could find and drank cocoa from the fireless heaters and listened to his cries. In the morning the Prince made them a speech about Destiny, and the God of his Fathers and the pleasure and glory of giving one's life for his dynasty, and a number of similar considerations that might otherwise have been neglected in that bleak wilderness. The men cheered without enthusiasm, and far away a wolf howled.

Then they set to work, and for a week they toiled to put up a mast of steel, and hang from it a gridiron of copper wires two hundred feet by twelve. The theme of all that time was work, work continually, straining and toilsome work, and all the rest was grim hardship and evil chances, save for a certain wild splendour in the sunset and sunrise in the torrents and drifting weather, in the wilderness about them. They built and tended a ring of perpetual fires, gangs roamed for brushwood and met with wolves, and the wounded men and their beds were brought out from the airship cabins, and put in shelters about the fires. There old Von Winterfeld raved and became quiet and presently died, and three of the other wounded sickened for want of good food, while their fellows mended. These things happened, as it were, in the wings; the central facts before Bert's consciousness were always firstly the perpetual toil, the holding and lifting, and lugging at heavy and clumsy masses, the tedious filing and winding of wires, and secondly, the Prince, urgent and threatening whenever a man relaxed. He would stand over them, and point over their heads, southward into the empty sky. "The world there," he said in German, "is waiting for us! Fifty Centuries come to their Consummation." Bert did not understand the words, but he read the gesture. Several times the Prince grew angry; once with a man who was working slowly, once with a man who stole a comrade's ration. The first he scolded and set to a more tedious task; the second he struck

in the face and ill-used. He did no work himself. There was a clear space near the fires in which he would walk up and down, sometimes for two hours together, with arms folded, muttering to himself of Patience and his destiny. At times these mutterings broke out into rhetoric, into shouts and gestures that would arrest the workers; they would stare at him until they perceived that his blue eyes glared and his waving hand addressed itself always to the southward hills. On Sunday the work ceased for half an hour, and the Prince preached on faith and God's friendship for David, and afterwards they all sang: "Ein feste Burg ist unser Gott."

In an improvised hovel lay Von Winterfeld, and all one morning he raved of the greatness of Germany. "Blut und Eisen!" he shouted, and then, as if in derision, "Welt-Politik—ha, ha!" Then he would explain complicated questions of polity to imaginary hearers, in low, wily tones. The other sick men kept still, listening to him. Bert's distracted attention would be recalled by Kurt. "Smallways, take that end. So!"

Slowly, tediously, the great mast was rigged and hoisted foot by foot into place. The electricians had contrived a catchment pool and a wheel in the torrent close at hand—for the little Mulhausen dynamo with its turbinal volute used by the telegraphists was quite adaptable to water driving, and on the sixth day in the evening the apparatus was in working order and the Prince was calling—weakly, indeed, but calling—to his air-fleet across the empty spaces of the world. For a time he called unheeded.

The effect of that evening was to linger long in Bert's memory. A red fire spluttered and blazed close by the electricians at their work, and red gleams ran up the vertical steel mast and threads of copper wire towards the zenith. The Prince sat on a rock close by, with his chin on his hand, waiting. Beyond and to the northward was the cairn that covered Von Winterfeld, surmounted by a cross of steel, and from among the tumbled rocks in the distance the eyes of a wolf gleamed redly. On the

other hand was the wreckage of the great airship and the men bivouacked about a second ruddy flare. They were all keeping very still, as if waiting to hear what news might presently be given them. Far away, across many hundreds of miles of desolation, other wireless masts would be clicking, and snapping, and waking into responsive vibration. Perhaps they were not. Perhaps those throbs upon the ethers wasted themselves upon a regardless world. When the men spoke, they spoke in low tones. Now and then a bird shrieked remotely, and once a wolf howled. All these things were set in the immense cold spaciousness of the wild.

§7

Bert got the news last, and chiefly in broken English, from a linguist among his mates. It was only far on in the night that the weary telegraphist got an answer to his calls, but then the messages came clear and strong. And such news it was!

"I say," said Bert at his breakfast, amidst a great clamour, "tell us a bit."

"All de vorlt is at vor!" said the linguist, waving his cocoa in an illustrative manner, "all de vorlt is at vor!"

Bert stared southward into the dawn. It did not seem so.

"All de vorlt is at vor! They haf burn' Berlin; they haf burn' London; they haf burn' Hamburg and Paris. Chapan hass burn San Francisco. We haf mate a camp at Niagara. Dat is whad they are telling us. China has cot drachenflieger and luftschiffe beyont counting. All de vorlt is at vor!"

"Gaw!" said Bert.

"Yess," said the linguist, drinking his cocoa.

"Burnt up London, 'ave they? Like we did New York?"

"It wass a bombardment."

"They don't say anything about a place called Clapham, or Bun Hill, do they?"

"I haf heard noding," said the linguist.

That was all Bert could get for a time. But the excitement of all the men about him was contagious, and presently he saw

Kurt standing alone, hands behind him, and looking at one of the distant waterfalls very steadfastly. He went up and saluted, soldier-fashion. "Beg pardon, lieutenant," he said.

Kurt turned his face. It was unusually grave that morning. "I was just thinking I would like to see that waterfall closer," he said. "It reminds me—what do you want?"

"I can't make 'ead or tail of what they're saying, sir. Would you mind telling me the news?"

"Damn the news," said Kurt. "You'll get news enough before the day's out. It's the end of the world. They're sending the *Graf Zeppelin* for us. She'll be here by the morning, and we ought to be at Niagara—or eternal smash—within eight and forty hours. . . . I want to look at that waterfall. You'd better come with me. Have you had your rations?"

"Yessir."

"Very well. Come."

And musing profoundly, Kurt led the way across the rocks towards the distant waterfall.

For a time Bert walked behind him in the character of an escort; then as they passed out of the atmosphere of the encampment, Kurt lagged for him to come alongside.

"We shall be back in it all in two days' time," he said. "And it's a devil of a war to go back to. That's the news. The world's gone mad. Our fleet beat the Americans the night we got disabled, that's clear. We lost eleven—eleven airships certain, and all their aeroplanes got smashed. God knows how much we smashed or how many we killed. But that was only the beginning. Our start's been like firing a magazine. Every country was hiding flying-machines. They're fighting in the air all over Europe—all over the world. The Japanese and Chinese have joined in. That's the great fact. That's the supreme fact. They've pounced into our little quarrels. . . . The Yellow Peril was a peril after all! They've got thousands of airships. They're all over the world. We bombarded London and Paris, and now the French and English have smashed up Berlin. And now Asia is at us all, and on the

top of us all. . . . It's mania. China on the top. And they don't know where to stop. It's limitless. It's the last confusion. They're bombarding capitals, smashing up dockyards and factories, mines and fleets."

"Did they do much to London, sir?" asked Bert.

"Heaven knows. . . ."

He said no more for a time.

"This Labrador seems a quiet place," he resumed at last. "I'm half a mind to stay here. Can't do that. No! I've got to see it through. I've got to see it through. You've got to, too. Every one. . . . But why?. . . I tell you—our world's gone to pieces. There's no way out of it, no way back. Here we are! We're like mice caught in a house on fire, we're like cattle overtaken by a flood. Presently we shall be picked up, and back we shall go into the fighting. We shall kill and smash again—perhaps. It's a Chino-Japanese air-fleet this time, and the odds are against us. Our turns will come. What will happen to you I don't know, but for myself, I know quite well; I shall be killed."

"You'll be all right," said Bert, after a queer pause.

"No!" said Kurt, "I'm going to be killed. I didn't know it before, but this morning, at dawn, I knew it—as though I'd been told."

" 'Ow?"

"I tell you I know."

"But 'ow *could* you know?"

"I know."

"Like being told?"

"Like being certain.

"I know," he repeated, and for a time they walked in silence towards the waterfall.

Kurt, wrapped in his thoughts, walked heedlessly, and at last broke out again. "I've always felt young before, Smallways, but this morning I feel old—old. So old! Nearer to death than old men feel. And I've always thought life was a lark. It isn't. . . . This sort of thing has always been happening, I suppose—these things, wars and earthquakes, that sweep across all the decency of life. It's just as though I had woke up to it all for the first time. Every night since we were at New York I've dreamt of it. . . . And it's always been so—it's the way of life. People are torn away from the people they care for; homes are smashed, creatures full of life, and memories, and little peculiar gifts are scalded and smashed and torn to pieces, and starved, and spoilt. London! Berlin! San Francisco! Think of all the human histories we ended in New York!. . . And the others go on again as though such things weren't possible. As I went on! Like animals! Just like animals."

He said nothing for a long time, and then he dropped out, "The Prince is a lunatic!"

They came to a place where they had to climb, and then to a long peat level beside a rivulet. There a quantity of delicate little pink flowers caught Bert's eye. "Gaw!" he said, and stooped to pick one. "In a place like this."

Kurt stopped and half turned. His face winced.

"I never see such a flower," said Bert. "It's so delicate."

"Pick some more if you want to," said Kurt.

Bert did so, while Kurt stood and watched him.

"Funny 'ow one always wants to pick flowers," said Bert.

Kurt had nothing to add to that.

They went on again, without talking, for a long time.

At last they came to a rocky hummock, from which the view of the waterfall opened out. There Kurt stopped and seated himself on a rock.

"That's as much as I wanted to see," he explained. "It isn't very like, but it's like enough."

"Like what?"

"Another waterfall I knew."

He asked a question abruptly. "Got a girl, Smallways?"

"Funny thing," said Bert, "those flowers, I suppose.—I was jes' thinking of 'er."

"So was I."

"*What!* Edna?"

"No. I was thinking of *my* Edna. We've all got Ednas, I suppose, for our imaginations to play about. This was a girl. But all that's past for ever. It's hard to think I can't see her just for a minute—just let her know I'm thinking of her."

"Very likely," said Bert, "you'll see 'er all right."

"No," said Kurt with decision, "I *know*."

"I met her," he went on, "in a place like this—in the Alps—Engstlen Alp. There's a waterfall rather like this one—a broad waterfall down towards Innertkirchen. That's why I came here this morning. We slipped away and had half a day together beside it. And we picked flowers. Just such flowers as you picked. The same for all I know. And gentian."

"I know" said Bert, "me and Edna—we done things like that. Flowers. And all that. Seems years off now."

"She was beautiful and daring and shy, Mein Gott! I can hardly hold myself for the desire to see her and hear her voice again before I die. Where is she?. . . Look here, Smallways, I shall write a sort of letter—And there's her portrait." He touched his breast pocket.

"You'll see 'er again all right," said Bert.

"No! I shall never see her again. . . . I don't understand why people should meet just to be torn apart. But I know she and I will never meet again. That I know as surely as that the sun will rise, and that cascade come shining over the rocks after I am dead and done. . . . Oh! It's all foolishness and haste and violence and cruel folly, stupidity and blundering hate and selfish ambition—all the things that men have done—all the things they will ever do. Gott! Smallways, what a muddle and confusion life has always been—the battles and massacres and disasters, the hates and harsh acts, the murders and sweatings, the lynchings and cheatings. This morning I am tired of it all, as though I'd just found it out for the first time. I *have* found it out. When a man is tired of life, I suppose it is time for him to die. I've lost heart, and death is over me. Death is close to me,

and I know I have got to end. But think of all the hopes I had only a little time ago, the sense of fine beginnings! . . . It was all a sham. There were no beginnings. . . . We're just ants in ant-hill cities, in a world that doesn't matter; that goes on and rambles into nothingness. New York—New York doesn't even strike me as horrible. New York was nothing but an ant-hill kicked to pieces by a fool!

"Think of it, Smallways: there's war everywhere! They're smashing up their civilisation before they have made it. The sort of thing the English did at Alexandria, the Japanese at Port Arthur, the French at Casablanca, is going on everywhere. Everywhere! Down in South America even they are fighting among themselves! No place is safe—no place is at peace. There is no place where a woman and her daughter can hide and be at peace. The war comes through the air, bombs drop in the night. Quiet people go out in the morning, and see air-fleets passing overhead—dripping death—dripping death!"

Chapter VIII

A WORLD AT WAR

§1

It was only very slowly that Bert got hold of this idea that the whole world was at war, that he formed any image at all of the crowded countries south of these Arctic solitudes stricken with terror and dismay as these new-born aerial navies swept across their skies. He was not used to thinking of the world as a whole, but as a limitless hinterland of happenings beyond the range of his immediate vision. War in his imagination was something, a source of news and emotion, that happened in a restricted area, called the Seat of War. But now the whole atmosphere was the Seat of War, and every land a cockpit. So closely had the nations raced along the path of research and invention, so secret and yet so parallel had been their plans and acquisitions, that it was within a few hours of the launching of the first fleet in Franconia that an Asiatic Armada beat its westward way across, high above the marvelling millions in the plain of the Ganges. But the preparations of the Confederation of Eastern Asia had been on an altogether more colossal scale than the German. "With this step," said Tan Ting-siang, "we overtake and pass the West. We recover the peace of the world that these barbarians have destroyed."

Their secrecy and swiftness and inventions had far surpassed those of the Germans, and where the Germans had had a hundred men at work the Asiatics had ten thousand. There came to their great aeronautic parks at Chinsi-fu and Tsingyen by the mono-rails that now laced the whole surface of China a limitless supply of skilled and able workmen, workmen far above the average European in industrial efficiency. The news

of the German World Surprise simply quickened their efforts. At the time of the bombardment of New York it is doubtful if the Germans had three hundred airships all together in the world; the score of Asiatic fleets flying east and west and south must have numbered several thousand. Moreover the Asiatics had a real fighting flying-machine, the Niais as they were called, a light but quite efficient weapon, infinitely superior to the German drachenflieger. Like that, it was a one-man machine, but it was built very lightly of steel and cane and chemical silk, with a transverse engine, and a flapping sidewing. The aeronaut carried a gun firing explosive bullets loaded with oxygen, and in addition, and true to the best tradition of Japan, a sword. Mostly they were Japanese, and it is characteristic that from the first it was contemplated that the aeronaut should be a swordsman. The wings of these flyers had bat-like hooks forward, by which they were to cling to their antagonist's gas-chambers while boarding him. These light flying-machines were carried with the fleets, and also sent overland or by sea to the front with the men. They were capable of flights of from two to five hundred miles according to the wind.

So, hard upon the uprush of the first German air-fleet, these Asiatic swarms took to the atmosphere. Instantly every organised Government in the world was frantically and vehemently building airships and whatever approach to a flying machine its inventors had discovered. There was no time for diplomacy. Warnings and ultimatums were telegraphed to and fro, and in a few hours all the panic-fierce world was openly at war, and at war in the most complicated way. For Britain and France and Italy had declared war upon Germany and outraged Swiss neutrality; India, at the sight of Asiatic airships, had broken into a Hindoo insurrection in Bengal and a Mohametan revolt hostile to this in the North-west Provinces—the latter spreading like wildfire from Gobi to the Gold Coast—and the Confederation of Eastern Asia had seized the oil wells of Burmah and was impartially attacking America and Germany.

In a week they were building airships in Damascus and Cairo and Johannesburg; Australia and New Zealand were frantically equipping themselves. One unique and terrifying aspect of this development was the swiftness with which these monsters could be produced. To build an ironclad took from two to four years; an airship could be put together in as many weeks. Moreover, compared with even a torpedo boat, the airship was remarkably simple to construct: given the air-chamber material, the engines, the gas plant, and the design, it was really not more complicated and far easier than an ordinary wooden boat had been a hundred years before. And now from Cape Horn to Nova Zembla, and from Canton round to Canton again, there were factories and workshops and industrial resources.

And the German airships were barely in sight of the Atlantic waters, the first Asiatic fleet was scarcely reported from Upper Burmah, before the fantastic fabric of credit and finance that had held the world together economically for a hundred years strained and snapped. A tornado of realisation swept through every stock exchange in the world; banks stopped payment, business shrank and ceased, factories ran on for a day or so by a sort of inertia, completing the orders of bankrupt and extinguished customers, then stopped. The New York Bert Smallways saw, for all its glare of light and traffic, was in the pit of an economic and financial collapse unparalleled in history. The flow of the food supply was already a little checked. And before the world-war had lasted two weeks—by the time, that is, that mast was rigged in Labrador—there was not a city or town in the world outside China, however far from the actual centres of destruction, where police and government were not adopting special emergency methods to deal with a want of food and a glut of unemployed people.

The special peculiarities of aerial warfare were of such a nature as to trend, once it had begun, almost inevitably towards social disorganisation. The first of these peculiarities was brought home to the Germans in their attack upon New

York; the immense power of destruction an airship has over the thing below, and its relative inability to occupy or police or guard or garrison a surrendered position. Necessarily, in the face of urban populations in a state of economic disorganisation and infuriated and starving, this led to violent and destructive collisions, and even where the air-fleet floated inactive above, there would be civil conflict and passionate disorder below. Nothing comparable to this state of affairs had been known in the previous history of warfare, unless we take such a case as that of a nineteenth century warship attacking some large savage or barbaric settlement, or one of those naval bombardments that disfigure the history of Great Britain in the late eighteenth century. Then, indeed, there had been cruelties and destruction that faintly foreshadowed the horrors of the aerial war. Moreover, before the twentieth century the world had had but one experience, and that a comparatively light one, in the Communist insurrection of Paris, 1871, of the possibilities of a modern urban population under warlike stresses.

A second peculiarity of airship war as it first came to the world that also made for social collapse, was the ineffectiveness of the early air-ships against each other. Upon anything below they could rain explosives in the most deadly fashion, forts and ships and cities lay at their mercy, but unless they were prepared for a suicidal grapple they could do remarkably little mischief to each other. The armament of the huge German airships, big as the biggest mammoth liners afloat, was one machine gun that could easily have been packed up on a couple of mules. In addition, when it became evident that the air must be fought for, the air-sailors were provided with rifles with explosive bullets of oxygen or inflammable substance, but no airship at any time ever carried as much in the way of guns and armour as the smallest gun-boat on the navy list had been accustomed to do. Consequently, when these monsters met in battle, they manoeuvred for the upper place, or grappled and fought like junks, throwing grenades, fighting hand to hand in an entirely

medieval fashion. The risks of a collapse and fall on either side came near to balancing in every case the chances of victory. As a consequence, and after their first experiences of battle, one finds a growing tendency on the part of the air-fleet admirals to evade joining battle, and to seek rather the moral advantage of a destructive counter-attack.

And if the airships were too ineffective, the early drachenflieger were either too unstable, like the German, or too light, like the Japanese, to produce immediately decisive results. Later, it is true, the Brazilians launched a flying-machine of a type and scale that was capable of dealing with an airship, but they built only three or four, they operated only in South America, and they vanished from history untraceably in the time when world-bankruptcy put a stop to all further engineering production on any considerable scale.

The third peculiarity of aerial warfare was that it was at once enormously destructive and entirely indecisive. It had this unique feature, that both sides lay open to punitive attack. In all previous forms of war, both by land and sea, the losing side was speedily unable to raid its antagonist's territory and the communications. One fought on a "front," and behind that front the winner's supplies and resources, his towns and factories and capital, the peace of his country, were secure. If the war was a naval one, you destroyed your enemy's battle fleet and then blockaded his ports, secured his coaling stations, and hunted down any stray cruisers that threatened your ports of commerce. But to blockade and watch a coastline is one thing, to blockade and watch the whole surface of a country is another, and cruisers and privateers are things that take long to make, that cannot be packed up and hidden and carried unostentatiously from point to point. In aerial war the stronger side, even supposing it destroyed the main battle fleet of the weaker, had then either to patrol and watch or destroy every possible point at which he might produce another and perhaps a novel and more deadly form of flyer. It meant darkening his air with airships. It meant building them by the thousand and making aeronauts by the hundred thousand. A small uninitated airship could be hidden in a railway shed, in a village street, in a wood; a flying machine is even less conspicuous.

And in the air are no streets, no channels, no point where one can say of an antagonist, "If he wants to reach my capital he must come by here." In the air all directions lead everywhere.

Consequently it was impossible to end a war by any of the established methods. A, having outnumbered and overwhelmed B, hovers, a thousand airships strong, over his capital, threatening to bombard it unless B submits. B replies by wireless telegraphy that he is now in the act of bombarding the chief manufacturing city of A by means of three raider airships. A denounces B's raiders as pirates and so forth, bombards B's capital, and sets off to hunt down B's airships, while B, in a state of passionate emotion and heroic unconquerableness, sets to work amidst his ruins, making fresh airships and explosives for the benefit of A. The war became perforce a universal guerilla war, a war inextricably involving civilians and homes and all the apparatus of social life.

These aspects of aerial fighting took the world by surprise. There had been no foresight to deduce these consequences. If there had been, the world would have arranged for a Universal Peace Conference in 1900. But mechanical invention had gone faster than intellectual and social organisation, and the world, with its silly old flags, its silly unmeaning tradition of nationality, its cheap newspapers and cheaper passions and imperialisms, its base commercial motives and habitual insincerities and vulgarities, its race lies and conflicts, was taken by surprise. Once the war began there was no stopping it. The flimsy fabric of credit that had grown with no man foreseeing, and that had held those hundreds of millions in an economic interdependence that no man clearly understood, dissolved in panic. Everywhere went the airships dropping bombs, destroying any hope of a rally, and everywhere below were economic catastrophe,

starving workless people, rioting, and social disorder. Whatever constructive guiding intelligence there had been among the nations vanished in the passionate stresses of the time. Such newspapers and documents and histories as survive from this period all tell one universal story of towns and cities with the food supply interrupted and their streets congested with starving unemployed; of crises in administration and states of siege, of provisional Governments and Councils of Defence, and, in the cases of India and Egypt, insurrectionary committees taking charge of the re-arming of the population, of the making of batteries and gun-pits, of the vehement manufacture of airships and flying-machines.

One sees these things in glimpses, in illuminated moments, as if through a driving reek of clouds, going on all over the world. It was the dissolution of an age; it was the collapse of the civilisation that had trusted to machinery, and the instruments of its destruction were machines. But while the collapse of the previous great civilisation, that of Rome, had been a matter of centuries, had been a thing of phase and phase, like the ageing and dying of a man, this, like his killing by railway or motor car, was one swift, conclusive smashing and an end.

§2

The early battles of the aerial war were no doubt determined by attempts to realise the old naval maxim, to ascertain the position of the enemy's fleet and to destroy it. There was first the battle of the Bernese Oberland, in which the Italian and French navigables in their flank raid upon the Franconian Park were assailed by the Swiss experimental squadron, supported as the day wore on by German airships, and then the encounter of the British Winterhouse-Dunn aeroplanes with three unfortunate Germans.

Then came the Battle of North India, in which the entire Anglo-Indian aeronautic settlement establishment fought for three days against overwhelming odds, and was dispersed and destroyed in detail.

And simultaneously with the beginning of that, commenced the momentous struggle of the Germans and Asiatics that is usually known as the Battle of Niagara because of the objective of the Asiatic attack. But it passed gradually into a sporadic conflict over half a continent. Such German airships as escaped destruction in battle descended and surrendered to the Americans, and were re-manned, and in the end it became a series of pitiless and heroic encounters between the Americans, savagely resolved to exterminate their enemies, and a continually reinforced army of invasion from Asia quartered upon the Pacific slope and supported by an immense fleet. From the first the war in America was fought with implacable bitterness; no quarter was asked, no prisoners were taken. With ferocious and magnificent energy the Americans constructed and launched ship after ship to battle and perish against the Asiatic multitudes. All other affairs were subordinate to this war, the whole population was presently living or dying for it. Presently, as I shall tell, the white men found in the Butteridge machine a weapon that could meet and fight the flying-machines of the Asiatic swordsman.

The Asiatic invasion of America completely effaced the German-American conflict. It vanishes from history. At first it had seemed to promise quite sufficient tragedy in itself—beginning as it did in unforgettable massacre. After the destruction of central New York all America had risen like one man, resolved to die a thousand deaths rather than submit to Germany. The Germans grimly resolved upon beating the Americans into submission and, following out the plans developed by the Prince, had seized Niagara—in order to avail themselves of its enormous powerworks; expelled all its inhabitants and made a desert of its environs as far as Buffalo. They had also, directly Great Britain and France declare war, wrecked the country upon the Canadian side for nearly ten miles inland. They began to bring up men and material from the fleet off the east coast, stringing out to and fro like bees getting honey. It was then that the Asiatic forces appeared, and it was in their attack upon this

German base at Niagara that the air-fleets of East and West first met and the greater issue became clear.

One conspicuous peculiarity of the early aerial fighting arose from the profound secrecy with which the airships had been prepared. Each power had had but the dimmest inkling of the schemes of its rivals, and even experiments with its own devices were limited by the needs of secrecy. None of the designers of airships and aeroplanes had known clearly what their inventions might have to fight; many had not imagined they would have to fight anything whatever in the air; and had planned them only for the dropping of explosives. Such had been the German idea. The only weapon for fighting another airship with which the Franconian fleet had been provided was the machine gun forward. Only after the fight over New York were the men given short rifles with detonating bullets. Theoretically, the drachenflieger were to have been the fighting weapon. They were declared to be aerial torpedo-boats, and the aeronaut was supposed to swoop close to his antagonist and cast his bombs as he whirled past. But indeed these contrivances were hopelessly unstable; not one-third in any engagement succeeded in getting back to the mother airship. The rest were either smashed up or grounded.

The allied Chino-Japanese fleet made the same distinction as the Germans between airships and fighting machines heavier than air, but the type in both cases was entirely different from the occidental models, and—it is eloquent of the vigour with which these great peoples took up and bettered the European methods of scientific research—in almost every particular the invention of Asiatic engineers. Chief among these, it is worth remarking, was Mohini K. Chatterjee, a political exile who had formerly served in the British-Indian aeronautic park at Lahore.

The German airship was fish-shaped, with a blunted head; the Asiatic airship was also fish-shaped, but not so much on the lines of a cod or goby as of a ray or sole. It had a wide, flat underside, unbroken by windows or any opening except along

the middle line. Its cabins occupied its axis, with a sort of bridge deck above, and the gas-chambers gave the whole affair the shape of a gipsy's hooped tent, except that it was much flatter. The German airship was essentially a navigable balloon very much lighter than air; the Asiatic airship was very little lighter than air and skimmed through it with much greater velocity if with considerably less stability. They carried fore and aft guns, the latter much the larger, throwing inflammatory shells, and in addition they had nests for riflemen on both the upper and the under side. Light as this armament was in comparison with the smallest gunboat that ever sailed, it was sufficient for them to outfight as well as outfly the German monster airships. In action they flew to get behind or over the Germans: they even dashed underneath, avoiding only passing immediately beneath the magazine, and then as soon as they had crossed let fly with their rear gun, and sent flares or oxygen shells into the antagonist's gas-chambers.

It was not in their airships, but, as I have said, in their flying-machines proper, that the strength of the Asiatics lay. Next only to the Butteridge machine, these were certainly the most efficient heavier-than-air fliers that had ever appeared. They were the invention of a Japanese artist, and they differed in type extremely from the box-kite quality of the German drachenflieger. They had curiously curved, flexible side wings, more like *bent* butterfly's wings than anything else, and made of a substance like celluloid and of brightly painted silk, and they had a long humming-bird tail. At the forward corner of the wings were hooks, rather like the claws of a bat, by which the machine could catch and hang and tear at the walls of an airship's gas-chamber. The solitary rider sat between the wings above a transverse explosive engine, an explosive engine that differed in no essential particular from those in use in the light motor bicycles of the period. Below was a single large wheel. The rider sat astride of a saddle, as in the Butteridge machine, and he carried a large double-edged two-handed sword, in addition to his explosive-bullet firing rifle.

§3

One sets down these particulars and compares the points of the American and German pattern of aeroplane and navigable, but none of these facts were clearly known to any of those who fought in this monstrously confused battle above the American great lakes.

Each side went into action against it knew not what, under novel conditions and with apparatus that even without hostile attacks was capable of producing the most disconcerting surprises. Schemes of action, attempts at collective manoeuvring necessarily went to pieces directly the fight began, just as they did in almost all the early ironclad battles of the previous century. Each captain then had to fall back upon individual action and his own devices; one would see triumph in what another read as a cue for flight and despair. It is as true of the Battle of Niagara as of the Battle of Lissa that it was not a battle but a bundle of "battlettes"!

To such a spectator as Bert it presented itself as a series of incidents, some immense, some trivial, but collectively incoherent. He never had a sense of any plain issue joined, of any point struggled for and won or lost. He saw tremendous things happen and in the end his world darkened to disaster and ruin.

He saw the battle from the ground, from Prospect Park and from Goat Island, whither he fled.

But the manner in which he came to be on the ground needs explaining.

The Prince had resumed command of his fleet through wireless telegraphy long before the *Zeppelin* had located his encampment in Labrador. By his direction the German air-fleet, whose advance scouts had been in contact with the Japanese over the Rocky Mountains, had concentrated upon Niagara and awaited his arrival. He had rejoined his command early in the morning of the twelfth, and Bert had his first prospect of the Gorge of Niagara while he was doing net drill outside the

middle gas-chamber at sunrise. The *Zeppelin* was flying very high at the time, and far below he saw the water in the gorge marbled with froth and then away to the west the great crescent of the Canadian Fall shining, flickering and foaming in the level sunlight and sending up a deep, incessant thudding rumble to the sky. The air-fleet was keeping station in an enormous crescent, with its horns pointing south-westward, a long array of shining monsters with tails rotating slowly and German ensigns now trailing from their bellies aft of their Marconi pendants.

Niagara city was still largely standing then, albeit its streets were empty of all life. Its bridges were intact; its hotels and restaurants still flying flags and inviting sky signs; its power-stations running. But about it the country on both sides of the gorge might have been swept by a colossal broom. Everything that could possibly give cover to an attack upon the German position at Niagara had been levelled as ruthlessly as machinery and explosives could contrive; houses blown up and burnt, woods burnt, fences and crops destroyed. The mono-rails had been torn up, and the roads in particular cleared of all possibility of concealment or shelter. Seen from above, the effect of this wreckage was grotesque. Young woods had been destroyed whole-sale by dragging wires, and the spoilt saplings, smashed or uprooted, lay in swathes like corn after the sickle. Houses had an appearance of being flattened down by the pressure of a gigantic finger. Much burning was still going on, and large areas had been reduced to patches of smouldering and sometimes still glowing blackness.

Here and there lay the debris of belated fugitives, carts, and dead bodies of horses and men; and where houses had had water-supplies there were pools of water and running springs from the ruptured pipes. In unscorched fields horses and cattle still fed peacefully. Beyond this desolated area the country-side was still standing, but almost all the people had fled. Buffalo was on fire to an enormous extent, and there were no signs of any efforts to grapple with the flames. Niagara city itself was being rapidly

converted to the needs of a military depot. A large number of skilled engineers had already been brought from the fleet and were busily at work adapting the exterior industrial apparatus of the place to the purposes of an aeronautic park. They had made a gas recharging station at the corner of the American Fall above the funicular railway, and they were opening up a much larger area to the south for the same purpose. Over the power-houses and hotels and suchlike prominent or important points the German flag was flying.

The *Zeppelin* circled slowly over this scene twice while the Prince surveyed it from the swinging gallery; it then rose towards the centre of the crescent and transferred the Prince and his suite, Kurt included, to the *Hohenzollern*, which had been chosen as the flagship during the impending battle. They were swung up on a small cable from the forward gallery, and the men of the *Zeppelin* manned the outer netting as the Prince and his staff left them. The *Zeppelin* then came about, circled down and grounded in Prospect Park, in order to land the wounded and take aboard explosives; for she had come to Labrador with her magazines empty, it being uncertain what weight she might need to carry. She also replenished the hydrogen in one of her forward chambers which had leaked.

Bert was detailed as a bearer and helped carry the wounded one by one into the nearest of the large hotels that faced the Canadian shore. The hotel was quite empty except that there were two trained American nurses and a negro porter, and three or four Germans awaiting them. Bert went with the *Zeppelin's* doctor into the main street of the place, and they broke into a drug shop and obtained various things of which they stood in need. As they returned they found an officer and two men making a rough inventory of the available material in the various stores. Except for them the wide, main street of the town was quite deserted, the people had been given three hours to clear out, and everybody, it seemed, had done so. At one corner a dead man lay against the wall—shot. Two or three dogs were

visible up the empty vista, but towards its river end the passage of a string of mono-rail cars broke the stillness and the silence. They were loaded with hose, and were passing to the trainful of workers who were converting Prospect Park into an airship dock.

Bert pushed a case of medicine balanced on a bicycle taken from an adjacent shop, to the hotel, and then he was sent to load bombs into the *Zeppelin* magazine, a duty that called for elaborate care. From this job he was presently called off by the captain of the *Zeppelin*, who sent him with a note to the officer in charge of the Anglo-American Power Company, for the field telephone had still to be adjusted. Bert received his instructions in German, whose meaning he guessed, and saluted and took the note, not caring to betray his ignorance of the language. He started off with a bright air of knowing his way and turned a corner or so, and was only beginning to suspect that he did not know where he was going when his attention was recalled to the sky by the report of a gun from the *Hohenzollern* and celestial cheering.

He looked up and found the view obstructed by the houses on either side of the street. He hesitated, and then curiosity took him back towards the bank of the river. Here his view was inconvenienced by trees, and it was with a start that he discovered the *Zeppelin*, which he knew had still a quarter of her magazines to fill, was rising over Goat Island. She had not waited for her complement of ammunition. It occurred to him that he was left behind. He ducked back among the trees and bushes until he felt secure from any after-thought on the part of the *Zeppelin's* captain. Then his curiosity to see what the German air-fleet faced overcame him, and drew him at last halfway across the bridge to Goat Island.

From that point he had nearly a hemisphere of sky and got his first glimpse of the Asiatic airships low in the sky above the glittering tumults of the Upper Rapids.

They were far less impressive than the German ships. He

could not judge the distance, and they flew edgeways to him, so as to conceal the broader aspect of their bulk.

Bert stood there in the middle of the bridge, in a place that most people who knew it remembered as a place populous with sightseers and excursionists, and he was the only human being in sight there. Above him, very high in the heavens, the contending air-fleets manoeuvred; below him the river seethed like a sluice towards the American Fall. He was curiously dressed. His cheap blue serge trousers were thrust into German airship rubber boots, and on his head he wore an aeronaut's white cap that was a trifle too large for him. He thrust that back to reveal his staring little Cockney face, still scarred upon the brow. "Gaw!" he whispered.

He stared. He gesticulated. Once or twice he shouted and applauded.

Then at a certain point terror seized him and he took to his heels in the direction of Goat Island.

§4

For a time after they were in sight of each other, neither fleet attempted to engage. The Germans numbered sixty-seven great airships and they maintained the crescent formation at a height of nearly four thousand feet. They kept a distance of about one and a half lengths, so that the horns of the crescent were nearly thirty miles apart. Closely in tow of the airships of the extreme squadrons on either wing were about thirty drachenflieger ready manned, but these were too small and distant for Bert to distinguish.

At first, only what was called the Southern fleet of the Asiatics was visible to him. It consisted of forty airships, carrying all together nearly four hundred one-man flying-machines upon their flanks, and for some time it flew slowly and at a minimum distance of perhaps a dozen miles from the Germans, eastward across their front. At first Bert could distinguish only the greater bulks, then he perceived the one-man machines as a multitude

of very small objects drifting like motes in the sunshine about and beneath the larger shapes.

Bert saw nothing then of the second fleet of the Asiatics, though probably that was coming into sight of the Germans at the time, in the north-west.

The air was very still, the sky almost without a cloud, and the German fleet had risen to an immense height, so that the airships seemed no longer of any considerable size. Both ends of their crescent showed plainly. As they beat southward they passed slowly between Bert and the sunlight, and became black outlines of themselves. The drachenflieger appeared as little flecks of black on either wing of this aerial Armada.

The two fleets seemed in no hurry to engage. The Asiatics went far away into the east, quickening their pace and rising as they did so, and then tailed out into a long column and came flying back, rising towards the German left. The squadrons of the latter came about, facing this oblique advance, and suddenly little flickerings and a faint crepitating sound told that they had opened fire. For a time no effect was visible to the watcher on the bridge. Then, like a handful of snowflakes, the drachenflieger swooped to the attack, and a multitude of red specks whirled up to meet them. It was to Bert's sense not only enormously remote but singularly inhuman. Not four hours since he had been on one of those very airships, and yet they seemed to him now not gas-bags carrying men, but strange sentient creatures that moved about and did things with a purpose of their own. The flight of the Asiatic and German flying-machines joined and dropped earthward, became like a handful of white and red rose petals flung from a distant window, grew larger, until Bert could see the overturned ones spinning through the air, and were hidden by great volumes of dark smoke that were rising in the direction of Buffalo. For a time they all were hidden, then two or three white and a number of red ones rose again into the sky, like a swarm of big butterflies, and circled fighting and drove away out of sight again towards the east.

A heavy report recalled Bert's eyes to the zenith, and behold, the great crescent had lost its dressing and burst into a disorderly long cloud of airships! One had dropped halfway down the sky. It was flaming fore and aft, and even as Bert looked it turned over and fell, spinning over and over itself and vanished into the smoke of Buffalo.

Bert's mouth opened and shut, and he clutched tighter on the rail of the bridge. For some moments—they seemed long moments—the two fleets remained without any further change flying obliquely towards each other, and making what came to Bert's ears as a midget uproar. Then suddenly from either side airships began dropping out of alignment, smitten by missiles he could neither see nor trace. The string of Asiatic ships swung round and either charged into or over (it was difficult to say from below) the shattered line of the Germans, who seemed to open out to give way to them. Some sort of manoeuvring began, but Bert could not grasp its import. The left of the battle became a confused dance of airships. For some minutes up there the two crossing lines of ships looked so close it seemed like a hand-to-hand scuffle in the sky. Then they broke up into groups and duels. The descent of German air-ships towards the lower sky increased. One of them flared down and vanished far away in the north; two dropped with something twisted and crippled in their movements; then a group of antagonists came down from the zenith in an eddying conflict, two Asiatics against one German, and were presently joined by another, and drove away eastward all together with others dropping out of the German line to join them.

One Asiatic either rammed or collided with a still more gigantic German, and the two went spinning to destruction together. The northern squadron of Asiatics came into the battle unnoted by Bert, except that the multitude of ships above seemed presently increased. In a little while the fight was utter confusion, drifting on the whole to the southwest against the wind. It became more and more a series of group encounters.

Here a huge German airship flamed earthward with a dozen flat Asiatic craft about her, crushing her every attempt to recover. Here another hung with its screw fighting off the swordsman from a swarm of flying-machines. Here, again, an Asiatic aflame at either end swooped out of the battle. His attention went from incident to incident in the vast clearness overhead; these conspicuous cases of destruction caught and held his mind; it was only very slowly that any sort of scheme manifested itself between those nearer, more striking episodes.

The mass of the airships that eddied remotely above was, however, neither destroying nor destroyed. The majority of them seemed to be going at full speed and circling upward for position, exchanging ineffectual shots as they did so. Very little ramming was essayed after the first tragic downfall of rammer and rammed, and what ever attempts at boarding were made were invisible to Bert. There seemed, however, a steady attempt to isolate antagonists, to cut them off from their fellows and bear them down, causing a perpetual sailing back and interlacing of these shoaling bulks. The greater numbers of the Asiatics and their swifter heeling movements gave them the effect of persistently attacking the Germans. Overhead, and evidently endeavouring to keep itself in touch with the works of Niagara, a body of German airships drew itself together into a compact phalanx, and the Asiatics became more and more intent upon breaking this up. He was grotesquely reminded of fish in a fish-pond struggling for crumbs. He could see puny puffs of smoke and the flash of bombs, but never a sound came down to him. . . .

A flapping shadow passed for a moment between Bert and the sun and was followed by another. A whirring of engines, click, clock, clitter clock, smote upon his ears. Instantly he forgot the zenith.

Perhaps a hundred yards above the water, out of the south, riding like Valkyries swiftly through the air on the strange steeds the engineering of Europe had begotten upon the artistic inspiration of Japan, came a long string of Asiatic swordsman.

The wings flapped jerkily, click, block, clitter clock, and the machines drove up; they spread and ceased, and the apparatus came soaring through the air. So they rose and fell and rose again. They passed so closely overhead that Bert could hear their voices calling to one another. They swooped towards Niagara city and landed one after another in a long line in a clear space before the hotel. But he did not stay to watch them land. One yellow face had craned over and looked at him, and for one enigmatical instant met his eyes. . . .

It was then the idea came to Bert that he was altogether too conspicuous in the middle of the bridge, and that he took to his heels towards Goat Island. Thence, dodging about among the trees, with perhaps an excessive self-consciousness, he watched the rest of the struggle.

§5

When Bert's sense of security was sufficiently restored for him to watch the battle again, he perceived that a brisk little fight was in progress between the Asiatic aeronauts and the German engineers for the possession of Niagara city. It was the first time in the whole course of the war that he had seen anything resembling fighting as he had studied it in the illustrated papers of his youth. It seemed to him almost as though things were coming right. He saw men carrying rifles and taking cover and running briskly from point to point in a loose attacking formation. The first batch of aeronauts had probably been under the impression that the city was deserted. They had grounded in the open near Prospect Park and approached the houses towards the power-works before they were disillusioned by a sudden fire. They had scattered back to the cover of a bank near the water—it was too far for them to reach their machines again; they were lying and firing at the men in the hotels and frame-houses about the power-works.

Then to their support came a second string of red flying-machines driving up from the east. They rose up out of the

haze above the houses and came round in a long curve as if surveying the position below. The fire of the Germans rose to a roar, and one of those soaring shapes gave an abrupt jerk backward and fell among the houses. The others swooped down exactly like great birds upon the roof of the power-house. They caught upon it, and from each sprang a nimble little figure and ran towards the parapet.

Other flapping bird-shapes came into this affair, but Bert had not seen their coming. A staccato of shots came over to him, reminding him of army manoeuvres, of newspaper descriptions of fights, of all that was entirely correct in his conception of warfare. He saw quite a number of Germans running from the outlying houses towards the power-house. Two fell. One lay still, but the other wriggled and made efforts for a time. The hotel that was used as a hospital, and to which he had helped carry the wounded men from the *Zeppelin* earlier in the day, suddenly ran up the Geneva flag. The town that had seemed so quiet had evidently been concealing a considerable number of Germans, and they were now concentrating to hold the central power-house. He wondered what ammunition they might have. More and more of the Asiatic flying-machines came into the conflict. They had disposed of the unfortunate German drachenflieger and were now aiming at the incipient aeronautic park, the electric gas generators and repair stations which formed the German base. Some landed, and their aeronauts took cover and became energetic infantry soldiers. Others hovered above the fight, their men ever and again firing shots down at some chance exposure below. The firing came in paroxysms; now there would be a watchful lull and now a rapid tattoo of shots, rising to a roar. Once or twice flying machines, as they circled warily, came right overhead, and for a time Bert gave himself body and soul to cowering.

Ever and again a larger thunder mingled with the rattle and reminded him of the grapple of airships far above, but the nearer fight held his attention.

Abruptly something dropped from the zenith; something like a barrel or a huge football.

CRASH! It smashed with an immense report. It had fallen among the grounded Asiatic aeroplanes that lay among the turf and flower-beds near the river. They flew in scraps and fragments, turf, trees, and gravel leapt and fell; the aeronauts still lying along the canal bank were thrown about like sacks, catspaws flew across the foaming water. All the windows of the hotel hospital that had been shiningly reflecting blue sky and airships the moment before became vast black stars. Bang!—a second followed. Bert looked up and was filled with a sense of a number of monstrous bodies swooping down, coming down on the whole affair like a flight of bellying blankets, like a string of vast dish-covers. The central tangle of the battle above was circling down as if to come into touch with the power-house fight. He got a new effect of airships altogether, as vast things coming down upon him, growing swiftly larger and larger and more overwhelming, until the houses over the way seemed small, the American rapids narrow, the bridge flimsy, the combatants infinitesimal. As they came down they became audible as a complex of shootings and vast creakings and groanings and beatings and throbbings and shouts and shots. The fore-shortened black eagles at the fore-ends of the Germans had an effect of actual combat of flying feathers.

Some of these fighting airships came within five hundred feet of the ground. Bert could see men on the lower galleries of the Germans, firing rifles; could see Asiatics clinging to the ropes; saw one man in aluminium diver's gear fall flashing headlong into the waters above Goat Island. For the first time he saw the Asiatic airships closely. From this aspect they reminded him more than anything else of colossal snowshoes; they had a curious patterning in black and white, in forms that reminded him of the engine-turned cover of a watch. They had no hanging galleries, but from little openings on the middle line peeped out men and the muzzles of guns. So, driving in long, descending and ascending curves, these monsters wrestled and fought. It was like clouds fighting, like puddings trying to assassinate each other. They whirled and circled about each other, and for a time threw Goat Island and Niagara into a smoky twilight, through which the sunlight smote in shafts and beams. They spread and closed and spread and grappled and drove round over the rapids, and two miles away or more into Canada, and back over the Falls again. A German caught fire, and the whole crowd broke away from her flare and rose about her dispersing, leaving her to drop towards Canada and blow up as she dropped. Then with renewed uproar the others closed again. Once from the men in Niagara city came a sound like an ant-hill cheering. Another German burnt, and one badly deflated by the prow of an antagonist, flopped out of action southward.

It became more and more evident that the Germans were getting the worst of the unequal fight. More and more obviously were they being persecuted. Less and less did they seem to fight with any object other than escape. The Asiatics swept by them and above them, ripped their bladders, set them alight, picked off their dimly seen men in diving clothes, who struggled against fire and tear with fire extinguishers and silk ribbons in the inner netting. They answered only with ineffectual shots. Thence the battle circled back over Niagara, and then suddenly the Germans, as if at a preconcerted signal, broke and dispersed, going east, west, north, and south, in open and confused flight. The Asiatics, as they realised this, rose to fly above them and after them. Only one little knot of four Germans and perhaps a dozen Asiatics remained fighting about the *Hohenzollern* and the Prince as he circled in a last attempt to save Niagara.

Round they swooped once again over the Canadian Fall, over the waste of waters eastward, until they were distant and small, and then round and back, hurrying, bounding, swooping towards the one gaping spectator.

The whole struggling mass approached very swiftly, growing rapidly larger, and coming out black and featureless against

the afternoon sun and above the blinding welter of the Upper Rapids. It grew like a storm cloud until once more it darkened the sky. The flat Asiatic airships kept high above the Germans and behind them, and fired unanswered bullets into their gas-chambers and upon their flanks—the one-man flying-machines hovered and alighted like a swarm of attacking bees. Nearer they came, and nearer, filling the lower heaven. Two of the Germans swooped and rose again, but the *Hohenzollern* had suffered too much for that. She lifted weakly, turned sharply as if to get out of the battle, burst into flames fore and aft, swept down to the water, splashed into it obliquely, and rolled over and over and came down stream rolling and smashing and writhing like a thing alive, halting and then coming on again, with her torn and bent propeller still beating the air. The bursting flames spluttered out again in clouds of steam. It was a disaster gigantic in its dimensions. She lay across the rapids like an island, like tall cliffs, tall cliffs that came rolling, smoking, and crumpling, and collapsing, advancing with a sort of fluctuating rapidity upon Bert. One Asiatic airship—it looked to Bert from below like three hundred yards of pavement—whirled back and circled two or three times over that great overthrow, and half a dozen crimson flying-machines danced for a moment like great midges in the sunlight before they swept on after their fellows. The rest of the fight had already gone over the island, a wild crescendo of shots and yells and smashing uproar. It was hidden from Bert now by the trees of the island, and forgotten by him in the nearer spectacle of the huge advance of the defeated German airship. Something fell with a mighty smashing and splintering of boughs unheeded behind him.

It seemed for a time that the *Hohenzollern* must needs break her back upon the Parting of the Waters, and then for a time her propeller flopped and frothed in the river and thrust the mass of buckling, crumpled wreckage towards the American shore. Then the sweep of the torrent that foamed down to the American Fall caught her, and in another minute the immense mass of deflating wreckage, with flames spurting out in three new places, had crashed against the bridge that joined Goat Island and Niagara city, and forced a long arm, as it were, in a heaving tangle under the central span. Then the middle chambers blew up with a loud report, and in another moment the bridge had given way and the main bulk of the airship, like some grotesque cripple in rags, staggered, flapping and waving flambeaux to the crest of the Fall and hesitated there and vanished in a desperate suicidal leap.

Its detached fore-end remained jammed against that little island, Green Island it used to be called, which forms the stepping-stone between the mainland and Goat Island's patch of trees.

Bert followed this disaster from the Parting of the Waters to the bridge head. Then, regardless of cover, regardless of the Asiatic airship hovering like a huge house roof without walls above the Suspension Bridge, he sprinted along towards the north and came out for the first time upon that rocky point by Luna Island that looks sheer down upon the American Fall. There he stood breathless amidst that eternal rush of sound, breathless and staring.

Far below, and travelling rapidly down the gorge, whirled something like a huge empty sack. For him it meant—what did it not mean?—the German air-fleet, Kurt, the Prince, Europe, all things stable and familiar, the forces that had brought him, the forces that had seemed indisputably victorious. And it went down the rapids like an empty sack and left the visible world to Asia, to yellow people beyond Christendom, to all that was terrible and strange!

Remote over Canada receded the rest of that conflict and vanished beyond the range of his vision. . . .

Chapter IX

ON GOAT ISLAND

§1

The whack of a bullet on the rocks beside him reminded him that he was a visible object and wearing at least portions of a German uniform. It drove him into the trees again, and for a time he dodged and dropped and sought cover like a chick hiding among reeds from imaginary hawks.

"Beaten," he whispered. "Beaten and done for . . . Chinese! Yellow chaps chasing 'em!"

At last he came to rest in a clump of bushes near a locked-up and deserted refreshment shed within view of the American side. They made a sort of hole and harbour for him; they met completely overhead. He looked across the rapids, but the firing had ceased now altogether and everything seemed quiet. The Asiatic aeroplane had moved from its former position above the Suspension Bridge, was motionless now above Niagara city, shadowing all that district about the power-house which had been the scene of the land fight. The monster had an air of quiet and assured predominance, and from its stern it trailed, serene and ornamental, a long streaming flag, the red, black, and yellow of the great alliance, the Sunrise and the Dragon. Beyond, to the east, at a much higher level, hung a second consort, and Bert, presently gathering courage, wriggled out and craned his neck to find another still airship against the sunset in the south.

"Gaw!" he said. "Beaten and chased! My Gawd!"

The fighting, it seemed at first, was quite over in Niagara city, though a German flag was still flying from one shattered house. A white sheet was hoisted above the power-house, and this remained flying all through the events that followed. But presently came a sound of shots and then German soldiers running. They disappeared among the houses, and then came two engineers in blue shirts and trousers hotly pursued by three Japanese swordsman. The foremost of the two fugitives was a shapely man, and ran lightly and well; the second was a sturdy little man, and rather fat. He ran comically in leaps and bounds, with his plump arms bent up by his side and his head thrown back. The pursuers ran with uniforms and dark thin metal and leather head-dresses. The little man stumbled, and Bert gasped, realising a new horror in war.

The foremost swordsman won three strides on him and was near enough to slash at him and miss as he spurted.

A dozen yards they ran, and then the swordsman slashed again, and Bert could hear across the waters a little sound like the moo of an elfin cow as the fat little man fell forward. Slash went the swordsman and slash at something on the ground that tried to save itself with ineffectual hands. "Oh, I carn't!" cried Bert, near blubbering, and staring with starting eyes.

The swordsman slashed a fourth time and went on as his fellows came up after the better runner. The hindmost swordsman stopped and turned back. He had perceived some movement perhaps; but at any rate he stood, and ever and again slashed at the fallen body.

"Oo-oo!" groaned Bert at every slash, and shrank closer into the bushes and became very still. Presently came a sound of shots from the town, and then everything was quiet, everything, even the hospital.

He saw presently little figures sheathing swords come out from the houses and walk to the debris of the flying-machines the bomb had destroyed. Others appeared wheeling undamaged aeroplanes upon their wheels as men might wheel bicycles, and sprang into the saddles and flapped into the air. A string of three airships appeared far away in the east and flew towards the zenith. The one that hung low above Niagara city came still lower and dropped a rope ladder to pick up men from the power-house.

For a long time he watched the further happenings in Niagara city as a rabbit might watch a meet. He saw men going from building to building, to set fire to them, as he presently realised, and he heard a series of dull detonations from the wheel pit of the power-house. Some similar business went on among the works on the Canadian side. Meanwhile more and more airships appeared, and many more flying-machines, until at last it seemed to him nearly a third of the Asiatic fleet had re-assembled. He watched them from his bush, cramped but immovable, watched them gather and range themselves and signal and pick up men, until at last they sailed away towards the glowing sunset, going to the great Asiatic rendez-vous, above the oil wells of Cleveland. They dwindled and passed away, leaving him alone, so far as he could tell, the only living man in a world of ruin and strange loneliness almost beyond describing. He watched them recede and vanish. He stood gaping after them.

"Gaw!" he said at last, like one who rouses himself from a trance.

It was far more than any personal desolation extremity that flooded his soul. It seemed to him indeed that this must be the sunset of his race.

§2

He did not at first envisage his own plight in definite and comprehensible terms. Things happened to him so much of late, his own efforts had counted for so little, that he had become passive and planless. His last scheme had been to go round the coast of England as a Desert Dervish giving refined entertainment to his fellow-creatures. Fate had quashed that. Fate had seen fit to direct him to other destinies, had hurried him from point to point, and dropped him at last upon this little wedge of rock between the cataracts. It did not instantly occur to him that now it was his turn to play. He had a singular feeling that all must end as a dream ends, that presently surely he would be back in the world of Grubb and Edna and Bun Hill, that this roar, this glittering presence of

incessant water, would be drawn aside as a curtain is drawn aside after a holiday lantern show, and old, familiar, customary things reassume their sway. It would be interesting to tell people how he had seen Niagara. And then Kurt's words came into his head: "People torn away from the people they care for; homes smashed, creatures full of life and memories and peculiar little gifts—torn to pieces, starved, and spoilt." . . .

He wondered, half incredulous, if that was indeed true. It was so hard to realise it. Out beyond there was it possible that Tom and Jessica were also in some dire extremity? that the little greengrocer's shop was no longer standing open, with Jessica serving respectfully, warming Tom's ear in sharp asides, or punctually sending out the goods?

He tried to think what day of the week it was, and found he had lost his reckoning. Perhaps it was Sunday. If so, were they going to church or, were they hiding, perhaps in bushes? What had happened to the landlord, the butcher, and to Butteridge and all those people on Dymchurch beach? Something, he knew, had happened to London—a bombardment. But who had bombarded? Were Tom and Jessica too being chased by strange brown men with long bare swords and evil eyes? He thought of various possible aspects of affliction, but presently one phase ousted all the others. Were they getting much to eat? The question haunted him, obsessed him.

If one was very hungry would one eat rats?

It dawned upon him that a peculiar misery that oppressed him was not so much anxiety and patriotic sorrow as hunger. Of course he was hungry!

He reflected and turned his steps towards the little refreshment shed that stood near the end of the ruined bridge. "Ought to be somethin'—"

He strolled round it once or twice, and then attacked the shutters with his pocket-knife, reinforced presently by a wooden stake he found conveniently near. At last he got a shutter to give, and tore it back and stuck in his head.

"Grub," he remarked, "anyhow. Leastways—"

He got at the inside fastening of the shutter and had presently this establishment open for his exploration. He found several sealed bottles of sterilized milk, much mineral water, two tins of biscuits and a crock of very stale cakes, cigarettes in great quantity but very dry, some rather dry oranges, nuts, some tins of canned meat and fruit, and plates and knives and forks and glasses sufficient for several score of people. There was also a zinc locker, but he was unable to negotiate the padlock of this.

"Shan't starve," said Bert, "for a bit, anyhow." He sat on the vendor's seat and regaled himself with biscuits and milk, and felt for a moment quite contented.

"Quite restful," he muttered, munching and glancing about him restlessly, "after what I been through.

"Crikey! *Wot* a day! Oh! *Wot* a day!"

Wonder took possession of him. "Gaw!" he cried: "Wot a fight it's been! Smashing up the poor fellers! 'Eadlong! The airships—the fliers and all. I wonder what happened to the *Zeppelin*?. . . And that chap Kurt—I wonder what happened to 'im? 'E was a good sort of chap, was Kurt."

Some phantom of imperial solicitude floated through his mind. "Injia," he said. . . .

A more practical interest arose.

"I wonder if there's anything to open one of these tins of corned beef?"

§3

After he had feasted, Bert lit a cigarette and sat meditative for a time. "Wonder where Grubb is?" he said; "I do wonder that! Wonder if any of 'em wonder about me?"

He reverted to his own circumstances. "Dessay I shall 'ave to stop on this island for some time."

He tried to feel at his ease and secure, but presently the indefinable restlessness of the social animal in solitude distressed him. He began to want to look over his shoulder, and, as a corrective, roused himself to explore the rest of the island.

It was only very slowly that he began to realise the peculiarities of his position, to perceive that the breaking down of the arch between Green Island and the mainland had cut him off completely from the world. Indeed it was only when he came back to where the fore-end of the *Hohenzollern* lay like a stranded ship, and was contemplating the shattered bridge, that this dawned upon him. Even then it came with no sort of shock to his mind, a fact among a number of other extraordinary and unmanageable facts. He stared at the shattered cabins of the *Hohenzollern* and its widow's garment of dishevelled silk for a time, but without any idea of its containing any living thing; it was all so twisted and smashed and entirely upside down. Then for a while he gazed at the evening sky. A cloud haze was now appearing and not an airship was in sight. A swallow flew by and snapped some invisible victim. "Like a dream," he repeated.

Then for a time the rapids held his mind. "Roaring. It keeps on roaring and splashin' always and always. Keeps on. . . ."

At last his interests became personal. "Wonder what I ought to do now?"

He reflected. "Not an idee," he said.

He was chiefly conscious that a fortnight ago he had been in Bun Hill with no idea of travel in his mind, and that now he was between the Falls of Niagara amidst the devastation and ruins of the greatest air fight in the world, and that in the interval he had been across France, Belgium, Germany, England, Ireland, and a number of other countries. It was an interesting thought and suitable for conversation, but of no great practical utility. "Wonder 'ow I can get orf this?" he said. "Wonder if there is a way out? If not. . . rummy!"

Further reflection decided, "I believe I got myself in a bit of a 'ole coming over that bridge. . . .

"Any'ow—got me out of the way of them Japanesy chaps. Wouldn't 'ave taken 'em long to cut *my* froat. No. Still—"

He resolved to return to the point of Luna Island. For a long time he stood without stirring, scrutinising the Canadian

shore and the wreckage of hotels and houses and the fallen trees of the Victoria Park, pink now in the light of sundown. Not a human being was perceptible in that scene of headlong destruction. Then he came back to the American side of the island, crossed close to the crumpled aluminium wreckage of the *Hohenzollern* to Green Islet, and scrutinised the hopeless breach in the further bridge and the water that boiled beneath it. Towards Buffalo there was still much smoke, and near the position of the Niagara railway station the houses were burning vigorously. Everything was deserted now, everything was still. One little abandoned thing lay on a transverse path between town and road, a crumpled heap of clothes with sprawling limbs. . . .

"'ave a look round," said Bert, and taking a path that ran through the middle of the island he presently discovered the wreckage of the two Asiatic aeroplanes that had fallen out of the struggle that ended the *Hohenzollern.*

With the first he found the wreckage of an aeronaut too.

The machine had evidently dropped vertically and was badly knocked about amidst a lot of smashed branches in a clump of trees. Its bent and broken wings and shattered stays sprawled amidst new splintered wood, and its forepeak stuck into the ground. The aeronaut dangled weirdly head downward among the leaves and branches some yards away, and Bert only discovered him as he turned from the aeroplane. In the dusky evening light and stillness—for the sun had gone now and the wind had altogether fallen—this inverted yellow face was anything but a tranquilising object to discover suddenly a couple of yards away. A broken branch had run clean through the man's thorax, and he hung, so stabbed, looking limp and absurd. In his hand he still clutched, with the grip of death, a short light rifle.

For some time Bert stood very still, inspecting this thing.

Then he began to walk away from it, looking constantly back at it.

Presently in an open glade he came to a stop.

"Gaw!" he whispered, "I don' like dead bodies some'ow! I'd almost rather that chap was alive."

He would not go along the path athwart which the Chinaman hung. He felt he would rather not have trees round him any more, and that it would be more comfortable to be quite close to the sociable splash and uproar of the rapids.

He came upon the second aeroplane in a clear grassy space by the side of the streaming water, and it seemed scarcely damaged at all. It looked as though it had floated down into a position of rest. It lay on its side with one wing in the air. There was no aeronaut near it, dead or alive. There it lay abandoned, with the water lapping about its long tail.

Bert remained a little aloof from it for a long time, looking into the gathering shadows among the trees, in the expectation of another Chinaman alive or dead. Then very cautiously he approached the machine and stood regarding its widespread vans, its big steering wheel and empty saddle. He did not venture to touch it.

"I wish that other chap wasn't there," he said. "I do wish 'e wasn't there!"

He saw a few yards away, something bobbing about in an eddy that spun within a projecting head of rock. As it went round it seemed to draw him unwillingly towards it. . . .

What could it be?

"Blow!" said Bert. "It's another of 'em."

It held him. He told himself that it was the other aeronaut that had been shot in the fight and fallen out of the saddle as he strove to land. He tried to go away, and then it occurred to him that he might get a branch or something and push this rotating object out into the stream. That would leave him with only one dead body to worry about. Perhaps he might get along with one. He hesitated and then with a certain emotion forced himself to do this. He went towards the bushes and cut himself a wand and returned to the rocks and clambered out to a corner between the eddy and the stream. By that time the

sunset was over and the bats were abroad—and he was wet with perspiration.

He prodded the floating blue-clad thing with his wand, failed, tried again successfully as it came round, and as it went out into the stream it turned over, the light gleamed on golden hair and—it was Kurt!

It was Kurt, white and dead and very calm. There was no mistaking him. There was still plenty of light for that. The stream took him and he seemed to compose himself in its swift grip as one who stretches himself to rest. White-faced he was now, and all the colour gone out of him.

A feeling of infinite distress swept over Bert as the body swept out of sight towards the fall. "Kurt!" he cried, "Kurt! I didn't mean to! Kurt! don' leave me 'ere! Don' leave me!"

Loneliness and desolation overwhelmed him. He gave way. He stood on the rock in the evening light, weeping and wailing passionately like a child. It was as though some link that had held him to all these things had broken and gone. He was afraid like a child in a lonely room, shamelessly afraid.

The twilight was closing about him. The trees were full now of strange shadows. All the things about him became strange and unfamiliar with that subtle queerness one feels oftenest in dreams. "O God! I carn' stand this," he said, and crept back from the rocks to the grass and crouched down, and suddenly wild sorrow for the death of Kurt, Kurt the brave, Kurt the kindly, came to his help, and he broke from whimpering to weeping. He ceased to crouch; he sprawled upon the grass and clenched an impotent fist.

"This war," he cried, "this blarsted foolery of a war.

"O Kurt! Lieutenant Kurt!

"I done," he said, "I done. I've 'ad all I want, and more than I want. The world's all rot, and there ain't no sense in it. The night's coming. . . . If 'e comes after me—'E can't come after me—'E can't! . . .

"If 'e comes after me, I'll fro' myself into the water.". . .

Presently he was talking again in a low undertone.

"There ain't nothing to be afraid of reely. It's jest imagination. Poor old Kurt—he thought it would happen. Prevision like. 'E never gave me that letter or tole me who the lady was. It's like what 'e said—people tore away from everything they belonged to—everywhere. Exactly like what 'e said. . . . 'Ere I am cast away—thousands of miles from Edna or Grubb or any of my lot—like a plant tore up by the roots. . . . And every war's been like this, only I 'adn't the sense to understand it. Always. All sorts of 'oles and corners chaps 'ave died in. And people 'adn't the sense to understand, 'adn't the sense to feel it and stop it. Thought war was fine. My Gawd! . . .

"Dear old Edna. She was a fair bit of all right—she was. That time we 'ad a boat at Kingston. . . .

"I bet—I'll see 'er again yet. Won't be my fault if I don't.". . .

§4

Suddenly, on the very verge of this heroic resolution, Bert became rigid with terror. Something was creeping towards him through the grass. Something was creeping and halting and creeping again towards him through the dim dark grass. The night was electrical with horror. For a time everything was still. Bert ceased to breathe. It could not be. No, it was too small!

It advanced suddenly upon him with a rush, with a little meawling cry and tail erect. It rubbed its head against him and purred. It was a tiny, skinny little kitten.

"Gaw, Pussy! 'ow you frightened me!" said Bert, with drops of perspiration on his brow.

§5

He sat with his back to a tree stump all that night, holding the kitten in his arms. His mind was tired, and he talked or thought coherently no longer. Towards dawn he dozed.

When he awoke, he was stiff but in better heart, and the

kitten slept warmly and reassuringly inside his jacket. And fear, he found, had gone from amidst the trees.

He stroked the kitten, and the little creature woke up to excessive fondness and purring. "You want some milk," said Bert. "That's what you want. And I could do with a bit of brekker too."

He yawned and stood up, with the kitten on his shoulder, and stared about him, recalling the circumstances of the previous day, the grey, immense happenings.

"Mus' do something," he said.

He turned towards the trees, and was presently contemplating the dead aeronaut again. The kitten he held companionably against his neck. The body was horrible, but not nearly so horrible as it had been at twilight, and now the limbs were limper and the gun had slipped to the ground and lay half hidden in the grass.

"I suppose we ought to bury 'im, Kitty," said Bert, and looked helplessly at the rocky soil about him. "We got to stay on the island with 'im."

It was some time before he could turn away and go on towards that provision shed. "Brekker first," he said, "anyhow," stroking the kitten on his shoulder. She rubbed his cheek affectionately with her furry little face and presently nibbled at his ear. "Wan' some milk, eh?" he said, and turned his back on the dead man as though he mattered nothing.

He was puzzled to find the door of the shed open, though he had closed and latched it very carefully overnight, and he found also some dirty plates he had not noticed before on the bench. He discovered that the hinges of the tin locker were unscrewed and that it could be opened. He had not observed this overnight.

"Silly of me!" said Bert. "'Ere I was puzzlin' and whackin' away at the padlock, never noticing." It had been used apparently as an ice-chest, but it contained nothing now but the remains of half-dozen boiled chickens, some ambiguous substance that might once have been butter, and a singularly unappetising smell. He closed the lid again carefully.

He gave the kitten some milk in a dirty plate and sat watching its busy little tongue for a time. Then he was moved to make an inventory of the provisions. There were six bottles of milk unopened and one opened, sixty bottles of mineral water and a large stock of syrups, about two thousand cigarettes and upwards of a hundred cigars, nine oranges, two unopened tins of corned beef and one opened, and five large tins California peaches. He jotted it down on a piece of paper. "Ain't much solid food," he said. "Still—A fortnight, say!

"Anything might happen in a fortnight."

He gave the kitten a small second helping and a scrap of beef and then went down with the little creature running after him, tail erect and in high spirits, to look at the remains of the *Hohenzollern.*

It had shifted in the night and seemed on the whole more firmly grounded on Green Island than before. From it his eye went to the shattered bridge and then across to the still desolation of Niagara city. Nothing moved over there but a number of crows. They were busy with the engineer he had seen cut down on the previous day. He saw no dogs, but he heard one howling.

"We got to get out of this some'ow, Kitty," he said. "That milk won't last forever—not at the rate you lap it."

He regarded the sluice-like flood before him.

"Plenty of water," he said. "Won't be drink we shall want."

He decided to make a careful exploration of the island. Presently he came to a locked gate labelled "Biddle Stairs," and clambered over to discover a steep old wooden staircase leading down the face of the cliff amidst a vast and increasing uproar of waters. He left the kitten above and descended these, and discovered with a thrill of hope a path leading among the rocks at the foot of the roaring downrush of the Centre Fall. Perhaps this was a sort of way!

It led him only to the choking and deafening experience of the Cave of the Winds, and after he had spent a quarter of an hour in a partially stupefied condition flattened between solid

rock and nearly as solid waterfall, he decided that this was after all no practicable route to Canada and retraced his steps. As he reascended the Biddle Stairs, he heard what he decided at last must be a sort of echo, a sound of some one walking about on the gravel paths above. When he got to the top, the place was as solitary as before.

Thence he made his way, with the kitten skirmishing along beside him in the grass, to a staircase that led to a lump of projecting rock that enfiladed the huge green majesty of the Horseshoe Fall. He stood there for some time in silence.

"You wouldn't think," he said at last, "there was so much water. . . . This roarin' and splashin', it gets on one's nerves at last. . . . Sounds like people talking. . . . Sounds like people going about. . . . Sounds like anything you fancy."

He retired up the staircase again. "I s'pose I shall keep on goin' round this blessed island," he said drearily. "Round and round and round."

He found himself presently beside the less damaged Asiatic aeroplane again. He stared at it and the kitten smelt it. "Broke!" he said.

He looked up with a convulsive start.

Advancing slowly towards him out from among the trees were two tall gaunt figures. They were blackened and tattered and bandaged; the hind-most one limped and had his head swathed in white, but the foremost one still carried himself as a Prince should do, for all that his left arm was in a sling and one side of his face scalded a livid crimson. He was the Prince Karl Albert, the War Lord, the "German Alexander," and the man behind him was the bird-faced man whose cabin had once been taken from him and given to Bert.

§6

With that apparition began a new phase of Goat Island in Bert's experience. He ceased to be a solitary representative of humanity in a vast and violent and incomprehensible universe,

and became once more a social creature, a man in a world of other men. For an instant these two were terrible, then they seemed sweet and desirable as brothers. They too were in this scrape with him, marooned and puzzled. He wanted extremely to hear exactly what had happened to them. What mattered it if one was a Prince and both were foreign soldiers, if neither perhaps had adequate English? His native Cockney freedom flowed too generously for him to think of that, and surely the Asiatic fleets had purged all such trivial differences. "Ul-*lo*!" he said; " 'ow did you get 'ere?"

"It is the Englishman who brought us the Butteridge machine," said the bird-faced officer in German, and then in a tone of horror, as Bert advanced, "Salute!" and again louder, "*Salute!*"

"Gaw!" said Bert, and stopped with a second comment under his breath. He stared and saluted awkwardly and became at once a masked defensive thing with whom co-operation was impossible.

For a time these two perfected modern aristocrats stood regarding the difficult problem of the Anglo-Saxon citizen, that ambiguous citizen who, obeying some mysterious law in his blood, would neither drill nor be a democrat. Bert was by no means a beautiful object, but in some inexplicable way he looked resistant. He wore his cheap suit of serge, now showing many signs of wear, and its loose fit made him seem sturdier than he was; above his disengaging face was a white German cap that was altogether too big for him, and his trousers were crumpled up his legs and their ends tucked into the rubber highlows of a deceased German aeronaut. He looked an inferior, though by no means an easy inferior, and instinctively they hated him.

The Prince pointed to the flying-machine and said something in broken English that Bert took for German and failed to understand. He intimated as much.

"Dummer Kerl!" said the bird-faced officer from among his bandages.

The Prince pointed again with his undamaged hand. "You verstehen dis drachenflieger?"

Bert began to comprehend the situation. He regarded the Asiatic machine. The habits of Bun Hill returned to him. "It's a foreign make," he said ambiguously.

The two Germans consulted. "You are an expert?" said the Prince.

"We reckon to repair," said Bert, in the exact manner of Grubb.

The Prince sought in his vocabulary. "Is dat," he said, "goot to fly?"

Bert reflected and scratched his cheek slowly. "I got to look at it," he replied. . . . "It's 'ad rough usage!"

He made a sound with his teeth he had also acquired from Grubb, put his hands in his trouser pockets, and strolled back to the machine. Typically Grubb chewed something, but Bert could chew only imaginatively. "Three days' work in this," he said, teething. For the first time it dawned on him that there were possibilities in this machine. It was evident that the wing that lay on the ground was badly damaged. The three stays that held it rigid had snapped across a ridge of rock and there was also a strong possibility of the engine being badly damaged. The wing hook on that side was also askew, but probably that would not affect the flight. Beyond that there probably wasn't much the matter. Bert scratched his cheek again and contemplated the broad sunlit waste of the Upper Rapids. "We might make a job of this. . . . You leave it to me."

He surveyed it intently again, and the Prince and his officer watched him. In Bun Hill Bert and Grubb had developed to a very high pitch among the hiring stock a method of repair by substituting; they substituted bits of other machines. A machine that was too utterly and obviously done for even to proffer for hire, had nevertheless still capital value. It became a sort of quarry for nuts and screws and wheels, bars and spokes, chain-links and the like; a mine of ill-fitting "parts" to replace the defects of machines still current. And back among the trees was a second Asiatic aeroplane. . . .

The kitten caressed Bert's airship boots unheeded.

"Mend dat drachenflieger," said the Prince.

"If I do mend it," said Bert, struck by a new thought, "none of us ain't to be trusted to fly it."

"*I* vill fly it," said the Prince.

"Very likely break your neck," said Bert, after a pause.

The Prince did not understand him and disregarded what he said. He pointed his gloved finger to the machine and turned to the bird-faced officer with some remark in German. The officer answered and the Prince responded with a sweeping gesture towards the sky. Then he spoke—it seemed eloquently. Bert watched him and guessed his meaning. "Much more likely to break your neck," he said. " 'Owever. 'Ere goes."

He began to pry about the saddle and engine of the drachenflieger in search for tools. Also he wanted some black oily stuff for his hands and face. For the first rule in the art of repairing, as it was known to the firm of Grubb and Smallways, was to get your hands and face thoroughly and conclusively blackened. Also he took off his jacket and waistcoat and put his cap carefully to the back of his head in order to facilitate scratching.

The Prince and the officer seemed disposed to watch him, but he succeeded in making it clear to them that this would inconvenience him and that he had to "puzzle out a bit" before he could get to work. They thought him over, but his shop experience had given him something of the authoritative way of the expert with common men. And at last they went away. Thereupon he went straight to the second aeroplane, got the aeronaut's gun and ammunition and hid them in a clump of nettles close at hand. "That's all right," said Bert, and then proceeded to a careful inspection of the debris of the wings in the trees. Then he went back to the first aeroplane to compare the two. The Bun Hill method was quite possibly practicable if there was nothing hopeless or incomprehensible in the engine.

The Germans returned presently to find him already generously smutty and touching and testing knobs and screws and levers with an expression of profound sagacity. When the bird-faced officer addressed a remark to him, he waved him aside with, "Nong comprong. Shut it! It's no good."

Then he had an idea. "Dead chap back there wants burying," he said, jerking a thumb over his shoulder.

§7

With the appearance of these two men Bert's whole universe had changed again. A curtain fell before the immense and terrible desolation that had overwhelmed him. He was in a world of three people, a minute human world that nevertheless filled his brain with eager speculations and schemes and cunning ideas. What were they thinking of? What did they think of him? What did they mean to do? A hundred busy threads interlaced in his mind as he pottered studiously over the Asiatic aeroplane. New ideas came up like bubbles in soda water.

"Gaw!" he said suddenly. He had just appreciated as a special aspect of this irrational injustice of fate that these two men were alive and that Kurt was dead. All the crew of the *Hohenzollern* were shot or burnt or smashed or drowned, and these two lurking in the padded forward cabin had escaped.

"I suppose 'e thinks it's 'is bloomin' Star," he muttered, and found himself uncontrollably exasperated.

He stood up, facing round to the two men. They were standing side by side regarding him.

"'It's no good," he said, "starin' at me. You only put me out." And then seeing they did not understand, he advanced towards them, wrench in hand. It occurred to him as he did so that the Prince was really a very big and powerful and serene-looking person. But he said, nevertheless, pointing through the trees, "dead man!"

The bird-faced man intervened with a reply in German.

"Dead man!" said Bert to him. "There."

He had great difficulty in inducing them to inspect the dead Chinaman, and at last led them to him. Then they made it evident that they proposed that he, as a common person below the rank of officer should have the sole and undivided privilege of disposing of the body by dragging it to the water's edge. There was some heated gesticulation, and at last the bird-faced officer abased himself to help. Together they dragged the limp and now swollen Asiatic through the trees, and after a rest or so—for he trailed very heavily—dumped him into the westward rapid. Bert returned to his expert investigation of the flying-machine at last with aching arms and in a state of gloomy rebellion. "Brasted cheek!" he said. "One'd think I was one of 'is beastly German slaves!

"Prancing beggar!"

And then he fell speculating what would happen when the flying-machine was repaired—if it could be repaired.

The two Germans went away again, and after some reflection Bert removed several nuts, resumed his jacket and vest, pocketed those nuts and his tools and hid the set of tools from the second aeroplane in the fork of a tree. "Right O," he said, as he jumped down after the last of these precautions. The Prince and his companion reappeared as he returned to the machine by the water's edge. The Prince surveyed his progress for a time, and then went towards the Parting of the Waters and stood with folded arms gazing upstream in profound thought. The bird-faced officer came up to Bert, heavy with a sentence in English.

"Go," he said with a helping gesture, "und eat."

When Bert got to the refreshment shed, he found all the food had vanished except one measured ration of corned beef and three biscuits.

He regarded this with open eyes and mouth.

The kitten appeared from under the vendor's seat with an ingratiating purr. "Of course!" said Bert. "Why! where's your milk?"

He accumulated wrath for a moment or so, then seized the plate in one hand, and the biscuits in another, and went in

search of the Prince, breathing vile words anent "grub" and his intimate interior. He approached without saluting.

"'Ere!" he said fiercely. "Whad the devil's this?"

An entirely unsatisfactory altercation followed. Bert expounded the Bun Hill theory of the relations of grub to efficiency in English, the bird-faced man replied with points about nations and discipline in German. The Prince, having made an estimate of Bert's quality and physique, suddenly hectored. He gripped Bert by the shoulder and shook him, making his pockets rattle, shouted something to him, and flung him struggling back. He hit him as though he was a German private. Bert went back, white and scared, but resolved by all his Cockney standards upon one thing. He was bound in honour to "go for" the Prince. "Gaw!" he gasped, buttoning his jacket.

"Now," cried the Prince, "Vil you go?" and then catching the heroic gleam in Bert's eye, drew his sword.

The bird-faced officer intervened, saying something in German and pointing skyward.

Far away in the southwest appeared a Japanese airship coming fast toward them. Their conflict ended at that. The Prince was first to grasp the situation and lead the retreat. All three scuttled like rabbits for the trees, and ran to and for cover until they found a hollow in which the grass grew rank. There they all squatted within six yards of one another. They sat in this place for a long time, up to their necks in the grass and watching through the branches for the airship. Bert had dropped some of his corned beef, but he found the biscuits in his hand and ate them quietly. The monster came nearly overhead and then went away to Niagara and dropped beyond the power-works. When it was near, they all kept silence, and then presently they fell into an argument that was robbed perhaps of immediate explosive effect only by their failure to understand one another.

It was Bert began the talking and he talked on regardless of what they understood or failed to understand. But his voice must have conveyed his cantankerous intentions.

"You want that machine done," he said first, "you better keep your 'ands off me!"

They disregarded that and he repeated it.

Then he expanded his idea and the spirit of speech took hold of him. "You think you got 'old of a chap you can kick and 'it like you do your private soldiers—you're jolly well mistaken. See? I've 'ad about enough of you and your antics. I been thinking you over, you and your war and your Empire and all the rot of it. Rot it is! It's you Germans made all the trouble in Europe first and last. And all for nothin'. Jest silly prancing! Jest because you've got the uniforms and flags! 'Ere I was—I didn't want to 'ave anything to do with you. I jest didn't care a 'eng at all about you. Then you get 'old of me—steal me practically—and 'ere I am, thousands of miles away from 'ome and everything, and all your silly fleet smashed up to rags. And you want to go on prancin' *now*! Not if I know it!

"Look at the mischief you done! Look at the way you smashed up New York—the people you killed, the stuff you wasted. Can't you learn?"

"Dummer Kerl!" said the bird-faced man suddenly in a tone of concentrated malignancy, glaring under his bandages. "Esel!"

"That's German for silly ass!—I know. But who's the silly ass—'im or me? When I was a kid, I used to read penny dreadfuls about 'avin adventures and bein' a great c'mander and all that rot. I stowed it. But what's 'e got in 'is head? Rot about Napoleon, rot about Alexander, rot about 'is blessed family and 'im and Gord and David and all that. Any one who wasn't a dressed-up silly fool of a Prince could 'ave told all this was goin' to 'appen. There was us in Europe all at sixes and sevens with our silly flags and our silly newspapers raggin' us up against each other and keepin' us apart, and there was China, solid as a cheese, with millions and millions of men only wantin' a bit of science and a bit of enterprise to be as good as all of us. You thought they couldn't get at you. And then they got flying-machines. And bif!—'ere we are. Why, when they didn't go on making guns and

armies in China, we went and poked 'em up until they did. They '*ad* to give us this lickin' they've give us. We wouldn't be happy until they did, and as I say, 'ere we are!"

The bird-faced officer shouted to him to be quiet, and then began a conversation with the Prince.

"British citizen," said Bert. "You ain't obliged to listen, but I ain't obliged to shut up."

And for some time he continued his dissertation upon Imperialism, militarism, and international politics. But their talking put him out, and for a time he was certainly merely repeating abusive terms, "prancin' nincompoops" and the like, old terms and new. Then suddenly he remembered his essential grievance. "'Owever, look 'ere—'ere!—the thing I started this talk about is where's that food there was in that shed? That's what I want to know. Where you put it?"

He paused. They went on talking in German. He repeated his question. They disregarded him. He asked a third time in a manner insupportably aggressive.

There fell a tense silence. For some seconds the three regarded one another. The Prince eyed Bert steadfastly, and Bert quailed under his eye. Slowly the Prince rose to his feet and the bird-faced officer jerked up beside him. Bert remained squatting.

"Be quaiat," said the Prince.

Bert perceived this was no moment for eloquence.

The two Germans regarded him as he crouched there. Death for a moment seemed near.

Then the Prince turned away and the two of them went towards the flying-machine.

"Gaw!" whispered Bert, and then uttered under his breath one single word of abuse. He sat crouched together for perhaps three minutes, then he sprang to his feet and went off towards the Chinese aeronaut's gun hidden among the weeds.

§8

There was no pretence after that moment that Bert was under the

orders of the Prince or that he was going on with the repairing of the flying-machine. The two Germans took possession of that and set to work upon it. Bert, with his new weapon went off to the neighbourhood of Terrapin Rock, and there sat down to examine it. It was a short rifle with a big cartridge, and a nearly full magazine. He took out the cartridges carefully and then tried the trigger and fittings until he felt sure he had the use of it. He reloaded carefully. Then he remembered he was hungry and went off, gun under his arm, to hunt in and about the refreshment shed. He had the sense to perceive that he must not show himself with the gun to the Prince and his companion. So long as they thought him unarmed they would leave him alone, but there was no knowing what the Napoleonic person might do if he saw Bert's weapon. Also he did not go near them because he knew that within himself boiled a reservoir of rage and fear that he wanted to shoot these two men. He wanted to shoot them, and he thought that to shoot them would be a quite horrible thing to do. The two sides of his inconsistent civilisation warred within him.

Near the shed the kitten turned up again, obviously keen for milk. This greatly enhanced his own angry sense of hunger. He began to talk as he hunted about, and presently stood still, shouting insults. He talked of war and pride and Imperialism. "Any other Prince but you would have died with his men and his ship!" he cried.

The two Germans at the machine heard his voice going ever and again amidst the clamour of the waters. Their eyes met and they smiled slightly.

He was disposed for a time to sit in the refreshment shed waiting for them, but then it occurred to him that so he might get them both at close quarters. He strolled off presently to the point of Luna Island to think the situation out.

It had seemed a comparatively simple one at first, but as he turned it over in his mind its possibilities increased and multiplied. Both these men had swords,—had either a revolver?

Also, if he shot them both, he might never find the food!

So far he had been going about with this gun under his arm, and a sense of lordly security in his mind, but what if they saw the gun and decided to ambush him? Goat Island is nearly all cover, trees, rocks, thickets, and irregularities.

Why not go and murder them both now?

"I carn't," said Bert, dismissing that. "I got to be worked up."

But it was a mistake to get right away from them. That suddenly became clear. He ought to keep them under observation, ought to "scout" them. Then he would be able to see what they were doing, whether either of them had a revolver, where they had hidden the food. He would be better able to determine what they meant to do to him. If he didn't "scout" them, presently they would begin to "scout" him. This seemed so eminently reasonable that he acted upon it forthwith. He thought over his costume and threw his collar and the tell-tale aeronaut's white cap into the water far below. He turned his coat collar up to hide any gleam of his dirty shirt. The tools and nuts in his pockets were disposed to clank, but he rearranged them and wrapped some letters and his pocket-handkerchief about them. He started off circumspectly and noiselessly, listening and peering at every step. As he drew near his antagonists, much grunting and creaking served to locate them. He discovered them engaged in what looked like a wrestling match with the Asiatic flying-machine. Their coats were off, their swords laid aside, they were working magnificently. Apparently they were turning it round and were having a good deal of difficulty with the long tail among the trees. He dropped flat at the sight of them and wriggled into a little hollow, and so lay watching their exertions. Ever and again, to pass the time, he would cover one or other of them with his gun.

He found them quite interesting to watch, so interesting that at times he came near shouting to advise them. He perceived that when they had the machine turned round, they would then be in immediate want of the nuts and tools he carried. Then they would come after him. They would certainly conclude he had them or had hidden them. Should he hide his gun and do a deal for food with these tools? He felt he would not be able to part with the gun again now he had once felt its reassuring company. The kitten turned up again and made a great fuss with him and licked and bit his ear.

The sun clambered to midday, and once that morning he saw, though the Germans did not, an Asiatic airship very far to the south, going swiftly eastward.

At last the flying-machine was turned and stood poised on its wheel, with its hooks pointing up the Rapids. The two officers wiped their faces, resumed jackets and swords, spoke and bore themselves like men who congratulated themselves on a good laborious morning. Then they went off briskly towards the refreshment shed, the Prince leading. Bert became active in pursuit; but he found it impossible to stalk them quickly enough and silently enough to discover the hiding-place of the food. He found them, when he came into sight of them again, seated with their backs against the shed, plates on knee, and a tin of corned beef and a plateful of biscuits between them. They seemed in fairly good spirits, and once the Prince laughed. At this vision of eating Bert's plans gave way. Fierce hunger carried him. He appeared before them suddenly at a distance of perhaps twenty yards, gun in hand. "'Ands up!" he said in a hard, ferocious voice.

The Prince hesitated, and then up went two pairs of hands. The gun had surprised them both completely.

"Stand up," said Bert. . . . "Drop that fork!"

They obeyed again.

"What nex'?" said Bert to himself. "'Orf stage, I suppose. That way," he said. "Go!"

The Prince obeyed with remarkable alacrity. When he reached the head of the clearing, he said something quickly to the bird-faced man and they both, with an entire lack of dignity, *ran!*

Bert was struck with an exasperating afterthought.

"Gord!" he cried with infinite vexation. "Why! I ought to 'ave took their swords! 'Ere!"

But the Germans were already out of sight, and no doubt taking cover among the trees. Bert fell back upon imprecations, then he went up to the shed, cursorily examined the possibility of a flank attack, put his gun handy, and set to work, with a convulsive listening pause before each mouthful on the Prince's plate of corned beef. He had finished that up and handed its gleanings to the kitten and he was falling-to on the second plateful, when the plate broke in his hand! He stared, with the fact slowly creeping upon him that an instant before he had heard a crack among the thickets. Then he sprang to his feet, snatched up his gun in one hand and the tin of corned beef in the other, and fled round the shed to the other side of the clearing. As he did so came a second crack from the thickets, and something went *phwit!* by his ear.

He didn't stop running until he was in what seemed to him a strongly defensible position near Luna Island. Then he took cover, panting, and crouched expectant.

"They got a revolver after all!" he panted. . . .

"Wonder if they got two? If they 'ave—Gord!—I'm done!

"Where's the kitten? Finishin' up that corned beef, I suppose. Little beggar!"

§9

So it was that war began upon Goat Island. It lasted a day and a night, the longest day and the longest night in Bert's life. He had to lie close and listen and watch. Also he had to scheme what he should do. It was clear now that he had to kill these two men if he could, and that if they could, they would kill him. The prize was first food and then the flying-machine and the doubtful privilege of trying' to ride it. If one failed, one would certainly be killed; if one succeeded, one would get away somewhere over there. For a time Bert tried to imagine what it was like over there. His mind ran over possibilities, deserts, angry Americans,

Japanese, Chinese—perhaps Red Indians! (Were there still Red Indians?)

"Got to take what comes," said Bert. "No way out of it that I can see!"

Was that voices? He realised that his attention was wandering. For a time all his senses were very alert. The uproar of the Falls was very confusing, and it mixed in all sorts of sounds, like feet walking, like voices talking, like shouts and cries.

"Silly great catarac'," said Bert. "There ain't no sense in it, fallin' and fallin'."

Never mind that, now! What were the Germans doing?

Would they go back to the flying-machine? They couldn't do anything with it, because he had those nuts and screws and the wrench and other tools. But suppose they found the second set of tools he had hidden in a tree! He had hidden the things well, of course, but they *might* find them. One wasn't sure, of course—one wasn't sure. He tried to remember just exactly how he had hidden those tools. He tried to persuade himself they were certainly and surely hidden, but his memory began to play antics. Had he really left the handle of the wrench sticking out, shining out at the fork of the branch?

Ssh! What was that? Some one stirring in those bushes? Up went an expectant muzzle. No! Where was the kitten? No! It was just imagination, not even the kitten.

The Germans would certainly miss and hunt about for the tools and nuts and screws he carried in his pockets; that was clear. Then they would decide he had them and come for him. He had only to remain still under cover, therefore, and he would get them. Was there any flaw in that? Would they take off more removable parts of the flying-machine and then lie up for him? No, they wouldn't do that, because they were two to one; they would have no apprehension of his getting off in the flying-machine, and no sound reason for supposing he would approach it, and so they would do nothing to damage or disable it. That he decided was clear. But suppose they lay up for him by the

food. Well, that they wouldn't do, because they would know he had this corned beef; there was enough in this can to last, with moderation, several days. Of course they might try to tire him out instead of attacking him—

He roused himself with a start. He had just grasped the real weakness of his position. He might go to sleep!

It needed but ten minutes under the suggestion of that idea, before he realised that he was going to sleep!

He rubbed his eyes and handled his gun. He had never before realised the intensely soporific effect of the American sun, of the American air, the drowsy, sleep-compelling uproar of Niagara. Hitherto these things had on the whole seemed stimulating. . . .

If he had not eaten so much and eaten it so fast, he would not be so heavy. Are vegetarians always bright? . . .

He roused himself with a jerk again.

If he didn't do something, he would fall asleep, and if he fell asleep, it was ten to one they would find him snoring, and finish him forthwith. If he sat motionless and noiseless, he would inevitably sleep. It was better, he told himself, to take even the risks of attacking than that. This sleep trouble, he felt, was going to beat him, must beat him in the end. They were all right; one could sleep and the other could watch. That, come to think of it, was what they would always do; one would do anything they wanted done, the other would lie under cover near at hand, ready to shoot. They might even trap him like that. One might act as a decoy.

That set him thinking of decoys. What a fool he had been to throw his cap away. It would have been invaluable on a stick—especially at night.

He found himself wishing for a drink. He settled that for a time by putting a pebble in his mouth. And then the sleep craving returned.

It became clear to him he must attack. Like many great generals before him, he found his baggage, that is to say his tin of corned beef, a serious impediment to mobility. At last

he decided to put the beef loose in his pocket and abandon the tin. It was not perhaps an ideal arrangement, but one must make sacrifices when one is campaigning. He crawled perhaps ten yards, and then for a time the possibilities of the situation paralysed him.

The afternoon was still. The roar of the cataract simply threw up that immense stillness in relief. He was doing his best to contrive the death of two better men than himself. Also they were doing their best to contrive his. What, behind this silence, were they doing.

Suppose he came upon them suddenly and fired, and missed?

§10

He crawled, and halted listening, and crawled again until nightfall, and no doubt the German Alexander and his lieutenant did the same. A large scale map of Goat Island marked with red and blue lines to show these strategic movements would no doubt have displayed much interlacing, but as a matter of fact neither side saw anything of the other throughout that age-long day of tedious alertness. Bert never knew how near he got to them nor how far he kept from them. Night found him no longer sleepy, but athirst, and near the American Fall. He was inspired by the idea that his antagonists might be in the wreckage of the *Hohenzollern* cabins that was jammed against Green Island. He became enterprising, broke from any attempt to conceal himself, and went across the little bridge at the double. He found nobody. It was his first visit to these huge fragments of airships, and for a time he explored them curiously in the dim light. He discovered the forward cabin was nearly intact, with its door slanting downward and a corner under water. He crept in, drank, and then was struck by the brilliant idea of shutting the door and sleeping on it.

But now he could not sleep at all.

He nodded towards morning and woke up to find it fully day. He breakfasted on corned beef and water, and sat for a

long time appreciative of the security of his position. At last he became enterprising and bold. He would, he decided, settle this business forthwith, one way or the other. He was tired of all this crawling. He set out in the morning sunshine, gun in hand, scarcely troubling to walk softly. He went round the refreshment shed without finding any one, and then through the trees towards the flying-machine. He came upon the bird-faced man sitting on the ground with his back against a tree, bent up over his folded arms, sleeping, his bandage very much over one eye.

Bert stopped abruptly and stood perhaps fifteen yards away, gun in hand ready. Where was the Prince? Then, sticking out at the side of the tree beyond, he saw a shoulder. Bert took five deliberate paces to the left. The great man became visible, leaning up against the trunk, pistol in one hand and sword in the other, and yawning—yawning. You can't shoot a yawning man Bert found. He advanced upon his antagonist with his gun levelled, some foolish fancy of "hands up" in his mind. The Prince became aware of him, the yawning mouth shut like a trap and he stood stiffly up. Bert stopped, silent. For a moment the two regarded one another.

Had the Prince been a wise man he would, I suppose, have dodged behind the tree. Instead, he gave vent to a shout, and raised pistol and sword. At that, like an automaton, Bert pulled his trigger.

It was his first experience of an oxygen-containing bullet. A great flame spurted from the middle of the Prince, a blinding flare, and there came a thud like the firing of a gun. Something hot and wet struck Bert's face. Then through a whirl of blinding smoke and steam he saw limbs and a collapsing, burst body fling themselves to earth.

Bert was so astonished that he stood agape, and the bird-faced officer might have cut him to the earth without a struggle. But instead the bird-faced officer was running away through the undergrowth, dodging as he went. Bert roused himself to a brief ineffectual pursuit, but he had no stomach for further

killing. He returned to the mangled, scattered thing that had so recently been the great Prince Karl Albert. He surveyed the scorched and splashed vegetation about it. He made some speculative identifications. He advanced gingerly and picked up the hot revolver, to find all its chambers strained and burst. He became aware of a cheerful and friendly presence. He was greatly shocked that one so young should see so frightful a scene.

"'Ere, Kitty," he said, "this ain't no place for you."

He made three strides across the devastated area, captured the kitten neatly, and went his way towards the shed, with her purring loudly on his shoulder.

"*You* don't seem to mind," he said.

For a time he fussed about the shed, and at last discovered the rest of the provisions hidden in the roof. "Seems 'ard," he said, as he administered a saucerful of milk, "when you get three men in a 'ole like this, they can't work together. But 'im and 'is princing was jest a bit too thick!"

"Gaw!" he reflected, sitting on the counter and eating, "what a thing life is! 'Ere am I; I seen 'is picture, 'eard 'is name since I was a kid in frocks. Prince Karl Albert! And if any one 'ad tole me I was going to blow 'im to smithereens—there! I shouldn't 'ave believed it, Kitty.

"That chap at Margit ought to 'ave tole me about it. All 'e tole me was that I got a weak chess.

"That other chap, 'e ain't going to do much. Wonder what I ought to do about 'im?"

He surveyed the trees with a keen blue eye and fingered the gun on his knee. "I don't like this killing, Kitty," he said. "It's like Kurt said about being blooded. Seems to me you got to be blooded young. . . . If that Prince 'ad come up to me and said, 'Shake 'ands!' I'd 'ave shook 'ands. . . . Now 'ere's that other chap, dodging about! 'E's got 'is 'ead 'urt already, and there's something wrong with his leg. And burns. Golly! it isn't three weeks ago I first set eyes on 'im, and then 'e was smart and set up—'ands full of 'air-brushes and things, and swearin' at me. A

regular gentleman! Now 'e's 'arfway to a wild man. What am I to do with 'im? What the 'ell am I to do with 'im? I can't leave 'im 'ave that flying-machine; that's a bit *too* good, and if I don't kill 'im, 'e'll jest 'ang about this island and starve. . . .

"'E's got a sword, of course." . . .

He resumed his philosophising after he had lit a cigarette.

"War's a silly gaim, Kitty. It's a silly gaim! We common people—we were fools. We thought those big people knew what they were up to—and they didn't. Look at that chap! 'E 'ad all Germany be'ind 'im, and what 'as 'e made of it? Smeshin' and blunderin' and destroyin', and there 'e 'is! Jest a mess of blood and boots and things! Jest an 'orrid splash! Prince Karl Albert! And all the men 'e led and the ships 'e 'ad, the airships, and the dragon-fliers—all scattered like a paper-chase between this 'ole and Germany. And fightin' going on and burnin' and killin' that 'e started, war without end all over the world!

"I suppose I shall 'ave to kill that other chap. I suppose I must. But it ain't at all the sort of job I fancy, Kitty!"

For a time he hunted about the island amidst the uproar of the waterfall, looking for the wounded officer, and at last he started him out of some bushes near the head of Biddle Stairs. But as he saw the bent and bandaged figure in limping flight before him, he found his Cockney softness too much for him again; he could neither shoot nor pursue. "I carn't," he said, "that's flat. I 'aven't the guts for it! 'E'll 'ave to go."

He turned his steps towards the flying-machine. . . .

He never saw the bird-faced officer again, nor any further evidence of his presence. Towards evening he grew fearful of ambushes and hunted vigorously for an hour or so, but in vain. He slept in a good defensible position at the extremity of the rocky point that runs out to the Canadian Fall, and in the night he woke in panic terror and fired his gun. But it was nothing. He slept no more that night. In the morning he became curiously concerned for the vanished man, and hunted for him as one might for an erring brother.

"If I knew some German," he said, "I'd 'oller. It's jest not knowing German does it. You can't explain."

He discovered, later, traces of an attempt to cross the gap in the broken bridge. A rope with a bolt attached had been flung across and had caught in a fenestration of a projecting fragment of railing. The end of the rope trailed in the seething water towards the fall.

But the bird-faced officer was already rubbing shoulders with certain inert matter that had once been Lieutenant Kurt and the Chinese aeronaut and a dead cow, and much other uncongenial company, in the huge circle of the Whirlpool two and a quarter miles away. Never had that great gathering place, that incessant, aimless, unprogressive hurry of waste and battered things, been so crowded with strange and melancholy derelicts. Round they went and round, and every day brought its new contributions, luckless brutes, shattered fragments of boat and flying-machine, endless citizens from the cities upon the shores of the great lakes above. Much came from Cleveland. It all gathered here, and whirled about indefinitely, and over it all gathered daily a greater abundance of birds.

Chapter X

THE WORLD UNDER THE WAR

§1

Bert spent two more days upon Goat Island, and finished all his provisions except the cigarettes and mineral water, before he brought himself to try the Asiatic flying-machine.

Even at last he did not so much go off upon it as get carried off. It had taken only an hour or so to substitute wing stays from the second flying-machine and to replace the nuts he had himself removed. The engine was in working order, and differed only very simply and obviously from that of a contemporary motor bicycle. The rest of the time was taken up by a vast musing and delaying and hesitation. Chiefly he saw himself splashing into the rapids and whirling down them to the Fall, clutching and drowning, but also he had a vision of being hopelessly in the air, going fast and unable to ground. His mind was too concentrated upon the business of flying for him to think very much of what might happen to an indefinite-spirited Cockney without credentials who arrived on an Asiatic flying-machine amidst the war-infuriated population beyond.

He still had a lingering solicitude for the bird-faced officer. He had a haunting fancy he might be lying disabled or badly smashed in some way in some nook or cranny of the Island; and it was only after a most exhaustive search that he abandoned that distressing idea. "If I found 'im," he reasoned the while, "what could I do wiv 'im? You can't blow a chap's brains out when 'e's down. And I don' see 'ow else I can 'elp 'im."

Then the kitten bothered his highly developed sense of social responsibility. "If I leave 'er, she'll starve. . . . Ought to catch

mice for 'erself. . . . *are* there mice?. . . Birds?. . . She's too young. . . . She's like me; she's a bit too civilised."

Finally he stuck her in his side pocket and she became greatly interested in the memories of corned beef she found there. With her in his pocket, he seated himself in the saddle of the flying-machine. Big, clumsy thing it was—and not a bit like a bicycle. Still the working of it was fairly plain. You set the engine going—*so*; kicked yourself up until the wheel was vertical, *so*; engaged the gyroscope, *so*, and then—then—you just pulled up this lever.

Rather stiff it was, but suddenly it came over—

The big curved wings on either side flapped disconcertingly, flapped again' click, clock, click, clock, clitter-clock!

Stop! The thing was heading for the water; its wheel was in the water. Bert groaned from his heart and struggled to restore the lever to its first position. Click, clock, clitter-clock, he was rising! The machine was lifting its dripping wheel out of the eddies, and he was going up! There was no stopping now, no good in stopping now. In another moment Bert, clutching and convulsive and rigid, with staring eyes and a face pale as death, was flapping up above the Rapids, jerking to every jerk of the wings, and rising, rising.

There was no comparison in dignity and comfort between a flying-machine and a balloon. Except in its moments of descent, the balloon was a vehicle of faultless urbanity; this was a buck-jumping mule, a mule that jumped up and never came down again. Click, clock, click, clock; with each beat of the strangely shaped wings it jumped Bert upward and caught him neatly again half a second later on the saddle. And while in ballooning there is no wind, since the balloon is a part of the wind, flying is a wild perpetual creation of and plunging into wind. It was a wind that above all things sought to blind him, to force him to close his eyes. It occurred to him presently to twist his knees and legs inward and grip with them, or surely he would have been bumped into two clumsy halves. And he was going

up, a hundred yards high, two hundred, three hundred, over the streaming, frothing wilderness of water below—up, up, up. That was all right, but how presently would one go horizontally? He tried to think if these things did go horizontally. No! They flapped up and then they soared down. For a time he would keep on flapping up. Tears streamed from his eyes. He wiped them with one temerariously disengaged hand.

Was it better to risk a fall over land or over water—such water?

He was flapping up above the Upper Rapids towards Buffalo. It was at any rate a comfort that the Falls and the wild swirl of waters below them were behind him. He was flying up straight. That he could see. How did one turn?

He was presently almost cool, and his eyes got more used to the rush of air, but he was getting very high, very high. He tilted his head forwards and surveyed the country, blinking. He could see all over Buffalo, a place with three great blackened scars of ruin, and hills and stretches beyond. He wondered if he was half a mile high, or more. There were some people among some houses near a railway station between Niagara and Buffalo, and then more people. They went like ants busily in and out of the houses. He saw two motor cars gliding along the road towards Niagara city. Then far away in the south he saw a great Asiatic airship going eastward. "Oh, Gord!" he said, and became earnest in his ineffectual attempts to alter his direction. But that airship took no notice of him, and he continued to ascend convulsively. The world got more and more extensive and maplike. Click, clock, clitter-clock. Above him and very near to him now was a hazy stratum of cloud.

He determined to disengage the wing clutch. He did so. The lever resisted his strength for a time, then over it came, and instantly the tail of the machine cocked up and the wings became rigidly spread. Instantly everything was swift and smooth and silent. He was gliding rapidly down the air against a wild gale of wind, his eyes three-quarters shut.

A little lever that had hitherto been obdurate now confessed itself mobile. He turned it over gently to the right, and whiroo!—the left wing had in some mysterious way given at its edge and he was sweeping round and downward in an immense right-handed spiral. For some moments he experienced all the helpless sensations of catastrophe. He restored the lever to its middle position with some difficulty, and the wings were equalised again.

He turned it to the left and had a sensation of being spun round backwards. "Too much!" he gasped.

He discovered that he was rushing down at a headlong pace towards a railway line and some factory buildings. They appeared to be tearing up to him to devour him. He must have dropped all that height. For a moment he had the ineffectual sensations of one whose bicycle bolts downhill. The ground had almost taken him by surprise. "'Ere!" he cried; and then with a violent effort of all his being he got the beating engine at work again and set the wings flapping. He swooped down and up and resumed his quivering and pulsating ascent of the air.

He went high again, until he had a wide view of the pleasant upland country of western New York State, and then made a long coast down, and so up again, and then a coast. Then as he came swooping a quarter of a mile above a village he saw people running about, running away—evidently in relation to his hawk-like passage. He got an idea that he had been shot at.

"Up!" he said, and attacked that lever again. It came over with remarkable docility, and suddenly the wings seemed to give way in the middle. But the engine was still! It had stopped. He flung the lever back rather by instinct than design. What to do?

Much happened in a few seconds, but also his mind was quick, he thought very quickly. He couldn't get up again, he was gliding down the air; he would have to hit something.

He was travelling at the rate of perhaps thirty miles an hour down, down.

That plantation of larches looked the softest thing—mossy almost!

Could he get it? He gave himself to the steering. Round to the right—left!

Swirroo! Crackle! He was gliding over the tops of the trees, ploughing through them, tumbling into a cloud of green sharp leaves and black twigs. There was a sudden snapping, and he fell off the saddle forward, a thud and a crashing of branches. Some twigs hit him smartly in the face. . . .

He was between a tree-stem and the saddle, with his leg over the steering lever and, so far as he could realise, not hurt. He tried to alter his position and free his leg, and found himself slipping and dropping through branches with everything giving way beneath him. He clutched and found himself in the lower branches of a tree beneath the flying-machine. The air was full of a pleasant resinous smell. He stared for a moment motionless, and then very carefully clambered down branch by branch to the soft needle-covered ground below.

"Good business," he said, looking up at the bent and tilted kite-wings above.

"I dropped soft!"

He rubbed his chin with his hand and meditated. "Blowed if I don't think I'm a rather lucky fellow!" he said, surveying the pleasant sun-bespattered ground under the trees. Then he became aware of a violent tumult at his side. "Lord!" he said, "You must be 'arf smothered," and extracted the kitten from his pocket-handkerchief and pocket. She was twisted and crumpled and extremely glad to see the light again. Her little tongue peeped between her teeth. He put her down, and she ran a dozen paces and shook herself and stretched and sat up and began to wash.

"Nex'?" he said, looking about him, and then with a gesture of vexation, "Desh it! I ought to 'ave brought that gun!"

He had rested it against a tree when he had seated himself in the flying-machine saddle.

He was puzzled for a time by the immense peacefulness in the quality of the world, and then he perceived that the roar of the cataract was no longer in his ears.

§2

He had no very clear idea of what sort of people he might come upon in this country. It was, he knew, America. Americans he had always understood were the citizens of a great and powerful nation, dry and humorous in their manner, addicted to the use of the bowie-knife and revolver, and in the habit of talking through the nose like Norfolkshire, and saying "allow" and "reckon" and "calculate," after the manner of the people who live on the New Forest side of Hampshire. Also they were very rich, had rocking-chairs, and put their feet at unusual altitudes, and they chewed tobacco, gum, and other substances, with untiring industry. Commingled with them were cowboys, Red Indians, and comic, respectful niggers. This he had learnt from the fiction in his public library. Beyond that he had learnt very little. He was not surprised therefore when he met armed men.

He decided to abandon the shattered flying-machine. He wandered through the trees for some time, and then struck a road that seemed to his urban English eyes to be remarkably wide but not properly "made." Neither hedge nor ditch nor curbed distinctive footpath separated it from the woods, and it went in that long easy curve which distinguishes the tracks of an open continent. Ahead he saw a man carrying a gun under his arm, a man in a soft black hat, a blue blouse, and black trousers, and with a broad round-fat face quite innocent of goatee. This person regarded him askance and heard him speak with a start.

"Can you tell me whereabouts I am at all?" asked Bert.

The man regarded him, and more particularly his rubber boots, with sinister suspicion. Then he replied in a strange outlandish tongue that was, as a matter of fact, Czech. He ended suddenly at the sight of Bert's blank face with "Don't spik English."

"Oh!" said Bert. He reflected gravely for a moment, and then went his way.

"Thenks," he, said as an afterthought. The man regarded his back for a moment, was struck with an idea, began an abortive

gesture, sighed, gave it up, and went on also with a depressed countenance.

Presently Bert came to a big wooden house standing casually among the trees. It looked a bleak, bare box of a house to him, no creeper grew on it, no hedge nor wall nor fence parted it off from the woods about it. He stopped before the steps that led up to the door, perhaps thirty yards away. The place seemed deserted. He would have gone up to the door and rapped, but suddenly a big black dog appeared at the side and regarded him. It was a huge heavy-jawed dog of some unfamiliar breed, and it, wore a spike-studded collar. It did not bark nor approach him, it just bristled quietly and emitted a single sound like a short, deep cough.

Bert hesitated and went on.

He stopped thirty paces away and stood peering about him among the trees. "If I 'aven't been and lef' that kitten," he said.

Acute sorrow wrenched him for a time. The black dog came through the trees to get a better look at him and coughed that well-bred cough again. Bert resumed the road.

"She'll do all right," he said. . . . "She'll catch things.

"She'll do all right," he said presently, without conviction. But if it had not been for the black dog, he would have gone back.

When he was out of sight of the house and the black dog, he went into the woods on the other side of the way and emerged after an interval trimming a very tolerable cudgel with his pocket-knife. Presently he saw an attractive-looking rock by the track and picked it up and put it in his pocket. Then he came to three or four houses, wooden like the last, each with an ill-painted white verandah (that was his name for it) and all standing in the same casual way upon the ground. Behind, through the woods, he saw pig-stys and a rooting black sow leading a brisk, adventurous family. A wild-looking woman with sloe-black eyes and dishevelled black hair sat upon the steps of one of the houses nursing a baby, but at the sight of Bert she got up and went inside, and he heard her bolting the door. Then a boy appeared among the pig-stys, but he would not understand Bert's hail.

"I suppose it is America!" said Bert.

The houses became more frequent down the road, and he passed two other extremely wild and dirty-looking men without addressing them. One carried a gun and the other a hatchet, and they scrutinised him and his cudgel scornfully. Then he struck a cross-road with a mono-rail at its side, and there was a notice board at the corner with "Wait here for the cars." "That's all right, any'ow," said Bert. "Wonder 'ow long I should 'ave to wait?" It occurred to him that in the present disturbed state of the country the service might be interrupted, and as there seemed more houses to the right than the left he turned to the right. He passed an old negro. " 'Ullo!" said Bert. "Goo' morning!"

"Good day, sah!" said the old negro, in a voice of almost incredible richness.

"What's the name of this place?" asked Bert.

"Tanooda, sah!" said the negro.

"Thenks!" said Bert.

"Thank *you*, sah!" said the negro, overwhelmingly.

Bert came to houses of the same detached, unwalled, wooden type, but adorned now with enamelled advertisements partly in English and partly in Esperanto. Then he came to what he concluded was a grocer's shop. It was the first house that professed the hospitality of an open door, and from within came a strangely familiar sound. "Gaw!" he said searching in his pockets. "Why! I 'aven't wanted money for free weeks! I wonder if I—Grubb 'ad most of it. Ah!" He produced a handful of coins and regarded it; three pennies, sixpence, and a shilling. "That's all right," he said, forgetting a very obvious consideration.

He approached the door, and as he did so a compactly built, grey-faced man in shirt sleeves appeared in it and scrutinised him and his cudgel. "Mornin'," said Bert. "Can I get anything to eat 'r drink in this shop?"

The man in the door replied, thank Heaven, in clear, good American. "This, sir, is not A shop, it is A store."

"Oh!" said Bert, and then, "Well, can I get anything to eat?"

"You can," said the American in a tone of confident encouragement, and led the way inside.

The shop seemed to him by his Bun Hill standards extremely roomy, well lit, and unencumbered. There was a long counter to the left of him, with drawers and miscellaneous commodities ranged behind it, a number of chairs, several tables, and two spittoons to the right, various barrels, cheeses, and bacon up the vista, and beyond, a large archway leading to more space. A little group of men was assembled round one of the tables, and a woman of perhaps five-and-thirty leant with her elbows on the counter. All the men were armed with rifles, and the barrel of a gun peeped above the counter. They were all listening idly, inattentively, to a cheap, metallic-toned gramophone that occupied a table near at hand. From its brazen throat came words that gave Bert a qualm of homesickness, that brought back in his memory a sunlit beach, a group of children, red-painted bicycles, Grubb, and an approaching balloon:—

"Ting-a-ling-a-ting-a-ling-a-ting-a ling-a-tang. . .
What price hairpins now?"

A heavy-necked man in a straw hat, who was chewing something, stopped the machine with a touch, and they all turned their eyes on Bert. And all their eyes were tired eyes.

"Can we give this gentleman anything to eat, mother, or can we not?" said the proprietor.

"He kin have what he likes," said the woman at the counter, without moving, "right up from a cracker to a square meal." She struggled with a yawn, after the manner of one who has been up all night.

"I want a meal," said Bert, "but I 'aven't very much money. I don' want to give mor'n a shillin'."

"Mor'n a *what?*" said the proprietor, sharply.

"Mor'n a shillin'," said Bert, with a sudden disagreeable realisation coming into his mind.

"Yes," said the proprietor, startled for a moment from his courtly bearing. "But what in hell *is* a shilling?"

"He means a quarter," said a wise-looking, lank young man in riding gaiters.

Bert, trying to conceal his consternation, produced a coin. "That's a shilling," he said.

"He calls A store A shop," said the proprietor, "and he wants A meal for A shilling. May I ask you, sir, what part of America you hail from?"

Bert replaced the shilling in his pocket as he spoke, "Niagara," he said.

"And when did you leave Niagara?"

" 'Bout an hour ago."

"Well," said the proprietor, and turned with a puzzled smile to the others. "Well!"

They asked various questions simultaneously.

Bert selected one or two for reply. "You see," he said, "I been with the German air-fleet. I got caught up by them, sort of by accident, and brought over here."

"From England?"

"Yes—from England. Way of Germany. I was in a great battle with them Asiatics, and I got lef' on a little island between the Falls."

"Goat Island?"

"I don' know what it was called. But any'ow I found a flying-machine and made a sort of fly with it and got here."

Two men stood up with incredulous eyes on him. "Where's the flying-machine?" they asked; "outside?"

"It's back in the woods here—'bout arf a mile away."

"Is it good?" said a thick-lipped man with a scar.

"I come down rather a smash—."

Everybody got up and stood about him and talked confusingly. They wanted him to take them to the flying-machine at once.

"Look 'ere," said Bert, "I'll show you—only I 'aven't 'ad anything to eat since yestiday—except mineral water."

A gaunt soldierly-looking young man with long lean legs in riding gaiters and a bandolier, who had hitherto not spoken, intervened now on his behalf in a note of confident authority. "That's aw right," he said. "Give him a feed, Mr. Logan—from me. I want to hear more of that story of his. We'll see his machine afterwards. If you ask me, I should say it's a remarkably interesting accident had dropped this gentleman here. I guess we requisition that flying-machine—if we find it—for local defence."

§3

So Bert fell on his feet again, and sat eating cold meat and good bread and mustard and drinking very good beer, and telling in the roughest outline and with the omissions and inaccuracies of statement natural to his type of mind, the simple story of his adventures. He told how he and a "gentleman friend" had been visiting the seaside for their health, how a "chep" came along in a balloon and fell out as he fell in, how he had drifted to Franconia, how the Germans had seemed to mistake him for some one and had "took him prisoner" and brought him to New York, how he had been to Labrador and back, how he had got to Goat Island and found himself there alone. He omitted the matter of the Prince and the Butteridge aspect of the affair, not out of any deep deceitfulness, but because he felt the inadequacy of his narrative powers. He wanted everything to seem easy and natural and correct, to present himself as a trustworthy and understandable Englishman in a sound mediocre position, to whom refreshment and accommodation might be given with freedom and confidence. When his fragmentary story came to New York and the battle of Niagara, they suddenly produced newspapers which had been lying about on the table, and began to check him and question him by these vehement accounts. It became evident to him that his descent had revived

and roused to flames again a discussion, a topic, that had been burning continuously, that had smouldered only through sheer exhaustion of material during the temporary diversion of the gramophone, a discussion that had drawn these men together, rifle in hand, the one supreme topic of the whole world, the War and the methods of the War. He found any question of his personality and his personal adventures falling into the background, found himself taken for granted, and no more than a source of information. The ordinary affairs of life, the buying and selling of everyday necessities, the cultivation of the ground, the tending of beasts, was going on as it were by force of routine, as the common duties of life go on in a house whose master lies under the knife of some supreme operation. The overruling interest was furnished by those great Asiatic airships that went upon incalculable missions across the sky, the crimson-clad swordsmen who might come fluttering down demanding petrol, or food, or news. These men were asking, all the continent was asking, "What are we to do? What can we try? How can we get at them?" Bert fell into his place as an item, ceased even in his own thoughts to be a central and independent thing.

After he had eaten and drunken his fill and sighed and stretched and told them how good the food seemed to him, he lit a cigarette they gave him and led the way, with some doubts and trouble, to the flying-machine amidst the larches. It became manifest that the gaunt young man, whose name, it seemed, was Laurier, was a leader both by position and natural aptitude. He knew the names and characters and capabilities of all the men who were with him, and he set them to work at once with vigour and effect to secure this precious instrument of war. They got the thing down to the ground deliberately and carefully, felling a couple of trees in the process, and they built a wide flat roof of timbers and tree boughs to guard their precious find against its chance discovery by any passing Asiatics. Long before evening they had an engineer from the next township at work upon it,

and they were casting lots among the seventeen picked men who wanted to take it for its first flight. And Bert found his kitten and carried it back to Logan's store and handed it with earnest admonition to Mrs. Logan. And it was reassuringly clear to him that in Mrs. Logan both he and the kitten had found a congenial soul.

Laurier was not only a masterful person and a wealthy property owner and employer—he was president, Bert learnt with awe, of the Tanooda Canning Corporation—but he was popular and skilful in the arts of popularity. In the evening quite a crowd of men gathered in the store and talked of the flying-machine and of the war that was tearing the world to pieces. And presently came a man on a bicycle with an ill-printed newspaper of a single sheet which acted like fuel in a blazing furnace of talk. It was nearly all American news; the old-fashioned cables had fallen into disuse for some years, and the Marconi stations across the ocean and along the Atlantic coastline seemed to have furnished particularly tempting points of attack.

But such news it was.

Bert sat in the background—for by this time they had gauged his personal quality pretty completely—listening. Before his staggering mind passed strange vast images as they talked, of great issues at a crisis, of nations in tumultuous march, of continents overthrown, of famine and destruction beyond measure. Ever and again, in spite of his efforts to suppress them, certain personal impressions would scamper across the weltering confusion, the horrible mess of the exploded Prince, the Chinese aeronaut upside down, the limping and bandaged bird-faced officer blundering along in miserable and hopeless flight. . . .

They spoke of fire and massacre, of cruelties and counter cruelties, of things that had been done to harmless Asiatics by race-mad men, of the wholesale burning and smashing up of towns, railway junctions, bridges, of whole populations in hiding and exodus. "Every ship they've got is in the Pacific,"

he heard one man exclaim. "Since the fighting began they can't have landed on the Pacific slope less than a million men. They've come to stay in these States, and they will—living or dead."

Slowly, broadly, invincibly, there grew upon Bert's mind realisation of the immense tragedy of humanity into which his life was flowing; the appalling and universal nature of the epoch that had arrived; the conception of an end to security and order and habit. The whole world was at war and it could not get back to peace, it might never recover peace.

He had thought the things he had seen had been exceptional, conclusive things, that the besieging of New York and the battle of the Atlantic were epoch-making events between long years of security. And they had been but the first warning impacts of universal cataclysm. Each day destruction and hate and disaster grew, the fissures widened between man and man, new regions of the fabric of civilisation crumbled and gave way. Below, the armies grew and the people perished; above, the airships and aeroplanes fought and fled, raining destruction.

It is difficult perhaps for the broad-minded and long-perspectived reader to understand how incredible the breaking down of the scientific civilisation seemed to those who actually lived at this time, who in their own persons went down in that debacle. Progress had marched as it seemed invincible about the earth, never now to rest again. For three hundred years and more the long steadily accelerated diastole of Europeanised civilisation had been in progress: towns had been multiplying, populations increasing, values rising, new countries developing; thought, literature, knowledge unfolding and spreading. It seemed but a part of the process that every year the instruments of war were vaster and more powerful, and that armies and explosives outgrew all other growing things. . . .

Three hundred years of diastole, and then came the swift and unexpected systole, like the closing of a fist. They could not understand it was systole. They could not think of it as anything but a jolt, a hitch, a mere oscillatory indication of the swiftness

of their progress. Collapse, though it happened all about them, remained incredible. Presently some falling mass smote them down, or the ground opened beneath their feet. They died incredulous. . . .

These men in the store made a minute, remote group under this immense canopy of disaster. They turned from one little aspect to another. What chiefly concerned them was defence against Asiatic raiders swooping for petrol or to destroy weapons or communications. Everywhere levies were being formed at that time to defend the plant of the railroads day and night in the hope that communication would speedily be restored. The land war was still far away. A man with a flat voice distinguished himself by a display of knowledge and cunning. He told them all with confidence just what had been wrong with the German drachenflieger and the American aeroplanes, just what advantage the Japanese flyers possessed. He launched out into a romantic description of the Butteridge machine and riveted Bert's attention. "I *see* that," said Bert, and was smitten silent by a thought. The man with the flat voice talked on, without heeding him, of the strange irony of Butteridge's death. At that Bert had a little twinge of relief—he would never meet Butteridge again. It appeared Butteridge had died suddenly, very suddenly.

"And his secret, sir, perished with him! When they came to look for the parts—none could find them. He had hidden them all too well."

"But couldn't he tell?" asked the man in the straw hat. "Did he die so suddenly as that?"

"Struck down, sir. Rage and apoplexy. At a place called Dymchurch in England."

"That's right," said Laurier. "I remember a page about it in the Sunday *American*. At the time they said it was a German spy had stolen his balloon."

"Well, sir," said the flat-voiced man, "that fit of apoplexy at Dymchurch was the worst thing—absolutely the worst thing that ever happened to the world. For if it had not been for the death of Mr. Butteridge—"

"No one knows his secret?"

"Not a soul. It's gone. His balloon, it appears, was lost at sea, with all the plans. Down it went, and they went with it."

Pause.

"With machines such as he made we could fight these Asiatic fliers on more than equal terms. We could outfly and beat down those scarlet humming-birds wherever they appeared. But it's gone, it's gone, and there's no time to reinvent it now. We got to fight with what we got—and the odds are against us. *That* won't stop us fightin'. No! but just think of it!"

Bert was trembling violently. He cleared his throat hoarsely.

"I say," he said, "look here, I—"

Nobody regarded him. The man with the flat voice was opening a new branch of the subject. "I allow—" he began.

Bert became violently excited. He stood up.

He made clawing motions with his hands. "I say!" he exclaimed, "Mr. Laurier. Look 'ere—I want—about that Butteridge machine—"

Mr. Laurier, sitting on an adjacent table, with a magnificent gesture, arrested the discourse of the flat-voiced man. "What's *he* saying?" said he.

Then the whole company realised that something was happening to Bert; either he was suffocating or going mad. He was spluttering.

"Look 'ere! I say! 'Old on a bit!" and trembling and eagerly unbuttoning himself.

He tore open his collar and opened vest and shirt. He plunged into his interior and for an instant it seemed he was plucking forth his liver. Then as he struggled with buttons on his shoulder they perceived this flattened horror was in fact a terribly dirty flannel chest-protector. In another moment Bert, in a state of irregular décolletage, was standing over the table displaying a sheaf of papers.

"These!" he gasped. "These are the plans! . . . You know! Mr. Butteridge—his machine! What died! I was the chap that went off in that balloon!"

For some seconds every one was silent. They stared from these papers to Bert's white face and blazing eyes, and back to the papers on the table. Nobody moved. Then the man with the flat voice spoke.

"Irony!" he said, with a note of satisfaction. "Real rightdown Irony! *When it's too late to think of making 'em any more!*"

§4

They would all no doubt have been eager to hear Bert's story over again, but it was it this point that Laurier showed his quality. "No, *sir*," he said, and slid from off his table.

He impounded the dispersing Butteridge plans with one comprehensive sweep of his arm, rescuing them even from the expository fingermarks of the man with the flat voice, and handed them to Bert. "Put those back," he said, "where you had 'em. We have a journey before us."

Bert took them.

"Whar?" said the man in the straw hat.

"Why, sir, we are going to find the President of these States and give these plans over to him. I decline to believe, sir, we are too late."

"Where is the President?" asked Bert weakly in that pause that followed.

"Logan," said Laurier, disregarding that feeble inquiry, "you must help us in this."

It seemed only a matter of a few minutes before Bert and Laurier and the storekeeper were examining a number of bicycles that were stowed in the hinder room of the store. Bert didn't like any of them very much. They had wood rims and an experience of wood rims in the English climate had taught him to hate them. That, however, and one or two other objections to an immediate start were overruled by Laurier. "But where *is* the

President?" Bert repeated as they stood behind Logan while he pumped up a deflated tyre.

Laurier looked down on him. "He is reported in the neighbourhood of Albany—out towards the Berkshire Hills. He is moving from place to place and, as far as he can, organising the defence by telegraph and telephones The Asiatic air-fleet is trying to locate him. When they think they have located the seat of government, they throw bombs. This inconveniences him, but so far they have not come within ten miles of him. The Asiatic air-fleet is at present scattered all over the Eastern States, seeking out and destroying gas-works and whatever seems conducive to the building of airships or the transport of troops. Our retaliatory measures are slight in the extreme. But with these machines— Sir, this ride of ours will count among the historical rides of the world!"

He came near to striking an attitude. "We shan't get to him to-night?" asked Bert.

"No, sir!" said Laurier. "We shall have to ride some days, sure!"

"And suppose we can't get a lift on a train—or anything?"

"No, sir! There's been no transit by Tanooda for three days. It is no good waiting. We shall have to get on as well as we can."

"Startin' now?"

"Starting now!"

"But 'ow about— We shan't be able to do much to-night."

"May as well ride till we're fagged and sleep then. So much clear gain. Our road is eastward."

"Of course," began Bert, with memories of the dawn upon Goat Island, and left his sentence unfinished.

He gave his attention to the more scientific packing of the chest-protector, for several of the plans flapped beyond his vest.

§5

For a week Bert led a life of mixed sensations. Amidst these fatigue in the legs predominated. Mostly he rode, rode with

Laurier's back inexorably ahead, through a land like a larger England, with bigger hills and wider valleys, larger fields, wider roads, fewer hedges, and wooden houses with commodious piazzas. He rode. Laurier made inquiries, Laurier chose the turnings, Laurier doubted, Laurier decided. Now it seemed they were in telephonic touch with the President; now something had happened and he was lost again. But always they had to go on, and always Bert rode. A tyre was deflated. Still he rode. He grew saddle sore. Laurier declared that unimportant. Asiatic flying ships passed overhead, the two cyclists made a dash for cover until the sky was clear. Once a red Asiatic flying-machine came fluttering after them, so low they could distinguish the aeronaut's head. He followed them for a mile. Now they came to regions of panic, now to regions of destruction; here people were fighting for food, here they seemed hardly stirred from the country-side routine. They spent a day in a deserted and damaged Albany. The Asiatics had descended and cut every wire and made a cinder-heap of the Junction, and our travellers pushed on eastward. They passed a hundred half-heeded incidents, and always Bert was toiling after Laurier's indefatigable back. . . .

Things struck upon Bert's attention and perplexed him, and then he passed on with unanswered questionings fading from his mind.

He saw a large house on fire on a hillside to the right, and no man heeding it. . . .

They came to a narrow railroad bridge and presently to a mono-rail train standing in the track on its safety feet. It was a remarkably sumptuous train, the Last Word Trans-Continental Express, and the passengers were all playing cards or sleeping or preparing a picnic meal on a grassy slope near at hand. They had been there six days. . . .

At one point ten dark-complexioned men were hanging in a string from the trees along the roadside. Bert wondered why. . . .

At one peaceful-looking village where they stopped off to get Bert's tyre mended and found beer and biscuits, they were approached by an extremely dirty little boy without boots, who spoke as follows:—

"Deyse been hanging a Chink in dose woods!"

"Hanging a Chinaman?" said Laurier.

"Sure. Der sleuths got him rubberin' der rail-road sheds!"

"Oh!"

"Dose guys done wase cartridges. Deyse hung him and dey pulled his legs. Deyse doin' all der Chinks dey can fine dat weh! Dey ain't takin' no risks. All der Chinks dey can fine."

Neither Bert nor Laurier made any reply, and presently, after a little skilful expectoration, the young gentleman was attracted by the appearance of two of his friends down the road and shuffled off, whooping weirdly. . . .

That afternoon they almost ran over a man shot through the body and partly decomposed, lying near the middle of the road, just outside Albany. He must have been lying there for some days. . . .

Beyond Albany they came upon a motor car with a tyre burst and a young woman sitting absolutely passive beside the driver's seat. An old man was under the car trying to effect some impossible repairs. Beyond, sitting with a rifle across his knees, with his back to the car, and staring into the woods, was a young man.

The old man crawled out at their approach and still on all-fours accosted Bert and Laurier. The car had broken down overnight. The old man, said he could not understand what was wrong, but he was trying to puzzle it out. Neither he nor his son-in-law had any mechanical aptitude. They had been assured this was a fool-proof car. It was dangerous to have to stop in this place. The party had been attacked by tramps and had had to fight. It was known they had provisions. He mentioned a great name in the world of finance. Would Laurier and Bert stop and help him? He proposed it first hopefully, then urgently, at last in tears and terror.

"No!" said Laurier inexorable. "We must go on! We have

something more than a woman to save. We have to save America!"

The girl never stirred.

And once they passed a madman singing.

And at last they found the President hiding in a small saloon upon the outskirts of a place called Pinkerville on the Hudson, and gave the plans of the Butteridge machine into his hands.

Chapter XI

THE GREAT COLLAPSE

§1

And now the whole fabric of civilisation was bending and giving, and dropping to pieces and melting in the furnace of the war.

The stages of the swift and universal collapse of the financial and scientific civilisation with which the twentieth century opened followed each other very swiftly, so swiftly that upon the foreshortened page of history—they seem altogether to overlap. To begin with, one sees the world nearly at a maximum wealth and prosperity. To its inhabitants indeed it seemed also at a maximum of security. When now in retrospect the thoughtful observer surveys the intellectual history of this time, when one reads its surviving fragments of literature, its scraps of political oratory, the few small voices that chance has selected out of a thousand million utterances to speak to later days, the most striking thing of all this web of wisdom and error is surely that hallucination of security. To men living in our present world state, orderly, scientific and secured, nothing seems so precarious, so giddily dangerous, as the fabric of the social order with which the men of the opening of the twentieth century were content. To us it seems that every institution and relationship was the fruit of haphazard and tradition and the manifest sport of chance, their laws each made for some separate occasion and having no relation to any future needs, their customs illogical, their education aimless and wasteful. Their method of economic exploitation indeed impresses a trained and informed mind as the most frantic and destructive scramble it is possible to conceive; their credit and monetary system resting on an

unsubstantial tradition of the worthiness of gold, seems a thing almost fantastically unstable. And they lived in planless cities, for the most part dangerously congested; their rails and roads and population were distributed over the earth in the wanton confusion ten thousand irrevelant considerations had made.

Yet they thought confidently that this was a secure and permanent progressive system, and on the strength of some three hundred years of change and irregular improvement answered the doubter with, "Things always *have* gone well. We'll worry through!"

But when we contrast the state of man in the opening of the twentieth century with the condition of any previous period in his history, then perhaps we may begin to understand something of that blind confidence. It was not so much a reasoned confidence as the inevitable consequence of sustained good fortune. By such standards as they possessed, things *had* gone amazingly well for them. It is scarcely an exaggeration to say that for the first time in history whole populations found themselves regularly supplied with more than enough to eat, and the vital statistics of the time witness to an amelioration of hygienic conditions rapid beyond all precedent, and to a vast development of intelligence and ability in all the arts that make life wholesome. The level and quality of the average education had risen tremendously; and at the dawn of the twentieth century comparatively few people in Western Europe or America were unable to read or write. Never before had there been such reading masses. There was wide social security. A common man might travel safely over three-quarters of the habitable globe, could go round the earth at a cost of less than the annual earnings of a skilled artisan. Compared with the liberality and comfort of the ordinary life of the time, the order of the Roman Empire under the Antonines was local and limited. And every year, every month, came some new increment to human achievement, a new country opened up, new mines, new scientific discoveries, a new machine!

For those three hundred years, indeed, the movement of the

world seemed wholly beneficial to mankind. Men said, indeed, that moral organisation was not keeping pace with physical progress, but few attached any meaning to these phrases, the understanding of which lies at the basis of our present safety. Sustaining and constructive forces did indeed for a time more than balance the malign drift of chance and the natural ignorance, prejudice, blind passion, and wasteful self-seeking of mankind.

The accidental balance on the side of Progress was far slighter and infinitely more complex and delicate in its adjustments than the people of that time suspected; but that did not alter the fact that it was an effective balance. They did not realise that this age of relative good fortune was an age of immense but temporary opportunity for their kind. They complacently assumed a necessary progress towards which they had no moral responsibility. They did not realise that this security of progress was a thing still to be won—or lost, and that the time to win it was a time that passed. They went about their affairs energetically enough and yet with a curious idleness towards those threatening things. No one troubled over the real dangers of mankind. They saw their armies and navies grow larger and more portentous; some of their ironclads at the last cost as much as the whole annual expenditure upon advanced education; they accumulated explosives and the machinery of destruction; they allowed their national traditions and jealousies to accumulate; they contemplated a steady enhancement of race hostility as the races drew closer without concern or understanding, and they permitted the growth in their midst of an evil-spirited press, mercenary and unscrupulous, incapable of good, and powerful for evil. The State had practically no control over the press at all. Quite heedlessly they allowed this touch-paper to lie at the door of their war magazine for any spark to fire. The precedents of history were all one tale of the collapse of civilisations, the dangers of the time were manifest. One is incredulous now to believe they could not see.

Could mankind have prevented this disaster of the War in

the Air? An idle question that, as idle as to ask could mankind have prevented the decay that turned Assyria and Babylon to empty deserts or the slow decline and fall, the gradual social disorganisation, phase by phase, that closed the chapter of the Empire of the West! They could not, because they did not, they had not the will to arrest it. What mankind could achieve with a different will is a speculation as idle as it is magnificent. And this was no slow decadence that came to the Europeanised world; those other civilisations rotted and crumbled down, the Europeanised civilisation was, as it were, blown up. Within the space of five years it was altogether disintegrated and destroyed. Up to the very eve of the War in the Air one sees a spacious spectacle of incessant advance, a world-wide security, enormous areas with highly organised industry and settled populations, gigantic cities spreading gigantically, the seas and oceans dotted with shipping, the land netted with rails, and open ways. Then suddenly the German air-fleets sweep across the scene, and we are in the beginning of the end.

§2

This story has already told of the swift rush upon New York of the first German air-fleet and of the wild, inevitable orgy of inconclusive destruction that ensued. Behind it a second air-fleet was already swelling at its gasometers when England and France and Spain and Italy showed their hands. None of these countries had prepared for aeronautic warfare on the magnificent scale of the Germans, but each guarded secrets, each in a measure was making ready, and a common dread of German vigour and that aggressive spirit Prince Karl Albert embodied, had long been drawing these powers together in secret anticipation of some such attack. This rendered their prompt co-operation possible, and they certainly co-operated promptly. The second aerial power in Europe at this time was France; the British, nervous for their Asiatic empire, and sensible of the immense moral effect of the airship upon half-educated populations, had

placed their aeronautic parks in North India, and were able to play but a subordinate part in the European conflict. Still, even in England they had nine or ten big navigables, twenty or thirty smaller ones, and a variety of experimental aeroplanes. Before the fleet of Prince Karl Albert had crossed England, while Bert was still surveying Manchester in bird's-eye view, the diplomatic exchanges were going on that led to an attack upon Germany. A heterogeneous collection of navigable balloons of all sizes and types gathered over the Bernese Oberland, crushed and burnt the twenty-five Swiss air-ships that unexpectedly resisted this concentration in the battle of the Alps, and then, leaving the Alpine glaciers and valleys strewn with strange wreckage, divided into two fleets and set itself to terrorise Berlin and destroy the Franconian Park, seeking to do this before the second air-fleet could be inflated.

Both over Berlin and Franconia the assailants with their modern explosives effected great damage before they were driven off. In Franconia twelve fully distended and five partially filled and manned giants were able to make head against and at last, with the help of a squadron of drachenflieger from Hamburg, defeat and pursue the attack and to relieve Berlin, and the Germans were straining every nerve to get an overwhelming fleet in the air, and were already raiding London and Paris when the advance fleets from the Asiatic air-parks, the first intimation of a new factor in the conflict, were reported from Burmah and Armenia.

Already the whole financial fabric of the world was staggering when that occurred. With the destruction of the American fleet in the North Atlantic, and the smashing conflict that ended the naval existence of Germany in the North Sea, with the burning and wrecking of billions of pounds' worth of property in the four cardinal cities of the world, the fact of the hopeless costliness of war came home for the first time, came, like a blow in the face, to the consciousness of mankind. Credit went down in a wild whirl of selling. Everywhere appeared a

phenomenon that had already in a mild degree manifested itself in preceding periods of panic; a desire to *secure and hoard gold* before prices reached bottom. But now it spread like wild-fire, it became universal. Above was visible conflict and destruction; below something was happening far more deadly and incurable to the flimsy fabric of finance and commercialism in which men had so blindly put their trust. As the airships fought above, the visible gold supply of the world vanished below. An epidemic of private cornering and universal distrust swept the world. In a few weeks, money, except for depreciated paper, vanished into vaults, into holes, into the walls of houses, into ten million hiding-places. Money vanished, and at its disappearance trade and industry came to an end. The economic world staggered and fell dead. It was like the stroke of some disease; it was like the water vanishing out of the blood of a living creature; it was a sudden, universal coagulation of intercourse. . . .

And as the credit system, that had been the living fortress of the scientific civilisation, reeled and fell upon the millions it had held together in economic relationship, as these people, perplexed and helpless, faced this marvel of credit utterly destroyed, the airships of Asia, countless and relentless, poured across the heavens, swooped eastward to America and westward to Europe. The page of history becomes a long crescendo of battle. The main body of the British-Indian air-fleet perished upon a pyre of blazing antagonists in Burmah; the Germans were scattered in the great battle of the Carpathians; the vast peninsula of India burst into insurrection and civil war from end to end, and from Gobi to Morocco rose the standards of the "Jehad." For some weeks of warfare and destruction it seemed as though the Confederation of Eastern Asia must needs conquer the world, and then the jerry-built "modern" civilisation of China too gave way under the strain. The teeming and peaceful population of China had been "westernised" during the opening years of the twentieth century with the deepest resentment and reluctance; they had been dragooned and disciplined under Japanese and

European influence into an acquiescence with sanitary methods, police controls, military service, and wholesale process of exploitation against which their whole tradition rebelled. Under the stresses of the war their endurance reached the breaking point, the whole of China rose in incoherent revolt, and the practical destruction of the central government at Pekin by a handful of British and German airships that had escaped from the main battles rendered that revolt invincible. In Yokohama appeared barricades, the black flag and the social revolution. With that the whole world became a welter of conflict.

So that a universal social collapse followed, as it were a logical consequence, upon world-wide war. Wherever there were great populations, great masses of people found themselves without work, without money, and unable to get food. Famine was in every working-class quarter in the world within three weeks of the beginning of the war. Within a month there was not a city anywhere in which the ordinary law and social procedure had not been replaced by some form of emergency control, in which firearms and military executions were not being used to keep order and prevent violence. And still in the poorer quarters, and in the populous districts, and even here and there already among those who had been wealthy, famine spread.

§3

So what historians have come to call the Phase of the Emergency Committees sprang from the opening phase and from the phase of social collapse. Then followed a period of vehement and passionate conflict against disintegration; everywhere the struggle to keep order and to keep fighting went on. And at the same time the character of the war altered through the replacement of the huge gas-filled airships by flying-machines as the instruments of war. So soon as the big fleet engagements were over, the Asiatics endeavoured to establish in close proximity to the more vulnerable points of the countries against which they were acting, fortified centres from which flying-machine raids could

be made. For a time they had everything their own way in this, and then, as this story has told, the lost secret of the Butteridge machine came to light, and the conflict became equalized and less conclusive than ever. For these small flying-machines, ineffectual for any large expedition or conclusive attack, were horribly convenient for guerilla warfare, rapidly and cheaply made, easily used, easily hidden. The design of them was hastily copied and printed in Pinkerville and scattered broadcast over the United States and copies were sent to Europe, and there reproduced. Every man, every town, every parish that could, was exhorted to make and use them. In a little while they were being constructed not only by governments and local authorities, but by robber bands, by insurgent committees, by every type of private person. The peculiar social destructiveness of the Butteridge machine lay in its complete simplicity. It was nearly as simple as a motor-bicycle. The broad outlines of the earlier stages of the war disappeared under its influence, the spacious antagonism of nations and empires and races vanished in a seething mass of detailed conflict. The world passed at a stride from a unity and simplicity broader than that of the Roman Empire at its best, to as social fragmentation as complete as the robber-baron period of the Middle Ages. But this time, for a long descent down gradual slopes of disintegration, comes a fall like a fall over a cliff. Everywhere were men and women perceiving this and struggling desperately to keep as it were a hold upon the edge of the cliff.

A fourth phase follows. Through the struggle against Chaos, in the wake of the Famine, came now another old enemy of humanity—the Pestilence, the Purple Death. But the war does not pause. The flags still fly. Fresh air-fleets rise, new forms of airship, and beneath their swooping struggles the world darkens—scarcely heeded by history.

It is not within the design of this book to tell that further story, to tell how the War in the Air kept on through the sheer inability of any authorities to meet and agree and end it, until every organised government in the world was as shattered and broken as a heap of china beaten with a stick. With every week of those terrible years history becomes more detailed and confused, more crowded and uncertain. Not without great and heroic resistance was civilisation borne down. Out of the bitter social conflict below rose patriotic associations, brotherhoods of order, city mayors, princes, provisional committees, trying to establish an order below and to keep the sky above. The double effort destroyed them. And as the exhaustion of the mechanical resources of civilisation clears the heavens of airships at last altogether, Anarchy, Famine and Pestilence are discovered triumphant below. The great nations and empires have become but names in the mouths of men. Everywhere there are ruins and unburied dead, and shrunken, yellow-faced survivors in a mortal apathy. Here there are robbers, here vigilance committees, and here guerilla bands ruling patches of exhausted territory, strange federations and brotherhoods form and dissolve, and religious fanaticisms begotten of despair gleam in famine-bright eyes. It is a universal dissolution. The fine order and welfare of the earth have crumpled like an exploded bladder. In five short years the world and the scope of human life have undergone a retrogressive change as great as that between the age of the Antonines and the Europe of the ninth century. . . .

§4

Across this sombre spectacle of disaster goes a minute and insignificant person for whom perhaps the readers of this story have now some slight solicitude. Of him there remains to be told just one single and miraculous thing. Through a world darkened and lost, through a civilisation in its death agony, our little Cockney errant went and found his Edna! He found his Edna!

He got back across the Atlantic partly by means of an order from the President and partly through his own good luck. He contrived to get himself aboard a British brig in the timber trade

that put out from Boston without cargo, chiefly, it would seem, because its captain had a vague idea of "getting home" to South Shields. Bert was able to ship himself upon her mainly because of the seamanlike appearance of his rubber boots. They had a long, eventful voyage; they were chased, or imagined themselves to be chased, for some hours by an Asiatic ironclad, which was presently engaged by a British cruiser. The two ships fought for three hours, circling and driving southward as they fought, until the twilight and the cloud-drift of a rising gale swallowed them up. A few days later Bert's ship lost her rudder and mainmast in a gale. The crew ran out of food and subsisted on fish. They saw strange air-ships going eastward near the Azores and landed to get provisions and repair the rudder at Teneriffe. There they found the town destroyed and two big liners, with dead still aboard, sunken in the harbour. From there they got canned food and material for repairs, but their operations were greatly impeded by the hostility of a band of men amidst the ruins of the town, who sniped them and tried to drive them away.

At Mogador, they stayed and sent a boat ashore for water, and were nearly captured by an Arab ruse. Here too they got the Purple Death aboard, and sailed with it incubating in their blood. The cook sickened first, and then the mate, and presently every one was down and three in the forecastle were dead. It chanced to be calm weather, and they drifted helplessly and indeed careless of their fate backwards towards the Equator. The captain doctored them all with rum. Nine died all together, and of the four survivors none understood navigation; when at last they took heart again and could handle a sail, they made a course by the stars roughly northward and were already short of food once more when they fell in with a petrol-driven ship from Rio to Cardiff, shorthanded by reason of the Purple Death and glad to take them aboard. So at last, after a year of wandering Bert reached England. He landed in bright June weather, and found the Purple Death was there just beginning its ravages.

The people were in a state of panic in Cardiff and many had

fled to the hills, and directly the steamer came to the harbour she was boarded and her residue of food impounded by some unauthenticated Provisional Committee. Bert tramped through a country disorganised by pestilence, foodless, and shaken to the very base of its immemorial order. He came near death and starvation many times, and once he was drawn into scenes of violence that might have ended his career. But the Bert Smallways who tramped from Cardiff to London vaguely "going home," vaguely seeking something of his own that had no tangible form but Edna, was a very different person from the Desert Dervish who was swept out of England in Mr. Butteridge's balloon a year before. He was brown and lean and enduring, steady-eyed and pestilence-salted, and his mouth, which had once hung open, shut now like a steel trap. Across his brow ran a white scar that he had got in a fight on the brig. In Cardiff he had felt the need of new clothes and a weapon, and had, by means that would have shocked him a year ago, secured a flannel shirt, a corduroy suit, and a revolver and fifty cartridges from an abandoned pawnbroker's. He also got some soap and had his first real wash for thirteen months in a stream outside the town. The Vigilance bands that had at first shot plunderers very freely were now either entirely dispersed by the plague, or busy between town and cemetery in a vain attempt to keep pace with it. He prowled on the outskirts of the town for three or four days, starving, and then went back to join the Hospital Corps for a week, and so fortified himself with a few square meals before he started eastward.

The Welsh and English country-side at that time presented the strangest mingling of the assurance and wealth of the opening twentieth century with a sort of Düreresque mediaevalism. All the gear, the houses and mono-rails, the farm hedges and power cables, the roads and pavements, the sign-posts and advertisements of the former order were still for the most part intact. Bankruptcy, social collapse, famine, and pestilence had done nothing to damage these, and it was only to the great

capitals and ganglionic centres, as it were, of this State, that positive destruction had come. Any one dropped suddenly into the country would have noticed very little difference. He would have remarked first, perhaps, that all the hedges needed clipping, that the roadside grass grew rank, that the road-tracks were unusually rainworn, and that the cottages by the wayside seemed in many cases shut up, that a telephone wire had dropped here, and that a cart stood abandoned by the wayside. But he would still find his hunger whetted by the bright assurance that Wilder's Canned Peaches were excellent, or that there was nothing so good for the breakfast table as Gobble's Sausages. And then suddenly would come the Düreresque element; the skeleton of a horse, or some crumpled mass of rags in the ditch, with gaunt extended feet and a yellow, purple-blotched skin and face, or what had been a face, gaunt and glaring and devastated. Then here would be a field that had been ploughed and not sown, and here a field of corn carelessly trampled by beasts, and here a hoarding torn down across the road to make a fire.

Then presently he would meet a man or a woman, yellow-faced and probably negligently dressed and armed—prowling for food. These people would have the complexions and eyes and expressions of tramps or criminals, and often the clothing of prosperous middle-class or upper-class people. Many of these would be eager for news, and willing to give help and even scraps of queer meat, or crusts of grey and doughy bread, in return for it. They would listen to Bert's story with avidity, and attempt to keep him with them for a day or so. The virtual cessation of postal distribution and the collapse of all newspaper enterprise had left an immense and aching gap in the mental life of this time. Men had suddenly lost sight of the ends of the earth and had still to recover the rumour-spreading habits of the Middle Ages. In their eyes, in their bearing, in their talk, was the quality of lost and deoriented souls.

As Bert travelled from parish to parish, and from district to district, avoiding as far as possible those festering centres of

violence and despair, the larger towns, he found the condition of affairs varying widely. In one parish he would find the large house burnt, the vicarage wrecked, evidently in violent conflict for some suspected and perhaps imaginary store of food, unburied dead everywhere, and the whole mechanism of the community at a standstill. In another he would find organising forces stoutly at work, newly-painted notice boards warning off vagrants, the roads and still cultivated fields policed by armed men, the pestilence under control, even nursing going on, a store of food husbanded, the cattle and sheep well guarded, and a group of two or three justices, the village doctor or a farmer, dominating the whole place; a reversion, in fact, to the autonomous community of the fifteenth century. But at any time such a village would be liable to a raid of Asiatics or Africans or such-like air-pirates, demanding petrol and alcohol or provisions. The price of its order was an almost intolerable watchfulness and tension.

Then the approach to the confused problems of some larger centre of population and the presence of a more intricate conflict would be marked by roughly smeared notices of "Quarantine" or "Strangers Shot," or by a string of decaying plunderers dangling from the telephone poles at the roadside. About Oxford big boards were put on the roofs warning all air wanderers off with the single word, "Guns."

Taking their risks amidst these things, cyclists still kept abroad, and once or twice during Bert's long tramp powerful motor cars containing masked and goggled figures went tearing past him. There were few police in evidence, but ever and again squads of gaunt and tattered soldier-cyclists would come drifting along, and such encounters became more frequent as he got out of Wales into England. Amidst all this wreckage they were still campaigning. He had had some idea of resorting to the workhouses for the night if hunger pressed him too closely, but some of these were closed and others converted into temporary hospitals, and one he came up to at twilight near a village in

Gloucestershire stood with all its doors and windows open, silent as the grave, and, as he found to his horror by stumbling along evil-smelling corridors, full of unburied dead.

From Gloucestershire Bert went northward to the British aeronautic park outside Birmingham, in the hope that he might be taken on and given food, for there the Government, or at any rate the War Office, still existed as an energetic fact, concentrated amidst collapse and social disaster upon the effort to keep the British flag still flying in the air, and trying to brisk up mayor and mayor and magistrate and magistrate in a new effort of organisation. They had brought together all the best of the surviving artisans from that region, they had provisioned the park for a siege, and they were urgently building a larger type of Butteridge machine. Bert could get no footing at this work: he was not sufficiently skilled, and he had drifted to Oxford when the great fight occurred in which these works were finally wrecked. He saw something, but not very much, of the battle from a place called Boar Hill. He saw the Asiatic squadron coming up across the hills to the south-west, and he saw one of their airships circling southward again chased by two aeroplanes, the one that was ultimately overtaken, wrecked and burnt at Edge Hill. But he never learnt the issue of the combat as a whole.

He crossed the Thames from Eton to Windsor and made his way round the south of London to Bun Hill, and there he found his brother Tom, looking like some dark, defensive animal in the old shop, just recovering from the Purple Death, and Jessica upstairs delirious, and, as it seemed to him, dying grimly. She raved of sending out orders to customers, and scolded Tom perpetually lest he should be late with Mrs. Thompson's potatoes and Mrs. Hopkins' cauliflower, though all business had long since ceased and Tom had developed a quite uncanny skill in the snaring of rats and sparrows and the concealment of certain stores of cereals and biscuits from plundered grocers' shops. Tom received his brother with a sort of guarded warmth.

"Lor!" he said, "it's Bert. I thought you'd be coming back some day, and I'm glad to see you. But I carn't arst you to eat anything, because I 'aven't got anything to eat. . . . Where you been, Bert, all this time?"

Bert reassured his brother by a glimpse of a partly eaten swede, and was still telling his story in fragments and parentheses, when he discovered behind the counter a yellow and forgotten note addressed to himself. "What's this?" he said, and found it was a year-old note from Edna. "She came 'ere," said Tom, like one who recalls a trivial thing, "arstin' for you and arstin' us to take 'er in. That was after the battle and settin' Clapham Rise afire. I was for takin' 'er in, but Jessica wouldn't 'ave it—and so she borrowed five shillings of me quiet like and went on. I dessay she's tole you—"

She had, Bert found. She had gone on, she said in her note, to an aunt and uncle who had a brickfield near Horsham. And there at last, after another fortnight of adventurous journeying, Bert found her.

§5

When Bert and Edna set eyes on one another, they stared and laughed foolishly, so changed they were, and so ragged and surprised. And then they both fell weeping.

"Oh! Bertie, boy!" she cried. "You've come—you've come!" and put out her arms and staggered. "I told 'im. He said he'd kill me if I didn't marry him."

But Edna was not married, and when presently Bert could get talk from her, she explained the task before him. That little patch of lonely agricultural country had fallen under the power of a band of bullies led by a chief called Bill Gore who had begun life as a butcher boy and developed into a prize-fighter and a professional sport. They had been organised by a local nobleman of former eminence upon the turf, but after a time he had disappeared, no one quite knew how and Bill had succeeded to the leadership of the country-side, and had developed his teacher's methods with considerable vigour. There had been a

strain of advanced philosophy about the local nobleman, and his mind ran to "improving the race" and producing the Over-Man, which in practice took the form of himself especially and his little band in moderation marrying with some frequency. Bill followed up the idea with an enthusiasm that even trenched upon his popularity with his followers. One day he had happened upon Edna tending her pigs, and had at once fallen a-wooing with great urgency among the troughs of slush. Edna had made a gallant resistance, but he was still vigorously about and extraordinarily impatient. He might, she said, come at any time, and she looked Bert in the eyes. They were back already in the barbaric stage when a man must fight for his love.

And here one deplores the conflicts of truth with the chivalrous tradition. One would like to tell of Bert sallying forth to challenge his rival, of a ring formed and a spirited encounter, and Bert by some miracle of pluck and love and good fortune winning. But indeed nothing of the sort occurred. Instead, he reloaded his revolver very carefully, and then sat in the best room of the cottage by the derelict brickfield, looking anxious and perplexed, and listening to talk about Bill and his ways, and thinking, thinking. Then suddenly Edna's aunt, with a thrill in her voice, announced the appearance of that individual. He was coming with two others of his gang through the garden gate. Bert got up, put the woman aside, and looked out. They presented remarkable figures. They wore a sort of uniform of red golfing jackets and white sweaters, football singlet, and stockings and boots and each had let his fancy play about his head-dress. Bill had a woman's hat full of cock's feathers, and all had wild, slouching cowboy brims.

Bert sighed and stood up, deeply thoughtful, and Edna watched him, marvelling. The women stood quite still. He left the window, and went out into the passage rather slowly, and with the careworn expression of a man who gives his mind to a complex and uncertain business. "Edna!" he called, and when she came he opened the front door.

He asked very simply, and pointing to the foremost of the three, "That 'im?. . . Sure?". . . and being told that it was, shot his rival instantly and very accurately through the chest. He then shot Bill's best man much less tidily in the head, and then shot at and winged the third man as he fled. The third gentleman yelped, and continued running with a comical end-on twist.

Then Bert stood still meditating, with the pistol in his hand, and quite regardless of the women behind him.

So far things had gone well.

It became evident to him that if he did not go into politics at once, he would be hanged as an assassin and accordingly, and without a word to the women, he went down to the village public-house he had passed an hour before on his way to Edna, entered it from the rear, and confronted the little band of ambiguous roughs, who were drinking in the tap-room and discussing matrimony and Bill's affection in a facetious but envious manner, with a casually held but carefully reloaded revolver, and an invitation to join what he called, I regret to say, a "Vigilance Committee" under his direction. "It's wanted about 'ere, and some of us are gettin' it up." He presented himself as one having friends outside, though indeed, he had no friends at all in the world but Edna and her aunt and two female cousins.

There was a quick but entirely respectful discussion of the situation. They thought him a lunatic who had tramped into this neighbourhood ignorant of Bill. They desired to temporise until their leader came. Bill would settle him. Some one spoke of Bill.

"Bill's dead, I jest shot 'im," said Bert. "We don't need reckon with *'im. 'E's* shot, and a red-'aired chap with a squint, *'e's* shot. We've settled up all that. There ain't going to be no more Bill, ever. 'E'd got wrong ideas about marriage and things. It's 'is sort of chap we're after."

That carried the meeting.

Bill was perfunctorily buried, and Bert's Vigilance Committee (for so it continued to be called) reigned in his stead.

That is the end of this story so far as Bert Smallways is

concerned. We leave him with his Edna to become squatters among the clay and oak thickets of the Weald, far away from the stream of events. From that time forth life became a succession of peasant encounters, an affair of pigs and hens and small needs and little economies and children, until Clapham and Bun Hill and all the life of the Scientific Age became to Bert no more than the fading memory of a dream. He never knew how the War in the Air went on, nor whether it still went on. There were rumours of airships going and coming, and of happenings Londonward. Once or twice their shadows fell on him as he worked, but whence they came or whither they went he could not tell. Even his desire to tell died out for want of food. At times came robbers and thieves, at times came diseases among the beasts and shortness of food, once the country was worried by a pack of boar-hounds he helped to kill; he went through many inconsecutive, irrelevant adventures. He survived them all.

Accident and death came near them both ever and again and passed them by, and they loved and suffered and were happy, and she bore him many children—eleven children—one after the other, of whom only four succumbed to the necessary hardships of their simple life. They lived and did well, as well was understood in those days. They went the way of all flesh, year by year.

The Epilogue

It happened that one bright summer's morning exactly thirty years after the launching of the first German air-fleet, an old man took a small boy to look for a missing hen through the ruins of Bun Hill and out towards the splintered pinnacles of the Crystal Palace. He was not a very old man; he was, as a matter of fact, still within a few weeks of sixty-three, but constant stooping over spades and forks and the carrying of roots and manure, and exposure to the damps of life in the open-air without a change of clothing, had bent him into the form of a sickle. Moreover, he had lost most of his teeth and that had affected his digestion and through that his skin and temper. In face and expression he was curiously like that old Thomas Smallways who had once been coachman to Sir Peter Bone, and this was just as it should be, for he was Tom Smallways the son, who formerly kept the little greengrocer's shop under the straddle of the mono-rail viaduct in the High Street of Bun Hill. But now there were no greengrocer's shops, and Tom was living in one of the derelict villas hard by that unoccupied building site that had been and was still the scene of his daily horticulture. He and his wife lived upstairs, and in the drawing and dining rooms, which had each French windows opening on the lawn, and all about the ground floor generally, Jessica, who was now a lean and lined and baldish but still very efficient and energetic old woman, kept her three cows and a multitude of gawky hens. These two were part of a little community of stragglers and returned fugitives, perhaps a hundred and fifty souls of them all together, that had settled down to the new conditions of things after the Panic and Famine and Pestilence that followed in the wake of the War. They had come back from strange refuges and hiding-places and had squatted down among the familiar houses and begun that hard struggle against nature for food which

was now the chief interest of their lives. They were by sheer preoccupation with that a peaceful people, more particularly after Wilkes, the house agent, driven by some obsolete dream of acquisition, had been drowned in the pool by the ruined gas-works for making inquiries into title and displaying a litigious turn of mind. (He had not been murdered, you understand, but the people had carried an exemplary ducking ten minutes or so beyond its healthy limits.)

This little community had returned from its original habits of suburban parasitism to what no doubt had been the normal life of humanity for nearly immemorial years, a life of homely economies in the most intimate contact with cows and hens and patches of ground, a life that breathes and exhales the scent of cows and finds the need for stimulants satisfied by the activity of the bacteria and vermin it engenders. Such had been the life of the European peasant from the dawn of history to the beginning of the Scientific Era, so it was the large majority of the people of Asia and Africa had always been wont to live. For a time it had seemed that, by virtue of machines, and scientific civilisation, Europe was to be lifted out of this perpetual round of animal drudgery, and that America was to evade it very largely from the outset. And with the smash of the high and dangerous and splendid edifice of mechanical civilisation that had arisen so marvellously, back to the land came the common man, back to the manure.

The little communities, still haunted by ten thousand memories of a greater state, gathered and developed almost tacitly a customary law and fell under the guidance of a medicine man or a priest. The world rediscovered religion and the need of something to hold its communities together. At Bun Hill this function was entrusted to an old Baptist minister. He taught a simple but adequate faith. In his teaching a good principle called the Word fought perpetually against a diabolical female influence called the Scarlet Woman and an evil being called Alcohol. This Alcohol had long since become a purely

spiritualised conception deprived of any element of material application; it had no relation to the occasional finds of whiskey and wine in Londoners' cellars that gave Bun Hill its only holidays. He taught this doctrine on Sundays, and on weekdays he was an amiable and kindly old man, distinguished by his quaint disposition to wash his hands, and if possible his face, daily, and with a wonderful genius for cutting up pigs. He held his Sunday services in the old church in the Beckenham Road, and then the country-side came out in a curious reminiscence of the urban dress of Edwardian times. All the men without exception wore frock coats, top hats, and white shirts, though many had no boots. Tom was particularly distinguished on these occasions because he wore a top hat with gold lace about it and a green coat and trousers that he had found upon a skeleton in the basement of the Urban and District Bank. The women, even Jessica, came in jackets and immense hats extravagantly trimmed with artificial flowers and exotic birds' feathers—of which there were abundant supplies in the shops to the north—and the children (there were not many children, because a large proportion of the babies born in Bun Hill died in a few days' time of inexplicable maladies) had similar clothes cut down to accommodate them; even Stringer's little grandson of four wore a large top hat.

That was the Sunday costume of the Bun Hill district, a curious and interesting survival of the genteel traditions of the Scientific Age. On a weekday the folk were dingily and curiously hung about with dirty rags of housecloth and scarlet flannel, sacking, curtain serge, and patches of old carpet, and went either bare-footed or on rude wooden sandals. These people, the reader must understand, were an urban population sunken back to the state of a barbaric peasantry, and so without any of the simple arts a barbaric peasantry would possess. In many ways they were curiously degenerate and incompetent. They had lost any idea of making textiles, they could hardly make up clothes when they had material, and they were forced to plunder

the continually dwindling supplies of the ruins about them for cover.

All the simple arts they had ever known they had lost, and with the breakdown of modern drainage, modern water supply, shopping, and the like, their civilised methods were useless. Their cooking was worse than primitive. It was a feeble muddling with food over wood fires in rusty drawing-room fireplaces; for the kitcheners burnt too much. Among them all no sense of baking or brewing or metal-working was to be found.

Their employment of sacking and such-like coarse material for work-a-day clothing, and their habit of tying it on with string and of thrusting wadding and straw inside it for warmth, gave these people an odd, "packed" appearance, and as it was a week-day when Tom took his little nephew for the hen-seeking excursion, so it was they were attired.

"So you've really got to Bun Hill at last, Teddy," said old Tom, beginning to talk and slackening his pace so soon as they were out of range of old Jessica. "You're the last of Bert's boys for me to see. Wat I've seen, young Bert I've seen, Sissie and Matt, Tom what's called after me, and Peter. The traveller people brought you along all right, eh?"

"I managed," said Teddy, who was a dry little boy.

"Didn't want to eat you on the way?"

"They was all right," said Teddy, "and on the way near Leatherhead we saw a man riding on a bicycle."

"My word!" said Tom, "there ain't many of those about nowadays. Where was he going?"

"Said 'e was going to Dorking if the High Road was good enough. But I doubt if he got there. All about Burford it was flooded. We came over the hill, uncle—what they call the Roman Road. That's high and safe."

"Don't know it," said old Tom. "But a bicycle! You're sure it was a bicycle? Had two wheels?"

"It was a bicycle right enough."

"Why! I remember a time, Teddy, where there was bicycles no

end, when you could stand just here—the road was as smooth as a board then—and see twenty or thirty coming and going at the same time, bicycles and moty-bicycles; moty cars, all sorts of whirly things."

"No!" said Teddy.

"I do. They'd keep on going by all day—'undreds and 'undreds."

"But where was they all going?" asked Teddy.

"Tearin' off to Brighton—you never seen Brighton, I expect—it's down by the sea, used to be a moce 'mazing place—and coming and going from London."

"Why?"

"They did."

"But why?"

"Lord knows why, Teddy. They did. Then you see that great thing there like a great big rusty nail sticking up higher than all the houses, and that one yonder, and that, and how something's fell in between 'em among the houses. They was parts of the mono-rail. They went down to Brighton too and all day and night there was people going, great cars as big as 'ouses full of people."

The little boy regarded the rusty evidences across the narrow muddy ditch of cow-droppings that had once been a High Street. He was clearly disposed to be sceptical, and yet there the ruins were! He grappled with ideas beyond the strength of his imagination.

"What did they go for?" he asked, "all of 'em?"

"They '*ad* to. Everything was on the go those days—everything."

"Yes, but where did they come from?"

"All round 'ere, Teddy, there was people living in those 'ouses, and up the road more 'ouses and more people. You'd 'ardly believe me, Teddy, but it's Bible truth. You can go on that way for ever and ever, and keep on coming on 'ouses, more 'ouses, and more. There's no end to 'em. No end. They get bigger and bigger." His voice dropped as though he named strange names.

"It's *London,*" he said.

"And it's all empty now and left alone. All day it's left alone. You don't find 'ardly a man, you won't find nothing but dogs and cats after the rats until you get round by Bromley and Beckenham, and there you find the Kentish men herding swine. (Nice rough lot they are too!) I tell you that so long as the sun is up it's as still as the grave. I been about by day—orfen and orfen." He paused.

"And all those 'ouses and streets and ways used to be full of people before the War in the Air and the Famine and the Purple Death. They used to be full of people, Teddy, and then came a time when they was full of corpses, when you couldn't go a mile that way before the stink of 'em drove you back. It was the Purple Death 'ad killed 'em every one. The cats and dogs and 'ens and vermin caught it. Everything and every one 'ad it. Jest a few of us 'appened to live. I pulled through, and your aunt, though it made 'er lose 'er 'air. Why, you find the skeletons in the 'ouses now. This way we been into all the 'ouses and took what we wanted and buried moce of the people, but up that way, Norwood way, there's 'ouses with the glass in the windows still, and the furniture not touched—all dusty and falling to pieces—and the bones of the people lying, some in bed, some about the 'ouse, jest as the Purple Death left 'em five-and-twenty years ago. I went into one—me and old Higgins las' year—and there was a room with books, Teddy—you know what I mean by books, Teddy?"

"I seen 'em. I seen 'em with pictures."

"Well, books all round, Teddy, 'undreds of books, beyond-rhyme or reason, as the saying goes, green-mouldy and dry. I was for leaven' 'em alone—I was never much for reading—but ole Higgins he must touch em. 'I believe I could read one of 'em *now*,' 'e says.

" 'Not it,' I says.

" 'I could,' 'e says, laughing and takes one out and opens it.

"I looked, and there, Teddy, was a cullud picture, oh, so

lovely! It was a picture of women and serpents in a garden. I never see anything like it.

"'This suits me,' said old Higgins, 'to rights.'

"And then kind of friendly he gave the book a pat—"

Old Tom Smallways paused impressively.

"And then?" said Teddy.

"It all fell to dus'. White dus'!" . . . He became still more impressive. "We didn't touch no more of them books that day. Not after that."

For a long time both were silent. Then Tom, playing with a subject that attracted him with a fatal fascination, repeated, "All day long they lie—still as the grave."

Teddy took the point at last. "Don't they lie o' nights?" he asked.

Old Tom shook his head. "Nobody knows, boy, nobody knows."

"But what could they do?"

"Nobody knows. Nobody ain't seen to tell—not nobody."

"Nobody?"

"They tell tales," said old Tom. "They tell tales, but there ain't no believing 'em. I gets 'ome about sundown, and keeps indoors, so I can't say nothing, can I? But there's them that thinks some things and them as thinks others. I've 'eard it's unlucky to take clo'es off of 'em unless they got white bones. There's stories—"

The boy watched his uncle sharply. "*Wot* stories?" he said.

"Stories of moonlight nights and things walking about. But I take no stock in 'em. I keeps in bed. If you listen to stories—Lord! You'll get afraid of yourself in a field at midday."

The little boy looked round and ceased his questions for a space.

"They say there's a 'og man in Beck'n'am what was lost in London three days and three nights. 'E went up after whiskey to Cheapside, and lorst 'is way among the ruins and wandered. Three days and three nights 'e wandered about and the streets

kep' changing so's he couldn't get 'ome. If 'e 'adn't remembered some words out of the Bible 'e might 'ave been there now. All day 'e went and all night—and all day long it was still. It was as still as death all day long, until the sunset came and the twilight thickened, and then it began to rustle and whisper and go pit-a-pat with a sound like 'urrying feet."

He paused.

"Yes," said the little boy breathlessly. "Go on. What then?"

"A sound of carts and 'orses there was, and a sound of cabs and omnibuses, and then a lot of whistling, shrill whistles, whistles that froze 'is marrer. And directly the whistles began things begun to show, people in the streets 'urrying, people in the 'ouses and shops busying themselves, moty cars in the streets, a sort of moonlight in all the lamps and winders. People, I say, Teddy, but they wasn't people. They was the ghosts of them that was overtook, the ghosts of them that used to crowd those streets. And they went past 'im and through 'im and never 'eeded 'im, went by like fogs and vapours, Teddy. And sometimes they was cheerful and sometimes they was 'orrible, 'orrible beyond words. And once 'e come to a place called Piccadilly, Teddy, and there was lights blazing like daylight and ladies and gentlemen in splendid clo'es crowding the pavement, and taxicabs follering along the road. And as 'e looked, they all went evil—evil in the face, Teddy. And it seemed to 'im suddenly *they saw 'im*, and the women began to look at 'im and say things to 'im—'orrible—wicked things. One come very near 'im, Teddy, right up to 'im, and looked into 'is face—close. And she 'adn't got a face to look with, only a painted skull, and then 'e see; they was all painted skulls. And one after another they crowded on 'im saying 'orrible things, and catchin' at 'im and threatenin' and coaxing 'im, so that 'is 'eart near left 'is body for fear." . . .

"Yes," gasped Teddy in an unendurable pause.

"Then it was he remembered the words of Scripture and saved himself alive. 'The Lord is my 'elper,' 'e says, 'therefore I will fear nothing,' and straightaway there came a cock-crowing

and the street was empty from end to end. And after that the Lord was good to 'im and guided 'im 'ome."

Teddy stared and caught at another question. "But who was the people," he asked, "who lived in all these 'ouses? What was they?"

"Gent'men in business, people with money—leastways we thought it was money till everything smashed up, and then seemingly it was jes' paper—all sorts. Why, there was 'undreds of thousands of them. There was millions. I've seen that 'I Street there regular so's you couldn't walk along the pavements, shoppin' time, with women and people shoppin'."

"But where'd they get their food and things?"

"Bort 'em in shops like I used to 'ave. I'll show you the place, Teddy, if we go back. People nowadays 'aven't no idee of a shop—no idee. Plate-glass winders—it's all Greek to them. Why, I've 'ad as much as a ton and a 'arf of petaties to 'andle all at one time. You'd open your eyes till they dropped out to see jes' what I used to 'ave in my shop. Baskets of pears 'eaped up, marrers, apples and pears, d'licious great nuts." His voice became luscious—"Benanas, oranges."

"What's benanas?" asked the boy, "and oranges?"

"Fruits they was. Sweet, juicy, d'licious fruits. Foreign fruits. They brought 'em from Spain and N' York and places. In ships and things. They brought 'em to me from all over the world, and I sold 'em in my shop. *I* sold 'em, Teddy! me what goes about now with you, dressed up in old sacks and looking for lost 'ens. People used to come into my shop, great beautiful ladies like you'd 'ardly dream of now, dressed up to the nines, and say, 'Well, Mr. Smallways, what you got 'smorning?' and I'd say, 'Well, I got some very nice C'nadian apples, or p'raps I got custed marrers. See? And they'd buy 'em. Right off they'd say, 'Send me some up.' Lord! what a life that was. The business of it, the bussel, the smart things you saw, moty cars going by, kerridges, people, organ-grinders, German bands. Always something going past—always. If it wasn't for those empty 'ouses, I'd think it all a dream."

"But what killed all the people, uncle?" asked Teddy.

"It was a smash-up," said old Tom. "Everything was going right until they started that War. Everything was going like clockwork. Everybody was busy and everybody was 'appy and everybody got a good square meal every day." He met incredulous eyes. "Everybody," he said firmly. "If you couldn't get it anywhere else, you could get it in the workhuss, a nice 'ot bowl of soup called skilly, and bread better'n any one knows 'ow to make now, reg'lar *white* bread, gov'ment bread."

Teddy marvelled, but said nothing. It made him feel deep longings that he found it wisest to fight down.

For a time the old man resigned himself to the pleasures of gustatory reminiscence. His lips moved. "Pickled Sammin!" he whispered, "an' vinegar. . . . Dutch cheese, *beer*! A pipe of terbakker."

"But *'ow* did the people get killed?" asked Teddy presently.

"There was the War. The War was the beginning of it. The War banged and flummocked about, but it didn't really *kill* many people. But it upset things. They came and set fire to London and burnt and sank all the ships there used to be in the Thames—we could see the smoke and steam for weeks—and they threw a bomb into the Crystal Palace and made a bust-up, and broke down the rail lines and things like that. But as for killin' people, it was just accidental if they did. They killed each other more. There was a great fight all hereabout one day, Teddy—up in the air. Great things bigger than fifty 'ouses, bigger than the Crystal Palace—bigger, bigger than anything, flying about up in the air and whacking at each other and dead men fallin' off 'em. T'riffic! But, it wasn't so much the people they killed as the business they stopped. There wasn't any business doin', Teddy, there wasn't any money about, and nothin' to buy if you 'ad it."

"But 'ow did the people get *killed?*" said the little boy in the pause.

"I'm tellin' you, Teddy," said the old man. "It was the stoppin'

of business come next. Suddenly there didn't seem to be any money. There was cheques—they was a bit of paper written on, and they was jes' as good as money—jes' as good if they come from customers you knew. Then all of a sudden they wasn't. I was left with three of 'em and two I'd given' change. Then it got about that five-pun' notes were no good, and then the silver sort of went off. Gold you couldn't get for love or—anything. The banks in London 'ad got it, and the banks was all smashed up. Everybody went bankrup'. Everybody was thrown out of work. Everybody!"

He paused, and scrutinised his hearer. The small boy's intelligent face expressed hopeless perplexity.

"That's 'ow it 'appened," said old Tom. He sought for some means of expression. "It was like stoppin' a clock," he said. "Things were quiet for a bit, deadly quiet, except for the airships fighting about in the sky, and then people begun to get excited. I remember my lars' customer, the very lars' customer that ever I 'ad. He was a Mr. Moses Gluckstein, a city gent and very pleasant and fond of sparrowgrass and chokes, and 'e cut in—there 'adn't been no customers for days—and began to talk very fast, offerin' me for anything I 'ad, anything, petaties or anything, its weight in gold. 'E said it was a little speculation 'e wanted to try. 'E said it was a sort of bet reely, and very likely 'e'd lose; but never mind that, 'e wanted to try. 'E always 'ad been a gambler, 'e said. 'E said I'd only got to weigh it out and 'e'd give me 'is cheque right away. Well, that led to a bit of a argument, perfect respectful it was, but a argument about whether a cheque was still good, and while 'e was explaining there come by a lot of these here unemployed with a great banner they 'ad for every one to read—every one could read those days—'We want Food.' Three or four of 'em suddenly turns and comes into my shop.

"'Got any food?' says one.

"'No,' I says, 'not to sell. I wish I 'ad. But if I 'ad, I'm afraid I couldn't let you have it. This gent, 'e's been offerin' me—'

"Mr. Gluckstein 'e tried to stop me, but it was too late.

" 'What's 'e been offerin' you?' says a great big chap with a 'atchet; 'what's 'e been offerin you?' I 'ad to tell.

" 'Boys,' 'e said, ' 'ere's another feenancier!' and they took 'im out there and then, and 'ung 'im on a lam'pose down the street. 'E never lifted a finger to resist. After I tole on 'im 'e never said a word. . . ."

Tom meditated for a space. "First chap I ever sin 'ung!" he said.

" 'Ow old was you?" asked Teddy.

" 'Bout thirty," said old Tom.

"Why! I saw free pig-stealers 'ung before I was six," said Teddy. "Father took me because of my birfday being near. Said I ought to be blooded. . . ."

"Well, you never saw no-one killed by a moty car, any'ow," said old Tom after a moment of chagrin. "And you never saw no dead men carried into a chemis' shop."

Teddy's momentary triumph faded. "No," he said, "I 'aven't."

"Nor won't. Nor won't. You'll never see the things I've seen, never. Not if you live to be a 'undred. . . Well, as I was saying, that's how the Famine and Riotin' began. Then there was strikes and Socialism, things I never did 'old with, worse and worse. There was fightin' and shootin' down, and burnin' and plundering. They broke up the banks up in London and got the gold, but they couldn't make food out of gold. 'Ow did *we* get on? Well, we kep' quiet. We didn't interfere with no-one and no-one didn't interfere with us. We 'ad some old 'tatoes about, but mocely we lived on rats. Ours was a old 'ouse, full of rats, and the famine never seemed to bother 'em. Orfen we got a rat. Orfen. But moce of the people who lived hereabouts was too tender stummicked for rats. Didn't seem to fancy 'em. They'd been used to all sorts of fallals, and they didn't take to 'onest feeding, not till it was too late. Died rather.

"It was the famine began to kill people. Even before the Purple Death came along they was dying like flies at the end of the summer. 'Ow I remember it all! I was one of the first to 'ave

it. I was out, seein' if I mightn't get 'old of a cat or somethin', and then I went round to my bit of ground to see whether I couldn't get up some young turnips I'd forgot, and I was took something awful. You've no idee the pain, Teddy—it doubled me up pretty near. I jes' lay down by 'at there corner, and your aunt come along to look for me and dragged me 'ome like a sack.

"I'd never 'ave got better if it 'adn't been for your aunt. 'Tom,' she says to me, 'you got to get well,' and I *'ad* to. Then *she* sickened. She sickened but there ain't much dyin' about your aunt. 'Lor!' she says, 'as if I'd leave you to go muddlin' along alone!' That's what she says. She's got a tongue, 'as your aunt. But it took 'er 'air off—and arst though I might, she's never cared for the wig I got 'er—orf the old lady what was in the vicarage garden.

"Well, this 'ere Purple Death,—it jes' wiped people out, Teddy. You couldn't bury 'em. And it took the dogs and the cats too, and the rats and 'orses. At last every house and garden was full of dead bodies. London way, you couldn't go for the smell of there, and we 'ad to move out of the 'I street into that villa we got. And all the water run short that way. The drains and underground tunnels took it. Gor' knows where the Purple Death come from; some say one thing and some another. Some said it come from eatin' rats and some from eatin' nothin'. Some say the Asiatics brought it from some 'I place, Thibet, I think, where it never did nobody much 'arm. All I know is it come after the Famine. And the Famine come after the Penic and the Penic come after the War."

Teddy thought. "What made the Purple Death?" he asked.

"'Aven't I tole you!"

"But why did they 'ave a Penic?"

"They 'ad it."

"But why did they start the War?"

"They couldn't stop theirselves. 'Aving them airships made 'em."

"And 'ow did the War end?"

"Lord knows if it's ended, boy," said old Tom. "Lord knows if it's ended. There's been travellers through 'ere—there was a chap only two summers ago—say it's goin' on still. They say there's bands of people up north who keep on with it and people in Germany and China and 'merica and places. 'E said they still got flying-machines and gas and things. But we 'aven't seen nothin' in the air now for seven years, and nobody 'asn't come nigh of us. Last we saw was a crumpled sort of airship going away—over there. It was a littleish-sized thing and lopsided, as though it 'ad something the matter with it."

He pointed, and came to a stop at a gap in the fence, the vestiges of the old fence from which, in the company of his neighbour Mr. Stringer the milkman, he had once watched the South of England Aero Club's Saturday afternoon ascents. Dim memories, it may be, of that particular afternoon returned to him.

"There, down there, where all that rus' looks so red and bright, that's the gas-works."

"What's gas?" asked the little boy.

"Oh, a hairy sort of nothin' what you put in balloons to make 'em go up. And you used to burn it till the 'lectricity come."

The little boy tried vainly to imagine gas on the basis of these particulars. Then his thoughts reverted to a previous topic.

"But why didn't they end the War?"

"Obstinacy. Everybody was getting 'urt, but everybody was 'urtin' and everybody was 'igh-spirited and patriotic, and so they smeshed up things instead. They jes' went on smeshin'. And afterwards they jes' got desp'rite and savige."

"It ought to 'ave ended," said the little boy.

"It didn't ought to 'ave begun," said old Tom, "But people was proud. People was la-dy-da-ish and uppish and proud. Too much meat and drink they 'ad. Give in—not them! And after a bit nobody arst 'em to give in. Nobody arst 'em. . . ."

He sucked his old gums thoughtfully, and his gaze strayed

away across the valley to where the shattered glass of the Crystal Palace glittered in the sun. A dim large sense of waste and irrevocable lost opportunities pervaded his mind. He repeated his ultimate judgment upon all these things, obstinately, slowly, and conclusively, his final saying upon the matter.

"You can say what you like," he said. "It didn't ought ever to 'ave begun."

He said it simply—somebody somewhere ought to have stopped something, but who or how or why were all beyond his ken.

Word Cloud Classics

Adventures of Huckleberry Finn

The Adventures of Sherlock Holmes

The Adventures of Tom Sawyer

Aesop's Fables

The Age of Innocence

Alice's Adventures in Wonderland and Through the Looking-Glass

Anna Karenina

Anne of Green Gables

The Art of War

The Autobiography of Benjamin Franklin and Other Writings

The Awakening and Other Stories

The Beautiful and Damned and Other Stories

Black Beauty

The Brothers Grimm 101 Fairy Tales

The Brothers Grimm Volume II: 110 Grimmer Fairy Tales

Bulfinch's Mythology: Stories of Gods and Heroes

The Call of the Wild and Other Stories

A Christmas Carol and Other Holiday Treasures

Classic Horror Tales

Classic Science Fiction

Classic Stories of World War I

Classic Stories of World War II

Classic Tales of Mystery

Classic Westerns: Zane Grey

Common Sense and Selected Works of Thomas Paine

The Count of Monte Cristo

Crime and Punishment

Don Quixote

Dracula

Dubliners & A Portrait of the Artist as a Young Man and Other Works

Emma

Frankenstein

Great Expectations

Hans Christian Andersen Tales

H. P. Lovecraft Cthulhu Mythos Tales

The Hunchback of Notre Dame

The Inventions, Researches, and Writings of Nikola Tesla

Jane Eyre

The Jungle Book

Lady Chatterley's Lover

Leaves of Grass

Word Cloud Classics

The Legend of Sleepy Hollow and Other Tales

Les Misérables

Little Women

Love Poems

Madame Bovary

Mansfield Park

The Merry Adventures of Robin Hood

Moby-Dick

My Ántonia

Northanger Abbey

Odyssey

Persuasion

Peter Pan

The Phantom of the Opera

The Picture of Dorian Gray

The Poetry of Emily Dickinson

Presidential Inaugural Addresses

Pride and Prejudice

The Prince and Other Writings

The Prophet and Other Tales

The Romantic Poets

The Scarlet Letter

The Secret Garden

Selected Works of Alexander Hamilton

Selected Works of Edgar Allan Poe

Sense and Sensibility

Shakespeare's Sonnets and Other Poems

Strange Case of Dr. Jekyll and Mr. Hyde & Other Stories

A Tale of Two Cities

Tarzan of the Apes & The Return of Tarzan

The Three Musketeers

Treasure Island

Twenty Thousand Leagues Under the Sea

Uncle Tom's Cabin, or Life Among the Lowly

The U.S. Constitution and Other Key American Writings

Walden and Civil Disobedience

William Shakespeare Comedies

William Shakespeare Tragedies

The Wind in the Willows and Other Stories

The Wizard of Oz

Wuthering Heights

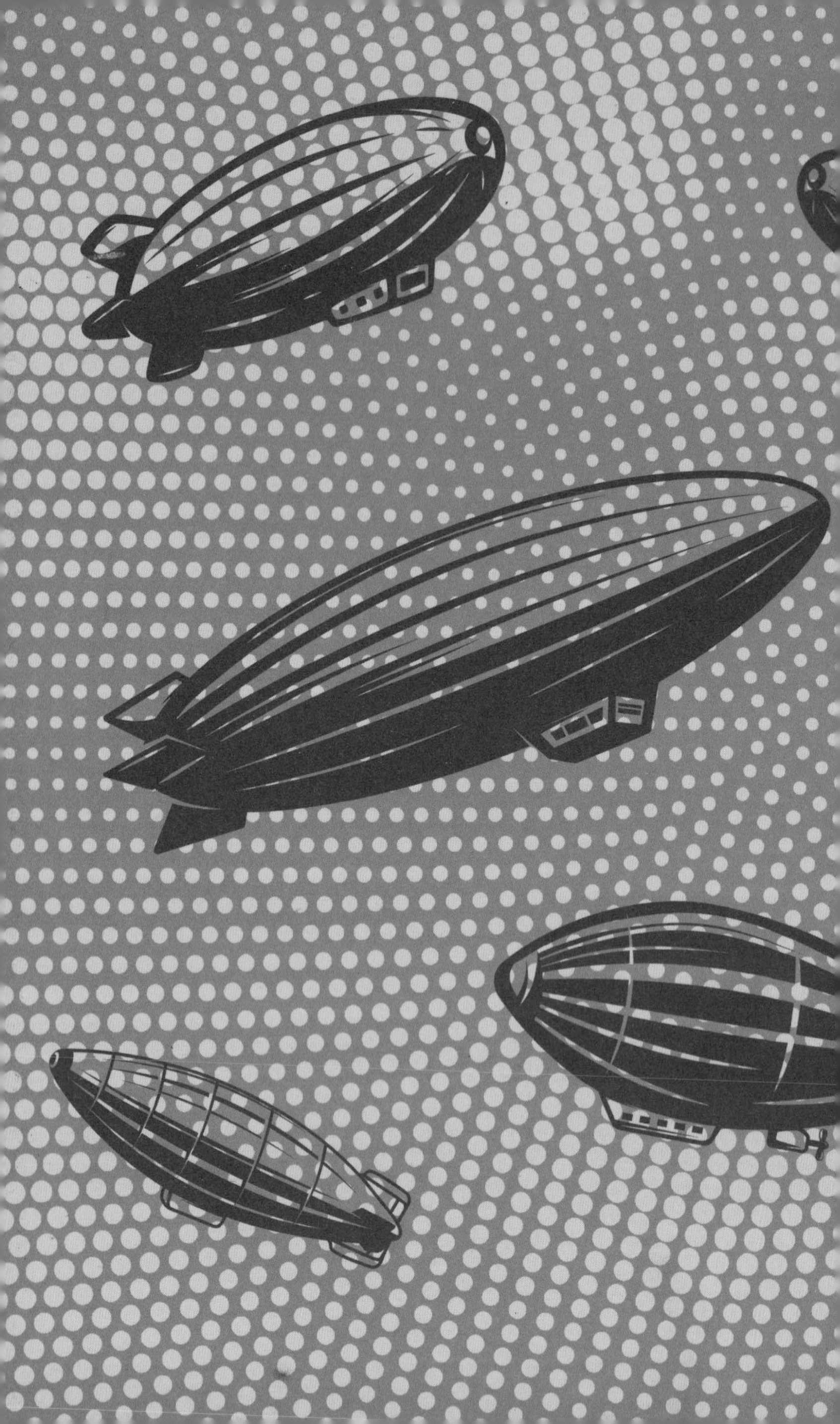